James Mackenzie
intrigued royalty . . .

The Queen of France
gave him his soubriquet de Wynter, for at 23 he already wore his family's mark—a shock of silver-pewter hair.

The King of Scotland
gave him his mission. So well known was de Wynter's way with a lady that the king thought him a proper envoy to bring back Margaret Douglas from England to Scotland where she belonged.

The King of England
wanted de Wynter out of England so that he could no longer court the Boleyn and Henry sent him to the Tower. The only way de Wynter could free himself and his life-long friends, The Companions, was to enter the Order of the Knights Hospitaller and be sent to Malta . . .

The Amira Aisha of Tunis
found him a shackled slave, a victim of high seas piracy, an ideal subject for her own schemes.

But
James Mackenzie
was man of destiny,
a Scot whose fortune
was guarded by

THE MER-LION

The Mer-Lion

Lee Arthur

WARNER BOOKS

A Warner Communications Company

To Edna

*without whom there would have been no Ramlah
. . . nor, particularly, any Lee Arthur*

WARNER BOOKS EDITION

Warner Books, Inc., 75 Rockefeller Plaza, New York, N.Y. 10019

 A Warner Communications Company

Printed in the United States of America

First Printing: July, 1982

10 9 8 7 6 5 4 3 2 1

Chronology of *The Mer-Lion*

1503   James IV of Scotland marries Margaret Tudor, sister of Henry VIII of England; *Seamus MacDonal arrives in Scotland from Ireland.*

1508   *The earl of Seaforth marries Islean, bastard daughter of James IV.*

1509   Henry VII dies, Henry VIII ascends throne of England, marries his brother's widow, Catherine of Aragon; *Islean, Countess of Seaforth, gives birth to a son, James Mackenzie.*

1512   James V of Scotland born.

1513   England and Scotland meet in the Battle of Flodden, James IV killed; *Berbers revolt in Tunisia, crown Hassan the Moulay and marry him to a Berber princess.*

1514   Margaret Tudor forfeits her regency, marries Douglas, earl of Angus; *heir born to the throne of Tunisia.*

1515   The Scots duke of Albany named regent of Scotland.

1516   The corsair chieftain, Barbarossa, murders his ally, the Sultan Selim of Algiers.

1518   Barbarossa confirmed as Beglerbey of Algiers by Suleiman.

1520   Henry VIII and Francis I of France meet at the Field of Cloth of Gold.

1524   Albany ousted as regent by Hamilton, Margaret Tudor and Douglas, returns to France; James V crowned king and imprisoned by Douglas.

1527   Siege of Naples lifted when Louise of France ransoms the French survivors; Henry VIII seeks a divorce from Catherine.

1528   James V escapes; Douglas exiled and divorced; Margaret Tudor marries Methven.

1532   *The earl of Seaforth assassinated in Edinburgh;* the Knights Hospitaler lay claim to Henry VIII's new palace, the late Cardinal Wolsey's Hampton Court; Anne Boleyn named Marquis of Pembroke, accompanies Henry VIII to the second Field of Cloth of Gold; *Barbarossa demands Aisha, princess of Tunisia, as his wife.*

1533   *The Great Games of the Amira Aisha held at el Djem in Tunisia from January 19 to 25; the sixth day a champion is named* and Henry VIII marries Anne Boleyn.

* Events italicized are fictional, occurring only in *The Mer-Lion*.

Characters

SCOTLAND

James Mackenzie, 4th Earl of Seaforth, son of the "Old Earl," husband to

Islean Stewart, Countess of Seaforth, bastard daughter of James IV, mother to

James Mackenzie, 5th Earl of Seaforth, reinvested by Claude, Queen of France, as 11th Lord de Wynter and 1st Baron Alais, father to

Jamie Mackenzie, disputed heir to the Scots titles of Seaforth, Alva and Rangely as well as Alais in France.

Seamus MacDonal, an Irishman, captain of the Seaforth guard, father to
Dugan of Alva
Derry of Rangely
Fionn and his sister, Devorguila, of Seaforth, both by Nelly.

Father Cariolinus, chaplain to the Seaforths

James IV of Scotland, King 1488–1513, husband of

Margaret Tudor of England, sister to Henry VIII, mother of

James V of Scotland, reigning monarch at this time.

Archibald Douglas, the "Marrying Douglas," stepfather to James V and father, by Margaret Tudor, of

Margaret Douglas, named and renounced heir to England.

John Stewart, Scots Duke of Albany, first cousin to James IV, regent to James V, heir in his own right to the Scottish throne.

Lady Ann Campbell, chatelaine of the Castle Dolour, near Alva, and third wife to

Lord Campbell, head of the southern Campbell clan

David Angus
David Ogilvy
John Drummond ⎫ Companions to James Mackenzie
Kenneth Menzies ⎬ when he was Master of Seaforth
Henry Gilliver ⎭ and later the 5th Earl.
George Cameron

Andrew Boorde, Englishman, visiting physician, law-breaker, and lecturer at the University of St. Andrews in Scotland.

ENGLAND

Henry VIII, King, brother to Margaret Tudor and Mary Tudor, unwilling husband to

Catherine of Aragon.

Anne Boleyn, Lady, daughter of the Earl of Wiltshire, sister to

George Rochford, husband to

Jane Rochford, Lady.

Mary Tudor, Queen Dowager of France, Duchess of Suffolk, wife to

Charles Brandon, friend to the king.

Thomas Cromwell, Master of the King's Jewels, rival of

Thomas Cranmer, Archbishop of Canterbury, successor to Wolsey, Cardinal.

John Skelton, Orator Regius and Poet Laureate to Henry VIII

John Carlby, Lord, Turcoplier in the Order of Knights of St. John of Jerusalem, Rhodes, and Malta

Thomas Notte, Captain of the King's Yeoman Guard, brother to

Walter Notte, Yeoman Gaoler, under command of

John Elstow, Gentlemen Gaoler, Tower of London

THE MAGHRIB (NORTHWESTERN AFRICA)

Don Federico, Captain

Eulj Ali, slave oarsman

John the Rob, an Englishman and unwilling passenger, chief of the the beggars.

Uruj Barbarossa, Beglerbey of Algiers, Corsair Chieftain, husband to

Marimah, first among four wives, mother of Eulj Ali.

Sinan the Jew, "Drub-Devil," of Smyrna, one of his lieutenants

Moulay Hassan, king of Tunis, father of

Aisha Kahina, daughter also of

Ramlah, Princess of the Berbers, half-sister to

Ali ben Zaid, son of the aged chief of the Berbers.

Hassan ben Khairim, slave dealer

Zainab, slave, and favorite handmaiden of Aisha

Artemidorius of Tralles, of Greece
Pietro Strabo, of Italy
Hamad Attia, of Gafsa, Tunisia
Al-wazier Yahiba, of Marrakesh, Morocco
Sheykh Beteyen ibn Kader, of Arred, Arabia
Ibn al-Hudaij, al wazier to Moulay Hassan, chief judge

⎫ Judges at the "Games"

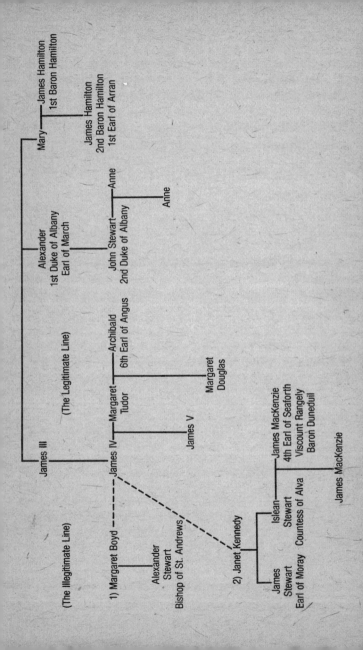

Table of Contents

PROLOGUE

**5 Shawwal, A.H. 939/
22 May, A.D. 1532**

The Maghrib
(Northwestern Africa)

Fear loosed his bowels and unhinged his knees.

Cowering, the messenger crumpled to the floor, face hidden in his hands. He had tried to surrender his packet in an anteroom, but as its contents were unknown, none would accept it. All knew full well that rewards were great for welcome words, but bad news often meant a short life for the bearer. A vicious kick propelled the man forward a scant body-length. Again. And again, as his blackamoor escort forcefully and frequently applied his leather-booted foot to the messenger's buttocks.

At the far end of the throne room, a gray-streaked, full-bearded man sat cross-legged on a divan, silken cushions piled about him, a naked scimitar spanning his knees. His hands—one living, one dead—were poised, statuelike, palm-down upon its gleaming blade. The single glimpse of those hands that the messenger stole unmanned him even more. The left hand was frozen forever in polished silver, the other hid its living flesh under a pelt of curly hair, the hue of which had earned the man his name—Barbarossa—the Red Beard. The very whisper of that name stilled noisy young children and made experienced merchantmen tremble. For three decades, this corsair chief had claimed the shipping lanes of the Mediterranean as his personal fiefdom, but that had not contented him. Like so many low-bred men, this son of a washerwoman (by a janissary-turned-potter) had royal dynastic ambitions. To achieve them, he would make alliances, break alliances, take partners, betray partners. He was even willing to wait until a certain girl-child grew to marriageable age. As a necessary step toward his goal, he had strangled his friend, the king of Algiers, in his bath. Barbarossa then bought his confirmation as the new Beglerbey of Algiers from the Ottoman sultan. It had cost him thousands of dinars, which he didn't begrudge. As the ruler of Algiers he could now demand that his trading partner, the Moulay Hassan of Tunisia, give him the bride of his choice: Aisha, heiress to the Moulay's throne. For eighteen years, since the day of her birth, Barbarossa had wanted to wed her. He could wait those few moments longer as her messenger amusingly humped the length of the room to hand over her answer setting the wedding date.

Eventually, even the longest stretch of marble floor must end, and the servile man came to the divan that blocked further progress. Blindly, the messenger held up the small leather packet in the general direction of the Beglerbey. One of those fearsome hands—the man dared not look to see which—plucked the message from his trembling grasp. But when the messenger tried to back away, the blackamoor's foot in the small of his back pinned him to the cold floor. In rapid succession, came a faint crackling sound as of a new-laid fire, the clash of metal fingers forming a fist, and the anguished howl of a wounded animal. Instinctively the messenger looked up . . . in time to see the scimitar descend.

Ignoring the blood and the body cleft near in two from crown to navel, Barbarossa stalked furiously through the sea of prostrate courtiers, each silently praying that he not be next. Only the blackamoor remained upright, following close on his master's heels, as Barbarossa growled his commands: "Prepare my ship. Summon Sinan the Jew; he will command in my absence. Tell my sons to follow me. Tell their mothers I go. Remind Sinan to heed the advice of Marimah. This mother of six of my sons is a woman of great wisdom. Would that I had listened to her words about the foolhardiness of proud princesses." This last he had not meant to say aloud, and he glanced around to check if the blackamoor had heard.

The black's face was bland. Not by the quiver of a muscle did he reveal the acuity of his hearing. He was a wise one, also. He changed the subject. "And the messenger?" he prompted. "Do you wish to send the body back?"

"Yes. No," Barbarossa corrected himself. "The message was never delivered. Do you understand?"

"If the master says day is night, or night day, even the sun must obey. The messenger never arrived, his message was not delivered."

Later, when the blackamoor returned with slaves to remove the body, one of them found, wadded up in a tiny ball, the piece of parchment that had already claimed one man's life and would eventually cost hundreds more theirs. He might have thrown the missive over the parapet to lie until the high tide, smashing against the rocks below, beat it into pulp and washed it out to sea, its message forever lost. But this the blackamoor could not permit. Marimah would pay well for such information. Confiscating the parchment, he examined it cursorily, then casually crushed it back into a ball and apparently tossed it into the sea; but his casting arm released nothing—the message lay tucked expertly in his palm.

What he had read— *"From Aisha, Amira of Ifriqiya and Tunisia, heir to the throne of the Hafsids, twenty-third in a line descended from Dido, Queen of Carthage . . . to Barbarossa, self-proclaimed admiral of the seas and self-made occupant of the throne of Algiers, son of Jacob the potter and Sara the laundress"*—raised the hackles on his own neck. He must dispose of this potentially perilous parchment quickly, but not, of course, without reading it first and committing it to memory. Marimah was not the only one who paid well for information about Barbarossa.

Eager to be about his own affairs, the black made short work of having the body hurled over the wall, to fall, twisting and turning, and then bounce and break upon the craggy escarpment. Even before the blood on the throne room floor had been mopped up, the crabs, the carrion-eaters of the sea, had begun to emerge from their water-washed crevices and fissures to feast upon still another in their diet of delectables cast with such frequency from the dizzying heights of the Beglerbey's palace above them. By the next low tide the carcass would have been picked clean, the bones washed away, banishing all evidence that a messenger had come from the princess of Tunisia.

That her messenger did not immediately return came as no surprise to Aisha. The bearer of such a challenge as she had penned must be considered a likely loss. She had, however, expected some sort of a reply. The dramatic return, for example, of the mutilated corpse of her envoy would have demonstrated the corsair's contempt

17

for the message. That was what she would have done. Of course, she reminded herself, Barbarossa was a commoner and couldn't be expected to observe proper royal protocol. That, at least, was how she attempted to explain the strange silence from Algiers. What troubled her sleep was the nagging thought that the challenge might never have been delivered. A cowardly messenger, fearful of his possible fate, might have shirked his duty and fled in the opposite direction. Until she received corroboration of delivery from her informant at the court of the Beglerbey, she feared she would suffer more than one restless night.

She took comfort in the knowledge that her beauty had not been marred by her sleepless nights. Her face was clear and unlined. Even innocent of kohl and rouge, it was exquisite, dominated by large, wide-spaced, darkly fringed eyes whose color changed with her mood, like a cat's, from green to gold. So captivating were they that the casual observer, caught up in their gaze, might overlook the telltale signs of pride, petulance and passion in her full lower lip and firm, pointed chin.

Aisha stretched luxuriously between the silken sheets of her couch, then sat up in one fluid movement, her silken mane of golden hair tumbling down about her slim shoulders like a living veil. She stretched again and stifled a yawn with the back of a small, long-nailed elegant hand. She slept in the nude. As her maids and her glass told her, her body was as beautiful as her face. Not an ounce of extra flesh blurred its grace. The breasts, although small and girlish, were high and rose-tipped, the waist uncommonly trim. Her hips and haunches were more boyish than she liked, a reflection of her youth, yet she detected a hint of curves that promised more abundance when she matured. One would have expected that, with her fair hair and chrysoberyl eyes, her skin would be pale; it wasn't. Not swarthy like her Arab father yet darker and more golden than her mother's Berber fairness. Indeed, long ago she had decided that the protected pallor of the seraglio was not possible for her. She courted the sun's paint brush by exposing her entire body to it until now she was from head to toe one golden glow.

She slid one long, slim leg out from under the covers, then heard from outside her chamber the clash of her bodyguards' crossed spears, their voices raised in a perfunctory challenge. Aisha settled back. Ramlah must be here. Only she would be about at this hour of the morning. After nineteen years of the sedentary life of a harem woman, Aisha's mother still followed her Berber training and rose before the sun.

Even before she kissed her daughter good morning, Ramlah blurted out part of her news: "Word's come."

"What word?" Aisha interrupted fearfully. No need to pretend unconcern with her mother. But Ramlah wasn't to be hurried. Settling down, cross-legged, upon her daughter's couch, she clapped her hands for service, complaining all the while at the dearth of good slaves these days. Only when Aisha's handmaiden had poured her a cup of sweet mint tea was Ramlah ready to satisfy her only child's curiosity. "My agent heard that your father's agents received word from an informer in Algeria that the messenger did deliver the packet to Barbarossa in person. And, my dear, the old man could not wait to read it in private; he must open the packet and break the seal right then and there."

"Then what happened?"

"What would you expect? He killed the poor bearer with one blow of his sword, practically split him in half. The old pirate seems very strong for his age; are you sure you won't change your mind?"

The look Aisha gave her mother spoke words, but Ramlah ignored it. As her daughter rose to dress, she ordered the slave to pour another cup of tea and watched critically. Only the best clothes, the best jewels, the best of everything—including a husband—were good enough for Ramlah's beloved daughter.

"You haven't heard the rest. A ship captain returned to port last night, and he claims he was stopped by a corsair ship. He was boarded and searched and all papers and correspondence on board were confiscated."

Aisha's eyes narrowed in thought, then widened as a possible explanation occurred to her. "Clever man! Barbarossa, you old schemer, I could almost like you. Almost, by your daring and resourcefulness, are you worthy of me." Ramlah's astonishment brought a laugh to Aisha's lips. Then, quickly, remorsefully, she brought her merriment under control. "He received my challenge all right, Mother. Can't you just imagine that old man reading it

19

aloud?'' She deepened her naturally low voice to the best approxi-
mation of a male's that she could, then aped the airs and manner of a
pompous, vainglorious, mock-heroic pretender to a throne as she
recited the words she had written to Barbarossa.

> *You assume me chattel, not equal, but I am neither. I am*
> *regal, descended from Dido through my patrimony . . . Kahina*
> *the prophetess/warrior-woman maternally. I choose my*
> *husband, not he me. Even if I were not princess, I would*
> *not consent. Even the Messenger of Allah (on whom be*
> *praise) was forbidden to take in marriage a non-consenting*
> *woman. The man I choose must be a prince among men. Are*
> *you he? Then, I set you a challenge. If you would have me,*
> *come win me. Prove yourself a king in combat against armed*
> *warriors, not unarmed rulers at their bath. Win against men*
> *who are your betters, and you shall claim the Princess and*
> *the throne of Tunisia as your own. Lose, and I claim your*
> *life—''*

"Yes, yes," Ramlah interrupted, "I know all that. I helped you
write it, remember? What does that have to do with sea searches?"
"Ahh, but imagine his reaction—"
Again Ramlah interrupted. Sometimes it seemed to her that her
brilliant daughter gave her no credit for intelligence. "I need not
imagine his reaction. He killed the messenger. What does—"
It was Aisha's turn to break in. "You forget, Mother. The
message then went on to say that his opponents would be worthy of
him for, and I quote, '*this competition shall be proclaimed in every*
mosque and every bazaar on this side of the Mediterranean and on
the other and will be open to all who by blood and bearing of arms
name themselves noble.' ''
"Aisha, you are being difficult. What is the connection?"
"As I see it, instead of acting as an ordinary man would, rejecting
or accepting my challenge out of hand, he set upon another course. I
think if we checked, we'd discover his men patrolling not just the
sea but every trade route out of Tunisia. Why? To forestall the
competition, of course. If the challenge were not proclaimed, none

20

would know of it. If none knew of the competition, none would come. Except Barbarossa. He could then claim his prize and enlarge his kingdom without risking his life or lifting a sword. I should be his by default.''

''But, you had already sent word abroad even before the messenger left for Algiers.''

''I know and you know that, but our corsair chieftain didn't. Do you think such a man would credit a mere woman with forethought and intelligence? Not he? But I wager he has discovered his mistake by now. The question is,''—Aisha's eyes glittered as if facing a wily chess master—''what will be his next move.''

She sprang to her feet and paced the floor, scattering her handmaidens to either side. If Barbarossa could have seen her striding about the silk-draped, fur-strewn room in all her naked, barbaric glory, he might well have changed his mind and attended the competition, thus changing the course of history. But he could not . . . and did not. He had discounted the descriptions of her charms as exaggerations.

The prospective competitors believed the tales of her tawny beauty, however, which gave fillip to their ambitious dreams of winning a throne at the colosseum at el Djem at the end of the month of Jamad I—at the time of the winter solstice half a year hence.

Naturally enough, this unusual competition became the talk of courts from one end of the Mediterranean to the other. Within the Christian world, jokes, sneers, and snide remarks about this woman, who so lacked pride and self-respect that she would marry a man simply because he won her, fell freely from the mouths of women who had been bought and sold, many while still in the cradle, for their marriage portions and estates. Within the Moslem world, there was much approbation for Aisha's actions. The only daughter of Sultan Suleiman the magnificent and his Roxelana, for example, regretted that she had not done something similar. She had chosen her husband from among a small, select group of nobles whose antics she'd secretly watched at the royal baths. At least, she thought, this princess's husband will come to her bed willingly, unlike mine, who had to be commanded by my father to divorce his former wife and marry me.

Some people escaped the gossip and speculation about the

21

competition. The Moscovites and the Brahmins, the Mongols and the Mings, the bushmen and pygmy were too isolated in 1532 by their distance from the center of the civilized world. Others, preoccupied by their own concerns, chose to isolate themselves. For example, those within the domain of young James V, King of the Scots . . .

BOOK ONE

The Mackenzies of Seaforth
A.D. 1503–1532

Scotland

CHAPTER 1

Scotland was not always insular. Forty-four years before, when the late King James IV came to the throne in 1488, he brought the sun out from behind a cloud to shine on Scotland, attracting the best brains and talent in Europe to his court. Each day another ship came into port, bringing an artist, poet, merchant, inventor, or another of the like, to flourish in an open, encouraging environment. Like Lorenzo de Medici, a continent away and a little more than two decades dead, James was an all-round prince, the first Renaissance man of his country, and a politician in the best sense of the word. A warrior who preferred peace, this lusty man, whom complaisant women delighted in bedding, chose as his first and only bride, in 1503, the drab, sharpish, elder daughter of his quarrelsome neighbor to the south, Henry VII of England.

Margaret Tudor came without eagerness to her husband. She was fourteen, less than half his age. From her vantage point in England, the English-Scottish border seemed the northern limit of civilization. But Margaret had been reared to do her duty to her dynasty. Besides, marrying the Scot made her a reigning queen and for once she would be able to outdo her younger, more popular, beautiful sister, Mary of England, her father's favorite. So she came to Scotland and assumed her place in his wedding bed. As a gesture toward the youthful inexperience of his bride on her wedding night, James removed the iron chain he had worn about his body constantly for fifteen long years in expiation for the death of his father. To Margaret's pleasure, he was a gentle, experienced lover. To James's surprise, his cold-seeming bride was loving, and lusted for the carnal aspects of her marital life. The next day James again wore his chain, but cold iron did not deter Margaret. She was soon pregnant—to her father's relish, and her husband's relief.

Another who came unwillingly to Scotland's shores the year of Our Lord 1503 was Seamus MacDonal from the glens of Antrim across the North Channel. As a lad of nine, the eldest of eight boys with whom he shared a bed, he had been wakened many times late at night by sounds of weeping and his father's angry whispers. Yet it came as a complete surprise one day when his father gruffly informed him, "Take your one clean shirt and get out'f my house. No more leaching off'n me, lad. I've sold you into service." The kicking, fighting man-child had to be dragged, while his pregnant mother protested, out of the peat-roofed, one-room cottage. He and his father hadn't struggled far down the path when his mother came running after. "Wait! Sean, let me at least give the child my blessing."

Reluctantly, the tall, giant of a man let go and Seamus flew back to his mother's arms. Hugging him against a belly swollen with its annual burden of bairn, and with tears streaming down her face, she smoothed back his shock of blond hair with a work-roughened hand and whispered fiercely, "Walk tall, my son. No man is your better. Do your duty as you see it, and may the merpeople watch over you."

"Aren't you finished, woman?" Her husband growled. "The ship won't wait forever. If we miss it, I'll ha' to give the two pieces of silver back."

"Hold hard, Sean. But a moment more. Remember, Seamus my love, my blessings go wi' you." Then, she held her son away from her. "Go. Tis better this way. Ireland holds no future for you, and Scotland may."

Seamus resisted no more but took his father's hand and went with him, turning and twisting to watch his mother wave for as long as she was in sight. In the village, they went straight to the wharf and then to a small fishing boat.

"Ho, Fergus, I bring me lad."

The man who came hurrying from the bow of the ship was thin

and wiry with the look of a man always harassed. "'Tis about time. We're about to cast off. Well, don't just stand there, lad, get ye aboard."

Without looking back, Seamus did as he was told and took a seat in the bow on a pile of much-mended nets. Within moments, the boat had left its moorings. Perhaps he only imagined or wished it so, but Seamus thought he heard his father's voice calling his name. He ran back astern across the slippery deck, but the boat was well out in the channel by then, and Sean MacDonal was nowhere in sight.

Across the North Channel they sailed, the boat not once throwing out its nets. Seamus's tears soon gave way to helpless retching as the waves tossed the ship. Shortly, land came in sight and the ship made its way up the Sound of Jura to the Firth of Lorne where the fishing was good; the hold was soon filled. The bow of the boat turned into the Loch of Linnhe, all the while moving closer to Ben Nevis. The snow-covered mountain, so much higher than the hills that formed the nine glens of Antrim, filled Seamus with awe. And well it might, for Ben Nevis is the highest mountain in Scotland. Nestled at its base was the small town of Seaforth, where the master directed his ship to dock.

Leaving the crew behind to sell their catch, the master made his way, Seamus's hand held fast in his, up to the mighty keep on the crest of Dun Dearduil, the Castle Seaforth, home of the Mackenzies. Once Seamus saw the sable banner with gold morse sejant flying from atop the highest tower, he went along willingly. After all, hadn't his mother's last words wished the merpeople to watch over him? A Mer-Lion on a banner wasn't exactly a merperson, but to Seamus it was close enough. Across the stone bridge and over the moat they went, making their way with the blessings of the captain of the guard through the gate house with its two circular towers joined by a battlemented portcullis. From there they entered an enormous court, a vast expanse of greensward surrounded by many-windowed walls. In the corner, there was a round tower; beneath it, their destination—the castle kitchen. For four pieces of silver, Seaforth on Dun Dearduil had bought itself an assistant to the spitdogs in the kitchen.

But not for long. Mer-Lion or no, Seamus refused to do dog's work. Within twenty-four hours, he had made his first attempt at escape. He had not reached the castle gate before he was brought back, whipped thoroughly, and set to spit-turning again. He was not deterred. On his next attempt, he made it all the way to the drawbridge before being stopped by the captain of the guard. Back he went, his bottom a mass of welts, to his place before the fireplace. Not for long. Again and again he tried. Eventually, he made it all the way down to the docks and was seeking passage back to Ireland when caught by the earl's men. Brought home, totally unrepentant, and looking the earl—the old one, a man in his fifties—straight in the face, Seamus vowed to continue to run away until he escaped the hated kitchens. The earl took this defiant boy at his word, for Seamus was set a new task—shoveling dung in the stables. The boy stopped running away. Once the earl discovered Seamus could clean the stalls of the famed home-bred gray destriers without needing to have these notoriously short-tempered animals removed, he was confirmed in his role of stableboy and the grays were made his special charge. Nobody envied him his new responsibility, but Seamus was happy and remained so for the next five years.

When the old earl died in 1508, his son, also a James Mackenzie, became the Fourth Earl of Seaforth . . . and promptly married the only acknowledged bastard daughter of King James IV, a woman almost half the earl's age. Seamus, the new assistant head groomsman, came forward to steady her stirrup when she dismounted within the Fountain Court of Seaforth on Dun Dearduil. One look upward into her eyes, so dark blue they seemed almost purple, made him hers for life; his allegiance unofficially but incontrovertibly changed from the Earl of Seaforth to his Countess.

It was Seamus who personally groomed her jennets . . . who contrived when she rode to be by her side . . . who was there to give her a leg up or a hand down when she hunted in the countryside. And when, within the year, she bellied up in pregnancy, Seamus devised a small basket-cart within which she could continue to ride out, himself riding alongside or handling the reins of the pony.

When in early 1509 the heir was born—James Mackenzie, Master of Seaforth, Viscount Rangely, Baron of Alva—Seamus managed to find an excuse to be absent from the festivities. And when the family went to Edinburgh to present the child at court to his grandfather, James IV, Seamus contrived to stay behind. His excuse was the gray destriers; his real reason was a mixed bag of emotions—love, jealousy, fear—all dominated by an illogical dislike of the child. Over the next several years, Seamus seldom saw the child since noble-born men-children in the sixteenth century stayed within the women's quarters while they were still dressed in feminine long gowns.

Although 1509 was remembered by Seamus as the year his rival was born, the Scots remembered it as the year King Henry VII of England, father to the young Queen of Scotland, Margaret Tudor, died. The honeymoon peace was over and the stage set for a major confrontation between two brothers-in-law: eighteen-year-old Henry VIII and a man twice his age, James IV.

James IV was a good king and a man Henry VIII might well have been wise to emulate in certain respects. James was a builder. The palace he designed at Holyrood, next to the Abbey of the same name, effectively turned Edinburgh into an exciting capital city with pomp and pageantry, tournaments, processions, and pilgrimages the order of the hour. Henry stole the ideas, even the buildings, of others.

James was innovator: his royal navy—the first Scotland could boast—was not many-vesseled, but its crews were freemen, deliberately choosing their life at sea. Their bravery was greater than that of press-gangs or chained oarsmen. Henry's aim was bigger and grander ships. James was merchant, encouraging trade with Europe. Henry cared nought for trade except that such enriched his treasury, enabling him to make war. James was administrator, taking men of learning and law into his Privy Council and paying them heed. Henry appointed men and then pitted them against each other, putting prime value on cunning and connivery. James was judicator; Henry, executioner. James was banker working hard to establish his country's currency and honest coinage. Henry debased both to pay for his war, and robbed the church to boot. James was statesman, marrying for the good of his country and then making peace with his father-in-law. Henry took his brother's widow as the first of six wives.

Both men were patrons of the arts, of sorts. Henry competed unfairly with the artists, writing songs and poetry and translations that his court must, of course, praise. James acknowledged himself no poet, but having his great-grandfather's love of poetry, he saw to it that his court offered shelter and patronage to those with real talent. Moreover, he granted a patent to two burgesses to establish Scotland's first printing press and then granted them license to print more than just works of law and theology—as was the case in England. Thus Scotland could read Henryson's retelling of Aesop's fables in a Scots setting and in the Scots tongue . . . Dunbar's poem in celebration of the king's Tudor bride, "The Thistle and the Rose" . . . and all of the works of Gavin Douglas, Bishop of Dunkeld. This son to the murderous Bell-the-Cat Douglas, and uncle to the Marrying Douglas, was first to translate the *Aeneid* directly from the original. From his *The Dukes of Eneados*, written in Scots, would later come the English version.

James was not without fault, however, as Margaret Tudor was first to proclaim. Not only did he keep her pregnant with babes that all died but one, but he left a spate of living natural children around his kingdom. (These latter did not endear him to his less fertile brother-in-law.) Moreover, James was quick to acknowledge offspring if there were at least a good chance that he was the father. He saw to it that the children of his official mistresses (first, Margaret Boyd, mother of Alexander Stewart, the Bishop of St. Andrews; and later, Janet Kennedy, mother of James Stewart, Earl of Moray, and the Lady Islean, Countess of Alva and Seaforth) received benevolences and estates commensurate with their status. Henry, less wisely, attempted to elevate his one bastard son above his natural born daughter, Mary Tudor.

That these two princes could not share their isle harmoniously surprised no one. Once the shrewd influence of Henry VII was gone, problems multiplied, beginning at the border. No longer did the English wardens suppress the wanton raids of English Borderers into Scotland, and James's wardens retaliated by ignoring the incursions by Scots into England.

Henry VIII compounded the problems by dabbling in European politics. In 1512, he joined with the Pope and the Emperor Maximilian in an alliance against France, Scotland's traditional ally. Against her will, Scotland was being pulled into a maelstrom not of her own choosing. Yet, it was a flaw in James IV's own character that brought Scotland to commit the folly of invading England.

James, though forward-looking, was in one respect an atavism: he was an honorable man. Honorable in the medieval, chivalric sense of the word. In the early summer of 1513, faced with an invasion by an English army, Louis XII invoked the Auld Alliance between France and Scotland; and his queen, Anne of Bretagne, named James her champion and sent him a token, a turquoise ring, to carry while he protected her honor. James IV did the only thing a true knight could do—he went to war to defend his lady's honor.

He issued his challenge and summoned his lords, the clans, and the Borderers. And the men came, for they loved their king. Thousands and thousands of them: barons, knights, free-holding lairds, farmers, laborers—common folk and nobles alike, plus all four Scots dukes, fourteen earls, and even three bishops. Seaforth was among those who answered the call. With him went Seamus MacDonal, now a big, blond giant of a horsegroom, who towered at least half a head higher than any of the other Seaforth retainers.

Men from all over Scotland assembled outside Edinburgh, beneath the protective walls of the castle. After hearing Mass in the Abbey of the Holy Cross, alongside Holyrood House, the king and his lords rode out and down St. Mary's Wynd. With him for a distance rode Margaret Tudor, the princess of England whom he had the day before named regent of Scotland as mother of the two-year-old James V. In her very pregnant belly reposed the assurance James needed that his dynasty would continue. As the king and his entourage clattered by with banners snapping in the wind, pipes and drums setting the measure, those living in the noble houses lining St. Mary's Wynd rode out and joined the procession.

Seamus, turning in his saddle, could see the Lady Islean standing on the steps leading down to the courtyard. She was joined there by Seaforth, who gravely took her scarf, tucked it into his sleeve as a token, and bade her good-bye. He did not wear full armor; he was going to war, not a tourney. And the horse his squire led was a cob, not one of his mighty destriers. Thus, mounting required no block and tackle, but simply a leg up. He leaned down from his horse to say something to the beautiful child who stood close to his mother's skirts. Whatever it was, it provoked a laugh followed by a kiss and then a salute. Then Seaforth was off, his men following after, under the six-foot-long Seaforth sable banner bearing a maned Mer-Lion, its forelegs ending in webbed paws, and, from the waist down, its body and tail that of a sea serpent.

Soon the procession reached Cowgate, or the southgate, either a misnomer, for there was no gate joining the city walls there. The phalanx of nobles and their minor entourages filled the street back as far as one could see. Now, the pipes and the drums were nearly drowned out by the cries and huzzahs of the people cheering their king and his glorious army off to victory. Outside the wall, the army joined up. And so sounded the first sour note of the show. So disorganized, so eager to join in, and so independent were they, that some of the troops came to blows as to which would have precedence. The spearmen, in their eagerness to go to war, pushed forward. Like a row of dominoes, each forced the one in front to tread on the heels of the man before him until the Scots army was literally forcing its king to rush to stay ahead of it. Seamus feared for a while that he might get caught in the crush. Later he heard reports that men had fallen and been trampled in the melee. That night, when James met with his assembled lords, he hailed the event as a sign to hurry forward in this goodly cause.

The cheers of the people stirred the blood of the warriors; making them eager to meet their ancient foe. And about them nature added her purple benediction: meadows of heather, spread like spilt wine—or, as some more cynical would have it, Scottish blood—across the hills and moorlands, with the feathery-leaved bracken in its russet glory enriching the scene. Seamus drank it all in. The hills, the sylvan settings, the clear streams, the heather—indeed, it was a glorious time to be alive. Cheerfully, willfully, agreeably, even eagerly, he and his fellows rode into war. Coming to meet them, perhaps less eagerly, but surely unwaveringly, was the English army under the command of Lord Howard, Earl of Surrey.

The two armies met on September 9, 1513, in England, near Flodden Field, at the base of Branxton Hill.

The cannons played overture to this battle, a deep thumping tympany serving as counterpoint to the high-pitched sounds of men preparing for war: the clash of metal on metal, horns blaring and wailing and just as shrilly replying, the cries of men seeking to cheer, rally, and bolster the confidence of their fellow men while striking a note of fear in their opponents.

Seamus never did understand what, if any, were the battle plans. He was too wrought up by the sudden realization that this was actually war; that he was in it; that he couldn't change his mind now and go back; and that, more than anything else in the world, he needed to piss just one more time. Just then the Borderers under the Earl of Home and the Gordons under their clan chief, the Earl of Huntley, advanced. The Mackenzies led by Seaforth went with them and Seamus forgot everything else but staying close to his lord. Down the hill they charged, fell upon a group of men, broke through them and surged on toward the English camp, stopping only to take prisoners. Then, though their leaders urged them on, many began to plunder the dead and the helpless, fallen living.

Seaforth's squire was among the fallen; and on the battlefield Seamus was given an impromptu promotion, confirmed while the army was stopped. As he watched, of a mind to ask Seaforth's permission to join in plundering, horsemen appeared on their flank. The English had struck back. Now there was fighting in earnest and men falling left and right. After the first furious moments, each side drew back to regroup; it was obvious they were well-matched, neither side having an advantage in men or position, and thus neither eager to renew the attack. So they stood facing each other like two angry dogs, their hair on end, their lips drawn back in a snarl, their motions stiff-legged as if to attack.

However, as the noises of the battle raging elsewhere grew even louder, there seemed to be an unspoken but mutual understanding between these two factions. Each side withdrew just a bit . . . and then some more, never relaxing their guard, of course. Finally to Seamus's surprise, the Scots were back at Branxton Hill. From there they could see, in dusty but vivid panorama, the course of the battle. It was a preview of Hell.

The sounds were deafeningly loud, and dominating all else were high-pitched screams that repeated and resounded and never ceased. The acrid smell of gunpowder clung to his nostrils, as well as the sickeningly sweet odor of blood. Dust rose from the battle, pierced now and again by brief slashes of lightning, the spark of metal on metal. No one in his right mind, thought Seamus, would voluntarily go down into that inferno. That, he saw with horror, was exactly what the Earls of Huntley and Seaforth planned to do. Like lemmings in sight of the sea, they threw themselves suicidally into battle. Down they went into the face of a rain of arrows. Horses fell, pulling down their riders, leaving large gaps in the line of spearmen. Once into the thick of things, dead Scots tripped their fellows up and made the way treacherous. Courage the Scots had in abundance . . . plus the strength of men whose leader fought alongside and among them, unlike the British whose king this day was in France, fighting a war more to his vainglorious liking.

But the Scottish spear on which James and the rest so relied had met its match in a better weapon: the bill, a six-foot-long shaft of wood topped with a combination ax blade and curving hook. Deftly the English billman lopped off the head of the spear before him, and then did the same to its owner. One and two, and one and two, and do it again. Slowly but methodically and invincibly, the wielders of these weapons advanced, using the steady, back-and-forth sweep of a scyther. Their harvest was death, and it recognized no rank. James IV himself, fighting on although shot full of arrows and with one hand almost severed at the wrist, fell victim to one swift stroke of a bill that separated head from neck.

Seaforth went down, too, victim to a blow that Seamus didn't see. Seamus panicked. He would have run if he'd known where to go. But in the chaos, there was no sense of left or right, north or south. There were only waves of fighting that one rode out as well as one could. Not knowing what else to do, he straddled the body of his lord. So large, vigorous and strong was he that he managed to foil four bills and kill the men who wielded them, until a blow from behind flattened him. When he fell, his massive body cloaked the smaller one of his lord's, shielding it from the British carrion who came at dusk to strip the corpses of the nobles. Seamus regained consciousness before all of the plunderers had passed but cannily played dead; however, his bladder could be denied no longer. Seamus pissed in his breeches, unwittingly wetting the lord of Seaforth beneath him.

When the British withdrew, chased by darkness back to their camp to celebrate victory, Seamus carried the body off the field and up Branxton Hill, intending to give it decent burial. He was surprised to find that some Scots were still stubbornly encamped there. The Home Clan, who had fought the vanguard of the British alongside the Gordons and Mackenzies, had refused to join in that last self-destructive charge into battle. When Seamus stammeringly inquired as to why the Borderers were there, Archibald, the third Earl of Home, gave the same answer he had given Huntley and Seaforth a few hours before: "He does well that does for himself. We have fought our vanguard already; let others do as well as we."

(Weeks later, tales circulated among the Scots that it was not a bill, but a spear wielded from behind by a man of the Home Clan that caused the death of the king. When Seamus was asked for confirmation because he had talked to Home's men before and after the final battle, he refused to comment. He spoke only of a debt owed the Border chieftain for the loan of a horse to carry home the corpse of Seaforth.)

From their position on high ground, the few Scots who remained spent a sleepless night—kept awake by the moans and cries of their fellows down on Flodden Field. Seamus would have gone down to attempt to succor them, but he was not sure that Home's Borderers would have let him return.

Down there, the vast majority of James's brave army perished. Twelve earls, three dukes, all of the bishops who had ridden into battle joined the king in death. Long live the new king . . . the two-year-old nephew of the man whose army had massacred the Scots, decimated the ranks of her nobility, and destroyed with one stroke most of her country's leadership.

At dawn when the first of the scavengers came out onto the battlefield, the hills around them were clean of surviving Scots. During the night, the Borderers had begun their way home. Seamus too, with the body of his lord tied on a horse.

The jostling of the horse roused the earl from his deep coma, and he moaned, frightening Seamus momentarily. Then, filled with joy, he would have cut his master loose to ride upright, but the semiconscious earl was aware enough to decide that riding tied was faster and surer.

Not until the battle was left far behind, did Seamus stop to make camp and to unloose Seaforth from his packhorse. Then it was time to examine the wounded arm. What he saw made him all the more determined to get the earl home as fast as possible. There had been great loss of blood. Seaforth's lips were blue, his face white, his hands palsied. The ropes cutting off circulation had stemmed the bleeding, and a clot of sorts had formed, but the clot was blackish, the edges of the wound purple and angry. Flies had been at it, too, and hung in clumps from it. Shooing the flies away was easy, but it was difficult to bathe the wound without starting the bleeding again. Seamus felt that a man needed all the blood he carried with him. "If the good Lord wanted us rid of our excess blood, he'd arrange regular fluxes for us like he does with our womenfolk." Once the wound was cleansed and bandaged, and the earl rested a bit, they were off again in haste to Scotland and the nearest of the earl's homes, that in Edinburgh.

As Seamus led the horse up St. Mary's Wynd, he was reminded that less than a fortnight before, they had left the Countess of Seaforth there in attendance on the pregnant Queen Margaret. Ten lances, or one hundred men, had gone with the earl, plus thirty mounted men, to join the largest army ever gathered together by a king of Scotland before or since. Now Seamus, the earl, and one borrowed horse were all that returned of the Mackenzie contingent.

Seamus surrendered his charge gladly to the anxious countess. Before he left, however, he blurted out the bad news of her king father and bishop half brother.

"The one loved me much, I'll sorrow for him on the morrow. As for the other . . ." The countess shrugged her shoulders expressively. "Time now for the living; my lord husband and my very faithful Seamus. Now, hie you to your bed. If you collapse here, 'twould take too many of us to carry you."

Seamus managed a weary bow in her direction. Turning to leave, he hadn't taken more than a step or two when her elegant, bejeweled white hand on his arm stopped him.

"Seamus," she said, her blue black eyes shining with unshed tears, "Seamus, how can I thank you for Seaforth's life?"

Seamus, for all his strength, was unable to cope with the emotionalism of a woman. He turned pink with embarrassment and failed to meet her eye. The two stood there at an impasse, until finally the lady took his enormous hand in hers and brought it to her lips. At the touch of her soft lips, the spell was broken, Seamus was released from his immobile state. "Lady," he stammered, "don't— It's late—I—"

"Yes, I know." But she didn't release his hand. "Get you to bed, dear, good, sweet friend."

Looking down into that loving face, he held his breath lest he follow his impulse and kiss her. He breathed a large sigh of relief when finally she released his hand, and he fled from the room like a guilty child. Instinctively he headed for the haven of Nelly's large bed in an alcove off the kitchen. Slaveys, seeing the look in eyes glazed with fatigue and suppressed emotion, made way for his lumbering progress; then, one hastened to alert Nelly to the return of her man. When she rushed to his side, she found him fast asleep, fully dressed, sprawled on his back across the bed. Her attempts to shake him awake went for nought. Pushing and shoving him about, she determined that he had no major wound. Having to be satisfied with that, she unlaced his boots and tugged futilely on one. It didn't budge. Nor were her efforts to remove his tunic more successful; his dead weight was too much for her body heavy with his child. Impervious to her efforts, he slept on, never knowing nor stirring when Nelly joined him in bed. Nor did he awaken when, before dawn, she crept from his side to rouse the kitchen staff. Through breakfast and supper he slept, totally oblivious to the sounds of a large staff preparing, serving, and cleaning up after meals eaten by a staff numbering in the hundreds.

CHAPTER 2

Daylight had dimmed and nighttime was upon them again when Nelly tried once more to awaken Seamus. He woke up swinging, thinking he was back in Flodden. Two months, even six weeks before, she could have dodged his wild blows. Not today. Not with his child due within the month. His cuff sent her reeling across the room to slide down against the wall like a sack of wheat, landing on her bottom with a loud "oof." Seamus, befuddled by sleep, watched dumbfounded for a long minute. Then, realizing what he'd done and immediately contrite, he leaped to his feet, walked out of his loosened boots, and fell his full length on the stones.

"Are you hurt, Nelly girl?" he asked, looking up at her from the floor.

She shook her head. "No thanks to you. And you?"

He looked at her, she at him, and both broke into laughter.

The lackey, at whose instigation she'd awakened her man, stared at the two as if they had lost their senses. And when they made no attempt to get up immediately, he cleared his throat self-importantly to get their attention. "Seamus, the lady sent me for you," he announced, his disapproval of these two big people sounding in every syllable.

"Aye, be right with you," said Seamus, reaching for his boots. While he put them back on, Nelly, with a flurry of white petticoats, rose awkwardly to her own feet. Reaching into the pocket suspended from a cord around her waist, she brought forth a small flask of wine and one well-squashed napkin containing a flattened slab of bread.

"Now, look what you've done," she began, but Seamus hushed her.

"Nay, Nelly, that's just the way I like it," he protested, manfully chewing off a big chunk.

Nelly wasn't mollified; her expression softened, however, as she saw how hard he worked at his chewing while trying to smile at her. "Aye, eat hearty. Drink, too. You been weakened by your long sleep judging from that love-tap you just fetched me."

With that, she gave him a cuff that sent him staggering on his way, for Nelly was as big for a woman as Seamus was for a man. Passing through the kitchen, he paused now and then to wash down the bread with a hearty swig of wine. The lackey, following close on his heels, twice ran into him. Seamus, in disgust, motioned him to lead the way up the stairs to the courtyard . . . only to call him back while he took a piss on the manure pile outside the mew doors. His audience, irritated at first by the delay, was impressed in spite of himself by the strength and duration of the man's relievings.

Finished, his codpiece tied and his points secured, Seamus followed his guide past the chapel and into the hall, behind the screen's passage, up the stair and into the upper chamber of the cross-wing and from there into the solarium. The room, the largest on the second story, was well lit and well peopled. Still a bit muddled, Seamus thought himself come to Bedlam, St. Mary's Hospital for the insane in London.

In the big four-poster bed in the middle of the room lay Seaforth, ignored by his men as they argued among themselves. The countess was deep in debate with Father Cariolinus, the aged family chaplain, and contending between themselves were two total strangers, both ill kept and shabby. The tonsured one Seamus surmised to be a priest–physician.

"God pray," he said silently, "let the man be a little skilled and not simply a horse-leech." Long before, Seamus had come to the decision that it would be better to die than be mangled at the hands of most so-called physicians.

The grubby priest was arguing animatedly with an equally dirty, little man of indeterminate age, his short robe stained, splotched, and grime-encrusted, his boots badly patched and run down at the heels, his stockings sagging about his scrawny calves. This was undoubtedly the priest's barber–assistant. That he had been admitted to this chamber boded no good for the earl.

For the past four hundred years, ever since a papal decree that no priest willingly shed blood, the gorier aspects of medical care had been relegated to a lay brother whose only real expertise with the razor might lie in shaving his priest's tonsure. Such a man bled the patient, drew teeth, and, as Seamus recalled queasily, sawed off limbs.

Off to one side was still a third stranger. His young, apple-cheeked face looked more used to laughter than serious discussion, and his appreciation of the good life showed in the way his fur-trimmed, red woolen physician gown bellied out in front. Belying the overall impression of softness and baby-fat were the firm, muscular hands he clasped before him. Except for his robes, he didn't look like any physician Seamus had seen before. Priest and barber argued over the juxtaposition of Jupiter with Gemini, determining the best time for bleeding. The stranger ignored them. Instead, he studied the subject of all the discussion—the Earl of Seaforth. Doped with opium—the room reeked of it—the man lay in his bed like one already dead. The pallor of his face was incongruous and frightening in a man who gloried in the hunt, the passage of arms, a tilt at the quattrain, and the breaking of a horse. For the first time, Seamus realized, the earl's famous prematurely silver white hair seemed appropriate, for today the earl looked every one of his forty-one years.

Seamus's presence was soon noted by the Lady Islean. Tall, lithe, she was so rosy-cheeked that the gap between her own and her husband's age was accentuated. Drawing Seamus close to the bed, she quickly outlined the situation in a low voice.

"We are all agreed that the wound has mortified." She drew back the quilt of wool from the arm and with a finger disturbed the bandages about the wound to let Seamus see the streaks of red and purple and black radiating out from the wound. The smell of rotting flesh was enough to make a strong man gag, but it seemed to bother the countess not at all.

"You get used to it," she observed as Seamus paled, continuing with her explanation: "We all agree that the arm must come off."

Again outwardly she showed no emotion. "But Father Cariolinus insists that such an act needs not only the sanction of the church but the services of the priest's assistant.

"I had heard," she continued, "that Andrew Boorde—over there—was in Edinburgh, and just now returned from studying at Montpellier, where he actually spent a week watching a surgeon dissect a dead man. It is an act forbidden by the father . . . and Father Cariolinus here, in turn, forbids such a man to touch the earl. Boorde was, it seems, once a Carthusian priest and even suffragan bishop of Chichester. The good father fears he would menace not just my Lord's body, but also his soul."

Seamus said nothing, but looked hard at Boorde, who could not fail to overhear and who returned the look in kind, breaking the stare with a slow, deliberate wink.

That decided Seamus. "Lady, if he is the man you want, he is the man you'll have. Leave the priests to me."

In two strides, he crossed the room to the priest and his assistant, collared one with each hand and quick-marched them toward the door. Totally flustered, Father Cariolinus scurried after, clutching in vain at the giant before him.

Boorde sprang to open the door before them, allowing the intertwined foursome to leave. Outside the door, Seamus shook his two victims like a terrier with a rat and pushed them down the hall. Gently but firmly he disengaged Father Cariolinus from his arm, picking him up and setting him down from the chamber door. "Go, priest, do what you do best. Say a few prayers for the man on the bed in there."

Seamus returned to the chamber and took a stand within the door, barring with his body any from entering. The quacks gone, the physician quickly took stock of the men left in attendance. All, he was sure, had seen their share of bloody limbs at the highly popular drawing-and-quartering of traitors and criminals on High Street. If anything, Boorde feared that instead of withdrawing in disgust, they might press too close. He cleared the room of all but Seamus, four gentlemen of the bedchamber, two servers to do the mopping up, and the patient. The Lady Islean he sent to supervise the cooking of a special salve needed when the sawing and burning were done.

If the earl had been conscious, Boorde would have sedated him with a drink of Malmsey laced with more opium. But an uncon-

41

scious man might choke on such; thus, a gag was made ready in case they might need it later. Building a fire in a three-legged pot he carried for the purpose, he laid out his tools: lancets, big, small and tiny, plus a medley of cauterers, a handful of which he put to heating in the little pot. Out of the sack also came needles and tongs of many sizes, as well as bodkins and stoppered bottles and drawstringed bags. Last of all, he drew out three serrated blades, selecting the largest, with the cruelest teeth. Carefully feeding his little fire until it burnt with a white-hot flame, he emptied one of his bags into a small metal crucible and hung that from the pot's handle.

While it heated, he launched into a monologue, as if lecturing apprentices:

"A fire in the chamber is good, to waste and consume evil vapors within the chamber. I do advise you neither to stand nor to sit by the fire, but stand or sit a good way off from the fire, taking the flavor of it, for fire does arify and dry up a man's blood, and does make stark the sinews and joints of man. In your bed lie not too hot nor too cool, but in a temperance. Ancient doctors of physic said eight hours of sleep in summer and nine in winter is sufficient for any man; but I do think the sleep ought to be taken as is the complexion of the man."

Seamus, still exhausted though he had slept the clock around and then some, had difficulty believing his ears. The smells, the heat, the deathlike earl—all this presided over by a merry man discussing the values of fire and sleep was too much. He had to get out of here for a second to breathe clean air.

"Physician," he interrupted, "is there aught else that you might need?"

The doctor looked about the chamber and nodded. "A table—a good, solid one, the length at least of that man there . . . and of the same width or more. And some wine. A Malmsey if you please."

Seamus felt like one released from Hell as he left the room, the two lackeys in reluctant tow. They had been drinking in the words of the doctor and were loath to leave. When Seamus returned with a trestle table brought up from the great hall below, the doctor was still carrying on.

"When you be out of your bed, stretch forth your legs and arms and your body, cough and spit." He demonstrated, then continued.

"After you have evacuated your body..." He paused. Seamus feared another demonstration, but the doctor wanted merely to check the temperature of the contents of the crucible. "Near at heat. Now, where did I leave off? Oh, yes. After you have evacuated your body and trussed your points, comb your head so and do so divers times in the day. And wash your hands and wrists, your face and eyes and your teeth, with cold water."

He stopped. The crucible was bubbling away, and from among his jars, he selected one, slowly emptying it into his concoction. The crucible hissed, and the room filled with the smell of roses. Seamus's stomach lurched, then steadied. As Seamus gently lifted the earl to the table and lashed him fast, the doctor sniffed, then savored the bouquet of the wine.

"A good vintage this, I ha' never had better. Oh, you'd best remove the bandages from his arm," he directed, then devoted himself to guzzling the wine.

Wiping his lips fastidiously on the arm of his gown, he upended the wine jug well above the furthest reach of the poison's streaking. The dregs he sloshed over his own hands to wash them. Just below the elbow, he made his first cut with the largest lancet, a bold brave stroke that caused blood to well up; whereupon the earl came awake, screaming. Seamus's hand over his mouth stilled further sounds, while the physician got up the gag. At Boorde's direction, Seamus let go. Seaforth opened his mouth to scream, and Boorde deftly popped in the gag. Whistling tunelessly, Boorde went back to work, cutting away as the patient's eyes bulged, and the veins and muscles in his neck stood forth in mute token to the strength of each muffled scream until finally, mercifully, he fainted.

Deeper the lancet probed, and the blood spurted. Undismayed, Boorde took up his white-hot cauters and slapped them on the wound. The smell of cooking flesh added to the nightmarish quality of the scene. Boorde, Seamus admitted, seemed to know well his business and didn't waste a moment. Other than the whistling, he made no sound until the flesh had been cut through all around and scraped from the bone. With the bone bared, Boorde took up his monologue where he'd left off, this time rhythmically punctuating his comments with a rasping stroke of his saw.

"Exercise is good...

"in moderation . . .

"do some labor . . .

"or play at the tennis . . .

"or cast a bowl . . .

"or poise weights . . .

"or plummet lead in your hands . . .

"or do some other thing . . .

"to open your pores . . .

"and to augment natural heat."

The bone was almost severed, and Boorde's forehead was beaded with the sweat of his exertion.

Seamus's shirt was sweat-soaked, too, but from tension. The sounds of the saw traveled to the bottom of his feet and back up his spine and set his teeth on edge. The others in the room seemed not the least unnerved.

Suddenly, arm and elbow separated. Ignored, the arm fell to the floor as all grabbed for the stump which, released of its anchor, flopped wildly about, strewing blood in a shower of gore upon all those grouped around the earl's improvised bed.

"Here, friend Seamus," Boorde said in good humor, "give me a hand with his lackahand." The doctor seemed pleased with his joke as he handed Seamus the large tongs, the curve of which fitted tightly around the wriggling earl's bicep. "Hold it steady now while I coat it with burnt lead."

Slowly he began to pour the rose-scented molten lead from its crucible. As the first drop dribbled onto the living flesh, the earl's body galvanized in one violent convulsion, then ceased moving. Whether he had fainted or died, Seamus couldn't tell, nor could he spare a glance at the moment. The hot lead on the moist flesh sent up a cloud of blinding steam. Eyes closed, holding his breath against the stink, Seamus steadied the tongs to hold the foreshortened arm upright lest the molten metal find its way onto other flesh.

Once the stump was coated to the physician's satisfaction, he put the crucible aside and declared the operation a success. "Of course," he admitted, cheerfully scraping moist bone chips from the blade of his saw with thumb and forefinger, "the patient probably will not live. However, occasionally one of mine does. Now, while we wait for the metal to cool before I bandage the stump, how might I be of further service to you?''

Andrew, first gentleman of the bedchamber, complained of a toothache. For him Boorde recommended, "purges and gargles if the ache is due to a descending humor. Chewing horehound root is the French remedy. But if the ache be due to worms, then impregnate a candle with henbane seeds. Sit you with the mouth open to allow the perfumery entrance. This will stupefy the worms and they will fall into the basin of water you place in your lap. Then catch them and kill them on your nail.''

Almost as an afterthought, Boorde warned, "Beware of giving over a tooth to be drawn out by the Pelican or the Davier. Pull one and pull out more, I always say.''

For another's insomnia, Boorde's advice was in keeping with his whole mien: "To bedward go merry. Let not anger nor heaviness, sorrow nor pensivefulness, trouble nor worry disquiet you. Be sure the windows of the house, specially of your chamber, be closed. When you be in your bed, lie a little while on your left side, but sleep on your right side, that troubles the heart less.''

As he went about handing out advice, Boorde was also quietly packing up his sack. At last, jabbing within the mouth of the comatose man with his forefinger, he deftly plopped the gag out into his other hand. As he did so, the earl moaned, and Seamus held his breath, silently praying the man would not awaken yet. With his free hand Boorde tested the heat from the wound. "Not yet time to bandage the wound.'' Tossing the gag into his sack, he laughed impishly. "Are you Scots less than other men? No one has asked about white leprosy. Do you men not use too much Venus acts or are you somehow immune? In France, many a physician makes his living treating these sad victims of love.'' The gentlemen of the bedchamber demurred for themselves but did have a friend in need of such a cure and so pressed the good doctor on.

"There are at least three cures, my friends: finely powder a root of gentian and mix it with its own juice and white vinegar in a poultice. Have you no gentian, use madder root but add a dram of sugar. Apply freely. However, many swear that the best remedy of all is the simplest: take a scarlet cloth and rub yourself well with it.

Then take a handful of mandragora leaves and do the same. Twice a day do this until the skin grows back pink and whole. But rub not too hard lest you get yourself in a different humor, for especially now should you avoid the usage of a harlot or whore."

Spitting on his forefinger, he tested the lead on the wound and announced it cool enough. As he bandaged, he continued his dissertation. "Avoid you harlots, they are unclean. Do not think you can tell from their smell whether they be in good health or not, for I will tell you the harlot's secret. She does stand over a chafing dish of coals, like my crucible there, and into it she puts brimstone and, using her skirts as a tent, perfumes herself. Later she smells clean, but she is not. If you do meddle with such a woman and then meddle with another, you shall burn not just yourself but the other as well. You, if so burnt, best wash your secrets two or three times with white wine and seek out a surgeon. If this goes untreated, the guts will burn and fall out of the belly."

As Boorde was speaking, John Nairn turned pale and suddenly clutched himself protectively. "Physician, is there no other cure?" he choked.

Boorde adjusted the final bandage on the earl's stump slowly and meticulously. Then, as if in deep thought, he answered, "I have heard of such a one. It's an anointment that sometimes has the desired results. But, alas, it is most complicated to make."

When he did not continue, Nairn pressed him on. "Good doctor, for a man in such extremity, no cure is too difficult to undertake. And my friend would be most eager to show his generosity for your trouble."

Boorde considered a moment and then nodded agreeably. "Well, then, for your friend. Take boar's grease and powdered brimstone—"

"Good doctor, go slow," Nairn interrupted, counting the first two items out on his fingers to commit them to memory.

"Powdered brimstone," said Boorde, "and the inside bark from a vine that grows in a churchyard. Add the greenish deposit scraped from a copper pot. Or if you have not copper, use brass or bronze. Then you must get five ounces of quicksilver . . . and another of fasting spit, but not all need come from the same man. Two or three of your—I mean his—fellows may contribute theirs too. Beat this together and apply to the sores."

Nairn would have left the room then and there to begin gathering the ingredients together, but Boorde called him back. "Now, this is a cure, as I say, for the pocky person who has taken his case from lechery. But, it is of no avail if the cause of the case is sodomy. The cure for that, young man, is truly extreme," and Boorde heartily clapped the young man on the shoulder. "A cure simple yet dire." He paused for effect. "Marriage."

The men all laughed, except for Seamus, who having kept his silence so far had had enough of this talk of sin, cures and ills. He wanted the earl back in his bed, the countess at his bedside. "Be you gossips finished?"

Boorde took the hint. "Yes, yes, friend Seamus, by all means we are through. Get your master back in his bed, and one of you summon your mistress." While the men followed his bidding, Boorde retrieved the now-lifeless forearm and hand from the pool of blood under the table.

Taking Seamus aside, he asked in a low voice, "Friend Seamus, do you think the duchess would give me this arm, seeing that the earl will not need it?" Seamus, shocked, didn't reply. Thoughtfully, Boorde manipulated the fingers one by one. "It's a good hand, a strong one, one that has probably served its owner well in life."

Seamus reached for the limb, but Boorde did not release it. "Nay, good Seamus, it's not what you think. I would not make this into a curiosity for the prying to see. I would have it to use to teach my students how their limbs work. I know the law forbids operating on the dead, but surely an arm freely given would not cause the authorities alarm." Seamus only stood there looking down at the grisly bloody remnant of the earl that he and the red-robed doctor clutched fast between them. Boorde with a sigh reluctantly released his grip. "You shall have it, my hand on it." Again the play on words pleased him and restored his good humor. He made Seamus just the slightest of bows and then returned to the bedside of his patient. Holding the arm at his arm's length, Seamus walked to the nearest chest, pulled out a cloth—a bright red one, he remembered later—and swaddled the bloody thing.

Just as he finished, the duchess appeared with a small ewer of salve clutched to her bosom like a magic talisman. Immediately, the doctor was again workmanlike, launching into the treatment of the patient. "The metal coating will fall off, lady, but do not worry. Wash the wound daily with vinegar or wine if you have it; sack is very good, too. Then apply the salve. . . ."

Seamus, his bundle in hand, stealthily edged his way toward the door as the physician continued. "He should awake soon. Dose him with opium. Within a day or two his wits may return. Fear not if he tells you his hand itches or suffers pins and needles. 'Tis a trick the 'Natural Spirit' plays on the body as it attempts to rejuvenate that which can't grow back."

The Lady Islean seemed not to hear. Her face had gone white as the featherbed; her eyes fixed on the smooth sheet that should have bulged from the presence of a lower right arm beneath. Seamus, grasping the clumsy bundle behind him, thought he'd never reach the door, then suddenly was through it.

On his way to the stair, he could hear the physician's hearty, healthy, almost happy voice follow: "Lady, if his wits do not return within the week, purge his head with a sternutation. White hellebore, if you can obtain it. Otherwise, simple pepper blown into the nostrils will effect a good sneeze. Do that daily until . . ."

Seamus raced down the stairs and into the great hall where he found the servers preparing for dinner. He slowed his pace, lest he draw untoward attention, but moved on with purpose and without pausing to be questioned in depth.

Once outside the hall, he paused, his shirt soaked with sweat. Taking a deep breath, Seamus for the first time faced the consequences of his action. Rescuing the arm had been instinctive, an impulse. Now what to do with it?

In desperation, he turned, like the good Catholic he was, to the Church. Since he accepted the Church's tenet that parts of the body were hallowed having partaken of the Sacraments along with the whole, what better caretaker was there for such a part? Let Father Cariolinus take the problem of the disembodied arm on his prayer-stooped shoulders.

Such was his feeling of relief that, almost jauntily, he tucked his lord's arm under his like a parcel of dead fish from the market. In the small antechamber off the chapel he found his priest. But not alone. The priest, the priest–physician and the priest–assistant had evidently continued the discussion that had begun in the solarium up above. Now, fueled by a goodly draught of the earl's piment, a sour, thin wine sweetened with honey, they waxed philosophical. Seamus, debating what to do, stood at the door, unseen and unheeded, and listened as the unsavory duo pompously lectured the older, holier family priest. Seamus, once he caught the drift, grew ever more disgusted.

What the priest–physician expounded, his barber–assistant, in a helpful echo, explained.

"Hippocratemus," began the physician priest . . .

"A learned man that, even if a Greek," confided the barber. "Discovered the immortal nature of man's complexion centuries ago."

"Better than a whole hundred years that was from our present time," came the envying murmur.

"There are four elements one should know,"

"Fire, air, earth, and water, they are."

"and these four elements have attributes . . ."

"Heat, cold, dryness, and moisture," mouthed the barber. "which fix the complexion."

An upraised hand stopped the barber's explanation before he could begin. The priest–physician leaned forward and looked the chaplain deep in the eye. "We in the Church who know our medicine—and that, my friend, after tonight shall include you—we no longer say complexion. We call it temperament." Leaning back, self-satisfied that he had made his point, he nodded to his assistant as if to say, now we go on, but Seamus had had enough. He knew not whether the doctor upstairs or the priest and barber downstairs were equally learned men or all quacks, or one the former, the others the latter. He didn't know and simply didn't care. He was sick up to his chin with all this medical talk. He wanted rid of the earl's arm, which minute by minute seemed to grow heavier; he could almost hear its blood pouring out.

Interrupting the threesome, he tried to keep his voice pleasant: "Ah, here you are. I've been looking the manor over for you. The Lady Islean wishes to do more than merely thank you, priest. She would have you and your assistant see the earl's Lord Controller, who is just without, in conference with the butler in the great hall. You are to tell the Lord Controller that the Lady Islean wishes you be paid"— he paused and mentally halved what he thought the countess would have wanted, figuring that between the chapel and the hall, somehow the amount would double—"twenty silver pennies for your labors. Of course, there is no hurry. If he be gone, I shall personally bring you those twenty pennies." The partners exchanged looks as if to say, better the controller. Avarice conquering their need to impress, these two exponents of modern medicine hastily took their leave.

Once the two had scurried out of sight, Seamus knelt before the white-robed Dominican friar. Silently, he held out his bundle toward the priest. Without thinking, Father Cariolinus took it and cradled it in his arms. He was about to unwrap the bright red swaddling when an unpleasant thought stopped him. "Is this his—?"

Seamus nodded.

The priest swallowed. It was one thing, he thought, to see a traitor drawn and quartered, his limbs chopped off, his guts spilled; that was just punishment seen at the distance of one's choosing. It was another to be handed a true live—no, not live, he corrected himself—a true fragment of a friend. He shuddered with revulsion and thrust the bundle back at Seamus, but Seamus's upheld palm stopped it.

The priest was perplexed. His duties as chaplain to the Seaforths had never exposed him to a similar situation. Despite belonging to an order devoted to scholarly work, Father Cariolinus had somehow avoided the byways of esoteric theoretical theology. Seaforth had requested as chaplain a man who was more living exemplar than learned sermonizer, and Father Cariolinus was well-suited to such a domestic role. One look at the frail, stoop-shouldered monk whose expression radiated inner goodness had persuaded Seaforth that this was a wise choice.

"What would you have me do with it?" the priest whispered.

"Could you not say some words o'er it?" Seamus whispered back.

"Words?" whispered the dazed priest aloud, at the bundle he cradled in his arms.

"Bless it, maybe. Give it a sprinkling of your holy water. This arm has done its share of deeds and not all them good, I warrant."

"My blessing? Yes, of course, and the holy water. Good thinking, friend Seamus. Follow me." Determinedly, he led Seamus into the chapel, through the nave and into the apse. Genuflecting briefly

50

before the altar, he went around it behind the rood screen, and into the sacristy. There, while poising the bundle upon his hip as would a mother with her babe, he took up a small purplish glass flagon. Still governed by some unspoken resolve and trailed by a puzzled but obedient Seamus, he returned to the sanctuary and proceeded to the baptismal font.

"Here, hold it," he commanded, holding out the arm. Seamus, before he could refuse, found himself again custodian of the arm in its wrappings—as red as a Scottish bride's finery. The priest removed the cover from the font and placed the flagon, after unstopping it, within its proper receptacle.

"Open the wrappings," the priest directed, and Seamus, although he wanted nothing more than to refuse, found himself unwinding the cloth from around the limb. Except for the contorted hand with its massive golden Mer-Lion ring, it looked more like a slightly hairy leg of mutton than the once-living arm of a man. The priest blanched and closed his eyes in disbelief as he murmured in Latin an almost inaudible prayer, then continued in Scots:

> "Hear, O Lord, the sound of my call; have pity on me, and answer me. Of you my heart speaks; you my glance seeks, your presence, O Lord I seek.
>
> Hide not your face from me; do not in anger repel your servant. You are my helper: cast me not off; forsake me not, O God my savior. Though my father and mother forsake me, yet will the Lord receive me."

Then, they waited. The priest quietly, motionlessly. Seamus, with growing impatience as the arm cradled cautiously in his hands grew heavier and heavier, and, it seemed to him, wetter and wetter. He strained his ears for a telltale drip, but the silence was complete. At last the priest, his eyes still tight shut, spoke again—still in Scots, but this time joyously:

> Blessed be the Lord for he has heard the sound of my pleading, the Lord is my strength and my shield.

In him my heart trusts and I find help; then my heart exults, and with my song, I give him thanks.

The priest appeared a different man. Drawing confidence from somewhere, he seemed to know exactly what to do. He began anew and this time in Latin. The words were familiar ones; and when he paused for a reponse, Seamus answered without thinking, then realized the priest was saying Mass. Gradually his voice grew stronger, he began to gesture and project as if to a gathering.

Seamus, puzzled, looked about. Perhaps others had entered the chapel. But no, the two men and the limb were alone. Turning his attention back to the priest, he realized the other had opened his eyes and, irritated, was looking at him. "Well?"

Seamus, bewildered, temporized with "Et cum spiritu tuo."

"Nay, I asked you a question. Do you agree?"

Agree? Agree to what? Seamus feared to ask. Instead, he nodded his head. But the priest wasn't satisfied. He hissed, "Say 'I do.' "

"I do," the giant rumbled back uncertainly; best humor the priest, he decided.

Cariolinus: "Dost thou renounce Satan?"

Seamus: "I do."

Cariolinus: "And all his pomps?"

Seamus: "I do."

Cariolinus: "Dost thou believe in God, the Father Almighty, Creator of heaven and earth?"

Seamus: "I do."

Cariolinus: "Dost thou believe in Jesus Christ, his only Son, Our Lord, who was born of the Virgin Mary, was crucified, died, and was buried, rose from the dead, and is now seated at the right hand of the Father?"

Seamus: "I do."

Cariolinus: "Do you believe in the Holy Spirit, the Holy Catholic Church, the communion of saints, the forgiveness of sins, the resurrection of the body, and life everlasting?"

Seamus: "I do."

Cariolinus: "This is our faith. This the faith of the Church. We are proud to profess it, in Christ Jesus our Lord. Amen."

Seamus: "Amen."

Cariolinus: "Is it your will that this arm be baptized in the faith of the Church which we have all professed with you?"

Seamus choked.

He stood there speechless as the realization sank in. Not only had he taken part in the Sacrament of Baptism for a dead arm, but he was also being made to stand godfather to it. Inside, he wanted to scream out his "No! Never! Not I!"; instead in answer to the priest's unwavering stare, he heard himself say, "I do."

The priest, sprinkling the holy water, sonorously pronounced: "Arm, I baptize you in the name of the Father, and of the Son, and of the Holy Ghost. Arm, go in peace, and may the Lord be with you."

Seamus, essentially a god-fearing man even less versed in theology than the priest, wondered if such a baptism might be considered blasphemy . . . and if so, what supernatural being could have taken possession of the priest. He shuddered to think what all of this might portend for the priest . . . himself . . . and Seaforth. The sooner this arm was disposed of the better.

The priest began to tremble. "Quick, wrap it up. I can't stand the sight of it," Father Cariolinus confessed. "Besides, someone might find us with it."

Fumbling with the now stiffening arm, Seamus held it in one hand, red wrappings trailing, while with his free hand he tugged powerfully at the Mer-Lion signet ring on the grotesquely flexed, yet rigidly inflexible, index finger. Suddenly, the finger bent, the ring came off. Rewrapping the arm quickly, he looked again to the priest for guidance,

"What now?"

"Now?"

"Now!"

"We give it Christian burial."

"Father, 'twould be madness. If we're caught, no one will believe we're burying the arm. They'll think us grave robbers."

"Then I suggest we not be found in a graveyard. We'll bury the arm in a place I know at St. Giles. Next week, when Seaforth dies, we can retrieve it and bury the arm and the man together."

"Father, do you know what you say?" groaned the new-made godfather.

"I know that arm has been baptized and blest. It deserves Christian burial and it shall get it." Once determined on a course of action, Father Cariolinus had the same fixation of purpose that makes men martyrs. "Give me but a moment to get my breviary."

"Father, have you no' said enough over this arm? After all, it is no' a man you're burying, just his arm."

The priest drew himself up to his full height, a head shorter than Seamus, and seemed so firm in righteous indignation that Seamus gave in.

"Father, while you do so, best get your black cloak also. Your white habit will give us away in the dark. But hurry," he called after the priest who had put action into words and disappeared behind the rood screen.

The priest returned walking slowly, like a man whose parole has been revoked, but properly cloaked and ready to leave. Seamus gave him no chance to change his mind. Firmly tucking the dead arm under his own left, he grabbed the priest's arm with his free hand and propelled the three of them forward and out of the chapel.

Keeping within the shadows of St. Mary's Wynd, they made their way past Blackfriars Wynd and the archepiscopal palace of Cardinal Beaton, the "Burning Beaton," who pursued heresy without mercy, swiftly consigning sinners to the stake. Seamus wondered what the cardinal would do if he knew that earlier that night one of his priests had baptized an arm and given it a spiritual mentor . . . and further that priest and godparent were on their way to bury the arm at Beaton's own cathedral. At the thought, Seamus so quickened his pace that the priest at his side soon gasped for mercy.

Once at St. Giles, they went past the graveyard and on to the church itself. The three massive doors to the south had all been fastened. Carefully picking their way—for there was little moonlight and the south vestibule had juttings of statuary—they finally stumbled onto the modest porch on the west with its smaller, unlocked doorway.

Inside, they faced complete blackness until their eyes adjusted. Father Cariolinus now became guide, cautioning Seamus in a whisper now and again to step up or down as they traversed the aisle and crossed the transept, their footsteps echoing loudly upon the marble floor.

"Where are we?" asked Seamus.

"Shush, not so loud. There's a brother somewhere about charged with keeping watch," the priest whispered. "We have just left the nave and should be under the tower about now. Trust me, I know where we go."

The church was large—206 feet long across the transepts—but it seemed four or five times that to Seamus. Finally, Father Cariolinus stopped, Seamus bumbling solidly into him. The priest went sprawling, sending something metallic crashing to the floor. Seamus dropped the arm, and somewhere within the church a door opened with a grating sound. Just so must the gates of Hell rattle, Seamus surmised, when they open to admit some poor sinner.

"Quick, Seamus, the arm," hissed the priest, "give it to me."

"I do no' have it," the giant rumbled back, busily crawling about on all fours, desperately searching the floor in circles about him with outstretched hands for that other hand. He touched something with his left hand, but before he could do more than grab, his right touched something also. "Is that your hand, Father?" he whispered, freezing in his tracks.

"What hand? You touch me not," came the whisper from behind him.

"Then, I've found something," Seamus whispered back, still absolutely immobile. Nearby he could hear the priest's robes rustling on the floor; in the distance, footsteps paced eerily, now ebbing, now advancing. Again and again, out of the corner of his eye, Seamus saw a stab of light, as if from a torch, pierce the darkness of the transept they had traversed.

"What is it?"

Seamus jumped, the voice was at his ear. "Feel down my right arm with your hand." He could feel the priest do as he was told.

"Ah, you found Seaforth's arm."

"Then, what the hell am I holding in my other hand?"

"Shame Seamus. No cursing before God's altar."

"Answer my question."

"You have both."

"*Both?*" Seamus screamed in a whisper.

"Of course. Hand them to me, I'll put them away."

It took all of Seamus's willpower to pass over first one, then the other of the two hands—both were so hard and so cold to the touch. Only when the second had left his grasp did the pain in his knees remind him that he had balanced motionlessly upon them for these many long moments. He would have risen, but the priest's hand stopped him. "Here, help me lift this up. Quickly! The brother comes."

With Seamus doing most of the heaving, the two of them lifted the heavy metal object above their heads and slid it onto the altar before which they knelt. As they did, the priest began chanting in a quiet voice.

"What are you doing? The watcher will be here," Seamus was frantic. "No time for that, let us out of here."

"Quiet! *Kyrie eleison,*" he chanted, then in an aside commanded, "Pray!"

"Ho, who's there?" called a suspicious voice from their left. The torch, raised high, cast its beam upon them, reflecting off the gleaming tonsure of the still-chanting priest, kneeling before the altar. Reassured by the sight, the brother came closer.

"*Ideo precor beatam Mariam semper Virginem, beatum Michaelem Archangelum,*" chanted Seamus, reciting the first thing to come into his head.

"Don't stop," Father Cariolinus demanded quietly. Ceasing his own chanting, he gathered his robes about him, then laid a heavy hand on Seamus's shoulder, using it as a crutch, simultaneously forcing the young giant to remain kneeling and praying.

"*Beatum Joannem Baptistim, sanctos Apostolos Petrum et Paulum, Omnes Sanctos.*"

As Father Cariolinus moved nearer the torchlight he was recognized. "What do you do here, Father, at this hour?"

"*Et te, Pater, orare pro me ad Dominum Deum nostrum.*" Seamus had come to the end of the confessional. What now? In desperation, he began over again, praying the brother would be too interested in the Dominican priest's explanation to notice the repetition.

"Not my idea, frater, his. Our earl, as you may have heard, has taken a deadly wound in the arm. They may have to amputate. Nothing would do but that Seamus would have me accompany him here to pray to St. Giles for the earl's safety."

"Aye, we have many who appeal to the Saint for succor for the

wounded"—despite his words the brother still sounded suspicious—
"but few come at midnight. And none in the dark."

"The Saints do not sleep, that's why the church is kept open, is it
not?" the father replied. "Besides, we did have light, but the giant
there stumbled over his own big feet and dropped it. Didn't you hear
the clatter? I feared it might wake the dead!"

"I heard something. But the only one you woke, I fear, was I. I
must have dozed off. Well, no matter. Do you stay much longer? I
can keep you company with my torch."

Seamus had had enough of prayers. Crossing himself reverently,
he slowly rose to his feet, his eyes slowly coming up level with the
metallic case he had just helped put in place. The reliquary was, on
closer inspection and in torchlight, a beauteous thing. Now Seamus
could understand how something so small could be so heavy. It was
covered with cloisonné in a rainbow of sparkling shades. Never had
Seamus seen its like, at least not up this close. He was a man more
familiar with kitchens and stables than altars within a cathedral.
And, under the circumstances, he preferred to save a closer inspection for some other time.

"Are you ready, my son?" the chaplain asked solicitously.

"Aye, father. More than." Approaching the two men, priest and
serving brother, he genuflected before the latter. "Your blessings,
lord bishop?"

The priest, flattered, opened his mouth to deny the title, then
decided if the foolish peasant thought he had the appearance of so
worthy a servant of Christ, why disillusion him. Instead, with a wink
for the chaplain, the brother unctuously gave his benediction to the
still-kneeling giant. Then, he ushered the two men out, conversing
the while with the chaplain regarding state of the Earl of Seaforth's
health. As they were leaving, Seamus turned to the brother and
asked, with genuine curiosity, "Does the Saint grant many of the
prayers?"

"Ah, the tales I could tell you," he sighed. "Of course, usually
only the prayers of those who buy and light candles are granted."

Seamus took the hint and reached into his nearly flat purse and
pulled out a coin. "Then light one for my lord, if you will, and say
a prayer for him."

"I will, and if you would hear of miracles, return tomorrow." The brother palmed the coin expertly and barely waited until the two men had descended from the porch before he assayed its quality between his teeth. Tin! He was disgusted. But then, what could he expect from a servant so ignorant and easily impressed as to think him a lord bishop. Of course, *I do look a bit like Beaton, especially about the middle,* he thought, patting himself heartily.

Seamus could scarcely wait until they were out of earshot to ask his questions. But Father Cariolinus would have none of them. "I am tired. I am not so facile as you with my tongue. Nor does twisting the truth come easy to me. Leave me to my rosary, I must ask forgiveness of God for my venal sins of this night."

Seamus was adamant. "Just one question, good father, only one."

Finally, the priest gave in. "Well, what is it?"

"The other hand? Whose was it?"

"St. Giles's, of course, to whom the cathedral is dedicated. The patron saint of cripples like our poor earl."

"But the cathedral has been here hundreds of years."

"I know. So, has the hand."

"I felt it. It was whole. And no more cold than Seaforth's."

"Blessed be the works of our Lord."

Seamus wasn't content. "How will we know which is which later?"

"By the feel."

"What do you mean?"

"Your hands will tell you. Your nose, too. The hand that rots will be the earl's."

"You mean I'll have to go back and get it out again myself?"

"Who else?" the priest replied in his most saintly, unperturbed voice. "You are the arm's spirtual guardian, aren't you?"

Groaning in reply, Seamus hastily crossed himself, wishing now that he'd asked the fat watch-brother to light a candle and say a prayer for the Irish victim of this night's work. The chaplain beside him paid him no heed; he was too busy saying his beads: 150 Hail Marys, 15 Our Fathers, and 15 Glory Be to the Fathers, as well. It would take him the whole trip back, and then some, to finish it.

Left to his thoughts and dwelling upon his new, totally unasked-for position in life as godfather to a dead right arm, he remembered that the Earl of Seaforth for the past four years had been a father himself. Not once, however, since his return with the earl's body hanging practically lifeless from the packhorse had Seamus caught sight of the boy. Of course, Seamus admitted to himself, he had not gone out of his way to look for the child. Worriedly he interrupted the priest, "Have you seen the young master?"

The priest would have to start his rosary all over again. Only a godly man such as the chaplain could have borne the interruption so patiently. "I did, I believe, see the child earlier this day."

"Not tonight?"

"Tonight? No. Well, let me think. No—yes, Yes! He was there when the physicians arrived. I remember asking him why he was up so late and if he had studied his catechism."

"Then, best say a prayer for him too, Father, if he suspected the purpose of these late night arrivals."

He quickened his pace until the priest had to run to keep up, Seamus saying his own prayer for Lady Islean. "Oh, God, no more. Father dead, husband wounded near unto death, do not let anything happen to her son."

Returning to the house on St. Mary's Wynd, Seamus organized a search, cautioning the servants not to let the lady know that there was any problem. Seamus wondered where he would go if he were small, confused, and fearful for his own father's life. To the mews! Inside that dark, but warm and somehow alive place with its rhythmic sounds of horses' chomping on hay, swishing their tails and stomping their feet. Seamus made his way to the stalls of his own favorites: the famous destriers. The tall grays. The "Great Horses" for whose breeding the Mackenzies of Seaforth were famous.

These enormous, awesome horses fascinated him, and unless his memory proved him wrong, they had always had a certain fascination for little boys as well. Seamus realized as he proceeded down the rows of stalls, answering the demands of outstretched velvety, curious muzzles, that he had not paid much attention to the Lady Islean's child before. Was it, he asked himself, because he couldn't bear to admit that another man had begotten a child upon his lady's body? By denying the child, was he denying Seaforth possession, above and beyond what Seamus himself had, of the Lady Islean?

He stopped short. Tonight was a night of unwanted revelations.

He loved the lady, and even, at one time, had wished Seaforth dead. But no longer. The trip back from Flodden Field, the scene in the solarium, and then the rite in the chapel followed by the ordeal in the cathedral—all these had cleansed Seamus somehow. True, he loved the Lady Islean. But did he lust after her still? Yes. He admitted that, too. Would he gladly give his right arm to Seaforth if he could have the lady in return? Yes, oh God, yes.

But such desires, he also knew, were the dreamings of simpletons. He had to face reality. If the lord lived (and Seamus for the first time realized he loved the man and wanted him to continue), Seaforth would be crippled, unable to lead the life he had pursued before. To tourney, to hunt, to joust, to dance, to fight, to make music, to do all the things he had been trained from childhood to do—these things were now out of the realm of possibility for James Mackenzie, Fourth Earl of Seaforth. Now, more than ever, he would need his lady wife. And she would need Seamus.

And if the earl didn't survive? Could Seamus hope that the daughter of a king, the widow of the fifth-ranking earl in the land, would look with favor upon a bought man, a serving man, a horsegroom? Could Seamus himself accept her alliance with a man as ill-born as himself?

Standing there, absently stroking a horse, Seamus vowed not to love his Lady Islean less but to attempt to love her husband more . . . and to forgive the child his father. The child! Seamus, disgusted with himself for his self-pity and introspection, remembered why he was here.

Down the line of stalls he went, to the big airy box stalls, three times the size of a standing stall, which each great horse needed just to be able to turn around. Each animal had to bear a full 700 pounds of man and armor while charging at great speed, turning with agility, responding with alacrity, not for just minutes or hours but for days on end. The bigger the horses were, Seamus had discovered, the more gentle they seemed to be, at least with him. Even those who knew to strike out on command with rear or forefeet at the enemy—and even to bite if needful—were, without exception and contrary to the other stablemen's belief, of the most even temperament. Even Dunstan, the famed stud named after the patron of horses, St.

Dunstan of the twelfth century, was gentler toward a child than one of the Lady Islean's jennets.

It was at Dunstan's stall that he found what he was looking for: a small, black-haired child with astonishingly blue eyes. Perched on the edge of the feed trough, he was hand-feeding hay, one blade at a time, to this horse that needed bales of such per day just to stay alive. Yet the mighty Dunstan, gravely and courteously, took each blade when proffered and chewed it properly to the child's satisfaction before James Mackenzie, Master of Seaforth and Viscount Alva, picked another sprig from the large mound of fresh-mown hay before him and laid it across the palm of his hand for the stallion to mouth.

"You don't fear that you overfeed him?" asked Seamus dryly, breaking the silence.

"Oh no, Master Seamus, I'm being very careful."

"I see what you mean."

Seamus hitched himself up and onto the trough alongside the child. For a while the two took turns feeding the horse. When Seamus, out of pity, cheated once—offering the horse a good five pieces—a small hand knocked the offenders out of his palm and into the stall. Poor Dunstan went after it, but the child jumped down and picked up the five contrary pieces. Looking up in the moonlight at Seamus, his eyes were dark and his countenance grave.

"Don't do that, Master Seamus. You, above all men, should know it's bad to overfeed a horse."

Reaching down, Seamus gripped the young boy under the armpits. A disquieting memory suddenly came to mind, but he put it from him. Hoisting the boy back into place on the trough, he said, "And equally bad to underfeed."

The boy digested that for a few moments. Then with a laugh he reached down and grabbed two handfuls of the grass and threw them into the air. As they came swirling down about the startled horse, Dunstan retreated. But hunger got the best of him, and freed from the restraint of his own good manners, he fell to eating heartily.

The two, the little boy and the giant of a man, sat there in companionship watching the earl's favorite charger attack his food as if it were an enemy to be conquered.

"Poor Dunstan," said the boy, "he won't eat heartily anymore."

Seamus was puzzled. "Why is that, my lord?"

"He'll have no one to exercise him. So we'll need cut back on his rations, won't we, Seamus?" And the blue eyes, so disconcertingly like those of the Lady Islean, challenged him to disagree.

Seamus took his time answering. For the first time, he was looking at his lady's son. The child was beautiful. The head well shaped, the eyes large and fringed with thick lashes. The nose—his mother's—might have been more patrician, but Seamus felt certain that it would lose its upturned pertness with maturity. The mouth was generous, the lips neither thin or full, the chin determined.

The body was that of a healthy animal. Vigorous, well exercised, and, except for legs a shade too long, well proportioned. Not an inch of fat was there that Seamus could see. Overall, the impression was of sturdiness, shoulders and thighs stretching his jerkin and tights. The legs were so well shaped, Seamus saw, that if they kept their proportions, they would one day make women grow wild. All in all, Seamus decided, he had never seen a more pleasing child.

The child awaited his answer. Seamus had too much sense to deny the truth, but he had an inspiration. "Yes, for the while we'll have to cut back. But only until your father chooses to ride him again. Of course, you and I could see that he's exercised properly, if you wish."

Jamie considered that, mulling it over before he answered. Seamus liked that. As one who, except for his swearing, was essentially laconic, he found it refreshing that the child didn't run on and on. Finally Jamie spoke. "Yes, I think that would be fitting. I'd like that but, more important, so would Dunstan. Are we then agreed?" Jamie smiled.

The unearthly beauty of that smile, so like his mother's, took Seamus's breath away. He only nodded. The child, contented, his world put in order at last, grew grave, looked Seamus full in the eye, and commanded, "Then help me down, Master Seamus. It is long past my bedtime, I must not tarry here."

Only as they were about to leave the mews did the little boy venture a question. "Will he live, do you think, Master Seamus?" Try as he might, the boy couldn't keep the catch out of his voice.

"He's a good man, a godly man, a clean-living man," Seamus temporized.

Jamie ignored the obvious, and seized upon the essential. "Is clean living important, then?"

"Oh, very."

"More than praying?"

Seamus fell back upon his area of expertise. "I don't know. But the horse with good habits, who eats temperately, getting neither thick nor thin, seems to live the longest and *heal* the fastest."

"My father never gets thick nor thin."

"No, he always stays just right."

"So he should heal fast. But just the same, I'll pray for him. Will you pray for him, too, Seamus?"

"With all my heart, my lord, and for your good mother as well."

There was a long pause. "Pray for me too, Seamus."

"For you too, my lord."

Content that the conversation had gone the way he wished, the child said no more, but left Seamus and started across the courtyard toward the outside stair that led up to the family's apartments. Seamus watched him for a moment, then turned about, to go to the comfort of his bed and Nelly's arms. Abruptly, he was grabbed about the legs by two very determined arms.

"Thank you, Seamus. I love you, Seamus. Good night, Seamus."

Before Seamus could say a word, he was released and sturdy legs propelled their owner back to the stairway. And as suddenly as had come that declaration from a child he'd ignored until now, so suddenly did Seamus transfer to her son much of the unrequited, useless love he'd lavished on his lady.

CHAPTER 3

The earl lived, a tribute more to his constitution than to his physicking. His mind healed less quickly. At first, he refused to believe his arm was gone, claiming it itched or the sheets felt cool to it. Only after he had reached out futilely with an invisible arm was he forced to acknowledge its loss. He found refuge in anger, but such rage could not be contained, spilling over to include all about him.

Since Seamus's strength was needed daily in the sickroom, his presence was tolerated, but he was reviled for his clumsiness and for having the audacity to rescue the earl from a good death on the battlefield. Boorde, whether present or not, was ignored, casually dismissed as a butcher in physician's robes. Seaforth refused to see or be seen by the Lady Islean whom he loudly and profanely blamed for his maiming. Though she covered her ears, still she heard and often fled the room in tears.

But it was a dead man who was the special target of the earl's hatred. Ten times a day or more, Seaforth consigned James IV to purgatory for his benighted leadership. And when the king's queen was delivered of a dead son, Seaforth professed himself glad, though his malediction sounded hollow. His little son Jamie alone was spared a fair share of curses, but only on good days. On bad days, when the missing arm ached unbearably, Jamie, like everyone else, suffered.

Eventually the entire household learned to avoid the sickroom as

64

much as possible on those days when anger gave way to depression; at those times a deep all-pervasive self-pity wrenched at the hearts of those who loved him, making them wish that the fury would return. He sat for hours luxuriating in his misfortune. A new book arrived? Too heavy to hold in one hand. Would he write instructions for the seneschal at Seaforth? The quill needed sharpening, a task for two hands. A little music perhaps? Impossible to tune a lute one-handed.

The one thing that presented him with no difficulty was filling and refilling his cup. In the morning he began with their best home brew. By midday the ale was replaced with canary or madeira. At night-fall, usquebaugh was his choice . . . smoky, tawny, heady . . . a potent distillate that could and did lay the strongest man low.

On a night no different from others, Seamus sat quietly in a corner. The earl was well into his fourth or fifth usquebaugh, though it was not dampening the fire of anger that raged through his nerve fibres. Occasionally he shouted a command for another flagon of brew, or a silk cloth to wipe his perspiring brow, just to see a serving man jump at his command.

The Lady Islean quietly worked at her tapestry frame in one corner of the huge room. When her husband bellowed, her hand would still for long minutes at a time. Eyes averted from the drunkard, she stared at the flames in the large stone fireplace or at the one joy in this new existence: young Jamie, playing with toy soldiers while sprawled on the fur before the fire. He took the part of first one, then another of the miniature wooden soldiers, long in need of fresh paint but beautifully carved and detailed.

The soldiers had belonged once to the Lady Islean's full brother, James Stewart, the bastard Earl of Moray, and many other royal tykes before him. Many a battle these soldiers had fought and won or lost. The armored knight rode a charger trapped with chain mail. The mounted esquire carried a spear with a knightly banner. The third, who wore no mail but went on foot and carried a long bow, was the five-year-old's favorite. Even though his armor was leather and his uniform was drab, he could go where horses could not and so often won the day with spear, sword, or bow.

"Scout, I, your king, command you to ride forth and locate the enemy," Jamie said, picking up the foot soldier.

"By your command, sire," he answered himself in a small quiet voice. He had learned long since not to disturb his father when he was drinking.

Jamie's tiny hand slowly slid the lowly sergeant across the rug and out onto the broad plain of the slate floor.

"Master Meredith, set up camp at the base of that hill yonder."

"Right away, sire," the esquire replied through his third-party voice. And Jamie moved him smartly over by the wolf's head at one end of the rug.

"As for you, Lord Lachlan," he said, reaching for the knight, "deploy your—"

An anguished howl and then a curse cut him short. The earl had lurched from his huge chair, and in three unsteady steps had managed to plop his stockinged foot down on the bowman. Surprised and in pain, he howled with rage and savagely kicked the tiny soldier into the fireplace.

Jamie rushed to rescue his man, but not fast enough. His humble soldier caught fire like kindling and the flames drove back the daring hand that would have saved him.

"Why did you do that?" the boy cried, tears blackening his blue eyes. "He didn't hurt you deliberately."

Seaforth desperately held onto the mantel with his only hand, in real need to steady himself, for not only did his head spin from the sudden exertion, but he was also taken aback by the look in his son's eyes. He did not, however, intend to be put on the defensive by one so young, so he quickly took up a theme he had preached before.

"Why do you play with toy soldiers? Why are you not practicing with real weapons? At your age, I could set a lance and run a course and wield a 'mercy'* with either hand. Hear that? With either—" His voice broke; he grew maudlin, "I'll never joust again . . . or ride to the hunt . . . or show myself at court again." With the mercurial change of mood drink can cause, he grew angered. "Hear me? I'm crippled, and you play with toys!" With that, the earl kicked the two remaining soldiers in the direction of the flames. The miniature squire had fought his last battle, but the wooden knight was rescued by the great andiron on the near side of the fireplace.

---

*The miséricorde, a straight, thin-bladed dagger used to give the coup de grâce to a fallen foe.

Jamie didn't wait to watch the second of his beloved soldiers turn to ashes. Instead, he lunged for his one remaining treasure and ran from the room without another word, the tiny nobleman squeezed tight in his hand.

"Come back here!" the father roared. "Do you hear me? Come back here before I take a belt to your bottom."

"Enough!" came the sharp retort from the corner of the room. Seaforth turned to see his wife descending on him, her skirts flouncing and fire in her eyes.

"Enough is enough! And you have just convinced me. Tomorrow I leave for my lands at Alva. Jamie goes with me," the Lady Islean snapped. "If you ever want to see either of us again, you had best forget what's gone for good and remember the living.

"Your arm is gone. Drink won't grow you another," she continued, stamping her small foot on the slate. "You are still young. You have your life before you. But if a missing arm is more important to you than your own son, so be it. Wallow in your own pity. Drink yourself into an early grave. At the rate you are going, there will be no one here to grieve for you."

With that, she turned on her heel and walked quickly from the room. Seaforth started to shout some still-unformed thought after her. But her angry words had pierced his drink-befuddled mind, and he wound up muttering a weak and illogical rebuttal to himself.

Not another drink passed his lips that evening as he sat for long hours deep in thought. When he finally made his way to his lonely bed, he refused to allow Seamus to help him undress. Instead, dismissing the man, he lay across the bed in his day clothes. Eventually, he slept, but only fitfully, waking at the first lightening in the east.

Without sending for Seamus, the earl exchanged slippers for boots, shrugged on a hunting jacket, tucking its empty sleeve into his belt. His riding boots felt good after his being so long without them. Skipping breakfast, he headed straight for the mews.

The first servant he spied he curtly ordered, "Saddle me that new bay mare, Excitress." The man started with surprise, then hurried off to do the earl's bidding. Seamus questioned the footman's orders at first but took no chances. However, in place of the fractious mare, he ordered the saddling of an aged gelding. It was no lady's jennet, yet no challenge to a crippled rider, either. When Seaforth saw which horse was led out, he opened his mouth to protest, then thought better of it. The groom, coached by Seamus moments before, offered his cupped hands to assist the earl to mount, and Seaforth even silently accepted that. He settled in the saddle as if in the lap of a long-lost friend. It felt good to be a man again. The reins held firmly in his left hand, he urged the horse to curvet a bit. Then, refusing the groom's offer to go with him, he put the horse through the high, narrow arch leading out into St. Mary's Wynd. Seamus, having sent word of Seaforth's doings to the Lady Islean, followed not long after on a heavy-built cob capable of carrying his substantial weight.

The street leading up to the ridge was both narrow and steep but cleaner than most city streets, however, for it was lined with the city houses or "lands" of Scottish lords, and their slops were thrown into wells built for the purpose, not out of the windows onto the street. This early in the morning, the street was practically deserted. The few men Seaforth saw were quick to tug forelocks, doff hats and bow as due his rank; the women curtsied and bade him a smiling good-morning.

People looked at him, of course, but not with cloying sympathy, nor the curiosity reserved for a freak. Instead, the looks were what any rich lord or handsome male would expect. Reassured but somehow disappointed that what he had dreaded had not occurred, he made his way slowly up the wynd. It seemed more gray and sombre than usual. Then, he realized why. The noble banners denoting their owner in residence no longer flew from the houses lining St. Mary's Wynd. He suppressed a shudder. Had all of these nobles fallen that day at Flodden Field? He and his wife had not discussed the subject, carefully avoiding all mention of it except for once, early on, when he'd asked her who had won. And of the king, her father. Her one-word answers had closed the matter until now.

At the top of St. Mary's, he turned left on High Street toward the castle perched like a bird of prey on the hill above the town. At the base of that hill was Old Town, his destination. As the horse moved forward into the street, it was surrounded by beggars. Those on his right, sighting his empty sleeve, fell back, but not those on the left. They pressed closer. Grabbing at his feet, his stirrup, his jacket, they brandished crutches, waved aged bloodied bandages, pulled back eye patches to show empty sockets as they entreated him to remember Flodden.

The beggars weren't to be ignored. Some no doubt were professional cripples. But just as many, he feared, were fellow victims. Not often did he or any other nobleman feel any kinship with the masses, but this was one of those rare occasions. He would have scattered some coins among them; but with one hand, he couldn't both control his horse and reach for his purse. Frustrated, he stared straight ahead and spurred his horse onward. His manner angered the beggars, who redoubled their protests. At the combination of his own frustration and their persistence, he grew angry. With a wrench of his right shoulder, he pulled his own empty sleeve out of his belt and flaunted it as best he could in the faces of the crowd, mockingly repeating their own words: "Ha' pity on me, a simple victim of Flodden." Sullenly the cripples pulled back, and he forged ahead, his sleeve waving grimly in the breeze.

Within a few minutes, it was Seamus's turn to try to forge his way through the crowd, not so easily put off, now that one victim had gotten away without a donation. Now Seaforth gained a sizable lead, passing swiftly and without opposition through the portal to the Old Tolbooth with its miscreants chained to the jougs outside and its jailors lounging on the high stairs above. Just before he reached St. Giles Cathedral, Seaforth came upon the Luckenbooths squeezed in between the cathedral and High Street. Turning in, he searched out a ramshackled stall built onto the row like some haphazard afterthought. After two or three hallos, the owner finally came out.

"I need soldiers carved, for a boy—" Seaforth began, but from the blank look on the old man's face, he could tell not a word said had been heard. Twice more he spoke, each time louder, but to no avail. Seaforth had come too far to accept defeat now. Not happily, he realized he must dismount so as to shout in the man's ear.

Wrapping the reins about his hand, he gripped the pommel with all his strength, then stood up in the stirrups. Keeping his weight on the left foot, he threw the other leg over. It took all his concentration to keep his balance. Bending his knees slightly, he lay down with his stomach across the saddle, kicked his left foot free, and slid ineptly to the ground. He caught his breath after the unexpected exertion and started to shout his errand all over again, but the old man raised a hand in protest.

"Don't shout, I can hear you fine, if'n you only talk slow."

Slowly, very slowly, the earl described what he wanted, one carefully enunciated word after another: "Item one, a footman, one hand high, dressed in boiled leather armor, his bow slung over his shoulder. Give him, too, a modern arquebusier with a flask of regular coarse gunpowder and a touch box with priming powder."

The carver nodded his understanding.

"Item two: an esquire, on a rounsey, but let the horse be better bred than most. The esquire of unusual size . . . wearing mail, his horse lightly armored, and have the left arm extended so that he may carry a banner or lead the knight's destrier on the right."

The carver nodded.

"As to the knight, the third figure. Mount him on a tall horse, a gray. Let horse and man wear full tourney armor. The horse cap-a-pie with plate armor white and plain, his neck covered with a crinet, a peytrel for his chest and flanchard for his thigh, and beneath caparisoned in white velvet ornamented with silver bells. Let the knight's face not show, but dress him in Maximilian armor with its grouped channels and flutings. Arm him with long sword and shield. As to the latter, I prefer neither heater nor kite-shaped, but a near rectangle with rounded corners and a notch in the upper right-hand corner for a lance. And let it be not curved around the body but concave, so it will best slip an opponent's lance. And upon it paint, per fess argent and sable, a bend charged with three annulets, all countercharged. And upon the helmet put you a Mer-Lion, mounted. Any questions?"

The carver nodded. "One arm or two, my lord?"

Seaforth's lips tightened. It was all he could do to keep from smiting the man, but he realized the carver spoke not in malice but in an honest desire to please.

"Two," he replied, then thought better of it. "No, make it one." As Seaforth abruptly turned on his heel, the sleeve restlessly flapped. Awkwardly he tucked it back under his wide belt.

"Flodden, my lord?" It was Seaforth's turn to nod.

"I lost my only son and my grandson too. They were all that I had," the old man said. "Was it in a good cause, my lord?"

Seaforth had no answer. How does one equate a turquoise ring sent by a queen from a foreign land . . . or, for that matter, an arm lost from below the elbow . . . with the loss of the next generation and two? He shrugged his shoulders, pulling the sleeve loose again. Let the carver interpret that as he chose.

The carver didn't press him. With fatalistic tolerance he returned to his lean-to. Outside, Seaforth gathered up his reins and faced a new problem—mounting his horse. The old man would be of no help . . . and there was no lady's mounting block about. A vault into the saddle? Out of the question, Seaforth realized. He was too weak even to walk home. Grudgingly, he faced and accepted the reality of his situation.

Retying his horse, he made his way into the stall and found a place to sit down and wait until his men found him, as he knew they eventually would. The carver hospitably offered the lord a glass of home brew. Though thin and sour, it was wet and potent, and Seaforth drained his wooden goblet and did not turn down a refill. The lean-to was small and cramped, strewn with unfinished pieces and untouched chunks of wood. It smelled clean and fresh . . . of sap and shavings . . . the scrape of knife on wood . . . the slow, steady rhythm both hypnotic and relaxing . . .

He slept until awakened by the stomping of a horse as Seamus charged into the stall, ready to do harm to the carver if aught had befallen his lord. A glance and a word sufficed to reassure. Seaforth found himself effortlessly boosted up into the saddle again by his giant of a squire.

As they prepared to ride off, Seaforth called a halt, turned back in his saddle and shouted to the old man, "Grandfather, to answer your question: Yes, it was worth it." He never knew whether he'd spoken loudly and slowly enough for the carver to understand, but he hoped the lie would in some small way thank the old man for his hospitality.

Seamus chose to return to St. Mary's Wynd by a different route, skirting the base of castle hill and totally avoiding St. Giles's Cathedral. He had not yet returned to retrieve the arm sharing St. Giles's reliquary. Coming out of Advocate's Close, Seaforth halted his horse. Here at last was one explanation for the dearth of able-bodied men in town. Fathers and husbands, children and women were rebuilding a wall that had been in ruins six weeks before.

Noting the earl's curiosity, Seamus said, "They began it, lord, when word came of the British victory at Flodden. The brave nobles"—his voice reeked of sarcasm—"fled to their castle keeps in the Grampians and Highlands. But few of the people followed after. Most of these Scots are of sterner stuff and would no' have it. Especially the women. They, I am told, made life so difficult for those who did no' go off to war as well as those who came back whole—" Seamus paused uncertainly, aware of his gaffe.

Seaforth seemed not to notice. "Go on, what did they do?"

"They stopped cooking and laundering, changing nappies and sleeping in the family bed, until their men agreed to build this wall they call the Flodden Wall. It surrounds the city from the base of the castle all the way round to Catlin's Hill and Arthur's Seat. Bless me, our only chance is to run out of stone soon—small chance that, damn it. Women like old Bess there—she with the broad beam and arms akimbo, who acts as if she built the wall herself—she'll have us building on and on and around Nor Loch. Oh, God, Bess's noticed us. Lord, she's a widowed lady who fancies me. Ride on, please, my lord, or I'm in for a hard time."

Seaforth touched spur to flank and Seamus fell in close behind. When they finally turned into the courtyard, Lady Islean came charging down the steps before he could dismount, to berate him for leaving the house alone so soon after rising from his sickbed.

Meekly he sat on his gelding, towering over her, allowing himself to be browbeaten like some errant little boy while he looked at his wife with fresh eyes, finding himself glad indeed to be alive. She was young enough to be his daughter, near twenty years his junior, and looked more Irish than Scots. A tendril of hair escaping her caul was so dark that it appeared ebony although he knew it was brown. Her eyes, wide set and thickly lashed, were of that blue that varies with the owner's mood. Right now, they flashed darkly of anger. Her cheeks, always at least slightly flushed with color due to her fair and thin skin, now glowed a becoming red.

Ignoring her words, Seaforth smiled. A long, slow smile that transformed his usually serious face and made it much younger. The Lady Islean, unprepared for smiles, stammered a bit with bewilderment. Pretending nonchalance—after all he had done it before—Seaforth dismounted by himself. By the time he had both feet on the ground, the Lady Islean had gathered her wits about her. She would have continued on, but he put finger to her mouth.

"I was not alone. Good Seamus watched over me. Now hush, lady. Stop sounding like a good Scotswoman." Draping his one arm about her shoulders, he led her toward the house. He laughed a little ruefully, "I don't know how good I am at one-armed push-ups, my dear, but if you'll bear with me, tonight I would give being a husband a try."

Not at all reluctantly, her own right arm encircled his waist. Her tone was demure enough, but the look in her eyes was wicked. "My lord, I think you've done enough riding for one day. Allow me."

CHAPTER 4

From the rear, bending over her cooking, Nelly didn't look due to pop out a babe any day now. Every now and again, however, she would arch her aching back and rub the small of it a bit. Stirring the large copper caldron in which she made her specialty, garbage, for the staff's evening meal was hard work. Seamus, coming up behind her, sniffed appreciatively. Nelly worked miracles with the giblets of fowl, the entrails of mutton, plus a thickening of bread and a handful of spices.

Seamus realized he hadn't eaten in hours, but the conversation he had overheard between Seaforth and his lady had stimulated an appetite other than that of his stomach, though the thought of them together still bothered him. Slipping his arms about Nelly, he cupped her full, straining breasts in his enormous hands. Gratefully, she leaned back against his strength, letting him support her weight as he nuzzled her neck.

"You've been on your feet enough for one day, love," he said. "Let someone else do the stirring. You come with me, and I'll rub your back. Your front too, if you like. What do you say, Nelly, me gal?"

She was tired. Hot too, but not for his body. Her hair was damp and curly with sweat, while under her kirtle, she could feel the droplets running down between her breasts, pooling in the crease of her swollen belly. It would be good to lie down, she thought. "Nanny Goodall says my time is almost upon me," she remarked,

74

resting her head on the comfort of his broad chest. "She says your pestering me could bring on the babe."

"Me, pester you?" He rubbed her nipples slowly and felt them grow hard under his hands. "What I have in mind will just relax you. Besides, are you no' ready to be rid of your burden?"

That she was, she thought. Whether he relaxed her or not, the slow, caressing movements of his hands were excellent persuaders.

Calling to Effie, a scrawny slip of a girl not yet in her teens, Nelly surrendered her spoon and let Seamus lead her away. She had gone no more than ten paces before she stopped. "Effie, mind you stir deep lest the stew crust on the bottom. And no tasting. And no more sugar, either. You've much too sweet a taste to be able to season garbage properly."

She would have said more, but Seamus's hand on her elbow was urging her toward the stone steps leading up to the courtyard. She looked surprised. "Not my room?" He shook his head, and led her upward, out into the courtyard, then beyond to the mews. As captain of the guard he was privileged to have a room to himself above the horse stalls. "We'll be more private there, this time of evening," he said.

The stairs were steep and Nelly out of breath by the time they reached his room. It was neat and orderly, like Seamus himself, its walls bare of adornment other than a crucifix, its furnishings crude and functional. But the bed Seamus had built to his own measure: extra long and extra wide.

Nelly sank back against the pillows and breathed in the good clean smells of horses and hay and leather, the smells she associated with Seamus. God, how she loved him. She knew, of course, about his other women, but in her deep love of him, she could even accept that. Especially since he was faithful to her whenever he was in residence at Seaforth or when the whole household traveled to Edinburgh. What he did at Rangeley, the Seaforths' estate in the moors . . . or at Alva, the lady's manor with its famous silver mines near Stirling . . . to this she resolutely closed her eyes and her ears and her mind. Of course, she couldn't ignore the fact that her rivals at Alva and at Rangely had within the year, in that order, brought forth men-children.

Nelly chuckled to herself, and fondly tousled the straw-colored hair of the man bending over her. How did he, she wondered, take the news that his firstborn was black-haired . . . and his second a redhead? Did he wonder if a fox had gotten into his chicken coop? Hers, she vowed, would have his father's hair. Not for a moment did she doubt this; nor that she would have a boy; Nanny Goodall had told her carrying high always meant a boy.

But now her mind was brought back to more immediate things. Seamus had unlaced her kirtle at both sides, and again at the front, and pulled it down off her shoulders. Nelly marveled that a gown made especially to cater to the needs of a woman large with child should lend itself so readily to removal by an amorous man. Half the time with her other kirtles, Seamus hadn't bothered to tug them off, but had simply pulled them up about her waist—her shift too— and had taken his pleasure that way.

Not today. With the kirtle off, he unlaced her shift and drew that down off her body. Big and bloated and as grotesquely out of shape as she was, Seamus seemed to delight more in looking at her body now than when she was flat-stomached and small-breasted. Men, she thought. Who'd ever understand them? Today, however, she was glad for this strange aberration of his; the cool evening air felt good on her bare skin. When Seamus, his clothes shucked off quickly, gently turned her over on her side and lay down behind her, she found the cool air before and the heat of his body behind strangely refreshing.

Then she felt his hand. His enormous hand that could be so surprisingly gentle and delicate slid over her shoulder and down her back, pausing at the small of her back to rub the pain from her tired muscles. Following her spine, it went lower, to finger the hair-fringed opening below her tailbone. Involuntarily she flinched. He felt her body tense, and his hand moved on, up over the round haunch presented so trustingly to him, to the vast belly beyond. As his hand, fingers widespread, lay lovingly on that mound, he could feel through the tight-stretched skin the strong, explosive movements of his child beneath. He could have lain there like that, feeling the life of the child yet to come with the sensitive hand of the born horseman, but his pisser had other ideas. His hand moved off her belly and down to that hair-covered crevice between her legs. She moved her leg to give him greater access, but it was his needs that were uppermost in his mind right now. And so his hand didn't linger. Instead, he lifted her leg higher, so that he could place his weapon alongside that crevice and between her legs. Without being told, she gripped it with all the strength of her legs. And then, he began to rock back and forth. He knew satisfaction would be slow coming from this makeshift excuse for the moist hot channel which he so preferred, but what other choice did he have.

After what seemed hours, he thrusting faster and faster to no apparent avail, Nelly took matters into her own hands. Literally. Heaving herself away from him, she rolled over and shoved him over onto his back. With a sigh, Seamus gave himself over to her capable hand. As he lay there reveling in the sensations arising from her capable caresses, his mind strayed. Was this what the Lady Islean was doing for her husband? He suspected, knowing his lady as well as he did, that that strong-willed young woman would not be content tonight to indulge in such one-sided love. Especially after her remark about riding.

The thought of Islean riding her husband brought forth a groan from Seamus. Nelly, thinking she had hurt him, stopped her ministrations. But Seamus quickly put her hand back where it belonged, and with a thrust or two of his hips persuaded her that she should continue as before. That done, he relaxed and let his mind go back to the manor's master bedroom.

He could imagine Islean undressing her husband. First, she would remove his boots. Seating him in the chair brought up from the great hall weeks ago, she would turn her back to him, gripping one booted leg after another between her own while his foot would rest against her rounded bottom to supply the push needed to pull the boots from his foot. The toes on Seamus's foot curled as he thought of his own foot resting against that sweet rounded bottom.

While she was removing Seaforth's boots, he would be struggling one-handedly to unlace his jerkin. She, seeing what he was about, would rush quickly to his aid and push his hand aside. Then, she would take her time, perhaps playing with the thick curly hair on his chest. And once the jerkin was off, Seamus could well imagine she would wickedly ignore the turbulence in his codpiece, but, instead, roll his hose down slowly, caressingly, her cool hands brushing against his inner thighs.

Seamus squirmed with delight. Nelly took this as a sign of pleasure and speeded up the movement of her hand. But Seamus put his hand over hers, and set his own much slower pace for a moment or two. He was so caught up in his own fantasy that he wanted to prolong his pleasure.

By the time his thoughts returned to Seaforth and the Lady Islean, she would have undone her husband's codpiece and let his manhood loose. Although Seamus had never seen Seaforth's erection, he was sure it wasn't anywhere near the size of his own enormous staff. And he was glad.

Mentally finishing with Seaforth, Seamus let his imagination undress Islean. Small but proud rose-tipped breasts . . . the curve of her narrow waist . . . the fullness of her womanly hips . . . the slight swelling of her belly, so unlike Nelly's beside him . . . her heavy bush of dark pubic hair. The thought of that almost brought Seamus to completion. He had to seize Nelly's hand and stop her while he desperately thought of something else. Breathing deeply and slowly, he forced himself mentally to arm the Seaforth guard: 58 spearmen carrying three weapons apiece; 58 plus 58 are 116 and another 58 made— Seamus wasn't all that good with his sums, and he had to concentrate: 6 and 8 made 14, carry the 1, 5 and 1 and another 1 made 7, bring down the 1.

By the time he'd counted spears, and then shields and helmets and arrows, the turbulence within him had subsided, and he could release Nelly's hand. In fact, he could urge it on again. As Nelly resumed her caressing, Seamus imagined Islean approaching the big bed in the center of the room. There, propped against the pillows, reclined an aroused Seaforth. Islean knelt provocatively on the side of the bed, then moved forward, throwing one leg over him. Still on her knees, she inched forward, straddling him, until the round white globes of her buttocks were poised just above his staff thrusting upward from its bed of hair.

Her triangle of pubic hair would be parted slightly, a touch of bright pink skin showing through. Slowly—Seamus held his breath—she lowered herself upon her husband and Seaforth arched his back in an attempt to meet her halfway. Then, Seaforth's staff disappeared within the dark curly hair. Seamus's own could be denied no longer. With a mind of its own, it jerked within Nelly's hand, and in ever-increasing spasms, it gushed forth in a crescendo of excruciating pleasure.

His chest heaving with the intensity of his efforts, Seamus couldn't move. He simply lay there, drained of all feeling from the waist down. Nelly raised herself up on one arm and looked down upon him fondly, as if he were but a child and she his mother. Their lips met in a kiss devoid of passion. It was she who broke it. Smiling down upon him, she whispered, "Get yourself dressed my love, and fetch Nanny Goodall. My time is upon me."

Nelly did not pop out her babe. The labor was long and hard. In the stable, Seamus kept himself busy cleaning tackle that needed no cleaning, and grooming horses that had not a single hair out of place, and trying desperately not to listen to the groans coming from above. Finally Nanny Goodall came down the stairs. "The child will no' be born without help. Go, you, Seamus, to the father and beg him the use of the bell rope for the night."

Seamus blanched. "What are you planning to do, pull the babe out like a foal from a mare?"

The woman laughed and gathered up her skirts to make the steep climb up again. "Nay, nothing like that. But fastening a bell rope to the girdle has been known to shorten childbirth. So, if you would quiet those groans and save your Nelly the pain of birthing what you planted in her belly, be on your way . . . now!"

When the priest was not to be found in the chapel nor sacristy nor kitchen, Seamus climbed the three flights of stairs leading up to the garret. In a room just outside the unmarried women's dormitory were the priest's quarters, so that his presence might act as a deterrent against unexpected male visitors and licentious behavior. He found Father Cariolinus squatting upon the simple pallet that served as his bed, awkwardly and laboriously mending his hose. Quickly Seamus explained his errand.

The priest sighed. "Not again. Sometime I think that rope spends more time on pregnant women than it does on the bell. Nanny Goodall does rely on it so."

"But does it work?" Seamus inquired anxiously.

The priest looked up from fastening his shoes. "Nanny Goodall seems to think so; I like to believe that my prayers are more beneficial."

"Could you say a prayer for my Nelly?" Seamus begged, following the priest down the steep stairs.

"Aye, I planned to. She's a good lass, that one. She it is who minds my wash and does my mending."

When the two reached the chapel, Seamus volunteered to climb up and unfasten the rope from its clapper. As he began, the priest remarked, "We have some unfinished business from your last visit here, friend Seamus."

Pretending he didn't hear, Seamus kept on climbing.

"The earl is going to live, Seamus."

The tricky part was untying the rope with one hand while keeping the bell from sounding.

"Looks like you could use another hand," the priest called up, then realized what he had said. Seamus glared down at him and would have said something about gallows humor but just then the knot came loose.

"Stand aside, father, I'm going to let it drop."

The priest began coiling the rope, but his mind was elsewhere. "Seamus, is it possible that God is punishing you through Nelly for breaking your promise to him?"

Seamus groaned, a deep masculine version of the sounds he'd heard earlier that night. The thought had occurred to him too, but now to have it said by the priest— It was too much. "What would you have me do, father?"

"The arm can't stay there forever." His face was calm, his voice that of reason, but the wringing of his hands belied his manner. "Fortunately, St. Giles's feast day is past. But suppose some sick person asks and receives permission to touch the relic . . . and the people open the reliquary and find two hands? Someone is going to put two and two together and come up with our late night visit to the cathedral."

Seamus gave in. "You take the rope to the midwife, I'll go rob the church."

"It is not robbery, Seamus," the priest protested in alarm. "That would be a sin. Besides, we put the arm there ourselves."

"Then why can't we go and tell Beaton what we have done and ask for the arm back so we can bury it?"

The priest looked troubled. "I wish it were that simple. But you don't know our Cardinal Protector Beaton. He might well consider our act, at best, desecration not just of the reliquary or the altar or the relic but the whole church." A note of hysteria entered his voice. "Suppose, just suppose, he considers it blasphemy? In Leviticus it says 'whoever blasphemes shall be put to death.' I know, I have heard him say it myself."

"Father, control yourself. No one in his right mind would accuse you of blasphemy." Seamus tried to think of something that would reassure the priest, but he was no more learned in theology than he was in midwifery. "What about your bishop, have you asked his advice?"

"No, I tried. But he is away visiting his monastery of St. Raymond of Penafort. Seamus," he confessed, "I don't know what overcame my judgment that night. Do you think I was possessed?"

"You, father?" Seamus laughed, a genuine laugh. "No father, of all the people, you the devil would avoid most. Whatever work you did that night was not the work of the devil, rest assured of that!"

The priest unclasped his hands with relief. "I pray you are right. But we must get that thing out of there before it begins to stink and draws the attention of the celebrants of the Mass."

"Do no' call my godchild a 'thing.'" Seamus pretended mock umbrage, but the priest took him seriously. "No, no, it's all right, father. I was only making a joke. Look, here's the rope. I'll get me a lantern and go fetch the arm back right now, this minute. You go pray for Nelly, and I'll meet you back in the chapel before Martins, or Lauds at the latest. And, father, say a prayer for me while you are at it."

The priest was at prayer when a pale, nervous Seamus returned with his burden. How long he'd been gone, the priest didn't know; when he was praying he lost track of time. But he could see the beeswax candles that Seaforth supplied for him had burned almost to the bottom.

"The same door was undone," Seamus reported, "and the brother did not skip a snore during the whole of my visit." He put his package on the altar and, though the priest protested, began to unwrap it. "No, father, I insist, you must look at this."

The last covering came off. "You have brought the wrong one!" exclaimed the priest in horror. The arm before him, although cool to the touch and grayish in color as if drained of blood, showed no signs of rot. It looked newly cut off.

"No, father, this is Seaforth's arm. Look, you can see the marks on the finger where he wore his signet ring."

"It can't be, Seamus. It has been a month or more since I baptized that arm. It should be ripe by now and sweet-smelling to high heavens. This must be the Saint's arm, it smells too fresh."

"Father, the other arm in the reliquary—it had a wound in its palm, and the wound bled when I touched it."

"A wound? Oh, aye, I remember. Saint Giles had his hand pierced by an arrow while protecting a hind from some hounds."

"Did they have to cut his arm off too, like Seaforth?"

"Oh, no, not till years later when he was dead. Then they divided up the body to sanctify as many altars as possible. Only because of Lord Preston—he of the Preston aisle in the cathedral—did we get the whole arm. Some churches only got a lock of hair, a tooth or toe. We were honored above most because ours was to be the cathedral of Scotland's first bishop." The pride in his voice vanished as realization sunk in. "Mother of God, what have we done?" He crossed himself and would have prostrated himself before both altar and hand if Seamus hadn't stopped him.

"Nay, father. Maybe it's a miracle, maybe no', but it must be a sign that what we did was no' evil work of the devil. Be that as it may, father, what do we do with it now?"

The priest looked panic-stricken. "I know not, I know not. Cover it up and let me think. No, thinking's no good. I must pray for guidance!"

While Seamus carefully rewrapped the arm in its red swaddling, the priest abjectly prostrated himself before the altar in prayer and invocation. He had scarcely begun the Litany of Loreto when Seamus, remembering his original purpose in coming to the chapel that night, took to his heels and fled for the stable. Entering the door, he listened hard. It was quiet. Carefully, he made his way up the stair, trying to make no sound lest he disturb those within. A knock at his door brought no results. Nor did a second. Finally, he pulled the latch string and let himself in . By the light of a candle, he could make out Nanny Goodall asleep in a makeshift pallet on the floor. Stealthily he approached his bed.

"Shush, you lummox, you'll wake the dead," came a tired but happy voice from its depths. "And where were you when your son was born?"

Seamus sat down carefully on the edge of the bed, his eyes only for the woman in it. "I was in church, if you must know. Are you all right?"

"I'm fine, but are you not the least bit curious about your son? He has a fine head of blond hair, you know," she gloated, moving the covers to one side so that Seamus might have a look. She opened the swaddling clothes a bit more. "And on his ribs, the selfsame brown birthmark his da' has."

"He's so small," was Seamus's awed comment.

"What did you think? He would spring from my belly big as you? He's a fine-sized child. Lusty. Healthy. With a good strong set of lungs. They must have heard his first cry on High Street."

Nelly exaggerated. However, word of his birth had preceded Seamus into the earl's bedroom. For when Seamus was summoned hours later at Terce, he was greeted with hearty congratulations: "And what did you name him?"

"Fionn. Nelly would have nothing else."

"Fionn?"

"An Irish name. It means fair of hair and of skin. She wants to make sure my other loves get the message and ne'er forget, her son was born straw-colored like me."

The earl laughed. "Women! Come, join me in a drink, we'll toast your new son."

The strong usquebaugh on an empty stomach, combined with a sleepless night, set Seamus back on his heels a bit. The earl, catching sight of his expression, was all sympathy and concern. Then, man to man, he confessed that he himself had had a sleepless night, too. Seamus, catching sight of the headdress lying casually alongside the bed, knew what he meant. Another time, he would have been filled with bitter envy, but somehow the events of the night before had been a catharsis, purging him of his lusting after the Lady Islean.

Whether the feeling would last, Seamus didn't know, but he was glad he could return Seaforth's confidence with an honestly felt "Then, my lord, perhaps congratulations are in order for you, too."

Seaforth laughed and admitted the possibility. In this mood of camaraderie, the two men descended the stairs to the great hall below. There they parted, but only temporarily, for Seaforth expressed a desire for the first time in weeks to look over his domain. Seamus, in turn, went searching for the chaplain. But he was not to be found. He had left early before Lauds, on retreat to the monastery of St. Raymond of Penafort, taking only one bundle, presumably of his vestments. Seamus had no choice but to return to the great hall and await Seaforth's pleasure.

Seaforth's inspection, later that morning, didn't take long, the two men scarcely able to stifle their yawns. As a matter of fact, once Seaforth had seen the job Seamus had done policing the guardroom, the earl would have been content to call it a day. But the two men had picked up a small dark-haired shadow. Jamie, playing the moth to his father's flame, kept his distance but stayed always within earshot. Seaforth, still ridden by guilt, was afraid to push the child for fear of estranging him even more. Instead, leading the way toward the stable, he launched into a long story of the day he graduated from pony to horse. Gradually, his voice became softer, so that Jamie, if he would hear at all, must move closer and closer. Both Seamus and Seaforth affected not to notice.

Softly as he spoke, Dunstan had heard a familiar voice, and he soon drowned out all other sounds with the importunings of his neighs. When that didn't fetch his master fast enough to suit him, he reared and struck at the stalls with his powerful front legs. An ass or a lesser horse would have kicked with his hind legs, but not this destrier who had been trained since a yearling to do the capriole and caracole—warlike movements that had crushed many a foot soldier's head beneath flailing forehoof.

Seaforth, with Seamus and Jamie close behind, hurried down the row of stalls until he stood before his favorite mount. A softly spoken "Ho, there" was enough to turn the raging stallion into an overgrown pony. His velvety muzzle pushed against Seaforth's chest until the earl put forth his hand and rubbed between the horse's eyes. Up and down the broad forehead he scratched, the horse closing his eyes like a woman delighting in foreplay. Then down over the broad cheeks, finally searching out that ticklish spot in the V beneath the chin. The horse's skin rippled with shivery pleasure, and he stood transfixed. Never stopping his scratching, Seaforth said, as if to himself, "Poor Dunstan. Poor horse. It shall break my heart to get rid of you."

Seamus and Jamie cried out with one voice, "No!"

Pretending not to have heard, Seaforth continued in the same sorrowful voice, "Better to break my heart than yours."

Jamie, all thoughts of his lost toys driven from his mind by the love of this horse, cried out in tearful protest, "No, father, you can't. I won't let you."

Seaforth pretended surprise. "What? You care for him, too?"

"More than anything in this world." Seaforth chose not to question the exaggeration. The exchange was having the desired result, healing the breach between him and the being *he* loved more than anything in this world.

"Then would you do something to save him?"

"Oh, yes, anything."

Seaforth squatted down to look his son in the eye. As he did, Dunstan, released from his spell, reached over the side of his stall and nuzzled his master's head. Ignoring the horse, Seaforth put his lone hand on his son's shoulder. "Then you must promise me to grow quickly. With only one hand, I cannot hope to handle this horse. But to confine him to a stall for the rest of his life is unfair to him. From the time he was weaned, he has been trained for but one thing—to serve his master. To carry him. To fight for him. Warfare and tourneys are the only things he knows. Without them, he will begin to pine and eventually will lose muscle, and then heart, and then he will die. You must save him from this."

"But I can't. I'm too small." The tears began to flow again.

"Today, yes. But soon you will be big enough. In the meantime, we will let friend Seamus"—Seamus, who thought he'd been forgotten, was startled to hear himself brought into the conversation—"substitute for us. But only until you're ready to take on the responsibility of being Dunstan's master. Agreed?"

The man and the boy looked long into each other's eyes. "Agreed," the small voice quavered and then without warning he launched himself at his father, throwing both arms about the man's neck and burying his face in Seaforth's shoulder. Seaforth's long battle training stood him in good stead, for instinctively bracing himself, he held firm through his son's assault and hugged him back lovingly, albeit single-handedly and a trifle awkwardly.

Seamus, looking down on the two of them, renewed his own promise to the Seaforths . . . not only to mother, but father and now son as well. He would serve as faithfully as Dunstan, for he knew that were he deprived of the right to serve this family, something good and noble would wither and die within him. Dunstan too must have sensed something had happened, for he left off mouthing the earl's hair and with a snort, nuzzled the head of the child.

When the two left the stable, Seamus trailed behind, but close on their heels. Seaforth had begun his heir's training and Seamus was committing it to memory. They began with a subject of primary interest: the care of Dunstan.

As Seaforth talked, he discovered he enjoyed his role as savant and teacher. That there was a sense of achievement and even satisfaction in feeding eager minds, regardless of the fact that one was that of a mere child, the other that of a servant.

Soon Seamus discovered his newfound position as pupil was not confined to the stable. That night after supper, he joined the family for vespers, conducted by another Dominican priest hastily summoned to temporarily replace the good father Cariolinus. Afterward, he was told to join the family in the solarium where he found himself cross-questioned on the care of Dunstan, the Lady Islean looking on with interest. Jamie too underwent scrutiny. So eager was Seamus to learn, to understand, to forget nothing, that he forgot that the Lady Islean listened and that his fellow student was so much younger than he.

Afterward, Seaforth, no longer seeking solace in a cup, had the two stand near as he brought out a book—a primer, beautifully illustrated with large initial gold letters on every page. For a quarter of the hour or so, the two boys—one a diminutive person of four, the other an overgrown giant of nineteen—learned their letters, the one reciting away in an eager soprano, the other more self-consciously in a basso profundo. Instinctively, like a good teacher, Seaforth demanded little this first night, moving soon from primer to lighter works.

So began the routine that would take them through the weeks ahead. First the meat, then the sweet. The works of those Scots,

Douglas, Kennedy, and Dunbar. Seaforth in his new mood would have avoided Dunbar, a man of morbid bent. But Jamie had seized upon one poem with delight and would pester his father to read it so that he might joyously join the chorus:

Seaforth: Our pleasure here is all vain glory
This false world is but transitory,
The flesh is broken, the Field is sly,

Father and son: *Timor mortis conturbat me.*

Seaforth: The state of man does change and vary,
Now sound, now sick, now blithe, now sary,
Now dancing merry, now like to dee

Both: *Timor mortis conturbat me.*

Although neither Seamus nor the Lady Islean joined in, they could not help but share looks with one another, knowing full well that such a poem well described the Seaforth of but a week ago . . . and the country as it was today.

Soon Seaforth had read aloud all the books in his library and must send in to Edinburgh for more. These few in turn were swiftly devoured, and agents to buy were alerted in France . . . and Rome . . . and even, via Brussels and Amsterdam, in England. But nothing would he touch on theology except it be *Bible* or *Apocrypha* or psalter. As for law, he ignored the modern ones, instead seeking out the works of the basic lawmakers, Plato and Socrates.

No man with a book or a manuscript or scroll or even a shard would be refused admission to the house on St. Mary's Wynd, most leaving with full purse and empty hand.

Soon, the ranks of scholars at St. Andrews University were regularly raided to teach the family Seaforth. Jamie thrived on his diet of ink and parchment and illuminated letters. Seamus, who had responsibilities in the stables for most of the day, remained, in comparison, unlettered. But he felt it no great loss. None of his fellows could read as much as their names, while he was able to read and write Scots and could cipher beyond a thousand.

At first, understandably enough, Seaforth emphasized mind over body. One day, however, Seaforth happened upon Seamus, down on his knees, attempting to teach the rudiments of swordsmanship to the child who was not much taller than his own sword. Seaforth said nothing, standing there and watching two totally inept swordsmen hack away at each other. But something must have been said between the two parents, for preparations commenced the next day for their departure to Rangely on Rannock Moor, although Seaforth let it be known that they would soon go from there to the castle on Dun Dearduil. Downstairs in the kitchen, the servants were pleased with the news. The Seaforths had stayed long in their town house, and their lackeys would gleefully see them go. As for the child, the solution, according to those below stairs, was fosterage, the usual answer to the training of young lordlings in arms as well as household manners. But, Seamus countered, what noble house worthy of the fourth in line to the throne, would accept a son whose father was crippled and thus unable to properly train another's son as fosterling in return? The servants had no answer to this, but the earl did.

Their stay at Rangely was not long, but long enough for Seamus to go to the clan Cameron to bring back the youngest of four orphan brothers, George by name. Tall and thin, with legs like a spider. He was self-contained, excelling in what he liked, and managing to ignore or avoid what he didn't. He was destined to be the bane of the schoolmaster's existence, since his hand was so poor none could decipher it. But among the serving wenches, he did much better— and at the age of twelve, George Cameron could boast of being first to add an offshoot of his clan to the inbred population of the Mackenzies of Seaforth.

Soon after George arrived, Seamus returned to Rangely with another boy orphaned as a result of Flodden—Kenneth Menzies, trim, soldierly and looking as athletic as his prowess over the next nine years would prove him to be. Grumbler, grouser, complainer—no job assigned did he like, yet each was done perfectly, to the last detail.

Seamus brought back two boys from another trip, an Ogilvy and an Angus, who instantly, apparently, hated each other. Nothing one did pleased the other, yet each of these black-haired look-alikes was lost if his fellow were sick abed or put to a different task.

Among the last to join the group was the bastard son of a local girl, Henry Gilliver—a quiet, shy boy whom his fellows quickly learned to shelter. He was a natural candidate for the church as Father Cariolinus's Dominican replacement soon discovered. But though Gilliver was agreeable to his joining a religious order, his mother was not. He was to be her support, her mainstay in life.

The last arrival soon ranked close to Seamus in the affections of the earl and countess, which would have surprised the red-haired John Drummond who considered himself in a typically deprecating manner as the "not as" boy. He was, he once said, not as strong as Angus, not as shrewd as Ogilvy. He was responsible, yes, but not as detail-minded as Menzies. He was growing mature, but if he lived to be a hundred, he'd ne'er be as sophisticated as Cameron. He never realized that although he had less of the good points of the others, he lacked altogether the bad points of each. Jamie's natural preference for this boy was encouraged by the adults about him. They appreciated that such a friendship could be good for both the leader and the led, the rich boy and the poor, the privileged and the responsible.

The addition of Drummond made the group complete: six plus Jamie, all with some degree of breeding and wits, too. It took time and a fight or two to establish the pecking order with Jamie on top by virtue of his mind and muscle as well as his position. Soon after, with the household belongings loaded onto twenty carts, they were off to Seaforth on Dun Dearduil over the bleakness of Rannock Moor.

For most of the boys this was the first extended trip in saddle . . . and the first saddle sores. Seaforth was not sympathetic. Seamus unguented the boys that night . . . and put them back up into saddle the next morn. Fortunately, a six-day trip rarely did permanent damage.

Within a month, a stranger—the first of many—disembarked at the Loch Linnhe and made his way to Ben Nevis and the Castle Seaforth. With his arrival, the children's vacation ended and their education began. He was an expert with the falchion, a short sword, about one and one half inches wide at the handle and four inches wide at the bottom—a handy thing and easy for a youth to wield as compared to the bigger two-handed sword. After the falchion, they must learn the ways of the flamberge, a sword with a wavy edge, requiring a different two-handed stroke. Once these two weapons were mastered, the swordsman left, soon to be replaced by another weapon master.

Seamus, whenever able, attended the lesson, volunteering to be the practice piece of the tutor. Although he took many a buffeting and to begin with showed much clumsiness in addition to great strength, he learned. Jamie, who loved him like an older brother, never laughed, nor did Drummond, who followed Jamie's lead, nor Gilliver, who knew better of his own conscience. Nor did Angus and Ogilvy, who, except for their own eternal internal feudings, were basically taciturn.

Only Cameron and Menzies—a natural pairing—made fun of the good-natured giant. But more than once Jamie and Drummond took on the pair—Gilliver not joining in, three against two not being fair—and pummelled them well. That stopped them.

Seamus took his own revenge when the boys came to learn horse care under his command. The horses whose stalls Menzies and Cameron must tend were not of the neat, cleanly kind who soiled in only one corner of their stall. Instead, they wallowed in their own droppings. The mucking out was a long onerous chore for the boys.

Over the next ten years, their education continued in schoolroom, in the castle courts, in the hills and country beyond.

They learned to ride the most infractious of horses—Seamus attending horse fairs to seek them out. Later, they were charged with the actual buying of mounts. The horsedealers put clever tricks upon them—with Seamus's blessing—pulling a colt's teeth to make it appear older, making a dull jade kick and curvet as if he had spirit by placing a burr under the saddle, attempting to foist off a dumb horse, or a deaf one, or a night-blind one as perfect specimens. The boys learned by these tricks, and then were set to selling back their bad purchases at other fairs. Menzies, with frank and honest air and boyish innocent looks, was best at such chicanery.

A knowledge of all weapons must be acquired, including those used in the tourney, both traditional and modern ones: to run fair at the tilt or to skewer the ring; to draw the bow—sighting below the target for distances up to sixty yards, and above it for longer shots. Angus was the best longbow man, loosing a dozen arrows in a minute at a man-sized target 240 yards away and hitting the mark with all twelve. Ogilvy was easily his match with crossbow, especially the prodd bow, which was light enough to set by hand and fired clay pellets. No moving target, not even the smallest bird that came within 120 yards, was safe from him.

Purely physical pursuits were encouraged, too: vaulting, running, leaping, wrestling, and swimming. Here, Cameron with his extremely long legs had the definite edge. Surprisingly enough, when it came to dancing—which every courtier must learn from almost the time he can walk—Cameron was the least adept and not at all graceful. Whether he was called upon to dance the allemande, the quick courante, the slow sarabande or the lively gigue, he simply had no music sense.

The making of music took up much of their time, all having to learn to sing—a delight before and after their voices changed, a mockery while puberty intervened. Yet the Lady Islean insisted her all-male chorus continue. And soon, she demanded that they learn to accompany themselves as well—on lyre and lute and cittern, a similar instrument but wire-strung and higher pitched . . . the harpsichord family including virginals and clavichord . . . the sackbut and trumpet and bombard. And each had his own flute, choosing either bass treble descant or soprano. Gilliver seemed to have the most musical bent except in one area: Cameron found his only kindred musical spirit when first he attacked the Scottish bagpipe.

Not just of wars and music did they learn, but sport as well. At hawking, Drummond, with his quiet, reasoned nature, struck a response in the fierce-tempered imperious birds of prey. Let him and any other cast the lure, and the bird—whether gerfalcon, merlin or kestrel—was sure to choose Drummond's. Tricking the birds by having Drummond scent another's lure never fooled the longwings. And the shortwings—eagles, sparrowhawks or buzzards—always returned to his outstretched fist, sometimes even screaming and refusing to land until he proffered his gloved wrists. Even Jamie's peregrine, a slate gray and white beauty raised from a fledgling, went as willingly to Drummond as to her master.

To play at tennis and to bowl on the lawn was demanded of them and to hunt not just for sport but for food on the table, using one day spear, another lance, a third bow or arquebus. And when the weather was inclement, they amused themselves learning all manner of cards and dice—from Trump and Primero to Hazard and Treygobet.

They learned to play clean, and to figure the odds. And one day, they were introduced to the scurriest rascal Seaforth could find, who taught them how to shave the six die so as to bar treys or cinques and to load die to make a high fullam so as to cast cinques or sixes.

At cards, they were taught how to cut, misshuffle, mark, or misdeal—to cheat as thoroughly as they had been taught how to play by the rules. Gambling, the Lady Islean gave them to know, was foolhardy unless one knew all the odds, including the black ones.

Beyond all this, the boys learned table manners, including the serving of their elders at table as pages do in a royal household. The art of conversation—both empty and enlightened—was not neglected. And although Seaforth Castle lacked for young maidens of the same breeding and age as the boys, Lady Islean's ladies-in-waiting were not at all loath to polish the charms of these young men. Older women can teach young males much, and at Seaforth they did. Between these ladies and the serving women, all of the boys were properly bedded early in their young lives and quite frequently after that.

But not Seamus. His Nelly saw to that. His was the task of fending off females. For all the freedom Nelly allowed him, they might as well be married. Then, within the year after Fionn was born, Nelly gave birth to another child, a girl whom the Lady Islean named Devorguilla after the patroness of scholars who founded the Scots college at Oxford in the thirteenth century and whose beauty was such that 250 years later, girls were still being compared to her.

Devorguilla lived up to her famous name. A fair-haired, green-eyed, oval-faced beauty, she won the hearts of the whole of Castle Seaforth, especially that of the Lady Islean, who found the little girl an antidote to the masculine features of the military camp that her husband was fashioning for his heir. When the boys sought out the countess, they were just as apt to find a young blond-haired head bent over the embroidery frame as an older dark-haired one. The boys, fierce warriors that they were becoming, made much of this winsome lass, and she became their mascot. She cheerily ran errands for them, interceded in their behalf when they'd offended the Lady Islean, acted as foil for their pranks and jokes.

Because she showed no favorites, loving them all equally, they made her one of them, accepting her presence wherever they were and including her in their games, explaining to her their jokes, and even confiding in her their dreams.

When she was tall enough to learn to ride, they combed the horse fairs for the perfect pony for her, gentled and schooled it just so, made its tack themselves, including a smaller version of their own workmanlike saddles, and then fought with one another for the dubious privilege of holding its bridle and leading the pony round and round the dusty tiltyard.

Once she had mastered the basics of riding, however, they made no excuses for her being a girl and insisted if she wished to ride with them, she must ride like a man and keep up with them. She did, and mastered the bow too, learning to falcon with the best of them. No delicate little thing, Devorguilla was growing up to be a long-limbed, statuesque beauty equally at home with the pursuits of the out-of-doors and with women's tasks indoors.

It was only natural that when the Lady Islean undertook to teach her seven male charges the art of writing love letters, all seven of their efforts were addressed to the beautiful Devorguilla. Only in the classroom was she left behind, and that because of the age difference. However, the Lady Islean undertook to teach the child herself. Her only rule: she must not let the boys do the lessons for her.

Although much of the emphasis at Castle Seaforth was on warfare and weaponry, the countess was adamant that the boys' minds not be neglected, and the earl seconded this. Everyone, including Seamus, learned that turning a good rhyme was as much required of them as was reading and writing in at least three languages: Scots, French—the language of courtiers—and Latin, the language of the Church and literature.

Those with any gift for foreign tongues were encouraged to master more: English, Italian, Spanish, even Greek. The courts of Europe being so inbred, a knowledge of languages was more than an asset, it was an absolute necessity for the up-and-coming young man. Seaforth and his lady never forgot that six of these young men had their fortunes to make.

As life would have it, the boy whose future was best assured, who needed to excel at this training the least, did the best. Perhaps because his parents expected no less of him. The others at first excused their own lack of success by claiming that the tutors gave more than a fair share of instruction to the son of the lord; eventually they had to admit that James Mackenzie succeeded because he willed himself to, working twice as hard as the rest. He was a natural athlete, one who never went through the gangly, awkward stage, having been born with the natural grace of a cat, and he was the masculine embodiment of his mother's dark-haired, blue-eyed beauty. Introspective, he had inherited a certain sternness and reticence from his father, which could dissolve readily enough, if the situation presented itself, into infectious merriment.

He lived, he loved (very well, judging from the sighs and glances of the serving maids), he led. To be with him was an excitement, a source of endless innovative delight, for his was a curious mind that perceived possibilities for fun or fantasy in the most mundane situation. He was daring but not usually foolhardy, asking nothing of his fellows that he did not demand of himself more rigorously, and accepting on his own head responsibility for all of his and his fellows' actions. The earl and the countess gloried in him, losing themselves in the wonderment every parent feels at seeing dreams fulfilled, immortality promised, but at the same knowing that bittersweet feeling that comes in watching one's only child grow to manhood.

As was the way with all noble households, the family moved frequently, dividing their time among Rangely and Alva and Edinburgh, but always coming back to Seaforth. Even there, however, they were not unaware of the doings in Scotland, although the mood of court and country was less cosmopolitan, more insular. Because of the Lady Islean and Jamie's proximity to the throne, much of their attention was focused on the doings of the royal family, specifically Margaret Tudor's. Like the rest of the nobility, they were astonished by her wedding the head of the Red Douglas clan, Archibald Douglas, the sixth Earl of Angus. In so doing, she forfeited her regency, according to the terms of the late King James's will. Thus, when the Estates summoned John Stewart, the Scots Duke of Albany, from his home in France to be regent, the boys understood why. And, versed as they were in heraldry and genealogy, they understood too why the Estates confirmed him as hereditary second in line to the throne.

They were, in their familiarity, not at all impressed by the knowledge that Jamie Mackenzie, their playmate, was fourth in line, through the bar sinister, before his mother and behind her brother, to that selfsame throne. They understood why Albany had beheaded Lord Home and his brother, both of whom were believed to have murdered James IV at Flodden. But they could not fathom why he had eventually agreed in 1517 to the return of the exiled Margaret and her husband to Edinburgh.

Indeed they were ready, three years later, to proclaim "I told you so," when word came of a fight in April 1520, between James Hamilton, Earl of Arran, and the Queen Dowager's husband. Almost nine hundred men faced each other on the streets of Edinburgh that day. Before they were through, blood greased the cobblestones of High Street, the noble thoroughfare that led from castle to palace. For a while the battle seemed to favor the Hamiltons, who in turn favored the Scots Duke Albany, now in France negotiating a treaty. Then another Home, he of Wedderburn, at the head of his own Border clan, charged through Netherbow Fort and threw his weight in with Douglas.

The Hamiltons broke and ran, between tall houses, down meandering wynds, through narrow closes. Who it was that first called this bloodletting fracas "Cleanse-the-Causeway" no one knew, but the term was too apt to disappear. It stood in typical Scots contrast to that sophisticated ensemblage of pageantry and pomp that took place the same year across the German sea in France, the Field of Cloth of Gold, where Henry VIII and Francis I first met in a most ostentatious display of wealth and jewels.

Fortunately, for Scotland's sake, the peace between England and France did not last. Each monarch took umbrage at the other's flaunting of riches; and shortly thereafter, the Scots Duke of Albany returned to Scotland, with France's blessing and a token force of men-at-arms, to drive the English south of Scotland's borders.

For three years more, the country enjoyed the blessings of good, solid, capable government under the wise eyes of this gallicized ruler, who spoke not a word of Scots. He managed temporarily to throttle the gross ambitions of the Marrying Douglas.

Sometime in 1524, the earl and countess judged, things went sour for Scotland. An army of Scots being led against the British refused to follow Albany beyond the Border. Angus and his wife, Margaret Tudor, who had seemed on the brink of divorce, reconciled. Henry Stewart, Earl of Moray, brother to the Lady Islean and third person in the realm after Albany and the child King James V, was set upon by persons unknown as he was leaving St. Margaret's Chapel near the palace's yard. Left to bleed from more than a dozen wounds, his death seemed inevitable.

Upon the heels of these ill tidings came a summons of Seaforth to court. Seamus was not privy to the conversation, but Albany's messenger was closeted with the earl and countess for close to an hour. Seamus was then called to the library tower, and Seaforth put the messenger in his charge with pointed instructions: "See to it that this man be fed and bedded—apart from the barracks so he is not bothered by idle questioning. He shall return to court tomorrow—give him that new roan palfrey."

Seamus opened his mouth to protest; the horse was Jamie's.

Seaforth continued. "You and your troop and we and the boys shall follow close on his heels. Take full half the household troop and see to it that they are suitably armed. They go with us as does the countess and two of her ladies. Tell the men to pack lightly. All our baggage must go on sumpter horses."

When Seamus would have left, the messenger in tow, Seaforth called him back. "This will be the boys' first trip to Edinburgh in years. Let's not worry them with unnecessary details. Devorguilla will be staying here. I'll make some excuse to the boys. You break the news to your daughter." The two men just looked at each other. Seaforth didn't envy Seamus his task, and Seamus knew it. He would rather have faced seven outraged young boys than his one willful, lovely daughter. So, he did what fathers have traditionally done under such circumstances. He immediately sought out Nelly and told her to tell her daughter the bad news.

The following day, the countess and her ladies on jennets, the earl on an iron gray rounsey, the lads on their palfreys made a bright show. Jamie had raised an inquiring eyebrow when he discovered the roan gone, but other than that said nothing.

As Seamus rode out of Seaforth at the head of the troop, he remembered another trip to Edinburgh before Flodden. The countess had been young, the earl whole, and the heir a mere child. Now, the earl's beard was as laced with strands of white and gray as was his strange gray white hair; the countess had ripened with age; and the child was a young man who shaved nearly every day and handled himself and the weapons of a knight with surety. Seamus, who had been an apprentice groom far back in the ranks of the troop, now rode directly behind the earl's standard bearer. He was a man of thirty with at least three sons that he acknowledged but so far no wife. Truly had he become the earl's right-hand man, advancing from squire to Captain of the Guard. When pressed as to why he'd not married, he laughingly asserted, "When I find another as fair as the Lady Islean, I'll jump me into the marriage bed."

The trip from Seaforth to Edinburgh, because of the women, was made in fairly easy stages, stopping first at Rangely on Rannock Moor where first the troop of boys assembled ten years before. Then on to Crieff and Drummond Castle where the Second Lord Drummond's welcome seemed a bit cold until he realized that his young kinsman might make a welcome addition to the court. When they left, after a tearful reunion between John and his mother, the Lord Drummond was almost effusive in suggesting that the lad come back soon.

Bypassing Stirling, although night was upon them, the troop pressed on to Falkirk and Rough Castle, one of the nineteen fortresses along the great Roman Antonine Wall, which once ran the width of Scotland. The following afternoon they rode into Edinburgh and through the Cowgate, which now was indeed a gateway, its great gates connecting the Flodden wall. Partway up St. Mary's Wynd and into the Seaforth tall house they went; the boys were eager to ride out again and investigate the town, but Seaforth reined them in.

"Tomorrow will be soon enough. Today, see to your horses . . . and I'll set you an exercise. How would you defend this house against a siege? He with the best plan will get Dunstan's next colt."

The young men scattered, the better to survey the house, its grounds and defenses. Angus and Ogilvy paired off, as did Cameron and Menzies, while Drummond and Gilliver waited for Jamie to take the lead. He took the reins of his palfrey from the footman and, instead of charging into the house, led the way to the stable. "Our best defense may have to be a quick strategic retreat."

Seaforth and his lady, arm in arm, more slowly made their way up the stair and into the house, Seamus following behind, to the solarium, the room of so many memories.

"Seamus, you and I have a visit to pay on Castle Hill tonight," Seaforth said, and laughed wryly. "I have been advised to come in disguise. How a man with my hair and but one arm and served by the tallest man in Scotland can move about without detection in this city boggles the mind. The citizens would all have to be blind."

"A cloak with a hood, perhaps," the Lady Islean murmured.

"And would you have Seamus ride like a hunchback?" he replied quickly. "No, we cannot hide; but you're right, we should not draw attention to ourselves. So cloaks and dark colors it will be. Under your cloak, Seamus, wear your mail, as will I, and carry your favorite arms. Between now and when we leave at dusk, keep the boys occupied and preferably out of sight. If you can't do that, at least keep them separated so that no head count can be easily taken by an inquisitive soul. Now, go and get what rest you can."

The earl sounded bone-weary. He and his wife looked as if they had come down a long road, and beyond the next turn, the end was in sight. Only they were not sure just what form that end might take, nor whether they truly welcomed it.

The family supped, earl, countess, seven boys, two ladies-in-waiting, and Seamus, in the upper hall that night. The boys were all ravenous and full of their plans, but Seaforth would not entertain any details until the next day. "How can you know how to defend the house when you have not seen it except in full day? Know you how often the watch comes by during night? Or how many traffic the Wynd when the city stirs itself? Is this the best thinking you can do? Faugh, and to think I trained you!"

Crestfallen and more than a little subdued, the boys said no more but bolted their meal and eagerly sought excuse from the table. No longer was it boy against boy, but the troop united against its teacher.

Watching them go, Seaforth could not contain himself. "Pray God, we don't need to put any of those plans into action. I tell you, Islean, I can feel in my bones that it's a trap."

"Hush, don't start thinking that. John Stewart was the king, my father's best friend, more than just a cousin. He is an honorable man. Look at him, at the number of chances he's had to take advantage of the child-king. He hasn't done it. Can the child's mother or stepfather say as much? I tell you James, Albany would not have sent for us, brought us out of the safety of your keep in the Highlands unless it was an emergency.''

"That's exactly what I fear. What kind of danger could there be that would find us safer here in the midst of our enemies, whoever they might be, than within our own castle walls? I don't like it. Not at all.''

Islean had no answer, and Seamus took advantage of the silence to make his excuses from the table. He needed assurance, not uncertainty, to make him feel right with the world.

Fortunately, the moon was near full that night, for Seaforth would have no lantern-bearer light their way, although he was more than willing to take a score of men—almost a quarter of their troop—with him. Only after assuring himself that a strong guard had been posted did he lead the men out. Their route was round about, following the Flodden Wall round to the base of the castle, then up through Lawnmarket, beyond the Luckenbooths and up High Street, the famed causeway, to the castle.

The drawbridge across the old moat was down, and they crossed to a strong battlemented gateway, defended by a massive door studded with iron bolt-heads. A murmured word to the guardsman, and the door swung silently open. Up they went, by a pathway cut into the solid rock, to the Portcullis Gate beneath the state prison. Better known as the Constable's Tower, it was part of the defense works erected by David II more than 150 years before. The walls were enormously thick, ten to fifteen feet, Seamus judged. He would have preferred to defend this citadel against attack rather than Seaforth's tall house. On the left, a flight of stairs ascended direct to the citadel; on the right, the road continued. When Seaforth cast about for some guidance as to which path to choose, a man, heavily muffled, stepped out of the shadows. "Pardon, monsieur, if you will follow me." Without waiting for an answer, nor even looking back, he took the more circuitous road, to the battery on the edge of the cliff overlooking the Nor Loch below.

There in labored Scots, heavily French-accented, the man advised the earl to dismount and have his men take shelter in the shadows amongst the cannon, while Seaforth—with Seamus close behind—

entered the guardroom. The room was bare, without fire, candles, or lanterns. Only an occasional ray of the moon lit their way to the benches drawn up to the trestle table in the center of the room. Their guide said nothing. Seaforth and Seamus were well content to keep the silence.

Soon came the muffled sound of a bolt being drawn . . . and then just the faintest protesting of well-oiled hinges. A draught of cold, dank air raised the hackles on Seamus's neck, and a voice from out of nowhere spoke: *"Le Comte? Albany, à votre service. Parlez-vous français? Votre homme aussi?"* At Seaforth's assent, there was the scraping of a wooden stool being drawn up.

"Good. French it shall be. I prefer always to speak under such circumstances without interpreter. It makes for better understanding. And secrecy. Your wife's brother, the Earl of Moray is dead. And has been dead for two weeks. We have hidden the news. Please, allow me to continue. *La reine* Margaret knows. She has brought her son here to Edinburgh, along with two hundred English gentlemen sent by King Henry. They plan his erection. The regalia have been sent for. The investiture will take place. And within a day or two of it, the estates led by the king's stepfather will tell my Frenchmen to leave, and I will go with them. Already I have been told that I shall be divested of my claim to the throne. That will leave only four others, now that Moray is dead, with a frail claim to it: Hamilton (who will assuredly be put to the horn after his part against Douglas in Cleanse-the-Causeway, at the first chance Douglas gets); the daughter of the queen, Margaret Douglas, a nine-year-old girl; your wife, and your son, not in that order.

"No, don't interrupt. To buy the Queen Dowager's assistance, and, through her, her son's consent to this, Douglas has agreed to give her the divorce she wants so that she can marry the well-hung stallion she fancies. But to do so, he has had to swear on holy relics that his divorce of wife number four was invalid. Which makes his marriage to five, *la reine,* equally so. That, of course, bastardizes his own daughter. Now follow closely, for the lives of your wife, your son, yourself, and your king may depend on it. As you know by the laws of primogeniture, a girl can inherit only if there is no male heir; a bastard can inherit only if there is no legitimate child. Compare you the rights of a bastardized daughter of a queen dowager against the son of a bastard, but *acknowledged*, daughter of the king! The College of Heralds would have to rule your son had the greater claim.

"I know you are going to scoff, but Seaforth, I warn you, never underestimate Douglas. He is a man who wants, above all else, power. Why else would he have taken *la reine* Margaret into his bed? The woman is silly, a shrew, not much more than a strumpet, but she has the blood of kings flowing in her veins, and she was named regent in the king's will." His voice was calm, matter of fact, which made his words all the more chilling to Seamus.

"Suppose something should happen to that son of yours? Your wife's claim remains valid. Suppose that something should happen to you *and* your son, that you should be victims of a freak hunting accident, for example. It would not be hard to arrange. A son might still be gotten on your wife—perhaps by the Marrying Douglas himself. This could be considered payment for his role in securing *la reine* her latest fancy. And if Islean should not happen to breed? Douglas has seen three wives to the grave, why not a fourth? And then, suddenly, our nine-year-old Margaret Douglas becomes a factor again, next in line to the throne. You do follow my meaning?"

Albany's voice changed. Seamus could almost see him lean closer, his face grow more serious, his eyes more intent.

"Do not mistake me. What I do tonight is not to save the lives of the family Seaforth. If that is a by-blow of our meeting, I am delighted. But my main concern is to save the life of the young king. Nine years ago, when I was first made regent by the estates, I took a vow to protect that three-year-old child and to save his kingdom. I do not take such vows lightly. Until released of them, I will fulfill them to the best of my ability. The best way I can protect young James's life is to make sure his death would benefit no one, except maybe the Seaforths. What I propose tonight will neutralize any advantages to the Seaforths and totally nullify Douglas's. Here, then, is why I sent for you. I propose you send your son with me to France."

In the silence that followed, Seamus thought that he could almost hear the sounds of Seaforth's brain digesting this information.

"For how long?"

"Until the young king sires a living child. I understand he has already been striving hard in that direction, but with no tangible results so far. Perhaps because his stepfather restricts the ladies he sees to those with a curiously similar history of infertility. Then, too, the Stewarts themselves are none too prolific. Look at you and your own wife. I might add, another bairn in the Seaforth cradle would not hurt matters, if it could be arranged. If not, then I suggest that the wait might be so long as the king is childless or your wife beyond the breeding age. That is if we don't want Douglas to extend his marrying ways to a dowager countess." Albany, typically Gallicly gallant, added, "Especially one as lovely as yours."

That gross redheaded Douglas and the Lady Islean? Seamus was sickened at the thought, but he waited in vain for the earl to protest. When the earl finally spoke, his voice was so well controlled that in the darkness one had no hint of his thoughts.

"What of you? Of all the candidates, you have the best claim. The estates acknowledged you once. They'll do it again if you wish."

"You miss the point. I don't wish. If I had desired to be king of this savage land, I could have been so at any time in the last nine years. A word to the right Frenchman, *et voilà*, the child is gone. Look at the example set us by our neighbors to the south. Richard III did not let two small nephews stand in his way when he wanted the throne. The murder happened the year I was born and still they have not found the bodies. Ah, well, you get my message. Perhaps if I had had a son . . . but I too am a Stewart; my heir is a little girl. Would I wish upon her the fate I foresee for your son or the little Douglas? No, my friend, I go back to France, and there I stay where the weather is warm, the food heavenly, and we all speak the same tongue. Your son—he speaks French? Good. Think it over. If you agree, I shall take him into my own home and treat him as if he were my son. My little Anne has always wanted a brother. The boy, I am told, is as fair as his mother. *Bon soir, messieurs*."

Sounds of the stool being drawn back and scuffling of feet on the pavement announced the interview was over. A door creaked open and closed, a bolt clanged home, and then the door to the guardroom opened wide and their guide beckoned them out. Their ride back to St. Mary's Wynd in the darkness was uneventful and silent. Each man was lost in his own thoughts. Only as they dismounted in the courtyard did Seamus put thoughts to words: "My lord, let us go back to Seaforth. There, I swear to you, all will be safe. My life on it."

"Seamus, you read my mind. Would it were as simple and easy as that."

He sighed and Seamus remembered that Seaforth was not a young man. Then the earl clapped Seamus on the shoulder. "Good night, my friend. I rely on you to keep silent about all this. Until we decide what to do, one way or another, I leave those other young rapscallions under your wing. Keep them on a close tether. I do not want them showing their faces about town as yet. No, don't see me up. We've both had a long day. Get you to your own bed."

Seamus was glad he was not the one who must relate the night's events to the countess. What sleep, if any, the earl and countess managed that night he didn't know, but when he sought out his own breakfast, the Seaforths had already called for theirs and summoned Jamie to join them. Once the other boys were up, Seamus set Angus and Ogilvy to spying out the lay of the land from the roof of the tall house. Menzies, suspecting there was work to do, made himself scarce. Cameron and Gilliver were put to polishing weapons in the armory while Drummond, on his own, made himself helpful in the stables.

Soon the shouting began. Exact words were indecipherable through the heavy door of the solarium, but one could tell that Seaforth and his son were arguing mightily. Now and again the shouting ceased, presumably when the Lady Islean spoke her piece. But the quiet was short-lived. Louder and louder the shouting grew. Once the door was flung wide and Jamie stormed out. But his father's "You ungrateful brat, get yourself back in here" turned the boy on his heel. His slamming of the door warned the world not to mistake his obedience for compliance. Only when word was sent upstairs that Albany's herald had arrived with a message, did the voices cease and silence reign. Soon word came to show the herald up to the solarium, an unusual courtesy rarely shown even to a herald. His stay was short; he returned downstairs almost immediately.

On his heels came the family. The countess was red-eyed although she managed a smile. The earl was stony-faced, but no more so than Jamie. His eyes were bleak blue, his chin set in a rare stubborn cast, and his lips, usually so generous with laughter, were tight with barely suppressed rage. Whatever the cause, obviously the younger Seaforth had not won, nor had his parents found joy in their victory. Not by word or glance did Jamie acknowledge Seamus's presence. Indeed, with head held high and shoulders squared, he marched right past his old friend as if on his way to meet the headsman in the courtyard outside. Seamus turned to follow after, but a soft hand on his arm stopped him. "Leave him, he goes to say good-bye to the boys and his own boyhood." Looking down on her saddened face, Seamus didn't need to be told; Jamie was going to France.

Taking Seamus aside, the earl confirmed it: "The Regalia has arrived. As Albany predicted, the erection takes place today in the Chapel Royal at Holyrood Abbey. Our presence has been ordered. Ours and our *boys'*. Albany worded the summons so as to give us a chance to circumvent it. We have here seven boys. Only one was meant, but six of the seven will attend. The other has another destination; he is to be a gift to Albany from his loving cousin, the Lady Islean. Think you that you can find a sumpter case large enough to hold such a gift?"

Seamus's voice shook with emotion, but he managed an "Aye, my lord. I'll find one."

"Good. Then choose you carefully three or four of your best men, men you would trust with your life . . . and my son's. Set them the task of delivering Albany's gift. Normally, I would have you do it, but your height distinguishes you too well. Tongues would wag if you were not in attendance on the Seaforths. Therefore, you too shall be at the investiture of our young king. Wear your brightest, most eye-catching garb. If you have nothing so bold, maybe I do. Although with those shoulders . . ." His voice died out as he considered the breadth of the man before him. "After all, it will not be our fault if those at the court think mistakenly that one of the boys you serve is James Mackenzie, Master of Seaforth. The earl managed a smile. "God forgive me, I shall not disabuse them of that thought."

CHAPTER 5

For eight long, silent years, Jamie was away. As a condition of taking him and protecting him, Albany had insisted that he go incognito and remain incommunicado for the duration of his stay in France. Albany did manage, now and again, to send word that all went well with the lad. But the Lady Islean, with feminine contrariness, lamented her son's not finding ways to circumvent her very own injunction that he never write.

Often, however, Seaforth and his lady blessed Albany's foresight. Events had, to a large degree, worked out as Albany predicted. Douglas had indeed taken power, filling the royal household with his own Red Douglas kin, from the highest offices to the lowest. No morsel of food, stick of wood, nor piece of linen entered the castle without a Red Douglas having his hand touched with silver. Douglas reveled in the riches and in the power. Determined to keep both, he installed the young King James V in the prisonlike Constable's Tower of the Castle of Edinburgh. His wife he sent off to exile of sorts to Stirling, still very much a married woman and evidently destined to stay that way. Shortly thereafter, another of Albany's prophecies was fulfilled: Hamilton was put to the horn for treason. The proclamation, signed "James R." in a youthful, florid script and duly sealed, was read by Marchmont and Albany heralds from above the crowd gathered at the base of the Mercat Cross outside St. Giles Cathedral. Hamilton's lands were forfeited to the king; his title tainted by corruption of blood disqualifying him, his heirs, and his heirs' heirs from inheriting it. With one stroke of the pen, James V erased Hamilton from the peerage and moved the Seaforths and his half sister Margaret Douglas that much closer to his throne.

For four years, from 1524 to 1528, Douglas made Scotland his personal fief. The king matured but still sired no heir. Then Douglas's world fell apart. The king escaped from Edinburgh by the very same subterranean passage that Albany had used when he came to confer with Seaforth. Riding furiously, without regard for his mount, he headed straight for Stirling, almost thirty miles to the west. At Queensferry and Linlithgow and again at Falkirk, he found fresh horses waiting, the best Scotland had to offer.

Galloping across the bridge with a hundred followers alerted and united behind his banner, he ordered the city gates closed behind him. Then he charged across the drawbridge into the castle, ordering the portcullis let down. Finally, he rode his horse up the castle stair, into his mother's chambers, and to safety!

This was the chance for those who hated Douglas to rally about the young king. Seaforth was among them. It was he, some said, who had been largely responsible for the king's escape from Edinburgh. Now was the Red Douglas's turn to be put to the horn for treason. To escape the inevitable, he slipped away with his daughter by ship to exile in England, forfeiting his estates. With her son's consent, Margaret moved swiftly to divorce and remarry; her choice—a young groomsman. Henry VIII, while offering refuge to his brother-in-law, refused to accept the validity of the divorce and forbade his sister to discard her husband. Now Margaret was skewered on the two horns of the bull: in Scotland she was Countess of Methven, in England still Countess of Angus. And the Pope adamantly refused to intervene.

For four years, she lived that way until in 1532 her young husband, tiring of his aged wife, strayed. Never one to suffer an empty bed, she soon found solace in the arms of one Colin Campbell. Soon word had it that she would like to free herself permanently of Methven—a plan neither king, her son, nor king, her brother, approved. Seaforth, now spending some time at court, was designated to speak to the Dowager Queen and to convey Parliament's refusal. The woman was furious. However, like a venomous spider, she had confidence that what escaped her net today would fall into it tomorrow. One thing was sure, she would be rid of Methven eventually.

Seaforth had his own problems. Three times in four years he had narrowly escaped the assassin's knife. He had forced himself to become even more skillful fighting left-handed, and once this had saved his life. Twice Seamus's vigilance had protected his master. Each attempt occurred when they were in Edinburgh to attend sessions of Parliament in the intricately corbeled Banqueting Hall of Edinburgh Castle. On the castle grounds Seaforth felt safe and also in his home on St. Mary's Wynd. Between them lay the danger. Therefore, each time he traveled he took a different route. On February 11, 1532, he journeyed home by way of Roxburgh's Close. As he and his men started their horses down, an equally large group of Borderers under the banners of Kerr and Turnbull rode up. With no room to turn around, the two passed single file, each man defensively hugging the wall to his left, his unarmed side. How the disturbance started no one could remember. But a horse kicked out, jostling another, who bumped into still another. Tempers, always stretched thin between Highlander and Borderer, flared. Words were said, blows struck, swords and rapiers drawn. Fortunately, the way being so narrow, little damage could be done. But the shouts and clash of steel on steel drew the curious to their windows up above to look down on an ill-lit group bumping and shoving and shouting as each attempted to make his way forward. When the melee was over, Seaforth's horse was there but his rider was not. Retracing their steps, they found him, lying alongside the steps leading up to Roxburgh's house, a crossbow's quarrel protruding from his eye. He had been killed instantly.

Straight about, Seamus, his men on his heels, charged, back up the Close to the house shared by Kerrs and Turnbulls. There in the courtyard they found the men still mounted, old man Kerr himself coming down the stairs to welcome them. A few terse words and Kerr demanded that Seamus search his men for the bow. It was not found, neither there nor in the Close. When questioned, the gate keepers at either end of the Close swore no one had entered or left after the two groups started in their separate ways.

Seamus knew not what to do nor whom to accuse. The Close was lined with town houses belonging to men who might have reason to see Seaforth dead, or whose patrons might want him removed. Lady Roxburgh, for example, was lady-in-waiting to the Queen Dowager. Then again, one never knew from day to day whether the Kerrs and Turnbulls were working for or against the English. So Seamus went home, carrying his lord's body before him, cradled in his powerful arms. He wept unabashedly, for Seaforth, for his lady, and for himself, for he had grown to love this man like a father.

The man he sent ahead must have prepared the Lady Islean for what had happened, for she waited in the courtyard. As best he could, he covered the dead man's gored eye with the palm of his hamlike hand—this much at least he could spare her—and clutched the body even closer to him. "Lady, I'm sorry. I tried—"

"I know, I know. Hush, no, don't blame yourself. You saved him for me many times before and would have done so again, but this time it was God's will—" She couldn't continue for a moment but must take a deep breath. Then, looking up at the man on the horse, towering so far above her, she smiled bravely and, tears running freely down her face, continued resolutely. "Now, that *he* is gone, it is time my son came home. Albany knows where he is. Send the message via him. But now, for the last time, bring my beloved upstairs. I would be with him for a while by myself to say my farewells. . . ." Her voice broke, her mouth trembled, and she muffled her sobs with her hand.

Seamus, dismounting swiftly, carried the still body of his lord up the stairs and into the bedchamber as he had done once before after Flodden. He had been younger and stronger then, and the earl lighter, but it was as if the years had never passed.

When on the following day Seaforth was laid to rest, Lady Islean's message was ready; it was succinct: Come home. It set the place and the time for his arrival: a cave on the Firth of Forth, no later than the last day of May. That the message arrived and was received, they knew. Whether it would be obeyed remained to be seen.

For seven days now, since their arrival on May 22, 1532, Seamus and his band of Scots kept vigil for Jamie in the dank cave on the craggy coast of the German Sea, just north of the Firth of Forth. At first, Seamus had proclaimed that the cave was ideal for their purpose. It was vast, gouged a full eighty feet deep into the rocks. And before it, on the sea's side, rose a marker easily visible from far out at sea: a mass of basalt emerging from the foam sixty feet high and shaped by nature into the likeness of a woman's spindle.

Beyond it, out where the estuary opened wide onto the German Sea, Bass Rock rose sheer nearly 300 feet out of the water. And beyond the white precipices of Bass Rock stood the towers and turrets and battlements of Tantallon that so dominated this portion of the firth. Tantalizing Tantallon. Scene of many an unsuccessful siege, with its three sides of wall-like rock and one of rocklike wall. And Tantallon was the stronghold of Archibald, the Marrying Douglas, the man with most to gain by preventing James Mackenzie from coming home.

To make certain no Douglas on Tantallon's battlements spotted their campfire, Seamus and his men maintained a cold, fireless camp the first night in the cave. Fortunately, the nights were growing shorter this season, and the sun did not dip below the water until long after the men's stomachs told them the evening meal hour had come and gone.

Eventually the multicolored sky stopped reflecting off the water, and darkness settled like a black velvet bag over the bay and the cave. With darkness came an increased watch for a signal from a French ship standing out to sea.

"There!"

"No, there!"

"Over there!"

Three sightings in as many seconds. But the signal light refused to stay in one place. Shining first here . . . then there . . . it danced about just beyond the reef.

"A ghost ship!" someone bleated.

Even in the darkness, Seamus recognized the last voice. It was John the Small, a good man in a fight, but too much given to fanciful ideas.

"No ship—ghost or no—could cover that much distance that fast," Fionn, Seamus's son, replied almost as soon as the frightening words were spoken. His youngest had a head on his shoulders that functioned like one more than double his nineteen years, Seamus realized with pride.

"Then what is it?" came the question from several puzzled and wary Scots.

I'd best squelch this talk, Seamus thought, or these lads will be a pack of jellyfish. Before he could speak, the light moved faster and became several lights. Now, it was not just beyond the reef. It had moved in closer. Then, to the watchers' bemused horror, the lights darted toward shore . . . just as swiftly moved back. The effect was hypnotic. No man spoke, no man moved. A loud crack, like the slap of an object upon the water, broke the spell. Then, the lights went out, one at a time, like candles being snuffed.

"Fireflies!" said Seamus. His voice brooked no opposition, allowed for no contradiction, invited no discussion. The talk, at least that within earshot, ceased.

A little later, he heard the scraping of sand behind where he sat. Then, a large familiar shape hunkered down beside him.

"Da'," Fionn said, "fireflies are land creatures."

When Seamus did not answer, Fionn continued, "The noise was made by a tail. I saw it, and I was not the only one." Getting no response, eventually Fionn moved on.

There were no more strange lights that night, but few men slept; they had already slept a goodly part of the day away. Although Seamus made work as best he could, not even he could keep a hundred pairs of hands busy. When hands are idle, mouths are not. The talk ceased when Seamus approached, springing up anew the moment he passed.

Seamus didn't have to be told of what they spoke. Mermaids and the diamonds and sapphires they wore. Jewels the size of a man's fist. Devil stones from the depths of the sea whose flashing facets were always just out of reach. Seamus knew all about it. Every Irishman had grown up to tales of men who, tempted and taunted by those elusive riches, followed the flickering lights farther and farther out to sea, there to be set upon by jealous mermen and sent to a watery grave.

Just as sure as he was born in a proper Irish home with two doors opposite to allow a proper fairy path through, he knew fear would keep most men ashore. The others would be planning a closer look at those jewels. Fingering the stone with a hole in the middle that he

110

carried to protect horses from fairy harm, he prayed that the mermaids would not come back.

That evening as the men choked down their cold rations with big draughts of ale, Seamus ate separately. One by one, his three sons separated themselves from the rest and came to sit or sprawl within arm's length of their father. Although born of different mothers, they were three of a kind and all of an age. Dugan, the oldest, was named for black baby hair, since fallen out and come in straw-colored like Seamus's; Derry, the middle one, for his once-red now fair head. Only Fionn, the youngest, was named fair and stayed fair. The names stuck, but no one teased the boys about their misnaming, for they, like their father, were big, brawny, giants of men. Seamus was proud indeed of these three boys, and he took them with him whenever he could.

Fionn broached the subject first. "Da', about the mermaids. Is it true if you catch one and take it home to wife, you will become rich and powerful?"

"Richer than the Earl of Seaforth?" Derry wanted to know.

"More powerful than the king?" asked Dugan, the oldest.

"Is that what they say?" Seamus mused. "I never met anyone who caught one."

There was another long, companionable silence while the three digested that. Again, Fionn reopened the subject: "Was there no' a French lord who married one?"

"Ah, yes, Raymond of Poitou. It was quite a story. Judge you for yourselves. It seems, a century or so ago, the count met this beautiful woman in the woods. Immediately he fell in love with her. And she with him. So, he proposed. She accepted on one condition: that he never attempt to see her on Saturday. The count agreed and they were married. Over the years, she gave him three sons and made him rich beyond his dreams. He grew old, but she did no'. He suspected the secret of her youthfulness lay in what she did on Saturday in her room. Overcome by curiosity and consumed by jealousy, he bored a hole in her door so that he might see what she did on this day. He was half pleased, half disappointed to discover she spent her time innocently enough taking a bath. He was about to leave his peephole when he saw this tail go flip-flop in the bathwater.

Thinking only to protect his wife, he drew his sword and charged through the door. There in the tub was a naked woman from the navel up . . . but from the navel down, she had a long, scaly fish tail. Since the count had broken his word, Melusine kept hers. She flew out o' the window and was ne'er seen again.''

Fionn it was, with the mind as quick as his mother's lovetap, who put his finger on the fallacy. ''Da' you say they had three boys?''

''Aye.''

''And the count did no' know his wife was a fish from the waist down?''

Dugan, once he was pointed in the right direction, was no simpleton either. ''Can you imagine sharin' your bed with a slippery fish and no' knowin' it?''

''Those nobles,'' guffawed Derry, ''must do it different from you and me.''

Seamus kept a straight face and continued drawing shapes in the sand. The other three picked their teeth—Fionn's mother had supplied the smoked meat and it was a bit stringy—or they scratched, since they shared the cave with sand fleas.

Again it was Fionn, who, like a terrier with a rat, refused to let go but must play with the subject till satisfied it was dead. ''They say the Seaforths could tell us a lot about mermaids if they wished.''

Seamus's head snapped upright. ''Who says?''

''Many, no' just one or two.''

''And what do they say?'' Seamus's eyes narrowed; he sensed real trouble.

Dugan, the oldest by three months, came to his younger brother's rescue. ''That long ago, a Seaforth found a mermaid stranded high up on the beach. Instead of killing her, he carried her down to the sea and let her go. She would have married him but he was already wed. So she told him the whereabouts of a treasure chest. To this day, whenever they need money, they just go dip in that chest.''

''That's no' all,'' Derry added. ''They say she gave him a ring carved with the figure of a Mer-Lion on it and told him, if ever he were in trouble, to turn the ring on his finger and a real Mer-Lion would come to the rescue.''

''You believe this?'' Seamus asked incredulously.

112

"I've seen the ring," Derry said, the other two nodding agreement.

Seamus, in the face of stupidity, turned sarcastic. "And if a Mer-Lion could come to the Seaforth's rescue, why did the beastie no' come to the mermaid's?"

Logical Fionn knew the answer to that. "Maybe she didn't have the ring with her."

Now, Seamus knew he was losing his temper, "But if the ring could have rescued him, why did he no' use it two months ago to escape his assassins?"

"Yes," Dugan agreed, "why didn't he?"

"Ninny," Fionn answered, "this Seaforth lost one arm, how could he turn the ring on his only hand?"

That did it. Seamus saw red. He wouldn't stand for his sons' making his lord's honorable wound a source for such speculation. He surged to his feet like a bear at bay, and his boys, who had felt the heavy weight of his ham-like hands before, scrambled for safety. Lowering his head purposefully, he stalked back into the cave. At the sight of his glowering face, all of his men retreated. On he came, until he had his whole troop backed up in the depths of the cave.

Then his men felt the full weight of Seamus's tongue:

"You make me sick, you and your talk! Mermaids, you say. And what would mermaids want with the likes o' you, you weasel-beaked sons of harlots. Faced with a middenhill full of drabs with their skirts around their waists, you would no' ha' the sense to untie your codpiece. As for a mermaid, dizards! Dodkins! Dolts! You would no' know one if you saw one. I'll be shit if I think you even know which end to make love to. If there be any but bairns among you, we'll find out the truth of this mermaid story. Here and now. Tonight. If the lights dare come back. Now get out of my sight."

The men scattered as best they might. For the rest of the evening they gave Seamus a wide berth.

The night came and went without event, as did the next and the next. It was only toward the end of the week that the men began to step less fearfully and talk more freely. It was not that tongue-lashings were new to them. In fact, it was almost a matter of pride with them that their Irish captain was the tongue-lashingest, evilspeakingest, most foul-mouthed fulminator in all of Scotland. Like a storm, they knew his anger would eventually pass. What they didn't know was when. Besides, by the end of the week they had another subject to keep minds and mouths busy. Would the new Lord Seaforth really come home? Would he, after eight years' absence and eight years' silence, answer his mother's summons?

Seamus didn't want to admit, even to himself, that their wait here might be in vain. Only a dullard, however, would deny that the young master was taking his good sweet time. If he did, indeed, arrive this night, it would not be one day early.

One way or another, with the young master or without, Seamus decided, he and his men would be gone before daybreak; their saddlebags were already packed. He couldn't wait to be gone. Then, one week to the night of their first sighting, the mermaids returned.

Passing among his men as they stared wide-eyed, fearful yet fascinated, out at the flickering, shimmering lights dancing so lightly over the reef and waving enticingly from deep within each breaking wave, Seamus did what came naturally to him in extremity. He swore. At the mermaids. At Frenchmen in general. At French seamen in specific. At young lords who keep their men waiting. At Douglases in Tantallon. At assassins of good, honest men. At anything and everything. Gradually, he could see the men relax and shift their attention away from the sea to their captain. His swearing they could deal with. It was the unknown that terrified them. Once he had completely loosened the hypnotic grasp of those lights, he would make his move; for he knew it would take more than words to quell their fear. It was time to challenge their manhood. Without pause, he raised his voice and called to the lights:

"Come ashore, you blinkin' scaly lasses. C'mon in here and meet up with some o' Scotland's finest. They're so hard up they'll be good for the whole night. You can steal the heart of every mother-lovin' son of them. Wink an eye and you can tow 'em out to sea like speared whales. C'mon in, I say, they're waitin' for you. Well, what's keepin' you? You fickle, slimy-tailed harlots o' the sea. Shake your tails and get on in here where we can get a look at you."

The men waited in silence as Seamus stood motioning the glimmering lights in toward the rocky shore.

"Well, if they will no' come to us, we'll go to them. Who is with me? That is if there are any but bairns among you. Or is that why the mermaids leave you alone? Do they know something I don't? Maybe those codpieces are empty. Or ha' you all been gelded? Who'll go? Or do I have to kick some buns first?

"Fionn, Dugan, Derry, get the boat ready to launch. Who else is man enough to row out and bring back a wife, or at least a jewel or two?"

Greed fought with fear, and greed won. John the Small stepped forward first. He was joined by one, then another of his coterie. Then by twos and threes and fours, they volunteered until Seamus had the entire troop from which to choose. Other than John the Small, whom he couldn't very well pass over, Seamus chose the least imaginative among them. Stalwart, steady types—ones you might call slow—and his own sons.

Dugan, as oldest and steadiest, he put in the bow. His other two sons he assigned to the prow with him. The three of them launched the boat with such great force that it sent waves out to meet the breakers head-on. At this, the lights retreated, moving, as the legend had it, temptingly out to sea. Seamus, who had in his time gentled many a nervous colt and wooed as many sensitive lasses, knew what to do. His voice like thick honey-syrup, he kept up a steady chatter as much to calm the rowers as to tempt any mermaids closer:

"Steady now, lads . . . gently does it. Pretend the ocean's a woman; keep your stroke long and slow, just the way she likes it. That's it. That's the way to do it. Nice and easy."

He let his voice die down until there was silence except for the protesting of oarlocks and the soft splash and drip of water as eight blades slipped into the water in unison. The lights kept their distance, but seemed to grow brighter.

Fionn took advantage of the pause to lean over and whisper, "Da', how do you do it?"

"Do what?"

Fionn was very serious. "Make love to a mermaid!"

"From the rear, I should think. Let me know if you find out."

"God, she's got my oar!" John the Small flung his oar from him and leaped to his feet. Oars crashed into each other, whipped about as rowers let go; the boat rocked crazily and the lights went out.

Suddenly, it was pitch black about them, the only sound the deep rasping breathing of frightened men.

Seamus's voice was soothing. "If there's a mermaid out there waiting to be ravished, we're willing, aren't we men? Lucky lassie, with a whole boat of Scotland's best to choose from. But let's not rush the lassie. Let's just sit here and let her look us over."

Gradually, the sounds of harsh breathing leveled out until all was silence except for the lapping of waves against the boat's sides. Then, like camp fires being lit in the midst of an army encampment, the lights came on again, one after another, even brighter than before.

"Okay, lads, let's try it again. Steady now, all together. That's it. See? The jewels are almost as good as won. Just a little further now." Seamus realized he was shouting against the roar of the waves as they grew higher and hit with more force, the closer they got to the reef. He signaled the men before him to weigh oars and pass the word. Anchors dropped fore and aft, and the boat swung between like a cocoon dangling between twigs being buffeted by the wind.

The mermaids kept their distance from the boat, at least at first. But gradually, when the boat didn't approach them, they came to it. Soon, the whole area about them was filled with diamonds of the deep that made the stars up above seem dim by comparison. Still, with hand signals, Seamus cautioned his men not to move, to keep silence. Their patience was rewarded. The lights came still closer, until they were treated to a show of beckoning jewels real enough to drive a man mad.

As the others watched, mesmerized by the flashing of jewels hither and yon, Seamus found his attention drawn to John the Small. He was leaning over the side, dangling something from a cord just inches above the water. As it swung back and forth twisting and turning, Seamus squinted and shielded his eyes from the spray misting his face. John the Small was using the Mer-Lion crest from his jerkin as bait.

Seamus roared with outrage. Men jumped, the boat rocked, and John the Small dived for his mermaid's jewels. He came up triumphant, the jewel held high in his upstretched hand.

"I've got it," he mouthed, his words lost in the surf.

Suddenly, as the men watched, envying their fellow, the lights blinked out, and John's jewel went dull. Then, John the Small flung the thing from him, his scream so piercing, the men could make it out in spite of the waves. He had expected a handful of hard, crystalline jewels and instead had closed his hand on a cluster of jellied slime, the parasites that grew upon the coral. When his mates pulled him back into the boat, his teeth were chattering. No one could make out what it was he tried to tell them. And later, he refused to talk about it.

As the men were attempting to dry him off, Dugan looked out to sea. "A signal, Da'," he shouted, "out there to our right." Sure enough, a light flashed again in the void. Seamus swore. In his desire to solve the problem of the mermaids, he'd forgotten their own signal lantern back on shore. He could not flash a light in return.

"Back to shore, and don't spare your guts, men," he shouted. The men jumped to it as he got anchors weighed, and the oars moved in earnest, rushing the boat headlong back to shore. Once there and getting confirmation from the watchers there that they too had seen the signal, Seamus struck spark with flint and lit his own signal lantern. Carefully covering it with an oiled cloth, he held it in his lap as he was rowed back out to the break in the reef. The absence of lights from the deep was a pleasant relief.

Once. Twice. His signal light flared. Then was hooded. And all waited.

From the black velvet void beyond the reef, there came an echo, a speck of light that repeated itself. Seamus, if he hadn't known what a sudden violent move could do to a boat, would have jumped for joy. Instead, he muttered what words of thanks were due, then set about rigging up the special oiled cloth shield he and his men had brought with them, to protect the lantern on three sides against watchful enemies eager to interrupt the ship, and later its longboat, now being guided by its light to the only known break in the reef.

Now, there was nothing else to do but wait. He wished he were back at the Seaforth Castle or Rangeley, or the Lady Islean's keep at Alva, or even the cave. His childhood trip from Ireland had soured him on the seagoing life forever.

Here, at the opening in the reef—the only passage through—all hands must man the oars to keep the sea from rejecting the boat and vomiting it back to shore like flotsam. Sleep being out of the question, and conversation virtually impossible over the roar of the surf, each man was left to his own thoughts. Seamus's began with the man whom he awaited tonight, the one he loved as a son; then as thoughts have a way of doing, they ranged further afield and deeper into time until he was back in Ireland and reliving the pain of his parting from his mother. Her face remained clear in his memory, but those of his brothers were a blur as was that of his father. Not for the first time, nor for the last probably, he wondered if that had been his father's voice he'd heard as the ship left.

Rough hands shook Seamus out of the past, the events of all that had happened twenty-nine years ago in 1503. Tonight was the last of May 1532, and he had his duty to do.

"The longboat comes, Captain," came the shout over the roar of surf on the reef.

For a long moment, Seamus saw nothing; his eyes were too befuddled with memories. Then came a glint. And another. The splash of oar in water. The boat was almost upon them. "Up anchor. Pull for your lives 'lest they breech us." Urged on by the lash of Seamus's cursing, his own boat barely cleared the opening in time to allow the French longboat through. Strain his eyes and squint as he might, he could not discern within the other boat the hoped-for passenger. Seamus knew better than to attempt to make himself heard across the water, so he simply signaled the Frenchmen with his light to follow toward shore.

As first one boat, then the other scraped upon the shore, eight long years of separation should be over. Seamus sat where he was. He couldn't force himself to move. Suppose Jamie hadn't come. Suppose he had changed. Suppose— Even as his mind made him miserable with speculation, through the babel of voices issuing from the other longboat one drew his attention. It was low-keyed but authoritative, rich but decisive. Seamus's French was frayed, so the words he heard had little meaning, but he recognized the voice. He'd obeyed its commands many times before. He rose to go to that voice, then realized it had come to him, its resonance muffled by a heavy cloak, its owner's face concealed by a hood.

"Is it you?"

The newcomer chuckled. "It is I."

"You've grown."

Although the man didn't approach Seamus's height, he was taller by a hand than many.

"I should hope so."

"Is it really you?"

Seamus read amusement in the glint of teeth that he glimpsed within the depths of the hood. "Do you need proof?" Two slender aristocratic hands, bare of rings, drew back the hood. In the moonlight, the man's hair shimmered in shades of metallic gray white. Seamus was dumbfounded.

"Had you forgotten, good Seamus? The hair is part of my Seaforth legacy."

When Seamus had come to Seaforth as a child twenty-nine years before, both the old earl and the young had been white-haired, but both were beyond middle age. Yet he had heard even then of the early graying that distinguished Seaforth men.

Satisfied that Seamus had seen enough, the man drew the hood back in place. And just in time. For an unctuous voice interrupted them, "My lord de Wynter? Your baggage is ashore. You understand I cannot tarry. I must leave now if we are to get back to the ship while still dark." Seamus heard the clink of coins as money changed hands. Then, the Frenchman, all effusive thanks, took his leave.

"You . . . are *the* de Wynter?"

"Ah, my fame has preceded me."

Indeed, it had! Such deliciously wicked gossip could not be contained within any one country's borders. The de Wynter was reported to have been both delicious and wicked, in and out of as many scrapes as he'd been in and out of beds. Men used a gruff tone of voice in disparaging him that clearly reflected envy. Women were more honest and less discreet. "I thought de Wynter was an Italian."

"With that name?" The voice switched to another language that could have been Latin.

When Seamus didn't respond, the voice resumed in Scots. "I did, indeed, spend some time in Italy. The winter we left, I accompanied Albany and 10,999 others on a campaign to conquer Naples. It was a fool's errand. In the year we were there, I learned much besides the language. Eventually, Madame Louise, the Queen Mother, paid

119

to have us evacuated." There was no emotion in Jamie's voice. He was all matter of fact.

Seamus was disconcerted, and protested this calmness in his own way. "Well, that's all behind you now, Jamie. Now you'll be Seaforth."

"Seaforth? Maybe. But not Jamie. There is another Jamie. Seamus, in your old age, your eyes are going bad. You have not noticed my little companion." He pushed a child out into the dim flickering light. Seamus thought for a moment he was seeing a ghost. Here was the Jamie of twenty years before.

"Who?"

"I told you. My son."

The child stared up at the giant of a man. At the look of bewilderment in those deep blue eyes, something inside Seamus was touched.

"Your son? You're married?"

"Do no' be putting words in my mouth."

"But his mother . . . who, we didn't hear—" He was cut short.

"Are you planning to spend the rest of the night in that boat, or are we going to be on our way? The message I received implied urgency. Or am I mistaken? Besides, I see three giants whose acquaintance I need to renew. But is there no fair young maiden with them? Did those three boys finally manage to lose their sister? No, don't tell me, I've got it. They married her off!"

Seamus suddenly found himself just as eager to be under way as de Wynter had been moments before. Somehow, he did not like the turn this conversation was taking. Devorguilla and Jamie, as a combination, was one thing. Devorguilla and the de Wynter—that thought bothered him. It made him curt. "No, Devorguilla's back at Seaforth." He turned on his heel. "Come, you're right. We should be on our way."

CHAPTER 6

The outrider wheeled his horse and came galloping back, pulling it showily but cruelly to a halt before Seamus. "Campbells, Captain!"

"No mistake?"

"With that red hair and those piggy faces?" The rider laughed, tossing his spyglass from hand to hand, then to his captain. "Come, see for yourself. They wear the wild myrtle, the old man's badge."

"Pudding pricks!" Would nothing go right on this journey? Seamus wondered. It had been two days since they had left the cave secreted behind Spindle Rock. Leaving the baggage to follow under guard, they had traveled light. With the child alternating riding before him or de Wynter—Seamus wondered if he'd ever grow accustomed to using that name—they had ridden cross-country, avoiding the lone castle or armed manor, keeping their distance.

Not even at Dumfermline, famous for its good fare and warm comfort, had they stopped, but had made a wide detour round the Tower Burn. Cold meat and lukewarm ale had been their supper. Then, in concession to the child, they had had a few hours sleep, and had more cold meat and even flatter ale for their breakfast. Fortunately, the child seemed used to sleeping in the saddle and did not complain, although now and then Seamus heard him speak rather querulously in French to his father.

Now, within six miles of their destination, the manor at Alva, their haste was undone. A Campbell baggage train barred their way.

121

Seamus, with de Wynter close on his heels, spurred his horse forward to the edge of the trees. There, across the River Devon, were the carts. Thirteen in all, an unlucky number he thought, with ten riders apiece.

Entrusting young Jamie to the care of Fionn, he tersely outlined the situation as he saw it to de Wynter and suggested that they wait here and let the train pass.

"Are we at feud with the Campbells?" de Wynter asked.

"Nay, at least we weren't a week ago. But with the Campbells, one never knows. They're a chancey lot, even for Lowlanders. And the Queen Dowager, Margaret Tudor—cursed be her name—is in love with one of them, not with one of us."

"That could be remedied. In the meantime, why don't we just ride out and ford the river?"

"Your mother made me swear to bring you to Alva undetected."

Giving a decidedly Gallic shrug, de Wynter said nothing more. Taking silence for consent if not approbation, Seamus passed the word that the men dismount, setting his son Fionn and two others on guard, at the edge of the woods.

Since there was no convenient clearing in which to gather en masse, they broke up into groups of three or four or five and searched out the least uncomfortable places to lounge and pass the time.

Seamus had no more seen to the overall disposition of the troop than whispered word was passed to him: You are needed up front. De Wynter was already there, his back braced against a convenient tree, a spyglass trained across the river, Fionn at his side.

Fionn explained. "Da'? Those carts are ours. I replaced the slat on the second one myself before we left Alva."

John Scott chimed in. "See the horse in the lead, Seamus? See how he holds back in the harness letting his fellow do most of the work? It's old Wat, I'd know him anywhere."

Then the third guard, not to be outdone, spoke up. "The drovers, Captain. Look close. They're from Alva, too. See the one bringing up the rear? Lazy Simon. Four lengths between him and the rest. By the time they get to their destination, the rest will have already been unloaded, and he'll have a hand unloading his. Three pence says I'm right."

Had Alva been raided? Seamus wondered. His thoughts swerved to Islean; what of her? Had she been captured or worse?

De Wynter, suddenly displaying great interest in calmly paring his nails with a small baselard, pitched his voice low to keep it from carrying beyond Seamus. "The logical thing to do is to continue doing nothing as we were. Give them time to pass before riding for Alva. But would your men sit still for that? Look behind you." De Wynter showed even greater interest in the shaping of his little fingernail. Seamus turned only to be confronted by the rest of his troop, who, sniffing out that something was amiss, had crept up to see for themselves. Grinning cheerily at the prospect of a fight, many had already made the transfer of their swords from scabbard to more accessible belt rings. After nearly thirty years in this country, Seamus still couldn't get over the natural bloodthirstiness of the Scots. Or, at least some of them, he corrected himself. The man beside him, his eyes veiled by heavy black lashes, seemed not at all eager to fight. Maybe, thought Seamus, the years spent abroad dallying with the ladies had sapped him of more than semen.

Continuing on in the same nonchalant tone, de Wynter said, "If we do ride out, do we fight to recover the baggage or ride hell-bent for Alva and your lady? Shall we flip a coin?"

Seamus couldn't believe his ears. This dawcock! Without thinking, he drew back his hand to cuff the supercilious bastard a good one, only to find the point of de Wynter's baselard at his throat.

"I wouldn't do that, good Seamus. Cool down, man, use your head. Something's wrong here. There are no wounded so far as I can see among the riders, nor do I see any within the carts. Seaforth men have always made a good account of themselves. They must not have been there when the raid took place! But then, why didn't the Campbells fire Alva? Look, the sky to the west is absolutely clear. Not a sign of smoke nor ruddiness."

Seamus looked into those clear blue eyes and, when the baselard was withdrawn, shook his head as if to clear it. "What are you saying?"

"Maybe there was a bargain struck: take the furnishings and leave the manor intact. I don't know. I do know that I do not particularly care to have the Campbells sleeping in my bedsteads or eating off my pewter. So, good Seamus, I suggest we deprive them of their loot." He rose to his feet, like a cat, in one silken motion, brushing off the twigs and fragments of weeds from his leathers.

"Come," he said and the big man lunged to his feet and followed after. "Show me the lay of the land." Back in the depths of the forest, with those who served longest here at Alva to assist him, de Wynter drew a crude map with the point of his baselard in the dirt.

"Divide the troop. Send twenty or so on our fastest horses upstream to cross at Dolour. Good Seamus, tell ten—no, make it fifteen—of your best fighting men to travel with me. The balance you will hold back to attack the rear."

Like the experts they were, the men quickly singled out the twenty freshest and fastest horses. These were caught up and ridden out by the lightest and best riders, each paring his equipment down to lighten the horses' load. At the last minute they were stopped by de Wynter.

"Something is untoward here. I should just as soon not advertise who we are until we know what the whole play is. So divest yourselves of the Mer-Lion badge before going into battle . . . and if you need a battle cry, let it be something bewildering. Cry"—and he smiled as if at a secret joke—"Hydaspes!"

The men were too well trained to question their lord, but as they rode off, Seamus could see them rolling that strange battle cry on their tongues.

Now, there was nothing to do but wait. De Wynter lay down, his back comfortably against a tree. His son did the same alongside. The two talked quietly in French, de Wynter gesturing lightly with his hands. Seamus caught a word now and again, but the gist escaped him.

At last, again with the uncanny grace that seemed so natural to him, de Wynter rose and brought the boy over to where Seamus sat.

"Seamus, your height is a giveaway. Stay behind and protect my son." De Wynter smiled, and this time the smile warmed his blue eyes. "However, it is only fair to warn you, that I have instructed Jamie to stay behind and protect you since you are, I told him, a very old man."

Seamus sputtered, "Old—?"

De Wynter was enjoying himself. His eyes gleamed, his voice savored his plans. "When we ride forth, the carters should instinctively

124

draw closer to protect themselves. We shall encourage them in this by going slow and making great show of arms. But being so few, we will not engage them; instead, we will ride past. They may either shift defensively or even come after if not satisfied with their present loot. In either case, in their concern for us, they will not be prepared for an attack on their rear. I assume you'll have one of your sons lead it. Remind me to have you tell them apart for me later. Once the Campbells are engaged by this rear attack, we, joining up with our other force, will take them from behind. The crab never fails. Remember? No? Seamus, I'm shamed for you. Alexander used it to defeat the Indian army at Hydaspes. Well, gentlemen, shall we go?''

Seamus decided this Scot was as bloodthirsty as the rest. In this at least, the years in France had not changed him. Setting his cap securely to conceal the telltale hair, de Wynter swung up into his saddle with ease. Taking up his cloak, he swiftly and expertly rolled it about his left arm as a makeshift shield. He checked the baselard to make sure it was well seated in the top of his boot. Then, brandishing his sword, he led the column into the water.

From Seamus's vantage point, he could see the Campbells react. Hastily pulling the clumsy carts up close, the men as one rode to the rear to face de Wynter's troop. Fifteen was just the right number. Large enough to inspire concern, small enough to seem unwilling to attack a superior force. As de Wynter and his men swept past, the Campbells followed, maneuvering their horses always between the strange riders and the carts, leaving their rear totally unprotected. Seamus whistled. His men led by Dugan swept out of the woods and through the ford. The Campbells, undecided, lost much time before rushing back to their rear. That, plus some mischievous Alva men, lost the battle for them. De Wynter and his now-reinforced group fell upon them from the other side. Caught by surprise in a pincer movement, the Campbells' defense collapsed. De Wynter, surveying the scene, came to a decision, his voice carrying over the water: ''Strip them down to their short clothes and put all in one cart. Drive it up to the fork and leave it where the Waters of Care and Sorrow come together. Then, head into the hills and make your way home. Keep your wits about you . . . and no gossiping within earshot of these. I want no reprisal raids if I can help it.''

Only when the Campbells were out of sight, did de Wynter signal

Seamus to ride forth, a small, sword-brandishing Jamie riding before him in the saddle. Already the carts had been reversed, lazy Simon this time in the lead. A short word from de Wynter and the man moved out smartly, setting a pace hard for the others to maintain. As they went, Seamus questioned the drovers. Then rode forward to report.

"They say your Lady Mother ordered them to do it. That she stood aside and let the Campbells strip the place, even pointing out things they had missed." Seamus swallowed hard. "Do you suppose she's gone balmy out of grief or something?"

"I propose to find out. How many redheads do we have among us?"

At Alva, a warning trumpet sounded at the first sight of the baggage train turning into the road leading up to the manor. Brazenly, the outriders, their red hair uncapped and wild myrtle badges worn prominently on their chests, rode into the cobblestoned courtyard to face a one-woman welcoming party. No frightened lady this, but a very angry Lady Islean.

As they drew to a halt in a semicircle, she launched her attack. "You Campbells, can't you do anything ri— You're not Campbell-grown! Shaun! Rob! What—what are you doing here, you're suppose to be with Seamus!" Her eyes widened.

"Seamus MacDonal," she screamed, "show yourself, man, or I'll ha' your hide nailed to my stable door." From back within the train, Seamus rode forth, another man falling in behind. A happy, flustered, suddenly younger Lady Islean picked up her skirts and ran to meet them.

Without a look, she went past Seamus and straight for the second man. A stream of emotions coursed her expressive face as she drank in the sight of the son she'd not seen in eight years. Tall, elegant, head held high, he was everything a mother could want in a son: "Jamie, my boy, give me a kiss and let me look at you."

With that fluidity that characterized his every move, Jamie dismounted. He would have kissed her hand but she was too fast for him, throwing her arms about him, pressing her cheek to his broad leather-covered chest. He froze. Not an emotion appeared on his well-schooled face as he fixed his gaze well over her head. Seamus,

126

watching the scene intently, thought—Nanny Goodall over tea later, tch-tched in agreement—that this was no fit greeting for a son to give his mother.

Rebuffed by the lack of response, Islean drew back shocked, hurt, bewildered by her son. "Jamie, what's wrong?"

"Wrong, madam?" Now he took her hand in his, kissed it courteously. "Wrong? Not a thing. You sent for me. As always, I follow orders. I came."

He might as well have struck her. Her eyes opened wide and she flushed with anger. "And not a day earlier than you needed to."

Not even her anger could strike a responsive chord. Smiling civilly, he agreed. "Not a day earlier; then again, not a day later. You will find, madam, that in the last eight years I have grown very punctual." Catching himself as if this line of talk might lead elsewhere, he gestured toward the train. "Besides I brought you a present, or did you not want your things back?"

Retreating a step to better look up at him without hurting her neck, she said, "Since you ask, no, I do not!"

Slightly taken aback, de Wynter waited for her explanation. She, enjoying herself, was in no hurry.

Seamus, looking from one to the other, was struck by how much alike the two looked. Refined, typically inbred Scottish faces they had. Pale-complexioned, high-cheekboned, finely chiseled, with deep-set eyes. Yet there was nothing masculine about the lady . . . nor anything feminine about her son.

Finally, with a quizzically upraised eyebrow, de Wynter conceded defeat. "You didn't want them returned?"

She was devilish. "No, not for a week at least."

"Not for a week," he repeated, letting her enjoy her fun, "at least?"

"At least." Then, in triumph she gave in. "I lent them to the new chatelaine of Castle Dolour, the third Lady Campbell."

He heard only what he wanted to hear. "Lent them? Has the mine played out? Are you in such sad need of funds, then? I would have helped—"

"No, no, nothing like that." She took his arm, and again he froze momentarily; then, keeping his distance as best he could, he allowed himself to be led toward the manor steps. She noticed his reaction but chose to ignore it. "No, I just don't want to eat off trencher bread two days hence."

He stopped. That didn't make sense. "But without your plate, that's exactly what we'll be doing."

"Here, yes." Her eyes sparkled, but she suppressed her delight. "But not when we attend the banquet Lord Campbell will be giving for James V." Lowering her voice conspiratorially, she continued, "Someone, it seems, has filled the king's head with stories about the excellent hunting to be had in the copse round Castle Dolour during June. Now you know and I know and Campbell knows that the hunting's really nothing exceptional, but the king doesn't know that. I won't tell and Campbell doesn't dare, poor man."

She pretended to sigh as if very much put upon, but she could keep a sober face no longer. Sucking her lip with delight, she rushed on. "So, he's coming. Within the week. And you know Castle Dolour—no, I guess you don't. Anyway, it's well named. Gloomy, dreary, dank, not fit for civilized people to live in. Fits the Campbells perfectly." Suddenly contrite, she added, "Except for Campbell's young bride. A lovely child, but she's beside herself. I really feel sorry about getting her into this. However, good neighbor that I am, I rode over and offered to help Lady Ann in any way I could. Well, when we took inventory of the place, I was shocked. What Campbell does with his revenues I don't know, but he certainly doesn't lavish them on decent appointments. So naturally I offered to lend her what she needs. Just as naturally, she invited me to attend the banquet in the king's honor... which I allowed myself to be talked into accepting. Campbell will be furious. What he says when he finds out I'm sure won't be fit for young ears. Speaking of which"—she had a disconcerting habit of abruptly changing the subject—"have you taken a dwarf into your service, or is that a child I see peering round from behind Fionn's back?"

The first genuine smile yet transformed de Wynter's face. Islean caught her breath. He was almost too beautiful, this son of hers, but the slight crookedness of the smile saved him from that. At the pain in her chest she remembered to take another breath. Even as she did, she made note that the child was the father's weak spot.

128

"You have spied out my other present." He left her with unhurried steps that seemed to eat up the ground, and reaching up, lifted the child down from the horse. Hand in hand, the one so tall, the other so small, they adjusted their gaits automatically to each other and returned to where she stood.

"Madame, may I present your grandson. Jamie, *votre grandmère*. He speaks only French. You'll have to teach him Scots."

She wasn't listening. Eight years of frustrated motherhood surged to the fore, she dropped to her knees. "Poor child. He's exhausted. You've dragged him across this countryside without adequate rest. No, don't contradict. *Allons*, Jamie." she reached for his hand.

Although the child couldn't understand one word in ten that she said, trustingly he loosed his father's hand and took hers. "You and I will go inside and find us some milk and pottage—or maybe you've been brought up the French way to prefer watered wine. Well, no matter. I'm sure we'll find something. Perhaps a marchpane rabbit being made for James V that the king will never miss. And I think I know where there might be a toy or two that would interest you: a knight on his charger and two of his men.

"Now, don't worry about your father. He'll have his hands full figuring out how to undo the mischief he's made." With her free hand, she gestured back at the baggage train, but looked nowhere except at the child staring fascinated back at her. "Although if he wounded any of those Campbells, I'm not sure just what we'll do. But that's a problem for men—right, Jamie?—not grandmothers and grandsons." With that, she and the child disappeared within the door of the manor, leaving the group of men to stare at one another.

Having let his guard down a bit, de Wynter let it down further. Shaking his head in disbelief, he asked Seamus, "She hasn't changed, has she?"

"Not so you can tell, but she's a brave one. Not quick to show how she really feels. Take the death of your father—"

At the sudden change in de Wynter, Seamus broke off.

"Now, then good Seamus," de Wynter began, changing the subject handily, "can we allow our lady to be more gallant than we? If she has decided to strip our manor bare for the sake of the Campbells, can we do less than rescue the baggage train from the rascals who took it from them . . . and deliver the train to Castle Dolour's door. Besides, I should like to ask the lovely, young child-bride if I might be of assistance.''

Though Simon might be lazy, there was nothing wrong with his hearing. Standing up, he yelled back up the line, "Turn 'em around, we're going back again.''

With the cracking of whips and the protesting of brakes, the train began to reverse itself with much cursing and yelling as the teams and wagons turned in the narrow lane. At the last minute, de Wynter rode back up to the manor steps where a footman stood with others of the household staff, watching in merriment. A word, and the man disappeared to return immediately, a cloth-wrapped staff in his hands.

"Seamus, this time we go announced. Here.'' A snap of his wrist shook the banner out. "Delegate one of those three miniature imitations of yourself to carry this thing.''

Gruffly, to hide his pride, Seamus ordered Fionn to go forward and take the banner. "But mind you,'' he whispered in a voice that could be heard in the next county, "don't drop it or I'll blister your backside so bad you'll sleep standing up.''

De Wynter gravely handed the six-foot-long banner with its snarling Mer-Lion to the eager young man who rested it on the toe of his boot, wheeled his horse smartly, and started off to the front of the train. Falling in behind the young man, who was easily his father's equal in height, if not in weight, de Wynter's shoulders shook with silent merriment at the thought of this man slung over his father's knee.

It was almost daybreak when they finally rode back into the manor's courtyard with its cold and sputtering torches. The lovely child bride at Castle Dolour had been so thankful, so appreciative of the kindnesses of both the Lady Seaforth and her very gallant son, so insistent that the troop rest after its long ride. "You fought all those bandits off all by yourselves—just the few of you? Why, my captain told me there were an army of them. Borderers, he thought. Desperate men, absolutely bloodthirsty. Would have cut their throats as soon as look at them.''

"Under the circumstances,'' Seamus tried to explain to the Lady Islean later that day, "it would have been bad manners to refuse.''

130

To which, the lady's first reply was a snort. "One drink or two doesn't take a whole day."

"Nay, lady, it doesn't," he was forced to agree.

"Nor does it get your jacket ripped!"

Seeing how the wind was blowing, Seamus didn't rise to the bait. Instead, he held his tongue.

Seeing that she would get no more of him, she dismissed him after giving instructions that he hand over the jacket to one of her ladies-in-waiting. "That is, if the girl you are currently bedding isn't handy with a needle."

Mary Nairn, one of her ladies-in-waiting, a child of fourteen, learned more by questioning Fionn, however. "Of course, he isn't privy to what went on in the hall, having been sent to the guardroom to keep company with the Campbell men-at-arms. But, according to the butler, Lady Ann had a bottle of her husband's best Madeira broached for the two of them. And later sent for another. One of the servers who brought the men ale claimed a lute was sent for, too. And the devil of a time they had finding one because nobody plays at the castle except the harper, and he's away with Campbell.

"Fionn also said that two times his father sent a message to the Great Hall asking word with his young master, and neither time did he get a reply. Finally, he took matters into his own hands."

The Lady Islean had visions of Seamus striding into the Great Hall, grabbing her son by the nape of his neck and hauling him out of the keep. Delicious. Served the whelp right. She hung on every word the girl said. "Go, tell me, what did Seamus do?"

Very seriously, Mary Nairn confided, "He started a fight."

Taken aback, the Lady Islean said, "With Jamie?"

"Oh, no, not with the young lord."

"Who then? Oh, my God, not with a Campbell. That would ruin everything."

"Not with a Campbell either. With Fionn! It was all pretend, but they rolled and struggled all over the floor, upset the furniture, broke benches. Made a terrible mess of the place according to Fionn. And so big is he and his father that the Campbell captain was afraid to try to separate them. One of his men tried. Got a fist in the eye for his trouble. Finally, the captain sent for the master, who came running. Once he had separated them, he had no choice but to take his two fighters home. And what a tongue-lashing he gave them. Fionn said he always thought that his father could curse with the best, but the young master did even better. Fionn tells me he learned all sorts of new words"—she dimpled—"but wouldn't tell me what they were."

Armed with these tidbits of information, the Lady Islean decided to beard her son in his bed. She had a breakfast tray made up and as insurance brought her grandson with her. He wouldn't, she was sure, understand what was said. First she knocked . . . then Jamie called . . . then the lackey pounded. But no answer. Indignation gave way to anger and then concern. While she and her grandson kept vigil in the hall, the lackey went for Seamus. "Break the door down," she ordered.

Seamus had been in the family long enough to occasionally question an order. "Why?"

"He must have been hurt in your brawl yesterday, he doesn't answer the door."

"But he's not here." Seamus calmly pulled the latch string, opening the door to reveal the bed hangings spread wide, the bedclothes roughly pushed aside.

Never one to be discomfited by anything she herself had done, the Lady Islean ignored her part in the whole embarrassing scene. "Where did he go? Not back to Castle Dolour?"

"After last night, he doesn't particularly care to confide in me." He hesitated a moment, then out of love for his lady added with pride in his voice, "The grooms tell me he insisted on selecting his own mount: a short-necked, deep-chested, short-coupled mare with little hooves, light bone, and a roman nose."

"He could have selected Dunstan, for all I care."

"Oh, well, I thought you wanted to know where he was going."

"Seamus, if you know and haven't told me!" Islean was losing her temper, he was happy to see. It was his way of getting revenge for her comment about his bed partner. He knew she knew that at Alva it was always Dugan's mother.

"Well, I don't know for sure, except—"

"Except what?" She stomped her foot. "You big oaf, don't you tease me. Speak up."

At the look on her face, he repented. "Except that only a horseman would have chosen her. And he for only one thing and not her looks: she's the ugliest dun you ever saw and the best cross-countrier. And they tell me he was wearing hunting leathers, not courting clothes.''

She was too proud to show her relief. "How do you know? Maybe it's all the fashion in France to ride ugly mares and wear hunting clothes when courting?" Taking her grandson by the hand, she swept down the stairs, her head high, the subject closed.

Again de Wynter rode in late after the household was abed.

This time, the lady had a page waiting for him with word to awaken her when he returned. However, by the time the page had wakened one of her ladies, the lady-in-waiting had awakened her, and she'd put on a robe de chambre and lit a candle to make her way down the hall of the transept, the door to his chamber was closed. Although she whispered his name in a voice loud enough to wake the household, and worked the latch string, she received no response. Nor did the door budge an inch when she tried it.

However, when he came downstairs at the crack of dawn, again dressed in riding clothes, she was in the Great Hall waiting for him.

"Good morning," she called, crossing the hall to the sideboard. "Come breakfast with me."

She lifted a lid on a pot, and the most delectable aroma escaped. His stomach reminded him that since his return to Scotland Wednesday night last, he'd eaten nothing but cold meats and stale ale. "I can offer you a pottage of eggs and fried onions." She replaced that lid and raised another, "Or pumpes." His mouth watered. He hadn't had pumpes since he'd left Scotland eight years before. At that moment a serving woman entered bearing a load of fresh-baked bread.

He knew he should be on his way, but a warm breakfast would not take long. Hooking a stool with his toe, he drew it up to the table. His mother, satisfied she'd have her long talk at last, was willing to bide her time. She ladled a large dipperful of pumpes into a bowl and handed it to him. "I think you'll like these. I made them myself, just the way you like them. With cloves and raisins—no mace, I remembered, and smoked pork."

She drew up her chair to the table across from him. "There's almond milk and rice sauce in the pitcher by your elbow." She watched him pour the thick sauce over the meat balls. "The sauce is already sweetened, but you, if I remember right," she said, passing him another bowl, "like your pumpes really sweet."

Not until he'd spooned more of the dark brown sugar all over the dish and taken his first bite, did she speak. "The king arrived yesterday." His mouth was so full he couldn't answer, but he thought, she's gone mad. These things were so tough he could barely chew them. She must have used only gristle and tough old smoked meat. His teeth were stuck shut. "Tonight is the banquet. I worked too hard to get us invited to not attend. You do intend to go, don't you?"

He could only nod. There was method to her madness. The pumpes were the best homemade gag he'd ever encountered. The most flavorsome, too, he had to admit.

"It is time that we talk, you and I, about several things. Your son, for example." Unable to speak, he glowered in reply, and Islean retreated. "Your father's death for another." Her voice grew gentle, her manner introspective. "The attack wasn't unexpected, you know. There had been at least three attempts before that I know of. I keep reminding myself that he was not a young man, but it's hard. He didn't act like a man turned sixty. But he'd had a good life, one arm and all. He did what he thought was best for you and me, though I didn't always agree. Not then, not now. But I have to know. Jamie, do you want to be king?"

De Wynter choked, whereupon she rose and slammed him in the center of his back with the flat of her hand until he held up a hand for mercy. Swallowing finally, he managed to gasp out, "Desist, desist, I beg you. I'll be black and blue and afraid to show my naked back to a soul."

"Good." Resuming her place, she returned to the subject. "You didn't answer my question."

He played with his horn spoon, turning it over and over between his long agile fingers. "Doesn't everyone want to be king?" he began sardonically, then thought better of that. For a moment she thought he was about to open up and confide in her. Then, he arose.

"Madame, you were right. The pumpes were excellent. Now, if you'll excuse me—"

"Answer my question!" she ordered.

There was a note of bitterness in his voice. "Does what I want make any difference? Did it eight years ago?" He turned to go.

"I have to know. I don't want to kill the king in vain."

"My God, you can't be serious."

She drew herself up to her full height and stared him in the eye. "I am. I have planned it well. Tonight my men will serve my food, on my dishes. It will not be easy, but it can be done. I am determined to resolve this matter that took my son from me eight years ago and that cost me my beloved husband. If this is the only way, then let it be so. And if the food fails, there's always my poniard." This was no weepy, hysterical woman, but a fully determined, vindictive mother fighting like a she-wolf to protect her own. Long minutes passed while the two took mental measure of each other.

Satisfied her words were not an idle threat, he finally spoke, choosing his words carefully. "No, I don't want to be king. Albany schooled me too well." He held up his hand to stop her from interrupting. "Do not mistake me. He upheld his part of the bargain." Again that note of bitterness crept into his voice. "He taught me how to rule, or, better yet, how not to rule. But there is in me one thing no good king can have—"

"Go on."

"A sense of humor."

"You're mad."

"Not at all. I can laugh at myself, and no king can do that without questioning his supposed God-given right to rule. So I beg you, spare your king. Good or bad, he is the only one Scotland will have if I have my choice."

"But what of your son?"

"Ah, yes, we mustn't forget Jamie, the latest in the line of illegitimate heirs. Albany tried to make me a Frenchman, and in many ways he succeeded; but I am still a good enough Scot to know the last thing this country needs is another child king. Look at our history. What good a king accomplishes he undoes by leaving as his heir an infant. It would seem to be Scotland's curse—to be ruled by regents. And I prefer my child to grow up, God and you willing, at Seaforth, not as a prisoner at Edinburgh or another of the royal castles. No, madame, solve your problem another way, but spare James."

"Then"—she took a deep breath, for what she asked of him was to deny his birthright—"renounce your claim. Tonight. Before the king and the court."

"Is that all it takes to save a king's life? Then, I do it gladly." He pulled on his gloves. "Now, if you'll excuse me, madame, I still have a great deal more work to do if the copse around Castle Dolour is going to yield up the magnificent hunting claimed for it by some gossip-monger."

He bowed and left, and she sat back in her chair. It had been almost too easy. Now all she had to do was get through this evening. Idly, she wondered if she could, indeed, have killed the king. She didn't know why not. She always contended a fast-acting poison not only didn't taste good but also wasn't in good taste. Besides being easily detected by the deaths of the royal tasters, it ruined a perfectly good banquet into which a lot of time and effort had gone. No, the poison she'd had in mind took its time about working. She'd just save the recipe for when Seaforth's murderers were found out. But enough of that.

Today, instead of concocting Nanny Goodall's never-fail recipe for sick dogs and cats—they ran away and died in the bushes—she could make sure her gown was ready for tonight. The pattern had come from Spain, the fabric from Byzantium via Venice, the silver thread spun from the ore of her very own mines here at Alva. The dress had been made at Seaforth; the embroidery done by Dugan's mother, a fine, robust woman who may well indeed have been the finest needle-woman in Scotland. What a shame to keep her at Alva. But now her work would be seen, for the court of King James had come to Alva. Here was Lady Campbell dying a thousand deaths over her state banquet and royal guests; Jamie spending his days out herding game toward a notoriously bad section for hunting; a whole court packing up and traveling miles upon miles; a lord known for his stinginess being forced to support for at least two weeks a most profligate court. Everyone was being discommoded so that the Lady Islean could have her dress stitched by the woman of her choice. It struck her funny bone! Would that a dress had been the only reason she had connived and engineered the banquet and that a hunted beast's life were the only life at stake.

"*Grand-mère, grand-mère, c'est moi!* It is me!" called a small voice in bad Scots. Leaning over the rail that lined the musician's gallery above the Great Hall was a dark-haired charmer. Looking up at him, she decided life had its compensations. Here in this child was her immortality. That tonight she would aid his father in renouncing his birthright bothered her not a bit . . . well, a little, but she vowed she'd make it up to him some other way.

Already she was beginning to review what boys of good birth she could entice to Seaforth to be companions to her grandson. "Come down, my love, I have a treat for you—pumpes." She signaled for the butler to take away the bowl from which she'd served the lad's father. "But not these my sweet. They were perfect for your father. But for you, we'll get fresh. Fresh, tender, chewable ones. And then you must tell me again all you remember of your mother."

CHAPTER 7

The wooden double doors to the hall were thrown open from within. There, framed in the opening, stood three bagpipers dressed head to toe in the blue green tartan of the Campbells. The courtiers, peering over their monarch's shoulder, oohed and ahhed and applauded. Never before had they seen anything like it! A whole suit of tartan! Many immediately decided they too must have the same. James V, King of Scotland, his hostess the Lady Campbell on his arm, was speechless. Not more than a month before, he had secretly ordered such a suit for himself in the red blue royal Stewart tartan. Now, here in a desolate castle in the Lowlands, before his suit even had been delivered, the Campbells had stolen a march on him. Treason! Treachery!

Before James could roar his wrath, the pipers shrilly drew breath to launch, with a wabble and a warble, into the *Bodaich nam Brigisean*, the clan's pipe music. Inside the massive three-story-high dining halls were more tartan-clad attendants. Poverty makes good mathematicians out of kings in constant need of borrowing funds. James, multiplying their number by the cost of his suit—2¼ ells of variant-colored velvet for the short coat at six shillings the ell, and three ells for the threws at four shillings the ell—the result made him gasp. His hostess interpreted his reaction as complimentary and preened accordingly. Carefully, she neglected to mention that the Countess of Seaforth had arranged for the clothing and supplied most of the attendants, too.

Despite the newly lime-washed walls, the hall itself was dark and gloomy. The windows of thin polished horn, sited up high, effectively kept out both light and enemy invaders. Rush dips and flares burning in crude sockets only emphasized the gloom. However, in honor of the royal guest, Lady Campbell had ordered down the candle beams. Diners above the salt would eat by fine beeswax candlelight. Lighting those below were candles of tallow that swiftly melted into rancid fat and overflowed the grease pans to drip onto the hats of those farther down.

At the far end of the hall, out of reach of wayward sparks from the central hearth was a low dais with—luxury of luxuries—four box chairs. Of the four chairs, only one was owned by the Campbells, the others lent by Lady Islean. The balance of the court made do squeezing onto bare, backless benches and low wooden chests, their hardness softened only by the spreading of a lady's voluminous multilayered skirts and petticoats.

No sooner had the court been seated than the dark brown home-brewed ale began to flow. As the pipers desisted with a wheezing bray, the trumpeters announced the arrival of the warner. Three men staggered under the weight of this two-foot-high masterpiece of sugar and plaster—courtesy of the Seaforths—which depicted the king with his crown of gold, hunting the hart on the copse with his court. Genuine plaudits and compliments greeted it, even from the royals; and the Lady Campbell, basking in the limelight, not only was glad Lady Islean had been delayed but prayed the countess might never make the banquet at all.

Even as the warner was completing its circuit about the hall, the trumpets sounded again for the arrival of the first course: a porpoise roasted whole, an entire salmon, a mammoth dish of stewed eels and oysters in Bastard Gravy, the king's favorite dish, as the Lady Islean knew. She had even helped make the gravy, carefully adding salt, pepper, sugar, and ginger to the mixture of ale and oyster liquid. Carefully she supervised as Lady Ann added, strand by golden strand, the precious saffron worth its weight in gold. Only when the gravy was pronounced just right, were the oysters lowered gently to bask in the spicy golden liquid. If things had gone differently, this was the dish Lady Islean planned to poison, the king being so fond of it that he never failed to eat at least two servings, and if it were particularly good, a third, or even a fourth.

Tonight was a four-helping night. Sated, James passed up the next several courses, not being tempted again until the swan was served. Its wings spread and tied open, its neck gracefully curved, its feathers, head and feet left intact although the meat had been cooked and minced and mixed with rice before being stuffed back inside. A piece of camphor held within the gilded beak was lit just before the bird, poised as if to fly, was carried in on a charger. Out of deference to his young hostess, the king allowed himself to be served a small portion. It was his experience that elegant as it was on the water, the swan at table was most often a tough old bird. Wonders of wonders, this swan was tender, moist and lightly spiced. It made James uncomfortable. Like everything here at Castle Dolour, the swan was too good, the servants too many, the servers too attentive, the ale too free-flowing. Only the hostess, to his way of thinking, was just right; she hung on his every word; blushed at his every compliment, and ignored her husband completely.

His host, on the other hand, James disliked more with every new proof of his wealth. Immediately, he began planning how to neutralize Campbell's obvious importance in this corner of Scotland.

The new Spanish ambassador to Scotland from the court of Charles V was also impressed by the magnificence of the banquet. Already he had begun mentally drafting his next report to his master. If minor lairds, which was what Campbell seemed to him to be, had such wealth, Scotland should be accorded a role bigger than that of a mere pawn in the international game of chess which the Holy Roman Emperor now pursued.

Oblivious to this little sallow-complexioned man in their midst, the court of Scotland was enjoying itself. Drunkenly and loudly. Servants, charged with filling the cups, went wary of the suddenly outstretched foot of knight or lady attempting to ease a cramp or pursue a caress. Hounds added to the confusion as, watching for droppings from the table, they grew ever more bold and fought among themselves for each tidbit. To add to the air of Donnybrook Fair, someone took it upon himself to add another armful of wood to the fire burning in the center hearth. It burned fitfully, the wood obviously being fresh-cut and giving off thick billows of smoke. Taking a roundabout route to reach the smoke-hole in the roof some thirty feet above, the smoke gradually engulfed the hall in a gray haze.

The king, whose eyes were smoke-sensitive and inclined to weeping, cursed himself for choosing Castle Dolour for a hunting trip. "The hunting best be good," he said to himself, "if I am going to have to put up with smoke-hole and outhouse. Outhouse! In this day and age—how old-fashioned! And if that hunting isn't good, I'll just take to my bed and extend my visit another two week. That will bleed Campbell's treasure chest a bit!" He smiled at his host at the thought, and pompous, stupid Campbell smiled right back.

Just then, James noted a stirring among the courtiers nearby. Many had half risen and were craning necks to get a better view of the other end of the hall, now totally obscured by smoke. James turned to his hostess for explanation. "Lady, have you planned entertainment for us?"

"Nay, sire. This is not my doing. I am as curious as you." Yet, no sooner had James's glance moved from her, than she bit her lip in annoyance at a sudden thought.

Like an apparition, the stout body of the chamberlain materialized through the smoke. Behind him came a couple more richly dressed than any seen at court. The woman was slender and regal in her bearing, holding her head high, her bejeweled hand resting ever so lightly on the arm of her tall companion. So extraordinary were her gown and parure that none spared a glance at the man dressed in black from the high heels of his satin shoes to the lofty plumes on his hat.

She wore nacre satin so heavily embroidered and reembroidered with gold thread that from the hips up not a thread of white showed through. From wrist to shoulder, the sleeves of her gown were slashed and lined with white revealing the tight, wrist-length sleeves of her tawny gold farthingale.

Unlike the fashion at court, her gown was not square cut nor low cut, but rose high about her neck, ending in a multilayered, gold-edged ruff very like a lion's mane, totally framing her pale, patrician face. Her dark hair was dressed high on her head and crowned with the first toque of jewel-studded gold velvet ever seen in Scotland. From her neck hung a heavy gold chain. At its end, with eyes of gold white diamonds, hung a Mer-Lion.

Murmurs of approbation accompanied her slow and stately progress. Even James was so taken aback by this singular beauty that he decided he was in love. A feeling in his gut told him so. One between his legs convinced him of it.

His dream was shattered by his mother. Margaret Tudor had glimpsed the jeweled ornament the woman wore between her breasts and interpreted it correctly. "It's Islean," she whispered to her son in a voice harsh with hatred.

Since that was her usual tone of voice when speaking of other women, he ignored it, concentrating only on what she said while never taking his eyes from the vision before him. "Who?"

"The Dowager Countess of Seaforth," she replied. When that did not elicit its intended result, she added triumphantly, "Your bastard half sister!"

Jamie closed his eyes and clenched them. He could have wept in disappointment. Another dream dashed. Again by his mother. For a moment he hated her, but then remembered she was indeed his mother. His voice was cold and devoid of emotion when he eventually replied, "Oh, her." Now, through disillusioned eyes, he could see the fine lines about her eyes. He guessed that she must be about his mother's age or older, but unlike the Dowager Queen, she didn't look it. He rationalized this by reassuring himself that Islean had not led the monstrous life his mother had: widowed early, separated from her son for years, all the tribulations that made her seek comfort in her cup. Without turning his head to look, James knew his mother's drink-glazed eyes had hardened, her face turned white and drawn with jealousy. She loved fine clothes and jewels but had had very few in her lifetime. James vowed that she should receive her due; the prelates had promised to pay off his annuity in a lump sum if he withdrew his mother's petition for a divorce. Once those monies came, he'd buy Margaret some trinkets and a dress with three changes of sleeves.

So closed was his face, that not by a grimace could mother, court, or half sister read his thoughts. He made it even blander as the couple came to a stop before him. Calmly, quietly, serenely, they awaited his notice so that the chamberlain could announce them, which really was not necessary. Margaret Tudor was not the only one at court to recognize the Lady Islean, but the identity of her companion prompted a buzz of speculation among the seated court-iers.

The king was in no hurry to satisfy their curiosity. Deliberately, he searched the Lady Ann's plate for a last morsel or two. Today, his astrologers had assured him, would be longer than yesterday; thus, there would be plenty of time for hunting later. Since that was so, he could play with this couple a while longer. Surreptitiously, he studied the man, who was much younger, obviously, than the Dowager Countess. Was Islean eager, like his mother, to take a younger man into her bed? Damn women, why couldn't they pick out one man and stay with him? Then he remembered: Islean's husband had been assassinated. Anyway, who was this fellow? In stark contrast to the Dowager Countess, his all-black outfit was without embroidery. Of course, well-turned legs like that could be shown off without stripings or patternings. But the cut, the fabrics, the fit—that took money, lots of it—but nowhere was there an embroidered badge of family. Not even a family crest or signet ring on the long elegant fingers.

King though he was, James himself would not have gone abroad without wearing the thistle of Scotland. Even when he went out among his peasants disguised as a humble tenant farmer, the Good-man of Ballengiech, he wore his signet ring. He turned it inward of course so it wasn't readily apparent; but it was still there if he should need to identify himself quickly. So who was this young man that he felt no need for such a device?

More openly now, James studied the face before him. The man was young, but there was something ageless about the expression on his high-bred face. Was it the eyes . . . or the arch of the brow . . . or the set of those thin lips? James could not decide. Islean had it, too. James settled back in triumph. He had solved the problem: the two before him were the dexter and the sinister of the same beauty . . . the two were sister and brother . . . no, mother and son.

As he studied them while pretending not to, they studied him quite openly. They saw a thin, young man; much younger than de Wynter in appearance if not years; dark of hair, which was not too profuse, the beard confined to his chin quite scraggly. His eyes were dark as was his complexion, which had been too much exposed to the sun. There were sun marks about his eyes and laugh marks about

143

his mouth. In all this, one could clearly see the legacy of his father. The sensuous mouth and the heavy eyelids were Margaret Tudor's most obvious contribution to her son.

It was his dress, however, that was shocking. From where they stood, they had almost a full view of his seated figure with its wrinkled hose, soiled doublet, the patched boots. But when he sat up and gestured to the chamberlain to announce them, he carried himself like a king, and his bearing demanded the respect due any monarch.

While the scrutinizing was going on, the chamberlain had availed himself of the opportunity to clear a small space in front of him on the thick sodden rushes littering the floor. Now, he smartly rapped his ebony stave of office upon the bare stone floor. The resulting crack was satisfyingly sharp. With it, the two sank down into low courtly obeisances:

"Your Majesty, Your Royal Highness, Duke, Lords and Ladies and Baronesses: The Earl of Seaforth, Viscount Rangely, Baron Alva and also of Alais of France—James Mackenzie—and the lady, his mother, the Dowager Countess, Lady Islean, also of Alva."

When he finished, having uttered the whole thing in one breath, the dowager bowed her long, regal neck still farther and her son doffed his large plumed hat. At once the king knew why this man had no need of embroidered badge of household. He, like his fathers before him dating back to the reign of the first Plantagenets, need only bare his head for all the world to know his name, rank, and lineage. Shortly after the age of sixteen, his thick, heavy mane of black hair had, like theirs, turned white. Not a dead white, nor an albino white, nor even a pure white, but a living lustrous white intermingled with shades and streakings of silver and pewter.

The murmurs of those who had wagered on the unknown's identity and won were now drowned out by the gasps of those who were seeing the famous head of hair for the first time. None were more obviously shocked than the two female occupants of the dais: Lady Ann, who had spent a long afternoon and evening in conversation with this man and had seen him only with his hat on; and Margaret Tudor, who was bound by her greatest single preoccupation to wonder if the hair elsewhere were white or black.

144

The king himself rose and came down from behind the table to raise the dowager countess to her feet.

"My court is honored by your presence and bedazzled by your appearance," he said. "Come join us at table."

Unceremoniously, he gestured at the Lady Ann and her husband to relinquish their places so that the Seaforths could have the seats of honor. Frantically, Lady Ann looked about for a stool for herself, but there was none. So she and her husband stood awkwardly, shifting from foot to foot while servants scurried about looking for seating for their master and his lady. Eventually, rough three-legged ones were brought up from the kitchen, but not before de Wynter had refused his chair and offered it to the Lady Ann. Gratefully, she sank into it, only to be treated to a glare from the Lady Margaret, who found herself seated, much to her dislike, between two women.

Reaching for her cup, as was her wont whatever the occasion, she studied the two men standing to one side. The two men were a study in contrasts. As Campbell ventured awkward conversation, Mackenzie appeared quite comfortable and at ease. Campbell was short and fat and gross. The man next to him was not a giant, but he was so lithe and lean that he appeared taller. His shoulders were wide, his waist narrow, his stomach flat, his buttocks small and squarish . . . and from what Margaret could see, his codpiece was not padded as Campbell's so obviously was. As for those black-clad legs, they were as shapely and well turned as any she'd ever seen, including— Margaret hesitated for a moment and then regretfully concluded— including her brother Henry's.

At last, to Campbell's relief, their stools came. But to Margaret's displeasure, de Wynter was seated to Lady Ann's left, which made it necessary to talk across her, if Margaret were going to satisfy her curiosity. Ignoring the young woman, Margaret spoke up rather more loudly than was called for.

"My lord, I could not help but hear you are titled in France as well as Scotland. I did not know the Seaforths had land on the continent."

"They did not," the man replied with a slight smile, but volunteered no further information.

"Then, these are new acquired?" Margaret continued, not at all undaunted.

"They are."

"Bought or earned?" Margaret's smile was brittle, her sneer obvious even to the naive Lady Ann.

"Earned, my lady."

"We too have congress with France, but I do not remember any great exploits by a Scots Baron of Alais. But perhaps that is because there were none?" Margaret was taunting him now. Challenging him. Seaforth, mentally weighing the advantages or disadvantages of taking up her gauntlet, remained silent for a moment. The Lady Islean watched him with concern; this was the first time she had seen her son at court, and she knew Margaret to be a formidable antagonist. She considered rushing into the fray herself, but she held her tongue. For eight years her son had been at a court known for its standards of wit and repartee; he must have learned something there to have survived at all.

"Queen Claude chose to give me another sobriquet" was his measured reply—not answering, yet not evading entirely the thrust of her comment.

Now, it was Margaret's turn to drop the subject or pursue it. Even in her slightly drink-befuddled mind, she sensed something amiss. The young man was, although polite enough, not at all cowed by her comments. And his reply was an open invitation for her. She feared she was not going to like the answer to her next question. But she put a bold front on it. "And what might the sobri—" Her thickened tongue twisted on the word. She started afresh. "And what might that name be?"

"De Wynter."

De Wynter. The court knew the name well. It conjured up different images for different people. Lover. Swordsman. Adventurer. Soldier. Horseman. Courtier par excellence. Men imagined setting a lance against him. Women envisioned his setting a lance against them.

The king was delighted. Here at last was a companion after his own heart. One who would provide sport and amusement and even a touch of competition. "Welcome to my court, cousin," he called over the heads of the Lady Islean, his mother and his hostess. Catching sight of the raw hungry looks on the faces of the latter two, he wondered which would bed him first.

146

James had no illusions about his court. Henry VIII's court might be known for its drunkenness, and Francis I's for its lavishness, but the court of James V was already known for the licentiousness and looseness of character of its women. The thought did not displease him. Poor he might be, but he had won a reputation of sorts among his fellow monarchs. Of course, he put a better face on it than did some of the gossips. They might call his court the royal brothel; he preferred to think of it as descending directly from the famed Courts of Love of olden days.

He wondered what the Lady Islean's reaction might be to the avaricious looks of the amorous females about him, but her face was most carefully schooled. He decided to do some probing on his own. "You have a most famous son there, lady."

"Famous, sire?" she replied quietly. "Infamous is more like it."

James laughed. Mothers were all alike. "You don't approve then, lady?" Islean wasn't sure of James's intent. She searched quickly for the proper answer; it would not do to answer the king ill-consideredly. "My approval was not sought, sire."

"And if it had been, would it have been given?"

"Alas, sire, I know not. Guide me in this. The king of France's queen evidently approved. Should I question her royal judgment?"

"Nay, dear lady. But I might." He came to a decision, one he knew would please his mother and his court. "You and your son shall have to bide awhile at court so that I may see for myself if my sister's judgment was correct."

This was not what Islean wanted. "Sire, I am sure nothing would please my son or me more. But we came unprepared for such an honor, having ridden over from Alva just for this great banquet." She nodded her congratulations to her host and hostess. "We had hoped to have words with you privately and then take our leave."

James could not believe his ears. She was refusing him. Not since he had been made king had anyone refused him anything, except those abbotts of course . . . and the Pope in the matter of his mother's divorce. But a mere subject, unthinkable! It made him more determined than ever. However, he didn't show his displeasure openly; he would exact payment from her or her son at some later moment.

"But, madam, I shall have no time for such a private conversation. I am going hunting. And now, madam—" Abruptly, he got to his feet, giving his chair a shove that sent it flying. The whole court rushed to rise. Taking his mother's hand in his, he left the dais while the others made hurried obeisances. Looking down on Islean's dark head before him, and at her son's white one just beyond, he spoke once more, and there was no doubt this was no request but a royal command: "Send for your clothes, madam. I would see how fit you and your son are to be in line to the throne."

With that, he and his mother swept from the hall. As the royal couple passed through the huge doors, the court quickly dispersed, elbowing one another if need be to clear the way to get to their chambers and change into hunting garb.

Islean and her son watched them go. "It would seem, dear mother, that the king is impervious to your charms."

"Ill-bred jackanapes," she snapped.

De Wynter laughed. "I take it you refer to the king. One fears you have too long been queen in your own court, Mother. You forget, one doesn't refuse a king."

"Or a Dowager Queen?" she replied, stung by his comment.

"Or a Dowager Queen," he agreed. "I suggest you send some of the men for our clothes. In the meantime, your grand entrance has failed to get us fed. Let me see if I can wrest some food from the staff in the kitchen before they devour it all. Will you join me?"

For a moment, she wondered if her son had lost his senses. Then her own sense of humor asserted itself. Bowing mockingly to her son she took his arm. "Better than that, I'll show you the way."

While the Lady Islean and her son commandeered food and drink from a startled kitchen staff, James and his court prepared for the hunt. At the last moment, a handful of ladies, including the Lady Ann and Lady Margaret, begged to be excused. The former claimed household duties to be done; the latter professed a headache brought on by overindulgence in her cups. The king accepted both excuses at face value; however, at the last moment he sent for his secretary and dictated a note:

> *Cousin:* That both our afternoons be not fruitless, it pleases me to offer you a sporting challenge, the meaning of which, to such an educated man as you, must be readily apparent. At the end of today's hunt, whatever I win in the woods

shall be yours. Whatever you chance to gain this day, you will share with me.

James Rex

The secretary was then instructed, after writing it out, to give it to a footman who was in turn to deliver it to Seaforth. "Who is he, sire?"

"De Wynter," replied the exasperated king.

"As you wish, sire."

Stalking to his horse, held tightly by an anxious groom, the king swung up into the saddle without assistance, signaled the groom to let go, and after letting his mount curvet a bit to settle down, spurred it forward, joining nearly a hundred huntsmen, both men and women. At least a dozen had bugles strung from straps around their necks to signal the hounds and hunters with their single-note short and long blasts. Both two- and four-legged hunters knew the codes that stood for a sighting, at bay, a change of direction, or a lost scent.

Many had taken the opportunity, while the king spoke so earnestly to his scribe, to check bowstrings and feathered shafts. Well they knew the king would permit no excuse for a missed shot when the fleet hart was driven back by the beaters directly into range of advancing hunters.

At this season, the hunting was carefree. There were no restrictions on the catch. From mid-September to early May was the closed season, and only does could be taken. But now, in mid-June, the bucks with their branched heads were as fair game as the sleeker and more succulent does. This condition removed some of the risk, for the bowman who brought down an antlered specimen during the closed season was disgraced in the eyes of his fellow hunters. And novices who tended to draw the bow at the first flash of tail need not be reminded of the penalties of overeagerness.

Three bold notes on the bugles signaled the opening of the kennel doors. The hounds, overeager and reckless from their long imprisonment, lunged off in all directions, baying and chasing imaginary spore. More bugle calls and not a few whippings were required to put the baying hounds back in line. When a semblance of order was restored and all were mounted, the buglers sounded the

149

strident notes that threw fear into the hearts of the four-legged creatures within their hearing. Deer darted down to the dales or up to the high ground where the beaters waited to turn them back. The baying hounds took off in a direction set by the fleetest, and the mounted archers and buglers followed in close pursuit. To the less experienced hunter it might seem utter confusion, but the old hands knew it mattered little at this stage of the hunt what direction was taken. So carefully had the beaters been stationed that no matter where the court galloped, there would be plentiful game fleeing the sound of bugle and hound.

Within minutes shafts were flying from quickly strung bows. Down went the stags that Englishmen called the red deer. And the pale-colored fallow deer, just turning to their spotted white hues for the summer. And the little roebucks, agile and graceful, who held mostly to the high ground until flushed by the worrying hounds or the blasts of buglers. Bucks and does alike, harried by the hounds at their heels, plunged to the sward, blood spurting from the shaft wounds that crippled their legs or stilled their hearts. They were left where they fell. The cutters who trailed sought out the grassy deathbeds and slit the throats while the bodies were still warm.

By the setting of the sun, so many deer had been slain that, when piled together, they reached higher than two men and farther across than the widest brook in the forest. All had had their necks slit, some after death and some dying as blood poured from severed jugulars. The blood purged, the carcasses could stand for several hours before putrefication set in.

The ritual of the cutting was performed by attendants summoned to the clearing where the deer were piled. Wielding sharp knives, they attacked one carcass after another in the same manner. A slit to open the slot in the neck. The second stomach seized, cut loose, and cleared of flesh. Off went the legs, hacked at joints. The hide was stripped from the body. The belly was laid open with one stab followed by a quick pull. Deftly the bowels were removed, and only the clumsy spilled any of the foul contents.

Moving to the other end, the gullet was gripped, and the wezand disengaged from the windpipe. Now the guts were yanked and the meaty portions neatly carved. The shoulder bones came out first.

150

Then the chest was halved. The shoulder filleted with practiced skill. After clearing the spine, the haunch was lifted high by one while another hewed it off. The thigh bones were stripped of their meaty muscles and set aside. Then, the head and neck came swiftly off in two pieces.

Now it was the hounds' turn. The lights, liver and tripe were flung into the bushes and quickly set upon by the howling pack. While the slavering beasts feasted and fought among themselves for the prizes, pieces of gristle-covered thigh bones were hung from nearby tree branches for the ravens and crows, which long since had learned to expect their fee at the end of the hunt.

There was much blowing of bugles and general merriment and the passing of flasks; then, swords flashed, skewering flanks and haunches for the trip back to Castle Dolour. Great and many were the compliments extended to their host, the surly, corpulent Lord Campbell. He for his part passed the presence of so much game off as commonplace. Secretly, he wondered by what miracle the copse that rarely yielded up a pair of carcasses when the Campbells hunted could yield up scores for the king. He also thanked the Campbells' patron saint for taking pity on his thin pocketbook; all this venison would easily feed the whole court the next day as Lady Ann would be relieved to hear.

Warmed by the wine and basking under the compliments of court and king, Campbell in an expansive mood found room for a kind thought for his young bride. Grudgingly he admitted she'd brought off the banquet earlier that day in fine style. Cheaply, too, judging from the accounting his controller gave him. Privately, Campbell thought all those tartan-clad servers were ostentatious. However, the king was impressed, and that was the thing these days if one were to make one's mark at court.

Perhaps he would give Lady Ann some trinket or two to show his appreciation. No, on second thought he decided that that might spoil the wench. A word of thanks should be sufficient. After all, he'd already done her favor enough by marrying her. In the meantime, his stomach reminded him that the effects of the feast had been transitory. He wondered what succulent foodstuffs she was preparing for the court right now.

Actually, the Lady Ann had her mind on something else besides food. But first, she must deal with her fellow stay-at-homes, including the Queen Dowager. Her four problems, however, solved themselves. Once the women had waved good-bye to the hunting party from the castle steps, then watched it pass through the barbican and cross over the moat, they spoke all at once, pleading exhaustion, headache, eye strain, then scattered like frightened quail, each going to rest in her room.

Once there, their indispositions vanished, and out came the traveling glasses, paint pots and jars. Hair must be smoothed and combs readjusted. Some even went so far as to change, mostly to gowns more low-cut than before, and be refreshed with perfume. Dame Sybil, first lady-in-waiting to Lady Margaret, was so carried away as to dab perfume between her breasts and then untie her sleeves and splash more in her armpits. She could afford to be so profligate; she had access to the royal perfumes.

Then, quietly, each stole from her room to seek out de Wynter. One searcher, the lord butler was later to relate, actually made her way up to the dormitory assigned to the men-at-arms. Another was found within the falconry. Still a third explored the depths of the stables. But de Wynter was not to be found—not in the now-deserted kennel, nor on the lookout's turret, nor in the library where the household's single book was kept, nor in the castle's pale excuse for a music room with its one unstrung lute and badly tuned harpsichord. What they did find, in one place after another, were their fellow searchers, who professed concern for horse, dog or falcon, the need for book, music, or a bit of fresh air. Whatever the excuse, it was quickly accepted as each searcher hastened to be on her way in pursuit of her quarry.

Lady Ann was first to find the elusive Lord de Wynter, having taken the simple expedient of asking her chamberlain his whereabouts. She could not believe his reply. "The kitchen?"

"Yes, my lady," he assured her. "He and his lady mother have been there the best part of the afternoon."

There he and the Lady Islean sat, the remains of their meal before them, the chaos of the banquet surrounding them. "Come, join us, my dear," called the Lady Islean merrily. "I'm keeping watch on my silver while my son is trying his hand at organizing the clean-up by your kitchen staff. A great general he may be, but he's no majordomo. Look, he has the baker preparing the cold meats for tomorrow's pastries—and the carver cutting the lard into flour for the pastry."

"Seemed very logical to me," de Wynter said as he watched the carver stirring up great clouds of flour and the baker futilely hacking away at a haunch.

Lady Ann was at first taken aback, but seeing that the Lady Islean found the scene amusing, she relaxed and permitted herself a smile. After all, both carver and baker had given her all kinds of trouble, obeying her orders grudgingly if at all.

"Well, then if you don't like my domestic abilities, Mother dear, I shall have to show my expertise elsewhere," de Wynter said. Raising his voice, he called to the three bagpipers sitting at a table in one corner. "Come, give us a tune. We shall have a ceilidh, if Lady Ann is agreeable," he said, smiling down on his hostess. Pushing tables aside, he cleared a space for them to dance. The bagpipers, with much wheezing and many false starts, launched into the Caber Feidh, the pipe music of the Mackenzies. Grinning with comradeship, de Wynter led the Lady Ann out onto their improvised dance floor. It was a fast pace he set, and at first Lady Ann had trouble keeping up, but then as she relaxed and gave herself up to the music and the man, she found the steps came back to her feet.

The music swirled about them, and she had eyes for no one but this man who never seemed to take his off her. When the bagpipes warbled their last and the Lady Ann sank into a low courtly curtsey, returned with an equally gallant bow from her partner, her eyes were bright, her cheeks flushed with pleasure, and she looked pretty for once. Then, about her came applause from the staff, the Lady Islean, and the woman standing at the foot of the steps leading up to the pantry outside the Great Hall.

"So here you are," was about the best the Lady Margaret could muster. Of all the places she might have looked, this would have been the last. Margaret Tudor had never set foot in a kitchen before. Certainly she knew what went on there, for many were the provisionings she'd approved.

Before she could get more than a fast glance at pots hanging from pegs, shelves laden with bowls, rough-hewn tables and benches, and a vast fireplace large enough to roast an ox, de Wynter had come forward to greet her.

"Welcome, lady, to our ceilidh. Will you give us the honor of a dance?" he asked, taking her hand in his and leading her out into the open space. On command, the bagpipers launched into "Campbells Are Coming." The staff, who had been drinking more than the dregs of the goblets they'd cleared, reacted like the Campbells they were, and began keeping time with hands and feet. Looking up into those pools of blue black that seemed to drink in her soul, Margaret promised herself that before the night was over, de Wynter would be dancing her tune. Then, with pointed toe and hand held high, she and her partner swept into the jig.

Lady Margaret truly excelled in dancing. She moved within the measure of the music, never following it, never leading it, but accepting it and its spirit as her own. Where the Lady Ann's dancing had been joyous and exuberant, the Lady Margaret's was controlled and polished. She never missed a step or a note. And tonight, she was well partnered. Even the Lady Islean, who fancied the Lady Margaret not at all, had to admit that in this woman, her son had met his match. At least on the dance floor.

The music of the pipes led the others too eventually to the kitchen, in time to catch the last few measures of the dance, and see Margaret bestow an impulsive kiss on her partner. Then, to Margaret's chagrin, nothing would do but that he dance a tune or two with the others. At last he sank down gracefully, chest heaving, on the edge of the table, and, looking at the flushed faces of his females, he called for ale. His thirst slaked, he swirled his mother out onto the floor. She had hoped to have a word with him, and when the pattern of the dance brought them together briefly, she warned, "She'll eat you alive."

Two steps apart and together again. "Who?"

Turn away once more, then come together. "You know who!"

And when they came together for a lively promenade down the hall, he laughed down at her, kissed her fleetingly, and said, "We'll see."

Between the dancing and the drinking, the ladies paid little attention to the time. Thus it was that none were waiting to greet the king and his hunting party when they rode proudly and triumphantly into the courtyard. Campbell was furious. He turned to his chief huntsman and signaled him to let loose a blast on his bugle. The sound echoed off the stone walls of the courtyard and castle but evoked no response from the castle ahead. Finally, the king urged his horse forward, right up to the castle itself. Motioning one of his men to open the door, he rode through, followed close behind by Campbell and the rest of the party. Into the Great Hall they rode, their horses stirring up clouds of dust from the rushes. A second blast on the horn brought the chamberlain scurrying.

"Where is everyone? Is this place under a spell?" shouted the irate king.

The chamberlain had never seen an enraged king, and he feared for his life, especially as Campbell's face, too, was bright red.

His eyes bulging, his heart pounding, his voice a mere squeak in his throat, the chamberlain stood there a moment trembling. Then he dropped his staff and ran for the shelter of the kitchen.

The king, without thinking, urged his horse forward to follow. Down the stone stairs bolted the frightened servant; behind, half sliding on his haunches as if going down a riverbank, came the king's horse. Straight into the kitchen he rode, followed by a torrent of men—some mounted, some not—to find a flushed Lady Ann standing hand in hand with de Wynter. And to one side, the others who also had been so ill disposed a short while before.

The Lady Margaret—just a wee bit tipsy—acted as if naught were amiss and came forward to grasp de Wynter's other hand. "James, get down from that horse and take you a partner. De Wynter is teaching us the steps to a new French dance, a pavane." Without waiting for a reply, she motioned to the bagpipers to resume their music.

When she used that tone of voice, James reacted like a little boy instead of a king; he did what he was told. Dismounting he took the hand of Lady Ann, and followed his mother meekly into the center of the kitchen. There, to the woeful wail of three improvising pipers, the King of Scotland was introduced to the newest dance from the courts of Europe. His court, taking his lead and not to be outdone, quickly joined in. The meat the king had been so anxious to display was left lying helter-skelter about the Great Hall and entrance way above.

That dance over, James would have withdrawn. But before he could do so, his mother brought him a tankard of potent usquebaugh. "Drink, my dear. Hunting and dancing are thirsty work." She was right, James decided, gulping the fiery liquor. The chamberlain, still most fearful and dubious of the king's actions, refilled the tankard with trembling hand. Part of that had gone the way of the first, when the Lady Islean claimed her half brother for the next dance.

Seeing the cold meats, the leftover pastries, the fresh-baked breads for the morrow's breakfast, more than one hunter chose to make himself a meal. The servants, although fully aware that tonight's depredations on their prepared food meant they must arise early on the morrow to replace the damage, did not dare protest. Instead, they drifted away to make themselves an early bedding.

Left to themselves, the courtiers explored the cellars, led by Campbell, who was well into his cups or otherwise would have objected. They found casks and tumbrels, beer and wine and ale and Scotch whiskey. These were trundled up from the cellar and casually broached, in many cases so awkwardly that half the contents drained out onto the floor.

James of Scotland's court was partying. When they did, they had no rivals in all the world, except maybe the wild Irish. They drank deeply, ate heartily, kissed frequently. As the king was trying to decide which female to bed that night—he had the Lady Ann on one arm, the Countess of Mar on the other, and neither was a truly smart choice tactically, considering one's husband was his host, the other's his chancellor—he suddenly remembered his challenge to de Wynter. Dragging the two equally tipsy women along with him, he staggered over to where the young man stood.

"Two stags I struck and a fallow deer, de Wynter. What do I win in return?" James leered. He knew what he would have done with the castle to himself and five women available—no, make that four, one was his mother. Blinking rapidly to clear his blurred vision, he swayed a bit from side to side. De Wynter had been drinking for far

156

longer than the king, but appeared none the worse. His eyes narrowed as he assessed the youthful monarch before him. Today was the first time he'd met his cousin. The stories bruited about Europe made him out to be uncouth, rough, and impetuous, but saved by a sense of humor. Tonight, de Wynter decided, was not the time to provoke him. Instead, he must appeal to that sense of humor.

"Do you like riddles, sire? Good. Then, I shall answer you one, but first answer me two:

> A vessel I have
> That is round like a pear,
> Moist in the middle
> Surrounded with hair,
> And often it happens
> That water flows there.

James's mind was befuddled. What had this to do with his challenge? Before he could answer, de Wynter came back with another: "And the second: *'Qu'est-ce que plus on quiert et moins on le troube?'* Now for the third: 'What was given me I gave to another, the first I shan't name, the second my mother!' Answer me the first two, I'll answer the third."

James could not think clearly. "I'll have to study on that," he finally managed to mutter. Then giving himself willingly into the hands of his two fair but equally drunken keepers, he staggered off toward the cask of Madeira.

Lady Margaret, in that brief span of lucidity some alcoholics experience before they black out, watched her son go. "Essentially good, but not tough enough to rule." De Wynter, at her side, said nothing. Then, the drunken haze descended upon her again.

"And what of you, James Mackenzie? Call yourself Seaforth or de Wynter, what of you? Are you a tough man?"

"I, madam? Nay, I am a Frenchman returned for a brief visit to his Scottish homeland. That is all."

Lady Islean, who had deliberately stayed close to her son all evening, overheard and her viscera quivered at his words. The Queen Mother was too drunk to be subtle. "How brief? Do you leave tonight or sleep here?"

"I sleep here. Unfortunately, lady, I know not where."

"That's no problem. I know where there's a bed big enough for two. Follow me." And the Lady Margaret, misstepping just a bit, set off for the upper chambers. De Wynter hesitated only a moment, then followed after.

CHAPTER 8

It was more whistle than snore: high-pitched, thin, unexpectedly reedy coming from such a robust frame. The many-layered bedclothes heaved with each long-drawn breath. Such was the noise the sleeper made that it drowned out the call of the watcher on the turret who sounded the first cockcrow at sunrise.

A strange scraping sound, ending in a hollow snap, finally awakened her. Not coming fully awake at once, Margaret reached out to confirm the presence of her bed partner. But though the sheets were warm to her touch, the other half of the bed was empty.

Now, fully awake, she sat upright and looked wildly about. The pillow was indented, the coverlets thrown back although the bed curtains remained closed. She had not imagined it. De Wynter, or someone—she wasn't sure who—had spent the night with her. Her abrupt actions started her head to throbbing, and with a gasp of relief she fell back against the pillows. Who was he? she wondered. And where was he? But what happened last night? That concerned her more. She reached down between her legs and felt for an unexplained moisture. Nothing. Bringing her finger to her nose, she sniffed. It smelled like herself. Then, she tasted it. Was it her imagination or was it more salty than usual?

Desperately, she searched her memory. But everything was blank after they left the kitchen. The last thing she remembered was setting de Wynter to stand guard while she relieved herself in the jakes. Then, all was black.

Again, that strange noise. Cautiously, she parted the heavy bed curtains and peeked out. There, not fifteen feet from her, with his back to her, stood a naked man busily shaving himself as his manservant held the glass. It must have been the stropping of the razor that she'd heard. Once she identified him by the hoar-frosted hair of his head, she made no move to shrink back behind her curtains. Instead, she boldly took inventory of the man before her. As he scraped his cheeks, the movement made the muscles in his back ripple. They were smooth and sleek, like those of a swimmer or fencer, not all knotty bunches like so many jousters'. His shoulders were wider than she remembered, or perhaps it was that his waist was more narrow. His buttocks were compact, his legs long and better-looking in the flesh than in his knitted hose. She wished he'd turn around. Could a man that good-looking behind, be less so from the front? From where she lay, she could see his partial image in the glass. At first she thought he was making faces at her, then she realized he was simply contorting his face so as to reach every curve of it with the straight edge of his shaver. Suddenly, he smiled and looked at her out of the glass. "Good morning, did you sleep well?"

Instinctively, like a little girl caught spying, she ducked back behind the protection of the bed hangings. She was lying there, trying to decide whether to get up, when the curtains parted and de Wynter sat down on the side of the bed. He hadn't bothered to dress. And there, not a foot from her hand, was the object of her imaginings of just a few minutes ago. Of course, in its relaxed state, it was hard to judge its full potential. But Margaret had seen many a man's staff in her time, and if she were any judge, this one would please her well and fit her nicely.

As if he could read her mind, he laughed. "Wait until tonight. In the meantime, I have sent for some ale and a crust of bread. You'll probably want to break your fast before we ride out."

"Ride out?" She couldn't think, not with him so close to her. "Ride out?"

"The hunt, madam, did you forget? The king, your son, hunts Reynard today." Taking her hand in his, he raised it to his lips. She could feel the warm breath on the back of her hand. As he murmured, "Come, let us mount," he kissed her fingers one by one, then turned her hand over and kissed its palm, "our horses and ride awhile in that fashion."

Then he was gone. Damn him, why didn't he come right out and say whether he'd had her or not? It made all the difference in how she'd act this day. If he hadn't she'd be coquettish, teasing him with the delight to come. If he had, she'd be possessive, promising him even greater excitement. What to do? Which to be? She bit her lip with peevishness.

She lay there for long minutes, listening to the rich, low murmur of masculine voices. Then the bed curtains parted again, and de Wynter poked in his bonneted head. "Madame, your breakfast has arrived, and your chaplain to bless you so you need not hear Mass; and your ladies await with a choice of three riding costumes. I think I've thought of everything. And I do think the green would do the most for your glorious coloring." He tipped his bonnet and withdrew. As soon as she was sure he'd left the room, she threw back the curtains to find all as he'd said.

Thanks to his planning, the Queen Dowager was just the slightest bit late arriving in the courtyard. When she did, de Wynter came forward with her horse as if he'd done this all his life. "I was right. Green is your color," he said.

Effortlessly he gave her a hand up into the saddle, gathered the reins, and placed them in her gloved hands. When her son rode up to her side, he looked terrible.

"Well, madam, if you're ready," he said in a voice heavy with sarcasm. Without waiting for her reply, he gave the signal to ride out. Amid the clatter of hooves on cobblestone and full forty hounds baying and straining at their couplings, the hunters gave rein to their mounts and headed out over the moat and down toward the river's edge. Fording at the shallowest spot, they set their horses at full gallop to the forest edge.

Within the trees, the hounds were loosed, scattering in all directions with their noses to the ground. The riders tried to stay close, waiting for the hounds to pick up the scent. Now a smallish hound cried the scent, and the senior huntsman bugled the rest of the hounds to the spot, giving them the correct track and signaling them to be off.

De Wynter stayed near the front of the riders, but not at the very fore. He had long ago learned that the first few horsemen tend to override the track when the sly fox doubles back. He picked out one or two of what he believed were the more reliable hounds and closely watched their every move, letting his horse pick its footing and direction.

Soon the fox was in full sight, the hounds going wild and switching instinctively from scent to sight. When Reynard broke at right angles, the baying horde would cut across and take the shorter distance, gaining rapidly on their prey with every stride. The fox headed straight for more difficult terrain, knowing he could slow both dogs and riders in rocky footing and heavy bush. First within sight and then out of it, he drove the hounds crazy while horses and riders straggled.

The chase was well into an hour long when de Wynter sensed that the dogs were confused and had even possibly lost the quarry. For the past week, he had made close acquaintance with this terrain. Surveying the landscape around him, he reined sharply right along a hedgerow and kicked his mount into full gallop. But quick as he had been, Reynard was quicker. A full ten leaps in front of de Wynter he emerged from the hedge going cross-country away from the hounds as fast as his short legs would take him.

De Wynter gave out the yell: "There he runs, ahoooooo!" An alert bugler picked up the cry and signaled the rallying call in the new direction. Dogs soon were driving past de Wynter's mount, albeit in full gallop, and the hunt slowly organized anew. Again de Wynter dropped back and let others, including the king and his mother and their flank of crack huntsmen, lead the way. They seemed not as sure as de Wynter that the hunt would settle down to a long chase, with the sly red prey wheeling and dancing and doubling back.

Well after midday de Wynter thought he saw what he had patiently awaited all morning. The riders were now closely bunched on the heels of the baying hounds, still on the scent and an occasional sighting. He wheeled his mount sharply left around a small hillock, drove hard down a natural draw, and made his stand directly in the face of the oncoming horde. He had only to guess correctly at what point the fox would break from the thicket and thrust his sword point

162

into his chest before the surprised animal could wheel and be off in another direction.

In an instant his eyes picked out a hole in the thicket rounded by the regular passage of fox or rabbit. And in another instant he was dismounted, his feet planted firmly, with sword in hand. Reynard never knew how his strategy failed him. He knew only sudden fear as he leaped from the thicket and directly onto de Wynter's sword.

Quickly he snatched the red beast by the tail and held it aloft just as the first of the hounds came bounding up. With one foot he fended off those who jumped the highest, all the while swinging the carcass to keep it just out of reach.

The king and a handful of other horsemen burst through the thicket and reined their mounts into a circle around the melee. Those who had horns blew them insistently, those who didn't added to the din with lusty "hallooooooos." When all were gathered, they dismounted, patted each dog on the head as they could get near them, and generally kept up the cacophony to make the thrill of the catch last as long as possible.

To the victor went the honor of skinning the prey. While two eager hunters spread-eagled the red beast by grasping all four legs, de Wynter took his "mercy" from his belt and slit him stem to stern. The hounds were now in a frenzy, knowing that the reward for their hard work was at hand. De Wynter quickly and neatly, despite the best efforts of the dogs, made incisions down the hind quarters and the forelegs, connecting these with the slit down the belly. Then, breaking the tailbone and adding a few deft slices around the base of the long, red tail, he sheathed his knife and grasped the tail. While the hunters holding the hind legs braced themselves, and were held around their waists for extra support, de Wynter gave a tremendous tug, skinning the carcass from tail to nose. As he held the pelt aloft amid wild cheering and horn blowing, the holders heaved the carcass to one side, where the hounds fell on it, fighting for pieces until the last bit of meat was consumed, the last bone carried off, and the last drop of blood licked from the well-trampled ground.

The congratulations extended to de Wynter were many and sincere. He wondered, as he had in the past, whether or not the back thumpings and rib pokings were worth it. Almost, he'd rather let the fox go to hunt it again another day. James was not among the well-wishers, he having stayed mounted through the entire melee.

Mentally, de Wynter shrugged the whole thing off as the king's prerogative. He had no time to think of the male member of the royal family. The distaff red-haired version had arrived, taken in the situation at one glance, and staked her claim. De Wynter's mount in tow, she urged her horse forward into the midst of the throng. He looked up at her, the pelt in his bloody hands, and smiled that smile that sent shivers of excitement down her back.

"The lady in green needs a touch of red on her costume," de Wynter said. Holding the pelt up, he added, "Perhaps a muff of fox?"

She pretended female dislike of the bloody pelt, but leaned over and whispered. "I already have a muff of red hair."

"I know," he said and winked. Then, slinging the red pelt over his pommel, he vaulted into the saddle. And with the Lady Margaret at his side, he led the hearty band back to Castle Dolour, alternating between a slow trot and walking, the horses being well lathered from the chase. But whenever the horses moved slowly, the Lady Margaret took the opportunity to brush her leg against his, or to lean over and allow her hand to rest possessively on gloved hand or broad shoulder or muscular thigh. No one could fail to notice. Not king, nor court, nor the Lady Islean. What de Wynter's mother thought of his so disporting himself with a woman her own age, no one could tell. However, if Seamus had been there, he would have taken one look at her eyes and warned his fellow servants to stay clear of the Lady Islean. Evidently de Wynter got the message on his own, for he made no effort to approach her now or later that day. Quite the contrary. He seemed to avoid her.

The hunt the day before, followed by the carousing in the kitchen and then today's lengthy exercise, left the court somewhat subdued. Most were happy to eat a light supper of venison, and, with a cup at hand, sit and talk about hunts of the past. De Wynter, lounging in the chair at Margaret's side, played with his glass and wondered if the evening would ever come to an end. Margaret thought much the same thing but for a different reason. The Lady Islean wondered if she'd ever get her private talk with James. Lord Campbell, off to one side, was making a hearty meal. The cold meats his wife had packed for him on the hunt were not enough for a man of his huge appetite. The Lady Ann, seated at the king's left, was too young to recognize honest fatigue as contentment. Instead, she thought her guests bored and racked her brain for some amusement. The pipers had left this morning, so there could be no dancing. Gaming was out if she had her way; Campbell was a bad loser, but a large wagerer. She'd go without new clothes next season if he lost heavily. Then she remembered the one lute the castle possessed and had the instrument delivered to de Wynter.

Margaret was delighted. What a clever girl, she thought appreciatively and smiled one of her most regal, approving smiles on the young hostess. Unfortunately, Lady Ann did not see it, but Campbell did and he preened himself in his wife's reflected glory. So what if she'd slept he didn't know where the night before. One night of sleeping alone is a cheap price to pay to hobnob with royalty.

"Sing us a French song," Margaret commanded.

But de Wynter shook his head. "No, I'm in Scotland now, let's have a good Scots tune." And before she could remind him that her wish should be his command, he launched into song:

True Thomas lay on Huntlie bank:
  A ferlie he spied we' his e'e;
And there he saw a ladye bright
  Come riding down by the Eildon Tree

Her skirt was of the grass-green silk   He bowed Margaret's way
                                               and none of the court
                                               could miss his point.

  Her mantle of the velvet fyne;
At ilka tett o' her horse's mane
  Hung fifty siller bells and nine

True Thomas he pu'd off his cap
  And louted low down on his knee:
"Hail to thee, Maggy, Queen of Heavens!   The whole court mur-
                                               mured, he was changing
                                               the song as he went along.
  For thy peer on earth could never be."

165

"Oh, no, Oh, no, Thomas," she said,
  "That name does not belong to me;
I'm but the Queen o' fair Elfland,
  That am hither come to visit thee.

"Harp and carp, Thomas," she said;
  "Harp and carp along wi' me;
And if ye dare to kiss my lips,

Margaret nodded her head and pursed her lips convincingly.

  Sure of your body I will be."

"Betide me weal, betide me woe,
  That weird shall never daunten me."
Syne he has kiss'd her rosy lips.

De Wynter put words to action, and the court applauded his daring.

  All underneath the Eildon Tree.

"Now ye maun go with me," she said,
  "True Thomas, ye maun go wi' me
And ye maun serve me seven years,
  Thru weal or woe as chance my be."

She's mounted on her milk-white steed,
  She's taken True Thomas up behind;
And aye, whene'er her bridle range,
  The steed gaed swifter than the wind.

O they rade on, and farther on,
  The steed gaoed swifter than the wind;
Until they reach'd a desert wide,
  And living land was left behind.

"Light down, light down now, true Thomas
  And lean your head upon my knee;

Never stopping his singing, and strumming, de Wynter gracefully sank to the floor at the Lady's Margaret's feet and leaned back against her knee.

Abide ye there a little space,
   And I will show you ferlies three.

> As he continued his song, he could from his vantage point take in most of the court. Especially those two most important to him. As he described the three ferlies, he felt his bonnet removed from his head. Margaret, feeling her wine and more possessive than ever, could not keep her hands from him. Not by quiver of any muscle or a break in his song did he reveal that he was not delighted to have her run her fingers through his silver-shining locks.

"But, Thomas ye sall haold your tongue,
   Whatever ye may hear or see;
For speak ye word in Elfyn-land,
   Ye'll ne'er win back to your ain countrie."

O they rode on, and farther on,
   And they waded rivers abune the knee;
And they saw neither sun nor moon,
   But they heard the roaring of the sea.

> James had evidently forgot his pique, for he leaned back in his chair and with one hand rested his cup upon the arm of the box chair. The other kept time lightly on Lady Ann's arm. De Wynter, remembering the challenge given in yesterday's note, had deliberately chosen a romantic, fairy-tale song in hopes that it would soften James toward him. The ploy had evidently worked. De Wynter unhurriedly continued on with

True Thomas's adventures in Elfland. Eventually, however, he cut
the ballad short for he feared he
might put some of the court to sleep.

He has gotten a coat of the elfen cloth,
  And a pair of shoon of the velvet green Margaret vowed, if her
                                          seamstresses worked all
                                          night, tomorrow de
                                          Wynter would wear
                                          slippers of velvet green.
And till seven years were gane and past,
  True Thomas on earth was never seen.

The song was done. The music stilled. The last echo of the young
man's baritone bounced off the rock walls of the Great Hall and died
away. Yet, there was no sound nor movement among his listeners.
Across the width of the hall, son and mother exchanged fond looks,
all disharmony momentarily banished. Then Lady Margaret, never
one to let the opportunity pass to be the center of attention, spoke up
in that artificially artful voice some women put on when they
attempt to impress, "True Thomas, indeed. Me thinks you might
better have changed the hero's name to Journeying James."

Her attempt at a joke fell flat. James, her son, flinched. Sometimes he wondered if she would ever learn to think before she spoke.
But de Wynter soothingly said, "I am indeed just your James."

Margaret, flattered, felt even more kindly disposed toward this
man. But the Lady Islean wondered how her son could stomach such
simpering and contrived wit. It was nauseating. Had she taught the
boy no higher standard than this, to fawn upon a woman who was
his mother's age and had slept her way through the court? Who dyed
her hair red regularly and had recourse to borrowed hair to augment
her own? Who laced herself tightly to overcome nature's sagging
and spreading? What was the boy thinking of?

Suddenly, it occurred to Islean that perhaps there was another
game being played here. Perhaps he didn't intend to renounce his
birthright. She almost gagged on the next thought: mayhap he had
marital plans for the lady. She realized she was holding her breath

and released it gratefully. For she remembered—who could forget?—that the Lady Margaret was not free to marry anyone, her divorce not being approved in either England or Rome. She was, and the Lady Islean savored the word on her tongue, nothing more than a harlot. But that didn't seem to occur to the young man across the hall who continued to drink in every word the Queen Dowager said.

The king lurched to his feet. "It's late. Boar tomorrow. Let's to bed." Taking the Lady Ann's hand between his own two, James looked down at her and the lust was clearly visible even to her husband's politically blinded eyes.

However, Campbell comforted himself with the thought of another night with the whole bed to himself. "Besides 'tis unwise to spend one's sperm the night before hard physical activity."

Rationalize though he might, he did not attempt to meet the eyes of the courtiers about him. They, seeing his wife promoted above her station and sensing Campbell's own elevation in the king's esteem, played a two-faced game. To his face they spoke only of his great hospitality and behind his back they joked that his hospitality was only matched by his wife—who not only opened her house to their king, but her legs as well.

Lady Ann was totally oblivious to all this. She was really and truly in love. Last night, she had received from the king, even in his sotted condition, the first romantic coupling that she'd ever known. Campbell's way was entirely different: no foreplay, simply rolling on top and rutting until satisfied, then falling promptly to sleep.

How all this would end, Lady Ann didn't know and wasn't prepared to consider at this time. For now, she was determined to enjoy the first few days of bliss she'd known since her parents had married her, over her wishes, to the head of this lowly branch of the Campbell clan; she looked not once in her husband's direction.

However, James was not about to leave the Great Hall without solving a small problem that had been nagging at him since he awoke this morning. Stopping before de Wynter and his mother, who had bowed low as their monarch passed, he gestured for de Wynter to come closer. "Cousin, last night. Did you ever reply to my challenge?"

"Indeed, sire," replied de Wynter with a straight face.

"I thought so. But I wasn't sure. I remember something about a riddle, would you know aught of that?"

"Aye, sire, I posed you three, one in answer to your challenge."

"Ah, yes, and their answers again?"

"An eye, a love-hole, and a kiss."

James fingered his sensuous underlip and wondered which was which. But he saw de Wynter wasn't about to volunteer it. Nor was James sure he wanted to know the answer.

"Yes. Right. Well, that solves that. Good night. Sleep well. You too, lady mother." He kissed his mother self-consciously on the cheek, then escorted the Lady Ann from the hall.

The Queen Dowager, holding precedence and eager for what was to come, prepared to hurry out after the king. But de Wynter held her back. "Give them a moment, we're in no hurry. We have the whole night before us."

The whole night, oh, God, she hoped so. Not for a long time had a man been up to her insatiable needs. Methven's stamina had first attracted her to him. Only after their hurried marriage, which turned out to be no marriage at all, had she discovered that unlike herself, Methven needed days and days of rest to restore his staying power. By that time it had been too late to undo the mock-marriage. However, James barely tolerated this groomsman turned stepfather. Eventually he had had enough of the upstart's airs and had commanded his mother keep the man out of the royal sight. Margaret was quite pleased to obey since it allowed her to introduce a little variety into her bed as she intended to do tonight.

De Wynter escorted her out of the room, up the broad stairs to the second-best chamber in the castle. There, she turned and would have wished him a temporary good-night, but he pushed the door open and led her in.

"You forget," he whispered in her ear, "I have no chamber of my own, so tonight, we both have to make do with this one. Dismiss your ladies-in-waiting, and for tonight, I shall act the maid for you."

The idea was impossible. Preposterous. Unthinkable. The next thing she knew, she had sent her ladies packing. The last thing she thought before she surrendered herself to his ministrations was to thank God she still wore her green hunting costume. She never wore stays and uplifter with it; they interfered with her riding.

"Now then, where shall I begin? At the top and work my way down?" he said walking around her slowly, as if considering a weighty problem, she pivoting with him. "Or at the bottom and work my way up?" And then leaning forward, he pinioned her between his arms. "Or start from the back and work my way forward."

As his lips came down on hers, she felt his fingers at the back of her neck undoing her ties. Suddenly, she was aware only of his lips. Soft and tender they were at first. Like butterfly wings, barely touching her own. Suddenly he was all masculinity, his lips hard and demanding, forcing her own willing ones open. Then she felt his tongue. Inquisitively at first, it licked at her mouth, till more boldly it proceeded forward. Almost as a prelude of what would come later on the bed, his tongue penetrated deeper and deeper. When he would have withdrawn, her lips savored that tongue, only reluctantly, bit by bit, allowing it egress.

He moved away from her slowly, and as he did, those facile hands left her, drawing her gown, now completely unlaced, off her shoulders and then, ever so slowly, down off her breasts. Each movement he made was a caress. She would have followed those hands anywhere.

Again his lips claimed her own, but this time they were not content to taste just her mouth, but also her eyelids, then down over her cheeks and onto her neck, finding that warm junction where neck and shoulder met. Nibbling as he went, he returned to her mouth, finding it open with ecstasy. This time, when his mouth claimed hers, she gave as good as she got; the kiss, long and deep, left both breathless when by some unspoken mutual thought, they separated.

Coming apart at the same time was her shift, whose lacing his hands had been undoing. With one swift move, he pulled it down, leaving her naked to the waist. Instinctively, she flexed her back to make those heavy breasts more upright. But he seemed unaware.

Instead, he inserted his strong fingers between her bare skin and her clothes and with one strong movement, as if skinning a fox, he pulled them down off her hips and let them fall to the floor. Then she stood there naked except for her knitted stockings that rose thigh-high. "Diana incarnate" he murmured and the Lady Margaret forgot that she was forty-three—an old, old woman in the world's view—the mother of one living child aged twenty, and three dead ones. She felt young and slender and virginal—a chaste Diana—as she was swept up like a girl into her lover's arms and carried to her own royal bed.

"My stockings," she said.

"Ah, the stockings. I forgot." Then, slowly, each movement a caress, he rolled first one stocking then the other down about her ankles. "Not all the way?" she managed to ask.

"Never. In France they determine how active a lover a woman is by how well she kicks off her stockings during lovemaking. I judge you can do as well as a Frenchwoman, *mais non?*" And Margaret, looking up into those gorgeous smiling eyes above those delicious lips, vowed those Frenchwomen would have nothing on her. If she had to remove those stockings one by one with her toes, they'd go, and long before her lover had withdrawn.

Surreptitiously, she worked one foot against the covers, but a hand on her thigh stilled her efforts. "Not fair, that's cheating. It must be your legs kicking high in passion that does it." The hand on her thigh moved slowly upward until it came to the juncture between her legs. To her surprise it continued upward to curl her red hair between its fingers. Margaret was glad she'd taken the extra time this morning to henna that hair, even though it had meant riding the first part of the morning with a damp crotch.

"Ah, your red fox muff? Shall I keep my hands warm in it, or would you have me give you something else to heat up?"

He had evidently untied his points while he played with first her stockings, then her crotch hair. And there in its enormous glory stood the expanded version of the tool she'd seen this morning.

"Or would you have me wait awhile?"

Margaret, for once, was glad she was no young thing like the Lady Ann. She didn't need anywhere near the amount of foreplay he'd already bestowed on her. She could feel the contractions within her already, and she knew she was wet and ready for him.

"God, don't wait. Let me feel you now." That was all the invitation he needed, and then he was upon her. And in her. And with her. And part of her. Throwing her legs about his narrow waist, she urged him on . . . and on . . . and on . . . until, locking her legs

172

about his waist, she took over the pace and drove him deeper and deeper. She thought she'd never get enough of him until suddenly she crescendoed. Contracting and rippling and feeling waves and waves of exquisite pleasure. But still he had not come. "Now, we wait awhile," he said, withdrawing. But as with his tongue, she didn't want him to vacate, and she fought him with clenched legs and crossed ankles.

"My dear," he said, looking down from above his outstretched arms. "In case you hadn't noticed, I am all but dressed. Allow me to remove this warm clothing; and I'll renew the attack shortly."

Then, as she reluctantly let go, he withdrew as slowly as his tongue had departed before, and she couldn't decide which was the more exquisite pleasure, the entering or the leaving. "By the way, my dear," he said, sitting up, his erection not noticeably depleted, "the next time we only roll them down to the calves."

Looking down, Margaret saw what he meant. Both feet were bare. And he thought French women were lusty!

Later that night, her naked lover in her arms, she discovered this was a man unto her own heart. He liked variety. So she was had with her her feet about his neck. "It's good for you to look up to someone every now and then," and she forgot her helplessness as, with every thrust, he drove deeper and deeper. Then, when they'd rested a bit, nothing would do but that she get on her hands and knees and allow him to use her like an animal. "James did command me to ride to the hunt, did he not?" he asked. But Margaret wasn't listening, she had all she could do to support her own weight while he, besides assaulting her with all his might, played with those enormous breasts that hung like dugs and overflowed his hands.

The next morning, she refused to be awakened, turning over on her side, her back to him. "No, you go," she said sleepily.

Her lover laughed. Kissing the cheeks presented to him, top and bottom, he said, "Shall I skip the hunt also, pleading fatigue?" She only moaned, and with feeble hand pushed his face away from behind. "Go away, let me sleep."

"Well then, until tonight. Sleep deep, my dear, I'll present your excuses to the king if you wish." She didn't reply. She was fast asleep. If she'd been interested, he wasn't sure he could have performed as promised. Yawning, he unbolted the door to let his own servant in, then the household servants with the tub and pots of hot water. Soaking in the deep tub, he decided lovemaking was hard work. He didn't look forward to another sleepless night of it, especially with Margaret. Shaving and dressing swiftly so as not to again awaken his royal mistress, he left the room to join the rest of the court.

The third day's hunt began as had the one before. A quick Mass, a hearty, but hastily eaten breakfast, the usual din of dog and hoof and bugle. There was no slackening of interest, for each day's hunt provided a different quarry and called for different stratagems. Nor was there any visible lessening of the service which the Clan Campbell was extending to the king and his court.

After the king had gone to bed, the revelry had been just as boisterous and just as lavishly ladled and carved as the night before. The singing and drinking had gone on until the least conscientious hunters finally called it a night and stole off to their beds. Now, with the boar hunt about to get under way, excitement overcame the need for more sleep and the aftereffects of partying, and all was right with the world. Or so it seemed to most of the king's court, who lived an exciting and somewhat carefree life for so long as the reigning monarch desired their company.

In the courtyard the buglers took their cue from the king, blasting the start of the hunt. Horses leaped and hounds dragged their kennel keepers out onto the meadow as hands and hankerchiefs waved farewell from courtyard and windows. As they neared the trees, the horses rallied round while the hounds were given the scent of the quarry with pieces of boar's hide saved from the last kill.

Every ear was tuned to the first baying that signaled the dogs' picking up the scent. This morning it took an inordinant amount of time. The bristly boars were laired-up, so great had been the din of the hunt the last two days.

The first hour was spent trying to stay close to the hounds, who had split into several groups. No singles were seen, the hounds long before having learned to respect the prowess of the mighty boar. Whether by design or chance, the king and his immediate cronies stuck close on de Wynter's flank. Today, thought de Wynter, the king was not going to grant him the advantage of foreknowledge of the terrain. Maybe, it was as well, making his task easier. An old adage among courtiers said that he who made his king look better fared better. Today, de Wynter was determined to make a pleased king of an obviously disgruntled one. For that reason, before the hunt, he had a private word or two with the chief huntsman, who was a Mackenzie, having been lent to the Campbells by the Lady Islean.

The grizzled old warrior-turned-hunter, being well versed in the noble art of venery, urged the lead hounds on with rousing shouts. Any hunter worthy of the name knew that hounds on the boar scent required special encouragement to work them up to that fevered pitch where they forget their fear of the tusked prey. Today, full forty of them were now furiously pursuing a scent, past a quagmire and straight for a great rock that had tumbled down from the beetling cliff above.

De Wynter knew the spot well. He and his men had spied it out just five days before. As he circled one way, the king right behind, he motioned others to complete the huge circle that encompassed rock, muddy pool, and bushes so thick a horse would have trouble penetrating them. It was the perfect lair for the boar.

The old tusker would be in there somewhere, and it would take some doing to bring it out.

As the hounds darted in and out of the bushes, howling their bay song, the rest of the full hunting party gathered round. While the ladies remained a discreet distance away, some of the men dismounted to beat the bushes and shout threats and entreaties. This was dangerous, for the boar might charge out at full speed, slanting off to cut down the first object it spied with its piggy eyes. Others, still mounted, with shafts strung in their bows, covered every foot of the bushy circle, straining their eyes to catch the first glimpse and get off the first shot.

With a crackling of underbrush, the boar burst from its cover, sending two hounds rolling and moaning. A loner, banned from the herd because of age and mean temper, it was huge, menacing, ghastly, when grunting in outrage. Arrows bounced off its bristly hide, serving only to infuriate it even more as its head swung from side to side taking licks at hound and horse. In a minute it was through the barricade and off at a furious pace, unscathed.

The horns and hallooing rallied the hounds and horses, and all sped off in pursuit. Each time the dogs caught up on its heels, the beast would wheel and deal out its fierce punishment. Each time, the arrows would sting it into further flight, but no one could get in that lucky hit through a red and beady eye.

Now it was a matter of tiring the menacing beast until it would stand and fight. The chase went on over hill and through wooded glen, every mile or so punctuated by a brief stand and much snorting and pawing of the turf as the boar tossed the worrying hounds from its flanks with flailing tusks. Still the arrows did not do their job. Occasionally a horse was lost when a fierce charge cut the legs from under a rider. Those with the stomach for more continued on foot, brandishing sword or bow. In his own mind, the king was not to be outdone this day by that Frenchified Scotsman—who made no secret of the woman he was bedding—nor by any other if he could help it. He spurred his horse close to the charging hounds. Always his arrows were among the first to pelt the rock-hard skull, some shattering and others ricocheting in all directions. It seemed to de Wynter that the king was displaying the same reckless courage that Seamus said had cost his father his life at Flodden, but there was little to be done about it except try to stay close lest he lose his horse.

Frothing and foaming at the mouth, its tusks reddened by the blood of the hounds, the crafty old boar finally picked a spot where it would make its stand. The Water of Sorrow at its back, an outcropping of rock alongside, it dug huge holes in the ground with its forefeet as it beckoned the bravest forward for mortal combat. Now the bows were put aside in favor of the swords, and fully half the hunters dismounted and took up the battle line.

James was one of the first to hit the ground, his sword drawn, the thrill of battle clear on his face. De Wynter stationed himself a pace behind the king's unprotected left, shouldering aside the Earl of Mar in order to gain the spot as the king, showing no fear, strode directly toward the snorting beast. The hounds worrying its flanks were hardly a bother now. The real enemy was man and his flashing steel. Six more paces to go, then the boar feinted a charge. James instinctively went to one knee, bracing the hilt of his sword on the ground. That was all the boar needed. It sprang. Ignoring the sword pointed at its broad chest, it went for the king, in its rush bowling him over. The sword wrenched from his grip, on hands and knees he swung about—the hunter now the prey of a fearsome brute. The boar wheeled and stood but arm's length away, roaring and shaking its head in great arcs, the blood-tinged spittle flying in all directions.

The king could feel the hot breath as it snorted, smell its fetid odor rank with musk, see the dirt clinging to the hairs around its porcine eye. He was mesmerized by its head; its tusks, sharpened by rooting and stropping on natural whetstones, appeared to him as long as any he'd ever seen before. Swept by panic, he would have turned and run as had most of his followers, but was held motionless by fear.

At that moment, de Wynter knelt down and bent close to the king's ear and said, "Well done. The beast is yours." The king didn't hear. De Wynter had seen men freeze like this before. He clapped James heartily on the shoulder and repeated his words. The blow broke the spell, the words made James look at his adversary again. As de Wynter had said, the beast was mortally wounded, and with its last resolve was standing with legs locked, fighting to keep from going down. A few seconds later it did, lurching forward until that ferocious head and gory tusks were but inches from the king. The hounds, seeing their prey go down, swarmed over the bristly carcass trying in vain to rip it asunder. From the chest, only the hilt of the king's sword showed, the blade having punctured lung and heart.

The courtiers, returning from shelters they had sought eagerly moments before, were loud and vociferous in their plaudits for the king. By the heartiness of their praise they sought to erase the king's memory of their cowardice. The king suffered their compliments in silence.

The hounds were leashed with great difficulty, and the chief huntsman, skilled in carving, stepped up and with one stroke hewed off the trophy head. Another cut a pole and sharpened one end. On it, the boar head was skewered and raised aloft amid shouts and bugle calls. As stirrup cups were passed among the hunters, the carver bent to his work, cutting out the entrails and organs and rending the carcass in half from neck to gristly tail. The halves were strung on poles slung between two horses. Then, the tired but proud hunting party remounted and began its slow, lengthy trip back to the castle.

De Wynter stayed safely and inconspicuously in the background. There he was approached by his mother. "Fool, you could have been killed."

"There was no danger. I had my sword," he replied quietly. He had worked hard for the past week, slept little, especially last night, and now in the aftermath of this showdown with the boar, the adrenaline that had sustained him was disappearing. He was not prepared to match mental swords with his mother. Fortunately for him and his resolve, she was not one to fall back on feminine wiles except as a last resort, instead attacking him frontally rather than playing on his guilt for scaring her half out of her wits, which he had also done.

His salvation came from an unexpected quarter. The king had pulled his horse aside and waited for de Wynter and his mother to come opposite.

"If you will forgive us a moment, Lady Islean, I would exchange a word with your son in private," Jamie said.

When the Lady Islean reined her horse back, the two men rode ahead in silence for a long moment. Then James looked into de Wynter's steely blue eyes. A smile broke out on his face. His right hand extended across de Wynter's saddle and they shook hands. "Cousin, we thank you for standing by us."

"Sire, I only did what any loyal Scot would do for his king."

"And as no other Scot today did. We won't forget. We are in your debt." With that, the king spurred his horse on toward the front of the pack.

The Lady Islean read the exchange from both looks and gestures, and urged her own horse forward. Now was the time to strike, while the monarch would be most receptive to her petition—and her son's. Soon she and the king were deep in conversation.

De Wynter knew he should ride forward and intervene, but his fatigue was too great. He swayed in his saddle. All he wanted now was a hot bath and a hard bed. And he'd settle for the latter. A man's bed. One empty of female softness. Unfortunately, de Wynter feared the Lady Margaret would have other ideas.

He was right. But neither reckoned with the Lady Islean, who, riding back from her talk with the king, saw her son lurch, then catch himself. She saw the glittering black blue eyes, the lines round

178

the mouth, and it didn't take a mother's heart to interpret the problem correctly.

"Not a word, my lord," cautioned the chief huntsman as he took de Wynter's horse by the bridle and led it off to one side. "'Tis the lady's orders."

He was too tired even to inquire which one. Giving himself up to the capable hands of this retainer of old, he allowed himself to be guided through the woods to the temporary camp set up by the men of Alva while they played at being servants of the Campbells. As the aged man ushered de Wynter into the makeshift, he was apologetic. But de Wynter, spying the neatly made-up pallet, waved the old man's words aside. Without bothering even to remove his boots or bonnet, he sank down on the bed and was fast asleep. The huntsman threw several soft, supple deerskins over the sleeper and withdrew to return to the castle to see to the hounds. For those well-trained boar hounds were not Campbell's either, but the pride and joy of the owner of Alva.

In the meantime, de Wynter's disappearance was noted by the Lady Margaret, who, already two thirds into her cups, feared the worst. Cornering her son, she accused him of doing away with her lover. The king, protesting that he knew nothing of de Wynter's whereabouts, answered her back in kind, and they were off in a royal row—he throwing up to her the hasty marriage between her and Methven, her drinking, her loose ways, her brother's conduct in harassing Scotland's borders. From out of the past he even dredged up her marriage to Douglas and all of that, but always returned to Methven. James hated the man. And he hated himself for not exercising his power and eliminating him. He was sure that his mother's mock marriage made him the royal butt of jokes throughout Christendom.

But she had quarrels and grudges of her own to air. Mostly, she berated him for the poorness of her wardrobe, the emptiness of her jewel chest, the poverty of her household—her lack of households. He must hear in detail how the rest of his court could change dwellings every few months, but not the Queen Dowager. She must need stay long after the place began to stink, for she had no other places to go.

Noting the presence of an interested bystander, she threw that up to her son too: "Unlike the Lady Islean there, I can't simply pack up my pots and pans, my furniture and furnishings, my clothings, my chapel, my silver—if I had any, which I don't—and move when the rushes molder and the jakes need emptying. I have no Seaforth or Rangely on the moors, or Alva. I have nothing. And all because you don't marry and fill up our treasury."

As usual, the Queen Dowager began to cry; the king felt guilty for there was truth in what she said; and the court, used to these rows among the younger and elder of the Stewart household, ignored the whole thing. But Islean took note of it, marking down all of the taunts and rejoinders. They might stand her or her son in good stead at some time.

De Wynter slept the balance of that day away and all of the night. Early the following morn, Fionn awakened him and apologized for not having a tub so he might have a bath; the Lady Islean had, however, sent him with a change of clothes from the castle, but no mirror. "If the lord wishes, I wield a smart dirk and will gladly scrape that stubble from about your chin," Fionn offered.

Fearing the worst from those huge hands, de Wynter gingerly surrendered himself to the young giant's ministrations. His misgivings were quickly allayed. Like so many other oversized men, Fionn had learned early his own strength and was forced to develop a gentle touch.

The king too had not lain abed this morning. He was already dressed and hearing his first full Mass since coming to Castle Dolour. To his chaplain's chagrin, the king was apt, in love of the chase, to neglect God. When the hunting was over, the chaplain saw to it that the next Mass the king received, he got sermonized in full measure. It did not leave the king in a good mood. Nor did the meal after.

The cooking, he'd noted, had been going steadily downhill ever since that memorable first feast. Until today, he'd been inclined to overlook it because of his fondness for his bedmate of the last several days. However, last night, the Lady Ann, taking advantage of her continuing reception in his room, had been too forward, even requesting that she be allowed to leave Castle Dolour and go with him to court.

The king had told her, however, that would never do. She had taken the news badly, crying and bewailing his treatment of her, and refusing for the rest of the night to let him play any of those charming games they'd enjoyed the previous nights. She would be no doe and let him chase her round the bed. Nor vixen hiding under furniture and jumping out into his arms. He'd had great ideas for this night when they would have relived the boar hunt. But the silly girl had other things on her mind, and the night was a total loss. Especially coming atop that row with his mother. He knew from sad past experience that making amends could cost his treasury a pretty penny. Just how much depended on what portion of the row she remembered.

So far this morning, both he and his mother had avoided meeting each other's eyes, but now he stole a glance at her profile in hopes of getting a clue to how she felt. What he saw didn't bode well: her eyes dull with bags below, her mouth set, her lower lip more prominent than ever, her hair pulled back under a coif and her face powdered more heavily than usual. She looked the martyr, but James feared he was the one who was going to suffer.

On the king's other side sat the Lady Ann, looking paler than usual. Her eyes were red and her mouth trembled as if she would weep. Only Lord Campbell seemed his usual surly self, although he did wonder why, when things had obviously gone so well, his fellow occupants of the dais seemed so unhappy. As for himself, he had never eaten so well, and he was gorging himself, for he feared the good food would not last once the royals were gone. He decided he would have to talk to the Lady Ann about that when she'd recovered from her royal fever and had come back to earth as the Lady Campbell she was.

Thus matters stood when de Wynter's presence was announced. He entered, dressed in shades of beige, from the palest of fawn to a rich golden hue, to a mixed reception. The king welcomed him—in hopes that the Queen Dowager would find in her lover a source of solace for her pique with her son. The Queen Dowager ignored him—how dare he let her suffer that way! The Lady Ann fawned upon him—desperately trying to make the king jealous. The Lord Campbell glared at him—how dare he make so free of the Castle Campbell, coming and going as he pleased.

Bowing low, de Wynter requested a few words in private with the king, who seized upon this excuse to leave the frosty atmosphere of the dais. Ordering the court to continue with their meal, he drew de Wynter with him, and the two made their way to the music room.

Before de Wynter could say anything, the king began. "I know what you wish," he said, not looking at his cousin, but idly playing a few sour notes on the harpsichord. If he had looked, he might have seen a startled look appear briefly then vanish from de Wynter's face. The king continued, "Your mother informed me of your desire to renounce your claim to the throne last night. I am of mixed emotions about it."

Abandoning the harpsichord, he swung around and looked de Wynter in the eye. "On the one hand, we are not particularly eager to have that snot-nosed offspring of the Douglases, my half sister, move any closer to the throne than she is now. It is a bone of contention, I admit, between me and the Queen Dowager. She would love it, and my stepfather would love it more. On the other hand, we should feel more comfortable not having a contender to the throne to our left during future boar hunts." Then, the king added, his smile taking some of the sting out of his words, "Besides, my future hunts would have more predictably happy results for me if you were back in France."

Now, it was de Wynter's turn. "Between you and me, sire, I should be happy to take ship tomorrow. Nor do I see why my lady mother places such emphasis on the matter. Although I gladly renounce my birthright, I should suppose that any moment now one of those fortunate ladies you favor might produce a solution to the problem of an heir. I understand that England is considering such a solution to her problem. Which, of course, is no surprise to you. Just look at the honors Henry has heaped on his bastard, Henry Fitzroy."

At James's look of inquiry, he continued, "Besides acknowledging the boy, the child has been made Duke of Richmond and of Somerset. Two significant titles, wouldn't you say? If I recall rightly, Richmond was Henry VIII's title before he succeeded, and Somerset had been the king's own dukedom as well as that of his grandfather. Then there was the lad's elevation to Lord High Admiral. You know, I have even heard of some plan afoot to make him King of Ireland." This was court gossip of the highest caliber, and King James was all ears. Briefly, he wondered how a man sitting way off on the Continent would know so much more of the doings in England, a land on James's own doorstep. James, for the first time, could understand why Francis I's ancestor had become familiarly known as the Spider King of France and Europe—and Francis had evidently inherited that trait from his great grandsire.

Now, de Wynter threw out a piece of gossip that might be the most revealing to his purpose: "The latest is the duke's proposed marriage. I understand that papal authorities have been sounded out and the Cardinal Campeggio himself has seen no moral objection to the duke's marrying the Princess Mary."

Only by the slightest narrowing of the eye did James reveal special interest in this direction, but de Wynter had been watching for just such a sign. James's reply was quite casual, however. "You seem quite knowledgeable of events in England—and in Rome."

"Sire, I have spent the past eight years in France," de Wynter said. "One learns to survive. As to Rome, that's easily explained. I was Albany's squire on the Italian campaign in '24. We took part in that ill-advised midwinter assault on Naples. There, besides developing a taste for rodents, I made some friends among the Neapolitans. Anyway, a year later, I was among the several thousand survivors evacuated by Madam Louise, the Queen Mother, who acted as regent for her imprisoned son."

"Ah," responded the king. "That's how you came to be called winter."

"Not really. Although it was certainly appropriate. No, the name was given to an early member of my line by Eleanor of Aquitaine at one of her Courts of Love. Whether it referred to his sangfroid or, more logically, this strange head of hair, I know not. Anyway, when Francis was ransomed a year later, in the flush of his freedom from Charles V, he gave honors and benefices and titles to his fellow survivors of the Italian campaign. That's when I received Alais. Actually it was Queen Claude's decision to renew the honorific of de Wynter."

"You still haven't explained your Roman connection."

"Oh that. One of the Neapolitan friends I made is now a prince of the Church. It was he who had occasion to describe Clement's unofficial reaction to the marriage of Mary Tudor."

183

There again, James's eyes gave him away. De Wynter was certain now. Mary Tudor was the object of James's interest. But de Wynter knew, he would have to lead up to the matter gradually.

"There is another solution," de Wynter said, abruptly changing the subject.

For a moment James feared his mind had been read. "There is?"

"You could take you a Scottish wife and produce a legitimate heir, one the whole country would welcome."

The king chuckled. Partly in relief. " 'Tis not a particularly original idea, cousin. Lives there a lord in this country with a marriageable gal who hasn't thrown her at me? And well though they might rally round such an heir, first let me make a choice among the women and I'll have the clans at each other." He laughed sardonically. "Such a marriage would make the Cleanse-the-Causeway look like good clean fun, the blood would run so."

De Wynter was not deterred by the king's response. "A foreign princess then? One who could swell your coffers?"

Now, the king was all ears. And his suspicions aroused. "You interest me, cousin, go on."

"Consider the possibilities. There is, of course, England. The Princess Mary Tudor."

Now, it was out in the open. Obviously this was James's hope. A marriage with England would mean a uniting of the two kingdoms on the one isle—under a Stewart. But James, de Wynter also realized, was not yet ready to reveal his dreams to a newfound cousin. Indeed, James went back, oh so casually, to fingering the tinny music piece.

"Her father and my mother are brother and sister," was his only response.

"No more consanguine than the marriage between brother and half sister which the Pope is prepared to bless in the case of Richmond and Mary. So, one could assume a papal dispensation would solve Scotland and England's problems. That is, if the Pope were as inclined to grant one for James as he is for Henry. There is the embarrassment of your mother's marriage to Methven to consider, you know.

"There is still another hurdle to cross if we get over the papal one. What assurance would one have, once thoroughly wedded and bedded, that Henry would not prevail again on the Pope and have his marriage to Catherine of Aragon annulled? With the mother put aside, would not the daughter be? And what if the king should beget himself an heir on this Boleyn girl he's so hot to marry. What, then, would already poor Scotland have purchased for its money?''

De Wynter had all the king's attention, and a small appeal to his for whom Boleyn served as maid of honor for about three years, tells me the girl, besides being an exotic beauty, is an enchantress. Clever, intelligent, witty, the type of woman who would appeal to you.''

De Wynter had the king's attention now, and a small appeal to his vanity did not hurt. Now, to capitalize on his advantage. "Unfortunately, Anne Boleyn is not available. But Madeleine of France is. She is everything that Anne is and more. Unlike Mary Tudor, her legitimacy is assured, her sons would rule—and France would not demand monies of you, as England has. Just the opposite. A full 50,000 crowns will be the princess's dowry.''

The talk of money stirred James as little else could. Fifty thousand crowns? For that, his mother'd forgive him anything. Even the murder of Methven—or two Methvens. But it would not do to let de Wynter know he'd struck a responsive chord. Besides, twice now de Wynter had mentioned, in veiled terms, of course, as England's demand that Scotland pay for the privilege of marrying their king to England's princess. If word were out in Europe—James didn't want to think on that—it would kill all chance of a marriage between Mary and himself.

De Wynter was continuing. "I have myself seen the girl. She is a lovely girl, and sweet but not lacking in a sense of adventure. One who would do anything to please her lord." His voice became more confidential; and though the two were alone in the dank empty room, James moved closer so as better to hear.

"Naturally, being the daughter of a renowned lecher and womanizer like Francis and his most prolific and fecund queen, you can be assured that the girl would not be a disappointment in bed. However, I assure you that French monarchs watch over the virginity of their daughters like the jewel it is. The Lady Madeleine would come to you ignorant of any other man.''

That, thought James, would be a novelty. Since Douglas began pandering to his stepson with cast-off leavings, James was more accustomed to well-used women. It might be nice to stretch a rich virgin.

Casually de Wynter reached into the pouch he carried at his side, and produced a small red leather box. "Perhaps you'd care to see her likeness?"

James as casually reached for the box. It fit comfortably within the palm of his hand. On its cover the fleur-de-lis of France was heavily stamped in gold. Within its black velvet interior was a small oval portrait. The girl's likeness he dismissed with a glance. "Sweet" adequately described it. But the frame. That was a work of art. Blue enamel with traceries of gold throughout and a studding of diamonds at the end of each golden tendril. At the top of the frame like a crown, a large pear-shaped pearl surmounted a cluster of rubies and diamonds in the shape of some exotic flower with leaves that were oval-cut emeralds.

James was impressed. The frame was priceless. If Francis should send such a gift as this just to tantalize the prospective bridegroom, the 50,000 crowns might be only the first offer. But it wouldn't do to seem too eager. Besides, there were negotiations under way for an Infanta from Spain—not to mention the English marriage. And the Hollander one. Ah, it was good to be young and unmarried if one were a king, even the king of a poor country.

In the meantime, the French princess must not be refused, nor her ambassador discouraged. Thus, James temporized, "Cousin, I am disappointed in you. A man with such a reputation with women should have been able to scare up more flattering words to describe such a young beauty. I shall keep this portrait with me always, to gaze on her—how did you characterize it?—her sweet face whenever my soul needs mending. As to the marriage itself. Though she is in truth a most desirable wife, and her dowry is—how would I describe it? adequate—I cannot at this time think of marrying this or any other princess."

He stopped with a woeful sigh, but he neither looked nor sounded sincere. De Wynter had not expected otherwise. A decision of this magnitude would take careful study. Francis knew it, too. This was only France's opening gambit. For, while Scotland was being offered one bride, Mary Tudor was being sought for the Dauphin. Marriage was as good a way as conquest to unite kingdoms. Francis with his brood of children had more confidence in marital maneuvers than martial ones. He had, after all, been notoriously unsuccessful in his attempts at the latter.

Since James was obviously expecting some response, de Wynter looked properly perplexed.

"Yes, indeed," James continued, "I've taken a vow not to marry until the matter of my mother's marriage is solved. Perhaps your friend, the cardinal?" By the time de Wynter wrote to Rome or to Naples or wherever the prelate might be, and got a response, whatever it might be, which was of no real import to James, weeks would go by. By then, James was sure he'd come up with another delaying tactic. These marital negotiations could drag on for years. After all, unless one were lucky, one married only once or at the most twice in one's life. Except for death in childbirth, women seemed immune to early ends.

In the meantime, it would be best to sever the relationship between Margaret and de Wynter. His mother, in her cups, was notably loose-lipped. An ardent lover who was in the employ of a foreign country might well learn too much from her. To accomplish the breakup would take some doing, the king already being in her bad graces. James suspected he would have to buy his way back into her favor with the French frame. Then, he had a inspiration. So diabolically clever was it that James very seriously came close to considering himself a diplomatic genius, especially when he heard what next de Wynter had to say.

CHAPTER 9

"Well, what did he say?" De Wynter had barely closed the door to the music room behind him when the Lady Islean was upon him.

"Not now, on our way back to Alva. How long will it take you to pack?" Although his words seemed to convey some urgency, his tone of voice was preoccupied.

"Why are you eager to leave?" Then, she couldn't resist the opportunity. "Don't you wish to renew your acquaintance with Margaret?"

He refused to rise to the bait; instead, he started off briskly. "The king has agreed to make my excuses for me."

The Lady Islean had to follow along at a good pace if she wished to continue the conversation. "I doubt that. He'd rather beard twenty boars than tell his mother something she doesn't want to hear. You should have heard the row last night."

"Oh? Tell me about it as we ride. As to my question?"

"To pack? Just a few minutes for my own clothing. Your father always insisted I be ready to move on at a moment's notice. But I had planned to stay and collect my belongings, taking them back with me. Not that I don't trust the Campbells."

"If I were you, I'd worry more about the Stewarts. In fact, I should assign one of the Alva housemaids to assist the Queen Dowager in her packing. From what I saw in her room, she has a habit of collecting loose objects."

The Lady Islean was shocked. Not at petty thievery—it happened all the time—but by the Queen Dowager? "She only has to admire and she'll be given what she fancies."

"With some sort of largess expected in kind. Mother, the woman hasn't two shillings to rub together. I felt her purse while she slept. It was empty. Her wardrobe? It's half the size of yours and many of the dresses have been turned. Her jewels are glass. But if you don't believe me, check the harpsichord in the music room. In it, you'll find two of your goblets and a salt that I retrieved from her room three nights ago."

Shocked, the Lady Islean twirled and began to retrace her steps, but de Wynter caught her by the arm. "Later, Mother. Those things are safe. It's the others I'd worry about."

"What do you suggest? That I strip the place while the king is still here?"

"How well do you trust the Campbells?"

The two stared at each other, so much alike other than that hair. Then, the Lady Islean dimpled and laughed. "Not at all. I'll do it. You see to the horses and carts."

To the courts' amazement and the Campbells' chagrin, servants began to remove the castle's furnishings—the chairs, the linens, the serving plates, the very kettles in which the many meals had been cooked—then the servants themselves clambered aboard clumsy conveyances and were driven away. Last to leave was the Lady Islean. As Fionn helped her mount her jenny, she was tempted to say something biting in the way of goodbye, but desisted when she saw the expression on the young chatelaine's face.

Lady Ann was mortified. And her husband was obviously furious with her. The king, guessing what had happened and realizing what was likely to follow, intervened. After all, he owed Ann something for those two nights, regardless of the disappointments of the third, that she had entertained him royally in his bedchamber. And so he made the Lady Ann a most low obeisance, and kissed her hand most tenderly.

Not looking at her at all, but at the red-faced head of the Campbell clan, he said, "You are a man most fortunate in your mate. I should wish myself to be as lucky as you when I take a woman to wife. Cherish your Lady Ann most carefully; we should be upset to discover that our royal visit had caused her any discomfort.''

The use of the royal "we" would, as he knew, impress the Lord Campbell. His words had the effect of a command. To reinforce his words, he slipped the small silver ring from his little finger and placed it upon her small thumb. "Take this token of my esteem, lady, and send it to me if ever I can be of service to you.''

Then, he mounted and rode off, leaving the young girl romantically holding the ring to her lips. It was the most precious thing she'd ever owned. Her husband, glowering next to her, waited not a minute longer than courtesy demanded, then turned about and stomped inside to seek solace in a large tankard of wine. If only he could find a cup from which to drink.

James, as he rode at the forefront of the royal caravan, thought to himself that his investment in that score of silver rings was wise; he must remind the Earl of Mar to order more.

James had not yet made it a habit to take himself up into the Highlands to visit the clans. But after seeing the wealth of the Earl of Seaforth, he decided he would soon rectify the matter.

The troop bound for Alva had not gone far when they were joined by another, de Wynter having rounded up the huntsmen from their temporary camp and, with the hounds running underfoot, started them back to their more familiar haunts. Amidst much barking and bugling and shouting the troops merged, organizing themselves with a few well-chosen words from de Wynter. With Fionn again bearing the Mer-Lion banner in the fore, the Mackenzies, lord, lady, and clansmen, returned from their first royal hunt.

To the Lady Islean's disgust, de Wynter did not immediately seek her out; not until he had ridden inspection on all of the wagons and horses and hounds, assuring himself that all was in order. It made no difference to Islean that that was exactly what her husband would have done. Finally, her son urged the ugly, surefooted mare forward, bringing her alongside the Lady Islean's jenny.

She had, during the time he was busy, gone from eager impatience to outright anger to calm resolve; she would wait and let him bring up the subject. She was tired of appearing the younger of the two.

But he seemed not eager to talk. Eventually, she broke the silence: "That's an ugly mare you ride."

"Is that what you wanted to speak to me about?"

"You know damn well it's not."

"Well, then, what would you like to know?" He was all agreeableness and she would have liked to turn him over her knee and administer a good paddling.

"You could start at the beginning," she replied, exasperated, "but perhaps that's too logical."

He reached over and put his hand on hers, his expression all contrite. "I didn't mean that as you took it. I really don't know how to begin; you're not going to like what you hear."

"He didn't agree to your renunciation of the throne?" was her shocked question.

"He didn't quite disagree. Wait, let me explain. The way he put it, he rather liked having two bodies—I had not yet told him about Jamie—between him and Margaret Douglas. He said he slept better that way. Besides, he liked having his heir near at hand here in Scotland."

"Well, that's just too bad. I'll ride right up to Mercat Cross in Edinburgh and announce my renunciation to the world at large. You'd better do the same. Comforting, indeed. Who does the bastard think he is?"

"Mother, you have it wrong. We're the bastards, remember?"

She ignored that. "Is that all he said?"

"Not exactly. He finally admitted he'd reconsider the matter if a way could be found to persuade Margaret Douglas to return to Scotland."

"You joke!"

"Not at all. That's what he said in so many words. However, he did understand our rightful concern for our own skins. He was sorry, of course, about the death of Albany's heir . . . and of your brother, the Earl of Moray . . . and of your husband." For the first time, his voice betrayed him, and Islean realized her son did care. It was her turn to reach for his hand. They rode awhile, hand in hand. Then, with his voice back under control, de Wynter continued. And this time, if anything, his voice was bitter. "And out of his great and real love for us, when I told him of my son, he refused to confirm Jamie as my heir."

"Oh, my God, no. He wouldn't, he can't. You've acknowledged the boy as your own."

"Mother, don't fight it. He's right. We can argue and protest as much as we wish, but only the king decides the succession, whether it be his own or a lowly earl's."

She was defeated. All her plans, her plotting, her work, all of it was undone by the will of one man.

He squeezed her hand. "But all is not lost yet, Mother. The king is agreeable to reconsidering the whole matter under certain circumstances."

Her eyes brightened; she still believed that right would always will out. "Anything. I'll deed him my silver mines . . . you can turn over Rangeley to him. All we need is Seaforth."

"That isn't what he has in mind, although I doubt that he would refuse them if offered. No, he has in mind that I personally persuade Margaret Douglas to return to Scotland."

"You're not seriously considering it?"

"Why not? I hear England's beautiful in the summer. Isn't it time that I see for myself?"

"Has the whole world gone mad? The Red Douglas would never let her go . . . nor would Henry. He uses her to keep Margaret, the mother, under control. Whenever he wants her to aid him in some scheme that's to Scotland's disservice, he promises to disinherit the Princess Mary and name Margaret Douglas heiress to England."

"Perhaps the daughter is tired of being elevated and then reduced in precedence. She might well wish to visit her mother. Be that as it may, I owe it to you and Father and Albany and all who have worked so hard to protect me during my youth . . . and to Jamie so that he takes his rightful place in Scotland. I have to give it a try."

He was right and she knew it. But she had trouble saying so aloud. Somehow putting thoughts in words made them so final. As they rode on, the two mounts matching their paces, she tried to force herself to say she agreed. He let her take her time. He was afraid she might ask what were the alternatives.

Finally, in so many words, she accepted the inevitable. "When do you leave?"

"That depends. Have you by any chance kept in touch with the rest of the companions?"

"The companions?"

"That was the name we boys gave ourselves, after Alexander the Great and his men. Gilliver objected since Alexander was heathen, but we voted him down. If they are still in Scotland and are at all willing, I should like to enlist their cooperation in this mad adventure of mine."

She thought a moment. "Drummond, I know, has taken service with one of the Bonnet Lairds. As for the others, I shouldn't be surprised if Seamus had kept in touch with them. You might ask him when we get back to Alva."

They rode on silently, companionably, the enormity of the task facing them uniting them again. Suddenly the Lady Islean began to chuckle. As her son watched, somewhat taken aback, she laughed outright. Catching sight of his expression, she managed to calm herself, then confided, "I've not gone mad. I just saw a picture of my son robbing the Queen Dowager of what she had already robbed, and she snoring through the whole affair. Imagine her puzzlement when she goes to look for her new possessions and can't find them. Think you she'll blame you?"

"Not funny, Mother," her son replied.

"Speaking of fun," she countered, "did you ever get your green shoes?"

He confessed, "Alas, I did. Unfortunately, the lady has too big an eye and the shoes would better fit Seamus."

"Give them to him. He'd love them. The green of the emerald isle, he is oft heard to say, is his favorite color."

"I would, but there's one problem. The green of these shoes is the most bilious I've ever seen."

"That's no problem. Seamus is color-blind."

Fionn, riding before them, overheard and thought to himself, Da' never told me about that.

CHAPTER 10

The Lady Islean was right. Seamus had known of the boys' whereabouts, at least generally speaking. That night, the three—Islean, de Wynter and Seamus—sat down to devise messages individually tailored to appeal to each of the boys as they remembered them.

To George Cameron went word that there was excitement to be had and a woman to seduce . . . to Kenneth Menzies, a challenge offering some hope of pecuniary rewards . . . to Angus and Ogilvy, a chance to outwit the English as well as outshine a fellow Highlander . . . to Henry Gilliver, the opportunity to serve Scotland and discharge a debt to the Seaforths. Only to John Drummond was the message blunt and without artifice: "I am embarked on a dangerous enterprise and I need your help. Come to Alva on the 8th if you possibly can. Signed, Jamie Mackenzie of Seaforth, Rangeley and Alva." To which the Lady Islean added in her delicate hand the word "please."

While Dugan, Derry and Fionn were off delivering the messages, those left behind began assembling the equipage the group would need for the trip. "Shall we figure on all seven of you, or how many?" asked the Lady Islean, expressing a concern all had felt.

But before de Wynter could answer, Seamus did: "Figure on eight. I go, too."

"Never!"

"Nay, not you," her son chimed in.

Their reaction was so immediate that the Lady Islean and de Wynter never knew who spoke first. But Seamus was determined. When the Lady Islean pleaded her inability to handle four hysterical women—his bedmates plus his daughter—if anything should happen to their man . . . and de Wynter asked who would protect the Lady Islean and young Jamie, only then did Seamus waver.

Reluctantly, Seamus agreed that his place was in Scotland. "But then you'll take one of my sons. Never let it be said that a Seaforth went into battle without a MacDonal there to protect his back."

But which one? All three, if Seamus knew his boys, would want to go, and each mother would demand her son stay behind. Finally, it was decided that such a decision be made by lot.

That settled, or at least put aside until the problem arose, the discussion returned to horses and arms and the men to go with them. De Wynter agreed to leave the choice of horseflesh to Seamus. "Except for the plain mare. She served me well during the fox hunt, and I have grown fond of her."

As for men, de Wynter saw no need for other than the original group, but the Lady Islean wouldn't hear of it. "You'll travel like a Seaforth. Let some of your friends serve as gentlemen-in-waiting if you wish, but nobody'd take Angus and Ogilvy for anything but what they are—bloodthirsty Highlanders. You'll go like a proper Scot earl. With dresser, cook, secretary, barber, chaplain—a proper entourage plus a score of men-at-arms."

She was determined, but de Wynter was equally so. He had to travel light. It was going to be difficult enough to get a small group safely and secretly across the border . . . and back.

"Why must you go secretly?" asked the Lady Islean.

Seamus and de Wynter looked at each other in poorly concealed amusement; then they realized she was not joking. "What do you have in mind, Mother?"

"You're going on this mission for James. Let him afford you some protection."

"He can't protect his own borders, lady," Seamus reminded her. "How can he protect a group of Scots once they're in England?"

"You forget, a herald has diplomatic immunity. Let James appoint you herald, and send you in satin tabard with messages to the English Court."

De Wynter impulsively hugged his mother. "You are a genius, Mother. Better yet, let the Lady Margaret send messages to her daughter. That will gain me entry to her presence."

Seamus, however, dampened their enthusiasm. "And how do you get the king to agree to all this?"

"Well," drawled de Wynter, lounging back in his chair, "I could work my charms on the Lady."

"Lady? Royal whore, you mean," was Islean's acid rejoinder. "Save your charms for England. A little token or two would do as much good."

Ringing for a lady-in-waiting, she sent for her jewel chest. When it was opened, Seamus couldn't believe his eyes. Never had he seen so many jewels in one place. Even de Wynter, who had had occasion to see the jewels of the Queen of France, was impressed. "So this is your weakness. I should have known your royal blood would surface somewhere."

Islean ignored him. She and the earl had argued about her passion for jewels too many times to allow for guilty feelings engendered by her own son. Instead, she brought out her treasures one by one. Immediately rejected were all those identifiable with the Seaforths—the Mer-Lion medallion she'd worn the night of the banquet; the heavy signet ring of the Earls of Seaforth, the one Seamus had taken from a dead finger on that night in 1513 not long after Flodden. "It's yours now, Jamie," she said, fingering it sadly.

He closed his hand about hers. "No, you keep it safe for my Jamie. Unless I succeed, it may be all the inheritance he'll have."

Nothing more was said, but the ring was set aside.

At last, with an exclamation of delight, Islean seized upon a bracelet a full two fingers wide—heavy with gold and sparkling with many small diamonds. "This should do it. Big, bright, and flashy. I never liked it, too gaudy."

While de Wynter examined it, Seamus protested. "It's too fine for the woman." With his big fingers he stirred among the many items still remaining in the chest and hooked one finger through a narrow bangle, a single brown stone hanging from it like a teardrop. "Why not this?"

The Lady Islean laughed. "That, my dear Seamus, is worth two of the other. There are few large diamonds in this world, and even fewer perfect brown ones.''

Seamus dropped the piece as if stung. De Wynter, retrieving it, examined the gem with the eye of a connoisseur, then casually dropped it back into the chest, ''She'd take it for tourmaline. Better the bracelet.''

Unsatisfied, the Lady Islean rooted again in the chest and found what she sought: a small, black velvet pouch. Opening it, she poured eight matched pearl studs into her hand. As she rolled them about in her palm, they gleamed softly. Then, she suddenly thrust them at her son. ''Here, they were a gift to my father from the musselmen of Grantown on Spey. However, they might serve Scotland better if you had them.''

He was impressed by their beauty, by their history, and by their evident importance to her. Her sacrifice was unnecessary, yet she wanted to make it. One, then another, he took from her hand. ''These two I'll take; keep you the others just in case.''

She pretended not to mind the loss of all of them if he needed them, but the two men could tell from the way she handled, gazed at, and fondled the six he left her that she was pleased her total sacrifice had not been needed.

Six days later, on July 8, the companions began arriving at Alva. The first to ride up the lane was Kenneth Menzies. Mounted on a spirited gelding and dressed in fine linsey-woolsey, he was the picture of the prosperous nobleman. Before he'd done more than kissed Lady Islean's hand and been welcomed inside to refresh himself in the Great Hall, Gilliver arrived.

He was thin and frail-looking as ever, but much of the innocence and naiveté had been erased from his countenance.

Rather than have each tell his story and de Wynter his own to each newcomer, it was decided to save them all for supper that night. No sooner had this resolve been made, than two more arrived to join the company. Racing each other on lathered horses that had been used hard, came Angus and Ogilvy. Or, wondered the Lady Islean as she watched their arrival from the leaning place built into the oriel window in her solarium, was it Ogilvy and Angus? Neither, she concluded, looked as though life had treated them kindly.

Drummond came next. He looked his role as professional soldier. He was dressed in hard-surface woolens and serviceable leather. His horse wore quiltings of fabric and was not flashy. Even its gait was economical. Only his weapons were out of the ordinary, as one would expect of the Master of Arms in service to a Lowland clan chief.

When the sun had gone down and they were into their third cup of ale with supper soon to be announced, the watchman sounded the warning, "A'horse, a'horse." Soon George Cameron strolled into their gathering with a handkerchief to his mouth and a dandified gait. "Am I late, dear me?" he said in a dulcet tenor. Then when they reacted with shocked looks among them, he laughed, amused at his jest. "Sorry, comrades. But Bertha was in labor and I was curious to see whether we'd finally get ourselves a boy."

There was absolute silence finally broken by the Lady Islean. "Well?"

He took the chair Seamus relinquished for him and looked about him at his fellows.

"Well?" the Lady Islean repeated in a much more forceful voice.

"What? Oh, the babe. Another girl. That's nine so far. Don't look at me. I don't conceive them. I'm just there for their begetting. Besides, there were two sets of twins."

His fellows howled. George, the ladies' man, had indeed surrounded himself with women. Nine babes and a wife. He tried to explain that he hadn't planned it that way, but the more he said, the more they laughed. Eventually, he gave up and escaped in the cup Fionn gave him. When their laughter subsided, it was his turn: "Now tell me how each of you has done."

"In the sequence of your arrival," interposed the Lady Islean, attempting to give the proceedings some order.

Kenneth Menzies, bowing an acknowledgment, began. "I know what I look like, but I'm not. I have me a half interest in the White Horse Inn off High Street near the Canongate. Of course, the gentlemen who come there to dice, dine, and drink don't know it. They think I'm a patron like themselves, only a bit more lucky. But I don't cheat." He bowed to the countess. "Thanks to you, I don't need to. Give credit where credit's due—it was the training I got at

Seaforth. Of course, the constables don't believe that for a minute."

In the silence that followed, Gilliver said, "I guess I'm next. I've just come from St. Andrews. Four years ago when my mother died, I went there to join Holy Orders. The archbishop, discovering my skills with pen and ink—I guess I owe that to you at Seaforth— excused me from many of the usual duties of a novice to make me his secretary. I wasn't quartered in the monastery. Instead, I stayed within the archbishop's residence. That gave me access to the town. There, I had the great honor to talk many times with Patrick Hamilton." He paused to lend emphasis to his words.

"I was there in February '28 when they burned him. I heard his screams. I saw the flesh melt from his bones. I smelt the reek of his burning. When a sudden wind picked up, I choked on his ashes." Gilliver had difficulty continuing. The others respected his emotion and waited patiently. "You know, I'd heard him preach, I'd read his thesis, the so-called 'Patrick Pieces,' and there wasn't a thing in there against the Church. He was simply against the corruption we see in the Church, and the immorality. Do you know a priest asked me the other day to stand godfather to his newborn child? All Hamilton wanted to do was get across the word that Man, made in the image of God, must be good . . . and that the power of Faith is boundless. For this and in the name of his supposed eternal salvation, they burned him."

Gilliver looked so disturbed that Islean half rose to go to him and comfort him in her arms. Gilliver didn't notice. "What could I do? I couldn't take orders under the circumstances. The archbishop released me from them, but insisted I take service with him, my knowledge of Latin and Greek serving him well."

The others sat silent, only the Lady Islean having a comment upon this. In her softest voice, she asked what they all wanted to know. "Are you reformed? Are you Lutheran?"

He broke down, crying his answer. "Hamilton showed me the way . . . but I've lost it. Oh, God, yes. How can I leave Holy Mother Church? My mother would curse me in Heaven if I did."

There was no answer to that. Instead, a long silence ensued while those at the table considered what he said. To most his agony seemed self-induced. Religion for them was something you were born into, lived with, tolerated as best you could, and, they hoped at the end, profited by. Religion was one thing there was no need to worry about.

The countess, determined to press on, broke the silence. "Angus, Ogilvy . . . Ogilvy, Angus . . . which came next?"

"I," came the response simultaneously from two deep voices.

Neither truly wanted to reply, but as Ogilvy used to take the lead when they were boys at Seaforth, it was to him that the rest looked.

He was, to say the least, laconic. "We went back to the clans. They found a place for us. Not fine it was: herding sheep. Having trained our dogs right, like Seamus taught us, we put our minds to aught else."

There was silence.

Angus continued, "We make the best Scotch whiskey ever to come out of the Highlands. Five still pots we have a-burning right now on fires of peat. Like Seamus taught us. And our whole produce is spoken for, for the next two years."

"Seamus, you didn't," was the best the Lady Islean could muster in a feeble remonstrance.

"Oh, aye, I did. But how well, we'll no' know till we taste the usquebaugh they're bragging on."

"You're on! Check our saddlebags."

Drummond came next. "I've little to say. I served with John Armstrong of Gilneckie in Eskdale."

"Were you with him at Teviotdale?" asked Gilliver, awe-struck.

Drummond smiled. Sweet Gilliver, so easily impressed. "Nay, but I know what happened, and it was not like the balladeers said. Certainly he got a loving letter from the king, but he was not betrayed. Armstrong rode there with a score of my fellow moss-troopers with but one thing in mind: to kidnap the king. I'd hold with no such thing, so he left me behind. But his fate was fitting. He was met, treachery for treachery, and outmatched. To my mind, he deserved his visit to the dyester's pole. But not his men. I knew them well and many were good-hearted men. Anyway, the gallows put me out of work, for I'd not ride with Kerr or Scott. So, that's why I'm here."

Good, honest Drummond, thought de Wynter. I wonder how well it will sit on him, this jaunt I propose. But if only one man I can have, this is he. That foolish Armstrong. A gem he had if he'd only listened to him.

Now, all eyes were upon him. It was de Wynter's turn. He knew once he removed the cap that whatever else he said would fall on deaf ears. Which was best. There were parts of his life that would not stand close scrutiny and which he preferred not be dealt with in any depth. Thus, in the most casual way he knew, he swept off his bonnet. The reaction to his silvery crest was as he had expected, he had seen it before. Then, while they attempted to digest that, he launched into his tale.

He covered his whole life, briefly, tersely, touching only high points, since his departure from Scotland. His life with Albany, his service in Italy, his ransoming, his return to France, his dubbing, his reputation with the ladies, in part unearned. "Unlike Cameron here, I have sired me no daughters. But I do have one son. That's why I sent for you."

While de Wynter explained his task, Islean left the room to return shortly with a young Jamie Mackenzie holding tight to her hand. Sleepy-eyed, he looked what he was: helpless and threatened, as all these men had been, with making his own way in the world. The sight of the child was all that was needed to set and strengthen their resolve. If they must capture Margaret Douglas—rape her, kill her, torture her, or whatever to protect the child's inheritance—they would.

Finally Drummond asked, "What do we call you? Jamie, or Seaforth or this new title of yours?"

For only a moment their leader paused, then looking at them, one by one, in the eye, he said, "Call me Jamie if you love me. To all others, I go by de Wynter."

The troop rode out three days later, but a much smaller group than the Lady Islean had envisioned. For many of the tasks that she had wanted to assign to servers the companions themselves felt they could perform. Thus was Gilliver the secretary and Devil's own chaplain; Fionn the barber; Drummond the farrier; Cameron the cook; Menzies the dresser; Angus and Ogilvy the provisioners. Only three of Alva's servants did they take, and those were essentially as men-at-arms, each to hold three horses if need be.

BOOK TWO

**The Companions
13 Muharram, A.H. 940 /
27 August, A.D. 1532**

England

CHAPTER 11

The two were going at it again, this time as cohorts, in a room on the inn's second floor.

"Why the hell doesn't Margaret Douglas stay put?" Menzies complained.

"Aye," Cameron agreed. "Three times now we've drawn up our plans, bribed the servants and—"

"Plans, hell!" Menzies interrupted, rising angrily to his feet and knocking over the wooden bench alongside the trestle table. "Three sets of jakes I've explored from the moat. Short straw or no straw, no more stinking jakes for me."

Cameron ignored Menzies but righted the bench and straddled it. "Each time we've everything set, she ups and moves away to 'visit' somewhere else."

"Maybe 'twas only coincidence," Gilliver interposed hopefully. If anyone else but gullible Gilliver had made the remark, he would have been greeted by hoots and laughter.

Instead, Drummond said kindly, "Nay, Gilly, I fear they have a point. Three times is too many times for mere coincidence."

Menzies eased himself up to sit atop the table. "I tell you, she knows we're after her!"

"She couldn't," argued Gilliver, never discouraged by being taken lightly. "None of us would tell and who else knows?"

Menzies snorted in answer, but Cameron replied, "Her mother and half brother, for two."

"The Queen Dowager wants her daughter back," Drummond reminded him patiently.

"A lot of other Scots don't," Menzies countered quickly. "And if Maggie's in her cups and in bed, she'll tell anybody anything."

Cameron laughed. "If we have to worry about all her drinking and bedding mates, we've half the males in Scotland to concern us."

Drummond coughed. The one thing they need not do was waste time on the royal lady's sleeping habits, especially with de Wynter present. "If James did not want his half sister back, why send us for her?"

De Wynter didn't turn from his spot near the window overlooking the innyard. "To give him an excuse, perhaps, to seize Seaforth and mother's estates."

Menzies slapped hand on thigh. "Of course! Look what he did to the royal architect, Hamilton of Finnant. The man was making a commission on every timber sold, every brick made, every pane installed. Mother of God, he grew richer with every palace James redid: Falkland, Stirling, Linlithgow—"

"Spare us a recital of the royal register," Cameron begged.

Menzies gave his friend a scathing look, then continued on. "The king would have us believe that instead of making plans for the new palace in Edinburgh that James commissioned, the architect was making plots to kill James. I thought at the time that Hamilton wasn't rightfully executed but that he was murdered. Now I know why."

Gilliver broke the silence that followed. "That doesn't make sense to me."

De Wynter turned and smiled on his naive friend, "Since he was childless, Hamilton's extorted money and lands reverted to the king. You must remember, Gilly, as far as the law of primogeniture is concerned, if we fail here, I too remain childless."

"All right, Jamie, let's assume someone—James, Margaret, whoever, it makes no mind at the moment—someone in Scotland wants us to fail. How do they, up there, warn Margaret Douglas down here?"

"I don't know that they do," de Wynter replied. "Maybe we're not being avoided. Maybe we're being lured into a trap. Putney,

Mortlake, now Barn Elms—each move progressively farther inland and farther away from a fast escape by ship.''

De Wynter's theory started a flurry of conversation. None had considered this possibility. Angus's voice cut through the noise; ''What would you have us do, then? Trip the trap like simple dawcocks?''

''No. I do suggest we test my theory. Make no play to capture her this time, and if she moves anyway, then we'll know for sure.''

Cameron nodded agreement. Now was his chance to try out on de Wynter an idea already broached to his fellows. ''Might there not be another way? Couldn't we persuade her to go with us willingly?''

''Go on.''

''She's a lass. We're men . . .'' A leer completed the statement.

If the rest expected de Wynter to laugh, they were disappointed. ''Possibly. Are you volunteering?''

''Well, me being a proven stud and all—''

Anything else he might have said was drowned out by a chorus of jibes with Angus getting the last word. ''I bet your wife was not sorry to see you go, you pecker-pusher.''

De Wynter ignored the laughter, gathering up his cloak and cap preparatory to going. ''Best keep your breeches on for a while, George. When I presented myself with the letters from the Queen Dowager, she couldn't have been more proper . . . nor more poisonously cold. In the meantime, let's see if she stays put if we do not try anything. Now, I must be getting back to Scotland Yard. I am invited to join king and court when they change residences tomorrow. He leaves Richmond for Hampton Court to check the progress of construction on the Great Hall. I suggest you follow his example and change inns.''

Sending Fionn before him to make sure the way was clear, de Wynter swung his great cloak about him and settled his plumed cap more closely about his head, making sure not a wisp of white hair showed.

Drummond, following after for last minute words, couldn't resist the opportunity. ''Jamie, why not dye it?''

''What? And go unremarked?''

''Seriously. What will you do when those French caps go out of fashion?''

"I should just have to start another fashion. No, I do not joke. You either make necessity work for you or you end up catering to it."

Drummond changed the subject. "We've been here more than a fortnight. You said we had to be back in Scotland by mid-September. Are you sure you're playing the waiting game for the right reasons?"

"You mean the Boleyn?"

"I mean nothing." Clear brown eyes met blue ones; the blue ones could not sustain the gaze. De Wynter turned and was about to step from the cover of the stairway and into the busy common room but a hand on his shoulder stopped him. "One more thing. A matter of curiosity. You seem preoccupied with the window. Did you see something?"

De Wynter shook his head. "No, but I should have. My ghost apparently has deserted me for the first time since we arrived in London."

"That's a good sign. You must have lost him." Drummond looked and sounded relieved.

De Wynter favored him with that rare, beautiful smile that made him look again like the Jamie of the past. "Let's hope so. By the way, if you are changing inns, you might try the one near Teddington. I hear their food is good, and you would be close to me at Hampton."

Drummond shrugged. English food could never be called good as far as he and his men were concerned. "You know us, one inn's the same as another. We'll leave on the morrow."

De Wynter nodded his approval, then checked his cap once again and wrapped his cloak tighter about his herald's tabard and left the room. Few noticed either his entrance or his passage, the room having grown hazy with smoke from a fire built up a few minutes before by a most helpful Fionn . . . using green wood just as he had done at the Castle Dolour two months before.

CHAPTER 12

The following morn, Henry VIII awoke long before dawn to the imperious, irritating pealing of church bells summoning him to matins.

Now that he had broken with Catherine of Aragon, his wife of twenty-two years, and toyed with breaking with the Holy Mother Church, he resented these pre-dawn awakenings. The din of the bells sharpened the pain in his head. What he would not give right then and there for a whole raw egg in a glass of Madeira. As hangover cure, it never failed; but no, the Church demanded fasting before Mass.

That was not his only deprivation. His bed, too, was empty, thanks to the Church. He heaved himself up into a sitting position. The movement set his head to throbbing, not improving his dyspeptic outlook on life in general and Anne Boleyn in specific. Not once had she shared his bed, preferring that he be celibate until divorced and she be chaste until queen. He had decided ruefully that Mistress Anne wanted him, but wanted his kingdom more. This well may be the supreme trade, he thought, a crown for her maidenhead. At least I'll be first. Let those others flock about her like dogs on the scent of a bitch in season. Get rid of one, another pops up: Percy, Ormond, that damn fool poet Wyatt, and now that young Scot herald. Sniff as they may, I, Henry VIII, shall pluck that maiden's head, or the man's! I swear it!

The bed creaked sympathetically as he swung his feet over the edge, gingerly resting them on the floor. But the cold of the bare wood soothed the fire in his gout-ridden left foot.

Setting his nightcap aright over red curls streaked with gray, and tugging his nightshirt down about his hairy haunches, he stood up; and as abruptly sat down again, grunting with pain.

"Damn foot," he muttered, looking down on the offending member with its purplish sausage where the big toe should be. "Damn king," he corrected himself, the waves of pain in his head making him wince. Nothing like pain to force one to be objective about oneself. This morning Henry suffered pain in double doses, head and foot. Not all of it was his own fault. Glutting himself at supper, draining all those tankards of ale, topped off with goblets of wine—these were his own doing. But not the dancing. That Anne and de Wynter's partnering had caused.

He gritted his teeth in unregal envy. Those two made a pair, both exotically colored, tall and slender, with an elegance and catlike grace his own ponderous body could never duplicate. As Anne and de Wynter demonstrated the latest dance from France, his sister Mary had sighed and whispered something to her husband, Suffolk. But Henry had overheard: "Such a study in contrasts—he light where she is dark and vice versa." When she added, "What a beautiful pair, so of an age," that had done it.

Spurred by the need to prove himself still young, Henry rose. Ignoring the warning twinges in his foot, he claimed Anne as his partner: "Come, mistress, master me this dance." The court applauded his wit; de Wynter, relinquishing her, bowed and withdrew.

What else could the bastard do? Henry had thought, gallantly accepting and returning the bow. Anne, delighted, led him through the steps of the pavane. He, like some young cockerel, must step out lighter and livelier with more elegantly pointed toe than had her previous partner. This morning he paid for last night's folly.

Henry groaned. He could imagine Anne's reaction to his suffering, her light, bright voice cataloguing his sins of last evening, leaving out no foolish or embarrassing detail from her diatribe.

Then, just when he was losing patience with her tongue, her throaty voice would change . . . her black eyes lose their snap . . . her red mouth curl into a smile. Then she would say something like, "*Mon pauvre roi*. No wonder your head aches. Outdrinking those

210

young gallants. Have you no pity? They look like milksops along-side a real man like you. Then, mercilessly to dance *cinque pas* about them! And you think you feel bad? Think of them, their pride made a shambles. You have outmanned them.''

To hear such praise he would gladly tolerate a thousand tongue lashings. If she'd only let him, Henry was sure he could outlove every one of them, too. Especially de Wynter. No man that slender, Henry decided, could have a proper man-sized pisser.

On that satisfying thought, Henry blew his nose resoundingly between two fingers and hawked up spittle from his throat, ejecting both in the general direction of the slop jar. As usual, he missed. God, how he hated using that thing. Even for pissing. If only his father had loved splendor less and creature comforts more when, after the great fire of '99, he'd rebuilt this palace. Wolsey had when he rebuilt Hampton Court. That the son of a butcher could build a better palace than the son of a king disturbed Henry. But he had to admit Hampton Court Palace was a much more fitting residence for a Tudor king than was Richmond.

It had been no surprise when the cardinal finally presented him with the palace and all its furnishings. "Wise move, Wolsey," he'd said. "'Tis not fitting for a mere prelate to live better than a king." However, out of his mercy, he had allowed Wolsey to occupy and enjoy the palace for the next four years while he completed the furnishing of it. At the Church's expense, of course.

Now, three years after that, three full years after *all* of Wolsey's lands were declared forfeit to the Crown, a claimant had turned up demanding ruinous back rents or return of the land under some sort of lease made with Wolsey. Henry refused to accede to either demand. Instead, he set his new archbishop to searching out a loophole. Cranmer ought be able to release his king from a simple lease, if not from marriage to Catherine.

Elsewhere in the palace, doors banged open and closed as lackeys alerted ushers of the bedchamber to summon gentlemen of the wardrobe to attend the king. While he awaited their presence, his thoughts dwelled on Hampton Court, a truly imperial palace. An individual jake for every important apartment. Bathing closets, too. No need for the tubs used here at Richmond.

Outside his chamber, word went down to the kitchen to bring water and bathing tub. Four men struggled upstairs, bearing the china-lined wooden tub with the king's royal arms engraved in the side. A stream of servants followed after, carrying pots of hot or cold water to fill it. Then this whole procedure must be reversed after the bath was over. The stairways of Richmond between kitchen and king were wet daily with spilled water.

But not at Hampton Court. Henry stretched vigorously without disturbing the foot that had temporarily slackened its throbbing. The more he thought of his new palace the more determined he was to keep it. If need be, he would meet the Turcopilier's demands, and pay rent monies to the Knights Hospitalers of St. John of Jerusalem.

No, damn it, I'll see them all in hell first, he laughed unpleasantly, or better yet, in the Tower. Kings shouldn't pay rent to the Church. What gall, pressing such claims years after I've started enlarging the place. I've even affixed the tokens of royal ownership. Twenty-seven and six it cost me—each!—for that robber baron of a stone carver to carve three lions rampant, holding up shields bearing my arms.

Then there's the cost of the bricks and the glass and everything else I've ordered. If it isn't already legally mine, Cranmer shall have to make it so, he resolved.

As much as he'd have liked to throw the Turcopilier into the Tower, it was all bluster. He feared, rightly so, that the Grand Master had friends in high places at the Vatican. With the Pope still considering the king's petition for a divorce, it would not do to unduly upset the Church. At least right now. However, whatever Henry wanted he would have, eventually. And keep till tired of it. But he was not yet tired of Hampton Court Palace. He consoled himself that the Turcopilier, John Carlby, was an Englishman. A loyal subject should be amenable to some sort of arrangement. But what?

Before Henry could decide, his attendants arrived. Truly important decisions demanded his attention: which doublet to wear, what color hose, a hat with plume or jewel or medal, and especially—his foot reminded him—what to do for shoes.

Once the king was bathed, shaved, preached at, and fed heartily, the court prepared to move up the River Thames to Hampton.

While Henry stood admiring the dignity of the River Thames from the steps of Richmond Palace, with Richmond Hill behind him, the gatehouse and wardrobe court before him, and the Maids of Honor row of houses just beyond, Suffolk approached him.

The son of Henry VII's standard-bearer, who had been killed in single combat with Richard III at Bosworth, Suffolk had dared, above his station and without permission, to marry Henry's sister. The same Mary Tudor who has been married and widowed within the previous year by that sickly dotard, Louis XII of France.

Although her remarriage to a commoner was treasonous, Henry pardoned the pair. After all, had not Henry's great-grandfather, Owen Tudor, been a mere clerk of the wardrobe to Henry V's widow before he married her and established the Tudor's dynasty? All Henry demanded was that the pair pay a king's ransom as recompense, as well as returning all the jewels and plate given Mary as her marriage portion. With that returned to the Tudor treasury, Henry relented, allowing the couple years to pay the recompense . . . at the usual usury rates, of course. Meanwhile Henry and Suffolk rousted together, jousted together, and wagered together, for of all of those who attended the king, only Charles Brandon, Duke of Suffolk, completely shared the king's love of jousting, and, because he did, shared Henry's heart.

This morning Suffolk greeted Henry with a proposal. Let there be a race to Hampton Court: the king and those courtiers using the royal barges versus those who preferred to ride cross-country. Coming from anyone else, the idea was dangerous, pitting king against courtier, but Suffolk knew his king.

Suffolk's idea challenged the king's desire for diversion, especially since Henry'd immediately conceived an advantage for his side that would guarantee his winning. "We shall await you at the gatehouse," he agreed, "if you do not drown first while fording the Thames."

"Fording the Thames? How so, sire?"

"Twould not be fair to use the king's bridges to best the king, would it? We shall send ahead and see to it they refuse you passage."

Suffolk chewed his lip a moment, then guffawed. "Agreed. At the gatehouse. If your barge does not swamp first, that is if it is ever launched."

The two men shook on it, pursuivants trumpeted it, heralds

announced it in voices as loud and clear as the very trumpets. The court, delighted and diverted, divided into two camps. Some to ride the tide, others their horses. The race was on.

Henry's party, arriving at the landing, was off to a slow start. Shortsighted, the king had not noticed that the tide was out, the usually strong, peaceful current replaced by a yellow muck spotted here and there with human dung and other filth. Henry could only fume and limp back and forth until the tide allowed landing of the royal barge, which was stalled mid-channel where the water was deep.

His only consolation was that Suffolk would not fare better in his fording of the treacherous Thames. Then, scores of servants in the livery of Suffolk and others, even Tudor white and green, emerged from the palace and descended to the river's edge. After removing their hose, they waded out shoulder to shoulder into the ooze. Several paces behind the liveried vanguard rode the courtiers, the few ladies riding cross-saddle rather than pillion. Each had her horse in hand, an equerry to either side. To the merriment of those ashore, many a lackey floundered farcically, in unexpected sinkholes, especially midstream. The riders alerted, however, made their way round without incident. Within the hour, Suffolk's contingent had forded the Thames. With a salute to their king, who was still unable to board his gilded barge, off they galloped, the few bright-colored velvet gowns among the tawny hunting costumes echoing the touches of fall foliage in sharp but pleasing contrast to the ombré green of the woods.

So engrossed had Henry been in the spectacle that he did not realize until too late that his sister, Suffolk's frail lady, would share the cabin of the royal barge while Mistress Anne rode horseback. One quick query revealed that de Wynter too had taken the more demanding course. Then, the king's rage and jealousy knew no bounds. His sister had all she could do to prevent his sending after Anne; taking horse himself; or wading out, muck or no muck, to board his barge. Only the fact that the tide was reversing itself kept him shorebound.

With the tide with them, the barge party had the advantage of nature as far as Teddington, where the influence of the tide on the Thames ceases. Thereafter they rowed against the current, but the royal barge had twelve burly oarsmen to a side. The offer of a piece of gold apiece made their adrenaline flow far stronger than the gentle Thames. The contestants using the river route had still another advantage over their horseback opposition: those who went on horse could win only by losing, and that closely. The fickle favor of their king was well known to all.

However, it was a beautiful day for a ride, a typically English late summer day. The sun, burning the mist off the meadows, gradually revealed gentle verdant hills to either side of a river valley flat and fat with plenty. A westerly wind promised continuation of this beautiful beginning throughout the day. It would be a hard ride, nonetheless, cross-country, rather than simply paralleling the river. All but daring women balked at this. To ride at more than a walk meant riding astride, as their Scottish sisters did to the North, instead of using the more usual, ladylike sideways seat. The side-saddle had not yet been introduced into England.

They rode out straight west, not turning southward until Isleworth. As they put the gray, forbidding, cloistered nunnery of St. Bridget's behind them, many a woman crossed herself, breathing silent thanks that she rode free that day instead of being sequestered behind convent walls. The riders' immediate goal was the parish of St. Margaret's, far inland from the river to their left. From there to Twickenham was less than two miles, most of it through broad meadows where all could ride abreast if the sheep grazing there would make way.

But first, passing from meadow to meadow, they must traverse such thick cedar groves that the sun was shut out, the wood dankly quiet. Going single file, or at most two across, the two score courtiers and as many attendants lost time here that they would have to make up if the race were to be close, between St. Margaret's and Twickenham, or again in Strawberry Vale.

As the procession strung itself out, de Wynter followed his natural preference: never to be in the crush of riders where his sword arm might be restricted. Instead, he and Fionn alongside, held back, letting others who were more familiar with the route, go before.

He was not, however, destined to ride so much alone. Within the bounds of the second grove of cedars, he came upon a trio of riders: George Lord Rochford, Mistress Anne Boleyn, and her dismounted equerry struggling with her stirrup leathers. Losing patience with the equerry, Anne's brother, Rochford, gave an oath and began to dismount.

Anne dissuaded him. "Nay brother, Jane will be spitting pins if you remain longer. The Scots earl here has no jealous wife. He will not refuse me his services while you ride on ahead."

Rochford, plainly relieved to be freed, with a "by your leave" hurried off to forestall the harangue he expected from his shrewish, shallow-brained wife. De Wynter had no choice but to come to Anne's assistance.

However, it took less than a minute or two to move the buckle up a notch. Anne, thoughtfully removing her foot from the stirrup and lifting her leg out of his way, raised her skirts unnecessarily high and gave de Wynter an unusually good look at her black-stockinged, shapely calf.

"Thank you, milord," she said, smiling down upon him. "Somehow, I felt sure you would be more successful with that recalcitrant buckle."

He arched an eyebrow questioningly before acknowledging her thanks with a slight bow, but he said nothing. Nothing need be said; with her cooperation and without pressure on the stirrup, the buckle had offered no resistance. As he gathered up her reins and handed them back to her, their fingers touched and lingered.

Slowly, deliberately, she withdrew hers from his. But she did not urge her horse forward. Instead, she waited patiently while he remounted, then moved her horse close beside his, her equerry falling in behind with Fionn. De Wynter couldn't help but wonder why the subterfuge had been necessary. In the past, she had sought him out brazenly, especially when the king was at hand—a practice potentially hazardous to his future. The element of danger, rather than discouraging him, added a fillip to his enjoyment of her attention. Besides, in her he found a woman seemingly impervious to his charms—something new to him. He was more used to keeping women out of his bed than luring them into it. That Henry had had no more success than he, simply whetted his desire for her.

As they rode silently along, he could appreciate her attraction for Henry. Not conventionally beautiful, in fact almost plain in repose, Anne's face was transformed when she smiled or talked. Then, one couldn't take one's eyes from her. Adding to her fascination was her vivid, almost exotic coloring: long black hair, enormous black eyes, and lips startlingly red against pale white skin.

Beauty alone could not have enslaved Henry VIII. There were many at court far prettier than she. Catherine Howard, her twelve-year-old cousin, for one. However, as de Wynter knew from having been skewered on it, Anne's wit was sharp, her mind even sharper. And she had that unique ability to concentrate totally on the person she was with, never looking elsewhere nor pretending to listen while thinking of other things. Thus, what one said to such an avid audience seemed wiser or wittier or more romantic or more humorous or more poetic than when said to anyone else.

In this lay much of her fatal attraction for Henry. Only with Anne Boleyn did he forget his gout, his failing eyesight, his corpulence. With her he felt young, whole, a great king, the prince among princes that he wanted to be. Part of his fascination with her, of course, was the fact that she refused her king what he wanted, while seeming to offer it to others. Not a man at court, de Wynter included, had she not flirted with; and not a one, de Wynter excluded, had resisted her coquetries. In this lay de Wynter's fascination for her. The two, each more used to being the hunted rather than the hunter, had at first been piqued by the other's reaction. Then annoyed. Then tantalized. Then as weeks went by, drawn irresistibly to each other.

The grove thickened, the way narrowed, and they went single file, he giving her precedence. But as soon as there was room, she paused, waiting for him to draw up beside her.

"Milord, may I say in all truth that that is the plainest, nay, ugliest mare I have ever seen?"

"Shush, Mistress Anne, not so loud. She thinks she's a beauty."

"Disillusion her," Anne commanded callously.

"I? Never. I think she's a beauty."

"Your knowledge of physiognomy does you not proud."

"Mistress, I protest. Knowing not that she is plain, she acts like a beauty, deceiving others into agreeing. A clever woman might do the same, don't you think?"

She changed the subject. "I was waiting for you. You have a tendency to linger behind. I feared, your being new to our country, we might mislay you."

"*Mislay*, Mistress Anne? That would be impossible to do. Besides, might it not be better if you should ride ahead and leave me behind?"

"Better for whom?" She tossed her head, surrounding herself in a cloud of hair.

"For the both of us. Think you the king won't hear of this?"

"Oh, but I mean he should. If no one tells him, I shall do so myself," she said, and she was serious.

"For God's sake, why?"

She laughed, not merrily. "I control him through jealousy. Catherine of Aragon never looked at another man, I never look anywhere else unless I am alone with him."

"My God, Anne, you live dangerously."

"How so?" She was genuinely curious.

"Such conduct could be named adulterous."

"But only after marriage, and I, in case it escaped your notice, I am still unwed."

"Is marriage what you want?"

"More than anything in this world."

"Then, Anne, wed me."

"You jest, sir!"

Neither knew who was the more surprised—she who thought him immune to her fascination or he who had thought himself so. But once he had blurted out his offer, he did not regret the impulse. He wanted her! Not since Jamie's mother had he so yearned for a woman. If this were love, then what he'd felt before had been merely young, puppy love in comparison.

"I mean what I say. Marry me, Anne, and come back to Scotland with me."

"No, do not say that," she whispered, her face growing pale. "Please God, do not love me. You must not love me. Only so long as you feel nothing for me nor I for you, are we safe!" The words came out, tumbling over one another in a rush of emotion, tears welling up in her eyes.

She would have urged her horse on to a faster pace, but he forestalled her, seizing the bridle and holding the horse back. "No, Anne, I must know. Are we, as you say, safe?"

"Yes, no, I mean, I don't know." She was confused, unsure of herself, totally unlike her usual, supremely confident self.

"You do know. Swear to me that you feel nought for me. Swear it if you can."

"I swear!" She bit her lip and fought her tears, but her chin was raised, her voice defiant.

He let go her bridle. "You have played me the fool."

Now it was his turn to put heels to his horse, but she called after. "No, wait! De Wynter! James! I beg you! It is not what you think."

He stopped and wheeled his horse about and waited for her to come up with him. As they rode on, side by side, the silence was tense. She broke it.

"If I explain, will you promise me never to bring up the subject again?"

"No, I cannot do that. I love you."

"Try."

He made no answer, but she took his silence for acquiescence. For long moments the only sounds disturbing the woods were the jingle of harness and hollow clop of hooves on lichened grounds.

"He gives me no choice. I dare not care for you."

"Why not? He cannot marry you. Will you go through life always as a mistress Anne, without home, husband, or children?"

"No. I shall have all that," she replied, her face set, her voice determined. "Eventually."

"Why not now?"

"Although he cannot have me to wife, he will allow no other to. One by one all the men I have cared for have been sent away or worse. Poor Percy. He dared ask permission to marry. He meant he wanted to marry me and the king knew it, but pretended to misunderstand. So Percy was married off to a simpering child, one mentally weak. She drools uncontrollably, especially when she eats. I hear he has lost much weight. Not she, she is with child again."

"Anne, no! I care not what happened to others."

"Sweet, gentle Ormond—to whom I had been promised in marriage by the king himself—had the temerity to show real love for me. So Henry raised him high, then rived him low. He was invited—an honor not to be refused—to cross lances with the king.

Not until he was handed a Sharp Lance Running did he discover this was to be a Joust a l'Outrance."

De Wynter whistled silently under his breath. He would not have liked to face the massive king, full-armored, in a joust to the death.

"So great was Ormond's fear, one could smell it. He could not hold his head high, much less his lance. He was unhorsed on the first pass but had been unmanned long before that. Again and again, Henry ordered him to his feet. Ormond tried, but his legs failed him. Eventually in disgust, Henry granted him the couvre-chef de mercy. I never saw my gentle Irishman again. He was exiled to Ireland and our marriage never again mentioned. Then, there was Wyatt—"

"Thomas Wyatt, the poet?"

"The same. He dared write a poem—"

"'Ye Olde Mule'?"

She laughed without merriment. "No, that was his device to save his life. It succeeded; Henry merely exiled poor Thomas to Castle Allington in Maidstone. A not-too-dreadful fate for having forgotten what he himself wrote.

"And what was that?"

"'There is written her fair neck round about: *Noli me tangere; for Caesar's I am!* And wild for to hold, though I seem tame.'

"James, the words of his poem were well said. Do you not forget them," she cautioned. "Wyatt escaped worse because of past poems, but Henry did not leave the matter at that. He made Thomas forfeit his library, remanded him of the right to write his poetry, and, to make matters complete, set Thomas's wife as his jailer to enforce the king's commands. Ah, if there is a hell on earth, Thomas has found it at Allington."

He simply smiled back at her and quoted in reply: "'Be it evil, be it well, be I bound, be I free, I am as I am and so will I be.' I, too, know Wyatt's work and I know I am in love with you."

"Then be warned, for 'I am as I am and so will I die.' And James Mackenzie, Scots Earl of Seaforth, I will be Queen of England. I stake my head and my heart upon it."

"Can nothing change your mind?"

"Nothing. I have waited too long. Six years too long. Sacrificed too much. No, I am set on this course wherever it takes me . . . and naught will dissuade me."

He looked at her, her head held high, her chin set defiantly, and more than ever he knew this was the woman for him. In her determination, her stubborn ambition, he saw himself . . . and his mother. The thought of Islean and Anne Boleyn meeting gave him pause.

The women would clash of course, both being strong-willed, but eventually would like and respect each other. Both were women of spirit, not content to accept what fortune allotted. Accept, no! Beg, bribe, buy, taunt, trick, scheme, seduce—yes! They were his kind of women, worthy of unselfish love, commanding admiration, evoking pride in a man.

A halloo from ahead interrupted his thoughts for the time being. Their tardiness had been noticed; they had been missed. A shout to the men riding behind, discreetly out of earshot, and the horses moved out briskly to catch up with Rochford. He, still smarting from the sting of his wife's sharp tongue, immediately took his sister to task, "Are you mad, Nan? The king will hear of this!"

"I can guess who will be the happy bearer of such ill news," she replied, smiling viciously at the sister-in-law who tarried out of curiosity just up ahead. At the age of almost sixteen, Jane Lady Rochford's face was already set in grim, unhappy lines.

During the next part of the ride, through the meadows and through the sheep to Twickenham, neither Anne nor de Wynter spoke much. They rode so close their calves would sometimes touch, neither of them seeking this nor avoiding it, but taking innocent delight in it. At other times as the terrain allowed, their mounts went at a gallop and side by exhilarating side cleared brook or hedgerow or hay rick. Rochford, watching close, saw once again his Anne, that barely remembered, quick-to-laugh, life-loving youthful sister, the hoyden of his past, riding, hunting, hawking, and willing to diddle his dandy though she remained chaste. Devoutly, he wished them gone from court and back at Hever. There, safe behind the moat, protected by crenellated battlements and machicolations, Anne could be just plain Nan again, Jane would regain her once pleasant mien, and old King Hal could be consigned to hell. Rochford laughed mirthlessly. If wishes were horses . . .

Past Strawberry Hill the troop cantered; there some less hardy women found excuse with their escorts to drop out and search for berries long out of season. The rest rode on to and through Strawberry Vale at a hard gallop and on to Teddington, where they breathed their mounts. An enterprising innkeeper at the Clarence served the courtiers cool ale and watered wine. Suffolk, before he left, tossed a coin in his direction. The coin was caught but when examined was found lacking, as the keeper's sour expression revealed. Anne, noting this, turned to de Wynter. "Pay him more if you love me, so that when I am queen, he will love me," she half teased, half pleaded.

"That is an atrocious argument for making one man pay another's debts," he said. Even so, he tossed the innkeeper a gold coin. Catching it and biting it in one motion while he genuflected obsequiously bespoke great practice on the keeper's part. As he watched the elegantly dressed riders troop off, their liveried attendants in tow, he hawked and spat after them, remarking to his gawking wife, "Did you see her? The one with the ribbon round her neck?" He spat again. "I knew her badge at once. The royal whore. Another visit from such as she and seven more guests like those stupid Scots we have housed within, and our fortune's made."

"Think you so?" his wife retorted, her voice a perpetual whine. "The Scots're animals. Refused to sleep on the two beds I made up fresh. Instead all seven slept on the floor on bedding raided from our other rooms."

"God's blood," the innkeeper swore, dropping his two coins into his purse with a satisfying clink and marching back into his inn prepared to do battle if necessary with the uncivilized but overpaying Scots upstairs.

For the rest of the way, Anne rode in the vanguard and flirted with Suffolk, whom everyone knew was discreetly safe. Not till they reached the three-story-high gatehouse to Bushy Park at Teddington did they discover they did not know the password. Though Suffolk threatened, the gatekeeper refused them entry. When a crowd of gapers and gawkers gathered, Suffolk ordered the group to ride roundabout to the next gate, that at Hampton Wick. Approaching it, riding hard, they saw and were seen by the flotilla of wherries and barges, including the gilded royal one bearing the king and his sister, her ladies-in-waiting and Henry's cronies and staff. As the two groups exchanged merry waves and shouted greetings, Henry had his leather-lunged herald shout "No entry" to the gatekeeper. Henry sailed on triumphantly, doubling his offer of reward to rowers and polesters.

As the stymied riders milled about before the wall, de Wynter studied it closely. It was, he decided, designed more to keep deer in than horsemen out. Summoning Fionn, who rode always in earshot, he explained his plan: "Stand you up atop your saddle since your mount has the broadest back. If I climb up on your shoulders, I can easily reach the top of the wall. Once over, I open the gates."

Fionn would have balked at being the one on top, but he was not loath to play the base to this two-man pyramid. "Anne," de Wynter admonished, "keep the gatekeeper and his man distracted." Without more ado, the plan was put into action.

So shocked was Suffolk at the sight of these madmen from Scotland, one balancing on a horse while another clambered up his body as if on a ladder, that he went speechless. Not so Mistress Anne, who asked, "Know you not, gatekeeper, who I am? See, there is my badge, the white falcon, and here is my name: Anne Boleyn."

"It's the king's whore," said one inside to another in a whisper never intended to travel so far.

Anne's face turned white, her lips tightened, but her voice never faltered. In dulcet tones, she continued, "I who have the ear of Henry—"

"And something else too," came that penetrating voice.

"... suggest, nay, command you, open the gate!"

Suffolk, sufficiently recovered from his stupor, added his harangue to hers, saying, "I, the Duke of Suffolk, husband to the Princess Mary Tudor, order you: Open the gate."

"Nay, milords, saving Your Grace, I ha' me orders," the same voice retorted loudly.

Suffolk shouted back, "And who might you be?"

"May it please Your Grace, I be Dick Whiting, gatekeeper first to his Eminence the Cardinal Wolsey and now to the King's most excellent Majesty, Henry the Eighth, King of England." His fellows within the gate cheered at the name of their good King Hal. Bolstered by their response, Dick Whiting continued, "I ha' me orders. His Majesty said the gates shall not open."

At that, the gates opened, gnashing and groaning and grating on ill-used hinges, to reveal a smiling de Wynter standing between. With a shout and a cheer, Suffolk's troop galloped through and on into Bushy Park. Hampton Court Palace lay but a mile and a half up ahead. Watching their dust billow, Fionn held de Wynter's horse as he mounted, "And without a thank-you or a by-your-leave."

The two men silently agreed: the English were a sorry lot, not at all civilized like the Scots. They had not time for further reflection. They were hurried on their way by an enraged gatekeeper and the half dozen pikemen also on duty, who charged out of the gatehouse, threatening death or castration to any who came within range of their weapons—formidable twenty-two-foot-long staffs with cruel barbed points on the end and tasseled rain spouts in the middle.

The first gate navigated, there was only one more to go—that at the entrance to the gardens just beyond the walled-in tennis court to the east of the tourney field. The "Flower Pot" gates opened with ease when the gatekeeper, not having been forewarned, knuckled under to Suffolk's first peremptory command. Through the garden they rode, taking care not to harm the topiary beasts that inhabited this make-believe wilderness.

Around the tennis court, past the walled and towered Tilt Yard, turning south at the Royal Mews, they charged until, with a spray of stone, they stopped upon the moat-bridge lined with heraldic beasts. The doors to the five-story brick Great Gate House were closed fast; however, the face of a Yeoman of the Guard could be seen peering out. At Suffolk's hail, the face withdrew. The twenty-four-foot-high, linen-fold paneled oak doors beneath the oriel window opened slowly and majestically to frame the broad yet majestic figure of Henry VIII standing, feet spread, hands on hips, laugh on lips, upon the carefully manicured turf of the Green Base Court within.

"Welcome," he roared. "Welcome to Hampton Court. Now, Suffolk, damn you, pay up."

CHAPTER 13

A lesser or greater man might have been nonplussed, not Suffolk; he shouted back as boisterously as he'd been addressed: "Pay what, sire? We never set the wager." Putting spurs to his horse, he led his troop across the bridge and through the deep gatehouse.

Henry stared hard at the approaching man, his face turning red. Suddenly it cleared, and as Suffolk dismounted, the king was upon him. "Damme," he said, hugging the duke in a grip that would have crushed a smaller man, "You're right. We never did. You've ridden your butt off in vain."

Suffolk hugged the man back, eliciting a "huuuuh" from the man-handled lungs of his monarch. "You've bribed your bargemen for naught!"

"Have I?" Henry's piglike eyes narrowed under the folds of fat that formed his eyelids. Then, his eyes widened, his whole face suffused with joy: "You're wrong! That's your forfeit for the race. You pay the bargemen. And Suffolk, I promised them double!" Henry roared, it was the kind of joke he loved.

Nothing daunted, Suffolk shouted right back, "With what? I still owe you 24,000 pounds for my wife. Release me from that and I'll pay the rowers triple." Henry stopped laughing. The court—sensitive to royal moods—ceased moving and talking immediately. All awaited his reaction. Only the horses dared breach the silence with an occasional stomp of hoof or slap of horsetail upon fly-bit rump, and one muffled nicker was echoed by a nervous twitter from an anonymous throat. Even the duke staring boldly at his king seemed frozen in space. Suffolk, privileged beyond most, had been shouted out of court before by his monarch and sent home to his wife in disgrace. Each time after suitable apology and waiting period, he was ordered back. Who knew better how chancy it was to brace Henry . . . especially during, before, or after an attack of gout.

Almost in slow motion, Henry with one of those big, broad, leonine gestures he loved, reared back and roared with laughter.

"Damn you Suffolk, you've done it again. Gotten the best of me. I'll just have to lend you the money to pay off me rowers." Falling upon Suffolk's shoulders, he hugged the man and the two pummeled each other and laughed until tears ran from their eyes.

When a king laughs, his court laughs. At first only in sniggers and titters and hollow guffaws, but laughter has a way of being contagious and building upon itself.

"You don't laugh?" said a quiet voice at de Wynter's side. Anne had taken advantage of the general hilarity to approach him again.

"I find nothing humorous in a monarch's promising a man and a woman they might marry; then, when they do, beggaring them with ruinous fines."

"Is that what they say in France?" She considered upon it. "Suffolk looks not like a beggar to me."

"Because of his clothes? Look about you. Is there a man or woman here who actually owns the clothes on his back? It's all a brave show made on usurer's money. Tell me, Mistress Anne, does your gown belong to you?"

Anne colored ever so slightly. Although possessed of a rare fashion sense enabling her to make do with simpler clothes, she, too, was hard put to maintain the gowns and jewels necessary to the image of promised consort to a man who spent 200,000 pounds a year on clothes alone, plus more on jewels. Anne, in the first few years of her waiting, had been financed by her Howard relations, especially her uncle Norfolk in hopes of future advancement. When the divorce did not come through, and the wedding appeared not near, those funds invested in what might be a nonexistent future dried up. Only last week she had been forced to call upon the services of a money-lender. She endeavored to think of the frighteningly strange man in the long black robes with oily black hair and the flat black hat as her financial advisor. He was, with his 50 percent interest rates—"Lower for you, my lady, out of love for His Majesty"—an out-and-out extortionist. However, to play out her game with Henry, she needed money.

No glimmer of this graced her face. "Of course it does. Can you say as much?"

"All mine, every stitch, every jewel. I owe no man nor woman . . . except you," he added, bowing slightly in her direction.

"Me? For what?" She was genuinely bewildered. He'd borrowed no money nor owed her for gambling. Quite the contrary. She recalled having borrowed from him and lost on a throw of the dice.

"For bringing me again to the good king's attention."

Henry, in the middle of still another hearty laugh, had looked over Suffolk's shoulder and seen Anne and de Wynter in conversation. The laughter died in his throat. He stiffened and pulled back from Suffolk, who, noting the change in Henry, stopped laughing and turned to see what was amiss. Like dominoes falling one on the other, the court in progression ceased laughing and started staring. Anne and de Wynter seemed unaware, he keeping his gloved hand resting lightly on hers.

But they were aware. The silence was too deafening. The unseen stares were too obvious. She was more concerned by the gradual tightening of his hand on hers. "Let go, you're hurting me," she said under her breath.

"Why, if you care for me, do you keep including me in this game you play?"

She did not answer immediately. The pressure on her hand increased inexorably. "I'll scream," she hissed through clenched teeth.

"What? And let Henry know I'm no rival of his? Not likely. I suggest you talk before I crush all six of the fingers on this lovely hand. Why me?"

"You're new to court." The pressure loosened ever so slightly; she could breathe again.

"Go on."

"Henry's coming this way."

"Hurry then." The grip tightened again.

Her chin went up, she held her breath. If only Henry would limp faster. But the pain in the vestigial sixth finger on her hand was too much. "Because you're beautiful enough for even the king to believe my interest real," she gasped. "And because you're safe from Henry."

Shocked by such an unexpected response, his grip loosened involuntarily, and she pulled free. Flexing her fingers within her glove, she decided none were broken.

"Safe?"

"Safe! I want to be queen, not a murderess. You're Scots Herald Ross. He wouldn't dare kill a herald." Still she did not look at Henry, making his way slowly through horses turning every which way, their riders jostling one another to make way for the king.

"Now, it's your turn to smile, milord, and mine to exact revenge. Watch!" Her smile was not lovely. The king was upon them.

"Mistress Anne, what do you here?" the king bellowed, his voice a mixture of anger and suspicion. Not at all discomfited, she smiled winningly down at her king, her eyes caressing him, "Sire, the Lord de Wynter here was just telling me the most fascinating news about yourself. Your songs—they are all the fashion at Francis's court."

The king's little eyes shifted their stare sideways to de Wynter. Serenely the Scots earl returned the English king's glare, the two men taking the measure of each other. Henry decided this Scot must go. De Wynter came to a similar conclusion: Regardless what Anne says, the king will have my head—herald or no herald—unless I am gone shortly.

"Oh?" grunted the monarch, veiling his thoughts as he continued staring up at the slender lordling, scarcely half his age.

De Wynter's voice could not have been more sincere, his lie more straight-faced: "Indeed, Your Majesty, they are played constantly."

Henry's songs, as Anne knew full well, were condemned to neglect at the French court on the general principle of Anglophobia. De Wynter had never heard one played; he knew not even what kind of songs the man wrote; they might even have been hymns. God damn Anne for getting him into this. But not by a muscle did his face betray his emotions. "Of course, both their Majesties have their own particular favorites."

Henry, interested in spite of himself, never objected to a little, or

228

even a lot, of ego-boosting; he even managed a semicivilized, "You must tell us more about it later."

Anne added impishly, "And show us the dance, too!"

Henry frowned; he hated all show-offs but himself. On the other hand, he was intrigued. "Dance?"

"One of your songs has been made into a new dance," she explained. She was exacting the last inch of revenge for her hurt hand.

De Wynter mentally condemned all trouble-making women, especially Anne Boleyn, to perdition, but not by a raised eyebrow did he betray that he had no idea of what she spoke. However, two could play this game as well. "I should be delighted to demonstrate at Your Majesty's pleasure. Especially if Mistress Anne will partner me." That, he thought, should get him off the hook. But Henry said neither yea or nay, only a noncommittal "Harumph," as egotism and jealousy warred within him.

Recognizing a dismissal when he saw one, de Wynter removed his hat with a flourish, bowed low over his saddle, and one-handedly set his horse to backing straight away as if the animal had eyes on its rump. It was an exquisite display of horsemanship, even Henry would concede that. It also elicited an appreciative impulsive response elsewhere. Jane, Lady Rochford, clapped. Just once, before her husband stilled her. She might be empty-headed, but he was not. It was courting disaster to champion one of Henry's rivals, especially if one were a member of the staunchly Catholic Howard family, even if only by marriage. Hiding her head in confusion, Jane could only hope the king had not heard. And if he had, had not seen.

But Anne Boleyn had both heard and seen. And as she gracefully dismounted into Henry's arms, in the process letting the whole of her body run the length of his, she smiled with almost evil delight, for there was no love lost between these two sisters-in-law, one quick-witted, the other slow. "Oh, I agree, Lady Rochford. The Scots do have a way with horses. And women, too, I hear. What do you think, sire?"

What Henry thought was both unspeakable and unprintable. But if thought could kill, Lady Rochford, de Wynter, and the horse would find themselves all in a common grave.

Anne continued to lean against him, her pelvis moving slowly to and fro, so daringly in public only because she was sure the court couldn't see. He stifled a groan; he was beginning to respond. Although the thick padding of his codpiece would prevent disclosure, inspecting the palace was going to be damned uncomfortable with one of his members swollen by gout, the other by lust.

"Tonight, Anne?" he begged.

"We'll see," she replied demurely. "Now, show me this magnificent Great Hall you are a-building," she commanded. Henry, proud builder that he was, was happy to oblige. With his Anne clinging to his arm, they made their way slowly—to allow for his sore foot—across the lush green turf toward the inner gatehouse. Anne looked up to check the time and stopped, shocked. There, below the oriel windows, below the astrological clock, below the bell which antedated Wolsey, was an undeniable reminder of the former owner. Defaced, but still recognizable, were Wolsey's arms in terra-cotta affixed to an archepiscopal cross, surmounted by a likeness of his red hat and supported by putti.

"Sire, I thought you intended replacing those?"

"What, the medallions? Never. I have always had a fondness for those roundels with their royal heads."

She thought him teasing her but was not absolutely sure. "Nay, not those. They are magnificent, especially the one of Augustus. It reminds me much of another wise king, I know." Her flattery, although obvious, was most pleasing. "Nay, sire, I refer to the panel above the gateway."

Although he knew well what she meant, he pretended ignorance, drawing her instead closer to the gatehouse and squinting up to where she pointed. "Oh, that. Yes, yes, indeed, I see what you mean. That does mar the facade, indeed. Yes, those arms should be replaced. But by whose? Mine are already in place on the outer gatehouse. By all rights, there should go the arms of the Queen of England. What do you think?" He studied her carefully, but Anne Boleyn's face was as well-schooled as that of any courtier, maybe better. Not by a quiver of her chin or a twitch of the cheek did she show that she seethed within. How dare he think that? Catherine of Aragon's arms up there? Never. Better to keep Wolsey's own than those of that Spanish prune. Even as she forced a smile to her lips, she vowed that Catherine's arms would never appear there. "Even such a queen would be overwhelmed by so great an honor."

"You think she would be very pleased?"

"Verily."

"Do you think she would honor me in return?"

"How could she do otherwise?"

"So you think the woman whose arms go up there should reward her king?"

She began to see his drift. "Even so!"

"By opening her bed to me?"

She laughed inside. For what he would have now, he was prepared to pay with future promises; first, make her queen, then he could have what he wanted. Six years of this had taught Anne how to handle the situation. Demurely, she curtsied and looked up at him with wide-open, innocent eyes. "Would the Queen of England ever refuse her bed to her rightful lord, the king?"

Henry grimaced. The answer could not have been more diplomatic nor its message more certain: make her queen and then he could have what he wanted. Abandoning all pretense, he looked down on her and spoke the truth as he knew it on this particular occasion. "Damme, Anne, I can't wait any longer. I must have you."

"And so you shall," she promised softly, "as soon as you rid yourself of your brother's wife. For our son will be no mere Henry Fitzroy, but a princeling worthy of his father's throne."

It was her standard speech, spoken as convincingly as an actor reciting his lines for the hundredth time and still investing them with newness. As she spoke, she stared into his face, its expression piteous in its lechery, yet she knew no pity. Instead, she compared it to another's. Both men were fair of skin, but Henry's, red-tinged by swollen and broken blood vessels, had been too much abused by wine; its features blurred by fat; its cheeks hirsute within short hours of shaving, the red stubble liberally laced with white. Of the two men, one was obviously best, the other somewhat bestial. But where one was kind, the other was king. She knew she would choose again as she had before: the royal over his rival. In that moment of decision, she spoke out impulsively. "I want you, my king. More than anything."

Henry misinterpreted her meaning, but his delight was so marked that she let him think hers were words of passion rather than ambition. So pleased was he with those meager crumbs from her, that he too made a decision. "Then, my dear, in honor of her whose arms shall soon go up there, we'll call this the Anne Boleyn Gateway." At her real surprise and expression of genuine delight, Henry grew more pleased with himself. Let de Wynter equal that, he thought.

Restored to a good mood, he placed her arm on his and led her within the gateway and under its vaulted fan roof. Then, leaning himself on the sturdy arm of his chamberlain, he mounted the stairs leading to the source of all the hammering, the Great Hall. As the court entered, chattering gaily, the noise ceased and the workmen perching on scaffolds a full fifty feet above them peered down curiously at a court staring up at them. John Molton, the Master Mason, sensed the silence, turned from arguing with an ill-dressed workman at the other end of the hall, 106 feet away, and trotted forward to greet his king fearfully. The workman followed behind.

Milton showed the king the progress made since last Henry had visited, the workman doggedly following after. Henry was in a good mood and was generous with his approbation. He approved the hammer beam roof going up, arch by richly carved oaken arch. The intricate Italianate foliage on the last beam was examined carefully and pronounced perfect; the workman still hovered nearby. The designs for the stained-glass windows were reviewed, the frames standing by ready to be lifted high within the brick walls: the workman scuffled his feet and waited patiently to one side. Then Molton led the way to his *pièce de résistance*, a sheet-sheltered structure twice a man's height. Flamboyantly, he tugged at the covering, and the sheet slid off to a chorus of admiring gasps to reveal a close crown atop a vane held by a great crowned lion, standing in the midst of painted and gilded vanes borne by fantastic carved beasts. Henry's jaw dropped, his mouth gaped.

Here in this louver for the central smoke vent had he found a crown worthy of his Great Hall. Like a child with a New Year's present, he must examine every detail, limping about the six-sided structure, fingering first a massive-maned lion tall as he . . . fierce dragon with tail lashing . . . sleek, snarling greyhound. Two by two the beasts stood at the corners of this hexagon, their immense size making the gilded vanes they bore seem ethereal. Finally, he stood back and nodded. "Well done, man."

The master builder gloated; such a work must be worth a large reward. The workman, hat in hand, cleared his throat and finding his voice spoke up. "Tain't been paid for, begging the king's pardon. I'll have me wages now, if'n it please Your Majesty."

The king limped over to where the workman stood his ground. The king's hearty clap on his shoulder shook the man a bit, but though he wavered, he stood firm. "You did that? My God, man, you impress us. But we should have known. Takes an Englishman to bring a beast alive. We sit at your feet in amazement." The man was dumbfounded. Never had he stood so close to royalty, and now to be talked to and treated like an equal, no, like a superior. He bowed his head in embarrassment, but Henry was not finished with him. "You give us an idea. Needham designed us a good roof, a great roof, but it lacks something. A touch of color, some light. There and there and there." Hundreds of heads craned to see where the king pointed, nodding sage confirmation of the king's great taste. "You will carve me lanterns, pendants to stand under each hammer beam . . . and others for the arches above."

"And my pay?" the man put forward hesitantly.

The king roared approval. "Just like one of our Englishmen. We talk of art, he of pounds and pence. Name your price, man; the king does not quibble."

Molton and the Lord Steward exchanged glances. It was up to the former to stall off payment while the Lord Steward of the Household, the Master of the Green Cloth, must find the funds to finally pay for each of the king's follies or favors.

Swallowing hard, the carver named his price.

"Agreed," said the monarch jovially. "Start work immediately. We should like to see samples of each by the end of the week."

"This week?" the man squeaked in dismay.

"Not enough time? Then"—the king fingered his upper lip in thought—"make it one this week, the other next. Now, don't just stand there man, hop to it."

Dismissed, Richard Rydge of London fled the scene, thoughts of his impossible deadline driving everything else from his mind, including the sums he was owed.

The king and his court moved on in royal inspection. Through the Great Hall to the annex at the east end, where foods would be served to the high table. Then down the stairs to the Serving Place where dishes would be received and inspected by the Chief Larderer, then passed on to the Chief Server. Onward they went to inspect the Great Kitchen in line with Wolsey's own, which had proved inadequate, although the cardinal's household had numbered over five hundred.

Under the Great Hall the king went to inspect his new beer cellar. A vast place it was, especially empty, twice the size of Wolsey's cellars, which had proved not nearly ample enough to store the household's daily beer ration. Take, for example, the maids of honor, who each received three gallons daily. One gallon both at breakfast and mid-day's dinner, half a gallon in the afternoon, and the last half at supper when she would also be served from the King's pitchers of wine. These were dispensed from the brick-vaulted crypt under the new Great Watching Chamber beyond the Great Hall. Here the Yeomen of the Guard were stationed overlooking the Kitchen Court and beyond that Wolsey's Chapel, which Henry was redoing, its ceiling being too plain for his taste, not at all indicative of heaven.

While the king made his leisurely inspection, another at Hampton Court Palace had been quite busy. The Scots Herald had continued backing his horse a bit farther, fuming the whole while. He had not missed any of the byplay . . . either between Anne and Jane Rochford, or Anne and her king when she dismounted. The girl, he decided, was a born vixen. Imagine showing such power over a man in broad daylight. De Wynter was no prude, but he was prudent. And she had been decidedly imprudent. As for Jane Rochford, Anne obviously thrived on other people's troubles. If they did not make enough on their own, she'd make some for them. Ordinarily, he would have avoided this kind of woman; he had no desire to court death. But with Anne, he found himself determined to win control over her and to force her to pay attention only to him.

His immediate concern was for tonight; he would indeed have all of her attention as he introduced an imaginary dance done to yet-to-be composed music for a poem of which he had never heard. Fervently, he prayed that that learned man, Wolsey, had had a library and that it was still intact. Not likely since the king had been industriously tearing down and building up much of Wolsey's famed "Happy Hampton," the massive pink brick palace whose fretwork of chimneys silhouetted against the sky rivaled Fontainebleau. But, if there were a library, wise Wolsey would have had copies of any and everything this vainglorious king'd ever writ. The task then: to select a poem, compose music to it, improvise some sort of believable dance to accompany it—by tonight. De Wynter feared the French Ambassador would not be pleased when he heard the reports of tonight's doings, but there was no choice in the matter.

Unfortunately for de Wynter's plans, Henry had indeed altered Wolsey's personal apartments to the south and east of Clock Court. Only one remained, a room lined high as the hand could reach with linen-fold oak paneling; above that with magnificent Italianate paintings of the Passion of the Lord; above that with a frieze of Wolsey's motto *"Dominus Michi Adjutor"* repeated over and over again; and above the frieze an ornate gesso ceiling alternating a Tudor Rose and the feathers of the Prince of Wales as centerpiece of each blue and red and gilt panel. The room was exquisite.

"We stored most of the manuscripts and books here, milord, those that the king didn't have put in his own writing closet. But His Majesty had it in mind to redo this room too, so everything was moved."

"Elsewhere in the palace?"

"I really couldn't say. But I doubt it. His Majesty's a great one for moving things from one palace to another."

Discouraged, de Wynter sought out his own quarters. As was typical of vagabond courts, his room was almost as hard to find as the nonexistent library. There, however, he hoped to find Fionn and devise some plan for the evening. To find Fionn, first he must track down the offices of the Lord Chamberlain of the Household, who had the ordering of quarters for more than a thousand men and women this day.

As was the case with everything at court, the assigning of quarters was done by order of precedence. As a Scots earl, de Wynter entertained no illusions as to his ranking at court. The understeward checked several lists before determining that de Wynter was quartered with the bachelor knights in the north range of the Great Gate House. Beyond that, the understeward could be of no help.

By trial and error and much questioning, he finally found his room—as he'd expected undesirably on an upper floor. However, by virtue of Hampton Court's having so many single rooms and his position as Scots Herald Ross to Margaret Tudor, he had it all to himself. The room was large, but devoid of all furniture except the bed.

Fionn was already there, having been assisted in his searching by many a helpful linen maid impressed by his size and very interested in where he might reside while the court was at table or busy for the evening. He had just begun unpacking.

"Best stop right there, we may not be staying the night," de Wynter said

"No luck?"

"None. Not unless we can find a way to search the king's own writing closet." The prospect did not faze Fionn, who held the king in lower repute than he did his Scottish Majesty.

"A note came for you." Fionn's voice was carefully noncommittal.

De Wynter arched an eyebrow in surprise, both at the news and the tone of Fionn's voice. He took the note without comment.

Puzzled, de Wynter studied the note. "Did you read it, Fionn?"

The young man laughed. "Nay, I have trouble enough reading Scots without taking on any foreign tongues."

De Wynter read it to him:

> The Right Honorable the Earl of Seaforth,
>> The King's Most Excellent Majesty has graciously given his Imperial consent to your Lordship's presentation of His Imperial Majesty's music tonight following the masque.
>>> The Lady Anne Boleyn

Penned across the bottom of the note, as if an afterthought, in a round childish hand identical to the signature was "C'est Bon!"

"What do you make of it?"

Fionn shrugged. The message seemed very straightforward to

him, but he humored de Wynter. "That you're to do your dance tonight after the masque."

"But I already knew that. And she knows I knew. Why take a risk that the king find her sending me notes for such a purpose, unless . . . *C'est Bon!*" He worried the phrase upon his tongue. "Of course, that's it! Continue unpacking, Fionn, and see if you can work your wiles on one of the linen maids to iron the tabard bearing the arms of Scotland's queen. I go to borrow a lute, steal a song, and invent an entertainment."

With the Great Hall still a-building, supper this night was held in Wolsey's Long Gallery, which was almost as long as the soon-to-be-completed Great Hall, but only half as wide. Thus tables could fit along only one wall of the length, and service was slow and clumsy. Still, there were two services from the sideboard, and two from the kitchen, and four changes of plates, many of which bore Wolsey's arms. Each course was preceded by a peal of trumpets and concluded by an extravagant set-piece, depicting Henry jousting or Henry hunting or Henry at tennis, or (and this won the pastry chef a gold piece) Henry in the royal barge racing and winning against a horseman.

Twelve trumpets and two kettledrums made the king's music. The wine flowed freely; the food, although not as good as that at Francis's court or even at Dolour, was plentiful and spiced enough to hide all but the aftertaste of decay. The highlight of the evening, however, came when a large pie was carried in. Four footmen it took to do it. And when the Master Carver cut into it, a score of bluebirds were released to fly about the room. Blinded by light, confused by smoke, lacking place to light or roost, they swooped low, befouling the tables and the heads of two of the startled diners. Just then, the Master of Falcons entered, followed by men bearing the royal Tudor birds as well as the white falcon of Anne Boleyn and those of the dukes in attendance. Then was great sport had by all as each hunter and huntress set his bird at its prey. Much gambling too, as those not hawking wagered on which shrieking hawk would get which fluttering bird, and which bold hawk would get the most helpless birds. The last was not a popular bet for the odds were low and the winner foreordained. Always Henry must win. Still, the Boleyn and the

Suffolks flew their birds deftly enough to keep some semblance of suspense.

When the last bird was downed, the last falcon whistled back to lure, the court moved on, leaving behind the bloodied remains of their feast.

For this evening, the entertainment was held in the Water Gallery, a styleless pile of pink brick, planned and executed by Henry VIII's royal architect and master builder. Although more properly a launching place and landing site for the royal barge, several hundred servants had hammered away the afternoon, hanging tapestries and arrays of gold and green silk from Wolsley's vast stores. Fresh greenery, leaning against the walls, transformed the chamber into a forest bower for this evening's masque.

A gay gossipy group made its way across the moat and down through the Pond Garden to the Water Gallery. Servants with torches lit their way; others stood at hand with ewers of wine lest any grow thirsty on the stroll down to the water's edge. During the short walk, the king and Anne Boleyn and a few others disappeared in full view of a conveniently, momentarily blinded court. De Wynter noticed and cursed it. All evening long he had had the king under surveillance, so as to keep count of the cups consumed. A sober king would see through his planned sham, a totally sodden king might sleep through it; a king drinking too much too fast grows nasty, while one who sips slowly but steadily should be merry and in good humor. Upon the king's humor depended the route de Wynter would take with his improvisation tonight; and upon that route and his reading of the king might depend his life. Now, the king had dropped out of sight!

The night was clear although unseasonably chilly. Most of the court, warmed from within, noticed it not at all. De Wynter did. His dress was for protection against wrath, not for warmth. The breeze whipped and penetrated the thin silk sleeves of his white shirt under the sleeveless white satin tabard embroidered with the Scottish queen's arms, quartered. Scottish lion rampant, English leopard passant-gardant, Stewart thistle, Tudor rose—picked out in thread of gold and gules, the latter the same shade red as his hose. He should have stood out for the boldness of his colorings, but not here, not this night. Not in the company of his fellow heralds—Richmond, Windsor, Lancaster, York, Somerset—for these English heralds in their gold and green and white and red, outglittered, if only by sheer numerical superiority, the lone Scottish envoy. In their midst he was less noticeable than anywhere else at court. Tonight, the English heralds and pursuivants, having official duties, occupied one end of the musicians' gallery with its panoramic view of the Water Gallery.

Servants moved among the throng of courtiers, refreshing the cups as all awaited the start of the entertainment. Finally, the four pursuivants' trumpets blared, and out of a mass of greenery sprang a group of wild men, gibbering and capering, hair in disarray, jerkins of rough-cut hide barely hiding Tudor livery. Crouching and jumping in a passable imitation of apes, they tugged on garlands of greenery, which pulled a marvelous mount into view.

Atop it, under the shade of a feather-leafed, orange-bedecked tree sat four men, one with the massive unmistakable form of the king. All were in disguise; their faces blackened, their court garb concealed under flowing robes, their hats Turkish turbans. Near spontaneous applause broke out, which grew more genuine as the men struggled to retain their precarious perches—hats as well—as the mount slithered, slipped, and lurched unevenly across the floor. On cue, the musicians began a weird, wailing, reedy music that to de Wynter's ear made the curl of a drunken piper sound good by comparison.

When the mount reached center stage, the "Turks" descended—the other three barely keeping the king from falling. Then, the four mimed a search for partners for the festivities. But when a slightly tipsy dame staggered out of the audience and hiccuping said, " 'Ow 'bout me?" she was courteously refused. Others among the court proffered their ladies—many ribaldly—but alas and alack, the "Turks" would have none of them. They continued searching behind curtains and hangings and among the greenery. But they found no ladies. Finally, the king mimed despair in broad gestures, beating himself on the chest, wiping tears from his eyes—taking care not to get blackface on his robes—and heaving great sighs. The court applauded heartily, for the king was a gifted pantomimist. Then, in the midst of his lamentation, an inspiration struck him. And the musicians replaced their hideous wailings with a suspenseful drumroll.

Gesturing to his trio of fellow Turks to follow, the king advanced threateningly toward the mount. Around it, he and his men marched, none too steadily. Then again, and after a pause to drain tall tankards, still a third time they weaved round it. Finally, waving his companions to stand back, the king dramatically drew sword—a good, English long sword—from beneath his robes, and struck the mount. Once, twice, thrice! With much creaking, the mount split in twain, and out danced four ladies to great applause.

They were all of a size, completely veiled except for their eyes. They pretended great fear of the king and his men, but seemed to calm as the lords made soothing sounds and each selected a lady, and led her to cushions strewn about the king's chair and new ottoman, a gift to Henry VIII from the Sublime Porte.

Now the masque within a masque began. From behind the mount came the Moorish dancers, or Morris dancers as they were more commonly misnamed. With bells on their feet and sashes about their waists, they did handstands and somersaults, cartwheeling and flip-flopping till their audience grew dizzy watching their whirligigs.

Hard on their heels came the king's Singing Men, mostly swarthy Italians and high tenors. One of their treacly songs drew such undeserved applause for its uneven quality de Wynter assumed it must be one of the king's own.

Truly genuine was the applause that greeted a thin little man with dancing black eyes and a nose pointed and sharp. Bowing and scraping and genuflecting, he accepted his applause modestly. Drawing paper from within his sleeve, he addressed the man in the chair. "Oh, great and noble Grand Turk, ruler of the Orient, searcher for truth, giver of gifts, I bring you a poem. With your kind permission?"

As the king raised a finger in approval, Skelton spoke out boldly so that all might hear, reciting a long wise honor of the king's stay at Hampton Court.

> Why come ye not to court?
> To which court?
> To the king's court
> Or to Hampton Court?
> Yae, but the king's court
> Is Hampton Court!

> All noble men, of this take heed
> And believe it as your creed:
> He who rises too high
> Plummets from the sky.
> Only the king stays.
> The king plays.
> The king prays.
> The king pays.
> Verilay!
> Your kind do obey.
> All noble men, of this take heed
> And believe it is your creed!

The applause rang out at these lines, but Skelton ignored the interruption, for his time allotted was short:

> Hither and thither, I wot not whither:
> Do and undo, both together.
>
> I blunder, I bluster, I blow and I blother:
> I make on the one day, I mar on the other;
> Busy, busy, and every busy,
> I dance up and down until I am dizzy.

With that he began pirouetting round and round and up and down. The king laughed, the court clapped, and nothing would do but that Skelton repeat his piece. After that, he must recite the king's favorite whenever at residence in Wolsey's palace:

To his Eminence, the former Cardinal Wolsey, where'er he may now be:

> He crieth and he creaketh,
> He prieth and he peeketh,
> He chides and he chatters,
> He prates and he patters,
> He clitters and he clatters,
> He meddles and he smatters,
> He glosses and he flatters;
> Or if he speak plain,
> Then he lacketh brain,

He is but a fool;
Let him go to school,
On a three footed stool
That he may down sit
For he lacketh wit!

The approbation was loud and general, and Skelton watched his audience closely. He who was stingy with plaudits would feel the bite of the poet's wit shortly.

All applause must eventually die. A coin-filled bag, token of the king's approval, was snared in midair by Skelton's thin talonlike fingers. A final bow and the poet laureate was off to quench his thirst. Throughout the entertainment, the king had not neglected his own cup. Now, when his part of the masque was to continue, he had difficulty getting up from his chair.

The ladies drew back, fearful, as their Moorish escorts dragged them to their feet with exclamations of lust. Pulling free, they would have run, but the king commanded them "Halt. Fear not. For I am not he whom you think I am." Throwing his Turkish robes from himself, he stood there bejeweled and befurred, living proof of that Tudor proverb, "Rich apparel, costly and precious, maketh a man lusty, comely, and glorious."

Suffolk, Norfolk, and Somerset followed suit. The ladies gushed great cries of joy and dropped their veils, revealing themselves proper Englishwomen; who did proper English obeisance to the king. The king himself unsteadily lifted Anne Boleyn to her feet, the others, their wives. The musicians struck up a lively dance tune, and the four couples formed themselves a set.

On cue, men appeared and pulled the mount out of the way. Not until the first dance was done did the chamberlain's staff knock thrice on the floor, inviting the rest of the court to join in. The food, the wine, the gout, and the day's activities had taken its toll on the king, for he soon sought solace in his chair, Anne on the ottoman beside him. As the dancing continued and his court made merry, his head nodded now and again, finally slumping against his chest. The usual six ushers appeared to lift the chair and carry it and the snoring king, who weighed close to twenty stone himself, to his chamber. At least two of his court were greatly relieved to see the king bed-bound; de Wynter for escaping making a fool of himself this evening, Anne for escaping making a mistress of herself in truth this night.

Officially, the evening was over. In twos and threes the court dispersed, but Anne Boleyn found her way barred by an elegant courtier in herald's tabard.

"Mistress, I am desolate. We did not dance."

"Be glad," she said. Noting their encounter causing raised eyebrows, she did not tarry but brushed on past him. He, not at all rebuffed, fell in beside her.

"Thanks to a timely note from a fickle lady, I spent the afternoon massaging a poet's ego and composing music to another's inferior rhymes."

"If I had known," she retorted, walking faster, "I would have watered the wine so he might have stayed awake and your afternoon not gone to waste."

Easily de Wynter matched his pace to hers. "Frankly, I was just as happy to see him off to bed. Weren't you?"

She was practically trotting now, as were the curious behind them. He merely lengthened his stride to accommodate hers. "Aren't you at all curious to know which song I chose?"

"I am not," she snapped back. "Now, let me be."

"Only if you promise to join me later in my room."

In shock, she stopped dead in her tracks, those behind them narrowly avoiding bumping into them. Drawing him away and ignoring the curious stares, she said, "You're mad, stark, raving mad."

He laughed. "Perhaps you'd rather I come to yours."

He took her by the elbow to lead her off, but she pulled free. "Don't even think of it."

"Then, it's settled. My room. Within the hour?"

"Keep your voice down, damn you," she hissed. "And don't hold your breath. I shan't be coming."

"Then, I promise I'll come search you out. And I'll make such a row 'twill wake even drunken Henry up."

She stopped again and stared at him speculating. "You wouldn't?" She corrected herself. "You would. Even if it were a sentence of death, you'd do this, wouldn't you?"

He took her hand in his and smiled, the teeth gleaming against his tanned skin. "I would. As to my death sentence, how long do you think I can wear this tabard?" He raised her hand to his lips, and entreated, "Anne, it's important. I must talk to you. Tonight."

"I don't know. I'll think on it. Now, let me be."

He raised his voice so that the curious would make no mistake: "My lady, I shall deliver your message of good wishes to my master, James of Scotland, immediately upon my arrival in Scotland. And if I see you not tomorrow before I leave, I wish you well."

She was taken aback. "You leave so soon?"

He nodded, then doffing his hat to reveal that thick silvery hair, he bowed and was gone, leaving her to stare after. Although she had known he must not remain in England long, womanlike she had avoided thinking on it. Now, faced with fact, she alternated between hurt and anger. How dare he make his plans without consulting her? How dare he be so matter of fact? How dare he leave her? That settled it. It would be she who sent him away, regretting every step he took, desiring nothing but his return to her. And she knew just how to accomplish this.

CHAPTER 14

Slowly, silently, the string tied to the latch tightened and drew taut, the bar-latch itself rising in response. Fionn, awakened by the first faint footstep outside the door, eased himself, dirk in hand, out of the bedroll placed strategically against the door. Alerted by Fionn's movements, de Wynter carefully slipped sword from scabbard and hid it among the bedclothes. The candle he moved noiselessly closer to hand, to be doused if need be. Then, he leaned back against the bolsters and pretended to read. He and Fionn had rehearsed for assassins and would sell their lives only dearly.

Although de Wynter reclined, feet crossed, apparently relaxed, his nerves were taut, his muscles tightened; catlike he could be up and first to strike the unwelcome visitor. He watched warily as the bar came free and the door moved inward. It stopped, blocked by Fionn's bedroll, then was forced open. Only the rustle of Anne Boleyn's skirts saved her from Fionn. De Wynter collapsed back on the bed and laughed with relief.

"Oh, it's only you." Ignoring the lackey as he restored dirk to sheath, she shoved the door closed behind her and leaned against it.

"Whom were you expecting, the Queen of England? Or had you forgotten you invited me?" De Wynter rose in one lithe move from the bed.

"Quite the contrary," he said. "We thought you had forgotten the invitation. Come in and welcome."

She ignored that, just as she ignored Fionn. "What an ugly room."

Compared to her own lavishly ornamented state apartment, it was. The walls were plain whitewashed brick, the floor covered with rushes, the window of bad glass undraped. There was no armoire, de Wynter's clothes hung from pegs in the wall. There was no fireplace, no chest, no chair, no stool, no bench, no place to sit. Only a bed in the center of the small room. Without waiting for further invitation, Anne Boleyn crossed the room and appropriated it, sinking deep into the featherbed mattress. De Wynter made do with the high but narrow windowsill; and Fionn, without being told, gathered up his bedding and slipped from the room, carefully pulling the latch closed behind him. A niche down the way would shelter him as he kept watch the rest of the night.

Neither Anne nor de Wynter seemed eager to breach the silence. She fingered the fine hangings of the bed with their Mer-Lions rampant embroidered all over. Thick and draft-proof, the silk inner and wool outer drapings were not in keeping with the rest of the room, nor were the featherbeds and quilts and pillows that made up the bedclothes.

"My mother's doing," de Wynter answered her unspoken question. "She insisted if I were to starve because of bad English food, I must at least sleep well."

"A considerate woman, your mother. I think I could like her."

"Eventually. I wager you'd both begin by hating one another though. Of course, there's only one way to be certain. Come back to Scotland with me."

"James, we've been through this before. Nothing is changed. And if that be the important matter you intend to discuss, I shall take my leave now." But she made no move to get up. Quite the contrary, she leaned back, bracing herself on outthrust hands, brazenly thrusting her bosom forward. With every breath she took, he became more conscious of it. She was dressed like a linen maid, in simple drawstring blouse, linsey-woolsey skirt and floor-length apron. But she invested even this commonplace outfit with elegance. Working her fingers within the covers, she drew back with an oath, her finger cut on the razor-sharp edge of de Wynter's sword. He was off the windowsill and by her side instantly, all contrite apologies.

"It's nothing," she said, attempting to hide the hand in her skirt. His hand would not be denied, and she was forced to yield hers up first for his inspection, then for his kiss upon the small cut. Then another.

"My mother taught me this, too," he said. "It speeds the healing."

When she made no move to pull away, he kissed the cut still a third time . . . then the tips of each of the other fingers, his lips lingering finally on that small fingerlet she normally tried so hard to conceal. His head bowed solicitously over her hand, his lips began retracing their path, gently mouthing each sensitive fingertip, until her lips grew envious of her hand.

But here, within reach of her hand, was his thick, lustrous mane falling over his forehead in waves of silver gray. She could imagine its soft silkiness. Without thinking, she reached out, one finger lightly tracing the curve of a wave. The slightest of caresses, a butterfly's touch, yet he felt it and looked up. Like Anne with her sixth finger, he normally hated to have his hair touched, but tonight was different. Tonight belonged to Anne Boleyn, and whatever she wanted, he wanted. He smiled. Approval of her caress, especially of her blouse, which had slipped off one shoulder, baring her alabaster skin. He promised himself that his lips would taste her there too, and elsewhere before this night was over. One inch and one caress at a time. First her palm, then her wrist with its pulse throbbing wildly.

"Your mother never taught you that."

"No, some things a man must teach himself."

She hated the women on whom he had practiced. Unable to resist any longer, she dipped her hand into those silky locks, letting them slip like silk through her fingers, only to catch them up again.

Nothing could be more innocent. He kissing her hand and wrist, she playing with his hair. Why then was she breathing more quickly? She shivered.

"You're cold. Here, let me draw the curtains and shut out the draft."

Before she could more than feebly protest, he had swung her legs up on the bed and begun pulling the hangings about them. As he did, he blocked out most of the light. She liked that. It seemed salve to her conscience. When he gently but firmly pressed her back against the bolsters, she yielded.

The hour was late, she was tired, the pillows invitingly soft. She was all acquiescence until his genuine concern spoiled everything.

"Your hand, does it still hurt?"

"Damn the hand," she exploded. "Let it fend for itself!"

"What? Is that jealousy, I hear?"

She could hear the silent laughter in his voice; it exasperated her. "I, jealous of my own hand?"

"Maybe your lips are?" Before she could reply, a gentle fingertip explored her lips, leaving them to ache for more.

"Or the curve of your proud neck?" Again a caress proved him right.

"Or the gentle slope of your shoulder?" Again, his hand accompanied his words.

"Or maybe your sweet breast?"

As his fingertips traced the outline of her small breast, she could feel her nipple react to the touch. A touch repeated, ever so slowly. And again. And again. And still again. It was too much. She tried to jest. "What are you, a one-breast man?"

"Ah, the other, the right is jealous." But his hand left not off its play; instead she could feel his warm breath through her blouse as his mouth sought its goal, gently sucking.

"No, no," she protested. "Not through the blouse. It will show."

His mouth refused to obey, but the hand fondling her other breast reached up and pulled undone the drawstring of her blouse. Then, with one quick shucking movement of that agile, strong hand, she found herself naked to the waist. Even in the half-light he could make out the turgid nipples rising so proudly from generous dark circles. One after the other, he licked at them, and they followed his tongue as slave follows master. But that was not enough. He would taste them fully. First one, then the other, his hand comforting the one neglected momentarily by his mouth. She reveled in it. Never had she been so aware or so proud of her breasts.

Her hands buried themselves in his hair while her chest arched up high to meet those now firm, now soft, now demanding, now biting, now barely touching, now drinking lips. God, she envied the wet nurse of this man. If he had been her suckling, never would she have

248

weaned him. He was driving her mad . . . but slowly. For he, too, savored each moment and would have worshiped at this altar forever. His hands, though, were not so easily satisfied as his mouth, and they would move upward to stroke her shoulders, downward to scribe each rib, span her waist, learn the fastening of her skirt, undo it, and travel on, love's journeyman, feeling beneath apron, skirt, and petticoat, a mounded belly, curved hip, dimpled navel.

Whatever his mind's reasoned plan, it was forgotten as his body took command. It must know her, surround her, encompass her, have her. Throwing his right leg across her, he came comeuppance, skewered on his own forgotten sword. The pain invoked a gasp as his blood spurted forth. With a curse, he dashed the sword from the bed, but the damage was done. His leg cut, the spell broken, the Boleyn freed. Rather, put in command. Rudely, crudely, she shoved him back on his bed. Her competent hands searched and undid his points, rolled down his hose, that she might know the extent of the damage. A moment and several rippings of fabric later and out of her fine linen petticoat she'd fastened a bandage of sorts.

He had lain still for this, but once she sat back, the bandaging done, he would have resumed what he'd begun.

"Nay, lie still till we make sure the blood is dammed."

"Damn the blood, it is only a cut."

"So you said of mine. Shall I, too, kiss you there and make you well . . . or would you have instead that which you seem to love so well?" Leaning over him, she inched her way upward, and then, her right breast in her hand, she teased his lips with it. Like a man dying of thirst, his arms surrounded her and his mouth found her breast. With each greedy suck, her insides contracted. Instead of growing weak and submissive, she grew strong and demanding. Let him know and submit and worship her, for she was woman, giver and denier of pleasure. Like mother with suckling babe, she inserted her finger between breast and mouth and broke the suction. He would have pursued his pleasure further but she would not have it.

"Lie still, you are too dressed. I would feel your skin on mine." Coquettishly, she took her time undoing his laces, opening his shirt. His points were already undone and could be saved for later. For now, she laid her head on his broad chest, her hair cascading over his arms and belly. Her lips moved more freely over his upper body, caressing the powerful muscles and investigating every part of his chest until finally her lips found one of his own nipples. He moaned as her teeth gently fastened on it. She stopped at the sound, fearing he was in pain, then sensing he was not, rolled her tongue about this fleshy reminder he was born of woman. He flexed his muscles to intervene; she quickly disarmed him. This time with a hand that strayed down to unloose his codpiece and unleash his manhood. De Wynter involuntarily flinched as her scorching lips followed the path taken by her hands: down over his chest, across his stomach and onto his belly. The curly hair under her cheeks she began nibbling, pulling it with her lips in playful nips.

She was a born tease. As her lips moved lower and lower, and his breathing grew faster, she deliberately began to work her way back up his torso, only to stop and return again and again to the most sensitive area.

She didn't need the half-light to see his response, it was butting itself against her.

"Anne, my God, please, don't..."

She had no mercy. Down his left thigh her mouth moved, nibbling and blowing lightly as the sensitive hairs on his leg transmitted their message back to de Wynter's brain. She would have thrown herself astraddle him and done the same up the other side but she had pity for his poor wounded leg, its blood soaking the featherbed. Instead her tongue moved to the soft, tender inside of his thigh. When he reached for her head to pull her up to his level, she countered with a firm grip on his wound, and in pain he fell back.

"I said to relax... and I meant it." She squirmed up his body, kissing where she willed, rubbing her breasts about him. Finally she looked down on him. His eyes glittered, whether from lust or love or bleeding she didn't know, nor did she really care. At this moment, he was simply man, and as such, wax in her hands. She chose to take him and shape him and mold him, but mostly play with him. Then let him ride away if he could and not regret her! She was determined that every time he shared bed with another woman, it would be Anne Boleyn's face before him, her breasts rubbing against his, her hands taking charge. Ride away and leave her, would he? Go back to his Scotland without so much as a by-your-leave? He'd see. Anne Boleyn was a woman not easily forgotten.

But she'd not sacrifice her close-kept, carefully guarded virginity for that. There was no need. She knew another way. One her brother had taught her years before. One that she'd used to bind Percy, Ormond, and Wyatt to her.

She reached for his sport. It jumped at her touch and pulled away, its owner stifling a gasp. But like a well-beaten pup, it came quick to heel and returned to her hand. To fondle and dandle and stroke was not enough, she must possess it, own it, make it hers, and so be mistress to its master. She slid down his body, caressing it with her lips as she went until those red lips were level with his red-tipped sceptre. Then, throwing a gore of her petticoat over it, like some devouring harpy, she engulfed it cloth and all. His body thrashed, his staff pulsed, and her teeth through the cloth tightened slightly. He froze in delicious pain, not to move again until she released him. She waited to make sure he understood that she, not he, was in control; then tenderly she loosed her grip, releasing him only to gently place a kiss directly on his most sensitive part. Alternating between pain and pleasure was, as Rochford had taught her well, a technique most women never dreamed of, much less used. More fools they, she thought, it always works!

As Anne's mouth played his member as if it were living flute, de Wynter forgot to think or speak. He could only feel and follow wherever she led. She was the conductor, moving from andante to allegro and back again, the petticoat providing now soft, now rough appoggiatura. He wanted her to stop. No, to go on forever. No, he knew not what he wanted. Whatever she wanted.

Anne delighted in her play, that much did she relish again being in command of man. In some ways, this compensated for the years she danced attendance, courting and fawning over Henry. However, the hour was late and the night short. The longer her absence the greater chance she'd be found out. Faster and faster she went, her soft lips like unholy succuba setting a lively pace until his whole body heaved to her rhythm. Satisfied, she sat back watching as he continued on to a final solo cadenza; Anne, gathering the petticoat close about his instrument, slowly fingered it until the cloth was saturated.

When next de Wynter opened his eyes, wetting lips parched from gulping for breath, Anne was calmly restoring her clothes to order. Her blouse decorously about her shoulders, the drawstring pulled tight, her hair curled up beneath her caul. With one lithe move, she slipped off her torn, wet petticoat. "I leave you a souvenir," she said, smiling down at him once more.

"I'll tie it round my lance, the next tourney I enter."

"Don't you dare."

"To tell the truth, right now I dare little."

"What of your leg?"

"What leg? You have numbed it and my other two as well."

"Such talk. Did your mother teach you that?"

He raised up on one elbow. "The question is who taught *you* that?"

She pushed him back down. The conversation was straying on difficult ground. " 'Tis a Boleyn family secret. Now I must be leaving. Unless there was indeed some matter of import you wished to discuss?"

"Oh, aye, that." He punched up the pillows behind him, the better to look her in the eye. "I need information."

"Say on."

"I need know where next Margaret Douglas will move."

"Why?"

"I can't tell you that."

"Then, tell me this: Why should I help you?"

He paused, considering. "Out of love for me?"

She laughed. "Was what I just did not enough? Greedy man. Very well, I bargain with you. I'll have the information for you tomorrow or the next...but you must agree to stay on at court another fortnight."

That he must consider. His needs conflicted. He had to know the Douglas girl's next stopping point if he were to return successful to Scotland. However, to stay even an extra day was tempting the fates. Yet what if there were a chance that this course that he and Anne had run tonight might be repeated? "Agreed. But remember, not where she is now—that I already know—but where she goes next."

"Yes, I heard you. Her whereabouts next. Why you should want to know that, I cannot imgine. She is very like her mother, big boned, clumsy, and bad of breath. A typical Tudor." Then she was between the curtains, her feet stirring the rushes slightly as she tiptoed across the room.

Between his wound and his wooing, he had no energy to go after. Instead, he slept, his clothes awry, the precious petticoat clutched in one hand. So he was found, first by Fionn, who came to warn him, then by Henry's Captain of the Yeomen of the Guard.

CHAPTER 15

Anne stormed into the king's writing closet like some raven-tressed, mourning-dressed avenging Fury, her somber gown—as she knew—merely heightening her exotic coloring. She looked ravishing, not ravished, frightening, not fearful. Immediately, Henry grew apprehensive. Suppose the spy were wrong? He consoled and congratulated himself on his forethought in summoning Thomas Cromwell as interrogator. If she were faultless, let the base-born councilor feel the scourge of her tongue.

Without appearing to, she took in the scene with one glance: Henry, still in his breakfasting robes, tankard in hand, lounging in and overflowing his too-small chair. Cromwell, who had been Wolsey's crony, stood at desk, dressed solemnly in marten-edged black, wielding a scratchy quill. De Wynter's serving man of the previous night, his hair disheveled, his clothes torn, his eye swollen shut, but—a good sign—not bound. Her eyes dwelled an extra second on de Wynter, standing relaxed and looking more rakish than rumpled, in slept-in, fought-in, ripped shirt-sleeves, open to the waist. The lace-edged, red-stained bandage was wrapped round his thigh, worn as elegantly as the king wore his blue of the Order of the Garter. Where, she worried, was the rest of that petticoat?

Forewarned by the oddity of the hour, Anne had predetermined her course of action. De Wynter's presence confirmed her fears. No meek milksop, she took the offensive.

Ignoring all but Henry, she curtsied deeply but briefly, not waiting to be bidden rise. "Sire, you awakened me."

There, she had done it again. Made him feel in the wrong. He cross-answered peevishly, "Madame, you hurried not a whit so far as I can see, yet I asked you come straight forth when I sent for you some time ago."

Her reply reeked of patient reasonableness. "I could not very well come in my dishabille."

He broke eye-contact, reacting like a child to that maternal tone of voice. "Well, why weren't you up?"

"I kept my bed this morning"—she allowed a trace of anger to enter her voice—"because I was up late last night on king's business."

"King's business?" Cromwell interjected in a voice hard and emotionless as the man himself.

Anne ignored the man, yet answered his question. "You have a spy at court." Henry's eyes narrowed—which one had she found out?

"I sought to discover his purpose. So I went to his room last night."

"You admit you went to his room?" Cromwell said.

"There I discovered he was not, as I feared, plotting death for my beloved king, but another. Or at least so I thought till now!"

"You thought . . . till now?"

Cromwell, Henry decided, sounded more echo than accuser.

"Yes, thought. Was I mistook, my dear lord?" she asked, moving forward and gracefully dropping to her knees at Henry's feet. "Or have these Scots dared raise hand against your imperial person?"

Her beauty, the apparent sincerity of her question took Henry aback. "Nay, madame, my person is fine—"

"Thank God. When I saw them standing there, I feared the worst."

"And well you should, madame," interjected Cromwell, unswayed by Anne's dramatics. "It is *your* person that is in danger."

Casually Anne rested one hand on the king's knee as she swung around to look at Cromwell. Henry could feel the heat of it penetrate his hose as she replied. "Lord Councilor, I assure you you are

mistaken. See? The Scot bears proof I can defend my person."
Without warning, her other hand brought forth from the depths of
her gown a small stiletto. As the king watched fascinated, she
restored it to its home within her well filled-out stocking. "Ask the
Scot, he'll tell you." Her stare dared De Wynter to dispute her.

Not he. He, too, would save his skin if he could, and if she wished
to cry attempted rape—not a hanging offense—let her. Better to
defend himself against that, than what actually happened. "Unfortunately, my leg is mute proof she is right."

Cromwell's head swiveled round as far as possible on his stubby
neck. "You attacked the lady?"

"Nay, she only thought I did. Like others of her sex, the lady was
overly quick to react when she thought her chastity under attack."

"It wasn't?" Cromwell persevered.

"Hardly. The lady has made it quite clear she saves her favors for
another. And I lack not for offers to forego my lonely bed." His
quick wits seized on a diversionary tactic. "Besides, I prefer to
share my bed with ladies, not she-cats who scratch and claw and
make demands. Oh, no, Your Eminence, I pity the man who takes
this lass to bed. Little sleep will he get. I know the type, totally
insatiable."

Two of his listeners breathed quicker in response to his words.
Cromwell, a man of base passions unsoftened by emotion, and
Henry, who had had no female release for too long. Anne, noting
their reaction, took up the cudgels.

"I, a she-cat? How dare you, you Scots barbarian. You would not
know a real woman if you met one, much less bedded her. I know
your type, too. You would have your women passive, apathetic,
lethargic, content to lie there with legs spread. Now, true Englishwomen,
we—" Her voice faltered. To say more might reveal too much.

"Are known throughout Europe," de Wynter smoothly continued,
"as the viragos you are. Strumpets more at home in a stew than at
court."

"Milord!" she protested, turning to the king with feigned shock,
her hand deliberately squeezing his thigh. "Will you let him impugn
our gentlewomen so?" Henry, bemused by the thought of a sexually
greedy Anne in his bed, only wished his Englishwomen were so

256

loose and lecherous as the Scot contended. However, no need to admit this to the braggard. No lack of offers had he had, eh? Well, no more.

"You puling cockatrice," he said, his own hand anchoring Anne's to his thigh. "Enough of your tainted tongue. One more word and I'll have your head, herald or no."

The silence that followed was prolonged, broken only by Henry's noisy sucking at his tankard. Finally, Cromwell intervened. "Sire, we still know not why the Lady Anne went to the gentleman's suite . . . nor why he admitted her. Then there is the matter of the evidence."

"Good point, Thomas."

Anne returned his suspicious gaze with the wide-eyed innocence of the hunted hind. Her voice too was soft and almost meek. "Sire, I told you. To unmask the man. To determine his evil intentions."

"Did you?"

"Indeed, I did," she confided. "The Lady Margaret Douglas. But whether to do for, or woo and wed, I know not."

To her surprise, Henry seemed not surprised. She could not know his spies had kept the Douglas girl always one estate ahead of the Scots for weeks now. This Henry was sure Anne had not known, which was to her credit. She now spoke at least partial truth. But how much?

Cromwell, the cynic, voiced his disbelief. "Lady Anne, you would have us believe you compromised yourself for another woman, a child yet?"

"I knew not that," she hissed, pure venom in her voice, "when I went there. I feared for my lord's life." Her story would not bear up under long questioning. It was time to hazard her trump. Turning to the king, she put on her most loving look, butter melting in her mouth. "Sire, I swear to you, he never even kissed me. I left his room as chaste as I entered it. Put me to the proof!" De Wynter never turned a hair, but Fionn misswallowed, and fell to gagging. He doubted any woman in the world could make such a statement as he had so warned his sister, Devorguilla, in his letters home.

"How——" The King licked his suddenly dry lips and started over. "How propose you to do this?"

"Send for your physician. I will submit me to his examination. But first, sire, spare me this man's gaze. Send him and his lackey away."

Henry's throat tightened. To know for sure, never again to doubt. He couldn't speak, he'd squeak; he nodded.

Cromwell was not so overwhelmed as he. "Sire, the evidence?" The king found his voice. "Not now, later!" Cromwell, silenced, could bide his time; he disliked the proud Anne more than any at court. For now, he would do his master's will and send for the physician and Anne's women. The Captain of the Yeomen Guard Henry charged with the care of the two Scots. To the question, "Here or the Tower?" Henry, aware once again of Anne's hand, this time almost imperceptibly inching its way up his thigh, shrugged. "Let Cromwell decide." An ungentle shove started Fionn on his way out the room; the guard stood by respectfully as the Scots lord made his leg to the English monarch. Already de Wynter was plotting how best to use his hidden pearls to secure assistance and release from prison. However, the tender scene before him—Anne sitting so subserviently at her monarch's feet while her fingers worked their magic near his well-padded codpiece—was too much for the Scot's sense of mischief. "Farewell, my sweet suckets; next time, remember, the lips!"

Anne barely stifled her smile. Henry started to rise to his feet to buffet the lordling who looked far too elegant for the Englishman's taste, despite his disarray. Anne's restraining hand, not to mention a head gone slightly woozy from too much ale on an empty stomach, curbed his momentum.

"Never. Never a next time. Get him out of my sight before I have his head. Cromwell, round up the rest of the rogues. I would have them all through Traitor's Gate 'fore vespers." The captain's grip on de Wynter's arm was steely as he ushered the man out of the room. Even as she watched him go, Anne was plotting how best to get him returned to court. But first, her own ordeal.

Long before she had felt her first flux, gossips had terrorized her with the gory particulars of losing one's hymen: the cruel impalement of her passage, the pounding, punishing pain culminating in one breathtaking stabbing spasm, the bloody flow bathing her tender tissues without relieving the aching soreness known to last for days afterward. Such talk had proved a telling incentive for remaining virgin. And she had. Now she prayed she need not experience the loss of her hymen to prove its presence. That it was there she had no doubt . . . nor that soon the king would dangle and dance at the end of her strings.

With the royal physician came his retinue: his barber assistants, his midwives, his herbalist, even a woman-witch. After them, Anne's women of the bedchamber trooped in. Her time upon her, Anne put on brave face, blew a kiss to her king, and led the way within to the king's retiring room.

Henry, his tankard replenished, quaffed deeply and again, in forlorn hope of clearing his head. Besides, his wait might be tedious. Bored, he reached for the papers left in the green velvet box for his perusal and approval by Cromwell who, despite being newmade Master of the Jewels, spent more time as king's amanuensis. The topmost paper was a note from one of Archbishop Cromwell's cronies. Its author, Browne, according to the inked scrawl in Cromwell's hand across the top of it, aspired to appointment to the Royal College of Arms. The message itself Henry read through twice, but in his ale-groggy condition, he could not fathom the purpose of it.

> We are unwilling to question the Royal Supporters of England, that is the approved descriptions of the Lion . . . Although, if in the Lion, the position of the pizel be proper, and that the natural situation, it will be hard to make out their retrocopulation, or their coupling and pissing according to the determination of Aristotle; all that Urine backward do copulate aversely, as Lions, Hares, Linxes.

Copulate? Retrocopulate? Who gave a damn how lions did it? Henry dropped the instantly forgotten note to the floor. What was taking the physician so long? If she were intact, one dextrous finger should determine that. God help the man if a too long fingernail should damage it; Henry had other plans for the splitting of that skin.

Idly, he reached for the next document, a letters patent creating a new peer, a Marquess of Pembroke, the date, witnesses, and recipient left blank for Henry to dictate later. Unfortunately, the lucky recipient's name drew a blank for the king. Then Henry recalled. Cromwell's idea. To reward his advocate, the Earl of Huntington, for efforts on behalf of Henry's proposed visit next week to France, to the Second Field of Cloth of Gold. Henry shrugged. Pembroke's holdings were not munificent, they would not be missed by the royal exchequer. Besides, Huntington might well be content with title without holdings. It was a thought, a good thought.

Henry was pleased with himself as he put this aside and picked up the next. It bore the seal of the Turcopilier of the Order of the Knights of St. John of Jerusalem, and its contents shattered the king's benevolent mood. Henry had little hope that Carlby was renouncing his claim. A quick skim told him he was right. The knight was adamant; he would have Hampton Court Palace or its rents immediately. Henry swore. How dare these gnats, protected by pope or position, annoy God's anointed king? De Wynter after his Boleyn, the Knight Hospitaler after his Hampton. "The devil take the two," he fumed.

Then he heard what he'd said. "That's it! Let the Hospitalers trade one for the other." With one stroke he would swat two gnats and be at peace. He pounded his tankard with glee, sloshing the ale over the sides and drenching his hand. He upped the tankard, drained it dry, and signaled for more.

The white-cauled, gray-faced, strung-thin midwife edged into the room bowing and scraping. Twice she hawked and hemmed before managing a tentative "If it please Your Majesty?"

"Well?" he prompted impatiently.

"The lady has not been known, she was intact."

"Was?"

His roar crumpled her like ancient parchment. *"Is!* I meant *is!"* Mistaking his yelp of joy for wrath, her nerves failed her and she fled the room, her full skirts swishing about her.

He never noticed. He would have kicked up his heels, but his gouty toe dissuaded him. Anne had been faithful. He would be first after all. How could he have doubted her? Would she forgive him? The last thought was sobering.

The letters patent! Of course. It took several tries to unwedge himself from his chair and get to his feet. Clutching the scroll in his sweaty fist, he limped across to Cromwell's desk. Seizing the quill, he laboriously inked in his fancy's name. Besot with ale, he forgot the final *e* on her given name.

He had barely finished when she entered, her face more pale than usual. Before she could make obeisance, he was upon her, swallowing her mouth with kisses. Wet, slobbery, spongy kisses. On top of unveiling and upending her bottom to the gaze and proddings of that man with his icy-cold hands, Henry's mouthings were too much; she wanted to retch. If he uses his tongue, I will vomit, she vowed silently.

Fortunately, Henry was too eager, childlike, to display his surprise and bask in her praise. Withdrawing from her mouth, he thrust the paper beneath her eyes. Her name drew her like a magnet. She could not believe her eyes. He had misspelled it. Her anger knew no bounds; all rational thought fled her head. "You cup-shotten cullion. Six years and still you know not that it is Anne with an *e!*"

"You don't like it." His lower lip trembled, tears welled up in his eyes. His Anne did not like her surprise. He stood there, a massive man, like a little boy, his joy gone awry. At that moment, she hated him.

"Oh, go sit down, rest your foot."

Obediently, he turned and did what she said while she took another look at the paper she held. Its significance did not come to her immediately. When it did, she swung from jubilation for what he had done, to realization of what she had done. She darted after Henry, grabbing his clenched fist in her two hands and then covered it with grateful kisses.

"No. Go away. You did not like my surprise."

"Sire, you wrong me. I loved it." Pushing him into the chair like a protective mother, her mind raced from thought to thought. Would he rescind it? Could she make amends? All the while she chattered on, "Henry, how can I thank you? Marquess. Not Marchioness. You do me too much honor. I am not worthy of your kindness." Sinking to his feet, she cradled his sore foot in her lap, gazing up at him with adoring eyes.

He was not mollified. "You called me names," he accused her.

"You deserved them," she chided him lovingly. "To tease your poor little Nan like that."

"Tease?"

"To make me think you meant this beautiful gift for some other Anne."

"Is that what you thought?" He brightened. "Did I do that?"

"Yes, you did." It was her turn to pout, all the time studying his response.

"Well, maybe so, but I didn't deserve names like those," he sulked.

He was going to be difficult. She would have to take drastic steps. But to be granted the title male—for that she would do much. On her own she would outrank most men and take precedence over all women except the royals. But this was only the first step. Give her another year and she would even take precedence over daughter, sister, and ex-wife. For now, she knew exactly what she must do.

"Come, sire, spread your legs. I would prove my love for you . . . the love of an insatiable succuba."

CHAPTER 16

The Captain of the Yeomen of the Guard would have his prisoners out of the palace, through the Pond Garden and into the Water Gallery, he hoped unseen. The fewer observers, the fewer questions asked, and the more fear each disappearance caused among the rest of the court. That was the king's rule, the captain's orders. But de Wynter was not one to be led off quietly like some complaisant suttee. Once he saw what was about, he determined to make his departure well known, since the more who knew, the sooner word would reach friendly ears in Scotland and France.

Spying a group of promenaders at the far end of the garden, he stopped short, creating havoc among his escort. Those beside him could not stop so soon, those behind charged into their slowing fellows, those before continued forward only to be halted by the noise behind. In the confusion, de Wynter saw his opening and sprinted back toward the gaily dressed courtiers, the captain lumbering steps behind.

"Ho there, Vaux," de Wynter ordered in a voice that would brook no disobedience. Without thinking, the earl so named stopped and looked back, his companions instinctively doing the same.

The captain cursed under his breath, the damage was done; the news of de Wynter's arrest was out in the open. "I will be right back," de Wynter said to the captain. "But first, my farewells to my fellows." The captain had no choice but let the Scots lord say his good-byes to the English ones, lingering perhaps a trifle longer than need be over the hands of the ladies as he took their leave in the French manner. Many a female English heart beat a little faster at the sight of that hoar-frosted head bent low and at the touch of warm, skilled lips upon the backs of their hands.

Addressing the group as a whole, he gave a deep and sweeping bow. "Fare you well, I'm off to be Tudor's guest and taste England's hospitality in the Tower. Tell Mistress Anne Boleyn I forgive her, and take care lest you join me there." With all those ears listening, he could only pray that one heard him rightly and would convey his words exactly to whom they were addressed.

From over his shoulder came the gruff, not unsympathetic voice of the middle-aged Captain of the Guard. De Wynter's message had not been lost on him, although it had been misinterpreted as de Wynter was sure it would be for most people. The captain, like most of England's middle and lower classes, was Catherine's man, considering her the rightful queen till death did her and the king part. If Mistress Boleyn, whom he privately considered the king's whore, had a hand in this arrest, then, so far as the captain was concerned, the young Scotsman could not be all bad. "Are you done, milord?"

"Quite. Lead the way, *mon capitaine*, I follow on your heels."

"Alongside would be better, if it please your lordship."

"If it pleases you, it pleases me. Forward we go, side by side." Tucking his arm within the captain's, the two marched off, very unmilitarily yet democratically, and the captain was secretly flattered. Many a prisoner had he escorted this route, and none had favored his guard with more than snarls or burning stares or icy disdain. To be treated with such camaraderie by a great lord was beyond his imaginings. Thus, once he'd seen his prisoner seated in the prow with Fionn secured aft and the barge underway, he hastened forward. Taking a place on the well-worn velvet-covered bench seat near de Wynter, he prepared to enjoy the twenty-one-mile trip down the Thames to the Tower. De Wynter resigned himself to enduring the man's conversation and hopefully turning it and the captain's attitude to his advantage. But he was to be sorely tested, for a subject of fancied mutual dislike sprung readily to the captain's tongue. "The Nan, she did you in, eh?" Misinterpreting de Wynter's silence as assent, he spat over the side and continued, "Forgive me spitting, but that woman's name leaves a foul taste on the tongue. You know, they say

264

she's tried many times to poison the good Queen Catherine, but each time, and sometimes just in the nick of, the poison's been found out. The whore's from Lambeth, you know—a well-known haunt of prisoners. We'll pass it by later and I'll point it out. Anyway, one day, mark my words, that witch-woman—they say she 'as the witch's mark plain as day on one hand—I predict, she'll get what she wants, take it from me, Thomas Notte. By the by, 'ow did she get you in this way? You make advances to 'er and she complain to the king?''

De Wynter seethed inside. To pull the man's foul-speaking tongue from his mouth would soothe the psyche but not lead to escape. Not trusting himself to speak, he schooled his expression and made mute denial, hoping his silence would discourage the man. It didn't. ''You mean she did the advancing?'' Notte whistled admiringly under his breath; it reinforced his faith in the immorality of the woman. ''Well, 'tween you and me, I wouldn't have said 'er no. She must be a saucy tumble to keep the king sniffing at 'er skirts for all these years. Besides, taking up lodgings in the Tower is a mighty high price to pay for not lifting a wench's petticoats. Of course, better the Tower than your head.''

De Wynter's self-control was about to give way. Somehow, someway, the man's backstairs chatter must be stilled. What was needed was a distraction. Not having one to hand, he invented one out of the work of the wind on the larches lining the far shore. ''Look! There!''

''Where?''

''Over there, in the larches.''

Craning his head and peering intently, the captain said, ''A deer? A big one?''

Why not? de Wynter thought, lying cheerfully. ''An enormous one. Never saw one bigger in my life.''

To de Wynter's surprise, the captain jumped to his feet, wildly but silently signaling the sweep to steer the barge in closer to shore.

Here was his chance, de Wynter exulted, watching the prow slowly, ponderously put about, like a sow wallowing in mud, obediently crossing against the current and moving southward. When the barge got within two body-lengths of the bank, he'd be over the side, through the water, and onto dry ground before anyone could stop him. Then, he dared any of these men to catch him.

Closer, closer the barge moved, de Wynter silently willing it even farther. Four body lengths, three . . . only one to go. As the boat inched forward, de Wynter slowly drew his feet back under him for that sudden surge up and over the side. Slowly as he moved, it was too much. The captain had not only the manners of a boor, but the instincts of a boar. De Wynter's barely perceptible movement triggered his alarm. He reacted instantly. "Poles in!" With whap and grunt, ten poles drove deep into the mud-bottom of the Thames, violently checking the movement of the barge. So fast and precise was the crew that de Wynter, as a soldier, although frustrated as a prisoner, admired their training. He also had to revise his chances of escape.

"Reverse course," the captain shouted to the sweep, then took his seat next to de Wynter.

The captain may have been animal-wary, but de Wynter had the canny sangfroid of a Scottish courtier fashioned in France. Reading and rightly interpreting men's faces was essential to survival in that den of deviousness; and what he saw in the captain's face boded no good for any future escape plans. So even as the captain was trying to trap the Scot—"Damme, missed 'im again! Sixteen points, you say, to 'is rack?"—de Wynter was ready with a counter gambit.

Smiling ingenuously, he made his confession, "Nay, not I. My eyes are a touch too nearsighted for that. But that young man over there, the corporal, he saw the stag. Let's ask him? Ho, corporal. A johnny on his toes like you must have seen the stag, he didn't have sixteen points, did he?"

The young man—an ambitious young sort quite taken by his own importance—wet his lips nervously as honesty and pride warred within him. "Why . . . ah, no. He didn't."

"Yes, that's what I thought, too." He'd gambled and won. Like most young men the corporal couldn't confess a failing. Now having no fear of contradiction, de Wynter knew he must win over the captain. "So it wasn't *the* stag? Tell me, what's so important about him?"

Almost persuaded that de Wynter had really seen something, the captain allowed himself to be drawn out, especially since he saw a way to repay his prisoner in kind. "Why, the old stag 'as such winning ways, he 'as the king's pardon and right to roam. No arrow for 'im if he tries to flee like there'd be for you. Of course, if we should shoot you dead, you could go join your King James—the fourth, wasn't he?—he who was killed at Flodden. He's over there in the Convent of Sheen. Then you'd see 'ow our good King Hal treats treacherous Scots. He wraps them up solid in a blanket of lead and keeps them in a lumber-room out back. You might just chew on that while I sees to me duties. I'll put yon Johnny on 'is toes to watch over you while I'm gone. It'll be worth 'is life if anything happens to you," he added in a voice that carried plain to the corporal's ears, motioning the younger man to take his place. With the captain gone, the corporal, uncomfortable about his lying, refused to let himself be drawn into conversation. The two men were left to their thoughts in a silence broken only by the splash of poles digging deep into the water and the drip of their release from the muddy grip of the Thames; the warmth of the English sun might have made the Scot drowsy, but not today. Today, he must escape and warn the companions. But the barge stubbornly stayed in the midst of the stream, and after a long while, de Wynter noticed that the banks they passed were more built up, less placid as genuine whitecaps broke the surface of the Thames here and there. The Thames was asserting her muscle, and with a string of commands the barge responded, poles stowed away and long oars taking their place. Escape under the circumstances was impossible.

With the patience of a man who has learned to change what he can, and endure what he can't, de Wynter allowed himself to doze lightly as if standing watch, knowing he would awaken at anything untoward.

The captain's appearance long after the sun had passed its zenith brought the Scot, catlike, to the alert, but only the slightest opening of his eyelids showed it. Actually, he would have gone easily back to sleep, but the sight of the slab of bread and flagon of ale carried by the captain kept him awake.

"Thought you might like to break your fast."

"My rumbler here seconds the thought." Hand on stomach, he stretched languorously and favored the captain with that rare smile that erased years from his face. Looking down on that boyish countenance beneath prematurely grayed hair, the captain realized for the first time how young was this man who journeyed to the

Tower, and he hated the king's whore even more. "Your lordship best cross yourself, just across the Thames there is Lambeth," he cautioned. "You will recall I told you of Lambeth. That's where astrologers and almanack-makers and mostly poisoners live. The whore hails from there. And anytime she goes home to visit 'er kin, you can bet the good Queen Catherine loses another of 'er poison-testing pets."

De Wynter had his mouth full of bread and could not protest, but the captain understood well the skeptical shake of his head. Coming closer, he took a seat and set out to convince the young man of the persecution of Catherine. "Who better than you should know how the whore works 'er wiles? If it's the poisoning you take exception to, you can believe it. All 'ere on the barge can vouch that Lambeth's the 'aunt of poisoners."

De Wynter was listening intently; more than that, he was looking over the captain's shoulder. Miracle of miracles, the barge was moving closer and closer to the shore opposite Lambeth. Let the captain rant and rave, de Wynter did not care, not if it meant a second chance at freedom.

"Look what happened not two years ago to the Bishop of Rochester, that holy man in 'is palace at Lambeth. He sent word down that 'is bread was stale, not tasty as it should be. The baker, he fixed that. Poison went into the next batch along with the leavening. The bishop escaped, 'aving been invited to dine with Cromwell, but the others in the household puked up their guts afore they died. You had to trail the spew to find the bodies. Seventeen was found that night, one a week later by the stench. And that doesn't count the poor people fed the trencher-meats at the gate. Well, you can bet they gave that cook what for over at Smithfield."

De Wynter's jaws worked mechanically; he could no more taste the bread than stop the captain's story. All the time, the barge crept closer to shore.

"The justices at Smithfield, they passed a special law just for that baker. Sat 'im down in his own caldron and boiled 'im up like a haunch of mutton. He was a fat man and 'is grease bubbled up and popped the skin and the smell was rancid. Those dogs that licked up the spills where the pot boiled over, they went mad. And when the stew bones, flesh and all, was thrown into the Thames, fish surfaced bellyside-up for a mile downstream. Such a user of poison was he, that Lambethman, that 'is flesh was steeped with it.''

Without thinking, he made the devil's horns with one hand to ward off the evil eye, then catching himself, crossed himself reverently. De Wynter started to put the rest of the loaf down next to the flagon, but the captain pressed him to continue. ''Eat. It may be a long time afore your next meal in the Tower. I 'as me a brother there and he says them who don't pay, don't eat. Unless your baggage catches up with you soon, your stomach'll soon be pressing against your spine. And if you wonder why we hug the Middlesex shore so close, it's not to fret you. I 'as no choice. My men know they keep the 'eretics in a cell atop the tower of Lambeth Palace. And if one goes too close, they can cast their spells on you from all that distance away. So, just you relax your vigilance and finish your meal. My lying corporal there has regretted 'is say on the stag and is ready to prove 'is devotion to king and me by shooting you dead if you move a step toward the wrong side.''

De Wynter didn't need to look around to prove the captain's veracity. His few short weeks on English soil had shown him these were temptable people burdened with a conscience. Easily might they sin and just as quickly regret it and attempt to make restitution. The corporal, he had no doubt, would be quick to pilch his hide. De Wynter decided to take the captain's advice. This time he savored all the flavor of the dark brown bread.

''Whilst you chew, you might give a gander at Westminster Abbey over there, what parts you can see. Too bad the palace blocks most of the view. I just hopes you don't get a closer look at it later. You know there's where they bury them they beheads at the Tower. No, I'm not funning you. 'Under the sword at the Tower, under the sward at the Abbey.' Them's the rules. Of course, you being Scots shouldn't mind that. That way you'd be united with your Scots Stone of Scone. Ah, I 'as your interest now. For truth, that's where we keep it, in the Abbey under the Coronation Chair. Of course, between you and me, I think all those Scots who've tried to steal it back were mad. Why bother with a stone, even if it was Jacob's pillow. Nah, me, I'd find me a lock pick and go for the pyx. You 'as heard tell of that, ain't you? That's the box wherein they keep the king's standards of gold and silver. I 'as ne'er seen it meself, but I hear 'tis kept in a special chamber carved out of stone, with a door made of stone and lined with the hides of men. Seven locks has that door and each a different key and seven different men keep one key each.

"Why do you wrinkle your nose like—ah, you smell the stink already. We're near the Tower. Just be glad the wind's behind us. No, don't look like that. That's not rotting men you smell, it's rotting fish from Billingsgate. Gads, earlier this summer the smell 'twas so bad, it wouldn't wash off. Had to wear off, it did. Only thing more foul is the tongue of a Billingsgate fish-hag. She'll scorch the stench off your back. So rank are some they could make a stone statue blush. The time to really see the fish market at Billingsgate is first thing in the morn. If you're lucky, you'll be housed in a cell overlooking the market. Wake you up early when the river teems with wooden fish bearing the catch up from the mouth of the river. On the banks, fish flop and people too. Slipping and sliding on the offal thrown on the ground. Enjoy it if you see it. Might be the only laugh you'll have before your own head goes flopping about on the Tower green."

De Wynter had finished eating, not a bit perturbed by the macabre talk of his warden, and now calmly wiped the crumbs from his lips on the sleeve of his shirt. The captain watched him admiringly. His tale flowed freely, for it was well rehearsed, having been delivered to all those he'd escorted to the Tower. Many it had sickened, and rare was the man who didn't turn white between the assault on his sensitivities and the offense to his senses. De Wynter was that rarity. Of course, the captain had no way of knowing that he addressed a survivor of the siege of Naples, a hell which made Dante's pale by comparison. The Scot's equanimity impressed the captain. Was the man really amused as he looked? Gad, that was gutty. He decided to confide in him, "There, see those wood things over there? Starlings they's called. They's be supposed to break the rush of water on London bridge but, God's truth, many's the careless boatmen broke on those piers. So I leave not the shooting of the bridge to just anybody. Meself takes the sweep to steer it through. As for you, you'll arrive at the Tower nice and dry. On the word of Thomas Notte, Captain of King Henry's Yeoman Guard. I suggests if you don't look down the shoot of the bridge, look you to either side but don't look up. There on the middle of London Bridge, that's where they hang traitors' heads to cure in the sun. Someday, I vow, the head of the Boleyn, she'll hang there. But I hope next time I pass, yours I'll not see. Fare you well, Scot, and if you should see at the Tower a Yeoman Warder, a Beefeater they's called, looks like me, that be me brother John. Usually I commend prisoners to him, but you're not like them, Scot, so don't you be taken in; me brother's not to be trusted. 'Course, none of the others is either. Well, good luck, your lordship. I wish you well.'' With a grin and a wave of his hand, Notte was gone, back aft to steer his barge safe just as he'd tried to do with his prisoner.

De Wynter, looking after him, feared anew for the safety of his Anne. If men like Thomas Notte were against her, she must tread the straight line. De Wynter's thoughts were stilled by the sudden sinking of the boat underneath him as the prow leaped into space and fell down the cascades between the piers of the bridge. For a long moment he exalted: the tower would not claim him. Then his hopes were dashed. The boat righted itself. He was not about to die. He would live to see the feared interior of those forbidding walls that had for four centuries dominated London.

CHAPTER 17

After successfully shooting the bridge's narrows, the barge plunged, yellow spray flying, into the Pool of the Thames, where the waves surged and heaved like the river it was. De Wynter did not see Notte again, at least not to talk to. The barge instead quickly threaded its way between wherries and other craft—hundreds of them, including one that could have been a king's flagship. Their destination dominated all, the sombre walls and the quadragon on the White Tower with its four dark cupolas, looking forbidding and impervious to escape.

At last the barge made fast at the base of St. Thomas's Tower with its infamous Traitor's Gate, that wood-toothed, yawning hole connecting the Thames to the Outer Ward of the Tower. As the yeomen struggled with the landing plank, de Wynter assessed his prison more closely. The Thames had been diverted round Tower Hill, creating a moat. Within that watery barrier rose outer walls better than five-men tall, broken here and there by towers and bastions. Eight of them he could see from where he stood, not including the keep atop the hill, their roofs bristling with pikemen, their sides studded with cannons. Up close, escape looked impossible. This was a fortress easily made fast from those without and probably from within.

The Romans were first to occupy this hill. The Saxons' King Alfred built upon their ruins. These then were the foundation of the first Norman Castle built by William the Conqueror. And here it still stood: the White Tower, so named for its coat of whitewash. From the day the first stone was laid for the keep, no monarch, including the current one, had failed to further fortify this already formidable stronghold. Over the years it had grown from fortress to fortified palatial prison.

The heavy gates swung open quietly. The demeanor of de Wynter's greeters, their total nonchalance, warned him that the charging of prisoners was routine for them. Through the arch beneath St. Thomas's Tower he was led, another portcullis swinging silently open before him within the Bloody Tower, and so through to the Inner Bail and Tower Green.

Dusk was upon them and torches flared here and there. Even so, it was light enough for him to make out the headman's block with its chiseled hollows for chin and chest, leaving a thin, neck-wide strip of stone to await the headsman's sword. In the dim light he couldn't be sure whether it had been fashioned out of mottled stone . . . or had those streakings come later? The thought did not rouse his spirits. Instead, he grew more pensive with every step taken toward that white hulk looming a full hundred feet in the air.

At the last moment, his escort veered left. Now he was surprised. His quartering was not to be in the White Tower itself, but in another, smaller, semicircular tower in the west wall of the Inner Ward. Up a narrow, winding stairway the strong hand on his arm propelled him, into a room on the first landing, not overly large, which took up all else of the first floor except the stairway. They left him there in the dark, to compose his soul or whatever, it being too cold and dank to do much else.

Feeling his way about the room, he discovered from barked shins and stubbed toes that he had table, stool, pallet on legs, and what would appear to be a fireplace. Retreating to the pallet, he hugged knees to his chest to conserve warmth and huddled upon the bare planks awaiting the pleasure of his keepers. Muffled noises outside aroused him, and shortly thereafter the door to his prison opened. The uneven light of the torch made the Yeoman seem grotesquely misshaped, but the identity of the bags and parcels could not be mistaken. His baggage had arrived. What of his companions? He prayed they had made good their escape.

The light hurt his eyes. Between his squinting and the torches flaring, the men who stood there seemed surrounded with a mystical aura. One figure among them separated itself from the group. Unlike the Yeoman Warders in their crimson skirts and sleeves outlined in gold, this man wore points and hose and jerkin and—more important to de Wynter—a mantle lined with marten. The closer he came, the less distinct were his features.

"Welcome, Your Lordship, to the Tower of London. Is there aught I can do to add to Your Lordship's comfort during your stay here?"

"Indeed. You might begin by lending me your cloak."

"A man with a sense of humor. Good, you will need it here."

"Where, if I may ask, is 'here'?"

"Beauchamp Tower, my lord. Now, the hour grows late and I have others to visit. Shall we proceed to business? As a prisoner of state, your charge for your keep, per day, is one and six. Considering the hour, we shall forgive today and commence tomorrow. If, however, you prefer ale to water, potage to soup, and wish to wash more than once a week, we charge accordingly. Is there anything I've left out?"

"The small matter of how I shall pay you. I am penniless." Not yet and not just for food did de Wynter plan to sacrifice one of his two pearls.

"Penniless? You have nothing? Not even in your luggage?"

"Come now, my Lord Gaoler, did not your searchers tell you as much?"

"And you have nothing on your person?"

"Nothing. They roused me from my bed. If you will lend me pen and paper however, I shall write to friends—"

"No, no writing."

He was to be kept incognito. The thought drove home the seriousness of all this, but he masked his concern, affecting cheerfulness instead. "Then I guess I shall just have to starve, if I do not freeze first."

"There was some mention of a silver collar..."

"My herald's collar? Gladly would I relinquish that, but unfortunately, I shall probably have need of it at my trial. I am to stand trial, am I not?"

"Suppose I lent it back to you if you should have some future use for it, in return for..." He considered a moment. "Your tabard?"

It was there! All was not lost! "Nay, that too I'll need. What of my crimson hat?" The gentleman gaoler, who planned to have all eventually, hesitated briefly, then struck the bargain. He and his guards withdrew but only temporarily, returning with lackeys bearing wood and bedding, a platter of food, and a large tankard of ale. Soon, de Wynter was ensconced as comfortably as this dreary prison would allow.

"And the collar?"

"Help yourself," he replied, his mouth full of thickly buttered bread.

"And the hat?"

"And the hat."

Straight to the right parcel the man went, swiftly extracting the collar and hat. De Wynter pretended deep engrossment in his food, but actually he watched carefully for a glimpse of brilliantly embroidered fabric—his tabard with its jewel-concealing cuffs. Other than the sight of that, nothing else offered him much consolation, especially if he were unable to communicate without the walls. Anne was his best, his only hope.

The next morning brought light but no sun to this westward-facing prison. From the slit windows he could make out much of London, secure within its city walls. And on the Thames, the fishing boats Notte had talked about. The Thames teemed with them as if boats had taken to spawning. The view from the other narrow opening was more grim, and its significance not lost on him. It was of Tower Hill with its dyester poles hanging heavy with rotting human fruit.

Turning inward, he examined his own surroundings more closely. He soon found traces of former occupants. Besides names and dates rough scribed on the walls, scratched in the chimney face and signed Burley was "Take no thought for the morrow, the morrow shall take thought for itself." In a recess made by the chimney, an unknown prisoner wrote with gallows humor, "This ill life we must endure, my poor grave be more secure." A third left him perturbed: *"Timor mortis conturbat me."* To put memories to rest, he started pacing, considering how best to make use of his two jewels... how to find out about his companions . . . how to learn the fate of Fionn and his whereabouts. Soon his feet settled down to a steady rhythm: ten steps north, five south, four west, eight east, four west, five south, and repeat again. With a shudder he realized he was inscribing a cross, but vary his pattern how he might, he always unconsciously came back to that.

For five days he existed so. Each day the gaoler arrived and silently directed the warders to supply the table, the hearth, and the bed. One of the men with him looked familiar, and de Wynter wondered whether he might be the John Notte of whom his brother had spoken. But de Wynter had no chance to question him, and the gaoler did not encourage talk. He did, however, accept a fine linen handkerchief in exchange for a nail. Then de Wynter could alternate his exercise with adding his own witness to the walls:

> How slow ye move, ye heavy hours,
> As ye were wae and weary!
> It wasna sae ye glinted by
> When I was with my dearie.

His sixth day in prison was that seventh day of the week which God blessed and sanctified, forbidding that anyone should work, and the routine changed. This time when the keeper arrived, he brought barber and soap and water. Once clean-shaven, de Wynter was urged to hurry his dressing. Taking no chances, he donned his tabard, then reminded his keeper, "My collar, my Lord Gaoler. A herald looks but half dressed without it . . . and you did have the payment of one hat."

"The problem is, Your Lordship, the hat looks not right without matching gloves." The two men locked glares, but de Wynter had no choice except to acquiesce. If his stay went on much longer, he feared the keeper'd have him stripped to breeches and hose. Once the gloves were turned over, the collar was produced from some hidey-hole on the gaoler's person. Clamping it about his neck took but a minute, and then de Wynter was ready to go.

Down the stairway they went and into the sweet fresh air of the green, the warmth of the sun stroking his shoulders and head. Again he was urged to move faster. In the daylight, de Wynter discerned another scaffold to his left, this one vacant of fruit. The headsman's block, he felt sure on second look, might once have been pristine;

276

now it was deep-stained. The keeper would not let his prisoner tarry, but herded him forward toward the White Tower. When William the Conqueror built his keep, he made it a mighty pile. The windows were set high in walls surmounted with turrets at angles. It was at least a hundred feet long, maybe more, and as much in width. De Wynter had in his time seen the castles of France and Italy and many a pile in Normandy, but none filled him with so much foreboding as did this plain, white mass of stone before him. They entered through a door in the south wall, turning at immediate right angles to mount a high winding staircase cut within the fifteen-foot-thick wall. Eventually they came out into a chapel. After the constriction of the stair, the chapel with its wide triforium, its barrel-vaulted ceiling, and its apse uplifted by stilted round arches would have seemed spacious if not for the massive, cubical-capitaled pillars breaking it up into so many aisles. Down the center they marched, their footsteps echoing eerily, bouncing from wall to wall. Although at no time during the past six days had his legs been shackled or his arms bound, de Wynter felt the pressure of history closing in about him and constraining his movements.

A thin man in bishop's miter stepped forth to greet them. "Archbishop Cranmer," the gaoler whispered. "Genuflect!" Afterward, de Wynter was able to study the man before him. A goodly man, harried by troubles—Harry's troubles. The feeble funning somewhat restored de Wynter's confidence. To be able to joke at all was a measure of the man. Cranmer, he thought, looked lacking in sense of humor. And lost within his rich robes. He was not one to have risen to this rank through purchase or friends, and thus must have earned it. An honest man is always dangerous.

"Do I address James Mackenzie?"

"Nay, My Lord Archbishop. You address James Mackenzie, Esquire, His Scottish Majesty's Envoy Extraordinary and Scots Herald Ross, the Right Honorable Earl of Seaforth." So did he offer his first gambit. Let the bishop accept this and he could claim diplomatic immunity.

"Before God, my son, there are no honorables or envoys. Each man stands on his own, identified only by his Christian name."

Gambit refused. What game was this English king and his archbishop playing?

"Granted, Your Grace, but I lay claim to diplomatic immunity by virtue of my mission to the Court of His British Majesty Henry VIII, bearing messages from His Scottish Majesty, James IV."

"My son, do you not hear us right?" Cranmer replied patiently. "We grant you your position and your immunity to civil trial. But here, my son, you stand before an ecclesiastical court."

De Wynter was shocked. "Ecclesiastical? Why, by God?"

"By God you shall be tried for breaking his commandments."

"Attempted rape? What commandment does that break?"

Cranmer ignored this. "Hear ye, James Mackenzie, the charges the Holy Mother Church has laid against you." Picking up a document heavy with wax seals and trailing ribbons, Cranmer commenced reading in that singsong, strung-together Latin used by too many churchmen. Since Latin was the language of Church, diplomats, and scholars—the universal tongue, if you would, of the Christian world—de Wynter early on had been exposed to it and later refined in it while incarcerated in Naples. Thus, though he might miss a technical word here and there, by concentrating, he could make out well.

What he heard, he swore he misunderstood. He was to be tried not for rape but for adultery; not for crimes in England but in Scotland; not with Anne Boleyn as partner but Queen Dowager Margaret.

"Your Grace, I ask the court's permission; but even if these accusations were true, what jurisdiction have you? These might be crimes in Scotland, what concern are they of England?"

Cranmer removed his glasses the better to see the elegant man before him. "Know ye not that His Imperial Majesty is named Protector of Scotland? That the Pope has agreed to appoint no Scottish bishops without his consent and that the Archibishopric of St. Andrews has been reduced to its ancient dependence on York which I represent." Cranmer's voice had been toneless so far, as if reciting by rote. Now it took on color. "Besides, your accusers are English subjects."

From out of the shadows stepped the young Margaret Douglas. She was as Anne Boleyn had described her and as de Wynter remembered: big boned and clumsy. Whether she had bad breath or no, de Wynter was sure he would never find out. There was a flush to her face and a vicious set to her mouth as well as a fiery look in her eye. Here was a female out to exact revenge. "On behalf of my mother, I accuse him," she said. "He took advantage of a woman's grief for loss of her husband, a queen's care for her country. He led my mother astray"—this was a fanatic who believed she spoke God's truth—"down the ways of irresponsibility, plying her with the drugs and seductions of the flesh. He made a god-fearing, loving mother and devoted wife into an avowed adulteress. Archbishop, judge you and punish him. Let him be dealt the Biblical punishment, let him be stoned to death."

"Hear also the woman's husband," intoned the bishop without change in inflection.

A tall man, an older, masculine, soft-fleshed version of the girl, stepped forward. It was Douglas, he who had made marrying an avocation. "Your Grace, before this court stands a man wronged by a lecher, a man who cries to you in the voice of loving husband and concerned father for justice. My wife, my daughter's mother, has deserted her marriage bed to cling to this man. I remind you, Your Grace, that the Lord God said, 'It is not good that the man should be alone; I will make him an helpmeet for him.' So says the Book of Genesis. Again in Genesis it says, 'Thy desire shall be to thy husband and he shall rule over thee.'"

Such pious mouthings coming from such a man? De Wynter could not decide whether to laugh or gag. A look at Cranmer decided him to do neither.

Douglas continued, "Your Grace, I rule not my wife who chooses to stay in the North sending her lover south to tempt my daughter to stray from her path of righteousness. My Lord Archbishop, I remind you that in the Gospel according to Mark, we are told 'What therefore God hath joined together, let not man put asunder,' and 'The woman which hath an husband is bound by the law to her husband so long as he liveth.' Need I remind you, Your Grace, that when Moses, according to Exodus, went down from the mount of Sinai, ten commandments did he speak, the seventh being 'Thou shalt not commit adultery'? Archbishop, judge you and punish him, stone him to death!"

De Wynter could restrain himself no longer, but his manner remained respectful, his voice cool and dispassionate. "The ninth commandment seems grossly neglected here. Then, too, does not John say, 'He that is without sin among you, let him first cast a stone . . . neither do I condemn thee: go and sin no more'?''

Cranmer eyed the man speculatively; such words bespoke more than casual knowledge of the scriptures. The other two had first to be rehearsed before they could quote so. However, such interruptions just delayed the foreordained course of this trial. "My Lord Gentleman Gaoler, have you other witnesses?"

"Ten, save your Grace, all kenneled here in the Tower."

De Wynter's pulse raced more quickly. The companions and servants were taken.

"Do they bear willing witness?"

"Nay, Your Grace, they remain stubborn though food and drink have been withheld from them."

"What do you suggest, My Lord Gaoler?" The archbishop addressed one man while covertly studying the elegant face of another. On the Scot's reaction to the keeper's answer depended the success of their plan.

"That they be put to the question. His Majesty's craftsman with rack and boot will shortly loosen their tongues."

A slight thinning of de Wynter's lips, the tightening of a muscle in the cheek—in these small signs did Cranmer find cause to rejoice. He had again advised the king right. Loyalty was the weakness of this man, his friends the key.

"Very well, My Lord Gaoler, I shall take that under advisement. Now, James Mackenzie, what say you in your defense?"

Feverishly he had been seeking some defense. Not in truth could he take shelter, that would condemn him out of his own mouth. Nor could he perjure himself by lying; if his men were put to torture the truth would out. Desperately, he seized upon a bold defense.

"Your Grace, what would you have me say? I cannot in good conscience stand by and let these slander the reputation of His British Majesty's good sister and his Scottish Majesty's revered Queen Mother."

He studied Cranmer's countenance. Not a whit had it changed. "Therefore I, as Margaret Tudor's emissary, challenge the Red Earl to Trial by Combat, the Jouse à l' Outrance. Let sharpened lances determine the truth of the—"

"Let it be recorded," interrupted the Archbishop, speaking over his shoulder to the clerk scratching away at his lectern in a deserted corner of the chapel, "the accused enters no defense."

"But—" De Wynter would have continued, but he was given no chance.

"So be it. I shall consult my God and my conscience and render my decision. Return him to his quarters."

"No!" de Wynter shouted. "I have not finished. Let me speak."

"Come, Your Lordship, if you cease your struggling, perhaps His Grace would allow you to see your men." All eyes sought out the archbishop.

That such a visit was part of the strategy to bend de Wynter to the king's will, none would have known by looking at Cranmer. His impassive gaze rested long and speculatively on the young Scot where he stood held fast in the grip of four burly Beefeaters. Personally, he regretted sacrificing another victim to the king's fascination with his Boleyn. However, what the king wanted was the archbishop's desire. Almost imperceptibly, Cranmer gave his consent.

"When?" de Wynter demanded.

Unseen by the herald, the keeper signaled the archbishop—all was in readiness.

"Would the present suit Your Lordship?"

"Very much."

"Good. My Lord Gaoler, you will conduct our young friend direct to see his men."

They did not retrace their steps. Instead, led by the keeper, they left the chapel, pacing the length of the banqueting room, de Wynter counting his steps off silently. It measured twenty-seven paces, an enormous room.

A door in the northeast corner revealed another stair built in the wall. De Wynter lost count of the steps as they made their way down into the depths of Tower Hill. Finally the stairs ended and they came out in a large room. But the torches carried by the warders revealed no Scots.

Bewildered, de Wynter looked to the keeper for explanation. Was this some sort of trick? Was he to be done away with secretly? The keeper forestalled his questions: "They be kept in the Little Ease."

Giving his torch to a fellow, he advanced toward a dimly lit corner of this windowless room tunneled out of solid rock. Grasping a ring in the floor, he gave a heave, opening a trap door, then gestured for de Wynter to advance. His first hint of what he would see was the stench. By the light of the torches held by his surrounding captors, de Wynter looked down into the upturned faces of his friends. They lay and crouched and sat in a small pit in the ground not big enough for all to stretch out, or high enough for any to stand.

"Jamie! Water! For God's sake, fresh air!" Some merely moaned. He knew not who cried what. "How long—?"

"They been down there since they arrived. They have not been out since, although we supply them with salt meat and water. They eat little but drink every drop. Their body heat turns the pit into an oven. How long will they last? They are strong young men, one or two might live out the next week."

De Wynter tried to push the menacing pikes aside so his men might escape, but strong arms held him back. "Let them out. They have done nothing. I am the guilty one. Take me to the archbishop. I shall confess." The keeper gestured his men to step back so he might let the door down.

"Drummond, Fionn, Gilliver," de Wynter called back over his shoulder as his warders pulled him back. "Have faith, I'll have you out." His promises were cut short by the hollow thump of the trapdoor closing with fearful finality. Returned to his cell, de Wynter lay dejectedly as the hours passed. The room grew dark. The fire on the hearth grew low, until merely smoldering, scattered coals. Still de Wynter made no move, lying still on his pallet. Even when the door opened and warders bearing torches entered, he did nought but cover his eyes with his forearm.

There came to his unwilling ears a medley of sounds. Logs being put in the fire . . . his furniture set back on its feet from where he had kicked it in helpless rage . . . the door opening more than once . . . and footsteps, many footsteps, scuffling about. With the closing of the door, the sounds died away except for the crackling of the fire. Then, a very faint rustle of cloth. Cranmer spoke.

"I take it you saw your friends and were not pleased," he addressed the still form on the bed. "The gaoler tells me you are prepared to confess?"

"Will it free my men?"

"No, I think not."

De Wynter was off the bed and on his feet like a snarling cat. But the archbishop remained unfazed and unruffled as the enraged lordling stalked him, mayhem being his object.

"Lift finger against me and you condemn your friends to die. The gaoler has his orders." With a stifled cry the defeated herald turned away, leaning dejectedly against the chimney place, staring unseeingly into the fire. Helpless. He was at the mercy of this man and his lecherous king.

"There is a way to solve our contretemps. Sit down and I will explain."

"I'd rather stand."

Cranmer chose not to object. "His British Majesty has sent me here personally to treat with you. First, let me make it clear you have no bargaining power. Your fate rests with me. I have in my possession eleven death warrants, signed and stamped with royal seal. And if I should wish, eleven confessions to confirm their righteousness. Yours has already been heard, and there are ways of making the most loyal friends and servants say what they think the court wants to hear. Which, as we both know, would be simple truth. But for what would you all be giving your lives? To save the nonexistent reputation of a harlot whose whoring is the talk of all Europe? Come now, my friend, you have better sense. The other side of the coin is—if one is convicted of adultery, what of the other? Is she not equally guilty? Naturally, his British Majesty would not, could not sentence his own sister to hang—"

"I thought stoning was prescribed."

"The advantage of hanging is that all voices quickly cease. You can see, His Majesty faces something of a dilemma."

"Good! Tell him to let us go free!"

"That would not satisfy the Douglases. No, if it were left to me, I would simply send you to join your friends and let you perish one by one in the Little Ease beneath St. John's Chapel Crypt."

"There will be talk—"

"There already is. Your melodramatic departure did not escape notice. It would be a matter of great embarrassment if the subject of your disappearance should come up during Henry's visit to France this week for the holding of the Second Field of Cloth of Gold."

"He should have thought of that before arresting me."

"What choice had he, the Pope's own proclaimed Defender of the Faith? Of course, the issue being ecclesiastical did not solve the problem of the immunities conferred by your tabard and collar. Naturally, no monarch in his right mind would kill an envoy, a messenger. That would border on an act of war. But killing an adulterer, that would be within his rights. And think how that would enhance His Majesty's own unblemished—"

"Ha!"

"Unblemished reputation. Then again, there is the matter of his sister. And the delicate negotiations for the marriage of the Lady Mary Tudor. You did, of course, know of them." Cranmer wished the man would turn round; his profile, though illuminated to its handsomest advantage by the firelight, helped Cranmer not one bit in judging how well his talk was being received. Despite that, it was time to come to the crux of the matter. No sign of this crossed the archbishop's face nor found its way into his tone of voice.

"It occurred to me, and His Majesty reluctantly agreed, that there might be a way, short of your deaths, to silence our gossips and confound our critics. For did not Our Lord Jesus address the adulterous woman, according to the Gospel of St. John, thusly: ' "Woman where are those thine accusers? Hath no man condemned thee?" She said, "No man, Lord." And Jesus said unto her, "Neither do I condemn thee: Go, and sin no more." ' "

Cranmer's voice died away momentarily. Then he began again, his voice tinged with real reverence. "Then did He not say also: 'I am the light of the world: he that followeth me shall not walk in the darkness, but shall have the light of life.' "

De Wynter listened carefully; what he heard puzzled and disturbed him. Standing upright, he turned and faced his judge. Cranmer's eyes were closed, the expression on his face genuine. Servant of king he might be, but he served another, less worldly monarch also. He was a true religious. De Wynter feared him more. The Church in the name of religion did most ungodly heinous things.

Cranmer opened his eyes and stared straight at him. "If you should follow Jesus . . ."

"Follow how?" De Wynter's eyes narrowed. In his gut, he dreaded this answer.

"Take orders. A genuine act of contrition. Then could no man criticize you, His Majesty and your Dowager Queen."

"No!" De Wynter's gut spoke.

"Think on it. Take as long as you like. But remember your friends. My Lord Keeper tells me one, he that is named Gilliver, might not make it through another day and night."

De Wynter groaned. What matter thinking on it? He had no choice. But still he might bargain. "And if I do, what of my friends?"

"The dyester's pole, unless—"

De Wynter clutched at straws. "Unless—?"

"Unless you were to act immediately and join an order based far from this shore. One in need of fighting men. Then I see no reason why your men might not depart with you."

"You have an order in mind." De Wynter accused him point-blank. "The Templars."

"That heretic group? Never. Besides, the next thing we'd know they'd have you in France at their temple there. No, we had another in mind."

"Well?"

Cranmer let him stew a little, but de Wynter, gambling for eleven lives, could well wait him out. Finally, Cranmer gracefully gave in. "We thought perhaps since you were so familiar with St. John—"

"No, not them. Not the Order of the Knights of St. John."

"I told His Majesty you'd know them."

De Wynter's voice was bitter. "Who does not know of the Knights Hospitaler late of Rhodes, now of Malta? You might as well sentence me and my men to death if you send us to defend that bare pile of rock out in the ocean."

"That well might be, but is it not better to die, sword in hand, the name of the Lord on your tongue, than at the end of a rope?"

De Wynter had no ready answer. The whole plan was so well thought out. An order of nobles, respected fighting men, one of whose canons was celibacy. What better proof and proclamation to the courts of Europe that this was a true act of contrition? Desperately, he sought for a loophole through which he might wiggle, but he knew there was none. Nor, if Gilliver's life were not to be wasted, could he take time making up his mind.

"If I were to agree?"

"The order would welcome you." And your fortune, Cranmer thought to himself. "We have the word of Sir John Carlby, the order's Turcopolier, on it. However, he offers you the haven of the order only if you join immediately."

"Immediately?"

"Tonight. So, James Mackenzie, what will you have? The life of a novice or no life at all? Make your choice."

Swallowing his pride, de Wynter opened his mouth to beg mercy; then, knowing it was no use, he swallowed his words and merely nodded.

"You agree then?" Cranmer was secretly delighted; already he could see Henry's reaction: Carlby appeased, Hampton Court saved, the too-desirable Scots herald gone, sailing to Malta on the same tide taking the King of England and Marquess Pembroke to France aboard the *Henry Grace à Dieu*, the selfsame ship that had a dozen years before, on the last day of May, taken Henry and Catherine to France.

"Know you then, the Right Honorable the Earl of Seaforth, James Mackenzie, that by token of this genuine act of contrition, the ecclesiastical court invoked this tenth day of October, in the year of our Lord 1532 is hereby adjourned, *res adjudicata. Dieu vous garde.*

"You will be taken directly to the priory of the hospices of St. John of Jerusalem, at the temple outside London near Westminster. Sir John awaits you there. And, my lord, do not attempt escape. Not till word comes you have arrived safely will your men be released."

"Will you at least raise the door, to give them fresh air?"

Cranmer considered. The thought appealed to his basic humanitarianism. "I see no problem with that. Perhaps you would even care to send a message, one personally reassuring?"

What to say to convince them not to fight, nor yet to give up hope. "Tell them I turned the ring on my hand and a roar was heard. Follow me!"

286

It was Cranmer's turn to be puzzled. "You turned the ring on your hand and a roar was heard?"

De Wynter nodded. "Don't forget 'follow me!' ''

"You have my word on it. My Lord Gaoler," he said, not raising his voice, "present yourself."

He might have said "Open Sesame," so promptly did the door open. "This man accompanies you. But he should not go half dressed. His collar, if you please. Send the bill for his keep to the Knights Hospitaler. For such a fighter as this, with ten men at arms, they should be willing to reimburse the king his generosity."

CHAPTER 18

On his way back up the Thames in a small but strong-poled, well-oared wherry, there was no Thomas Notte to spend de Wynter's time and fill his ears with such tidbits of information as that his destination was originally the seat in England of the Order of Templars, The Poor Knights of Christ and of the Temple of Solomon. When they moved elsewhere, the buildings passed into the hands of the Hospitalers, who leased all but the consecrated buildings to certain professors of common law, half of whom formed a society known as the Middle Temple, the rest the Inner.

From the river, Notte would have been quick to note that of greatest interest were the large, elaborate gardens where partisans of the Houses of York and Lancaster plucked the living badges that gave odor to that famous hundred-year-long series of "cousin wars" known as the War of the Roses.

As the wherry landed, thousands of starlings, roosting in the tree-lined approach to the Temple Church, took umbrage at being disturbed and took wind in a storm of flutters and angry calls.

"They be back," said the Yeoman Warder, who looked like Thomas Notte. "They be like the ravens at the Tower. Too lazy and well fed ever to take their leave for long. They say that if either starling or raven permanently disappear, it will mean the fall of the Temples of Law or Tower of London."

The Temple, although not a fortress, was indeed much like the Tower, both actually being a composite of buildings with a central

288

core. The Norman castle-keep for the Tower, the Norman round-church of St. Mary for the Temple. De Wynter's destination now was the hospice. It resembled an inn, but its windows were palisaded with wood tempered hard as metal, the ends of which were buried within the casing of the window. The doors, made of plank atop plank, bolted and banded, could have withstood fire or siege. The floors and walls were of stone, the ceiling twice a man's height. De Wynter feared he had exchanged one prison for another that had no fireplace to ward off the cold of the coming night.

For the next hour or so, he came to grips with reality. He would join the Order and persuade his men to do the same, that way saving all their lives. The Scot knew the order by reputation. There was no more fearsome fighting band in all of Europe. They and they alone had fought Suleiman the Magnificent to a stand-still, wrestling an honorable retreat from the victorious Moslems at Rhodes. Then they had traded with the Holy Roman Emperor: the defense of Tripoli for the archipelago of Malta with its satellite island of Gozo.

He could handle the fighting well. The religious life would probably not be unduly onerous. But the celibacy. That would take getting used to. De Wynter, being honest with himself and remembering well the way his body had its own way when denied release within woman, felt sure his body would take care of itself. But music, dancing, feminine company—these would be far more difficult to forego. Besides, the strict arbitrary discipline of life in the order was something he detested. He had been his own man too long to curtail his actions at the whim of someone else.

The creaking of the door gave him notice that his solitude was to be interrupted. He barely dared hope that Cranmer would keep his word so promptly, but he was mistaken. The archbishop wanted quickly to rid the Tower of all trace of these potentially diplomatically dangerous Scottish guests.

As the men entered the room, Drummond and Fionn supporting Gilliver between them, de Wynter cursed himself. For love of a woman he had tarried too long at Hampton and his men had paid the price. They were pale and gaunt, their faces mangy with straggly beginnings of beards. Most had lost weight, and their garments hung from them. Their bodies reeked, dank hair to bare feet, of human waste. Yet never had de Wynter been happier to see them or quicker to take each in his arms and hug them close. To Gilliver they gave the bed; the rest, once the greetings were past, squatted uncomfortably on the floor. As usual the others deferred to Drummond, who, next to Gilliver, personified the group's version of human perfection.

"We thank you for getting us out, Jamie."

De Wynter did not spare himself. "What else could I do? I was the one who put you in. Believe me, my friends, not for all the wealth in the world, not for my son Jamie nor my country, would I have knowingly subjected you to such an ordeal."

"We knew that. We can guess how you had us put in." Drummond grinned knowingly and de Wynter loved him again. "But how did you get us out?"

"That was the easiest part. All I had do was make a small promise."

Menzies was the first to voice his suspicions. "What small promise?"

"The king and his archbishop on behalf of country and Church have seen fit to attempt to disgrace me. They charged me with adultery—"

Cameron interrupted approvingly, "Good for you, you made the Boleyn."

"No, as matter of fact, I did not."

"Then who—?"

"Margaret Tudor." He could almost enjoy their cries of outraged amazement.

"Her?"

"What's new about that?"

Drummond, not easily diverted from the scent, returned to the point. "You mentioned a small promise?"

"To join the Order of the Knights of St. John of Jerusalem and Malta."

The others were stunned by such news, all but Drummond. "That seems not a very small promise to me."

It was as if he and de Wynter were the only two in the room.

"In the weighing, it seemed small."

"As compared to what? Our lives, perhaps?"

"Perhaps." To deny the truth would have been fruitless; besides, a touch of guilt might make his task easier. "Think on it. On the one

290

hand, scandal and disgrace whatever the results of the trial. On the other, a life of adventure, of travel to exotic lands, rich ransoms, all the fighting I could ask for, and all in the name of Our Lord Jesus Christ and His Apostle, St. John.''

"You never struck me as a particularly religious man," Drummond observed, not fooled at all by the fake enthusiasm de Wynter had mustered.

"Comes a time in every man's life when he grows closer to his Maker.''

"Amen," came the weak response from the pallet. Gilliver had roused at the speaking of his Savior's name. Raising himself onto one elbow with great difficulty, he looked the face of death, yet his eyes glowed with the fervor of a zealot. "Jamie, I beg you, let me go with you. I too would fight for Christ.''

De Wynter hurried to his side. "Lie back, little friend, save your strength." Gilliver was too exhausted to protest, but one hand clutched his friend's sleeve with surprising strength, not letting go until he had extracted a promise that he too could join the order.

De Wynter, staring down at his weakened friend, cursed himself for what his lusting had done to one who had trusted him totally. Never again, he vowed silently, will your love for me cause you anguish. I swear it.

"And what of us, Jamie?" Drummond asked.

De Wynter paused a moment or two to compose his thoughts, for here came the ticklish part. "Are we not companions?" he temporized.

But Drummond cut through to the quick. "Was that small promise more inclusive than you mentioned earlier?"

De Wynter couldn't trust himself to speak; instead, he shrugged in that typically Gallic way he had. The rest read the answer aright. Not for a long moment did anyone speak; then it was usually taciturn Angus:

"I ha' always wanted to see more of the world than our wee highlands.''

"Aye," confirmed Ogilvy.

Drummond, too, could put a brave face on it. "Fighting for God would be a welcome change. I think I'd like that.''

"Talk of travel and fighting all you want," Menzies groused, "but you all forget to mention that the order's celibate.''

"Celibate?" Cameron protested, horrified. "You mean as in no women? Jamie, I beg you, tell me it isn't so!"

The others smiled in spite of themselves at the look of desolation on their lusty companion's face. But before de Wynter could answer, the huge door to the room creaked open, and in walked a knight wearing a floor-length surcoat, a red cross boldly emblazoned upon chest and back. He was not a young man, nor particularly old. But his face belied the more youthful-looking body. It was a face stamped with character, sharply chiseled, weather-beaten. The eyes told of worldly things they had seen and dangers they had survived. There's a battler, de Wynter thought. He's a tough one hiding behind the cloth. He would never best you with his size, but with his head. And that's the kind to have on your side when the going is rough.

The knight surveyed the room. The group looked a sorry sight, but no one knew better than John Carlby how desperately the order needed fighting men. Having been nearly decimated by the forces of Suleiman, the order was beleaguered. Driven from their fortress on Rhodes, the remnants of the order were attempting to fortify Malta, make it their new headquarters. The need for fighting men had convinced Carlby to abandon his claim to Hampton Court. It was a claim—no one knew better than he—which was somewhat spurious and would have been nearly impossible to press, especially through Henry's own courts.

Despite their bedraggled appearance, Carlby decided it had been a good trade: one tenuous claim surrendered in return for eleven men, at least seven of whom looked to be more than familiar with weaponry.

"I am John Carlby, Turcopolier to the Order of St. John of Jerusalem, Rhodes and Malta. I bid you welcome, brothers, to the service of our Lord Jesus Christ. Now, if you would be so kind as to introduce yourselves . . . ?"

The leader, Carlby knew without having to be told, was James Mackenzie. Even though he was prepared, the sight of that famous mane of hair took Carlby by surprise. He had expected white hair, not mingling shades of silver and pewter. This was indescribable. This was de Wynter hair. Watching the leader, he listened carefully as one by one, in order of precedence, down to the lowest serving man, the others named themselves.

Drawing on his long experience as leader and armorer of fighting men, Carlby decided himself well pleased by his catch, except, perhaps, for Edward Gilliver. Yet, he admitted, the order needed its share of the religious as well as the warring, and maybe this clerkly type might find a place within the hospital from which the Order derived its pseudonym of "Knights Hospitalers."

The naming over, Carlby explained the initial taking of vows would occur this very night, but first, each man would be given a chance to bathe and dress. One by one, the men were ushered from the large room and led to smaller, individual rooms. The spartan nature of the cells brought home the fact that soon they would join a monastic order, one not known for indulging the softer needs of the body and human nature.

Having bathed and shaved earlier, de Wynter now had time to consider on how to extricate himself and his followers from this mess. Henry VIII with one stroke of the pen could free them. Would a petition to him be heard? Not a chance. But perhaps to the Holy Father himself? A letter to his friend the Cardinal of Naples, secretary of the Curia, might open a legal means of egress from the order. Then, too, he had friends, influential female friends. Not to mention a mother who would raise heaven and hell to see him free. But would Scotland's king and dowager queen be quite so willing to lend support when the threat of scandal hung over their heads? No, he must work within the Church if he would leave the Church.

Pounding on his door brought a serving brother to the grill. "If you please, a quill and ink. I need to collect my thoughts and leave instructions for the care of my estate." Seeing nothing wrong with such a natural request, the brown-robed, barefooted monk was soon back with writing implements.

The petition to Clement VIII took most thought. It must be obedient and respectful while subtly proving his unfitness for Holy Orders. The letter to the Prince of the Church was more plain-spoken, going into the matter in great detail. The third letter gave him the greatest trouble. It was addressed to his mother. Besides requesting that she forward the other two, he must reassure and comfort her and at least partially confide in her. At the last moment, he added a loving postscript to his son.

Folding the two letters bound for Europe as flat as possible, he put them within that addressed to his mother. At the last minute, he took up quill again and penned an agonized message to Anne, assuring her of his love and begging her to go to Scotland where he was sure he would be able to join her later. This letter too was flattened and placed within the covering one. The whole was then sealed with wax. How he would get it to her he wasn't sure. But for the delivery of this precious packet, he was well prepared to sacrifice one or more of his two pearls.

Working with teeth and nails, he tore open the lining of his tabard and transferred the two lustrous, nacre gems to his purse.

The peal of bells tolled matins soon enough. Doors opened, and the eleven candidates were accompanied to the chapel by brothers of the order. Only those of noble birth would be received as novice knights. The others would be initiated into serving orders as lay brothers. The companions—all but Gilliver who was bastard—proceeded forward to be draped in enveloping floor-length chasubles of blood-red silk. Red is the color of love, especially the love of martyrs, a fate pursued avidly by the Knights Hospitalers. The others wore robes of loose brown sackcloth, similar to those worn by the ordinary monks escorting them.

The chapel was small, but ornately presented. Stained-glass windows depicting feats of the Hospitalers defending Jerusalem filled one wall of the room, floor to ceiling. The moon shining through them gave pale suggestion of their sun-struck brilliance.

John Carlby, the highest-ranking member of the order at present in England, headed the processional toward the small but richly endowed altar where vessels glinted in golden hues. The silken white robe of the Turcopolier shimmered in the candlelight as he moved up the aisle. At the apse he met another procession, that of monks chanting in Latin, with the high priest in their midst. The two fanons of the bishop's miter streamed down over shoulders familiar to de Wynter, the thin, bowed ones of Archbishop Cranmer.

Seated on the bishop's throne against the center of the back wall, Cranmer permitted himself a small smile of approval. Henry VIII would indeed be pleased by the works of this day and night. Even the Holy Father himself would be forced to approve this slight stretching of ecclesiastical precedent, especially if he were never notified of the circumstances.

294

Cranmer made mental note to remind Carlby that these initial vows could be overthrown within the courts of the Church if any word got out that the candidates had been coerced. It was up to Carlby to intercept any messages and foil any gossip. Cranmer had done his part, delivering eleven men in return for a quick-claim release of all rents for Hampton Court Palace.

The mass was beginning, and thoughts of all else fled the mind of this devoted churchman . . . but only temporarily.

At last, the Call to Holy Orders began:

"Let those come forward who are to be accepted into the Order of the Knights of St. John of Jerusalem," intoned Carlby, naming the six robed in red, one by one. Each answered as prompted, *"Adsum,"* and moved forward to kneel before the seated Cranmer.

"Let those come forward who wish to serve within the Order of the Knights of St. John of Jerusalem," Carlby continued, naming the five brown-robed men, who knelt in a second or outer circle beyond the six noble-born.

"Do you know these men to be worthy?" Cranmer rhetorically questioned Carlby.

"As far as human frailty allows us to know, I do know, and I attest them to be worthy of the charge and honor of this office."

"Thanks be to God," said Cranmer. "Let us remember, however, what Saint Paul spake to Timothy, admonishing him, 'Lay not hands hastily upon no man, neither be a partaker of other men's sins.' Thus, lest one, or several, be mistaken in their judgment of their righteousness or err through affection, the opinion of many must be asked. And so, whatever you know of their lives or character, whatever you think of their merit, make it known now freely. If, therefore, anyone has anything against one of these, before God and for the sake of God, let him come forth and speak in confidence."

De Wynter had opened his mouth to speak out when Cranmer silenced him with, "Nevertheless, let him be mindful of his own condition. Speak, dearly beloved brethren, are these men worthy?"

"They are worthy," replied the deep bass voices of the whole communion of monks. Cranmer paused, letting those words echo throughout the stone interior of the chapel. "Then, beloved sons whom our brethren have chosen to be accepted into the community of this order and of the Holy Catholic Church, I exhort you: preserve in your behavior the integrity of a chaste and holy life. Know what you are doing; imitate what you administer; see that you mortify in your members all sin and concupiscence. Let the order of your life be a delight to the Church of Christ so that neither I, for promoting you, nor you, for accepting such great office, shall be condemned by the Lord, but rather that we shall merit to be rewarded. Which may He grant us through His grace.''

''Amen,'' came the chanted response.

Cranmer turned to the altar and knelt, leaning on his faldstool. At the whispered admonition of Carlby, the eleven men prostrated themselves, resting heads on joined forearms. Within the kneeling congregation, one voice began the Litany of the Saints, the rest chanting the responses.

Then, Cranmer bid all to rise and the candidates to come forward. De Wynter and Drummond . . . Menzies and Cameron . . . the rest also two by two, Fionn bringing up the rear. Upon the head of each, Cranmer rested his hand lightly. When the last had passed, Cranmer said, ''Let us pray, beloved brethren, to God the Father Almighty, that upon these His servants, He may multiply heavenly gifts; and that what they have undertaken through His gracious condescension, they may accomplish with His aid. Through Christ our Lord.''

''Amen.''

''The Lord be with you.''

''And with your spirit.''

''Approach me.''

One by one the candidates approached, in order of precedence, Cranmer reaching forward and taking their two hands between his. ''Do you promise me and my successors reverence and obedience?''

De Wynter's mouth tightened but he said nothing.

Cranmer tightened his hands as much as possible upon the unwilling ones between his, yet his strength was not great enough, de Wynter's resolve being greater, to force a response. Then, Cranmer nodded as if having heard a whispered response and leaning forward, still holding the Scot earl's hands in his, he kissed him on the right cheek, saying ''May the peace of the Lord be always with you.''

Releasing de Wynter, he signed for the next to approach, and so they did, one after another, each promising obedience and reverence.

Finally, Cranmer arose and blessed the new members of this fighting order. "May the blessing of Almighty God, the Father, the Son, and the Holy Ghost, descend upon you, that you may be blessed in the priestly order, and that you may offer for the sins and offenses of the people propitiatory sacrifices to Almighty God, to whom is honor and glory forever and ever."

To which all replied, even de Wynter, "Amen."

CHAPTER 19

They left the chapter house within the hour, to sail on the onflooding tide. Shooting the bridge by torchlight was even more heart-stopping than in daylight, yet the bargemen of the order, trusting in God, made less to do of it than had Notte. As daylight slowly diffused itself from within a bank of purple clouds and the face of the White Tower was touched with gold, the scene in the pool was gradually revealed. More than 900 vessels could find docking space within this great pool—Upper, Lower, and Middle—yet in the half-light, it looked more like a ship's graveyard; the deserted wintering hulks there, their masts and spars bare, their sails full-furled, resembled unfleshed skeletons, not sailing ships.

All except one—a spectacularly red-and-gold ship of the line—it bustled with lights, and the sounds of voices wafted eerily across the waters of the pool. From behind de Wynter's shoulder came the disembodied words of Carlby: "Harry, by Grace of God, King of England, sails upon the tide for France. He attends there the Second Field of Cloth of Gold, may God bless his endeavors and have mercy on the wife he leaves behind, as he is accompanied by another."

Not by gesture or grimace did de Wynter display his dejection; instead he seemed lost in study of the Thames. Beyond the entrance to the Millwall Docks where the *Henry à Grace Dieu* was loading, were landmarks of a different kind, also indicative of the king's rule: gaunt gibbet posts bearing bones of pirates left to bleach and dance to the music of creaking chains.

Once beyond these, the lower portion of the yellow pool channels the river into wayward and eccentric habits, broadening and curling, and seeming at every turn, especially when the tide comes in, more like a long chain of lakes than a river. With so much meandering and moving about, it seemed only natural to give every straight stretch of the river the name of Reach: Limehouse Reach, Greenwich Reach, Blackwall Reach, Bugsby's Reach, Woolwich Reach, Gallion's Reach, and so on until they reached the most magnificent reach of them all: Gravesend.

There the novice knights boarded the merchant ship *Annunciata.* Thence to Yantlet Creek was fifteen miles, from the Creek to the Nore Lightship another five nautical miles, and then they would be at sea. And still de Wynter had found no way to expedite his messages, the monastic brothers manning the barge being incorruptible. His only chance appeared to be the ship's husband. This land-agent, who had seen to the berthing, repairs, and provisioning of the ship for the owners, was the only one who'd leave the ship at the Nore, just before the open seas. In the space of moments de Wynter managed to press upon him both pearl and packet and secure his promise to send the letter north by messenger.

Unknown to de Wynter, his knightly shadow had seen the exchange. Before the ship's husband disembarked, he was further enriched, and the packet had left his possession and found its way into Carlby's purse.

The *Annunciata* left sight of the beacon ship at 5:00 A.M. on Friday, October 11, 1532. With luck—prodigious amounts of it—she would return to England by mid-December. Part of her problem was her captain. Although the compass's "constant needle" had guided ships for more than two centuries, there was no compass aboard the *Annunciata.* Her hoary captain had sailed with Columbus on a voyage where the needle failed. He could still—forty years later— remember the fear that failure had engendered. Ever since, he'd put his trust in the sun, the moon, the stars, landfalls—not the navigator's needle. Thus, on this journey to the Mediterranean, he chose to hug the coast of Europe rather than striking due south.

Across the Channel to Calais they went, getting a preview of the reception planned for the English king and his entourage. From there, they leap-frogged to Le Havre and thence to Cherbourg and on to Brest. Now, a long stretch of sea faced them as they worked their way, using both lateen sail and slave power across the Bay of Biscay. Finally, striking the coast of Spain to the east of La Coruña, they tacked close to shore and slowly made their way westward to the outermost tip of the Holy Roman Empire's landmass. At La Coruña, they took on water, and the passengers disembarked, ascending to the top of the Torre de Hercules. Don Federico was tempted to sail without them, so that he might squeeze on a few more tons of cargo to trade for candy wine on Cyprus. Only the fear of pirates made him sound the horn to summon the Hospitalers back to the ship. Those twelve fighting men might make all the difference in repulsing a pirate attack.

Once the *Annunciata* reached Gibraltar, a choice would have to be made: to take the fast, risky southern route or the safer, longer, northerly one to Cartagena, passing between Valencia and the Balearic Islands and up to Barcelona, across the Gulf of Lions to Marseilles, through the Ligurian Sea, keeping Corsica to starboard, down the boot to the tip and through the straits of Messina, thence due east to Greece and then south to Crete. Going this way would take twice as long, forcing a return trip during the fierce storms that lashed the Mediterranean from mid-November to April. The ship's captain, Don Federico, had tasted the winds of Solano, the hot, dust-laden winds that make men giddy and irritable and a crew almost unruly. It was not a pleasant choice.

On the other hand, the shorter route would take the *Annunciata* perilously close to the coast of Ifriqiya where Barbarossa laid up for the winter in Algiers, his fleet divided between his own capital and neighboring Tunis. Not before Tripoli, that fortress on the mainland under the protection of the Knights Hospitalers, would this merchant ship find friendly port.

Deliberately, Don Federico did not make up his mind. A word in his sleep overheard by one of his youthful bed partners and Barbarossa might be alerted. It was common knowledge that Barbarossa had his spies, even in English ports, plus a communications chain, stretching from one end of the Mediterranean to the other, that notified Algiers of departure date, destination, sailing plan, and most especially cargo manifest.

The *Annunciata*'s cargo was a mixed one. The usual woolen

goods, and a few great barrels of Scots whiskey, an experiment. But most of the space below ship was taken up by weapons from the fine armament shops in and around London. And beggars—a large contingent of them.

Nothing pleased the captain less than the bunch of dirty, thieving beggars in his hold. He had reluctantly taken them aboard and agreed to drop them off at the first possible port only because their transport meant ready money and sailing clearance. The king's men had been eager to pay a nice sum to get these beggars out of England.

"Clap them in jail," suggested the captain, but the king's justice had demurred.

"We have need of our jails for traitors and criminals, not beggars. Besides, they have friends among the people."

The ship was cramped. Jammed with cargo and sailors and slave-oarsmen and passengers. Only one cabin existed, and that, occupied by the captain and his two cabin boys, was small and roughly furnished. Even if the captain had offered it, the Hospitalers wouldn't have accepted, preferring to rig up clean-smelling quarters on deck.

Carlby didn't wait for their arrival in Malta to start testing his new recruits' knowledge of weaponry, languages, and religion—the three things they needed to know to succeed in the order. The serving brothers were no more adept at any of the three than he expected, except for Gilliver, whose knowledge of religion proved exceptional, and Fionn, who'd been well coached by Seamus in weaponry. As for the novice knights, he was gratifyingly surprised. Only in religion did he find them less than totally proficient; that and the Arabic tongue. The latter he set out to rectify immediately:

"You have an advantage, being Scots; many of the Arabic consonants will come easily to your tongue. Take *ra*, for example, it's rolled as you do your *r*s, not fricative as in English. *Kha* is another good one. It's sounded like the *ch* in *loch*. The only trouble is sometimes *kha* initiates a word. Try and say *loch* backward and you'll see what I mean.

"As in most languages, the commonest verbs in Arabic are irregular, but it has fewer than most. One thing you'll find confusing is that the verbs *have* and *be* do not exist. Also, verbs have no tenses, only two forms which show completed or incomplete actions. Since my only goal is to make you able to understand and command the slaves rowing in our galleys, most of whom are Arabs, not to turn you into Arab scholars, we'll concern ourselves here only with the spoken language, not bothering with the written one. That's too confusing, for one reads and writes Arabic completely opposite to English—going from right to left. Numbers, however, go from left to right as ours do. Repeat after me: *affamsu* . . . the sun; *albahru* . . . the sea; *arrajulu* . . . the man; *yadun* . . . hand; *paynun* . . . eye; *zamrun* . . . wine; . . .''

He found his pupils a mixed lot. Some, such as Angus and Ogilvy, would never command more than a passing knowledge of the tongue. Others, such as Drummond and Menzies, struggled hard and made slow progress. Cameron learned those words he thought would be beneficial to him, such as *beautiful, love,* and others that would work on women. De Wynter and Gilliver were the stars of the group, the latter because of his scholarly bent, the former seizing upon these studies as a narcotic to quell his troubled thoughts. Upon these two, Carlby lavished much time, even going so far as to begin teaching them to read and write the Semite tongue.

During the course of the lessons, Carlby also taught them of the order and its troubled history. Once there had been nine Langues, or houses with a common tongue. However, the numbers of the order had dwindled to such an extent that several Langues had been forced to combine with others. The English one, for example, now also encompassed Scotland. The rivalry between those two nations created more than a few headaches for the Turcopolier, or ''Pillar'' of the English Langue.

When Suleiman the Magnificent had driven the Knights into the sea off the Isle of Rhodes, he had allowed the remnants of the order to escape, knowing they had no home and believing they would disband and never be a problem again. However, Charles V of Spain, the Holy Roman Emperor, listened to the Knights' pleas for help and granted them the Maltese Archipelago in exchange for their promise to defend Tripoli against the Ottomans. He also exacted the payment of one Maltese falcon each year, a formality which would continue to affirm the fact that Malta was under the suzerainty of Spain.

Thus it was that Philip Villiers de l'Isle Adam, the order's

Grandmaster, was able to issue a rallying cry throughout Christendom, calling for additional men to help the order build Malta into a powerful headquarters. And for the same reason, John Carlby had been in England trying to raise funds as well as manpower.

A genuinely religious man, Carlby believed with all his heart that God had made him one of the survivors at Rhodes. And now he believed just as fervently that Henry VIII had been used by God to the good of the order.

Normally, the *Annunciata* would have stopped to trade at Lisbon, the richest town in Europe, but that city had been nearly leveled by an earthquake the year before and disease was still rampant. Instead, Don Federico set sail for Cabo de São Vicente, the huge rocky plateau with red brown precipices rising sheer above the sea. After rounding this cape, the *Annunciata* had choice of ports: Sagres, founded by Henry the Navigator as headquarters for his explorations of the African coast . . . or Cadiz, the Gadir of the Phoenicians and Gades of the Romans, and the fortress-city guarding the river-route to Seville. Here, the beggars the ship carried might well be sold, as the Spanish were always in need of slaves. However, one of Don Federico's wives lived here, and to enter Cadiz might result in a lengthy delay.

Don Federico decided it would be wiser to head straight for the Straits of Gibraltar. Between the ocean and the inland sea run strong currents, and uncertain winds cause serious problems for sailing vessels; Don Federico ordered all canvas furled and the oars out.

Three of the serving men and Angus and Ogilvy suffered with seasickness, but the other companions were weathering the voyage reasonably well. De Wynter, himself an excellent sailor, tried to amuse himself with card games in his spare time. Tiring of these, he played games of dominoes with Gilliver and Carlby. Winning can grow boring, especially if one's opponents are not one's match. Carlby, seeing this, suggested he explore the nooks and crannies of the ship. "Now would be a good time to go below, before the hold gets so befouled with the stench of wet wool and dirty men that one can take no more than a few minutes without coming up for air."

The fetid air assailed de Wynter's nostrils before he reached the third rung of the ladder. He pressed on and came across the band of beggars chained to one another and to the masts and bulkheads.

Sickened at the sight, he was also fascinated by the hapless group who immediately tried to practice their wiles on him.

Among the group were dommers, who "swallowed" their tongues and pretended to be dumb. Others were truly deformed individuals, either born that way or deliberately mutilated by their parents so that they might beg. There were contortionists who could twist their bodies grotesquely. And one other—a pickpocket whom the king's constables had thrown in with the beggars, a short, wiry, monkey-faced man, to whom the others seemed to look for leadership.

"You there," de Wynter said to him. "What are you doing down here?"

"You addressed me, lord? John the Rob at your service." The man attempted within the confines of his chains to bow and scrape. "To answer your question, your good King Hal has sent us south for our health. But somehow the captain of this fine sailing ship did not get the message right. Instead of 'Land them in Spain,' he heard 'Hand them in chains.' Perhaps you could inform him of his error, milord?"

His followers tittered. Even de Wynter was amused by the cheek of this swarthy son of England. "Rest assured, I shall give him your message."

"Oh, we'll rest all right. Nothing much else to do in this stinking hole. Fare you well, lord," John the Rob called after the departing Scot. "Come back and visit us anytime."

The insolence of the man, his cheerfulness under such circumstances, the wry grin on his wizened monkey-face lingered in de Wynter's mind and later that day, he questioned the captain about the beggars.

"Why the chains, you ask? To save the ship from their thieving hands. They'd steal the bread right out of your mouth. I've seen their like before. The only way I takes them is chained hand and foot."

"But some are crippled."

"The cripples are the worst."

"But where would they go? We're in the middle of the ocean."

"They're like magicians, they'd disappear in thin air."

Faced with such stupid stubbornness, de Wynter made up his mind to get the beggars freed. To this end, he broached Carlby.

"That hole is really foul. An absolute stink-hole. Perfect breeding ground for the pox. In fact, I would not be surprised if the smells coming from down there weren't the cause of Angus and Ogilvy's sickness."

The condition of a bunch of beggars bothered Carlby not at all. No man who had lived through a Moslem siege as he had at Rhodes would be bothered by man's inhumanity to man. But if the condition of the beggars should affect that of his new recruits, that was a different story. With de Wynter following on his heels, Carlby was off to beard the captain. A word from this martial churchman and the beggars were set free to clean themselves up, as well as the filth in the hole. Once clean, they were under orders to stay that way.

"And if I see one of you above deck, I'll clap you back in chains and, if you are able-bodied, set you to rowing," the captain threatened.

As the beggars hastily and loudly protested their good intentions, John the Rob caught de Wynter's eye and dropped him a wink. De Wynter was not surprised the next day to find the wizened little man standing alongside him as he leaned against the rail and watched the coast with its squares of white houses topped with colorful chimney pots.

"What are you doing up here?"

"Same as you, milord, admiring the view."

"I wouldn't think any view worth the risk of being rechained."

"No, nor of rowing. Look at those wretches, any one of them would gladly change places with one of us down in the hold. No, milord, not for any view—even of the Sultan's seraglio unveiled— would I risk rowing. But to say a word of thanks for your help . . ."

De Wynter was embarrassed, especially when John the Rob continued. "And if ever we beggars may be of help to you, make this sign, holding the little finger so, the pointer crooked like this."

Although de Wynter brushed the idea off lightly, the little man refused to scurry back to shelter until de Wynter had proven he could duplicate the gesture. Then, the beggar-chief was gone without another word, flitting from shelter of bale to protection of barrel. With a final wave, he was gone from sight.

De Wynter turned his survey to the galley and its slave-rowers. Chained six to a twenty-foot oar, they rowed, ate, slept, and defecated where they sat in irons. These are the fortunes of war, de Wynter reminded himself. He was glad John the Rob had not been discovered above deck. He did not think the beggar would last long if forced to strain muscles for hours at a time, with whips cracking about arms and backs that faltered. Especially favored for flogging, de Wynter observed, was a slim redhead who felt the whip over and over again yet was not cowed.

The slaves worked well in unison, muscles bulging and breaths gasping as each stroke fairly shot the ship ahead toward the straits. Sometimes the oars flashed even though the sails were full of wind. Don Federico was running against the calendar, as Carlby had explained.

Finally, the whipmaster sounded the drum, signaling an all-too-brief rest period. But many of the men exchanged one kind of work for another, carving bones or pieces of wood scavenged from heaven knew where.

"They're making scrimshaw," Carlby said, joining him. "They hope to sell it to a mujmil at the next port for food or clothes or even freedom. Faint chance of that last. But hope dies hard, and they all carve in the belief it might someday buy them their freedom."

"Are they any good?"

"Oh, yes. Come see for yourself."

The best of the carvers, de Wynter soon discovered, was the redhead, not much older than himself. With a piece of broken chain-link and a bent carpenter's nail, he had transformed pieces of bone into wondrous animals, the likes of which de Wynter had never seen.

After watching him perform during several rest periods, de Wynter struck up a conversation with him, though the oarmaster stayed nearby and kept a greedy ear open to the entire conversation.

"Where did you learn to carve such animals?" de Wynter asked in his halting and limited Arabic.

"The carving I have done since I was a little boy, *al rabb;* the animals are common to my native Ifriqiya. Like this one I work on now."

"May I see it?"

The redhead handed up the carving—less than the length of a

306

man's finger, half lion and half fish—and waited expectantly for the reaction.

"You have actually seen one of these?" de Wynter asked incredulously.

"Other than on the chests of your companions?" The redhead grinned, his white teeth shining against his sun-blackened skin. He gestured broadly. "Out there are many wonders. Keep the toy, as *radika* from me to you, you of the *Jamid Ja'da*."

At that the oarmaster shouldered his way past Carlby and held out his hand, demanding the carving. "That is not his to give. What the slaves carve is rightly mine to keep or sell as I see fit."

"*Ju'al*," spat the redhead, standing up in his chains and threatening the oarmaster with his fist. His fellow oarsmen joined him.

"Now you've done it," Carlby said to de Wynter, interposing his body between oarsmen and oarmaster. "Promise them *tajziya*, or we'll have a riot on our hands."

At the sound of the Arabic word for reward, the oarmaster stopped struggling within Carlby's grip.

"*Tajziya?*" he asked, all smiles and proper respect.

De Wynter dipped desperately into his purse, forgetting that it had been emptied back at the Tower. He drew out the single object inside, his mother's pearl. However, to save lives, it was a cheap price to pay. He handed it over to Carlby. One look at its lustrous perfection and the oarmaster licked his thick, negroid lips with anticipation.

But Carlby shook his head. "Put it back, man, that's too much. Way too much for one single carving."

The oarmaster, seeing his pearl escape him, offered the other carvings as well. When Carlby refused them, too, as not enough, the oarmaster in desperation said, "Him, too," pointing at the redhead. "He can carve you many more wonders. Carvings and carver, for one small pearl. That is a good bargain, *al rabb*."

Carlby hesitated, assessing the situation. It was the best bargain possible under the circumstances. It got them out of a dangerous situation at the lowest possible cost. "Agreed, but let it be *ruqba*," he said, taking the pearl from de Wynter.

The oarmaster demurred, but avarice must have its way.

"*Ruqba,* it shall be, but the slave cannot be released until Malta. I must have him at the oars to meet our schedule."

The bargain was struck, de Wynter surrendering his pearl for four carvings—that of his Mer-Lion crest, a giraffe, an elephant, and a crocodile—and one redheaded carver.

The Scots earl, as he followed Carlby up out of the galley-way, was more interested in discovering the meaning of *ruqba* than the identity of his new slave.

"*Ruqba* is a gift with a proviso attached. Under Islamic law, your gift of the pearl returns to you if anything happens to your slave—or to the oarmaster himself. Contrariwise, if you should die, the slave reverts to him. So guard yourself well."

Little did Carlby know it, but the slave de Wynter had just purchased was worth his weight in pearls to one inhabitant of the Beglerbey's seraglio in Algiers. Marimah, the most favored of Barbarossa's four wives, would pay any price for her only son, Eulj Ali.

Luckily for the oarmaster and the captain, they, too, did not know the true worth of the slave just sold to the Scot. It would have struck terror in their hearts and Don Federico might well have reversed his course out of fear of the redhead's father.

Eulj Ali, however, had been too shamed by his capture to inform anyone of his identity. In what had been his first captaincy, he had ventured too close to the coast of Caramania. Rounding a heavily wooded promontory, his little ship came in full sight of the *Mystical Rose.* Eulj Ali had no choice but flight. Putting up his helm, he scudded before the breeze, but the *Mystical Rose* goose-winged her two great lateen sails and turned in pursuit.

Even as free men rowing, Eulj Ali and his companions could hold their own for only so long before the galley's twenty-seven oars to a side, nine slaves to an oar, and the lash of the whipmaster would make a difference. Soon, the prow of the galley overhung the stern of the little ship. Escape was impossible, to fight was suicide. Eulj Ali ordered the lowering of his sail, the dipping of his banner. He and his companions were immediately cast in irons and within the month sold at the world's largest slavemarket in Venice.

Eulj Ali was neither frightened nor awed by his new master, de Wynter. However, as the whip struck his fellows and bypassed him, he realized he was indeed within the debt of the *al rabb.* A debt he resented and vowed to discharge at some future date if Allah allowed.

De Wynter, upon returning to the deck, instructed John Drummond to keep an eye on the boyish red-haired slave in the galley, explaining that he had just bought his service but could not claim his prize until they reached Malta. They were to report to him if the oarmaster applied the whip too generously or otherwise punished his man.

The Seaforth servants and especially Fionn, born into Seaforth service, wondered why their master had bought a slave when he had four servants at hand. They themselves, though they would die for him, were men who had chosen to serve him, and were fed and clothed by him in addition to receiving a small stipend at the end of each year of their service.

Steering eastward, the *Annunciata* hugged the coastline to the north, Don Federico fearing that some of Barbarossa's ships might be lurking within the Straits of Gibraltar. With sails and oars, she could outrun a pirate vessel if close to a safe port.

Once clear of the Straits, next stop would be Gibraltar. Here Don Federico hoped to unload the beggars and get word of the pirate fleet's last sighting. Out of Gibraltar, he must make the decision: to go by the long but safe north route, or due east past the pirate stronghold at Algiers.

Gibraltar, one half of the Pillars of Hercules and the key to the Mediterranean, crouched like a wary lion upon a huge rock. Connected to Europe only by a sandy isthmus, it was nominally Spanish, but very cosmopolitan and heavily Moresco because of its strategic location as a crossroad of shipping among three continents. Jebel Tarik, as the Moors called it (rock of Tarik, the Berber) was a welcome sight as first its towering cliff and then its city hove into view.

Don Federico wasted no time in trying to rid himself of the beggars. The Spanish commandant had other ideas, and men at arms turned the beggars back at the end of the gangplank. A few brave ones who jumped overboard that night and made for shore were hauled from the water and put to death. The rest resigned themselves to staying aboard until the next port was reached, John the Rob among them. He was too clever to risk his life on an uncertainty.

As fresh water and food were taken aboard, traders came to make offers on the cargo, to sell information and slaves, to peddle goods to the passengers or buy scrimshaw at bargain prices from the rowers or the oarmaster.

One of those who boarded, posing as a *mujmil*, was a spy for Barbarossa. Normally his job was to identify the cargo and its worth and pass this information along to pirate ships waiting in the Mediterranean. But today such thoughts were driven out of his head by the sight of a slave—a red-haired one sitting quietly on his oar bench. A knowing glance passed between the two.

Within minutes, the spy was back on shore arranging for the departure of three speedy *firkatas*, rowed by freemen avaricious for his promised reward. One was bound for Algiers, another for Venice, the third to straddle the shipping lanes outside Tunis. Their instructions were simple: "Intercept any and all pirate vessels you come upon. Pass the word that Barbarossa's son, Eulj Ali, is aboard the *Annunciata*, heading toward Cyprus from Gibraltar, route unknown."

The first day out of Gibraltar, the wind being favorable and the ship's motion giving him a false sense of security, Don Federico made his decision. He continued east straight across the Mediterranean, straight into the waters most thickly infested with pirate ships.

Partly, it was Carlby's fault. Don Federico had consulted the Knight Hospitaler who had sailed the Mediterranean most recently. Carlby, knowing the pirates should be wintering, chose to get to Malta at least two weeks sooner by going the shortest, potentially riskiest route.

The second day, a halloo rang out from the lookout on top of the mast. A corsair galleo of sixteen oar banks coursed dead ahead. Don Federico, his heart sinking, barked his orders, "Helmsman, hard aport! Boatswain, unfurl all canvas. Oarmaster, double the stroke."

The wily captain hoped that with his greater number of oars he could slide past the pirate ship without taking more than one broadside, and once past the enemy ship, could pick up a large lead while it tacked and came about.

The strategy might have worked had not Eulj Ali and other Moslems been among the oarsmen. Suddenly, they lost their rhythm, fouling their oars, disrupting the beat—effectively preventing the ship from moving out smartly.

The slight delay enabled the corsair galleon to veer to starboard and pass close by the virtually unarmed merchant vessel. The first volley of cannon fire shredded the main mast, tumbling canvas and splintered wood and lookouts to the deck. Don Federico knew the day was lost. He could no longer outrun the pirates, and there was not a friendly port anywhere near.

Carlby, de Wynter, and the ship's captain tried valiantly to organize the resistance to the boarding. When it came, though many fought gamely, there was little chance of repelling the attack. One by one the Christians surrendered or were cut down. Only one pocket of resistance remained. The Knights, the serving brothers of St. John of Jerusalem, and a swarthy, funny-faced, elfin man fought tenaciously. Even so, they were slowly backed against the rail and would have been chopped down if not for a command from Eulj Ali. "Hold, there. Let them live! Those thirteen brawny backs will put gold in your pockets at the slave market in Tunis. And the nobles can be ransomed!"

The pirates disengaged. Their scimitars properly bloodied, their bloodthirsty lust vented on beggars, servants, and sailors, they were willing to listen to greed, an able persuader. Now it was the Christians' turn.

Recognizing defeat, they obeyed Eulj Ali's order to "throw down your weapons and live to be ransomed." Bound together hand to hand, they sat forlornly on the deck while the corsairs directed the cleaning up of their prize. Canvas was folded and stowed away, great chunks of the broken mast thrown overboard. Blood sloshed from the deck, and bodies of the dead and seriously wounded were unceremoniously heaved over the rail to feed the carrion-eaters who constantly trail ships.

Among de Wynter's group, two of the Scots servants had their wounds examined. At a gesture from Eulj Ali, they were scooped up like so much trash and heaved screaming into the sea. John Carlby bowed his head and intoned the last Sacrament while the bound group sat penitent. The screams rose in frequency and pitch, then were cut short. Carlby interrupted his prayers to utter but one word:

"Sharks!" De Wynter silently swore to exact vengeance for their deaths.

While Moslem slaves and Christian seamen changed places at the oars, others were transferred in irons to the hold. Then, as the unfortunates sat or lay in bilgewater, the crippled ship set partial sail, and under the flogging of a familiar whip wielded by a new oarmaster, they headed toward Algiers. Their new captain was a boyish redhead.

Eulj Ali had had little difficulty convincing the first men to board that he was son of their leader. The resemblance between father and son was too well marked, especially the luxuriant flaming red beard. Wielding his chains like a feared "Holy Water Sprinkler," he had flailed away, wreaking havoc among the Christian crew, stopping only when he saw resistance lessening and the single knot of noblemen left. Having at least partially repaid his debt to the Scot by saving his life, the corsair thought nothing of having him locked in irons to be ransomed or sold as fortune would have it.

In the hold, John the Rob's experience came to the fore. It was he who showed the closely chained men how to lift their arms in unison when eating the miserable scraps they were thrown. How to drink in unison and in uniform amounts so that relieving their bladders could be done as one. How to sleep, alternating heads and feet so that broad shoulders did not rob them of room, and the peculiar choreography in which every other man had to step over the chains, bring them up and over his back and head and then, in unison, lie down head to foot. Only in this way were the chains prevented from buckling and doubling on themselves, and cutting shorter what little give they offered.

The physical discomfort was one thing. The worry about their fate was another. Carlby reminded them, "Boast not about being in Holy Orders. Suleiman has vowed to kill any Hospitaler found in the Mediterranean. And Barbarossa," he pointed out, "has served his time at the oar in the order's galleys."

CHAPTER 20

Mercifully, even with less than full sail, the trip to Algiers took but three nights and two days. The merchant ship with its firkata escort moored alongside the new dock at Al Penon, the fortress-island built and held by the Spaniards until Barbarossa tore it down around their heads in 1530. Now, two years later, with the help of thousands of slaves, many of them the former Spaniard inhabitants of the island, Barbarossa was rebuilding the fortress and simultaneously constructing a jetty connecting island and mainland. When it was completed, Algiers would have a large harbor of its own and would no longer need to use Tunis for the wintering of its fleet.

Brought up from the Stygian darkness of the hold, and still chained hand-to-hand, the prisoners were marched, walking sideways, crablike, toward the city. When one tripped and fell, to the catcalls and jeers of the onlookers, the others could only drag him along until he regained his feet. The last remaining Scot serving man—except for Fionn—fell once too often. A scimitar ensured he would never get up. The headless body bounced about, spewing blood on the fellow prisoners as they dragged it with them—a grim reminder of what happened to one who was less than surefooted.

Their destination soon loomed above them: the Jenina built by Barbarossa on the site of the palace once occupied by his assassinated Moorish predecessor.

Iron cages, less than a man's height, hung here and there from tree or beam, tower and turret. Inside crouched men, dead or dying

313

of thirst and starvation. To the Christians' horror, their group stopped just below a cage where one emaciated man was devouring the death-bloated remains of another. Above the great arched entrance to Barbarossa's Jenina, hundreds of heads and even more skulls were mounted on spears, the flesh being scavenged from the newer ones by great blackdaws. Amidst this mute and terrifying testament to the cheapness of life in the Barbaresco state of Algiers, the captives were glad to reach the comparative safety of the dungeons.

That night, while the prisoners from the *Annunciata* thirsted unattended in the windowless dungeons carved from stone below the Jenina, there was much merriment above in the Court of the Four Domed Chambers. There, intricately stuccoed walls, ornate window shutters, and lavish wood paneling rivaled in richness the sumptuous, overelaborate furnishings. That Barbarossa was unaware of his son's rescue and was still searching for him did not dampen the feasting. Eulj Ali, his four wives and his mother rejoiced in food and wine and, when he was up to it, in the vigor of his *jima* with one or more of his wives, as Marimah looked on fondly.

It was not until the following day that Eulj Ali, his mother, and his father's most trusted lieutenant, Sinan the Jew of Smryna, sat down to discuss the fate of the prisoners. Marimah wanted to wait until the Beglerbey returned before any decision was made. Eulj Ali protested; the decision, like the captives, was his. "They must be freed. I have no choice," Eulj Ali finally declared. "I am indebted to the *jamad ja'da* for my life."

"Who?"

"The *jamad ja'da*. Wait till you see him, Sinan. You'll agree the name fits the owner, for never on a young man did I ever see such a head of hair: white and gray and silver and damascene steel."

Sinan the Jew, looking on silently, found his interest piqued.

"A young man?" Marimah persisted.

"Of an age with me. He travels under this sign," Eulj Ali said, fishing his carving of the Seaforth crest from out of one of the many voluminous and secret pockets within his robes. As Marimah turned the small Mer-Lion over in her hands, Eulj Ali continued, "He bought me and protected me from whippings. I am in his debt, he saved my life."

"As you saved his," she retorted.

"He is a Hospitaler," was Sinan the Jew's quiet addition to the conversation.

Marimah reacted violently, throwing the small carving from her as if it had come alive and mauled her hand. "A Hospitaler?" she shrieked. "You saved a Hospitaler?" Fear, shock, anger, despair warred within her.

Eulj Ali could not meet her eyes; instead, he bent to retrieve the carving. Damn the Jew. He had hoped the secret would hold until the Christians were safely gone.

As if Eulj Ali had spoken aloud, Sinan the Jew responded impassively, "If I knew of this within minutes of your arrival, how long, think you, before word reached the Beglerbey?"

Marimah nodded vigorously; Sinan was right. Eulj Ali only stared coldly at his father's lieutenant. Not even months in the galleys had made him subservient to authority.

"There is a way . . ." the slow, nasal voice of Sinan suggested as he met, unblinking, the stare of his master's favorite son, a man only the foolhardy dared to offend.

Marimah, concerned for her son and fearful of her husband, clutched at the hope the man held forth. "Anything. Just tell us."

Ignoring her, since she was only a woman, even if mother to Eulj Ali, the lieutenant waited, staring at Eulj Ali. Only when he slowly and reluctantly nodded did Sinan proceed. "There is a way to save their lives and appease the Beglerbey's wrath while repaying the Moulay Hassan's daughter for her high-handed refusal of Barbarossa's offer to take her in marriage."

Eulj Ali had known nothing of the marriage offer or its aftermath. Diverted and alarmed, he stared at his mother with narrowed eyes. "My father would replace one of you? Which one? Not you, I trust?" A spy in his father's bed was an invaluable asset to a younger son with contentious brothers. Meeting his stare, Marimah saw smoldering in her son the same violence that Barbarossa was so quick to vent. Marimah had lived through Barbarossa's spasms of rage, however, and her son's did not frighten her unduly. She worried only that the Amira Aisha might change her mind and accept Barbarossa's offer. Marimah had spent too many years talking, coercing, threatening, coaxing, bribing, and whipping her fellow wives into order. The thought of removing one and introducing another into the seraglio did not find favor with her. Moreover, secretly she applauded the young princess's posture of independence.

Eulj Ali's face contorted with anger when his mother did not respond quickly enough to please him. Then Sinan the Jew's nasal voice insinuated itself between mother and son and averted possible violence against the mother by the son. "Your mother would not be forced out. All know she is the favorite of the Beglerbey." Ignoring Eulj Ali's sigh of relief as merely an indication of his immaturity, the Jew continued on imperturbably. "All I suggest is a way to use this matter to our advantage. The young princess not only rejected our benevolent Beglerbey's offer of marriage, but also challenged him to compete for her hand. Against others. Any others, providing only that they be of noble birth. Naturally, Uruj Barbarossa will not demean himself to compete with untried men whose only claim to virtue lies in the blood of their fathers and forefathers. However, is it not written that he who owns the slave also owns all that belongs to the slave? And are you not *muraquib* to the *jamad ja'da* and his fellows? If you enter one or all of these captives of yours into the contest and one of them wins, the prize is yours. If any or all lose, then they die. It is as Allah wills."

Marimah was anxious. "What of the Sultan of Sultans? What if Suleiman finds out?"

"Let him. Let him discover that the Moulay Hassan of Tunis harbors Knights Hospitaler. How long, think you, the Moulay will survive when his son-in-law is of that proscribed order? I have thought it over. No way may we lose, we can only win."

Marimah was not convinced. "What of the order? Suppose they get wind of this and exact revenge?"

"With what? If my voices tell me right, they scour the continents for new recruits. Think you they will dare storm Algiers or even Tunisia? Nay, they huddle on the barren rocks of Malta and pray that we ignore them."

Eulj Ali, having adopted the plan almost instantaneously, was eager for details. "How will you accomplish this?"

"I won't, you will. Is there a good-looking one among them who would impress a woman? Perhaps this *jamad ja'da?*"

"He is the most beautiful, but there are one or two others. Why do you ask? For yourself or our plan?"

Sinan the Jew ignored the discourtesy of his friend's son in alluding, even faintly, to the corsair's predilection for men. "If one is attractive enough, our work may be done for us. We sell him and his friends—as a lot—at the slave market in Tunis. Already the market is being dried up by the princess's agents who buy and buy and buy. If, however, by the time we get there, she has bought all she needs, we can enter them in the contest under the aegis of one of our Berber friends."

At first flush, Eulj Ali could find no fault with the scheme and he agreed to ship the Hospitalers out the next day to the slave markets at Tunis. But before they were dispatched, Sinan the Jew demanded a look at them.

"Shall we go now?" Eulj Ali asked.

"You two go," Marimah said. "I have things to do."

At the foot of the steps to the dungeon, the two men were met with cries of "Water! Water!" from the several cells that held the knights, servants, freemen, beggars, and sailors. Eulj Ali suddenly remembered he had not given orders to feed and care for the prisoners, and he bellowed up the stairway, "Bring water and food for these miserable curs. And be quick about it!"

With a scurrying of many feet, both food and water were shoved through the small opening in the bottom of the barred doors that provided the only light into the cells.

Going from cell to cell, Eulj Ali quickly assessed the damage and concluded that other than being parched and weak, the lot of them would soon recuperate. The beggars, he noted, seemed hardly bothered at all by the lack of food and water. And when he came to the cell holding de Wynter, their eyes locked in a mutual mixture of respect and hatred.

"A thousand pardons, *al-rabb*," said the redhead. "I was so glad to be home that I did not extend the courtesies of my home to you." And from his lips came a taunting victory laugh.

"I shall remember it," said de Wynter, noticing Eulj Ali's companion for the first time. Ignoring Eulj Ali, the Scot and the Jew silently took one another's measure while thirst-crazed, hungry men, slurping water and gulping unchewed food, filled the dungeon with the bestial noise of some hellish menagerie. De Wynter, staring into those hooded eyes, felt his hackles rise—as if in the presence of evil incarnate—and he knew terror.

"I would have a better look at him," Sinan finally said, without looking elsewhere. "Bring him out here and let me assess his true worth."

Only too well the redhead knew the real meaning of Sinan the Jew's request. He wished to assess the man as a sex object, not as meat for the slave market. Nonetheless, Eulj Ali had to admit, sometimes the two were the same.

However, Sinan's liking for men frequently left his partners disfigured. That would not do for de Wynter, Eulj Ali decided. "No! Let him be. We want him in good shape when he arrives in Tunis. In fact, if I catch you near him, I'll cut off that thing that causes you so much trouble." He also changed his mind about sending Sinan alone with the prisoners on the four-day journey to Tunis.

The following day the prisoners were marched from their cells back to the harbor. Still in chains which bound them one to another, they were herded aboard a fifty-foot barcha especially fitted out for speed. Instead of a hold, the usual construction for this type of Mediterranean vessel, she had now but a raised walkway down her middle, with rowing benches and oars below it on either side. Each bench, six to a side, was built for three oarsmen, 36 in all. With any kind of a breeze at all this vessel, equipped with a triangular sail, and with oars plying at a good rate, could outrun anything in its size class and most that carried far more sail.

The pirates used the ship, the *Sea Devil*, for getting messages from ship to ship, or from Algiers to Tunis or Cairo, and occasionally, as on this trip, to carry a prize catch to the closest slave market, the huge one at Tunis. Although it was necessary to arrive at market with slaves in as good physical shape as possible, why feed them for more days than necessary?

De Wynter, Carlby, and the rest of the Christian captives were lined up in single file down the length of the raised walkway. A huge, hairy man passed down the line with a heavy set of pincers snapping the irons in two between every third man. Each threesome was then shoved onto a rowing bench with a second corsair snapping a leg manacle onto the left ankle of each prisoner.

In de Wynter's threesome, as the luck of the draw dictated, were Fionn and John the Rob, who stuck as close to de Wynter as possible. Fortunately for them, Fionn had muscles to spare and compensated for John the Rob's lack of weight as they pulled at the oar.

De Wynter looked about from his low vantage point. No shelter from the boiling sun or angry storm was provided them nor any place to recline. To rest, one leaned forward on one's arms on the heavy oar. Remembering the squalid conditions in which the oarsmen labored aboard the *Annunciata*, de Wynter prayed for a short trip.

If, as Carlby supposed, their destination was a slave market somewhere, probably at Tunis, de Wynter had no intention of spending the rest of his days as a slave. Like a true fighting man and survivor of Naples he had already begun to plan an escape at some undetermined moment in the not-too-distant future. "By my mother's memory, mate," John the Rob said to de Wynter, "it looks like we're in for a rough go, eh?"

"So it would seem, friend," de Wynter replied. "My guess is that we'll not long be at sea; we are taking on too little water. We might even be back on land in three days if the breeze holds. Pass the word. Maybe it will give heart to some of these poor wretches."

He considered for the moment mentioning their probable destination, then decided against it. No need to cause them any more dismay at this stage.

"And tell them to behave themselves or we'll all feel that hairy bugger's whip, I daresay."

John the Rob casually leaned forward and called guardedly to Ogilvy, "The white-haired one thinks we'll be where we're goin' in three days. Pass it on. And tell me men to mind their bloody manners lest we all get the bloody whip or worse."

The highlander spoke quietly to his oar mates and leaned forward, in turn, to pass the word. A whip, cracking across his back, forced his scream. A voice—a decidedly English voice—practiced in being heard over creaking oarlock and howling wind yelled, "There'll be no talkin', y'hear? Nary a word! Or ya'll feel the bite o' me little

319

friend here." With that this renegade Englishman cracked the long bullwhip over his head in rapid fire succession in every direction, just to put the fear in them all. And with most, he succeeded.

"Now ye pulls when I say 'pull,' and ye rests when I say 'hold.' Do it right and we'll get along just fine. I see ye slackin' and ye gets me whip. Any questions?"

"Yes, sir," spoke up John the Rob, "where do we sl—" The crack of the whip cut off the word, the frayed tip biting through his tattered shirt, and the balance of the blow falling across de Wynter's back.

"I said no talkin'. Can't ye hear?" the hairy one roared.

"I was only answerin' yer questi—" Again the whip cracked and caught John the Rob's back, though de Wynter sensed its fall and leaned away from its full force.

"No talkin' means no talkin'. Understand?"

A few heads nodded, but nobody answered; John the Rob was too busy swallowing the bile pain brought to his throat. Satisfied, the hairy one went forward to help cast-off while the prisoners leaned on the oars, resting their heads on their chained arms.

The plank was pulled aboard, great hemp ropes slipped off their moorings, and the sail untied though not hoisted aloft. The few kegs of water were rolled up the walkway and tied down near the cabin. Bags holding bread and rolls were stocked on top of the kegs and weighted down with marlin spikes and extra pulleys.

Striding down the walkway, the whipwielder roared, "Let's see what kind a lily-livered seaman ye are. Pull those oars into your guts, then straight up, then push. Altogether now. Pull. Up. Push, me hearties."

And the ship took its first lurch away from its rocky mooring.

"Pull. Up. Push. Bend to it, ye landlubbers." A dozen times he repeated his rhythmic cadence and despite some oar fouling and general mishandling of the cumbersome pieces of timber, the ship was gliding well out from those still moored.

"Now, over here." He cracked his whip high over de Wynter's side of eighteen oarsmen. "Dip those oars in the water and hold 'em there." Again the whip cracked, this time over the other eighteen. "And over here ye keep on the same as before. Pull. Up. Push. Pull.

Up. Push. Get yer backs into it and bring her about, ye no good scum."

Slowly the ship swung round and headed out of the harbor.

"Now we does it the other way, me hearties. We pushes away. Then lifts. And we pulls."

Again there was some fouling up, primarily from the beggars to whom the oar and rowing were totally foreign. But being chained in threes actually helped the three dozen slaves soon achieve a semblance of rhythm. As the *Sea Devil* began to make headway, the crew of eight scrambled about hoisting the great triangular sail and securing its moorings while one heavyset man of the sea handled the steering oar and the captain stood on the walkway shouting directions.

The sail billowed out and de Wynter could feel the ship fairly leap forward. And while it lessened the strain of each pull on the oar, it kept the oarsmen on their guard lest the blades catch in the rushing water and rap them smartly on chin or chest.

It was two hours after they had cleared the great harbor at Algiers that the oarmaster finally cracked his whip and yelled, "Hold!" To a man, the rowers dropped exhausted on their oars, their backs aching to the point of torture and their hands already showing blisters.

A ten-minute break and the whip cracked again. "Up an' at 'em, ye lazy louts. Push. Up. Pull. Push. Up. Pull."

The midday sun dried the salty sweat on their arms and necks, for though the ship's headway was creating its own breeze, little of it reached the lower levels where the oarsmen labored. Some had collaborated with their chained partners to rip their shirts open or all the way off, though de Wynter and some of the more experienced sailors knew it was better to have some cover from the burning sun and, later, the night air.

Every two hours a crewman passed down the rows with a bucket of lukewarm water and a common ladle. One ladle apiece, and if any slopped in their eagerness, a lash with the whip. When the ten-minute break was up, back to the oars. Many a bladder ached for relief, but was forced to hold out as long as possible. The steady back-and-forth motion created a kind of euphoria, a trancelike state with aching muscles responding mechanically, but the chains cut sharply into the wrists of anyone who fell too deeply comatose.

An hour before sunset, the oarsmaster cried, "Hold." They had made excellent headway all day, for the wind had held and the oars had plied at a steady, punishing beat. The captain of the *Sea Devil*, who had been reminded more than once that first day by Sinan the Jew that Barbarossa would have his head if the prisoners were not in fit shape when they reached Tunis, had decided to feed them and let them rest their weary muscles.

A large keg was rolled out on the walkway and a crewman smashed in its lid with a heavy mallet. Picking the splintered wood out of the liquid contents, a fair amount of which had spilled onto the planks, one crewman ladled out a stew lumpy with congealed grease while two others held bowls and passed them to the eager oarsmen. No spoons. Just bowls, which each trio soon learned to bring to their mouths in unison.

This was, for most of them, their first taste of salmagundi, a hearty concoction which was a favorite with Mediterranean pirates, but which could be made only the first few days out of port or when they had just captured a merchant ship with a full larder. This particular batch of salmagundi had been prepared in the kitchens at Al-Penon, Marimah's idea to keep the prisoners in good health.

Into the huge cooking kettle had gone turtle meat, pigeon, pork, and duck, cut into chunks and marinated in spiced wine beforehand. In, too, went cabbage, mangoes, boiled eggs, palm hearts, onions, olives, grapes, and anchovies. Plus copious quantities of garlic, salt, pepper, mustard seed, oil, and vinegar.

Salmagundi was best when served piping hot. But the makeshift galley on the *Sea Devil* did not have a fireplace sufficient to heat up the stew, and it was served warmed by the sun, with the gobs of grease clinging to the vegetables and chunks of meat. Not a man among the prisoners thought it anything but delicious as he gobbled and slopped it down in rapid fashion, hardly attempting to chew the tougher chunks. The bowls were gathered up, and the oarmaster strode down the center walkway brandishing his whip.

"Awright, ye slop hogs, on yer feet, and make it snappy, or I touches up yer backs with me leather."

The men staggered to their feet, the stronger helping the weak.

322

"Now ye takes yer turn at the trench," the hairy one bellowed, "and if ye misses a drop, ye'll stand in place all night, so help me."

Eager hands ripped open britches and loosed streams of urine into the narrow trough that ran along the hull on either side. Each in turn relieved himself and resumed his standing position. Crewmen drew buckets of sea water from over the side and sloshed the troughs which sloped from forward to aft, the resulting foul mixture running out holes cut in the sides of the ship for the purpose, and which could be plugged in the event of foul weather and heavy waves. There being no provision made for relieving one's bowels, the men simply sucked in their guts and refused to respond to their natural urgings. De Wynter, for one, wondered what effect the greasy and spicy salmagundi would have on their intestines.

"Ye can thank the captain for givin' ye a chance ter sleep. Meself, I'd work ye through the night. Mind I'll make up for it when the sun comes up, so ye best make the most o' it," taunted the oarmaster. "Down ye go, and I dinna want a head up till mornin'," he said and cracked his whip for emphasis.

Down went the heads upon aching arms resting on huge oars. Exhaustion let them sleep despite the cramped, uncomfortable position and the aches from back, legs, and arms. They slept with only minor stirrings during the night—a cramped leg shifted here and a head turned to the opposite side there when a crick in the neck grew too severe. The dawn broke all too soon and the prisoners were allowed to stand and stretch and use the trench. Ladles of wine were handed out, and each man was tossed a chunk of bread, already beginning to sour. Then it was back to the oars, steady two-hour shifts, followed by ten-minute breaks for water and rest. The wind was holding and the crew seemed satisfied with their progress. Even the oarmaster seemed more lenient with the whip and tongue. And in the late afternoon came another shipping of the oars, mugs of ale and pieces of bread, another piss call and blessed rest for the night.

John Carlby was suffering as much as any man aboard. Not as young as de Wynter and his fellow novices, and not as accustomed to the rugged life as were John the Rob and Fionn, he relied on an inner faith that kept him going hour after hour at the oar without losing the peaceful expression that was an inspiration for all within sight of him. He had survived the battle at Rhodes, he would survive this latest twist in the road he was sure God had set for him. This was merely another test, albeit a strenuous one, of his belief.

His experienced eye told him that Tunis was indeed the probable destination as he and de Wynter had surmised. And within a few more hours the sail would be slackened so that arrival could be effected in daylight hours. He knew, too, that the oarsmen would be forced once more to the oars, bringing the ship to her moorings more gently than could the ship's huge triangular sail, which was fine for straight running but difficult to maneuver in the harbor. And just before he passed out from utter exhaustion he remembered details of the harbor—bigger than the one at Algiers, and better protected from the elements. And he remembered visiting the slave market, the distaste and revulsion he had felt upon seeing humans sold as livestock. The tall minarets, the bargaining street merchants, the call to prayer at dawn. It was a colorful, and yes, a sinful city in many ways, a reflection of the depraved man who was its monarch.

Leaning on their oars, the slaves slept. Carlby but fitfully for he was troubled by a collage of dreams of turreted Moslem cities and of stark church-fortresses and of dark rock-hewn dungeons. Everywhere he looked there were people, some with hauntingly familiar, long-dead faces, others with cold, indifferent, strange countenances. Through it all loomed a ship, a monstrous one that grew and grew and that refused to move within the sea no matter how hard he rowed and rowed and rowed . . .

He heard a cry. At first he thought he had uttered it, then realized it came from a lookout posted on the top of the tiny cabin. Carlby could not discern immediately what all the clamor was about, though he craned his head as far as possible without being detected, and strained his ears to catch the excited conversation. The crewmen were gathered at the aft rails, pointing and gesticulating at the water.

Peering through the oarlock, Carlby could see what had upset the crew: a myriad of lights trailed the ship, sparkling and twinkling within the depths of the waves, and lighting up their wake with a greenish white glow that was both beautiful and eerie. There wasn't a man among the crew who hadn't listened to, and told, tales of the mermaids who trail ships, enticing sailors with their fiery jewels, causing some to dive overboard and disappear. The watery enchantresses were reported to have led ships onto the rocks so that they might add to their treasures of gold and jewels and men.

The lights now engulfed the ship from stem to stern, the wet hull reflecting the phosphorescent glow onto the water and making it appear brighter than ever. Some of the crew drew back from the rail, while others, fascinated though frightened, could not resist the allure of the spectacle. Facing aft as they were, Carlby and about half of the prisoners watched and listened, though few knew what was happening.

"What's got 'em so excited, milord?" John the Rob whispered across to de Wynter.

"It's the lights," de Wynter answered. "Some say they are mermaids flashing their jewels. Others say it is reflection from the hide of some giant sea monster below. Who knows?" he said with a grin, knowing that John the Rob's wild imagination would take over, and enjoying the jest. At best, de Wynter knew in his heart that a logical, natural explanation existed. He would have to ask Carlby when they were unchained from these damnable oar stations. Carlby did indeed know, and he suspected the captain was holding out the truth from his crewmen for reasons of his own. The lights were gammari. Shrimp. Billions of miniscule floating crustaceans joined together in huge schools, each giving off its own tiny phosphrescence, and the whole adding up to a formidable light-emitting body. Just why the mass seemed to twinkle and sparkle Carlby had never learned, but his scholarly mind told him it had something to do with reflection and prismatic phenomena as the waves and the ship's wake brought angles into play.

As suddenly as they had appeared, the lights disappeared behind the speeding ship. The voices quieted, though the stories continued. One had actually seen a mermaid. Another saw a circle of shimmering diamonds in the shape of a crown. And one pooh-poohed the others with his tale of having seen the monster's green tail rise out of the water during a similar sighting of the lights off Gibraltar three years earlier.

Carlby and his fellow prisoners drifted back to sleep, less worried about strange lights in the sea than how to survive another day at the oars.

De Wynter woke just before dawn. He, too, had dreamed. The

same dream as before. He was riding up the Ben Nevis to Seaforth on Dun Dearduil. There stood two women waiting for him, a small boy standing between them. The one woman, he knew without seeing her face, was his mother. The other he was sure was Anne Boleyn. But even though he urged his horse first to a trot then to a canter, finally to a gallop, the castle seemed no nearer, nor the other woman's face clearer. Always, just as he was sure another stride of the horse would enable him to make out his loved one's face, he awoke.

A slowing of the ship, preceded by sharp commands and squealing block and tackle, told him the huge sail was being furled. No doubt they would stand off the harbor entrance at Tunis until daylight and use the oars to bring her in. His muscles ached at the thought. But at least it would be a short turn at the oars, no more than half an hour he judged, remembering how long it took them to clear the harbor at Algiers.

He raised his head cautiously and looked around in the dim light shed by the lamps that had been placed on the walkway. Most of the men were still mercifully asleep, but he saw Carlby and a few of the others carefully stretching arms and legs, trying to get their circulation going. Satisfied, and not wanting to raise the wrath of the oarmaster who might be keeping an eye on them, de Wynter again rested his head on weary arms and waited patiently for dawn.

The sun had not yet risen above the waves when the crack of the whip and a bellowing voice roused them and bade them stand. After queueing up at the narrow latrines, the men stood in place while watered sour wine and stale bread were doled out and promptly wolfed down. Then it was back to the oars, the men alternating as they spit on their blistered hands and rubbed them to ease the soreness and give themselves a decent grip. The sun was warming their backs as the cadence was struck and the ship moved gracefully toward the harbor entrance. Within it, evidently, the ship could not steer a straight course, for the sun threw its rays first over their right shoulders and finally straight in their faces as the steering oar slanted them directly toward the colorful and massive piles of houses, mosques and ancient stone structures that rose from the water's edge in a long, crenellated line.

The sudden whir of mighty wings caused the prisoners to glance skyward, some frightened, some cautious, some merely curious. Hundreds of pink flamingos, disturbed by the ship, had taken wing. Through the oarlocks, the outer rowers saw a sea of pink to every side as the ship moved toward its moorings. Even hardened sailors were moved by the sight, John Carlby remembered. De Wynter, having read about the wondrous sight, realized what he was missing.

This was Al Bahira, the little sea connecting the Gulf of Tunis to the city, a few miles to the southwest. The shallow water here was ideal for the great birds, but hazardous for navigation. The steersman, with lookouts posted forward, had skillfully guided the ship through La Goulette, a narrow channel that offered ships their only real entrance. To the rowers' right rose the shadowy hills of Cap Bon. To their left the ruins of Carthage. And behind their hardworking backs, the city itself, at a distance of fifteen kilometers or so.

The air was calm now, the sea wind having dropped. The oppressive heat, even in the fall, settled in around the ship, and the oarsmen perspired more heavily with every stroke. The Carthaginians had been smarter than the early settlers of Tunis, or Thunes, as the Phoenicians called it. They had sought out higher ground and a small natural harbor for their city while Thunes, its predecessor, had been built on low ground rising only a few hundred feet above the sea, and situated between two lakes, Al Bahira and Sebkha es Sedjoumi, an inland saltwater lake. By its location, it was excessively hot and humid in summer and cold and blustery in winter.

Across Al Bahira they rowed, the cadence slowing as they neared the docking area. The sounds of the busy city could be heard over the splash and creak of the oars. Finally, the oarmaster barked the command to raise oars, a few minutes later to dip oars and to back water, finally to ship oar. Gently, expertly, the *Sea Devil* nosed alongside the great stone pier jutting out into the lake.

Again the prisoners were bade to line up on the walkway that ran the length of the ship like a wooden backbone, and crewmen snapped links into place, making them once again a long human chain. A plank was thrown across to the pier, and single file they made their precarious way across.

Street urchins taunted and threw pebbles at the chained prisoners, who were marched from the *Sea Devil* to a nearby prison built to hold slaves until they were ready for the auction block. They had but to navigate two and a half of the irregular souks which marked the lowest part of the city, nearest to the sea. This was the edge of the native city, or medina, walled by stone some forty cubits high and strengthened by turrets at regular intervals.

Now, some three hundred years past its prime, Tunis was experiencing the slow decline that would someday tumble its great wall and reduce the once colorful and exciting souks, the market stalls, to repositories of cheap, shoddy merchandise.

As passersby ignored him—slave chains were all too common in this city—de Wynter indulged his own curiosity. Ahead he saw turrets of what must be the Great Mosque, framed in the foliage of olive trees.

Beyond it, and higher still, near the middle of medina, sat the Dar al Bey, home of the ruler and the site of state occasions. The hill blocked from his view the last of Tunis's three wonders—the Bardo Palace, harem of the Beys, built early in the fifteenth century about two kilometers from the center of the city.

Then the slaves arrived at a low stone structure with tiny barred windows and not many of them at that. While the captain went inside, the prisoners were herded together under guard of the crew. De Wynter could hear the captain haggling over the price he must pay for cells. Then the captain motioned the slaves to enter the doorway and they followed him down a dank corridor, made a few sharp turns and stopped in front of two cubicles with open doors. Each man was cut free from the next and shoved roughly into the tiny cells, half the group in each one.

The young Scottish earl looked around his new place, noting the rings set all round the walls for the purpose of chaining prisoners, and was grateful that the captain, maybe under orders from Eulj Ali, was not going to keep them in irons. The doors clanged shut and were secured. This time de Wynter and Carlby were in the same group and glad of it. They sat with their backs to a wall and discussed their situation. John the Rob stationed himself near the door and attempted to engage the guard in conversation, mostly offering him promises of silver for a bucket of drinking water.

According to Carlby, they would be bathed, fed, and generally well cared for during their stay in these cells. To bring a proper price as slaves, they would have to appear healthy and not too shabby. When the slave auction would be held and how long they would stay in the cramped cells, he didn't know. Maybe a week, maybe no more than a few days, judging by the haste the captain had insisted on.

The cells were so small, the men alternately sat or stood. Eventually they were taken two at a time to a common washroom and doused with buckets of water while they attempted to clean themselves with rough, strong soap. Leaving the bare room, distinguished only by the drain in the middle of the floor, each man made his first quick trip to a void room with several excreta-soiled holes in the floor, which, judging from the echoes, were actually deep wells. The smell kept any from lingering. On leaving, they were handed white ragged strips of bleached muslin to loop between their legs and tie around their waists.

Their spirits raised, the prisoners whiled away the balance of the afternoon dozing or talking quietly, the beggars even practicing some of their sleight-of-hand. Water was passed around once. And from somewhere, probably one of the local souks, came a tin of salve for their blistered hands and a bottle of oily hair dressing and a crude comb. Not until all others had made use of the latter was it passed to the beggars, who, John the Rob confided, had head-lice.

Shortly after the muezzins called the faithful to prayer for the fourth time that day, slaves brought in a single earthenware tub of food and left it sitting in the middle of the floor. There were no utensils, only hands. Some would have dug right in, but Carlby and de Wynter, acting quickly, stopped them. The food must be portioned out fairly.

When the emptied crock was removed, the next problem to be solved was floor space. Eighteen bodies did not fit comfortably in a room less than four paces by five paces. Especially when those bodies stretched out on the floor. De Wynter solved that one. He simply split the group in two—one half was able to stretch out full length for a time while the others sat, leaning against the opposite wall, each group alternating every three hours.

Having sat, then stretched out, then sat again through the dark hours on the uncomfortable stone floor, de Wynter slept only fitfully and was awake when the first call to prayer wafted clearly over the still city. *"Allahu Akbar,"* he translated, "God is most Great."

Then, to de Wynter's surprise, the call broke off. Not once during his captivity had he heard the Imam cease the Adhan before completed.

Carlby too looked puzzled. What dire calamity had struck the city to halt the first call to prayer of the day?

CHAPTER 21

No natural calamity in the city had caused the break in the call to prayer. It was just a maniacal game played on certain prisoners by the depraved and deranged ruler of Tunis, the Moulay Hassan. In the Palace of the Harem, called the Bardo, the Moulay too heard the clarion call. His annoyance at having his sleep disturbed quickly gave way to pleased anticipation of what would happen later that day to the poor unfortunate who had mistaken the dawn and mistimed the call to prayer. But now was the perfect time to begin again where sleep had intervened and stopped his play with his bed partner.

With a move surprisingly fast for such an obese man, the Moulay pulled the bed clothes away to reveal the naked body beside him. It was that of a child of not more than 10 or 11, scarcely past puberty. The slave had been a gift from Barbarossa, accompanying his proposal of marriage to the Princess Aisha, and had been chosen to appeal to the Moulay's well-known debauched taste.

The child was indeed a rarity—as the Moulay noted with awakened desire—neither all male nor all female it had organs of both. Where the Bey's gaze traveled over the cringing slave, his small, pudgy, brown hands followed. Then lunging atop the child, he pressed his fat slobbering lips against the tender, dry, childish mouth, suppressing the child's scream.

Up above the palace, the living gargoyles of Tunis shivered on the city's minarets as they continued to watch for the first ray of the dawn. At the Moulay's direction, the call to prayer in Tunis had evolved into a deadly game. Each slave purchased for the game was given ninety days in which to be first to spot the dawn and begin the first Adhan of the day, the chant, *"Assalatu Khairum Hinan Nawn* (Prayer is better than sleep)."

The game was simple, having but three rules.

The first provided suspense. Which and how many of the miserable slaves would win another ninety days of life and of competition?

The second gave the populace variety. The unsuccessful slave was executed on the ninety-first day. To the delight of the people of Tunis, the Moulay himself decided on the means of death, and his inventiveness was such that word of these public executions had spread throughout the Mediterranean. Beheading English-style or burning at the stake in the French manner were too tame for him. He preferred his victims to die slowly and noisily. Some he had trussed and turned on a spit so that the flesh blistered and charred; then they were doused with water so as to prolong the suffering. Impaling was another favorite, especially for a slave who was small and skinny. The weight of his own body would slowly drive the sharpened stake higher and higher up into his body.

The third rule of the game gave the loser a fitting punishment. The slave who wrongly woke the people of Tunis by issuing the call prematurely lost his tongue.

Naturally, there was great competition among the unfortunate slaves to be first to spot that initial streak of the dawn's first light. And frequently, a slave started the chant prematurely—as had happened this morning—desperately gambling that the elusive ray would flash the same instant. If his timing were perfect, hundreds of voices joined his own, his life extended for another three months. Sometimes, as had happened this morning, the solitary voice faltered . . . broke . . . and silence was restored to the city. The Tunisians, appeased by the public spectacle of detongueing, had grown accustomed to such false awakenings and stoically had learned to turn over and go back to sleep or to indulge themselves in other pastimes, as the Moulay was doing.

Today's unfortunate was an English yeoman captured by Barbarossa's pirates and sold to the keepers of the Great Mosque better than two months ago. Cringing, he could hear the booted footsteps of the guards slapping against the tiles of the courtyard as they approached the base of the minaret on which he perched. They would not bother to climb up and drag him down, he knew. Instead, they would wait for him to descend as he would have to do one day, one way or another.

Edwin Godwin pulled his scant rags around his still-strong body to ward off the chilling gusts sweeping in off the Mediterranean and wished himself back in his native England. Desperately, he pondered his fate. Fear of falling had kept him awake through the early morning hours, and fear of failing had fooled his eyes into believing they had seen a lightening of the sky in the east.

Now, he had three choices left to him: to cling to his perch and eventually, growing light-headed from lack of food and drink, topple off to his death upon the tiled courtyard seventy-five feet below; to end his misery quickly by throwing himself off the minaret; or to make his way down the stairs and surrender to his fate.

Tempering his decision was the knowledge that from among the speechless victims of the Moulay's game came a selected few members of the mute bodyguard of the princess, his daughter. If one were young and strong, once the stub of a tongue had healed, life as a member of this elite group was reported to be easy and luxurious. "Suppose her bodyguard is full . . . or I am not thought young and strong enough?" He shook his head to clear away such defeatist thoughts. He had gambled and lost with his premature chant; he would have to gamble again.

Then, even as he inched his way around the parapet toward the opening to the stairway, a streak of light seemed to pierce the darkness. Here was a second chance and even if false, he could lose his tongue but once. His voice rang out surprisingly clear:

"God is most Great! God is most Great!
  I bear witness that there is no god but God,
  I bear witness that Mohammed is the Apostle of God.
  Come to prayers.
  Come to good works.
  Prayer is better than sleep.
  God is most Great! God is most Great!
  There is no god but God!"

In the depths of the bed in the Bardo, the Moulay halted his thrusting and raised his head: it was the same voice. The Moulay was furious. Then, the single voice was drowned by a chorus of voices, their chanting filling the air: "God is most great. I bear witness that there is no god but God."

Now the Moulay was indeed maddened. The call was genuine; the slave had escaped his fate. But worse than that, the interruption had robbed the Moulay's unstable manhood of its ability to continue. As the slave stared in terror, the lust-filled features above him twisted into a mask of rage and the slave rightly feared for his life.

But then, the monarch remembered the night before. Not for many years had he been able to so sustain and prolong his lustings. It was the novelty of this boy–girl's body. Such novelty might serve him well again. As such, he decided he would be foolish to take the child's life. Even as he prepared to tell the slave as much, he was interrupted again. By a sound. More a clearing of the throat than a cough. The Moulay froze. His voice, high-pitched, was menacing: "Who loves life so little he dares disturb the Moulay?"

The oily face of the roly-poly eunuch quivered with fear, but the voice, his most unctuous, gave no hint of it. This was not the first time he had interrupted his master in his devoirs, but each time he feared that it might be his last. "It is audience day, Magnificence."

The Moulay sighed and rolled over onto his back. Released, the youthful slave bolted from the bed for the door. The eunuch instinctively grabbed for him, but the Moulay shook his head, allowing the child to go.

Approaching the bed, the eunuch knelt. Quickly, with the speed of one doing familiar tasks, the eunuch deftly put slippers upon his master's chubby feet. And then, with the eunuch's help, the Moulay sat up.

While the city's inhabitants, like all Moslems throughout the world, made their obeisances to the East, touching their foreheads to the floor in worship of Allah, Tunisia's ruler yawned and watched as the eunuch knelt between his knees. Gently, the eunuch lifted his master's flaccid member with his left hand and pointed it toward the bejeweled crystal night-soil jar he held in his right hand.

As the stream of urine swished noisily in the urn, the Moulay looked about him. The heavy silk hangings, the thick rug with its famed blue Kairouan design, the cushions embroidered with gold thread, the copper braziers burning merrily to make the room warm

334

as noon—everything that he saw pleased him. He loved this place from the depths of his being. He much preferred its light, airy, decidedly effeminate beauty to that of the Dar al Bey, his official residence in the center of the medina. Here amid splendid gardens nestled away from the heat and stink of Tunis, he had privacy to indulge his wildest perversions.

Besides, the Dar al Bey meant too many unpleasant memories for the depraved monarch.

As the heir apparent, the first forty years of his life had been spent at the Dar al Bey, mostly confined to the small but luxurious one-room "Prince's Cage," in a remote spot in the palace gardens. His companions had been aging concubines, confirmed sterile, the droppings of his father, the Moulay Hamid. Other than food, the prince found his only pleasure in sex, especially in the company of his male slaves and guards. His environment, if not his genes, turned him into a confirmed homosexual before his youth had progressed to manhood.

The big break in his wretched, boring existence came as the result of a revolt by the savage Berbers in the south. Surging out of their mountain holdings with surprise as their ally, they quickly overcame all resistance in the oases and tent cities of the outlying tribes.

Soon they moved on the capital city of Tunis itself, took it by storm, killed its ruler, Moulay Hamid, and took the victors' revenge on both inhabitants and property.

But the Berbers were no city dwellers. Having plundered to their hearts' content, they were soon restless for the cool, clean air of their mountain homes. The problem was how to return and still retain their hold on Tunis. The answer lay in sacrificing one of their dutiful daughters for the good of the whole tribe.

Released from the Prince's Cage, Prince Hassan was led into the throne room. There, frightened and bemused by the fierce looks of his captors, he was married to a Berber princess named Ramlah. And then, in accordance with Berber custom, the two were taken to a bedroom for the consummation of the marriage before the eyes of the tribe's elders. It was then that the Moulay Hassan learned what a powerful aphrodisiac fear could be.

The brief coupling over, the prince could barely control his nausea. But all thoughts of his stomach fled when he saw his wife's father, a wild mustachioed man, start toward the bed. Fear made him deaf to the man's words. It was the Berber princess who heard the request, and, in utter disgust for her new husband, surrendered to her father the bloodstained sheepskin from the marriage bed.

Without another word, not even a glance backward at the newly-weds lying on the bed, the father spun around and left with his fellows to hang the bloody trophy on a pole before the palace gates. Thus was the grand and glorious Dar al Bey reduced to just another Berber marriage tent. The ancient custom was supposed to prove to the world the sanctity of the bride and the manliness of the husband. In this instance, it was only half right.

Alone at last with his young bride, the Moulay could no longer contain himself and spewed out the contents of his stomach over the bed, himself, and the glistening beautiful body of his bride. To compound matters, the prince broke into tears.

Perhaps if she had been older and wiser—or not a Berber—Ramlah might have swallowed her pride and taken him in her arms and comforted him, winning a husband by acting the mother. But the reeking vomit, the tears and the animal-like nature of her *lailat al-jilwa* were too much. She leaped from bed and fled the room. When she fled, she left behind all chance of ever reaching rapprochement with the Moulay.

Weeks went by without the two seeing each other. Restless though they were, the Berbers still camped outside Tunis. They seemed indifferent to the fact that the Moulay and Ramlah maintained separate living quarters.

Then, the news swept the city. The young princess was with child. With that, the Berbers packed up and left. The succession to the throne was assured.

Once the Berbers were gone, the Moulay prepared to indulge himself as never before had been possible while confined to the Prince's Cage. And his indulgence included neither his wife nor a harem of women.

His first step was to find other living quarters—far away from the accursed Dar al Bey. The Palace of the Harem, once emptied of its feminine inhabitants, he decided, would best satisfy all his needs. Far enough from the city, yet close enough for him to maintain control, it would be redecorated and replanted to suit his own tastes and staffed with a choice selection of unusual slaves and guards.

His plans formulated, the Moulay sent for his bride. He received her in an anteroom just off the huge audience chamber. If she felt fear, she did not show it, refusing to prostrate herself before him. In the duel of stares, he was first to look away. Totally unnerved by her demeanor the Moulay found himself staring at her belly. Was it his imagination or was it distended with child? His child! His son was growing there. The thought gave him courage.

"Now hear me, woman," he blustered. "This child you bear must be a male. I command it. Do you every procedure known to man to assure it. Make no mistake, I will have you watched night and day, and shall punish your first wrong move." His insane giggle gave his threat peculiar potency, yet the Berber princess did not deign to reply. Uncertain how to interpret her silence, the Moulay hastened on with his tirade. "You will live here at Dar al Bey, confined to the harem wing and its gardens, while I live elsewhere. The guard will kill you if you attempt to leave without my permission. Now get out of my sight."

The queen eyed her husband as if he had just crawled from beneath a rock. Then, to the Moulay's relief, she nodded and walked unhurriedly from the room.

For a woman used to the free life of the Berbers, the very thought of confinement in a seraglio was distasteful. But the reality was worse even than her imaginings. The harem quarters just beyond the court of the black eunuchs had been left to deteriorate as the former Moulay, growing senile, lost his lust for life. The rooms smelled dank, unused; the tapestries and wall hangings had grown moldy; dust and spider webs were everywhere; mice had made nests within the couches, their droppings covered the rugs. The grounds were even worse. The gardens were forests of weeds. The fountains had fallen over while the catchpools, green with scum, now hummed as fertile breeding places for mosquitoes.

As she stood, dismayed at her surroundings, she heard screams in the background. Retracing her steps, she flung the harem doors open only to find her way barred by guards. The screams, torn from many male throats, rose and fell and stopped and started anew. Hastily closing the doors, she fled into the garden and there, burying her face in her robes, tried to keep out the sounds of her husband's handiwork.

The Moulay had issued orders that no male relative of his was to live past noon that day. Throughout the length and breadth of the palace and the city, soldiers of the new monarch sought out and slew royal brothers, uncles, and cousins.

One of the younger uncles had had the resourcefulness to make his way to the harem wing. Dashing past the startled guards, he ran through the rooms to the gardens. There, ignoring the startled woman, he flung himself at the stone wall. He had almost scaled it when he was hauled down by his pursuers and hacked to pieces before her eyes. As the coup de grace, one of the soldiers skewered on his scimitar the sightless head, tongue lolling from its gaping mouth. They would have left the headless, twitching remains behind, but the queen blocked their path.

"I could have you beheaded for entering my quarters," she reminded them. "But I see the blood-lust upon you, and you are not yourselves. I shall forget I have seen you, but first get that wretched thing out of here. Now! Go!"

Suddenly aware of where they were and who she was, the soldiers quickly grabbed the royal relative by its heels and dragged it out, its neck spitting a trail of blood behind it.

Thus were Tunis and its queen introduced to their new Moulay. When the slaughter was over, the heads were brought before him as he sat on his throne at the head of the marble stairs in the Court of the Stone Lions. There, one by one, each head was displayed and identified, its owner's name checked off on a scroll. Then, the head was added to the stack in the center of the courtyard.

When the last head was placed on this pyramid of staring eyes, protruding tongues, and hideously distorted faces, the heap of human heads towered above the Moulay's own. The flies buzzed about the drying blood clinging to flesh and bone. The Moulay Hassan, his feet shuffling in the pool of blood that was spreading on the courtyard tiles, slowly circled the heap, talking first to one and then another of his dead relatives.

His ghastly one-way conversation with the heads was interrupted by a slave, carrying a small casket. Kneeling before the Moulay, the slave opened it. Within was the still sweet-smelling head of his father, the Moulay Hamid.

"Ah, there you are," cooed the Moulay. "The party would not have been complete without old father himself, now would it?" Reaching out, he stroked its cheek, recoiling as the flesh fell away from the skull. At the Moulay's direction, the slave carefully removed the skull and placed it at the very top of the pyramid of heads.

The new Moulay giggled with delight and demanded an accounting of the slaughter. "One hundred forty, *jalala al-malik*," murmured the gray-bearded recorder of the scroll.

"Speak up, man," shrieked the Moulay. "How many?"

"One hundred forty."

"You needn't shout, man, my head can still hear . . . unlike those over there." The Moulay snickered. Then a new thought struck him. "Including the Moulay Hamid or not?"

"No, *jalala al-malik*, not including him. I did not think to count him."

"But you should have. He, too," the Moulay giggled, "was a relative. The closest relative I had. And he is dead along with all the others. But I live! And no one"—he looked about him—"no one will ever tell me what to do again."

He returned to his skull pyramid, pulling a tongue here, pushing an eye out there. Then his voice dropped as he confided in his dead relatives, "I would have destroyed the Prince's Cage, you know, but I may have need for it. A thing grows in my queen's womb, and if it is a boy—" He had no need to finish. Everyone knew what he meant.

And as is the way with courts and courtiers, the queen sequestered in her harem back in Tunis was informed of his every word, and especially what was implied as the fate of her child if a male.

The queen's duty to tribe, country, and husband dictated she produce a boy. So she slept with a sword under her bed, ate only the flesh of male animals, drank no milk (which is the fruit of the female), and put aside her silky garments in favor of the heavy wool robes of a man. Even though she did all these things, she could not discipline her thoughts. And they dwelled on having a daughter.

When the midwife, crouched low beside the birthing chair, caught the bloodied body of the babe and began to moan, the queen knew her prayers were answered. The babe was female. The child was named Aisha, after the favorite wife of Mohammed, Messenger of God, to whom the queen had prayed.

"I name you also Kahina after your Berber ancestress, the princess–prophetess, who drove the Arabs out of Carthage centuries ago. May you, my daughter, do the same."

The Moulay neither came to see the babe nor even acknowledged formally that there was a child. Abhored and ignored by her father, the little Aisha blossomed under her mother's doting care. At about three, she began to realize that she was special, a princess, a beautiful one at that, and she cajoled, charmed, and commanded her servants into allowing her a surprising degree of freedom within the palace.

By the age of six, she had the run of the Dar al Bey. No hiding place or hidden nook had escaped her notice. The servants, accustomed to seeing her run gaily up and down the corridors with her token bodyguard—patient, unintelligent, unimaginative Ahmed—in tow, seldom took notice of her comings and goings. Poor hapless Ahmed, who had trouble enough just keeping up, could not manage to keep track of where she went. Even he was forbidden to enter her favorite place, a garden just beyond the harem itself, barely within the seraglio proper, and adjacent to the long-vacated Moulay's apartments. Here, she soon discovered, she was safe from friend, slave, and even mother. No mere mortal dared enter these grounds without serious second thought, and Ramlah avoided anything to do with the Moulay as if he were leprous.

As Aisha's freedom elsewhere was curtailed and her education expanded, the garden became more and more her refuge. One day when forced to begin learning Turkish, the language of the enemy, she fled here from the harem. "Isn't it enough I know Berber and Arabic? To learn that—" She searched for an epithet and could find none apt, so spat vehemently. Absently, she began, as she often did, to tease the carp that still lived in the pool. Over the years she had with patience and instinct tempted their curiosity until the gold and red and red gold mottled fish came to explore her teasing fingertips. From there it had been a simple matter to teach them to feed from her hand. The placid things learned quickly to allow her to scratch

340

their shimmering bellies with one hand while they fed greedily from her other hand. Today they had only begun to eat when an enormous shadow darkened the water and sent them scurrying. Turning about, the little girl saw a short, rotund man wearing the largest turban she'd ever seen. Atop it was an even larger crimson feather that trembled in the breeze and would have wafted away but for the jewel almost as red and almost as brilliant that held it fast. The man's face, although set in a smile, troubled her. Its lips were fat, its eyes small, its chin wreathed with fat and its skin oozing perspiration. Yet there was something about the face that was familiar, reassuring. It was this quality that misled the child.

"You charm the fish well," the man finally said.

"Better even than Ahmed, and his people were fisherfolk," she boasted.

"Ahmed?"

"My bodyguard."

"I see no one."

"He's not here. He's out there"—she gestured vaguely, sweepingly—"somewhere." She giggled. "Probably he's asleep."

"You should be tired, too. It's hard work coaxing the fish."

"Me, tired? Never. I could play games with the fish for hours."

He paused, irresolutely for a moment, then, unaccustomed to denying himself anything, asked, "Have you ever played Naked Frog? It's my favorite game."

"Is it fun? Would you teach me?"

"Gladly. But to learn it we must go inside."

Trustingly, the little girl placed her small hand within the pudgy grasp of her new friend and the two went inside.

Hours passed and Ramlah grew first concerned with Aisha's absence, then fearful, then hysterical. Eventually, a search turned up a sleeping Ahmed outside the entrance to the gardens of the Moulay. The gates were barred from within. Only Ramlah's tongue and the lash of the captain of her bodyguard, a Berber left behind to protect her by her father, persuaded the petrified slaves to break in. The garden was empty.

Not so the second chamber within. There on a low couch sprawled a small, still form, its clothes scattered about, its nether region splattered with gore. And glaring at the intruders from just beyond the child was an irate, near-naked Moulay, his fat forearms resting familiarly on the naked child's chest.

Ramlah, overcome with a murderous rage that rendered her speechless, stood frozen as he screamed epithets at her, her bodyguard, and at the whole world for disturbing him at his pleasure.

It was the word pleasure that restored Ramlah's voice. "Pleasure, you say? What monarch is so sick as to seek pleasure upon his daughter's body?"

The Moulay blinked and shook his head. Then came the realization. In his quixotic impulse to taste a female after devoting himself exclusively to men for years, he'd ravished his own flesh, his own daughter, his only heir. He had enjoyed the child's resistance and enjoyed her screams, but he was not so depraved and without compunction that he could simply continue to lie there. He drew back, and Ramlah's Berber captain resolutely strode forward, picked up and carried the bloodied body of the still-unconscious child from the room. Suddenly Ramlah grew seven feet tall as she looked upon her husband with loathing. "Know you what you've done today. Incestuous monster, Mohammed—upon whom be praise—will bar you from heaven's gates. On Earth, no monarch will speak well of you; no slave give you shelter. You are mad. You have committed the unspeakable sin, you have lain with your daughter. And if you so much as speak to Aisha again, word shall reach my father. Then, once more, the Berbers shall be down upon your head, and this time they will cut off that thing you misuse so, cook it before your eyes, and stuff it down your throat! And I shall cheer them on, for you little, stupid, crazy man, you have deprived your country of a future and condemned your own line to extinction. Your daughter may rule but she is no longer a virgin and can never wed, thanks to you. Think long on that, oh Moulay Hassan, daughter-ravisher!"

She turned on her heel and left the room. Back in her own quarters, she gazed down into the unconscious face of her daughter, its pale cheeks streaked with tears and its eyes blue-shadowed. Fearfully, she patted the cheeks hoping to rouse her gently. Aisha awoke screaming. Before her eyes, Ramlah saw something flicker and die in her daughter. Aisha awoke, prematurely a woman at age six. Never again did the halls of the Dar al Bey echo to a child's carefree laughter or thoughtless giggle. With one brutal thrust, her father had made Aisha a woman. And though neither mother nor daughter spoke of what had happened behind the doors of the Moulay's apartment, every night for months, even when sleeping in her mother's arms, Aisha awoke screaming.

From that day on, she put away her dolls, her toy dishes, every reminder of eventual motherhood. Instead, she dressed like a boy and demanded she be treated as such. Particularly, she insisted that she be sent to school as if she were a prince.

At the Prince's School, maintained at the Dar al Bey as at every major Arab palace for the purpose of educating the sons of royalty and the nobility, Aisha was the only pupil. Quickly and eagerly she learned, at the feet of the wisest and most scholarly men in the land, to read, write, and speak classical languages in addition to her mother's native Berber and her father's Arabic tongues. Mathematics. Astrology. Geography. History. Aisha mastered them all, plus the languages of Tunisia's erstwhile allies, the hated Turks and despised French, taught her by slaves from those countries purchased for the purpose and later resold at the vast slave market in Tunis.

In the harem she learned to sing, to dance, to play the three-stringed guitar, to do needlework and painting, and to use cosmetics: henna to make her long, thick mane gleam like molten gold, and kohl to make her large almond-shaped eyes seem even darker and more unfathomable.

Her first visit to her mother's tribe was at age seven. There as a Berber princess, she was to be taught to think for herself, to hunt and shoot, to wield knife and scimitar, to ride both camel and speedy desert horses. But first, she had to live down her Arabic heritage and prove herself to her peers, a group of children as fair-haired as she.

Unfortunately, nothing at the Prince's School had prepared her for the rough-and-tumble in-fighting that Berber children seem to absorb with their mothers' milk. She was no match for even the youngest of them that first summer. Her beatings were frequent and severe, but, as one of the elders privately noted, fair, and so the tribal elders allowed them to continue.

Dry-eyed and tight-lipped, she took her blows and got up, dusted herself off, and came back for more. Slowly, grudgingly, she won the respect of her tormentors, if not for her fighting ability, at least for her courage. By the end of her first season in her grandfather's camp, her Berber cousins had begun to lose interest in such one-sided fights. By the end of the next season, an unspoken peace was made, which was just as well for the Berbers. Aisha, or Kahina as she was called here, had used her time in Tunis to good purpose, learning wrestling holds from slaves, purchased for that purpose and then killed for touching the body of the royal lady. With these lessons behind her, Kahina did more than hold her own; she won victories.

With the fighting out of the way, Kahina's quick wits and book-learning gave her a decided advantage among the Berbers, and soon she had earned her rightful position as leader of the children. Among those who had looked on and followed her progress was one who became a fast friend: an uncle ten years her elder, Ali ben Zaid, born to her grandfather in his seventieth year by a young slave woman.

Over the course of the years, as the two grew closer and closer, the Berber elders, by their noninterference, expressed tacit approval of the relationship. Nothing would have pleased them more than to have the succession to the throne reinforced with still more Berber blood. Of course, technically, the two were within the proscribed degrees of consanguinity as enumerated by the Prophet, which the elders agreed, was a matter for the mullahs to settle; first, the girl must agree to the marriage. With that in mind, the elders voiced no objections to Ali's request, in Aisha's fourteenth year, that he accompany the princess back to Tunis. Indeed, the gray-hairs smiled secretly within their beards and exchanged knowing looks. And one even suggested that they take a more roundabout route back, visiting others of her people along the way. "Let her," confided one to another, "see how well Ali ben Zaid is accorded respect by others of her people and she will see him in a new light."

This was Aisha's first visit among her nomads and she savored every moment of it—from her arrival in camp with a flurry of sand thrown up by her fierce horsemen of the desert to the last sip of the sweet mint tea drunk in her honor at the feast on the eve of her departure. So smoothly did everything go that only gradually did Aisha become aware how much all this depended on Ali's ability to lead and organize. Moreover, his skill as a horseman and warrior greatly impressed her people, as did his obvious deference to her.

She could practically read the message in the eyes of her beholders; "If this ferocious warrior and proud horseman accords this girl-child such respect, she must indeed be worthy of ours." Thus did their curiosity change to esteem; aloof distrust become admiration. Having accomplished this, the darkly handsome Ali and his slender, boyish-looking companion took their leave and rode off toward still another oasis. Aisha knew that given enough time, she could bind all the Bedouin tribes to her banner. Time was the problem. Two days here, three days there, and fewer than a hundred tribesmen had she met. At this rate, she would have to travel all of the year to meet even half of her people. She vowed that eventually she would do just that.

Leaving Gafsa, the most northerly of the oases in the Great South of Tunisia, Aisha turned her horse's head eastward, straight toward the capital. Instead, Ali suggested they go by way of Redeyef some seventy kilometers away, a more circuitous route but not too far out of their way. The morning sun was only two hours in the sky. They had plenty of time, even with a halt at midday, to get there before dark and then take the road to Tunis. Aisha was in no hurry to return to the constricting life of the seraglio, not after tasting freedom among the Berbers and Bedouin. Quickly, she reined her mount away from Tunis and followed Ali's lead. At first, they rode through lush green grass strewn with fragile-looking flowers which spread like rich carpets upon the desertlike steppe, drawing sustenance from underground springs. But soon the path grew rugged. Redeyef was situated in rough, mountainous terrain among the foothills of the Lower Steppes. To its south lay Moulares, with its phosphate mines, and the Djebel Alima caves where the Caspian people worked and lived.

Along the way, Ali suggested another detour which would take them through the impressive gorges of the Oued Seldja not far from the Algerian border. Two summers before, Ali had visited this natural wonder with friends, and his young mind remembered with awe the sheer rock walls and cascading streams.

Leaving their escort behind, they tethered their horses at the foot of a reddish cliff, and the eager pair entered a narrow cleft, making their way upward on foot. It was a relief just getting down off the horses and stretching their legs, though climbing was difficult. Following the stream through rocky walls, Aisha and Ali soon reached the natural amphitheater that Ali remembered so vividly.

As they stepped into the lush green meadow, Aisha gave a startled cry. At the far end of the small amphitheater where the cliffs rose 200 meters above the stream, hung the misty ribbon of a waterfall of such beauty that it took her breath away.

"I've never seen anything so beautiful," the young princess whispered.

"Nor I," replied Ali. "I wanted you to see it, so that we might share its memory."

"Oh, thank you," Aisha said as she turned and placed her full lips on his in a quick, but grateful kiss. Ali's arms went about her tiny waist. Hers instinctively went over his broad shoulders and circled around his neck.

With infinite patience, savoring the touch, the young couple explored each other's lips. Gradually, the kiss grew more intense as each was awakened to the other's need. Then Ali broke the kiss and the silence almost simultaneously. "Forgive me, princess," he blurted out as realization of what he had done came to him. "I had no right to do that. I forgot you are the Princess Aisha—"

Her fingertips on his lips silenced him. "Hush. No more of that. I am your friend Kahina, remember? Besides, it was I who started it. I couldn't help it, it is so beautiful here."

It was her turn to become silent as he covered her hand with his and kissed those quieting fingertips one by one. Almost shyly, she asked the question that was foremost in her mind. "You did like it, didn't you?"

"Of course, I did," he replied, abandoning her fingertips and seeking once again the slightly parted lips of the girl he now knew he loved and had always loved.. Aisha did not resist the gentle pressure that seemed to float her down into the deep, lush grass. Ali's surprisingly soft and gentle lips moved now to her closed eyes, then to the slightly upturned nose, the gleaming lobes of her ears, the softness of her neck, always returning to drink again of the woman he desired.

Even as he did, one hand moved gently but firmly down her shoulder to come to rest on Aisha's budding breast. At the touch, even through her burnoose, Aisha shivered. Ali interpreted it as a signal to continue giving pleasure. His hands now gently, lovingly cupped the firm, young mound and moved in rhythmic circles. For Ali, it was a moment of unbelievable beauty. A moment which hung in the eerie stillness of nature's amphitheater for a frozen eon . . . and then was shattered. By a whisper.

"Ali," Aisha whispered in his ear. "Ali, don't. I beg you. No more." Although the memory of her painful first penetration had faded over the years until it was but a shadow in the back of her mind, the rest of her brutal ravishment remained indelibly etched on her psyche. Now, Ali's lips on hers, his hand on her breast, recalled thick, merciless lips forcing her mouth open, a tongue filling it, making her gag, hard hands cruelly tweaking her little girl's nipples, and then—she couldn't bear to remember; she couldn't bear Ali's caresses.

He misinterpreted the tears welling up in her eyes. "I've hurt you, my love."

"You? Hurt me?" She laughed bitterly, and now the tears flowed unchecked. "No, not you. Never you. I'm the one who must hurt you." Again her fingers stilled the lips about to protest. "Believe me, Ali, I do care for you. And I would that I were other than what I am. If I were someone else, anyone else—a slave girl or *raqisa*, I could come shamelessly but gladly into your arms—" Her voice broke, and a moment passed before she could get it under control. "But I am not. I am my father's daughter. And because of what he has made me, I can never know a love like yours."

Her eyes flashed, her face grew bleak, and her mouth hardened. He was not sure of what she meant, but he did know that before his very eyes she had changed from innocent maiden to cruelly astute royal. This change in her countenance must have been mirrored in his, for suddenly her expression softened. Once again she was the young girl he had known for these many years.

"Ali," she whispered, "believe me, I do love you. But in the only way possible for me to love you—as my brother."

Ali, choked with emotions that fought his ability to reason, gave a little sob, and moved away, lying back and staring unseeingly at the limitless sky. Time went by before Aisha leaned over and rested her head on his shoulder. "Ali, I'm sorry, I truly am. But if you'd like, you can kiss me again."

He groaned. As much as he wished to do just that, he knew he couldn't trust himself to stop just there. It was her turn to misinterpret his reaction. "Ali, are you sick? Should I get help, tell me—"

He forced a smile to his lips. "No, little princess, my sickness is incurable."

She couldn't meet his eyes.

"If you are ready, Aisha, we had best go back."

Slowly, they rose to their feet and, without a word, began the walk back down the canyon. Her hand reached out and joined with his as, without speaking, the two slowly wound their way back to the horses to ride on toward Redeyef and the safety of company. Aisha had learned one valuable thing: here was a man she could trust.

Although Ali would never forget their tryst in the gorge, Aisha seemed to have banished it from her mind. At least, she never once spoke of it, talking only of her meetings with the Bedouin. This was Aisha's first breath of the heady fumes of royal power, and she found the prospect of more intoxicating. It made the restrictions on her freedom of movement in Tunis even more onerous. "I shall not even be able to see you as often as I wish, Ali."

He was taken aback. "Why not? I'm your uncle!"

Aisha laughed. "Oh, suddenly, you've remembered that," she teased him.

"Only when it's convenient to remember it," he shot back. "Now, tell me, why can we not see each other whenever and wherever we wish?"

"Because in Tunis, I can see you only when you come to see me at the seraglio."

"You mean you don't come and go as you choose?"

"Hardly. It would not be safe for me, a woman, to go out in the streets. I live the life of a princess in prison. A comfortable prison, but a prison all the same."

She touched heels to her horse's flanks and put him to a canter as if already fleeing the confines of the harem. Ali and her escort had no choice but to follow after, but already Ali was looking for a solution to Aisha's problem.

Less than a week after their return to Tunis, Ali presented himself at the Dar al Bey with his plan for creating the *al Ikwan*, a bodyguard for the princess, selected from among the slave *muezzins* muted by the Moulay's command and even by his own hand. Ali judged, rightly as it turned out, that these refugees from the game-of-call-to-morning-prayer would feel no love for the father and would learn loyalty to the daughter. Besides, it took a strong, tough man to live through such an ordeal. The tongue tied to a horse's tail and pulled out by the roots in a gruesome tug of war. Or else cut off with a red-hot sword, causing and cauterizing the wound simultaneously. Or ice was brought down from the Atlas Mountains, to remove the tongue, layer by layer by layer, in a long agonizing ordeal. There was no limit to the Moulay's insane creativity when it came to torture.

Ramlah was quick to point out the obvious. "The slaves' very silence is an obstacle to your plan. How do you speak with men who once spoke many tongues and now can only ululate like babies?"

Aisha agreed. "I shall never speak in ughs and arghs or cackles and croaks."

"You needn't," Ali replied. "Their minds are whole, they will understand you."

"Think you, uncle, my people will fear and respect men who talk with growls like beasts? How would that make me safe within the city? No, I'll not have it. Find another way."

Ramlah agreed. "Even if you do, she will still be a woman surrounded by men. That gives my daughter freedom?"

"It does. Remember, Aisha, our visit to the tents of the Taureg? You could not tell one from the other. I propose everyone, including you, go veiled as the Taureg men do, leaving only your eyes uncovered. Veiled in such a way, not even the Moulay will know if his daughter is present or absent from any particular group."

Both Ramlah and Aisha accepted veiling as a way to forestall any possible objections from the Moulay. Still, language presented a barrier to the adoption of the plan. But not for long. Within days, Ali had solved the problem of the myriad of many languages among the slaves by adopting Sabir, that polyglot language of the Crusades, as the official tongue of command. With its roots in Spanish, Arabic, French, and Italian, all but the English already understood much of it. Once all could understand Ali, he would teach them to speak without words, in the lingua franca of the mutes of the bazaar. From then on, they would be forbidden sounds and must sign with their hands.

To this, Ramlah and Aisha quickly agreed, and her personal guard, the *al Ikwan*, was established. Within months, it numbered more than three dozen, all speaking with their hands. The more intelligent of the group learned to signal with their eyes as well, and these, numbering less than twelve, formed an elite corps of body-guards and officers.

Thus, without words, the group might stop and start and turn and move as one. The effect was frightening to those who watched it. It was witchcraft to many of Aisha's people. Their fear became the force's most potent weapon. In this way were mute slaves transformed into silent masters.

Once he became a member of the group, no man left it except through death. So that the group remained small, the standards for admission grew ever more strict over the course of years. Aisha and Ali and the elite ones attended every public detongueing, watching carefully and critically how each *muezzin* withstood the hot or cold torture, the tug of war, the long-handled cutter that more tore than cut a facile member from a gagging throat. Then, afterward, the two, uncle and niece, would compare the degree of barbarity of the detongueing with the courage shown. Only after both had agreed the slave to be worthy and the elite corps had concurred, would a slave–*muezzin* be chosen to join the group. As far as Aisha was concerned, Edwin Godwin could not have chosen a worse morning to wake the city with his false call to prayer. Today was audience day. Adding a detongueing to her schedule meant she would have to forego the slave auction. That might be just as well. The Moulay liked to choose for himself the replacements for his game-of-morn-ing-call. She dared not bid against him, not until the problem of her marriage had been solved. If angered, the Moulay was capricious enough to change his deranged mind and ship her off to Algiers to the Barbarossa. Aisha remembered, from one of those rare meetings when she had been forced to join her mother as she endeavored to persuade the Moulay not to accede to the corsair's request, how astutely and cruelly he had pointed out, "What difference could bursting a piece of skin make to that son-of-a-nobody? He would still be marrying a princess and taking his place alongside kings."

"You're right. That lack of a 'piece of skin' might be of real benefit to him," Ramlah agreed, cleverly turning the Moulay's observation against him and capitalizing on his fear of Barbarossa. "Once married to Aisha, the corsair could use it as a legitimate excuse to bring about your death. The crime? Incest . . . rape . . . child-ravishment . . . whatever he wills."

The Moulay hadn't thought of that. Turning white, he asked, "What else can I do?"

"Challenge him to come and win her . . . in competition with others."

"Competition?" The idea had appeal for him.

Even now, Aisha could hear her mother's purring voice expounding their idea. "Think of it, mighty Moulay, hundreds of men fighting naked with strange weapons that tear and rip before killing, all for the honor of being allowed to wed your daughter."

"Suppose not many come. They might not like to die just for her hand."

Ramlah's inventiveness was up to the challenge. Silencing her daughter with a glance, she went on smoothly. "Then we'll fill out their ranks with slaves. In the nude, no one can tell a free man from a slave."

"Do they all have to die fighting?"

"Not all, some will die as you choose."

"I choose? How?"

"You shall do as the Roman emperors did. When one falls in defeat, you will give the signal for life or death," she promised. Sharing this city with her husband, she had been forced to learn how to appeal to the worst in his character—those attributes that had come to the surface on his release from the Prince's Cage and smothered what few good qualities he had once possessed. "Yes, mighty one, you shall decide how those defeated die."

She had captured his imagination. When he licked his full, lower lip nervously, the two women knew the day was theirs. Let him think on this for a while, and soon no power on earth could dissuade him. Ramlah's soft, soothing, subtle voice continued, describing in broad strokes—let his imagination fill in the detail—their plan to restore the partially ruined Roman amphitheater of al Djem in the

351

South, and to hold the games there. Games in the Greek, Roman, Arabic, Berber, and other even more bloodthirsty traditions.

Aisha found her own nostrils flaring, her pulse racing and her throat growing dry as she listened to Ramlah's words. She was, after all, her father's daughter, although one looking at the two would have found it hard to believe. He was short, thick, gross, and swarthy; she was tall and almost boyishly thin, although beneath her Taureg robes were more curves than one might have supposed. Hidden too was her hair, that thick, silken mane of molten gold that was her glory. Her green brown eyes, wide-spaced, dark-fringed and almond-shaped, looked out from under proud, high-arched brows. Only the mouth with its full lower lip bespoke the passionate nature and near barbaric emotions that father and daughter shared—he giving vent to them, she holding them in close rein.

As Aisha recalled the skill of her mother's manipulation of the Moulay, the second and true call to prayer interrupted her thoughts. So similar were the two voices that uttered the calls, they might have come from the same throat. She hoped so. Then there would be no detongueing today. However, if that were the case, then this *muezzin* would be one to be aware of and to watch for when he, as all did, finally faced her father's pincers.

CHAPTER 22

Six days a week, Aisha joined her mother in the three-hour ritual of the three baths in the harem's ornate ones. The seventh day, Audience Day, a Thursday, she had less leisure, so she used instead the austere bath within her own quarters. This, like the larger one, was heated by the Pompeiian system with boilers of copper beneath the floor. Stepping out of her only apparel, a pair of high-heeled panttobles of velvet, she walked down the steps of her marble bath and into the hot, steamy, water.

When immersed, she held out one hand. Wordlessly, a eunuch knelt and handed Aisha the scroll listing the cases to be heard this day. Quickly, she surveyed them. On the surface, none seemed too complicated. If she brooked no delay nor interruption nor tirade, the audience should be over long before the slave auction began. That is, if she heard the cases herself. If the Moulay should appear, the audience could last all day or less than an hour. That man in his *majanna* might do anything.

Clearing her mind of all thoughts, she left the bath and surrendered her body to her slaves' ministrations. Her nails were buffed, her feet pumiced, her hair washed and combed dry, then her forelocks braided and strands of diamonds entwined, her brows plucked, her lashes brushed with kohl, and her lips stained with a flower petal.

Only after completing her toilet did she don drawers of white see-through silk, a shirt of the same, the sleeves reaching to the wrist, the bodice open to the waist. Over that a sleeveless waistcoat, slit up the front, fell to the floor. Round and round the eunuch circled her, holding the wide embroidery-encrusted waist-wrap spread between his hands, to form her two-hand-high *kamarband*. Bracing herself by leaning on two eunuchs' shoulders, she stepped into her boots.

Critically, she surveyed herself within the polished silver of her mirror. Plain. Simple. Perfect. She would not change a detail. Lastly, her eunuchs draped her in a white, woolen *burd* that hid all but her face, her hands, and her white kid boots. She was ready to appear in public. As she left her quarters, she was joined by Ali and six of the *al Ikwan*. The Amira Aisha did not appear in public without bodyguard.

Thursday audiences started an hour after sunrise, and, with only a brief break for lunch, lasted as long as there were cases to be heard. Those heard last often received short shrift from a *gadi* eager to see the long day end. Since any Tunisian could demand his case be heard, the naive started lining up outside the courtroom long before dawn, hoping to be first. The experienced paid their bribe to the right official and had their case scheduled early in the day—the list Aisha perused.

On this Thursday, as usual, the bribes were in, the docket was set, everything appeared routine—until the Moulay and his entourage arrived at the Dar al Bey with much clattering of horses' hooves. The Moulay himself never went on horseback, but rode in a huge sedan chair complete with protective fringed top and balanced on three poles. Six runners at a time alternated, changing on the move, to keep up the steady pace . . . somewhere between fast walk and trot. They edged the sedan chair up to the stool's level so that the Moulay, without undue effort, might simply step out. Making a litter from their crossed hands, two blackamoors seated and carried him up the stairs and into the palace, through the first court and the next.

Finally, without his feet once touching the floor, he entered the courtroom. Had people known that their deranged monarch would be the judge, far fewer of them would have chosen this day to present their cases. The Moulay's entrance created pandemonium as everyone at once attempted to go from sitting cross-legged on cushions to totally prostrate, face-flattened against the tile-covered floor.

As always, the Moulay found his subjects' discomfiture amusing. Let his subjects be properly humble when in the presence of their ruler. Viciously pinching his blackamoor mounts he started them toward the dais just as Aisha and her escort entered from the side door. Without a moment's hesitation, Ali and the *al Ikwan* prostrated themselves. Aisha too settled gracefully to her knees and bowed her head. Pleased by his daughter's proper attitude, he allowed his bearers to seat him upon the cushioned couch on the dais, then beckoned his daughter to her seat upon a cushion at his feet. Only then might his subjects resume their places around the perimeter of the room.

The people buzzed excitedly but in muted tones, then ceased as the wazier stepped forward:

"By the grace of Allah, the court of *jalala al-malik,* the Moulay Hassan, is open to all. Come ye and seek ye the justice of the Moulay."

The court crier called the first case to order. The accusing party stepped forward, bowed and prostrated himself, then rose and gave brief testimony. When he strayed from a strict recitation of the facts, he was prodded with a pointed stick by a court official stationed behind him. At his second lapse, his case was dismissed. Next case.

Accusatory testimony given, the defendant stepped forward to tell his side. He was also allowed to rebut the testimony just given. No questions were asked of either party and no witness testified.

"Guilty. Call the next case." Such was the Moulay's manner of judging. The Amira fumed and seethed but said nothing.

About two hours into the session a strikingly beautiful woman awoke the Moulay from his doze when she begged the court to force her husband to take another wife. Even the Moulay Hassan was taken aback; seldom did a man with one wife resist taking more wives.

"If the court please," she testified, "I am my husband's only wife. My days are spent performing household chores, my nights on giving him pleasure. I am with child for the fourth time in as many years. When I am not with child, I must submit to his needs even during those times when most wives are excused. I love my children and my husband, but I would share my responsibilities with another.

"I ask that the court order my husband to take another wife so that we may divide household and conjugal duties between us especially when one of us is carrying his child. And," she concluded, "if he refuses to select a second wife himself, I request the right to select one for him."

There was a mild murmuring around the room as the woman returned to her little circle of friends and sat awkwardly down on her cushion. She was perhaps five months with child, proving her point and winning sympathy from the courtiers, if not the court.

A young man, the reluctant husband, stepped forward. *"Jalala al-malik,* I love her too much to share that love with another. I will buy extra servants for her. I will grant her nights off during her cleansing cycles. But do not," he pleaded, "force me to take a wife who could get no love from me whatsoever. It would not be fair to the woman, nor to me."

He was motioned back to his seat. The Moulay had made his decision, and out of his perversion came a judgment worthy of Solomon.

"Bachir Ali, you make a mockery out of marriage," the Moulay said in a stern voice. "You should have listened, as any good husband would, to your wife."

The audience tittered guardedly, for it was well known that Moulay Hassan ostensibly paid no attention whatsoever to his own wife.

"Since you did not ease her plight," the Moulay continued, "she is no longer yours. She will be married into a harem of many wives where, as she requests, her duties will be lessened. Her children will be cared for. Her lovemaking will be only occasional. As for you—your slate will be wiped clean. Before the sun sets tomorrow, find or buy two wives and do not make the mistake again of letting love blind you to your duty."

As the courtiers gasped at such a fantastic verdict, the stunned couple flew into each other's arms and wept openly. She wailed, "Why did I complain?" while he could only repeat, "No. No. Never." The two were separated by officials and led from the room.

The buzzing in the courtroom did not die down quickly. Not by a blink of the eye, however, did Aisha show sympathy for the couple; she had none. Both woman and man in her opinion, were weak; the judgment was fitting. It also speeded the cause of justice. Many a case yet to be heard was quickly settled between litigants who wished to avoid the possibility of a verdict such as this. When the holder of the docket called out the next cases to be heard, only the bitterest and most vitriolic came forth; the rest quickly announced that their differences had been resolved without benefit of the court.

At last, as the sun reached its zenith, the Moulay sent a eunuch scuttling off to the kitchen, "Tell the Vizier of the Third Kitchen that I would eat as soon as this next case is heard." Yawning, the Moulay indicated the court should continue. Consulting his list, the crier nasally intoned, "The man Ibrahim versus the Sheikh Hatim."

From the back of the room came two black-turbaned Berber tribesmen, one clutching a scroll containing his charge, the other grasping the scroll of his defense. Surrendering his scroll to an official, the accuser salaamed—kneeling and bumping his head twice on the tile floor, then prostrating himself fully in front of the Moulay. He wore a tattered robe, tied at the waist with a bit of rope, and shabby simple desert sandals, while the accused stood by in a snowy white robe with a bejeweled and tasseled belt about his middle.

The accuser rose to his feet and began, "Know ye, O great and gracious Moulay, that I, Ibrahim, son of Mahamma, of the tribe of Zeyd, did while at a horse fair in Kairouan, approach the Sheikh Hatim to ask that he allow his stallion to service my chestnut mare, Sherifa, the love of my life and the pride of my tribe. Know you, Moulay, that this mare has shared my tent since the day she was foaled. No mare has a broader forehead, a finer muzzle, a more intelligent eye. To see the beautiful ears that spring from her well-maned foretop, to watch them respond instantly to everything she spies, that, O Moulay, is to know true beauty."

A sharp jab from the pointed stick hastened his speech. "But know ye, O Moulay, that even though he swelled with pride at my request, the Sheikh Hatim did hold back the services of his stallion in the hopes of my offering to pay for that which should have been mine by right with no ransom. Naturally, I refused. And later that day, I sent my wife to him with a plea that he reconsider."

Like a Greek chorus, the courtiers nodded in unison. Such was the right and proper course to take in such a situation.

"The Sheikh Hatim took my wife into his tent and used her."

The courtiers again nodded. The sheikh was within his rights.

"But then he sent her back with his refusal, claiming my mare was unworthy of his stallion."

The courtiers shook their heads. If the wife were worthy of the sheikh, then the mare was worthy of the stallion.

"I refused to take no for an answer, and when the sheikh and his tribe left the fair, I followed them on my mare. At their first campsite, I again approached the Sheikh Hatim, reminding him that in the desert no man can refuse the services of his male to one who has need of him. Reluctantly, the sheikh agreed, but demanded a stud fee."

Even Aisha gasped. This was gross discourtesy. To ask pay for such service at a fair was one thing, but on the desert it must be given freely. The Moulay merely yawned again. Not only did animals bore him, but so did tribal law. The only laws he recognized were his own.

"This stud fee I refused to pay, O Moulay," said Ibrahim, "though, in truth, if I had the amount he demanded, I could have bought a foal or even purchased another mare rather than breeding my beloved Sherifa. And so I left his camp. But the stallion, unbeknownst to me, smelled the heat of my mare, broke his tether and followed us into the desert. While I slept in the arms of my wife in my tent, the stallion, more knowledgeable of the courtesies of the desert than his master, did mount my spirited mare."

Aisha nodded approval. The stallion did well.

"The ensuing squealing and snorting awoke me from a deep sleep," Ibrahim continued, "and at this point the men of Sheikh Hatim tracked the stallion to my camp. I protested my innocence; they did not believe me. Instead, they took the amount of the stud fee from my meager possessions: my wife and my trusty cross-wound bow, and also the mare.

"Know ye, O Moulay, that in this I claim the Sheikh Hatim's men were wrong. First, by desert custom he should have given freely of the services of his stallion. Second, he should not have had his pleasure with my wife unless he intended his stud to do the same to my mare. And lastly, his men should not have taken in fee the love of my life. I beseech you, O Moulay, direct Sheikh Hatim to return my mare to me."

So ended the tale of Ibrahim; now Sheikh Hatim rose in his own defense.

"Know ye, O Moulay, the magnificent and the just, that I, Sheikh Hatim, have in my possession a bay stallion with black points, a Kohlanee, descended from one of the five mares of the prophet Mohammed.

"I ask you, O Moulay, should I, the owner of such a horse, allow him to waste his seed on an Atterbi mare, a drudge among horses, but little better than a donkey? She was a small thing, and scrawny, for the man does not have enough wealth to feed his mare well, let alone his family.

"Yet even so, as a Berber, I might have lent the services of my stallion except for one thing. The mare's feet. Three were dark and one was white. Remember ye, O Moulay, the teachings of our forefathers on the markings of a horse—four white feet are good; a star is very good; two white hind feet and a star are nearly as good. And to have the two near feet white is excellent because one then mounts over the white. Good, too, is the near hind foot when it is white. But beware of the off hind foot alone being white. This is the mark of a bad horse. It can cost you your life. Your enemy will overtake you and slay you. Your son will be an orphan. Know ye, O Moulay, as I stand before you and Allah, the mare's off hind foot was white."

As one, the courtiers rolled their eyes in horror. Well they knew the teachings of the elders on the markings of a bad horse.

Having made a telling point, in his opinion, Sheikh Hatim continued his defense. "Not content with my refusal, the man Ibrahim sent his wife to me. She begged me that I agree, saying that the man had no sons and his mare had no foals. Out of pity, I took the woman into my tent that her husband might indeed have a son, even if not of his own seed. But still I refused to breed the mare. My stallion leaves his mark on his get; everyone seeing the star descending down between the flaring nostrils would know."

Knowing looks confirmed that such was indeed the way of Arab horses.

"After we left the horse fair, we made camp at an oasis many miles to the west. Right on our heels came the man on his mare, with his poor wife on a mule. Again he begged me to service his

359

wretched mare, demanding, as was his right, that I agree to such an ill-fated mating.

"Courtesy and custom left me no choice, but I decided to test him to see how highly he valued this breeding. I asked of him a nominal, truly paltry stud fee, but only to test him, as Allah be my witness. He refused. Before he left my camp, he swore that one way or another he would have a foal of my stud. Fearing he meant to steal my jewel, that night I tethered Jafar, for that is the stallion's royal name, with an iron chain around his hind fetlock. The chain I passed through the tent cloth and secured with a stake driven well into the ground beneath the felt upon which my wife and I sleep when traveling."

Turbans bobbed up and down applauding his wisdom.

"That night, Ibrahim crept into my tent and insinuated his body between myself and my wife, first pressing gently against her and then against me to make room in the middle. He then slit the felt and freed the stake, crept out of the tent and led Jafar away with the chain draped over his haunches.

Heads nodded in approbation of such true Berber daring, that midnight caper in the bed.

The Sheikh disabused them: "But Ibrahim did not call out his triumph as is the practice of the desert. Neither did he wait for us to waken. Instead, like a jackal, he stole away with my valuable stallion and made a mating with his mare. Too late my men rode into camp and opened his tent. Inspired by the performance of my virile stallion, he was riding his woman."

"Ibrahim feared for his life, and well he might, for the life of a horse thief in the desert is forfeit. He begged my men to spare him, offering all his possessions if only they would let him live. They rightly took his wife, his bow, and the mare, and left him—miserable excuse for a man that he is—the mule to ride woman-style. O Moulay, since I and my men acted with good conscience, we ask you to confirm us in the property taken to redeem the life of a common thief."

The Moulay, hungry and bored, wasted no time on deliberation or consultation with court officials, not even Aisha. "Both have defied custom, neither is worthy to be a horse breeder. Geld the stallion and dispatch his gonads to the Dar al Bey. As to the mare—deliver her by the sword of her unborn foal and make her barren. If she lives, return her to her owner; otherwise I affirm the Sheikh Hatim in his possession of the Spanish-made arquebus and of the wife. Case closed."

With that the Moulay clapped his hands, and the huge doors of the Court of Justice swung open. Led by the Vizier of the Third Kitchen, dozens of servants staggered in under the weight of mammoth copper trays, and every man in the room—accusers and accused, friends and witnesses, hangers-on and courtiers—hastened to find a place at one of the trays.

Since Aisha could not eat in public without unveiling, she excused herself and, accompanied by her bodyguard, left the room. The Moulay, of course, was served first—but only after a large blackamoor tasted each dish for poison—and washed each bite down with wine, the drink banned from the tongues of law-abiding Moslems.

While the court ate, many speculated on what the Moulay would do with the sizable testicles of the stallion Jafar. Some said they would be spitted and roasted; others held out for boiling, noting that the resulting juices made a potent and invigorating drink. A few kept their thoughts to themselves, greatly aiding the appetite and digestion of their neighbors.

The meal ended with sherbet, then the giant trays were removed. The Moulay's indigestion—a direct result of overeating and drinking—he blamed on the strain of sitting in judgment. And the next few cases received severe if not vituperative resolution!

The case of the dowry: One of a loving couple was sterile, the marriage voided, now the fathers squabbled over the return of the dowry. The Moulay ruled the dowry would become the property of the palace. Next case.

The case of marital rights: A harem wife complained she was not getting her rightful turn with her much-bedded husband. He countered that she was past her prime and was lazy in bed. The Moulay ruled the man should sleep with no woman for an entire month, and then might return to his harem ways, only if he shared himself equally among all his wives. Next case.

The case of the slaves: A wealthy landowner claimed a merchant had offered two of his slaves freedom, and then had shipped them to a foreign port and resold them. He asked for two new slaves in return. The merchant denied all in the name of Allah, and asked the Moulay to take his life if he were lying. The Moulay did. Loud were the thanks of the landowner for the privilege of assigning two of his best servants to duty at the Bardo for life—his punishment for letting the two slaves escape in the first place. Next case.

Consulting his list, the crier found every name crossed off. Audience Day was at an end. He was about to announce this when the doors to the left of the dais swung open and Aisha finally reentered the courtroom. She had been consulting with Ramlah. The two had concluded this was the chance they had waited for to make public and official the competition to which the Moulay had so far only privately agreed.

Behind Aisha came but two of her mute bodyguards, both veiled, and dressed all in white. Ali had disappeared . . . to attend the slave auction. Aisha's eyes never left her hated father's. When but five paces from him, she stopped and prostrated herself. Motionless, she waited an almost interminable length of time until he squeaked permission for her to rise. She remained obsequiously kneeling.

Her voice when she spoke was even more submissive. "O Moulay, I come before you as a humble supplicant. I am six years beyond the age of maturity, yet I have no husband, an unjustice to you and our country."

The Moulay's eyes narrowed. What was she up to? Was she canceling the competition? Or—his heart pounded—was she about to accuse him of her ravishing? She wouldn't dare, he blustered to himself; knowing full well that this offspring of a barbaric Berber was capable of anything unless he stopped her. She and her mother had made a bargain, and they must live up to it. In desperation, he rose to his feet, and in a voice shrill with fury, he shrieked at her, "You shall have a husband all right. Chosen by competition in a public contest with you as the prize for the winner. The losers, I shall deal with . . ." His voice faded off while he considered how he had planned to deal with them . . . with sword and mace, fire and cobra, lions and spears, ropes and water. And more. And more. He slavered in cruel anticipation.

Aisha could not believe her good fortune. Without coaxing or coaching, he was announcing the competition just as Ramlah had predicted. She prayed someday she could so well predict and control the man who became her husband. She had to bend her head to hide the triumph on her face, barely suppressing it in her voice, "Your wish, O Moulay, is my command. But a public contest?"

He forgot that the idea was not his, that the preparations had already begun, that this was a potentially dangerous thing to do politically. Instead, he heard the quaver in her voice and gloried in the sight of her head bent low before him. Indeed, she would marry and with a man in no position to complain if he received slightly used goods. Then the Moulay would be free to deal with that mother of hers. Too many years had that woman held him in thrall. Her punishment would be the slowest, most excruciating he could devise. He'd show her—and her daughter—that he was more than just a man. He was *malik!*

"A public contest," he proclaimed pompously, grandiosely, "and one open to all. To Berber and Arab. To noble, to slave."

The court, already agog, grew still more excited. If this were true, the Amira Aisha could become the bride of any one of them. The Sheikh Hatim listened, more eager than most. Gladly would he trade a four-legged stud to become stud to the Moulay's daughter. But the Moulay's next words gave him a chill. "Remember, you go to the winner. The losers come to me."

While the courtiers had sat contentedly, sipping their tiny cups of scalding hot black coffee and second-guessing the Moulay's judgment, within the Souk al Berka de Wynter and the others squatted stoically and endured another day. First, the emptying of the slop bucket, then the replenishing of the water gourd, then the doling out of unleavened bread baked in coals until black and brick-hard. After that, nothing, until late afternoon and the second meal of the day, couscous, followed by a night of sleeping in turns.

John the Rob, who had claimed unopposed the unwanted place before the door and next to the slop bucket, was first to hear the commotion down the hall. "Milords, gentlemen, and other folk," he announced cheerfully, "methinks breakfast is being served."

He was wrong. Instead, under close guard, the prisoners were let out of the cell and shoved into a double file, then led two by two down the passageway to the latrine, where their soiled loincloths were taken away. In the washroom each was doused with a pail of water. Sleeking their wet hair back as well as they could, they were led, still wet and still naked, into a shed. There, a group of black slavers awaited them. To one side lounged Eulj Ali, the captain of the ship, and a short, squat black man whose ornate robes and bejeweled curved dagger attested that he was no mere underling. Under his wary eye, each slave was led forward for the blacks to examine quickly and curiously. "Open your mouth, show me your teeth, move on . . . look up, look down, move on."

Over the monotones of the examiners, de Wynter, waiting his turn, could hear the thick voice of the black: "*Al-rabb*, I warn you, I run a quality auction here, and my customers know it. They expect my merchandise to be clean and healthy and able to do a good day's work. So even though I sell yours on consignment, if any one is diseased or infirm, my men will reject him."

"Fear not, *jallab*, these are healthy," Eulj Ali replied, working an ivory toothpick about within his mouth. "And look, there is the one I told you about. Is he not a beauty? Even wet, you can tell his hair is strange-colored."

The auctioneer looked where Eulj Ali pointed, then gestured for a man to move de Wynter out of line. Instinctively, de Wynter shrugged aside the guard's rough hand and stayed put. The black smiled, showing big square white teeth.

"A man of some spirit, as well." Two pairs of ironlike hands on wrist and bicep persuaded de Wynter that he wished to move out where the black could look him over.

Slowly, the black studied the naked man held angrily immobile for his inspection. Like the professional merchant of flesh he was, he looked first for that sign of class, that elegance so few bodies have. This one had it, he decided. Then, he looked for how the parts of the physique blended together. The well-shaped head was held disdainfully high upon its strong, corded neck, flowing into broad shoulders above a wide, deep-spring chest that tapered swiftly into narrow waist and slim hips. The legs were long and lean and limber, with little hair and that so light it barely showed. That pleased him. His customers disliked body hair.

Moving around behind the slave, he noted the strong back, still bearing a mark here and there of the oarmaster's whip. They would fade, he decided, tracing them with one finger, as de Wynter flinched at his touch. Approvingly, he ran his hands over the small, flat buttocks that clenched involuntarily as he separated them.

Walking around to face the slave who stared expressionlessly over his head, the black reached up and gripped the chin, forcing that well-chiseled aristocratic face from side to side. Still watching the slave's face he let his free hand move down the breastbone to the flat belly and then still lower. At first, only by the hooding of those frosty blue eyes did de Wynter acknowledge what the man's hand was doing so slowly, so thoroughly.

At last, the black stepped back, smiling. Still watching de Wynter, he addressed the two lounging onlookers and delivered his professional appraisal. "As you said, a beauty, a *rawa* indeed, even without the spice of the silvery hair. Only two faults do I find. The first, his height. Many of my more prosperous customers prefer such slaves to be small and especially weaker than themselves. The Moulay, for one, might look at this man, but he would not buy him. You, Eulj Ali, would be more his size."

"And the other fault?"

"A trifle and easily remedied with a slit of a knife. Like that you double his selling price. Of course, you would have to postpone the sale for awhile."

Eulj Ali and the captain exchanged avaricious glances. "How long?"

"He's young and healthy. He'd heal in two, three weeks or so."

Eulj Ali, sucked on his toothpick considering, then regretfully shook his head. "No, we can't wait. Sell him as is."

"But you will let me hold him out and sell him with the wenches. Selling this gem with that dross will weaken his price."

Before Eulj Ali could speak, the captain answered. "All or none. Those were my orders, those are your orders. If someone wants the *jamad ja'da* bad enough, he'll pay for the rest and get himself a bargain the while. These are all good stock—young, strong, able. Not a real shirker in the bunch except maybe the monkey-faced one. For being new to the oar, they made excellent time. Yes, indeed. They'll sell, all right. If your striker talks them up properly."

The black salaamed. "As you wish, *al-rabb*." Taking one last appraising glance at de Wynter, he signaled his guards to let the slave rejoin his fellows and become part of the herd. With his fellows, he was classified as indoor or outdoor material, had a number written in ink on his back, was given a fresh loincloth and moved out of this building and into a walkway open to the sky and lined with pens. Made of rough-hewn planks and heavy posts, there were at least a dozen of them, one after another, and not all of those de Wynter passed were full of men. De Wynter and the others were all herded into one pen, at the far end of the row. From between the planks they could look out onto a square of the city itself.

Carlby answered the unspoken question: "The slave auction, my friends. I've seen one much the same, but larger, in Venice. A few words of advice: follow orders, no matter how silly or unpleasant. And for God's sake, don't fight them, not with a gesture, a look, anything—"

"You, in there," hailed the captain from outside the pen. "No talking." To add force to his words, four of the guards climbed to the tops of the four corner posts and perched there, flicking the whips they carried.

Again from without the pen, the captain spoke. "No sitting. No fighting. No shitting. The first one who dirties himself gets a flogging. The same with any who try to climb out. When your turn comes, move smartly up on the block and heed the striker's instructions."

With that, the captain stalked off to find himself a good vantage point for the auction. The slaves in the pen had an excellent one. Without, the square was filling up with colorfully-robed men. The absence of women was noticeable, especially in the rumble of masculine voices. Even as the slaves were staring at the prospective buyers, the latter showed no eagerness to examine the slaver's wares.

Soon, the gate swung open wide and the guard deftly hooked the nearest slave, Fionn, round the neck with a wooden crook. One tug and Fionn followed, leaving the pen. As de Wynter and the others crowded close and stared through the space between the planks, one man, with the permission of the guard, demonstrated for his son how to prod a man's calf to test for muscles . . . to pinch his belly to check for fat . . . to determine his age by opening the mouth and checking the teeth . . . to prove him man by pulling aside the loincloth and rolling the balls within one's hand.

As the man did, so did the boy; Fionn, remembering Carlby's words, stood impassively while he was fingered. Finally, the father and the boy conferred, the latter evidently pestering the former to take some action. When questioned, the guard explained the conditions of sale. This provoked a heated discussion that ended with Fionn being returned to the pen, the prospective buyers turning away.

Within the square, drums began to growl, and slaves spread thick carpets at the base of the block, where the view was best, for the more affluent buyers. As other slaves, serving coffee, passed among the crowd, the drums picked up their beat, finally sounding a tattoo. On cue, the sumptuously dressed black stepped out onto the block.

"*Sbah al skir.* May the peace of Allah be with you. Welcome on behalf of the house of Hassan ben Khairim, your servant. This market I declare officially open and under the protection of the *Jalala al-Malik,* the Moulay Hassan—the blessings of Allah be upon him.

"Ah, my friends, I have such wares to show you today, I know not where to start. The men are young and brawny and superbly muscled. The women—ahh, such women—small and curvy and suitably muscled where it counts, down here. Within the group we sell today we have learned men, warriors, laborers, scribes and savants, gardeners—the full selection you expect when you attend a market of men conducted by the house of Hassan ben Khairim, your servant.

"But within this group, if you look close—and if you do not, I shall be sure to point them out—are such gems as I rarely have the honor to present to you. A giant of a man, blond, and muscled like none you've seen before. Two men's hands could not encompass the muscle in his arm. With a guard like that, any woman would be safe . . . except maybe from him. A flick of the knife solves that.

"Then, there is another, a man with a face on him that would make any child laugh. His hands, how fast. They juggle, they gesture, they make things disappear. I know; I had two bejeweled daggers before I met him . . . and look at me now, lucky to have one, luckier still to be alive.

"And then, there's the learned one who reads and writes Arabic like an *imam*, a man with a thousand tongues. The man who could be many things to his master: tallyman, majordomo, scribe, agent, whatever a man could wish. And this one is young enough and attractive enough that he could serve his master *night* and day.

"Ah, but speaking of which, there is another. My friends, I tell you this and I speak true. If I had my way, I would hold him back and sell him with the wenches, but his owner refused. This slave's beauty is such it would make the women look bad and the owner—ah, if I could just name him—the owner has twenty times as many women here to sell as he has men. He fears financial disaster if he allows you to compare men and women. It is for this reason that I announce a departure from our usual practice. Today, the House of Hassan ben Khairim, your servant, does what no flesh market dares. It sells the women first. *Muraqib*, bring out the women."

His shrewdness was apparent the moment the women were ushered out. None among the twenty was an outstanding beauty. The *mu'min* among them were veiled, the *fakir* were not. But it made little difference. Most of these women were there for resale. The corsairs' raids on the mainlands to the north of the Mediterranean had ceased until spring; until then, there would be a dearth of fresh, virginal, white women to sell.

The striker did the best he could, but the wares went slow and the bidding was low. Only one woman was stripped and she looked better dressed and was struck down to the last man who'd bid before he saw her naked. He, in turn, tried on the spot to try to resell her, but his fellows only laughed at him and called for the male beauty to be put on the block.

The black was a master at reading and playing the crowd. Bowing in apparent obedience to the mood of the crowd, he clapped his hands and shouted, "Bring forth a blond."

The official tallymaster, checking his sheets, called forth a number. From somewhere beyond de Wynter's pen, a group came forward with a blond slave, easily the size of Fionn. But this was a man well past his prime and going to fat with a look on his face that denoted unintelligent submission. Stumbling slightly, he was thrust onto the block, and the striker began his singsong chant.

When that slave was struck down to a new owner, another blond took his place, a much younger man. The black's plan became evident. He had whetted the crowd's appetite early on for a particular slave, now he was serving up similar ones, each progressively better in quality than the preceding one. The last of a dozen or more blonds had stepped up on the blocks and been struck down when the black came forward and gripped the slave by the arm. "Good, isn't he? Well, my friends, I have one that's still better.

"But first, I have some blacks brought all the way across the desert to be sold here. And, my friends, so green are they that I dare not sell them without warning you: take the word of a negrito, these aren't fit to enter your door. But, if you are looking for slop cleaners or dung shovelers or offal scrubbers, here are your men. What do I hear? One or all . . ."

Whenever the bidding slackened, the black's agents would move within the crowd drumming up excitement. Or the black himself would remind his prospective customers that the best was yet to be sold. The best he referred to were no longer engrossed in the auction. Less carefully watched than before—their guards' attention drawn elsewhere—the slaves found that so long as they made no sudden moves nor spoke too loudly, they were free to hunker down or lean on the fence and talk among themselves.

Thus it was that they never saw the single file of white-robed white-veiled figures insinuate themselves against a wall at the back of the crowd. But Eulj Ali and the captain did. Within seconds the captain had jumped down from his vantage point to pick his way slowly but steadily through the crowd. Getting to the base of the auction block took half as long as catching the black's attention. Once done, the captain spoke quietly but forcefully: "Put them on sale now!"

"It's too soon, they'll bring more later," the black protested.

"Do it now, or I'll do it myself." The captain was not joking.

"As soon as these last are sold," the black agreed reluctantly even as the striker closed the sale.

A slap of a black slave's hand stung the big drum to hum, and again, and again, quickly joined by others. The crowd hushed expectantly. All eyes focused on the black, who in turn saluted the crowd.

"My friends, you have been too generous today. My tallymaster assures me that already today the sales of the house of Hassan ben Khairim, your servant, have set a new record for the off-season. And so I ask myself, how do I reward and thank these too generous patrons of mine? Ah, you have guessed my plan. You will remember I spoke of a blond giant? A funny-faced man? A scribe who I am informed is also a physician? A *rawa?* It is time to present them to you.''

He clapped his hands and the group in and around the first pen were galvanized into action. The guards up above used their whips to roust the slaves and herd them just inside the gate to the pen. At the last minute, using whip and crook, four were singled out and pushed and tugged and prodded to one side. Four lengths of cloth, each with a slit in the middle for a head, were passed over the fence for these four slaves to wear. In the meantime, the black was addressing the crowd.

''My friends, who among you is content with the running of his house? Not I, for one. And if I were not running this sale for the house of Hassan ben Khairim, your servant, I would be out there preparing to bid on this next group. For, my friends, within this group is every man needed to turn your house into such a paradise as the rest of us shall not know until we go to join the Apostle of Allah—upon whom be Allah's blessing and peace—within the Garden of Allah—exalted be he! Within moments, my friends, you shall see such men as would make the *houris* in the Garden of Allah—exalted be he!—shiver with delight. And these men, all young, all strong, all able, are hard, nay, willing workers.

''Now, I know, my friends, that for some of you it may be inconvenient to replace your whole staff at this time. And others among you have smaller establishments for whom all these''—he gave a quick signal, and the slaves began mounting the block single-file, ''gardeners and sweepers and cooks and bakers and launderers and food servers and bath attendants—all these may be too many. Then, you, my friends, might wish to join with your neighbors in bidding on this group. For by order of the consignee, this group will be knocked down all or none!

''No, no bids yet!'' the black said quickly pretending to be remonstrating with some eager buyer within the crowd, ''for you have not seen all. There are four more to come, but first, look these over. Number 227, come forward.''

Angus sullenly walked forward, to be flexed and prodded and turned about. Number 228 was Ogilvy, and he must do the same. One by one, each was called forward to have his virtues extolled except for 241, Gilliver.

Apparently puzzled, the black walked about him, staring at him from, first, one direction, then another. ''Now, don't be fooled by this one, my friends. He looks scrawny. In fact he is scrawny, but within that feeble body is the perfect—what? My friends, rarely am I at a loss, but this time, I confess I am. Help me out.''

The suggestions thrown out were as obscene and inventive as the Arab mind could conceive, and the crowd laughed a bit harder at each. The black was pleased. A relaxed, jovial crowd was more apt to spend big. His plan was running smoothly. It was time to produce the last foursome of the day.

''Yes indeed, my friends, an excellent fly-whisker he'd make, especially for the blond giant I told you about. But now, my friends, tell me true, are these not the best thirty-two slaves you've seen in a long time?'' The black's agents within the group led the clapping, much of which was genuine.

The slaves did make a good appearance, obviously cleaner and healthier and better-fed than most of the wretched souls bid off that day. And being mostly fair-skinned, young, well-exercised males, they gave an impression of strength and ability. ''And now, my friends, what you have been waiting for. The funny-faced man!''

John the Rob stepped up on the block and tripped on his robe, going sprawling across the platform and into the group of slaves, who stopped his momentum and pushed him back on his feet. Whether accidental or deliberate, no one could tell, but the crowd laughed uproariously at him, and the frown on the black's face disappeared. ''As I said, my friends, the funny man. Can you not see him entertaining you and your harem on those hot sultry nights when the sirocco blows? Next, the blond.'' On cue, Fionn stepped up and his robe was at least as much too short as John the Rob's had been too long. In its skimpy depths, Fionn looked twice his size. With one grab, the black ripped it off to reveal the muscular body

371

below. The crowd began murmuring, black eyes glinted under the headrobes, and consortiums were formed to bid on this group.

"And the learned one."

Carlby stepped up on the block. "What language would you hear him speak?" The crowd called them out, one after one upon another, Carlby replying in kind. Then, he too was pushed back in line alongside John the Rob and Fionn.

Now, at last, it was de Wynter's turn. But he was no sheep to be meekly led off to slaughter. Disregarding Carlby's orders, he turned and attempted to escape. But the guards were well trained; they had dealt with obstreperous slaves before. They also knew bruises made now would not show until the following day, thus they did not attempt to handle him gently. From the black's vantage point up on the block, he could see the short-lived struggle, but his unctuous voice gave no hint of it.

"And now, within moments, you shall see him whom his owners call *Jamad Ja'da . . .* and you shall know why."

Finally, escorted by two burly guards, de Wynter was half carried, half led up onto the block. At the sight of that pale halo of hair, clinging in soft curls to his head, the onlookers gave out that weird half moan, half mew with which Tunisians express approval. The crowd surged forward, even the wealthy buyers getting to their feet, their coffee cups abandoned to be trampled on by the onpressing crowd. Only Eulj Ali and his captain didn't move, nor did the silent ones leaning against the wall. Eulj Ali, who had been studying them, spoke into the captain's ear: "The White Ones over there. Have you taken a good look at them?"

"What for? When you've seen one *Ikwan*, you've seen them all," the captain answered.

"But they say the Amira herself is sometimes among them."

The captain took a second look at the silent ones, a long, speculative look. "That may be, but unless close enough to see their eyes, there's no way—except maybe size—to tell the Amira Aisha from the others."

"Sssh, not so loud. Someone might hear you."

"They're all interested in the icy-haired one; besides, why so much interest in the Amira?"

"I'll tell you later. The bidding's about to begin."

The black chose to conduct this auction himself. "Now, my friends, who will give me 3600 shekels for the lot?"

There was silence in reply. "Come now, my friends, has Shaitan got your tongues? Who will start the bidding on this remarkable group? The only one of its kind in the whole of Ifriqiya. Why, those four in the front are worth that much themselves. What do you say?"

A voice from out of the crowd called, "Half that!"

"Half? My friend, this is a travesty. A mere 50 shekels apiece for such prime flesh? Who will give me more? . . . I have 60, do I hear 70?" With a nod from still another buyer, the bidding was on. At 100 shekels apiece, the bidding slowed, and no matter how much the black cajoled, no more bids were forthcoming.

"My friends, what must I do to make you realize what a prize this group is?" he asked, walking around the perimeter and staring out at the crowd. On cue, one of his agents shouted, "Disrobe him."

The crowd liked the idea. Amid cries of "Yes," and "Strip him," and "Shuck the slave!" and "Off with his robe!" the black bowed his obedience to the crowd's wishes and waved de Wynter's guards forward. "Bring him out here by himself and let us see every inch of that magnificent body."

The first tug removed the robe. "Look at him. You can tell this is a hot-blooded animal. See how clean the lines, how smooth the muscles, how firm the skin. And look—little hair. This is no hairy beast in need of daily body-shaving to keep him well groomed. And need I remind you, no stubble to prick and scratch and ruin his master's fun."

The second tug removed the loincloth. "Look, my friends, a young bull with the blood of royalty coursing through his veins, its seed stored in his sack. Think you of the fine young slaves he might sire if you should so wish. Now, I ask you, who will bid four thousand shekels for this group?"

Two, four, a dozen shouted at once—to be silenced by a piercing whistle. The crowd fell silent. They had heard that whistle before. Slowly, like waters parting, the crowd split in two, leaving a path through which walked the silent ones. Without a word, the leader advanced to the foot of the block and held up a small tablet to the black. Perusing it swiftly, he grinned broadly, showing square, white teeth back to the molars. Reverently he kissed it and announced,

"My friends, *al-rabb*, the house of Hassan ben Khairim, your servant, is honored to declare the bidding closed, the slaves sold to Ali ben Zaid, *amir l'al-assa* of the men of the Amira Aisha, may the blessings of Allah be upon her."

"How much, Hassan?" a *mutajasur* called out from the anonymity of the crowd.

The black hugged the tablet to himself and smiled beatifically. "The last bid plus 25."

"Only 25?"

"Twenty-five hundred! Sixty-five hundred shekels in all!" So great was his excitement, he did a little dance as the slaves were led down from the block, de Wynter still struggling vainly.

"Be careful of them," the black cautioned. "They are the most expensive meat I've ever sold!"

Eulj Ali and the captain hugged one another at the news. Never in the latter's wildest dreams had he thought the slaves would go for that much. Even as he was hugging and pounding his redheaded fellow, he was doing some fast mental accounting. At 6500 shekels less the black's 20 percent—which he would split fifty-fifty with the Moulay—with 50 percent set aside for Barbarossa, that left nearly 2000 to split, share and share alike, between himself and his crew! And already the captain knew what he was going to buy. A certain wench the black had shown him, who was being fattened up before going on the block.

"You collect the money and meet me at dusk at the coffeehouse in the souk of perfumes," Eulj Ali ordered, turning on his heel and melting into the crowd.

As the crowd dispersed, gossiping about the record price paid for the *jamad ja'da*, he and his fellows were being herded back into their pen under the surveillance of the fully veiled silent ones. De Wynter, last to leave, was last to reenter, being shoved inside like the enraged animal he resembled as he turned on his guards. Too late. The gate slammed closed in his face. As the prisoners milled around inside, Carlby and the others trying to calm de Wynter, John the Rob lending his robe as makeshift loincloth. Guards remounted the corner posts, and these were not half-naked blacks but heavily robed men of undetermined race, armed not with whips, but formidable spears.

Cooler heads among the group, notably Carlby's and Drummond's, physically prevented de Wynter from doing anything rash. They sat on him to keep him from attacking one of the guards or attempting to scale the fence to escape. While Fionn and the others held him down, Drummond and Carlby conferred, then Carlby approached one of the four guards. "*Salaam, janab.* May your slave ask of his master some water, perhaps some bread, and some shelter from the sun?"

The guard did not answer. Switching from Arabic to Sabir, Carlby repeated his request, no response. Spanish, French, Italian. It made no difference. The guard did not answer. Nor staring up into his veiled face could Carlby decide whether the black-eyed man had even understood. While he was debating what language to try next, the gate swung open and four nervous blacks entered. One carried a waterskin, two between them an enormous copper tray of what looked like dough balls, and the fourth headcloths plus a loincloth which he tossed in the general direction of de Wynter before fleeing the pen.

Later, as the men licked fingers and lips, having stuffed themselves to satiety on the meat-filled *hlalims,* John the Rob sidled up to Carlby.

"Sir priest—"

"Don't call me that. Forget that I am other than a slave like you."

"As you wish. Do you note that the guards do not speak, yet all act as one? And we got all you requested?"

Carlby shrugged. "Maybe someone outside the pen heard."

The smaller man leaned back and stared up at the guards, who returned his stare just as intently. "Maybe, but I have my suspicions..." With that, he got to his feet and wandered over to the gate, where he could peer through the planks and watch the goings-on within the walkway. It was he who first saw ben Khairim escorting a white-veiled one up the walkway.

Without undue haste, he strolled over and hunkered down next to Carlby. "The new master comes. Best watch our friend lest he do something rash."

Carlby nodded. Casually, so as not to draw unnecessary attention to himself, he got to his feet. Kicking Drummond's foot surreptitiously, he beckoned the man to join with him. The two moved, as if haphazardly, toward where de Wynter sat alone, arms hugging his legs, forehead on knees.

He didn't move a muscle when the two stood over him, but he knew they were there. Without looking up, he spoke: "It is time, is it? Well, it had to happen eventually. Thank you, but don't worry. I will do nothing rash. Not now. Not when your lives could be endangered." He turned his head to one side so that he might look Carlby in the eye. "But if I find a time when I cannot stomach it, pledge you not to stop whatever action I take."

Carlby squatted down before him. "De Wynter, others have found such a life bearable."

"I am not others." De Wynter's frosty eyes echoed his words.

"Jamie, mayhap it will not be as you think," Drummond suggested.

De Wynter laughed silently. "No? Why did Ali ben whatever pay better than double the best price paid before? Do you think he wants perfect rowers?"

Before he could say more, the gate again swung open. This time it stayed open. Blacks with crooks in their hands advanced and deftly snared one slave after another and drew him out into the walkway. There, irons were clamped on wrists, and the slaves were linked up; only Carlby, de Wynter, and Drummond remaining behind. Ali ben Zaid entered the pen then, and with the spears of the four guards lending emphasis to his gestures, summoned them forth. Reluctantly, the three rose to their feet and walked forward. They too were linked to the human chain; and then, prodded by spear point, the three dozen moved to leave the slave market.

But they were stopped by the slave dealer. "With your permission, *al-rabb*, the former owner of these slaves would like to share his newfound wealth with its source and give one of them a small memento."

At Ali's inquiring look, the black hastened on. "A mere trifle. A carving. A good luck charm, no more. Look, your man can see for himself it is harmless." And he handed it over to the nearest silent one, who examined it incuriously and quickly, and turned it back to the black. With Ali's concurrence, the black handed it over to its rightful owner, uniting de Wynter and the Mer-Lion again. With his charm held fast in his hand, de Wynter followed helplessly as the three dozen slaves were marched out the gates of the auction house, through the medina, to the Kasbah and whatever fate awaited them.

CHAPTER 23

That night was spent at the Kasbah, that sprawling combination of soldiers' barracks, slaves' quarters, and government offices where the day-to-day business of managing the country went on without the Moulay's immediate attention. To the slaves, the quarters seemed luxurious since each man was able at last to stretch out full length on straw spread over a cold stone floor.

The slaves woke semirested at the call to prayer at daybreak. Slop buckets were removed, water was passed out for hasty washing as well as drinking, and slaves brought food. One skimpy threadbare robe, two loincloths and a pair of rope sandals were issued each. From a square of patched cloth and a length of old rope, each man fashioned a head covering. Finally, the men were chained, neck to neck, a scant three feet between. Escorted by silent ones on horseback and followed by supply camels, the human chain departed by a side gate out onto the square facing the Dar al Bey, where Aisha and Ramlah were enjoying the three-hour bathing ritual preparatory to attending the Great Mosque.

The narrow streets, usually thronged with people, were practically deserted for it was Friday, the Moslem Sabbath, and the shops were shuttered. The only ones they passed were slaves and now and then a Jewess wearing her *kufia* or sugarloaf hat, loose jacket, and tight-fitting trousers. The point of a silent one's spear kept the slaves from ogling the women openly.

377

Whenever the crooked lane opened into a square, the slaves could see the graceful white minarets of the city's hundreds of mosques silhouetted against the cloudless cerulean sky. While passing near the Roman reservoir, they came close enough to the Mosque al Ksar, the oldest in Tunis, to hear the sonorous chanting of the owners of the shoes lined up outside the doorway.

Passing through the poorer quarters of the city, the slaves saw many a bloated belly supported by spindly legs. There were worse things in Tunis than being a well-cared-for slave. As they left the city gate, they turned not toward the east where the brilliant blue of the sea rivaled that of the sky, but southward toward the interior.

Soon, the slaves tramped past the last few signs of civilization and into a broad plain dotted with groves of olive and palm trees. Their welcome shade was sorely missed a few miles farther to the south when the group reached near-desert. The parched, sunburnt plain was coursed by numerous *oueds*, about which they must detour or laboriously traverse, not easy when walking so close to the man in front.

Mostly they walked single-file, picking their way over rocks deposited by rampaging waters running off the Bysacene and Zengitane mountains and flooding the plain during the rainy season. The salt crusts left by the evaporating water were cruel to the feet, and while trudging through them, the slaves were grateful for their rope sandals.

Off on the horizon, the slaves could see a long line of ragged and fantastic peaks, at least fifty kilometers high. Their eyes were playing tricks on them, for the Djebel Zaghouan Massif rose only two kilometers into the air, although it seemed much higher because of the flat plain that stretched to the base of the slope.

A piercing whistle called the first halt. While the guards faced Mecca and prayed silently, the drovers noisily forced their camels to kneel, the first human voices the slaves had heard since they left the city behind. The slaves, too, would kneel. But as they had learned the hard way while crossing the *oued*, no one moves independently of his fellows when chained neck to neck. Carlby, who had commanded many a slave chain in his time, realized the silent ones were not about to give directions, so he took command. "On the count of three, all squat. Hold onto the shoulders of the man before you, that will give you purchase. One . . . two . . . three!''

The camel drovers passed goatskins of tepid water that must be tilted, squeezed, and squirted in the general direction of one's mouth. De Wynter finally captured some and to him it tasted better than King Hal's best Madeira. Wiping his splattered face on his forearm, he watched to see how Drummond, to his left, would fare with this damnable Arab contraption. John the Rob, to his right, having drunk already, was searching the ground for large pebbles.

''Pass me that one there,'' he said, pointing to a rock about the size of a fig, near de Wynter's left foot. ''And that.''

Others seeing his interest, passed the round stones within their reach down the line to the beggar. One of the silent ones, noting the activity of the slaves, came over to see what was afoot.

''If you're going to brain one, here's your chance,'' de Wynter observed.

The beggar only grinned. ''Watch this.'' Within seconds one, two, three, four, six of the rocks had flown up into the air and begun circling effortlessly under the spell of the beggar's hands. The silent one watched a few moments, then walked away, only to return with three of his fellows.

''You have made a conquest,'' de Wynter said, looking up at the quartet of guards staring, almost hypnotized, above their veils at the whirling stones.

John the Rob said nothing, simply changing the juggling configurations. Evidently, so long as he was willing to juggle, the guards were willing to watch. When one rock slipped from his hands and fell noisily to one side out of his reach, one of the guards helpfully retrieved it and handed it back to the beggar.

Just then, the whistle sounded. Not one of the white-robed ones objected when John the Rob gathered up his rocks and, making a pouch of his spare loincloth, tucked the ends through the cloth encircling his thin waist.

Again on Carlby's count, the men, leaning one on the other, dragged themselves to their feet. Before they started off, Drummond via de Wynter asked John the Rob, ''What was that all about?''

"Later. And watch what you say. Our guards may be silent, but there's nothing wrong with their hearing."

The caravan was soon under way again. The silent ones' destination was Kairouan by nightfall of the second day out. Though it was the fabled holy city of northern Ifriquiya, the guards knew where there were women to be wooed silently and wine to be sipped noisily within the cool shade of one of the city's many mosques.

That first day, the weary caravan plodded through the sand and salt for fourteen hours, with but brief stops for water or prayer, and once for a quick meal of biscuits and dried dates, washed down with water from a local well worked by a donkey. A transverse beam with stone weights at either end was rigged over the well. The small desert donkey pulled a rope attached through a pulley to one of the weights. As the donkey moved away from the well, a makeshift leather bucket was raised to the surface, where a man tipped it with a rope, allowing the water to spill into a container, or in this case directly into a trough. When the animal walked back toward the well, the goatskin bucket dropped back into the well and was refilled.

The poor dumb thing, de Wynter thought, watching the donkey move back and forth, He has made the trip so many thousands of times, he no longer needs supervision. With a grimace, de Wynter saw the similarity to his own situation.

As darkness approached, the caravan came to a halt, the slaves again being allowed to kneel. This time on Carlby's count, the results were less ragged and uncomfortable. A tent was pitched for the owner of the whistle, and fires were built; soon the aroma of coffee drifted the slaves' way.

One of the camel drovers brought out a skin of flour—to which a little water and salt were added—and pounded it to mix the dough within. Big handfuls were then shaped into cakes. He raked some embers out of the fire and in their place dropped the cakes of dough. When heat-seared on one side, they were turned over. Finally, a hollow was scooped out in the sand under the embers, and the dough buried there with a covering of hot sand and embers.

After what seemed like hours to the watching hungry slaves, the cakes were dug up and the sand and ashes brushed off. When cool enough to handle, they were distributed among the slaves, along with a handful of dates and goatskins of water. With practice, more of the water went into de Wynter's mouth and less on his face. His cake of dough was soggy, Drummond's brick-hard. Both agreed the consistency was like sawdust, yet they tasted like manna.

Exhaustion precluded any other talk. But, tired as they were, they slept fitfully, being forced to lie spoonlike on their right sides because of the neck manacles. The heat of their close-pressed bodies kept off some of the cold night desert air.

At dawn they were almost glad to be roused from their sandy beds. Gladder yet when they stopped an hour later for water and another handful of dates.

Their midday meal varied not one whit from that of the morning, but their puffy, reddened eyes could make out shapes shimmering on the horizon. The heat haze made Kairouan's crenellated ramparts and white minarets look more mirage than real. The city itself seemed to rise out of the air rather than resting on higher ground like most cities. Perhaps that was what led to her name, Kairouan, "Caravan of the Desert" in the tongue of the Moslems who built her.

Lagging feet felt lighter and spirits lifted as the city took form in front of them. And by sundown, their blistered feet, rope-burned and lacerated by their sandals, trod the hard stones of Kairouan's streets. Past nineteen mosques, and countless shrines of marabouts, or holy men, they were marched, straight to the courtyard in front of the Great Mosque. There the camel-riding drovers kicked their mounts to kneel before the well. This was no ordinary well. Its designers had provided comfortable drinking for all—man and beast. Around its perimeter were ledges of varying heights and depths, calculated to fit hooves and paws as well as the knees of kneeling thirst-quencher. The guards helped themselves first to the cool liquid, then came the horses, then slave drivers and camels, finally the prisoners. Custom called for humans to touch the water only with their lips, and the parched prisoners who attempted to splash some of the cool water on their faces and arms received smart cuffs from their silent guards as the well's guardians harangued them to drink, not bathe.

After all had drunk, the guards, without any apparent discussion, led their train to the left, into a narrow, seldom used lane. Eventually, they came to a cleared area before the great wall separating the medina from the rest of the city. Here was a natural prison. The brick wall, some 500 years old, had windowless abutments jutting from it. One man or two, thanks to the walls, could keep a hundred closely chained prisoners from escaping. At the same time, the curious and beggars could not get close.

After a meal of goat meat, milk, and bread, the prisoners took a more lively interest in their surroundings. The guards were gathered off to one side, silently devouring a meal no more varied though more plentiful than that of the prisoners. The camel drovers, having wolfed their food, made themselves comfortable leaning against their kneeling beasts. All was somnolent.

Now John the Rob had his chance. Out came his round pebbles and up they flew. Soon, one drover got to his feet and then another. Finally all seven had formed a semicircle around the juggler.

"Quickly," John the Rob muttered out of the side of his mouth to de Wynter. "Ask the nearest one where we are."

"Who cares?" de Wynter whispered back. "I want to know where we go."

"Fine, ask him, but be quiet about it."

"Al Djem," was the sibilant reply.

"Where the hell is that?" de Wynter whispered back. A gesture in the general direction of the south was the quick reply. The drovers, torn between fascination for the flying stones and the prisoners' demands for information, grew restless. John the Rob began adding objects his fingers had found and stored within his pouch—a date, a stick, a link of chain—and the drovers hunkered back down. "Ask why the guards don't speak," came John the Rob's terse instructions.

Stealing a look to make sure no guard was nearby, the drover made a cryptic cutting movement of two fingers before an outstretched tongue. No more need be said. And the drovers decided already they'd said too much. They got to their feet and scurried back to the safety of their cud-chewing beasts.

Meanwhile, the guards were involved in some spirited, though silent, discussion, their hands gesticulating rapidly. Finally, one of them rose and went to his saddlebags. The matter of contention, whatever it was, was settled by throws of bone dice passed from hand to hand. One last throw and half of the guards hurried off to dig clean robes out of their saddlebags.

For the first time, the prisoners saw guards unveiled and in the flesh. Some were dark-skinned, but most light, one even fair. All had the lean, hard, muscular look of fighting men kept trim. If all were naked, one could not have told guard and prisoner apart. Scrubbing hands with sand, polishing teeth with a twig, one or two scraped away at their facial hair with a sharp dagger and the aid of a polished tray. Robed and reveiled, the six disappeared into the night, leaving their spears behind.

Four remaining, unrolled blankets to sleep, the other two standing first watch. The prisoners, having shared with one another the information gleaned from the drovers, soon fell asleep, too, one after the other like a stack of spoons.

Kicks woke them. The guards were back and Ali ben Zaid was very much in command. When the long line moved out again, traversing crowded, crooked lanes, their chains roused no interest, not even from children. At last, they turned into a wide avenue leading to the Bab Djedid, the eastern gate in the Great Wall. Every caravan heading toward Sousse and the other coastal cities must pass between those two enormous wooden doors, as did those bound for al Djem and the smaller inland villages that dotted the Sahel. At this hour, the line of slaves was just one of many trying to get through the gates. Falling in between a camel train and a flock of bleating sheep, many hid their breakfast dates within their loincloths to be chewed later when there was less dust.

A few miles along the well-traveled road to Sousse, Ali ben Zaid turned his mare's nose southward into the bleak desert terrain and headed straight as an arrow to al Djem. Dutifully the line of slaves followed suit. For five hours with no respite, the caravan trudged across the now-burning desert, the scorching sun climbing from just above their left shoulders to straight overhead. A quick midday prayer and water break served only momentarily to interrupt the tortuous journey.

They plodded along on uneven ground, straining to keep in step so the neck rings did not start their sores to bleeding again. Sand fleas had invaded their clothing during the sleep by the wall. Soon everyone, guards and slaves alike, was rubbing and scratching in a vain attempt to dislodge the pests or relieve the itching of their bites. The slaves, forced always to cooperate, dug and scratched at one another's back. But too much of the torment was beyond the reach of these tethered men.

By midafternoon another apparition, pinkish as the setting sun rose sharply from the sand atop a low plateau to take shape on the horizon dead ahead. De Wynter rubbed his eyes, then looked again. It was the Colosseum of Rome. A mirage. Yet it did not quiver and disappear. Quite the contrary, with each step they took the colosseum loomed larger.

Onward the slaves marched, each hour bringing the ruins into sharper focus. For twelve hundred years this great stone and mortar amphitheater had withstood the burning sun and driving sand storms, her great stone arches mellowing to a golden pink. Three tiers of superimposed arches rose thirty-six meters into the air, the height of twenty grown men. Decorated columns separated each arch. Roomy galleries formed a cross under the arena itself. In the passageway leading from the galleries to the arena, the ruins of a statue of Marcus Aurelius gazed down benignly.

As the slaves moved ever closer, they could see the remains of the Town of Thysdrus, once one of the richest cities in the whole of the Roman province of Ifriqiya. Alongside the amphitheater, dwarfed by its immensity, stood the ruins of vast villas, once the pride of rich olive growers; the scraggly remains of those same olive groves grew now in clumps to the east of the amphitheater. The villas they passed were desolate. Or sheep and goats and chickens took possession of rooms whose walls gleamed still with fragments of brilliantly colored mosaics.

Off in the distance, a second amphitheater could be seen. This one smaller and older than the one at al Djem. Where Romans trod, monuments rose, and these long outlasted the halcyon days of the Roman Empire.

The caravan was now close enough to hear the sounds of construction and see workers scurrying in and out of the upper tiers of the great amphitheater. On they marched directly into the shadows cast by the great oval which measured nearly 150 meters at its widest and 120 meters across its narrowest dimension.

CHAPTER 24

Controlled by their neck rings, the slaves moved one by one through the main entrance to the colosseum, past the two guards there, up one ramp, then down another. The interior of the colosseum was cool, a welcome protection from the burning sun that for hours had scorched their thin robes. Then, blinking, back out into the sun they walked and into the central oval where their neck chains were removed. Free of one another, like sheep, they stayed together, only looking about independently.

What they saw offered little hope for any escape. They were virtually sealed in, surrounded by a wall twice a man's height. If one surmounted that wall, the only exits were openings high up on the second and third tiers. To jump was suicidal. If one survived, unscathed, how could he avoid the guardposts the slaves had seen as they entered the area? No wonder chains were not needed to retain the slaves.

However, if they put in a full day of hard labor and obeyed the few rules the *muraqib* described—no shirking, no resistance, no backtalk, no sexual activity and no attempting escape—they could have the run of the lower area.

The slaves had not been freed from their fellows for more than an hour before the first escape scheme was hatched. The beggars, misled by the apparent paucity of guards, were its authors. John the Rob, hearing it, decried it but his people insisted. Finally, unable to reason with them, he threw up his hands and admitted defeat. "Have

385

it your way. But I warn you, you will not win free." Despite him, they made their attempt.

The next morning when the slaves emerged from their underground quarters, eleven crucifixes greeted them, each with a beggar affixed. Then, to the accompaniment of groans, shrieks and pleas, the balance of the original three dozen worked at rebuilding the walls.

"There must be some way to help," de Wynter said as he and John the Rob manhandled a large block up into place.

"No," the beggar grunted. "Don't risk yourself. They chose not to heed my warning."

For the rest of the day the incessant mewlings of the sun-bloated lumps drummed home the message: Do not try to escape. Eventually, one by one the carcasses fell silent, and those still living rejoiced secretly that they need no longer hear the disharmony of the dying.

The crucified served their purpose. Escape was not so loosely talked about. However, John the Rob used his juggling to elicit tales of underground passages from the freemen who worked at the amphitheater for wages. Causeways led, or so his informants said, from the amphitheater all the way north to Sousse, constructed to remove the bodies of Christians, slain by gladiators, for Christian burial. But though the prisoners searched the underground galleries over a period of weeks, no walled-up openings or tunnels could be found. Despairing of this approach, Angus and Ogilvy organized a tunnel dig. The first few feet had been dug and shored up by night when the *Ikwan*'s routine search uncovered their work. Since no one man admitted being the tunnel engineer, all twenty-five men sharing this cell were punished: three days without food, one without water.

Even with adequate food and water their days were pure torture. When not set to replacing huge blocks fallen from above, they wielded crude shovels and pickaxes in an attempt to erase the debris blown into the arena over centuries. Day after day, the guards picked up the pace. Time, for them, was not limitless. Studying them whenever possible, John the Rob pieced together their language and puzzled out the story. Within the month, the *rafi as'sa'n* would hold a great event here. As to what that might be, speculation was rife, ranging from a revival of the gladiator bouts to intertribal contests.

Each morning they vowed to meet that night and devise an

escape plan. Each night, after tending to the bruises and blisters of their fellows, they gladly abandoned talk to seek blessed sleep on the damp stone floor.

Twice each day they ate in the center of the arena—at daybreak and again at dusk. The food was plentiful, served in huge trays carried out by blacks staggering under the weight. Squatting about the tray's rim, the slaves found it became second nature to roll rice into balls and dip bread into hot rancid camel's butter and pick meat and vegetables from sour soup. They preferred not to know or ask what meat it might be. And when the meat was semiovoid with a finely linked spine down the side, they chose to pretend it was fish they consumed. Not a man among them would not have gladly given a year of his life for a jug of ale, warm, hot, or cold.

With hundreds upon hundreds of slaves working, the lower tiers of the amphitheater were gradually restored to some of their past glory. Those above were shored up and made structurally safe. Other than that, no attempt was made to return those tiers to former grandeur. Evidently the Moulay and/or his daughter did not expect to fill the amphitheater to capacity.

Fortunately, the silent ones were not sadists. They assigned slaves to work best suited to their abilities. Thus, Gilliver and John the Rob, both small and apparently weak physically, were assigned less onerous finishing work—the polishing, painting, scrubbing concentrated on that section once reserved for upper-class Romans. Marble seats were fitted with soft cushions; mosaic tile floors were pieced and patched and polished; the walls, too sadly decomposed to be restored, were covered with istabraq.

For the royalty, a whole suite of rooms was being readied. Adjacent to the box overlooking the amphitheater were two resting rooms, each with couches and low marble tables. As John the Rob described them, it was easy to imagine these rooms with their floors strewn with fur rugs, their couches piled high with cushions, their tables covered with foods and flagons of wines. Gilliver it was who told with awe of the comfort stations nearby, the marble seats laved by warm waters heated by boilers below.

Unknown to the slaves working within the amphitheater, beyond the confines of the arena, a camp was growing. Day by day, men arrived, together with their slaves, horses, trappings, tents, armor, and women. The females, they were immediately told, must go, or else the lord himself and his retinue must leave. No women would be allowed within the camp of the contestants by order of the Amira Aisha.

"However," Ali ben Zaid or one of the eunuchs would be quick to add, "we should be delighted to escort your women to Sfax. There, at the princess's expense, they may await the results of this competition."

Most of the contestants, many of whom had bankrupted themselves to get here, had no choice but to agree. One lord, however, actually did depart in a huff.

The women, depending on their status, were seated in litters or mounted on donkeys or camels for the trip to Sfax. There, they were temporarily housed in a makeshift seraglio. Once the games began, at Aisha's order, they were to be loaded into crude carts and trundled back to Tunis to be sold at the Souk al Berka under the white-toothed grin of that green-turbaned merchant of flesh, Hassan ben Khairim.

Most of the slaves lost count as each day melted into another, but not Carlby. Two days after the Moslems celebrated their Sabbath, he held Mass. That same day, he made a scratch on the wall to keep track of the weeks. One Sunday, consulting his wall, he announced, "Give or take a week, by my calculations we are two weeks past the feast of St. Andrew and have but two more weeks till the feast of the Nativity."

The announcement was greeted with silence. Nothing brought home to them more vividly the forlornness of their situation. Gilliver, in particular, took it hard. Since Islam considered Jesus Christ merely a prophet, the slaves could expect no celebration on his birthdate. Thus, Christmas Eve found work going on as usual. Twenty-three of them, as they had for the past few weeks, left the arena proper to work in the palace complexes soon to be occupied by the Moulay and his daughter.

De Wynter and Fionn were left behind to help in the clearing of the upper tiers of stones. It was obviously make-work since so few men could make little dent in the destruction caused over a thousand years. Why Fionn was singled out, no one knew. But de Wynter's special treatment they had come to accept. Soon after they arrived at al Djem, they realized that though de Wynter was clothed, fed, washed, slept, worked as hard or harder than the rest, he was more closely watched than the others. Thus no one was surprised that he was not let out of the tight security of the amphitheater.

Today, at the palace, some of the slaves were set to laying carpets from Kairouan or hanging fine tapestries from Djerba. Others unpacked pottery from Sousse, marble pieces from Chemtou, furs from Tabarka, linens from the Nabeul. They had not quite finished when whistle and gesture rounded them up. As they left the palace, a troop of white-robed horsemen escorted two litters through the first gate and into the court of the White Eunuchs.

The next morning, no guard kicked them up at daybreak, nor were they taken from their cells to eat in the arena. Instead, at midmorning food was brought to them: fresh fruit, goat's milk and the meat-filled *hlalims* they had not tasted since Tunis. Taking advantage of this unaccustomed leisure, Carlby and Gilliver took turns quoting psalms to each other; John the Rob practiced his juggling; others mended sandals; most, especially de Wynter and Fionn who still did daily the back-breaking stone-carrying labor the others had long since finished, slept.

And these were the two that the silent ones insisted rake the sand covering the arena floor. Putting their headcloths and robes aside, the two worked rapidly and companionably under the warm sun. Over and over again they did the job, their *muraqib* never being satisfied. The smallest ridge must disappear, lumps must be broken or buried, the rake marks must be erased until the sand began to resemble that left by the tides on the beaches of Tunisia.

Their labors were noticed but ignored by the three who entered the royal box up above. Each was dressed as was his wont when away from Tunis: Ramlah in Berber skirt and jacket and veilless headdress, Aisha and Ali ben Zaid in the enveloping white of the silent ones. No one spoke for a long moment as the two women admired the miracles Ali had wrought since last they visited the ruins.

"Son of my father," Ramlah declared, "if the Prophet had had you at Medina during the Hejira, his mosque would have been built in half the time." Aisha was not so effusive, but the sparkle in her eye was all the thanks Ali sought.

A Berber, he was modest, so he changed the subject. "What do

389

you think of this?'' He pointed to an amethystine amphora with black figures circling it. "We found it when we excavated one of the shrines below."

"It's beautiful, as is all that you have done."

Ali ben Zaid leaned on the wall surrounding the box and looked without seeing at the figures below. "I would that those I was doing this for were worth the effort." Dropping his veil, he faced the women. Young in years, he had that ageless look the desert bestows on its favorite sons. His lean, sharp face, all angles and planes, was dominated by a hawk nose that belied the sensitivity of his mobile mouth. His look was bleak, "I warn you, they are not!"

Aisha said nothing, but Ramlah protested, "These are the cream of the—"

He cut her short to hawk and spit down below. "Cream? Clots of soured cream perhaps. With the exception of one or two—one of whom I swear I have seen before—there is no man in that camp worthy of being in the Amira's presence, much less her bed." He spat again. The *muraqib*, who always kept one eye turned in his commander's direction, motioned the two slaves to go forward and smooth the sand below the royal box.

Ramlah, agitated, argued with him. Still Aisha said nothing, thoughtfully studying the man who was uncle and bodyguard, friend of her youth and her totally devoted slave. When he said nothing more, she was forced to. "And what would you have me do? Cancel the games?"

"No, open them wider."

"How?"

"The Moulay spoke of a public contest open to slaves—"

Ramlah interrupted. "He never actually meant—"

"Pretend he did!"

"You can't actually suggest that my daughter—"

"I do. Unless she wishes to marry so far beneath her, she will look up to a whore."

"The contestants are that bad?" Aisha asked.

"Worse!"

"You do not suggest this without a plan."

In answer he directed her attention to the arena where the two raked, the muscles in their arms and backs rippling smoothly and rhythmically under the golden brown skin. Ramlah was confused. Not Aisha. She considered them carefully. "And what of their faces?"

"The blond would satisfy most women; the other would satisfy anyone. He is a beauty. I myself had to fight my attraction to him. And outbid the whole of the slave market for him."

Money was no concern of Aisha's. "Would he compete?"

"Does he have a choice? No, I understand what you mean. Yes, I think so, provided the incentive is right."

"Incentive—what incentive?" Ramlah interrupted. "Is not the hand of my daughter enough?"

"Obviously not, Mother. So what do you suggest, Uncle?"

"That if he wins, he'll no longer be your slave."

"And what then? Do I free him, just like that, to walk away from here if he chooses, without marrying me?" The scorn in her voice would have shriveled other men. Not Ali, he knew his Amira too well.

"Not at all. You will have promised only that he will no longer be *your* slave. Sell him to me. Besides, Islamic law states you may not marry your own slave or bondsman."

She stared at him for a moment and then her eyes changed; he knew she smiled behind her veil. "You are, Uncle, more than a miracle worker, you are a genius."

"Aisha, you're not taking his plan seriously?" Ramlah said.

"I am, I am." She took another look at the two at work down below, backing away erasing their footprints in the sand.

"Aisha, you cannot. The Moulay will forbid it."

"Why? He announced the competition open to all in audience. Besides, he is the son of a woman bought in the markets, as was his father before him, and their fathers before them. There is more slave than royal blood in me, at least on his side. No, Ramlah, a slave husband might be the answer to all of our problems. I think, Uncle, that your plan is well made."

Ramlah bit her lip and was silent. Then, her face brightened. "What chance has a slave against free men?"

"Daughter of my father, take a good look at those slaves. Not an ounce of fat between them. I walked them here by way of Kairouan, chained neck to neck. They work seven days a week at hard, muscle-building labor, and sleep on a stone floor with no more mattress than a single thin robe. They are fed just enough to survive, no more. No wine has passed their lips, nor coffee; only fresh water or goat's milk. They are in excellent physical condition.''

"And what of their spirits?"

"Unbroken. I left the taming of them to you. I promise you—nay, I wager you—if you accept these slaves into your competition, one will win."

Her curiosity was piqued. "Which one?"

"I shall write his name on a tablet and seal it to be opened on your wedding night. Five thousand shekels to your ten says I shall be right."

"Done." The Amira looked down again at the men below, then gave the ancient urn a push, toppling it into the arena to smash into a thousand pieces in the path of the two rakers. Startled, they looked up at what was to them just another silent one. But Aisha liked what little she could see. "I would see them clean shaven. Can it be done?"

Ali laughed. "If I can rebuild a ruin, I can shave a beard. It will be done."

"When?"

"Tonight. They are due for bathing and delousing anyway. I'll just add barbering to that."

"I would be there; let me know when." She continued staring at the two slaves painstakingly raking up the pieces of purple and black pottery. The only sound was the slow, methodical swish, swish of sand being smoothed once again by the two young men in the arena.

"The urn was chipped. Replace it." She turned on her heel and left the box, Ramlah and Ali following.

Back in their cell, Carlby awaited their return to celebrate in hushed tones a solemn Christmas Mass, handing out crumbs of bread he had saved from his meager ration. De Wynter felt no Christmas joy, only hatred toward his captors. As John the Rob's dextrous hands massaged some of the soreness out of his back, de Wynter pitied the Order of St. John of Jerusalem if he were typical of their novice priests. On second thought, he decided he did not care a whit for them either.

The massage was interrupted by the arrival of a group of silent ones. Opening the cell door, they waved the prisoners out. Footsteps quickened when they saw that they were headed for the washrooms. Although there were luxurious baths within the colosseum, designed for the ancient gladiators, the slaves made do with something far less fine and didn't care. Under the silent ones' watchful eyes, especially two large almond-shaped ones, the slaves stripped.

Plunging their hands into bowls of strong-smelling soap, they lathered themselves from head to toe. Fionn and de Wynter claimed the privilege of being first to be rinsed. "We were, after all, the only ones this day to do an honest day's work."

The others' outrage was more for show than honest protest, and the two were pushed to the front of the line. As de Wynter stood under a hole in the ceiling, slaves up above loosed a torrent of sun-warmed water over his head. None of the baths he'd ever had in his life felt as good as this one. So long as the water poured over him, he was content to stand and relish it. But the other slaves would hurry him up. If the soap dried before one rinsed, the suds had to wear themselves off over the next few days.

When he finally emerged from under that beautiful water, he was handed—wonder of wonders—a rough cloth with which to dry himself. As he was toweling himself off, he had the sensation of being stared at. Yet looking about, he saw no one but his fellow slaves and the usual guards. Shrugging his shoulders, he dismissed the feeling.

He had not yet finished drying off when a silent one beckoned him into the next room. More wonders. There waited a team of barbers. Their methods were rough but thorough. Within minutes he had been stripped of his beard and his head lightened by several inches of excess curl. A clean loincloth, robe, and new sandals made him feel like a new man again. He moved almost jauntily at the head of the group as it was being escorted back up the stone-walled corridor. The feeling that he was being watched prevented his noticing they had taken a new turn, were going a different way. Every cell here was empty. When the guards stopped and unlocked one of the doors, he swallowed his protest. What the hell, what difference what cell they were in, a cell was a cell.

"Not so!" stormed John the Rob, who had left his juggling stones in the other cell. And Carlby regretted the loss of his makeshift calendar. That was not all they'd left behind. Where once they had been twenty-five, they were now ten: the seven companions, plus Fionn, Carlby, and John the Rob.

The following day, those ten prisoners were marched out into the arena, whose carefully swept sands now bore the impress of playful night winds. They came to a halt before the royal box, which held the same three figures as the day before. Ali ben Zaid stood, came forward, and unveiled. To the slaves' amazement, he was young, handsome even, in a dark, somber way. To their further amazement—for they had thought him a mute like the rest—he spoke to them, his voice rich and resonant:

"You have done well rebuilding this arena. How well remains to be seen, for the test of such a place is best judged by contest among participants. Therefore the *rafi as'as'n* have commanded me, let the arena be tested." At his signal, a silent one dropped an armload of weapons onto the sand from the first tier.

"Let me warn you: the weapons are blunted, you should not be able to hurt one another. But he who fights less than vigorously shall be punished. Now, you may begin."

There was a mad joyous scramble among the ten for weapons. First baths, now weapons. They felt like men again. The pairings off were done without words: De Wynter and Drummond, Angus and Ogilvy; Cameron and Menzies; and Gilliver sought out John the Rob, the two being of a weight, although the latter was not well skilled in weaponry. Fionn and Carlby, the only two left, gave each other a devil-may-care look and fell to, Carlby making up in skill for the advantage Fionn's size gave him.

Hack, slash, lunge, parry, counter and thrust . . . over and over they did it, and the smiles on their faces were fashioned of sheer joy. No one had to urge them on, all the frustrations of these hellish days of slavery were being spent. Aisha, Ali, and Ramlah watched intently. Ali with the eye of a man, Ramlah with that of a Berber woman, and Aisha with the view of a warrior.

Ali's whistle ended the duels. Even blunted weapons can be dangerous in the hands of a skilled opponent, especially when one is out of practice. Such was the case with the Terrible Ten, as John the

Rob called them. "Terrific is more like it," Cameron complained, but the word Terrible stuck.

Those ten slept well that night, all but de Wynter. For the first time in weeks, he dreamed. The same dream that had haunted him while aboard ship: the two women standing with a child in between. This time as he rode toward them, a white-robed wraith intervened. Still, he could not see the second woman's face.

Waking, he lay there and thought long of Scotland, his mother, his dead father, and especially of his son. By now, they would have learned of his admission to the order and of the fate of the *Annunciata*. With no demand for ransom, they would have decided him dead or worse. He prayed James V had kept his royal word and named the boy heir. Recalling that beautiful young face, he felt a pain in his chest and tears in his eyes. Desperately, he thought of Anne Boleyn, but tonight her memory was no comfort to him.

Again the next day, after a morning spent heaving stones from one tier to another, they were given access to the weapons. The day following, half-wild horses were driven into the arena "to test its footing," Ali explained. Gladly the men accepted the challenge facing them, John the Rob proving to be, once mounted, an unshakable jockey. That night, a tired but happy group of horsemasters compared bruises and boasts. Carlby, consulting his newmade calendar, passed the word that tomorrow would be the start of the new year, 1533. The men grew silent. In England there would be the traditional New Year's gifts. In Scotland, toasts to the end of one year, the start of another. Angus and Ogilvy kept their more potent usquebaugh just for this purpose. Here in al Djem in the country of Ifriqiya, there was nothing. Gilliver, seeing their sad faces, reminded them, "We have each other . . . and Christ."

It was little consolation. That night in de Wynter's dreams there was no threesome to tantalize him. Instead, the lovely and fascinating Anne Boleyn called to him from the depths of her bed. She lay there naked, her legs finally spread wide for him. Even as he approached her, another man—coarse, grayish of hair, broad of shoulders—would have intervened but he was pushed aside as a white-haired man climbed into bed with the ripe Anne Boleyn.

De Wynter woke. For the first time in weeks, his manhood had asserted itself. Hunger and exhaustion dampen one's other bodily needs. But not tonight. Tonight for the first time in years, his body had made its demands known . . . and satisfied them.

CHAPTER 25

Two more weeks went by, the days swiftly, the nights fitfully. Mornings were spent heaving building blocks about to restore a small portion of the third tier. Afternoons were devoted to swordplay or work with the horses that now docilely accepted the Arabic bridle, a noose about the muzzle.

Nights seemed to crawl by. Not even nightly showers helped. All, de Wynter soon discovered, were troubled by the same type of dreams. Carlby, the priest, was no exception. "We are human, you know. Look at the late, great Wolsey. Fathered three or four children, the latest while he was archbishop. Let my mind say chastity all it wants, the body will have its way. Besides, it's the food that's our problem. Don't look at me that way. Haven't you noticed? Less rice, more meat and vegetables and fresh fruit. Milk more often than water. If I didn't know better, I'd swear we were being fattened up for some—" He bit off his words. The men looked at one another, each wondering what the other was thinking.

Drummond was first to speak. "You don't mean"—he swallowed hard—"human sacrifice?"

Carlby chuckled cheerlessly. "No, not that. It's not the Moslem way. Human targets, maybe, but not sacrifice."

"But do targets need weapons?" That was Angus.

"Or horses?" (Ogilvy.)

"Or to be fat?" (Cameron.)

"Or to be clean-shaven?" (Menzies.)

397

"If not targets, what else?" John the Rob inquired.

"Bodyguards?" Gilliver hazarded. The others nodded. That seemed plausible.

"She has the silent ones for that," Carlby said, pointing out the obvious.

"Lots of them," Menzies added glumly.

The silence was deafening. Finally, Drummond said what all were thinking: "Participants."

No matter how they turned it, tested it, twisted it, and tortured it, the premise was valid. Everything fit too neatly. The monies paid at the auction. The purposeless work. The weaponry practice. The horses. The food. The daily bathing and shaving. The change of cell. Everything.

De Wynter, who had been silent throughout all this, finally spoke. "There is one way to find out for sure."

"How?" The rest spoke at once.

"Ask."

"Who?" "When?" "You?" The questions jumped at him.

He did not answer them, launching instead into another subject. "Have you noticed when we practice, there are always three or none in the box?"

They nodded. They were aware of the watchers.

"One we know is Ali ben Zaid, the head of the guard. And the woman might be his wife or handmaiden."

"No," John the Rob interrupted. "She is too arrogant, she carries herself too proudly. A beggar can tell nobility every time. Besides, I have seen him defer to her."

Carlby agreed. "She is most probably the queen. She is certainly too old to be the princess."

"Then," de Wynter asked, "who is the third one, the other silent one?" At first thought, the possibilities seemed endless. On second, most of those seemed silly or stupid.

"Fionn, did you notice the hands when the vase was broken while we raked sand?"

"No. Oh, I suppose I saw them, but they did not strike me as unusual."

"Look at them tomorrow."

"Why?"

"They are very small hands—"

John the Rob interrupted, "So are mine." The others laughed. John the Rob was very vain about his hands and boasted, "They be the best, the fastest, the prettiest hands in the land."

"That's right," Gilliver chimed in. "Many men have small hands."

"And boys," said Cameron with a leer.

"How many men, or boys, paint their nails?"

"And if that is the Amira herself?" Drummond wanted to know. "What difference does it make?"

"All the difference."

Drummond pressed the point. "So what do you propose?"

De Wynter leaned back on his bed of straw, arms folded behind his head, and smiled cryptically. "I propose we get some sleep and tomorrow unveil the lady." He closed his eyes, the subject was closed. His companions accepted the inevitable and prepared to sleep.

Not Carlby. Kneeling by de Wynter's bed, he spoke quietly so others need not hear. "Couldn't you ask the *Amir l'al-assa* instead of taking whatever chance you plan? He might talk."

The blue eyes opened wide and looked deep into his. "Tell me, priest, would you believe whatever story he chose to tell a slave?"

Staring down on that too-beautiful face, its eyes closed again as if in sleep, Carlby wrestled with his conscience for a moment, then confessed, "No, I fear not."

The eyes flew open again and de Wynter grinned boyishly. "Neither would I. That's why I propose to see for myself. Now, priest, get some sleep . . . or at least let me. This may be the last I get for a while."

The following day, de Wynter, though asked repeatedly what were his plans, refused to say anything except a "You'll see."

Later, however, when he had the chance, he took Fionn aside and asked, "Remember the gatehouse at Bushy Park? Could we do it again?"

The blond giant considered a moment, then broke into a big grin. "We can give it a try."

"Good. When I give the signal."

That afternoon, when the weapons had been surrendered and the horses driven in, de Wynter and Fionn began trying some of the less dangerous tricks they had done as boys, dismounting and remounting with their mounts at a gallop. Before the three occupants of the royal box knew it, there were eight attempting stunts. Some of the horses shied, others stopped short, but Fionn's, a big lumbering mare with yellow teeth, seemed impervious to the actions of the giant-sized fly that insisted on landing and leaving her broad back. De Wynter's mount was not so stolid, but his firm hands persuaded her to keep gamely on without missing a stride. To one side, Carlby and John the Rob sat watching the fun, too, although John the Rob remarked deprecatingly to his companion, "Them tricks look easy."

"Practice plays tricks on your eyes, my friend. Those boys have done those tricks a thousand times to make them look that easy."

"Well, if you say so . . ."

"I do. Save your neck. Don't try—now what are those two up to?" Carlby was watching Fionn and de Wynter. The two had been exchanging horses on the run, but now both rode one, Fionn's mare. Even as Carlby spoke, Fionn brought his mare to a stop before the royal box, and onto his shoulders climbed de Wynter. While Carlby watched unbelieving, de Wynter was over the wall in one catlike move and into the box. Two strides took him to the side of the alarmed Amira who had stood instinctively when she saw him vault the wall. Before she knew what he was about, his strong brown hand ripped off her veil. In that one instant, de Wynter knew he was looking at a face one couldn't forget—one as cold as it was beautiful. Soft, yet hard. Young, yet old beyond its years. Simple, yet haughty. But above all, beautifully, maddeningly desirable.

He had planned to demand she tell him her plans for them. He had rehearsed it many times in his mind. But being this close to such enticing lips drove all logical thought from his mind. Instead, he seized her and kissed her hard. The lips may have looked soft and luscious, but under his they were unrelenting—cold and immune to the demands his warm, hungry ones made.

Fierce with anger, Ali's hands cruelly pulled de Wynter from the princess. She stood there, white-faced with shock, her eyes blazing. She did not even deign to acknowledge his kiss by wiping it scornfully from her mouth. Instead, with a hand that trembled imperceptibly although she willed it not to, she replaced her veil. To de Wynter she said coldly, "Do not ever touch me again."

To Ali: "Punish him."

To her mother, who had stood aghast and disbelieving as this tragicomedy unfolded before her eyes, Aisha said, "Come. We are finished here."

The silent ones had charged the box and poured into the arena: The slaves below were hauled down from horseback and herded at spearpoint down the ramp leading to their cell.

De Wynter had made no effort to fight off either Ali or the others. Instead, he smiled and shook his head at his own foolhardiness. The kiss could not possibly be worth the punishment. However, he thought to himself, I should have thought of that earlier.

Ali in his agitation gave oral orders. "Take him below. In a cat cell by himself. I'll see to him later." Not waiting to see his commands obeyed, Ali followed after his Aisha. That this slave had so defiantly violated her was my fault, Ali berated himself. All my fault. I was the one who suggested the training in weapons, the horsemanship practice. But I'll have my revenge.

Down one ramp de Wynter was taken, then another, a flight of stairs, more stairs, and then into a warren of narrow cells. Left, right, right again, then left. He lost track of the turns. Finally, he was thrust into a small cell. The only source of light, the torch, disappeared with his guards. Wryly, he remembered his exploration of the Tower. This cell, he decided—his outstretched arm reaching easily to all three walls—was more like the pit his companions had had to endure. But here, though there was plenty of room to stand, there was none to lie down.

Instead, he could but crouch or squat or sit with legs bent tight. He settled down as best he could for what might be a long wait. In the hours—or was it days?—that followed, he recited every poem he knew. Then he translated each out loud, one by one, from Scots into English, French into Italian, Latin into Spanish, then switched around. He tried one into Arabic, but the language, he decided, did not lend itself to rhyming or else he was not fully master of it. When his throat grew parched, he damned himself for wasting his spit by speaking out loud.

Eventually, he slept. Not long, he thought, but he was thirsty and cramped when he woke. As he moved to relieve the cramp, he disturbed the other occupants of this underground prison. He could only hope that that rustling sound meant mice, not snakes nor large-sized vermin. Awkwardly he climbed to his feet within the confines of his cell, and stood for a while dancing up and down to start his circulation moving and to discourage any unwanted creeping, crawling visitors. The dust he disturbed swelled about him like a cloud of smoke and set him to coughing feverishly. He would have given much for a drink of brackish water. At last, he slept again.

How many days he spent in that cell he couldn't guess. Once he heard sounds in the distance and feared his rescuers had become lost in the maze, so he called to them. The echoes of his voice were his only reply.

He was asleep when they finally came for him. The point of a spear woke him up. The light of their torches dazzled his eyes.

"*Jamad ja'da,* you sleep soundly," said a voice not far from his ear.

He opened his mouth to make a witty reply, but nothing came out.

"I assume," Ali ben Zaid continued, "you would like to come out and stretch your legs."

De Wynter could only nod; his swollen tongue couldn't answer. Nor was he sure his legs would respond if he tried to rise.

"Maybe even have a drink with me?"

The sound of water pouring into a cup stirred the crouching man. Frantically his hands clawed at the bars of his cage while his eyes searched for the cup he knew was out there somewhere. Yet, even under this impetus, he could not force his throat to speak.

"There is only one problem."

De Wynter's blue eyes focused now on the dark brown ones looking at him over the folds of the veil. Ali had his full attention. "The princess has been defiled by your touch. She would have had those lips of yours sewn together permanently, but I dissuaded her." Ali did not care to remember that angry discussion. "She has agreed you be freed from this cell and given water, but only under one condition."

The blue eyes had not once looked anywhere but at his own.

"You are to enter her contest. Hundreds of men will compete. Most will die. Chances are you will, too."

The blue eyes didn't even blink.

"But, I am not finished. You and your friends—The Terrible Ten, I believe you call yourselves—you all will compete. Those of you who live through it will no longer be the Amira's slaves. I assured the Amira you would agree. Nod if I am right . . . and then I'll give you water."

The blue eyes stared fixedly into his, then just as Ali was about to give up hope, they partially closed as the man laboriously nodded his head. When they reopened, they seemed to have gone dead, as if the light behind them had been extinguished. Ali could not meet that stare. Getting to his feet, he issued orders.

"Open the door. Bring the cup here and give him a drink. Not too much. Now, you two lift him up to his feet. You will have to carry him, I fear. More water. Not too much. He'll be sick." The rest was a blur to de Wynter.

Finally, he was back in the cell he had shared with his friends. The daylight forced him to squint. Gratefully, he sank down onto the bed of straw, relishing the feel as though it were a featherbed. The anxious looks about him told him he must be a frightening sight.

Drummond, kneeling down and adjusting the straw to make a better pillow for his friend, asked, "Was the kiss that good? Was it worth it?"

Good, kind, unimaginative Drummond. De Wynter managed a smile. "No."

CHAPTER 26

If Carlby had warned him as he crouched in the cage with nothing to do but sleep that he would sleep little . . . or that once his ordeal was over, he would sleep around the clock, de Wynter would have laughed in the priest–physician's face. But when next those blue eyes opened, it was once again daylight. The first face he saw was the kind, open one of Drummond.

"Welcome back. Thirsty?"

With the support of his friend's arm, de Wynter drank greedily, pausing only long enough to ask, "How long?"

"That you slept? A full day."

De Wynter shook his head, then drank more.

"You mean before? Six days. Finished?"

As Drummond eased him back onto his straw bedding, the other eight gathered around.

"Are you up to answering a few questions?" That was Carlby's solicitous voice

He couldn't look them in the eye. How can you tell your friends that to save your own life, you have risked theirs? That by so doing he had given them a chance to win their freedom did not ameliorate his crime.

"Do you know where you were?"

"In an animal cage . . . under the floor of the arena."

"Ali swore we'd never see you again. Why did he change his mind?"

"I don't know."

"Don't you?"

In his weakness, his face betrayed his every thought, his internal struggle. Finally he confessed. "I agreed to their terms."

Carlby persisted. "Speak up. What terms?"

De Wynter was saved from answering by Drummond, who turned angrily on the older man. "He agreed to compete, that's what. You know that's what they wanted. John the Rob read their signs."

Carlby ignored the outburst. "Did you?"

De Wynter could not look the priest in the eye, instead nodding his head wearily.

"And if you win?" Carlby was insistent.

"I would be freed."

Angus spoke up unexpectedly. "Now that seems no bad deal to me!"

"Nor me," Ogilvy confirmed.

"I agree. Me too." All seemed to speak at once.

"You don't have to marry the Amira?" Carlby hung in there like a terrier with a rat.

"It wasn't mentioned."

"And why should it be?" Drummond continued to protect his friend. "A princess wouldn't marry a slave!"

"Not very likely," John the Rob agreed.

Still Carlby persevered. "Were we mentioned?"

De Wynter did not have to answer as guilt, grief, agony chased each other across his unguarded face. But he did. "Mentioned and included."

He was not prepared for his friends' reaction. They were smiling and pounding each other on the back. De Wynter could not believe his eyes. They acted as if he had just done them a favor. If he could believe his ears, their only regret was that the princess would not be at stake. Fionn, of all people, confessed that he had visions of sharing the Amira's harem in an orgy of fruit and wine and writhing female bodies dancing to the strains of horns, drums, and strange stringed instruments.

John the Rob agreed. "I could look forward to a life where the only thing I would need to steal would be a kiss." His attempt to make his monkey-face the picture of passion set the others to laughing.

Cameron proclaimed, "Once set free, I may just turn around and woo the princess yet. From what I saw, she looked ravishing."

Menzies retorted, "Ravishing is right. That's the only way you'll ever know a princess. As for me, I ache only for the fight."

"Aye, Angus and me, we're with you on that. We want no parts of that lady. Of course, my idea of a good fight does not include performing in a bloody circus."

"Aye, give Ogilvy and me a castle to defend, up there where the mountain breezes keep a man cool and comfortable, and we'll make the hills ring with our swords."

The rest were astonished. They did not think of those dark, dour Highlanders as harboring such poetic thoughts.

Of the group, only Carlby was silent. Drummond took him to task. "What of you, priest? Will your religion keep you from joining us?"

Carlby snorted. "Not likely. I am committed to fighting the heathen wherever I find them. I only pray that only heathens face my sword—"

"Don't ask 'em their religion," was Angus's practical advice.

Ogilvy seconded it. "If you don't know different, they'll all be heathens to you."

Carlby smiled his agreement. He knew wisdom when he heard it.

Later that morning, the group resumed its normal workday, rebuilding the third tier. Down in the shady part of the arena, some of the contestants had assembled in the cool of the day to test their skills. De Wynter, his chest heaving, his arms numb with an exhaustion more the result of his ordeal than the rebuilding, stumbled and sank to the ground, resting against one of the larger blocks. Rest periods were forbidden, but the silent ones made no move to prod him back to his feet. Instead, they let him sit and catch his breath and watch the contestants below.

What he saw did not bode well either for the Terrible Ten nor, for that matter, for the Amira's marital future. The slaves had imagined the event would attract younger sons of noblemen who thirsted after adventure, knights who might have fallen on hard times, young and athletic scholars eager to make their mark in the world. But no, this motley crew might claim noble blood but they showed little of it.

There was a killer instinct about them, and they were older. Much older. The average age seemed to be about thirty. Their faces bore scars, and their arms and backs bore testimony of many a nick with a blade or crush with a mace. The Scottish earl decided that he and his fellows would face tough fighting. But, he reminded himself, they had youth on their side. And Ali's conditioning. When the contestants returned to the camp to relax and sip wine during the heat of the day, the slaves were being issued weapons. De Wynter, whose drawn face testified to his exhausted state, was excused—the others being set two on one in threesomes. The royal box was empty this day as the Amira and her mother supervised last-minute preparations of the palace set aside for the Moulay and his harem of little boys. However, Ali ben Zaid was present and he summoned de Wynter to his side.

"Your friends know?"

De Wynter nodded.

"And they agree?" He took de Wynter's silence as acquiescence. "Good."

He turned to leave, but de Wynter had a question. "Amir *l'al-assa*, when do we join the contestants in camp?"

"You don't. You will not live there. Later, you and I will visit it so you may see what you compete against, but you remain here in the slave quarters." The two men looked deep into each other's eyes as if taking measure of the other. De Wynter had no choice but accept the man's word as final. As he turned to leave, it was his turn to be called back by a question. "Know you anything about camels?"

"Nothing."

"Then learn fast. Tomorrow, camels instead of horses."

"Ali ben Zaid? If you hate me so, why do you do this?"

The dark eyes above the veil were inscrutable and for a moment de Wynter thought the man would refuse to answer. Then, Ali spoke: "I would rather a slave win than scum!"

Impulsively, de Wynter held out his hand to this man who had just subjected him to the ordeal in the cage. Ali hesitated just a second before taking it. A handshake had not the same meaning in the Arab world, but these two were in agreement.

That night, forewarned, the slaves pooled what little they knew of camels, mostly what they had gleaned on the long trip from Tunis via Kairouan to al Djem. It was precious little.

Ten men against one camel. The fight was lopsided, for only the camel knew what it was doing. And what it was doing was failing to cooperate. She spat, she bit, she kicked, she spewed her cud a full five feet, showering the dignified Carlby with green slime. As he stood there, shocked, wiping the glop from his eyes, garbled croakings and cacklings—unmistakable sounds of laughter—issued from behind the veils of the silent ones.

"Almost," Carlby admitted later that night, wrinkling his nose as he caught a vertigial whiff of that odorous slime that had saturated his hair, "almost it was worth it just to discover the *Ikwan* are human."

Although Ali had the responsibility for the restoration of al Djem and the actual running of the games, Aisha herself planned the contests. And she plotted some unlikely and unpredictable ones. Assured there would be blood aplenty, the Moulay had gladly washed his hands of all preliminaries to the games and stayed in Tunis. Besides, he liked to be out from under the queen's disapproving eye, free to indulge unhindered in his debaucheries in the Bardo.

Thus, until the games actually began, the Amira and Ali were able to make crucial decisions without fear of contradiction, other than from Ramlah. However, the queen's prime concern was—as it had been since her own bloodied wedding day—to see the throne secured for a Berber-blooded dynasty. To accomplish this, Aisha must marry and give birth to a male heir. To achieve this end, Ramlah would accede to almost anything, including slave participation in the contest.

The games proved to be more complicated than originally envisioned. Were it not for an immense corps of eunuchs and slaves, unlimited sums of money, and the resources of one of the wealthiest countries in the world, they could not have been held. But by dint of meticulous attention to detail and the smooth-running organization of the beardless ones, all was coming to fruition on schedule . . . except for one thing. Aisha, whether deliberately or accidentally, had made no provision for her wedding week.

Ramlah took this on as her special province. She discarded

hundreds of sheepskins until the perfect white one was found for the marriage bed. When Aisha protested, "No need for special care there; no sheepskin will be displayed after my wedding night," Ramlah only smiled and said, "Be quiet, my child. There are ways if husband and wife are agreed." Aisha looked askance but held her peace.

The final week before the start of the games, the roads to al Djem were thronged with people and animals. Messengers heading elsewhere were long delayed or forced to go cross-country to avoid the herds of food on the hoof—mile-long camel trains bearing provisions and the utensils needed to cook and serve it to several thousand people of many different stations. Food was only part of what was requisitioned and brought: rugs, hangings, pillows, cushions, beds, divans—everything needed to restore a few of the villas of al Djem to satisfactorily luxurious substitutes for the Bardo and the Dar al Bey. Although the Amira and the Moulay actively discouraged visitors—for different reasons—those that would come must be accommodated along with their staffs.

Finally, one last caravan assembled in Tunis. More than 150 ships of the desert grumbled noisily under enormous loads of goods. Twenty slaves, ten to a side, shouldered the carrying bars of litters as large as a room, and twenty more men trailed close behind to exchange with the bearers every five miles. Easily a thousand slaves brought up the rear and as many horse-mounted guards walked to either side of the caravan but 500 meters away so that the dust cloud they raised would neither mar the view nor disturb sensitive royal nostrils.

The Moulay had decided to make a great sacrifice: to go direct to al Djem with no stops at coastal ports, no sumptuous overnight accommodations. To ease his suffering, slaves were sent ahead along the royal route to wait with sherbet to cool the royal throat, wine to drown the royal thirst, delicacies to tempt the royal appetite. The only stop occurred at Sousse, when four fifths of the journey was behind them, and this only so that the Moulay might receive gifts of gold from the tribes of the South who had been exhorted to demonstrate materially the honor conferred by having their *Jalala al-Malik* travel among them.

At last, on January 12, in the year of our Lord 1533, but by

Moslem count, the fourth day of the month of Jamada II in the year of the Hejira, 939, the Moulay arrived at al Djem on his first trip ever taken out of Tunis, there to be greeted by a Berber-Arab princess. Hated father and unloved daughter had come together to preside over history's most bizarre mating game. To watch and judge, as inside the gigantic oval game board called al Djem, players from every corner of the Mediterranean sharpened their moves and dreamed of being kinged.

CHAPTER 27

The quality of the free-willed contestants did not improve materially in the weeks after Ali had first condemned them roundly to Aisha and Ramlah in the all-but-deserted arena.

However, there were more of them daily. Five days before the contest began, they numbered more than 100, not counting the slaves. Each day, more men approached the Gate of the Gladiators leading into al Djem. There, scribes, seated cross-legged before low wooden writing tables, took down each man's name, age, country, and whatever proofs he might have of his noble blood. He was then measured and weighed. If accepted by one of the dozen elite of the *Ikwan* as a valid entrant, the man must then swear on *Bible*, *Torah*, or *Koran* that he was free to take a wife. In the case of the Taureg, who admitted already having two wives, an *imam* was summoned so that the man might divorce those far-distant wives by the formula first decreed by the Apostle of Allah. Aisha was not prepared to be wife number two, three, or four.

The criteria for acceptance were few. First, a man must be whole; loss of a limb or castration was cause for invalidation. Second, he must be of proven noble birth or own the armor, horse, and trappings thereof. Third, he must swear on the book of his religion that he had no other wife. Fourth, he must sign his name—or make his sign—on a scroll painted in elaborate Arabic.

Those who asked what they were signing were assured it was an agreement that once one entered in the actual competition, he would

411

not withdraw. In actuality the scroll was the result of weeks of work by the *ulama*. In the most elaborate, convoluted, subtle, devious terms possible, it committed the signer not just to compete so long as he was able, but, win or lose, to relinquish to the Amira and Moulay his future. One particular clause might even be interpreted to mean that each signer accepted the Islamic faith as an entity . . . and as his own. To have come this far, few entrants, even those few who could read Arabic, chose to read it, much less cavil at signing the scroll. Instead, they made their *X* or scrawled their names and rode off to join the great tent-city that sprawled ever farther into the desert.

Two days before the games, the list of entrants had swelled to more than 145. That day, Ali and de Wynter, wearing the white garb of the silent ones, rode off to inspect the camp of the contestants. De Wynter, who was young and healthy, had quickly thrown off the effects of his ordeal underground and, in fact, today rode the wild mare he had conquered in the arena. Naturally the twosome was surrounded by other mounted *Ikwan*. These Ali took more for protection than escape-prevention. If he read this fakir right, the presence of the other slaves still back in the arena would stand hostage for the *jamad ja'da's* behavior.

The original plan was for the tent city to grow up around paths set like the spokes of a wagon wheel, thus giving easy access from the city to the amphitheater and back. However, the contestants themselves had wrought havoc on the organizational plan. A tent assigned to a spot deemed by its haughty owner to be inferior in view or orientation to the sun was moved left, right, back, or forward.

The long straight access lanes planned soon became short, crooked ways. As Ali and his men navigated these, the Amir *l'al-assa's* eyes grew stern above his veil. De Wynter was glad for his own veil although he had smelled these smells before: the typical rotting food–fecal smells that perfumed most of the cities of Europe. Despite the assignment of slaves to clean up horse dung and bury other refuse, the contestants insisted on tossing garbage wherever they wished, of squatting and watering at will, of letting their followers, even the four-legged ones, do the same.

Here and there, of course, there were oases of sanity and cleanliness within the city. One, on the outskirts, was that of the Taureg who chose to camp with, not in, a city of contestants. The other, almost in the center, was an elaborate establishment that belonged to a small wiry redhead whom Ali pointed out without comment. De Wynter's eyes widened and he choked. But under orders not to break the mute law of the *Ikwan*, he swallowed the words *Eulj Ali* before they passed his lips.

Only temporarily. Once free of the camp, Ali asked the cause of his distress. De Wynter hesitated, weighing the benefits or disadvantages of sharing his knowledge with the other. Then, praying that naming the corsair would buy his fellows some advantage later, the Scots earl identified the redhead as Barbarossa's son. When this information was passed on soon after to Aisha, she bristled. "Obviously, he has been sent by his father," she surmised.

"What if he entered on his own?"

"I care not. How dare he enter my competition?" Her usually attractive face was twisted into an ugly mask. "These games wouldn't have been held except for his father's message. Think you I would marry the son? I would kill myself first."

"What would you have us do?"

"Kill him first, idiot!" Instantly she regretted the rashness of her tongue. "No, I didn't mean that. The killing part, yes, the other no. Ali, if you love me, you must see that he does not win."

"But he looks to me like one of the few good competitors."

"That may be. But marriage to him would be catastrophic for Tunisia. We would be handing over our country to his father. He must not win. You must arrange it. And if you don't, I will," she vowed emphatically.

Ali could only share her sentiments. "I shall do what I can, short of murdering him. Would you bring his father's wrath down upon Tunisia? If the son dies other than in the competition, we could be sure of reprisal."

"Perhaps we might find another wife for him." He wasn't sure what she meant, but he liked neither her words nor the look on her face. If he were Eulj Ali, he would depart the camp immediately, or, if he remained, sleep lightly.

Ali left Aisha's surprisingly austere quarters, those she had selected for herself rather than those outfitted for her by Ramlah. His own, he decided, were much more elaborate. But then, he had the women of his harem to consider. These concubines—he dared not take a wife—would turn any quarters into a haven, a harem of posh luxury.

The slaves within their even more austere quarters were delighted with de Wynter's news. Gladly would any one or all of them slit Eulj Ali's gut for him. Looking around the stone room with its ten pallets of stone, de Wynter remembered the luxury he had seen within the camp of the contestants. "They, at least, have means to combat the cold." The slaves did not. They were forced to burrow into the straw to keep warm, being allowed neither fire nor extra clothing. Their main concern, however, was weapons. Although each fought all day with sword and mace and dagger, the weapons were blunted. Nor did each man get the same weapon every day. As Carlby, made Turcopilier of the Order of St. John as much for his knowledge of weapons as his birth, reminded them, "A blunt sword maims, not kills. A strange sword must be mastered before it can maim, much less kill. We are handicapped before we begin."

All but John the Rob drank in his words as if they were the breath of life. John the Rob, as he knew full well, was paying now for a childhood slanted more toward cajoling or stealing alms rather than earning them at weapon point. Carlby had tried to teach the beggar the fundamentals. And against a clod, the beggar might win. Against a trained swordsman, he'd be skewered. Therefore, against Carlby's general principles, he agreed when de Wynter offered to show John the Rob a couple of tricks which no gentleman or knight would ever use, but which, in this case, the Turcopilier agreed, might give the beggar a fighting chance against a more experienced opponent.

Of greater advantage to the beggar and the rest would have been foreknowledge of the games. But on this Ali ben Zaid refused to comment, having been sworn to secrecy by the Amira. No use telling the slaves that already, by virtue of their unorthodox training, they had knowledge of the games. Or at least of those Ali knew were in the offing.

Early, Aisha had informed everyone that the exact makeup of the games would be a closely guarded secret. Only she knew in detail what each day was to unfold.

Carlby, appointed tactician of the group by de Wynter, requested of the Amir *l'al-assa* that he, Carlby, be allowed to discuss the weapons of the group with the person who supplied them. The man he was taken to meet, Carlby was surprised to see, presided over a good-sized establishment, but not really so large considering that close to 175 men would compete. The weaponmaster told him that all weapons for the games would be issued here, but that the slaves could not be fitted for them in advance. Here, a note of uncertainty entered his voice.

Carlby was deeply disappointed by these words, then, spying the anvil and firebed of a forge, his hope was restored. Upon closer questioning, the weaponmaster admitted to having made and weighted weapons. "If we were to each handle the same weapon and then determine our likes and dislikes and make you a list—"

He was interrupted. "I cannot read, *al rabb*. Your plan will not work." Whatever suggestions Carlby made, the weaponmaster turned aside as impossible. Totally frustrated, the Turcopilier left the armory. However, something about it preyed on his mind. That night, at food, Carlby realized what it was. There were really too few weapons in the armory for six days of competition. Had he been able to see the huge pens of animals just outside the amphitheater, he might well have solved his dilemma. Then again, he might have worried less about his fellows and more about his own ability to survive the games.

The following day, the slaves were brought out to sign the scroll. Without thinking about it they lined up in order of precedence:

"James MacKenzie, fifth Earl of Seaforth, of Scotland. No proof of nobility. Age 24."

"John Carlby," (no mention of his priestly rank) "of England. No proof of nobility. Age 32."

"John Drummond, of Scotland. No proof of nobility. Age 23."

"George Cameron, of Scotland. No proof of nobility. Age 24."

"Kenneth Menzies, of Scotland. No proof of nobility. Age 23."

"David of the clan Angus, of Scotland. No proof of nobility. Age 23."

"David of the Clan Ogilvy, of Scotland. No proof of nobility. Age 22."

"Henry Gilliver, of Scotland. No proof of nobility. Age 22."

"Fionn MacDonal, of Scotland and Ireland. No proof of nobility. Age 19."

It was John the Rob's turn and the rest watched him closely. Taking a deep breath, he stepped forward. "John the—" He cleared his throat and started over. "John, Richard's son, of England. No proof of nobility. Age 32."

The scribe, reviewing his records, noted duly, "No man has proof of nobility. What demonstration have you that you are of noble blood?" The slaves, puzzled, stared at each other in confusion.

Ali ben Zaid, prepared for this, stepped forward and emptied a pouch on the low writing table. "This!" The gold coins danced about the table, several rolling off to be chased by scribes, weighers and measurers.

The scribe avariciously fingering the one coin he had recovered, swallowed hard and reluctantly added it to the gleaming pile before him. "Proof accepted. Let them be weighed and measured and sworn."

Ali intervened. "No need for that, they are slaves. Let them sign the scroll. Then, let the gold be distributed among all of you, including these." Addressing the astonished slaves, he added, "After you sign, you may name that which a gold coin would buy for you this night."

He was surprised and pleased at the alacrity with which the slaves signed the scroll. He had hoped that promising each the satisfying of a desire would keep them from reading it. What he did not know was that the slaves feared he would change his mind and make them take the oath, which Carlby as a priest and Cameron as a married man could not do.

Then, they named what they would have: six wanted women; Gilliver and Carlby each a *Bible*, John the Rob six absolutely spherical, totally identical balls. Only de Wynter was silent.

"What?" Ali asked, secretly pleased the slave had not named a woman, which would have been difficult to explain to Aisha. "There is nothing you would have before you risk your life?"

"Could you transport a son or a king's mistress thousands of miles to here?"

"Nay, you know not even a *djinn* could do that. But you could buy that which would make their memories fade."

"Ah, but I wish just the opposite. No, your money cannot buy what I desire."

Despite his words, a bottle of potent *lagmi*, a palm wine, and four pottery cups arrived on the tray bearing the two books and six balls that the other three had requested. The half dozen who had requested women were quartered elsewhere, their desires sated by Ali ben Zaid's own concubines. For a long time, the bottle sat ignored on the tray. Then John the Rob removed the wax seal. "What the hell, tomorrow we may die; tonight, let's numb the thought."

De Wynter swirled the honey-colored liquid around in his cup, then echoed John the Rob's sentiments. "What the hell, here's to numbness!"

There was not enough wine to do that. And that night he again dreamed of those three figures. The same dream as before. But this time, his horse refused to move forward. Spur it, beat it, no matter what he did, the horse would not take him closer to his loved ones. Unknown to himself, that night in his sleep, he cried out a woman's name, but the three who shared his room never revealed it.

Within the camp of the contestants, women were absent; Aisha's decree had seen to that. Therefore, no reasonably young slave boy was safe while the *lagmi* flowed without stop. The contestants lounged in their tents munching on *merguez*, hot grilled sausages spiced with hot peppers and cumin, that called for a swig of *lagmi* with every bite.

Camel-calves and whole sheep roasted over spits, sending their tantalizing aromas throughout the camp. Couscous bubbled in enormous hammered copper pans while cooks roasted peppers and tomatoes on the red-hot coals. To one side, *yo-yos* soaked in thick lemony honey syrup before receiving a final dusting of grated orange rind. And while the food cooked, native musicians played and the wine flowed. This would be a night to be remembered . . . or not, depending on the *lagmi* consumed.

The Moulay followed no such austere regimen. He expected and received the same dishes he would have supped upon in Tunis at the Bardo. For him, candy wine to wash down scrambled eggs with hot sausage and peppers. Piece by piece he fed *brik*, the paper-thin turnovers filled with ground lamb and white eggs, to his latest favorite. Lamb kabobs and pigeon pie, a chicken tajine and fish cooked in almond paste, oranges and marinated radishes—this was the second course to be followed by five more. Between each

417

course, there was sherbet to clear the palate and more wine. Not even in his deepest alcoholic stupor did the Moulay forget to make obeisance to the letter of the Prophet's law—never to let the first drop of wine pass his lips—he fed it lovingly to his favorite, the her/him.

Elsewhere, in another restored villa, in the quarters of the Amira, Aisha was the unwilling participant of the first of six rituals—"Ordeals, you mean," Aisha complained under her breath—that culminate in a Berber wedding. Aisha had used every argument she could think of to avoid them, but Ramlah was adamant, even appealing to Ali ben Zaid. The latter's obvious shock at the proposed breach of tradition had been convincing; Aisha had reluctantly agreed.

She had not agreed, however, to stifle her giggles when her *ama*'s paintbrush daubed henna on a ticklish left foot. Ramlah frowned reprovingly and Aisha bit her lip and tried to suppress her laughter. The *ama* appealed to the queen, "She fidgets so I cannot guarantee keeping the lines straight."

At Ramlah's genuine concern lest the charm would be marred, Aisha swallowed her laugh and smoothed the smile from her face. She even tried to hold her foot rigid in the *ama*'s lap while she painted the *ukda*, a charm against the foot straying from the paths of goodness.

To forget the feel of the tickle, Aisha thought about the morrow, Day One of the competition. The contestants would compete in the Greek manner—nude, their bodies oiled, without weapons. Her nostrils flared as she thought of her trip to the slaves' showers. Fifteen times as many broad shoulders, narrow waists, and muscular buttocks would she view on the morrow. But would any approach the bodily perfection of those two fair-haired ones?

As the *ama*, finished with the first charm, began to paint the other foot, Aisha speculated on why the Olympians must compete nude. Aisha had to smother another giggle, Ramlah's disdainful snort adding impetus to her resolve. What, she wondered, would the judges do with that hermaphrodite who presently shared the Moulay's feast and couch? Disqualify her/him for her feminine organs . . . or admit him/her for his masculine ones?

418

Two down, two to go. The *ama* had finished with both feet, now for her palms. Because these were even more ticklish, the charms painted there were less intricate than the maplike traceries adorning the Amira's insteps. On her left palm went a red egg, symbol of woman and fertility, on the right, a red arrow, symbol of man and potency.

Seated behind a curtain was the *hafiz* Ramlah had hired. Taking as his subject the broad one of marriage, he began reciting from the *Koran* in a thin, reedy singsong. He had scarcely begun when Ramlah grew furious. His text was not one to inspire a reluctant bride.

"From the fourth Surah as revealed at al-Madinah, between the end of the third year and the end of the fifth year,

Verse 23:

> Forbidden unto you are your mothers, and your daughters, and your sisters, and your father's sisters, and your mother's sisters, and your brother's daughters and your sister's daughters and your foster-mothers and your foster-sisters and your mothers-in-law and your stepdaughters who are under your protection born of your women unto whom ye have gone in—but if ye have not gone in unto them, then it is no sin for you to marry their daughters—and the wives of your sons who spring from your own loins. And it is forbidden unto you that ye should have two sisters together, except what hath already happened of that nature in the past. Lo! Allah is ever Forgiving. Merciful.

Verse 24:

> And all married women are forbidden unto you save those whom your right hands possess. It is a decree of Allah for you. Lawful unto you are all beyond those mentioned, so that ye seek them with your wealth in honest wedlock, not debauchery. And those of whom ye seek content by marrying them, given unto them their portions as duty. And there is no sin for you in what ye do by mutual agreement after the duty hath been done. Lo! Allah is ever Knowing, Wise.

Verse 25:

And whoso is not able to afford to marry free, believing women, let them marry from the believing maids whom your right hands possess, Allah knoweth best concerning your faith. Ye proceed one from another; so wed them by permission of their folk, and given unto them their portions ...

With 176 verses to the Surah called "Women," why pick these three? At first, Aisha thought the selection chosen out of ignorance. Now she wondered. Was Ramlah trying to warn her through the words of the *Koran* against the slaves?

Just then, the *ama* finished. Ramlah gave her alms and sent alms to the hafiz with thanks for his inspirational reading. As she hoped, once paid, he stopped his recital. The two women were now alone, except, of course, for the usual handmaidens and eunuchs and slaves that shared the quarters of the royal.

"Tell me, Mother. Do you not find something contradictory in the painting of primitive charms during the reciting of the *Koran?*"

Ramlah looked pained. "Of course not. Before we had the revelations of the Apostle of Allah—upon whom be Allah's blessings and peace—we had the charms. The two tonight depict continuity, just as you and I depict the continuation of the blood of our fathers."

Aisha examined the egg on her left palm, cracking it into hundreds of pieces by simply clenching her fist ... the same with the right. "These symbols do not seem very solid," she observed.

"Their appearance deceives you. The egg must break to produce the offspring; the arrow, though collapsed, springs back. That is what your grandmother would say. I say, try washing them off before you complain of their impermanence."

Aisha stared at her mother. "You mean I shall go through the next week with these marks on my hand?"

"At least the next week, maybe longer, your skin being so fair. You did not ask why we use the henna. That too is symbolic. Of the blood which makes the two of you one." Here, Aisha snorted inelegantly but effectively. Ramlah frowned at her daughter and continued on as if never interrupted, "And which each of you must be willing to shed for the other, the wife in childbirth, the husband in battle."

Aisha vowed to herself, once her mother was gone, to aid the disappearance of these blood-red symbols with an application of pumice. To her dismay, scrub though Zainab, her maid, might, the henna lost little of the brilliance of its hue.

Later, Aisha lay naked and sleepless between the silken sheets of her enormous bed, brought in pieces from the Dar al Bey and re-assembled here. By the light of the braziers, just beyond the thin bed hangings, she slowly opened and closed her hands, watching egg and arrow shatter and spring forth renewed. She found both disquieting. When Zainab arrived the next morning upon the final words of the *muezzin*'s call, Aisha was already awake.

BOOK THREE

**The Great Games of Aisha
11 Jamad II, A.H. 939/
19 January, A.D. 1533**

al Djem

CHAPTER 28

At daybreak, 180 contestants, including the ten slaves, were awakened by the call to prayer by *muezzins*. Some staggered from their beds still drunk. Simple food awaited them: bread, fresh-churned butter, camel's milk, cold meat, fruit, plus strong coffee and sickly sweet tea with mint, but from fear or hangover, many did not eat.

When slaves gave cry to the-call-to-play, the men gathered with their retinues outside the Gate of Gladiators. As their names were read off by the scribe, the contestants—but not their attendants—were admitted through the Gate of Gladiators. Once inside, they were ushered down a ramp into a large barren chamber and told to strip. "No clothes, no weapons, no jewels, not even *ukda* or crucifix or Taureg veil will be allowed within the arena. The only exception, a band for your hair, we will supply."

The reaction was immediate. Since men when swearing and making love are most comfortable in their native languages, de Wynter and the others identified Spaniards, Greeks, Latins, Frenchmen, Byzantines, Slavs, Africans, and more. So multilingual was the group that ten slaves, speaking Scots and English, did not stand out.

Not until the goose-fleshed group of naked men emerged onto the sand-strewn arena floor to stand gratefully in the warmth of the sun, did the tanned, athletic bodies of the slaves mark them as different from the generally pallid, battle-scarred, heavy-muscled men about them. Ali, from his place, standing behind Aisha, was not surprised to see several paunches and one or two bodies outright fat. Aisha, veiled like a silent one, had expected that gazing on 180 naked men would be exciting. She realized, to her surprise, that secretly watching de Wynter and Fionn bathe had had far greater appeal. Would that still hold true, she wondered, and vowed to find out.

As the contestants milled about at one end of the arena, six men in long purple robes, followed by three times as many burly seminude slaves, appeared at the far end. Whether it was the dignified mien of the judges or the cruel scourges carried by the *mastigophorae*, their whip-bearing assistants—something silenced the contestants. The voice of the white-turbaned judge, speaking Sabir, rolled and echoed throughout the arena.

"Welcome to the Great Games of the Moulay Hassan—with whom may Allah be pleased—and his daughter, the Amira Aisha Kahina—with whom may Allah be content. We six wearing the purple serve as judges; the Moulay Hassan—with whom may Allah be pleased"—the judge pointed up to the royal box, its central seat conspicuously empty—"has graciously consented to be the chief judge of us all. Our decisisions will be final. Permit me to introduce my colleagues. From Greece, a direct descendant of contestants in the early Olympiads, *al jalala* Artemidorus of Tralles. From Rome *al jalala* Pietro Strabo. From our own city of Gafsa, *al jalala* Hamad Attia. From Marrakesh, in the land of Morocco, *al jalala al wazier* Yahib. From Arred, in Arabia, *al jalala* Sheykh Beteyen ibn Kader. Myself, I have the honor to serve as *wazier* to the Moulay Hassan— with whom may Allah be pleased—Ibn al-Hudaij."

So impressive, so dignified, so formal seemed the judges that the contestants discounted the purpose of the whip-bearers as ceremonial. When Ibn al-Hudaij spoke up again, saying, "If any man wishes to withdraw his name from the scroll, let him speak now before the games begin and the scroll is sealed!" no one stepped forward. Not even the slaves who were forestalled by threatening movements among the silent ones looking down from the first tier just above them.

"Seal the Scroll, close the gates, let the games begin!" the judge ordered.

426

"And now," the white-turbaned one continued, "let the rules of today's competition be announced. The blessings of Allah be on him who competes."

Artemidorus of Tralles, wearing a wreath of leaves upon his brow, stepped forward to outline in detail that which had been kept secret until now.

"Today, you recreate the Pentathlon, exactly as it was performed centuries ago in the stadium at Olympia. First, the discus throw, then, in this order, jumping, the javelin throw, running, and wrestling. Five events in all. One winner of each event. The five winners will be excused from tomorrow's contest, but no others. You will each compete in the three events of your choice, no more, no less."

Two assistants stepped forward holding sandglasses. "While the sand in this glass runs, you may ask questions of the judges about the events, so that you can choose. When this runs dry, the other will be overturned; while the sand in it runs its course, you must sign and obtain three tokens from the five scribes behind me."

The questions would have begun then, but the judge held up his hand. Not his hand but the forward motion of the whip-bearers quelled their voices. "Let me warn you, the events are limited. If you have not signed up and received tokens for three events, you will be assigned arbitrarily to whichever event is still open. One hour from now, the games begin. Now you may ask questions."

The floodgate was opened. Was the jumping over hurdles? Would the javelin throw be judged on accuracy? Was the jumping standing or running? How far was the run? No holds barred in the wrestling? And so forth.

The slaves instinctively gathered together looking to their leaders for decision. De Wynter's classical education had its advantages. "The Greeks arranged their contests logically—remember?—alternating the use of arms and legs with the last event requiring the whole body."

"Yes, but," Drummond reminded him, "no athlete in ancient times competed in more than one event, especially not on the same day."

"No time for that type of talk," Carlby interrupted. "Our immediate problem is signing the ten of us up for thirty events—"

427

"Suppose," de Wynter suggested, "one need not sign up individually for each event, but could sign others up? That would give us a numerical advantage."

"Might work," Carlby admitted.

Drummond volunteered to check with the white-turbaned one. He was back shortly. "The rules do not prohibit it. But only three names at a time."

De Wynter clapped him approvingly on the back. "Good. Now, while you were gone, we all agreed the most popular events are likely to be those closest to modern warfare: javelin throwing and wrestling. The least popular and last to be filled would be the first event, the discus throw; let's not even bother to sign for that. So who is our fastest runner?"

All were momentarily disconcerted by that non sequitur.

Then, Carlby saw his point. "Right, we send our fastest man to try to be first in line for wrestling. Our next fastest to javelin, and so forth."

All eyes turned to Cameron. "I'll do my best. Whose names do I give?"

"Mine," said Carlby. "I've wrestled my way round the Mediterranean. I may not be massive, but I'm tricky."

"Bet we English could show you a trick or two," John the Rob chimed in. "I may be small, but I'm slippery. There isn't a hold I can't wiggle my way out of. Sign me up, too."

"And I," said Drummond.

"Aye, add my name to your list," Fionn said.

"But that makes four," Gilliver pointed out, "and Cameron can only sign up three."

"Let me get in line to sign up for the wrestling also," Fionn volunteered. "What I lack in speed, I make up in size. Judging from the size of some of those contestants, a little muscle backing him up might be of value to Cameron as well."

Then Angus spoke up. "As long as you are going to be there, sign me and Ogilvy up."

"Now, Drummond, you or I—which of us will be able to secure a place in the javelin line?" de Wynter asked, smiling on his friend. "We have not run against each other in a long time. Who today do you think would win?"

Carlby settled that question. "You both better go. There will be at least six or more of you, not including me. I am no marksman with thrown weapons."

De Wynter agreed. He could, from their youth, name at least six such marksmen: "Myself, Drummond, Ogilvy, Angus, Cameron, and Gilliver."

"If there's room, add my name to the list, too," Fionn spoke up.

"Why not? But we'll need another runner."

"Let that be me," John the Rob spoke up. "I be good at running, having run from the king's guards all my life."

"Menzies, you and Gilliver sign up those who would run," de Wynter directed.

Carlby, Gilliver, John the Rob, Menzies, Cameron, and de Wynter himself opted for running. The same for jumping, with the exception of de Wynter, who said, "No, strangely enough, I think I'll go for the discus, better preparation for the javelin throw."

Fionn nodded consideringly. "Good point. I, too, should prefer the discus."

"Jamie, let me sign you up for it," Gilliver pleaded. De Wynter, studying that solemn, determined face turned so lovingly toward him, had to agree.

As did Carlby, who immediately spoke up. "You do that. I shall measure my own lungs by running to be first in line for the running."

Dourly Angus observed, "That leaves me and Ogilvy to handle the jumping, which we can handle nicely."

As the last handful of grains of sand poured down the funnel-shaped tube, they reviewed their entries:

Wrestling: (Cameron to make the entry) Carlby, Drummond, and
  John the Rob
  (Fionn to make the entry) Himself, Ogilvy, and Angus

Javelin throw: (De Wynter to make the entry) Himself, Ogilvy and
  Angus
  (Drummond to make the entry) Himself, Gilliver and Fionn
  (John the Rob to make the entry) Cameron

Jumping: (Angus to make the entry) Gilliver, Carlby and John the Rob

  (Ogilvy to make the entry) Cameron and Menzies

Discus: (Gilliver to make the entry) De Wynter, Fionn and Drummond.

If their calculations were correct, Menzies, Ogilvy, and Angus would compete in the discus throw by default.

Ramlah and Aisha fidgeted nervously. Would the Moulay never appear? As far as they were concerned, if he made just one single appearance to bless the games with his presence, he could then happily disappear forever so far as they were concerned. Ramlah finally sent a messenger to ask his pleasure.

Even as the royal women awaited husband and father, down below in the arena, contestants rushed, pushed, shoved, elbowed, and tripped to be first in their respective lines.

While officials scurried back and forth across the arena, slaves dug up and raked over one section of the arena floor, creating a pit as landing area for the jumping event. For the two throwing events, in another area of the vast arena, measurements were taken and precisely marked with pegs driven deep into the clay beneath the sand. At both ends of the arena, preparations for the stade run were underway, with starting blocks being sunk into the dirt at one end and a finishing line marked at the other, with boxes supplied upon which the judges would stand so that they might better see the winner as he breasted the tape.

Elsewhere, and quite close to the lines of contestants, a mound of dirt, a balbis, was raised, centered between two boards set in the earth, these to indicate rear and front boundary lines for the contestants.

Once these preparations were finished, the slaves withdrew, leaving holes, hills, and boxes marring the smooth sand of the arena. Those contestants who chose to enter but one event and let fate decide the others were limbering up within the open spaces.

The lines of contestants had been long, especially those for wrestling and javelin throwing as the slaves had accurately predicted. However, the scribes were well organized and had evidently memorized the contestants' names, thus speeding things up. So when Cameron, third in line since he'd been tripped on his way, named Carlby, the scribe supplied "England." For Drummond, "Scotland," and for John the Rob, a blank. Then Cameron remembered. "Oh, my God, he used another name, what the hell was it?"

Fionn, fifteenth behind him, saw Cameron's problem and called out, "Who?"

"John the Rob, his full—"

"John, Richard's son!"

Cameron breathed a sigh. "John, Richard's son," evoked a reassuring response, "England."

Delays like this were common throughout the registration period, and as a result, the sun had risen much higher than the royals had expected before the games began. However, that gave the Moulay time to arrive. A blast of many ram's horns signaled his tardy arrival, his current favorite mincing at his side, but there was no seat in the royal box for the her/him. Then one must be procured, otherwise the Moulay threatened to go home to Tunis.

As Ramlah and the Moulay argued about how high the stool should be compared to the queen's and the Amira's, the latter nudged Ali, who signaled the *kuddam* to sound the twisted horns again. The contestants, watching the doings in the royal box, actually outnumbered those seated within the amphitheater, not including the silent ones and slaves, of course.

Ibn al-Hudaij needed no audience but his master, the Moulay. For him, the *wazier* cupped his hands to his mouth and announced in his most stentorian tones:

"Let the games begin! *Jalala al-malik*, I have the honor to present to you today the reenactment of games which first honored a god and then emperors. First in Greece, later in Rome, and then 2000 years ago in this very glorious amphitheater in the heart of Tunisia. Give us, O Moulay—the blessings of Allah be on you—your permission to begin these games!"

While Ibn al-Hudaij waited breathlessly for his master's answer, the Moulay and Ramlah continued wrangling over which stool the favorite should sit on at the Moulay's feet.

A wazier doesn't tell a Moulay to stop bickering and pay attention to the matter at hand. Not if he values his head. All Hudaij could do was repeat even louder, "O Moulay, give us your blessings to begin these games."

The Moulay, annoyed, waved his *wazier* to be quiet. The latter seized upon this as his permission to commence.

"Let the games begin! And may Allah look with favor on those who compete, the judges, the assistants, and the spectators themselves, upon whom may Allah be pleased."

The Moulay reluctantly responded to the cheers of the sparsely filled arena . . . and the more enthusiastic ones of the contestants. "I welcome you to this grand occasion. May Allah look with favor on all who are involved."

He sat down. As did Ramlah, half a head lower, and Aisha, one quarter head lower than that, and the favorite, a token lower than that. A *muezzin*, chosen out of hundreds for the carrying quality of his voice, cried out, "The first event, the discus throw, ninety-four contestants. Each to make three throws—one with the light, one with the medium, one with the heavy. The winner to be he who throws any of the three the greatest distance, so long as it remains within the boundaries, and so long as he commits no foul in the act of throwing. The order of throwing has been determined by a drawing overseen by the judges. *Al jalala* Artemidorus of Tralles, the game is yours. May Allah bless him who competes."

Another great cheer went up. The spectators settled into their seats. The contestants crowded around the balbis. The measuring umpires took up their positions. And the first thrower stepped up on the raised mound, palming the light discus first in his left, then his right hand, and back again, trying to get the feel of it; for no contestant had been allowed to handle the carefully sized and weighted discus beforehand. Several sets of three were neatly piled under the watchful eye of the starter.

Planting one foot firmly on the top of the mound, the other halfway down its front slope, the first thrower leaned back until much of his body was horizontal, curled himself like a spring with the discus at his back, and with a mighty spring and twirl heaved the object toward the center of the arena. A cheer rose from the crowd, this being the first toss, and the measurers quickly descended on the landing area and marked the precise spot with a peg, while noting the exact distance on their official scorecards. De Wynter had no way of knowing whether or not this was a worthy throw, but it made him wonder if he could match it.

The athlete fouled on his second toss, his foot coming to rest just over the front line. His third toss was nowhere near as long, being made with the heaviest of the three discs. Now he could only wait and see how ninety-three others fared. The strategy of winning was quite apparent to de Wynter now. A bad throw or foul on the first throw could perhaps be rectified by a superhuman toss of the medium-weight disc. But it was most unlikely that anyone would win with the heaviest. To make matters worse, the critical first throw had to be done without benefit of practice.

The crowd's interest waned as athlete after athlete took his three turns, and it became clear to even the most unobservant that there would not be a winner until after the midday break. But interest was revived an hour into the discus event when the first call for the jumping contest was announced from the opposite end of the arena.

Gilliver, with his frail body, stood out in a sea of athletic and heavily muscled bodies, as he made his way, along with John the Rob, Carlby, Cameron, and Menzies, to the jumping area. Menzies was concerned because he was also entered in the discus event, and he might have a time conflict. But de Wynter had told him not to worry about it until he saw what number he drew in the jump, and as luck would have it, his was a low one.

"The second event is the Great Jump," the crier intoned for the benefit of those few spectators interested enough to leave their goblets of wine and their animated conversations. "One hundred and two contestants. The winner, he who clears the greatest distance in a running jump followed immediately by a standing jump. No foot may protrude over the starting line. No jump will count unless finished in a standing position. And no steps may be taken between the two jumps. Each contestant to have one try. May Allah bless him who competes."

The first jumper was called to the starting area, and staring intently at the long dirt pit ahead, ran swiftly down a marked path leading to the takeoff line, marked by a timber buried in the ground. In his hands he carried two metal weights with handles for gripping. As he toed the starting board and flew into the air, he heaved the

433

weights forward in his arms, tucked his feet up under his chin, and sailed through the air. Approaching his landing spot, he threw his arms and the weights backward, affording him a better-balanced landing. From his crouched landing, he straightened, took a deep breath, crouched again and from a standing start, repeated the maneuver with the weights. The measuring crew moved in quickly, figured the distance from the nearest premarked spot, and recorded the jump as being seven meters, five decimeters, and three centimeters—about nineteen feet.

"What do you think? Do the weights help or hurt?" asked Menzies of Carlby.

"I think it depends," Carlby replied, "on how big you are through the chest. If you're slight, I don't think so, but the weights may help heavy-chested ones. Let's watch a few more before we decide."

They watched the longest distance rise to over eight meters by the time Menzies had his go at it. He had decided to forego the weights, feeling that his unfamiliarity with them might cause him to lose his balance. (Carlby, on the other hand, needing every advantage he could get, privately decided to try the weights.) Down the approach track the handsome Scot sped, hitting the takeoff board just right, and windmilling his arms as he flew through the air. Clearly it was a good jump, Carlby saw, and he gritted his teeth and muttered low encouragement as Menzies straightened for the standing jump, then crouched and leaped forward. He almost outjumped his balance point, teetered precariously for a second, then got it under control and straightened up. The judge ruled a good landing, since the imprints were clean and no other part of his body had touched the dirt. Down on the scorecard went a new record of nine, seven, and two—a full twenty-six feet. With a clap on the back from Carlby, Menzies was off to find de Wynter.

The earl was very much involved when Menzies arrived at the balbis. De Wynter had his foot planted on the mound, was twisting into a tight coil, and letting fly with the first disc. It was a creditable throw, but at thirty meters, four decimeters, a meter short of the best thus far. Now came the real test: to outdo his first throw with a disc a kilogram heavier.

He did it! But only by four decimeters. Not enough. With the heaviest disc of the three, he fell far short of his first throws.

"Don't worry, you've got two more events to go," Menzies consoled de Wynter.

"And you?"

"Leading the jump, but it may not hold, it's still early."

"Drummond?"

"Not good enough," de Wynter replied. "Ogilvy's next, then you. How do you feel?"

"Not bad, though not nearly as comfortable about this as the jump," Menzies answered.

"Well, it may be," de Wynter said, "that we'll all have to compete tomorrow. A day of rest would be nice, but, frankly, compared to rebuilding that tier, competing seems easier."

Ogilvy stepped onto the mound, looked down at the unfamiliar disc, fidgeted his feet, and finally, with adrenalin pumping, threw a fluke. The round object flew farther than any before him. His second and third throws resulted in fouls, but his fellow slaves didn't care as they pummeled his bare back with enthusiasm.

Menzies executed his three throws with typical precision but none were beyond de Wynter's, let alone Ogilvy's. Angus did creditably, but his longest throw landed outside the markers and could not be counted.

Fionn worriedly whispered to de Wynter, "What would you have me do if Ogilvy's throw still leads when it is my turn?"

"Do your best," de Wynter answered. "Someone else might still do better than Ogilvy. If you don't and they do, we'll lose out altogether. Beat him if you can."

At the jumping pit, John the Rob and Gilliver gave it a good try, but fell far short of Menzies's mark. Carlby came not close at all; he was clearly past his prime for such pure athletic contests. Cameron jumped among the last, having drawn the seventy-eighth spot. Good athlete that he was, he just barely missed taking the lead.

Leaving Gilliver behind to see if Menzies's mark would hold up, the other four made their way around the perimeter to see how the discus event was going.

"How do we in this one?" Carlby asked of de Wynter

"Ogilvy still leads with Fionn yet to throw. I've advised Fionn to try and beat the mark. What do you think?"

"How many more to go?"

"Five after Fionn; one's big and might easily beat Ogilvy, or even Fionn."

"Yes, I see your point," he said, nodding his head as though to make his agreement more emphatic.

They watched anxiously as the final throwers set out to beat Ogilvy's mark of thirty-one meters, one, and five. Four throwers tried and failed. Then Fionn calmly stepped onto the balbis, palmed the disc a few times, took his stance and executed an excellent throw, just short of Ogilvy's mark. Another good throw. Same result. Drawing on that extra strength they all knew he had, Fionn managed to throw the heaviest disc nearly as far as his first throw. But still Ogilvy held the lead—by design or accident? The next two had no more success. With still two to go, the next bested Ogilvy's throw by more than a meter, dashing the slaves' hopes of their first win. They were still very much alive in the jumping area, where Menzies still led and only four yet to jump. Through narrowed eyes, they watched one come within half a footprint. When the final measurement was made, Menzies's distance had held and eighteen arms all managed to participate in lifting Menzies to the broad shoulders of Fionn and Ogilvy, for a victory dance.

The official crier's voice rose above the din to announce the winners of the first two events: "In the discus, the winner, with a throw of thirty-two meters, two decimeters, nine centimeters: Zeno, of the Isle of Crete. In the jump, the winner, with a distance of nine meters, seven decimeters, and two centimeters: Menzies, of Scotland. To allow you time to eat and rest, the next event, the javelin throw, commences in two hours. May Allah be with you where you go."

The crowd did not wait for the royal family to depart, but filed quickly out of the amphitheater and off to villas and tents, to dine and dally and rest. Many had found the Olympian games too slow and tame for their nature, and the seats too hard and uncomfortable for their posteriors.

Ramlah, for one, had enjoyed the morning. Not many an Arab woman, nor less-protected Berber, had seen so many naked men. Did not Mohammed tell believers to hide their pudenda from knees to waist from the view of women? Fortunately, for the sake of the games, few contestants were orthodox or even Moslem. However, Aisha had paid special attention to only a few of the contestants: the silver-haired one; the giant Fionn, whom Ali had so strongly recommended; a handsome Taureg from the desert country to the west; a magnificently muscled black;' and since they were there, those other tanned bodies that always surrounded the silver-haired one. One other one she watched—with loathing—Eulj Ali, the son of Barbarossa.

If he won, he would be excused from tomorrow's games, and that would not do. Tomorrow, gladiators fought. Nothing would please her more than seeing a sword through the redhead's heart. She wished she could arrange a special opponent for Eulj Ali, someone against whom he would have small chance of surviving. But the judges had demanded all draws from the gold dish be honest. Not yet was she ready to overrule these respected men. Not yet. As for Eulj Ali, she would hope for the best: the worst for him. In all honesty, however, she had to admit that he did have a masterful physique, with his father's red hair seeming to flow, uninterrupted, from his head to his beard to his full chest and in a narrow line down to surround his studlike genitals. She reminded herself Arabs hate body hair.

The Moulay Hassan too had enjoyed the morning more than anticipated. He could get used to watching naked athletes run and jump and contort their bodies. He too had been attracted to the beautiful pale-haired one, finding it curious that his head was hoary but his body hair dark, only barely tinged with multi-grays. He found this one quite stimulating. To enjoy himself until he got back in his villa, he sent for two boys from the group brought to al Djem for his own purposes.

The "Terrible Ten" spent the rest period sequestered in their own quarters, eating sparingly from the fruit, meats, and breads provided for the athletes, and resting on their pallets.

These hardened fighting men marveled at what they considered the tameness of the first day's events, calling them, "Womanly!" "Unmanly!" "Perfect for children and cowards." And more. De Wynter and Carlby said nothing. But each knew what the other was thinking, Perfect for Gilliver. Only because nine men had deliberately done more than their share had the frail young man survived the trip to and the days at al Djem. If tomorrow's games were Roman as suspected from the lineup of the judges, it followed that they would be gladiatorial. If gladiatorial, they might be competing to the death, Gilliver's death.

"But if Gilliver should win today—" de Wynter didn't have to say it. Gilliver would be excused on the morrow.

"How? The events are based on individual effort."

"Except running." de Wynter reminded Carlby. "Suppose we were to crowd out some of his faster competition? Anyway, it's worth a try."

That it might cost Cameron his own chance to escape, neither thought worth mentioning. Carlby was too much the priest; de Wynter too long the leader of the companions, who thought first of others. Which was why de Wynter had agonized so about his choosing to escape the cage by involving the others. Of more immediate concern was the wrestling contest. "Suppose two of us are paired?" Carlby wondered.

"Enjoy it. At least we'll fight clean; more than I can say for the others. Did you see—" His comment was cut short by the rattling of the cell door, an announcement by the silent one that the men were to come out. The games were about to resume at the javelin range. *Muezzins* announced the starting order; Cameron, Angus, Drummond, and Fionn in the early throwing, and de Wynter, Gilliver, and Ogilvy toward the end.

Aisha and Ramlah were back in their seats, but the Moulay was absent as were many of the morning's spectators when came the official call for the javelin throw: "One hundred and ten competitors. The winner will be he with the longest throw—without foul from the starting board—that is nearest to the center line drawn from the great post in the middle of the arena. One throw by each contestant. May Allah bless him who competes."

The javelin was the height of a tall man, one end fitted with a metal point. Before making the throw, the contestant fitted an amentum, or throwing loop, to the shaft near the balance point. Placing the index finger, or the index and middle fingers, in the loop and balancing the shaft on his thumb, the throw was made by a rapid thrust forward and upward, the body and legs, as well as the arm and shoulder, playing major roles in the execution. The purpose of the amentum was to increase the carry and to impart a slight rotary motion which helped to stabilize the flight, and thus control its direction.

The same balbis used for the discus event was also used for the javelin. One step over the front board resulted in a disqualification. In one detail, the javelin event was to differ from that in the earliest Olympics. The judges had agreed to forego the usual three throws and allow just one per contestant. The reason was that no other event could be staged during the javelin throw because this arena was shorter than the original stadium at Olympia. In Greece, a jumping or running event could be staged simultaneously with the javelin throw without fear that one competitor might spear another contestant with the deadly six-foot shaft.

In quick succession the throwers were called to the balbis and made their single throws. Cameron easily outthrew the first eight, his long legs and arms coming into play as though the javelin was the spear he had thrown all his life. Angus didn't really stand a chance. Drummond threw it well past Cameron's mark, but not as well centered. Fionn got his fingers fouled up in the loop and saw his strong throw veer off and out of the boundaries.

This was de Wynter's golden chance and he knew it. He watched Drummond's lead disappear several times over. And when he stepped onto the balbis, centered the loop, and tried to recreate all the positions and moves in his mind, he felt quite at home. So used was he to his hair, he forgot how it distinguished him. So he never knew three pairs of royal eyes—the Moulay finally having rejoined the group—plus those of one Berber and one hermaphrodite watched his throw with special interest.

It was a thing of beauty, sailing two lengths of the shaft past the farthest peg and not far off the center line. It held the record for long minutes, until, in an absolute fluke, a strong but awkward thrower stepped up and actually hit the post inches beyond where de Wynter had thrown.

Gilliver performed about as expected, and Ogilvy made a long but off-the-mark throw; the hopes of the "Terrible Ten" in this event were dashed.

As the winner was announced by the crier—a Spaniard by the

name of Balberus, with a throw of 65.6 meters—slaves removed the great post from the center of the arena, leveling out the mound of dirt and removing the boundary timbers that constituted the balbis. Other slaves placed five gaily decorated poles at intervals in holes already bored in a row of timbers sunk in the earth across one end of the arena. At the far end, a ribbon was stretched taut between two poles about twenty meters apart.

When all was in readiness, the *muezzin* cried, "The next, the stade race. One hundred and forty-four contestants. The distance, the length of the stadium. To be run in five heats of twenty each. Four contestants have drawn byes in the heats, and will move to the finals with the heat winners. The ultimate winner will be he who breasts the tape first in the finals. Impeding another runner will result in disqualification. May Allah bless him who competes."

None of the "Terrible Ten" were lucky enough to draw byes. And, as fate dictated, Gilliver was in a heat by himself. In another heat were de Wynter, John the Rob, and Menzies. Carlby and Cameron were matched in still another heat.

"Rotten luck," Carlby said to de Wynter. "They bunched us up in just three heats, and poor Gilliver is all by himself. No way to help him now."

"Well, we got one break," de Wynter said. "Menzies and I can try to help John the Rob. Especially Menzies. Since he's already won, it won't matter if he gets himself disqualified."

The first heat was soon called, and twenty athletes took their places, five between each set of poles. Carlby noted that they were assigned specific starting spots. With a blast on a ram's horn, they leaped from their crouched position on all fours and sped down the 150-meter course, seeming to Carlby, though his vantage point was not good, to break the ribbon en masse.

The second heat saw Gilliver finish in the middle of the pack, still puffing like a blowfish when he rejoined the group at the starting line. The third pitted de Wynter, John the Rob, and Menzies against seventeen other eager runners. And, in trying to help the beggar, both athletes had to slow up, and all three wound up out of the top finishers. The fourth heat held none of the "Terrible Ten." Cameron bested Carlby and all others in the final heat, his long legs churning and his chest thrust out to reach the tape a split second before his closest rival.

It was really a five-man race in the finals, the four byes turning out to be just mediocre runners. Cameron, who had had the least rest of any of the nine, was last off the starting block, but picked up ground with his long strides down the center of the arena, and outfought the third heat winner in the final two meters to win the stade race and the accolades of the crowd.

Immediately the clean-up crew was back in the arena, sweeping, raking, and laying down two bands of salt in wide circles near the center. These completed, they drew even larger circles of salt. These would be the lines behind which all but the four wrestlers, the judges, and umpires must remain.

The crier announced Cameron as the winner of the stade race, no one mentioning the fact that Scotland had now recorded two victories on the first day.

"The final event of the day, Greek wrestling. Ninety competitors. Each to compete until defeated. The matches to be from standing starts. Three clean throws constitute a win. The decision of the judge will decide the throws. Pairings in the first round will be decided by draw before the judges. Additional draws will be made after each round, with byes where necessary. May Allah bless him who competes."

The pairings of the first forty-five matches revealed none of the group matched against another of his fellows. Carlby explained why it was to their advantage that this was to be standing wrestling. "The main things to look out for are leg holds and tripping. Once the opponent gets you on one leg, he has you at a great disadvantage. Trips over an opponent's leg could put you off balance in a split second. The best defense is to be leaning forward, keep the arms moving so that the opponent cannot grab them easily, and stay on guard against sudden lunges for the legs."

Carlby had drawn the seventh pairing. But with matches going on simultaneously in the two rings, his was really the fourth that the group watched. But it proved an eye-opener for them. From the first instant when the umpire dropped the bright red cloth, Carlby was in the air and grabbing for the nearest leg of his opponent. So surprised

441

was the poor fellow, who had instead expected the usual sparring and feeling out before an actual move was made, that he failed to retract the leg. Carlby gripped it firmly in both hands, and, with a mighty heave, literally toppled the athlete on his back. A clean fall, the judge signaled. Back at it again! Carlby's opponent, his confidence shaken, took two more quick falls without ever laying a serious grip on the Englishman.

Fionn was paired in match number thirteen with a moderate-sized man who knew what the sport was all about, but who just couldn't stand up to the brute strength of the young giant. In fact, after the second fall, his opponent refused to continue, having landed heavily on one shoulder, which he continued to hold in pain. Fionn was declared winner by forfeiture.

Ogilvy, Drummond, and John the Rob, in that order, also won their first round matches. Only Angus, who drew a very tough and experienced opponent, went down to defeat after a good match tied at two falls apiece.

Forty-five names went into the gold bowl and were drawn in pairs for the second round; the single name remaining in the bowl earned its owner a bye.

Again in these matches no two members of the group were pitted against each other, a matter of luck that de Wynter hadn't counted on and that Carlby ascribed to Divine Providence. Only some of their opponents had they seen in the first round, since the others had performed in one ring while the slaves were wrestling in the other.

"Any more of those tricks up your sleeve?" Drummond asked Carlby. "I could use one this time around."

"Try the same opening move I did," Carlby said. "If you are fast enough, you should get the first fall. After that, your opponent must think defense, rather than offense, until he can catch up with you. Try it. It should work. Any other trick I might show you would take too long, and your opponent might see us at it."

Ogilvy drew the first match of the group in the fourth spot, and despite his strength, he went down to defeat at the hands of a skilled wrestler. John the Rob was not quite so quickly dispatched by a much heavier man who used his weight successfully to offset the beggar's darting moves.

Carlby got by his second-round opponent after a grueling match that remained tied at two falls apiece for so long that the judge called a halt to the match and awarded the decision to Carlby on the basis of his greater aggressiveness.

Drummond's opening move failed, and it left him open for a counter-move that had him on the floor almost instantly. He did manage one fall, but was eventually defeated by a worthy opponent.

Now only Fionn had a shot left at the next round. His opponent was a lighter but quicker man, who gained the first two falls before Fionn realized he must tire the man out and slow him down. Risking a disqualification, Fionn bluffed, faked, tantalized, played defense until his man grew both tired and frustrated at not being able to finish off the giant Scotch-Irishman. Fionn then used his greater strength to record three straight falls.

Carlby and Fionn advanced to the next round of eleven matches, with one man drawing a bye. Fionn survived. Carlby, showing the effects of a rigorous day, went down three and two. Fionn got through still another round and made the quarter finals. The six winners met in three matches that may well have done the original Olympics proud. Fionn, now well over his head as far as foul-experience went, lost a heartbreaker to Eulj Ali, a dirty fighter; and the final three were put in a draw to see who would gain a bye. The lucky Turk rested while Eulj Ali and another battled it out in the semifinal. He came on refreshed, totally expecting to finish off Eulj Ali's victor in three straight falls.

The crowd, which had been quiet, had come alive for the final few bouts, a lot of wagers being made and paid. The Moulay, easily bored, left. Ramlah and Aisha, delighted when Eulj Ali finally lost, found themselves without a favorite to cheer on. They stayed only because they did not want to drag Ali ben Zaid away.

The final event pitted two worthy opponents—the Turk with a heavy-slung belly, but short legs that gave him great balance, and a tall, rangy Nuba wrestler from Western Tunisia. When the Turk bent forward, his great belly seemed to act as a shield, protecting even his knees. On the other hand, the Nuba was one of that renowned clan who had wrestled practically from the time he was born, and his unorthodox style and strange gruntings were enough to throw fear into any opponent.

The crowd came to its feet for this one. And more than one contestant was glad he didn't have to meet either foe.

The Nuba scored the first fall, bending from the waist until his head nearly touched the floor, then driving up underneath the huge belly with his head and grasping for the knees. Down went the surprised Turk. Fall one. Back came the Turk with a trick of his own. With surprising agility, he suddenly dropped to his hands and scissored the Nuba's leg with his short, stubby, powerful ones, bounding back to his feet as his hands came off the dirt, leaving the olive-skinned Nuba lying on his side for a few moments in disbelief. The judge hesitated, never having seen such a move, then signaled a clean takedown.

Now wary of each other, the two circled and pawed and grunted. The crowd urged them on; the contestants watched in awe. The Nuba had an edge in conditioning, and the longer the match went, the more tired the Turk became. His forte was weight and a rounded body that was well oiled and hard to grasp. His foe was the more agile, being able to leap straight in the air for half the Turk's height, and circling constantly to make the tiring Turk pivot.

Like a cobra the Nuba struck, grasping a pudgy arm and going into a fiendish spin. Again the judge consulted briefly with his fellow judge, and announced a clean takedown. Two and one in favor of the Nuba. The Turk was beginning to heave his chest in an effort to give his lungs more air. And the Nuba flew around him in great leaps and lunges, now screaming and punctuating his lunges with staccato outbursts. Like a wounded boar, the Turk backed and parried, covered up and sidestepped. The Nuba saw an opening. It was all over.

The crier announced the winner even as one *muezzin* after the other called the faithful to prayer.

CHAPTER 29

Sobriety reigned throughout al Djem that evening, except, of course, at the villa of the Moulay. After the her/him sipped the customary, perfunctory first drop of wine, the Moulay grabbed the cup, relaxed his throat and drained the cup to the dregs in one long gulp, then held out the cup for more.

"You know," he confided to his attentive her/him, "they told me, no, they *promised* me, there would be blood. I should have known better. You can't trust a word a woman says. I sat all day long on that damn hard seat and all I saw were great big fat men running and jumping with their little things hanging down or flapping around. Disgusting. Men's bodies are so ugly. Did you see that one wrestler? He had a belly out to here. Killing him would make the world better, at least to look at."

The Moulay giggled and drank, the her/him refilling his goblet as the Moulay prattled on. "Tomorrow had better be better and bloodier or I'll call off the games and go home. That'll fix her and her mother!"

Within the camp of the contestants, more than one battered warrior wished the Moulay would do just that—end the games. Throbbing muscles begged for it. But the Amira had no pity for them. Only herself. Tonight, she underwent the second of the six rituals. Tonight was the Night of the Bath.

In the Berber tents of centuries ago when these marriage rituals were formalized, water was such a luxury that one would not dream

445

of wasting a drop to clean one's skin except to proclaim to the world a father's great wealth. When the Berbers adapted Islam, with its emphasis on cleansing, the ritual became a religious rite. No normal prospective Berber bride would face the night of the first bath with anything but delight. Certainly not with repugnance as Aisha did.

It was not the bathing that bothered her; it was its connection with marriage. As hers grew closer, Aisha grew more convinced: she did not want to marry. The bloodthirstiness planned for the rest of the games was to please and placate the Moulay, of course; but it might serve her as well—by emulating Cadmus, who sowed the dragon's teeth and reaped armed men who killed one another until but five were left. Tonight, if Aisha had her way, those five would have continued to strive until all were dead. With the games Aisha could indeed have her way. Without a prospective bridgroom there need be no bride. It was that simple.

The very thought of a man touching her made her flesh crawl. Once, Ali had kissed her. Only love of sister for brother had saved his life. Just as surprise had saved the slave. She could still remember the feel of his lips on hers! It made her feel unclean.

"You're wiping your lips again," Ramlah observed. "And with the right hand. That's a good sign. It means love will come before children."

Aisha dropped her hand from her lips as if her lips were red-hot coals, and rubbed the palms of her hands on her robe, to no avail, of course.

"Come and bathe. That will take your mind off him."

"Him? Him who?" Aisha demanded, her eyes growing dark with anger.

"The slave, of course."

"Which one? There are thousands of slaves in Tunisia."

"You know the one." Ramlah hesitated at the look on her daughter's face. "Forget I said anything. Come, the baths await us."

Head held high, Aisha stalked from the room, followed by her cheetah, refused her litter, and charged like an avenging warrior, straight toward the baths, her silent ones hurrying to keep up.

Ramlah smiled as she seated herself in her litter for the short ride to the nearby baths. Better to feel any emotion, even anger, than to be frozen inside. Ramlah, too, remembered the kiss, and thought what a couple they would make, he with the hair the color of ice, she with the ice hidden inside. Ramlah sighed. She did not envy that slave if he were chosen. Please Allah, that would be his problem and Aisha's. Pray the blond who seemed more tractable were chosen; it would solve many problems. Including hers: getting her daughter wedded and bedded within the week. But first the Night of the Bath.

For this one evening plus the one after next, Ramlah had ordered the restoration of the great Roman Bath near the amphitheater. In its day, it had been alive with water—frothing in fountains, cascading down stairs, sweeping under arched walkways. Warm water. Cold water. Hot water. Water and its stone counterpart, marble. Marble so satiny to the touch, pleasing to the eye, soothing to the soul.

Today, centuries later, there was still water, but not so much of it. Many a slab of marble was cracked, many a column lacked its capital. Still the bath proclaimed its opulent ancestry in the grace of its arches, the chasteness of its facade.

Aisha's bodyguards had been turning away visitors from the huge structure since late afternoon. The only ones admitted were the *asiras* —handmaidens of the Amira and her mother—who brought armloads of towels and baskets of soaps, oils, dyes, sponges, pumice, and gold combs and brushes of all sizes. There, too, came undergarments of the finest silk, caskets of jewels, sandals of gleaming pearls and kid leather, and as many flowing robes in as many colors as are ever seen in a Tunisian sunset. Other *asiras* carried pillows for the princess to lie against, rugs for her to walk upon, and bowls of fruit and jugs of wine to assuage her hunger and thirst during the lengthy bathing ritual. Finally, all was in readiness for Aisha. While the handmaidens waited, many played a four-handed clapping game, as their mothers had before them: "I am an *asira*. I serve the Amira. Asira, amira . . . amira, asira, in the dark which is which."

Young as they were, if they stopped to think of it, in their way Aisha's *asiras* knew they were lucky to be in her service. The work was easy compared to what many of the other slaves had to do. The Amira and her mother were not unkind mistresses, all things considered. Other than for Zainab, her favorite, Aisha showed no partiality among them, nor special feelings toward any of them. They were a taken-for-granted necessary part of her life. So long as she was not kept waiting overlong, nor made bored by their idle gossip, her voice was rarely raised, her all-encompassing power seldom exercised.

In truth, more than one of them harbored strong feelings of a different kind toward the princess. Their unnatural manless lives created unanswered stirrings in developing bodies, and Aisha became their focus. Their daily ministrations to her beautiful body fed the flickering flames of their desires. Half worship, half love, some felt; but others harbored deeper longings that at times became torture. Though they worked hard to be the best at massaging the curvaceous firm body of the young princess, or even the softer, more mature body of her mother, the very act and the restraint they had to muster as their inner passions welled merely piled frustration on frustration until their only relief was a surreptitious finger in the dark of night. That, or a hurried and unsatisfying mock-union with another of the *asira* in a hidden nook or on a straw pallet when eyes were closed in sleep on every side.

Zainab knew. She, who was the trusted favorite of the Amira, knew the longings of *asiras*. She, too, could have been a body-worshiper of Aisha, complete with the frustrations of loving an untouchable. But years before she had made her decision; and the princess had chosen, for her own reasons, to look the other way. Zainab could and would have her man. Or men, as she sometimes chose. After seeing that her charge was safely and comfortably in bed for the night, her time was her own, and the body that rejected women made good use of that free time. Often she gave thanks to Allah not only for giving her an insatiable appetite for sexual union, but also for somehow miraculously freeing her from the bother of bearing children. No matter how much and how varied the semen she milked into her contracting vagina, she remained barren. Motherhood, which would certainly have jeopardized and probably destroyed her position with the Amira, remained a thing for others who little enjoyed the preliminaries, and who deserved the fulfillment even less.

Jealousy tainted Zainab's relationships with the other *asiras*. However, so far, no other *asira* had gained the confidence of the exalted one. Zainab took pains to see that her challengers were few, and that those who dared were discredited.

Thus, as always, it was Zainab who walked just behind the Amira on the short journey to the baths this night, then waited with the princess for the arrival of the queen's litter. Trailing Ramlah were a dozen *asiras*, some of whom carried the last-minute preparations for the ritual. This one being so different from other baths, who could guess in advance every last item the queen might demand?

Through the arched entrance the party moved in unison, each step precisely in tune with the other, like some long-rehearsed procession; down a long hallway with arched openings on either side; and into a special suite of rooms deep in the heart of the ancient structure. Silent, almost unseen, the bodyguards stood rigid at attention, spaced at regular intervals down the hallway. Only one moved—to take the leash of the cat when it was handed to him.

Turning right into a gleaming tiled reception room, half of the group veered off, depositing their burdens on long marble benches while the rest proceeded to the next room. Here, Aisha stood quietly as her handmaidens stripped her of her clothes, hanging them neatly on golden hooks mounted in the wall. She moved sinuously on into the third room, heavy with steam billowing from heated rocks which were being doused with water from the pitchers of the *asiras*.

Quickly her lithe body took on beads of the moisture-laden air, combining with her own body heat and perspiration to cleanse her pores of the day's dust and her internal impurities. Torches, pressed into brackets on every wall, added to the heat, providing flickering rays of light that danced and bounced off her small, jutting breasts and hard, gently rounded buttocks. Zainab marveled, for the thousandth time, at her mistress's perfectly formed body, understanding anew how some of the other *asira* could fall so completely under the spell of this desert enchantress.

Ramlah waited in the reception room for the Iman with tonight's readings and wished that she were undergoing the seven-night ritual herself.

A few minutes in the steam-filled room was all Aisha wanted. Then she walked quickly into the first of three bathing rooms, stepped down, through the clouds of steam, into the sunken marble bath. Not once did she worry about the water being too hot. More than one elbow would have tested it and pronounced it just right for her royal body.

Sponges laved her shoulders and arms, while many hands soaped, rubbed, scrubbed her upper body. When her skin fairly smarted from the gentle abrasion, hands helped her to her feet, and as she stood knee-deep in the now-sudsy water, those same hands worked their magic on her hard belly, her well-muscled buttocks and thighs, and on down her legs until she felt the familiar sensation of gentle fingers separating her toes and brushing her nails and cuticles with small brushes.

At this, Aisha widened her stance so that the hands could gently separate her nether lips and cleanse her secret orifice, a gentle shiver running through her as the soft cloth brushed momentarily against her most sensitive part. And almost as pleasantly, two hands separated her cheeks while slim fingers worked the bar of soap high up in the crevice, as Islam demanded, lingering briefly where the muscles gathered in a tiny, sensitive circle.

Next, a tepid soaking bath laced with goat's milk. Hands gently but forcefully helped her down until only her face remained above the white liquid. And all the while, the hands rubbed her skin . . . from back to front and top to bottom. Nor was her face ignored. Fine sponges soaked up the liquid and squeezed it over her forehead and eyelids and cheeks and neck. Again and again. Until Aisha could fairly feel the diluted milk soaking into her pores and enriching them.

Without so much as toweling off, she moved into the third and final bath, shivering as the cool water shocked her overheated skin. As always, she thrilled to the tingle which the sharp change in temperature produced. The hands now patted and slapped rather than rubbed. Her whole being vibrated and responded. Then many hands lifted her to her feet, to stand and drip on a sleek leopard skin, before thick towels briskly rubbed and patted her dry.

Still damp, but eager to continue, she herself led the way to the massage table. There, surrendering all towels willingly, she laid herself facedown on the cool marble and gave herself up to the skilled, oiled, warm hands of the two masseuses. One attacked her neck, the other her feet, to erase every sign of tension. They had to double their efforts when a dry voice from without the room began again: "From Sura II, 'The Cow,' revealed at al-Madinah in the first two years of the Hejira and preceding the battle of Badr. I recite these to remind you of rights and duties of a married woman."

Resting her forehead upon the back of her crossed hands, Aisha sought to shut out the sounds of the Iman's aged voice as he recited from memory those verses chosen by himself and her mother for her edification as woman and bride-to-be. Even though she could not totally blot him out, other images fought for supremacy in her thoughts. An egg and an arrow: meshing, separating, joining. A blond giant and a slender strange-haired one, the two so alike in manner, though so different in appearance. Then again to the egg and arrow. Both important, yet so different; the one solid, the other tenuous. Without thinking, she flexed and reflexed the henna-painted hands hidden from her eyes. Discovering herself at this, she determined to concentrate on the Iman's voice:

They question thee, O Mohammed, concerning menstruation and marriage. Say: it is an illness, so let women be during their times and go not in unto them 'til the flow ceases and they are cleansed. But when they have purified themselves, then go in unto them as Allah hath bidden you. Truly Allah loveth those best who have a care for cleanness. Remember, your women are tilth given unto you for you to cultivate so go to your tilth often and plow well and good and send good deeds before you for your soul."

Aisha shuddered at the comparison; the slave women apologized effusively, thinking they had mistouched a nerve somewhere. The Iman continued blithely, serenely on:

"Those who forswear their wives must wait four months before going in unto them; then if they change their minds, lo! Allah is Forgiving, Merciful, a Knower of men and their minds. Too, if they decide upon divorce, lo! Allah is Forgiving, Clement. Women who are divorced shall keep to themselves apart three monthly courses. Nor is it lawful for them that they should conceal that which Allah hath created in their wombs. For if they bear fruit, their husbands would do better to take them back in that case if they desire reconciliation. For women have rights

451

similar to those of men over them in kindness, but men are a degree above them. So good women are obedient. Allah is Mighty, Wise. But women, too, have rights. If divorce be pronounced twice, then a woman must be retained in honor or released in kindness. It is not lawful to make them await your pleasure. Nor is it lawful for you that ye take from women aught of that which ye have given and endowed them. If ye have divorced her the third time, then she is not lawful to you until after she hath wedded another husband. Then if the other husband divorce her, it is no sin for her to rejoin her other man. Allah is Hearer, Knower. He giveth you to divorce for He knoweth men, yet three times must ye speak the words. This, too, He commands that hasty words do not unmake a marriage. For think ye that Allah giveth you first marriage, then divorce. Fear Allah, for He knoweth men better than they know Him.

Anyone knowing Aisha could predict her reaction to such words. Never had she acknowledged any man her superior. An equal, perhaps, as in the case, almost, of Ali. As the Iman had intoned the command for obedience, her head had risen as neck muscles went rigid. Angry words came to her lips to be suppressed only with great effort. Nor, as the Iman continued merrily on to divorce, did she grow much more relaxed. Only a man may divorce, never the woman—a patent unfairness as far as Aisha was concerned. Wisely, Ramlah signaled the Iman to desist. To have him continue on, as was normally done, detailing the suckling rights of children, would do this reluctant bride no benefit. Grateful for her release from listening more, Aisha allowed a robe to be thrown loosely about her magnificent shoulders, and she strolled into the dressing room where her grooming continued.

Her hands and feet were attacked simultaneously by *asiras* who specialized in this endeavor, pushing back cuticles, deftly running pointed wooden utensils along the undersides of her nails, rubbing the ends with pumice and polishing the surfaces with pieces of sheepskin sewn over pieces of wood. Now others applied colored gloss while helpful mouths gently blew it dry. Aisha did not watch, lest her good mood be soured by a glimpse of the hennaed symbols on her palms.

Her long, lustrous hair was rubbed, strand by strand, between towels that were replaced every few seconds by dry ones. Spiced oil spilled lavishly into palms was then rubbed into each strand until her head reflected the torchlights. And practiced fingers twisted her mane into dozens of tiny ropes fastened at the ends—Berber fashion— with multicolored beads. In Aisha's case, tourmalines of rare red and blue and green and brown and not a single ordinary black.

Rouge was applied to cheeks and nipples, kohl to her eyebrows and upper lids, powder over her body, a drop of perfume here and there. With the benefit of frequent practice, Zainab and the slave girls had refined to ultimate perfection the promise of healthy beauty.

Their ministrations completed, the handmaidens held the silken drawers for the Amira to step into . . . fastened about her proud-breasted form a loose-fitting sheer tunic . . . draped over that, a multicolored robe even more sheer, so that it accentuated more than concealed. Finally, over all, a gold-encrusted robe with tight-fitting midriff and flaring skirt.

Admiring the results, Ramlah nodded her approval. "No princess, Berber or Arab, was more beautiful." The kiss she gave her daughter was as much token of love as benediction. "Fear not, my daughter, no man can resist such loveliness."

"That, Mother, is hardly the problem. You have it backwards." With that, Aisha swept from the room to seek her litter for the return to her villa. There, to the mournful strumming of a zitar, she paced the floor. To spend her days watching nude men play games, her nights listening to old men singsong the *Koran*—these did not appeal in their passivity to her active mind and body. Nor did thinking about two slaves who, in all probability, would never survive the next few days. She needed something to do, to occupy her mind, her emotions.

A clap of her hands summoned a slave to bring Ali.

Love, admiration, lust—all warred within him and betrayed their presence in his eyes as he gazed upon this woman who could never be his. Tactfully, she ignored his response, pretending, as she had for years, that their relationship was as passionless on his side as it was on hers. Quickly, she got to the point. "Remember our trip together through the oases to meet the tribes? I vowed then to do it again. I have decided now is the time."

"Now? In the midst of the games?"

She was impatient; Ali had a tendency to always take her so literally. "Of course not, but immediately afterward. What better way to introduce a consort to his peoples? To help us plan it, I would have maps of the region, lists of the tribes and their elders, suggestions for gifts. There is so much to do and so little time to do it in. Especially since I would not have the Moulay know of this." For the first time in weeks, genuine enthusiasm sounded in her voice. For that he was glad. But to plan a trip through Tunis, one of such scope as she described, could not be done in the short time they had left. Ali said as much.

"How can you say nay without trying first?" Aisha demanded. "Begin the preparations. If need be, I can delay my departure a day or two or three. But I am going. I have made up my mind."

When she used that imperial tone of voice, Ali knew better than to argue. He could only hope that once she saw the unfeasibility of her desires, she would be more reasonable. However, he said none of this. "Your will be done, Princess. I shall start immediately."

"Good. Go. And sleep well." He was dismissed. But not into the arms of his concubines. Instead, as he knew she knew, the lamps would burn late into the hours of the next day as he began putting her wishes into actions. She, too, was awake late, making mental inventory of the gowns she would take, the jewels she would wear, the horses she would ride, the slaves she would need.

Only one thing would she not be able to decide for herself: which man would accompany her. As the zitar continued its sad song, she paced the floor. A man, a husband. Why must a woman marry? Was one of those wretches in the camp more fit to rule than she who had been educated to this role for all of her life? It was unfair. Not only would a husband usurp her right to rule but marriage would also rob her of the one threat she and Ramlah possessed to hold the Moulay in check—disclosure. Perhaps she might have to make her move to oust the Moulay sooner than she had planned—maybe as soon as the day after her wedding night. It would be her own grandfather who would come to collect the sheepskin. If he were to find it free of blood, and if he were to be told the truth . . . ? Aisha's eyes sparkled, and her pulse quickened as she imagined the Berbers, gathered en masse for her wedding, swooping down once again to oust a Moulay. But then the realist within her chided her: "Silly child, even if you, your *Ikwan*, and the Berbers were victorious, would the people rise up and support you, a mere woman? Or would they lie down and send for the Barbarossa?" She knew the answer as well as she knew her name.

She threw off the gown that hampered her stride. The stinging of the beaded ends of her plaited hair whipping about her shoulders seemed like caresses compared to the torture of her thoughts. Deliberately, she forced her thoughts elsewhere, to the trip. The trip . . . what better way to unite the tribes behind her than to come to them as a young bride with a champion of champions riding at her side? Barbarossa's illusion of invincibility would fade beside the reality of a man they could see, touch, and—she sucked in her breath with excitement—even challenge to compete.

It would work, she thought, snapping her fingers in delight and rousing the dozing zitar player to sudden discordant wakefulness. With surprising kindness, Aisha dismissed the girl and, with a twinge of regret, recognized that this trip would not be as devoid of political necessity as the other journey had been years ago. Unbidden, thoughts of a narrow, grass-covered gorge came back to mind, the memory of a kiss and a man's hand, warm and gentle on her breast. But that she forbade herself to ponder. She must think about gowns, jewels, horses, and slaves. Slaves. Again her treacherous mind led her astray. To thoughts of another kiss. Of blue, unbelievably blue eyes looking laughingly down into her own. Of arms holding her tight and immobile. Of some small object beneath his rough tunic bruising her breast. She had forgotten about that. What was it he wore about his neck? To wonder was to find out. Again a clap of the hands and a summoning.

Not long thereafter, de Wynter and his group in their rough quarters were rudely awakened from the deep sleep of the physically exhausted. As they scrambled to their feet, eyes blinking in the bright torch light, Ali strode up to de Wynter and held out his hand. "Give it to me."

"Give what? I have nothing."

"What you wear about your neck. I would have it."

Now fully awake, de Wynter opened his mouth to protest, then thought better of it. Ali was obviously agitated. Silently de Wynter reached into the neck of his tunic and pulled out the small carving of the Mer-Lion that hung from a thong made of threads laboriously unraveled from his tunic and plaited together. Before de Wynter could remove it from around his neck, Ali seized it and jerked, breaking the cord. With the Mer-Lion in his possession, he turned on his heel, leaving behind a group of stunned slaves.

"Now, what do you suppose that was all about?" Drummond asked of no one in particular. And received no answer back. Just when de Wynter had decided he'd begun to understand his captors, they did something so bewilderingly irrational. Why wake a man up in the middle of the night to get a charm he could have had the following morn? Ali asked the same question of his Amira as he handed her the small carving, but he too expected and received no answer. Instead, he was dismissed without a thank-you as Aisha studied the small carving she held in her hand. Never had she seen such a strange-looking animal. In a way it reminded her of its owner: proud, ferocious, different from others. When at last she fell asleep that night, the Mer-Lion was still clutched in her hand.

CHAPTER 30

The next morning, at daybreak, the *muezzin*'s call to prayer was reinforced within the slaves' cell by the play of a silent one's spear upon the bars of the door. The noise did not cease until even the deepest sleepers of the group acknowledged and decried it. The men sat up reluctantly and painfully, nothing new in their lives; so they had awakened every morning for weeks. But today, Menzies and Cameron gleefully, deliberately leaned back upon their pallets, bidding their friends a sardonic farewell.

Their triumph was short-lived. The silent ones seemed unaware that any had been excused from competition this day. A spear's point in the junction of the shoulder and neck persuaded both the agile and the quick to rise and join the rest for a trip to the slop room, then to eat a plain breakfast, as usual, except for portions that seemed unusually generous. Still gnawing at the hard-baked bread, they were on their way to the arena.

At the same time, within the tent-city of the other contenders, whip-bearers began a clean sweep through the camp, rousing those who, failing to heed the *muezzin*'s call and nursing sore muscles, had stayed in bed. As the men stumbled, limped, and hobbled out from their tents, a few noticed that at least a handful of their fellows had struck tents and disappeared with servitors. "Into the desert," said one. "Afraid," agreed the other.

As they gulped thick black coffee and a thick sweet mint tea with their meats, breads, and fruits, not a few envied those shrewd enough to run away. That was their opinion until they arrived at the arena. Atop each of six of the Corinthian mural columns, a head leered down, its tongue lolling uncontrollably. The flesh, not yet finished yielding up its fluids, had already begun to swell within the skin. Flies danced about the tongues and clung in thick clusters to the eyes. The contestants quickly averted their gaze and passed into the arena, the gate closing with frightening finality after the last one.

Within the chamber of the gladiators, that barren cold room, the men who gathered were somber. Again they were told to disrobe. Again they entered the arena shivering, welcoming the sun's heat. Again the royal box was only partially occupied: by Aisha, her mother and Ali ben Zaid. At the Amira's feet, lay al Abid, the cheetah, the Amira's almost constant companion since the royal box had been invaded by a slave within the last month. Al Abid did not, as a matter of course, make her presence known to the contestants below.

This time the Roman judge was in the forefront of the officials. "Today, of course, we honor the winners of yesterday . . . as tomorrow, those will honor today's winners and grieve for today's losers." With that, five pair-drawn chariots charged into the arena. "Let those who won enter the chariots and accept the salutes of those who lost."

The contestants watched silently as the winners—Menzies and Cameron, the Spaniard and the Nuba—entered their chariots. The fifth chariot remained empty but for its driver until a silent one entered the arena, carrying a head upon a pole. It was obviously one of the six who had welcomed the contestants from its perch on a column above the gate. The silent one seated the pole in the spear holder of the chariot.

Trumpets sounded, whips cracked, and gaily plumed horses leaned into their harnesses. These authentic recreations of Roman chariots were drawn by magnificent pairs of bays, grays, and chestnuts. Standing astride the single axles with reins wrapped about their waists were the five slave-charioteers, their long gold-embroidered capes flowing behind them while the long plumes of their pointed helmets whipped about in the breeze.

Alongside each driver clung one of yesterday's winners—or at least the four living ones—who wrenched arms and dug with clenched fingers at the sides of the chariot in an endeavor to keep balanced and upright. Their task was made no easier by the deliberate inexperience of the charioteers whose instructions had been brief but to the point: Keep your horses at a gallop or die when you dismount.

The horses, unnerved by the sounds and crowds of men, rolled their eyes and bumped one into another. Men stationed all along the perimeter of the arena on the first tier were there to jump down and cut free the horses if a chariot crashed against a wall or overturned. Ali ben Zaid and the Amira would be incensed if any horse should die.

Twice around the arena the chariots careened to the applause of the spectators, the blaring of trumpets, the neighing of horses and screams of the four frightened passengers.

"If so they treat winners," de Wynter observed to Carlby, "I fear their care of losers."

Carlby said nothing. De Wynter could have been reading his own mind.

The remaining contestants, standing in the center of the arena, silently pivoted with them, fascinated by the lurching of the chariots, hypnotized by that grisly reminder of the evanescence of triumph.

Upon command of a stentorian voice, the chariots halted, and their passengers dismounted on shaking legs. Two of the winners, the non-slaves, were ushered up into a box opposite that of the royal one, there to watch the proceedings in comparative comfort. The two slaves were ordered to join their fellows. The fifth's head was returned to his watchtower to leak and ooze upon the marble column below.

Once the chariots had departed and the winners had been taken to their places, the Roman judge continued: "Today's events would make Rome great again and return the glory of al Djem to her. Samnite will fight Samnite, Thracian Thracian, Myrmillone against Retiarius. One match of each will go on simultaneously, beginning one hour from now and continuing until a rest period midday, then resuming until the last match is concluded.

"Two of yesterday's winners will be excused from all exertion today. Another two have been assigned to assist the Ali ben Zaid and the silent ones as commanded by our mistress, the Amira Aisha. The fifth chose not to join us for reasons of cowardice. He and another five who tried to flee look down upon us from above the gate of the Gladiators. Pity not those, but fear for yourselves, for you who fight not well today will have your heads added to the ranks of onlookers above the gate." His listeners, already at the alert, stiffened further.

"I remind you of the scroll you signed, the scroll which has been sealed, the scroll which has been sent to the Holy City of Kairouan for safekeeping. In it was your promise to fight to the death, if necessary, to earn the right to become the husband of the Amira Aisha. However, in the spirit of the vestal virgins of Rome of ancient times, the Moulay Hassan himself has agreed to accept within his hands the option of sparing a fallen opponent's life. I warn you, *mujalid*, fight bravely. And if you should fail, appeal not for yourself to the Moulay. He shall condemn you. Only your opponent may successfully sue for your life . . . and he only if the fight were worthy. For woe befall the two who fight halfheartedly; the Moulay warns that a dagger shall leave each halfhearted indeed.

"I bid you retire to the chamber of the gladiators to prepare yourselves for today's contests. In the interest of fairness, the Amira Aisha has offered that insofar as possible each man shall be able to elect to fight as he will. Choose well, O gladiators. And let the blessings of Allah be on him who competes."

The contestants, aches and pains forgotten, silently turned and retraced their steps into the bowels of the arena. The two women in the royal box, in the meantime, drank deep of sweet mint tea and decided for the sake of their complexions to have the velarium—wide sun-strips—hauled across the arena above the royal box to block out the rays of a sun more ferocious than that of the day before. That such shade might endanger the combatants did not occur to them. Even if it had, it would not have overly concerned them, and Ali was not there to advise against their impulsiveness. He had gone with his mute escort to brief the occupants of the chamber of gladiators.

"The judges have decided that there be four types of combat, duplicating as nearly as possible the four most important classes of Roman combat. You thus may choose, first, to be a Samnite. He wields a two-edged sword and a square scutum or shield, each the length of his arm. For protection, he wears a wide-brimmed helmet, a leather guard for his sword arm, and metal thews on his left leg. He goes naked to the waist and wears a short skirt bound at the waist with a leather belt. His is the most protective armor, but such armor is burdensome, the sword heavy and massive. The bouts between Samnites require strength and endurance. Let the blessings of Allah be on him who competes as Samnite.

"Or, you may choose to emulate the Thracian, who carries the sica, a short, curved sword, and the buckler, a round shield which is smaller and lighter than the scutum borne by the Samnite. The Thracian wears a less massive helmet, a cloth tunic with wide leather belt studded with metal, and a leather guard for his right arm. Skill with sword and shield are asked of the Thracian, woe to him who has neither. Let the blessings of Allah be on him who competes as Thracian.

"The third class of Roman combatants is the Myrmillone or fishman, so named for the fish-shaped crest he wears on his casque, with its narrow pierced visor that protects the face but interferes with vision. Light is his sword, small is his buckler, and no armor burdens his body. Agility and coordination are demanded of the fishman, who must be able to evade and avoid his opponent, the net-thrower man. Let the blessings of Allah be upon him who competes as fishman.

"The fourth type of combatant is the net wielder, or Retiarius, of which I just spoke; he performs naked except for his broad metal-studded leather belt. He carries a net to cast and catch his opponent; a cord, attached, allows him to retrieve his net and cast it again and again. The net wielder is further armed with a trident, a long three-pronged fork with which to jab, slash and stab. Of all the combatants, he who wields the net fights from a distance, but his weapons, being foreign to most of you, will require mastering, unlike the swords of the other three. Let the blessings of Allah be upon him who competes as net wielder. Combatants, you have until the last grain drains from this glass to choose your weapons and armor. Hail *Mujalid*, I salute men soon to die!"

"Maybe not." De Wynter's words were spoken quietly, but no one within earshot, including Ali, doubted his resolve.

The slaves retired into a corner, ostensibly to consult with their weaponaire, Carlby. In actuality, all had but one thought: Gilliver.

461

None needed to be told that regardless of the type of combat, Gilliver would be about as ineffective in the arena as one of the flies now glutting itself on the head of yesterday's victor. One look at Gilliver's face, and all knew he was equally aware that to step out onto the arena meant certain death. Menzies forestalled any comments by turning to Gilliver, an arm about his shoulders, and saying, "Henry, I think Ali ben Zaid looks upon you with favor. Do you take advantage of this to beg of him that Cameron and I be allowed to stay with our friends during the combats. Speak softly and sweetly to him that he may agree to your request."

Gilliver, flattered, vowed to do his best and left the group to search out Ali ben Zaid. Once Gilliver was out of earshot, de Wynter hugged Menzies to him. "You do my mother proud."

Cameron interrupted, "No, I demand the right. Let me be the one."

Menzies, his mind made up, would not hear of it. "Use your head man. There is no way that Henry can grow long spindly legs like yours overnight."

Carlby listened to this exchange in amazement. "What on earth . . . ?"

Drummond, amused, patiently explained. "Menzies and Cameron, not content with winning the competiton in the arena, now must compete with each other."

"What for?"

"For the honor of saving Gilliver's life by taking his place."

"But why? He seemed proficient enough in the practice bouts."

Drummond laughed. "With blunted sword, he's a demon. Give him a real weapon and he'll lay it down and bare his breast for your blow. Henry, you see, takes his religion more seriously than most, maybe even you. God has commanded, 'Thou shalt not kill,' so Henry won't, not even to save his life."

"I had no idea."

"Sir priest, you see before you in the person of Henry Gilliver the makings of saint or martyr. Menzies and Cameron and the rest of us have no objections to the saint part, but, damn me, he becomes martyr over our dead bodies."

"Methinks he isn't the only one with a martyrlike bent," Carlby replied sourly. He had found in Drummond's remarks an implied comparison that was not flattering to the Hospitaler–priest.

Drummond tolerantly agreed. "Between you and me, you might well be right. But habits of a lifetime are hard to break, and for so long as I can remember, the companions have fought Gilliver's fights for him. We are to each other the brothers most of us never had. Blood couldn't make us closer."

"Even Angus and Ogilvy?"

Drummond laughed loudly. "They more than others. Of course, for all we know, Highland lassies being so loose-kneed, they might well be bairns of the same laird."

Angus and Ogilvy, who said little but heard much, favored Drummond with a glower. While Drummond and Carlby had talked, the matter of the masquerade had been settled.

"It should work," de Wynter said, "the helmets will disguise Menzies's hair and hide his face. That, plus the clothing he wears, should make detection impossible. Besides, who would suspect one of yesterday's winners as being stupid enough to risk his life for another?" De Wynter's loving smile belied his words as he gazed upon Menzies with affection.

Carlby, still annoyed by the unfortunate comparison between his and Gilliver's faith, couldn't resist commenting. "If Gilliver is as you say he is, how do you intend to persuade him to give up his place and risk another's life?"

Drummond hooted. "Sir priest, have you learned nothing of us during the time we've been together? Henry Gilliver worships not one but two gods. The first, the heavenly father above; the other, our brother de Wynter."

De Wynter was not amused, his raised eyebrow warning Drummond of as much; however, he acknowledged the justice of the remarks. "Leave Henry to me, I'll see he agrees."

Carlby abandoned that line of questioning. "All right, so Menzies can double for Gilliver, thanks to the helmet. How do you propose to have Gilliver pass as Menzies?"

At the sobering faces about him, Carlby felt remorse for what he'd done, although he consoled himself with the thought that imperfect as his motives had been for asking such a question, the reality of the problem must be addressed.

Fortuitously, a crestfallen Gilliver, bearing a pair of plume-bedecked helmets, returned to solve their problem. "Ali ben Zaid refused. He has other plans for Menzies and Cameron. When we get our weapons, you're also to draw swords from the weaponmaster. These are your helmets. You are to stand guard at the gate of death opposite the gladiators' gate. If any should try to follow as a corpse is carried out, the two of you are to prevent it.''

No one could have been more surprised than Gilliver at the jubilation with which his message was received. While de Wynter took Gilliver aside to explain the plan, the rest took their places at the end of the line of contestants, many of whom had already been armed and attired and had departed for the arena. Discovering this, Carlby, unpriestlike, cursed under his breath the love for Gilliver that had endangered the rest of them. As far as he was concerned, Gilliver might be spiritually strong, but to refuse to kill proved him weak in the head. After all, how many Crusaders, Hospitalers, and Templars had answered the call of Pope, taken up the sword, killed and been killed in the name of Christ? Were they admired by this group? No. But for a weakling—with what Carlby suspected were heretic leanings—the rest were willing to sacrifice their lives and Carlby's too, for that matter. The gray eyes, that watched as Gilliver's attitude changed from shock to anger to reluctant assent, were neither warm nor friendly. Drummond, noting the set of Carlby's face, could have sworn he read hostility on it, then decided he must be mistaken. Gentle, naive Drummond was unable to believe a priest capable of such feelings.

As the last in line, they had to take what weaponry was left: three Samnites, two Thracians, two net-wielders, one fishman. So intoxicated were the slaves by their spirit of sacrifice that each waited for another to make first choice. But Carlby, smarting from his imagined slight, was in no such self-sacrificial mood. He felt left out, but somehow responsible for these young men. Seeing a vacuum of leadership, he filled it.

"Who are our strongest?" the priest asked. "Fionn? Drummond? You, de Wynter? Then, you be the Samnites. Angus and Ogilvy, you're almost as strong—the Thracian's role should give you no trouble. John the Rob, you and I make up what we lack in strength in cleverness and trickery; let us wield net and trident. Which leaves the fishman for you, Menzies. Any objections?"

"None so long as I need not face one of you two in the arena."

464

"No one can vouchsafe that."

Menzies shrugged. "So when should Gilliver and I make the exchange?"

The end of the line had almost reached the weaponmaster; their options were decreasing by every step they took closer to the weapon racks and the entrance to the arena.

De Wynter spoke up. "A diversion, that's what we need. John, what say you that we let the rest proceed us, we bringing up the rear. Then we can try out our swords while still here in the changing room. While all eyes are on us, Gilliver and Menzies can exchange helmets. Once helmeted, no one can tell them apart."

He was right. The few mute guards bringing up the rear, as well as those within the entrance to the corridor, were quick to swivel at the sounds of steel clashing upon steel . . . almost as quick to intervene and separate the two swordsmen, then herd all the slaves down the corridor and into the arena to join the rest of the contestants. Carlby, watching Menzies stumble and feel his way down the corridor, his vision blocked by the fishman's helmet, suddenly realized what he had done. How dare he call himself priest! By all rights, he—not Menzies—should be sacrificing himself. As they entered from the darkness into the brilliance of the arena and stood blinking trying to adjust their eyes, Carlby offered to exchange places with Menzies.

"Nay, Carlby. I appreciate what you would do, but you are priest, not companion. Never would Gilliver allow a priest to take his place. Besides, if we couldn't figure out a way to make Gilliver grow eight inches overnight so Cameron might substitute for him, how would you propose we age him near a score of years to fit your battle-scarred body? Nay, thank you, but I am the man for the role. What you could do, if you would, is help me adjust this faceguard. I dare not remove the helmet to do it myself, yet I cannot dare to fight the clumsiest of netmen without being able to see."

Carlby gratefully seized upon the chance to be helpful and, foreswearing practicing with net and trident, helped bend the faceguard to fit Menzies's face. "Menzies, what you do is noble. Aren't you just the slightest afraid?"

"Noble, hell. Afraid, yes!"

Ali ben Zaid, who had been watching for the slaves' appearance, frowned when he noted that both Fionn and de Wynter were armed as Samnites. Although he saw the two slaves attempting to adjust the helmet without removing it, other matters prevented him from recognizing the incongruity of their actions and questioning them.

The slaves, like all the other contestants, had walked half to the left of the statue of Marcus Aurelius and half to the right. Thus, de Wynter, Drummond, Carlby, and Menzies had joined the single file of gladiators stretching from the left of the entrance all the way round the arena to the base of the royal box, where sat the whole of the royal family plus the Moulay's familiar; Fionn and the others had done the same on the right side.

Under the circumstances there was a possibility that Fionn and de Wynter might face each other in combat. Ali, not relying totally on the will of Allah, took steps to prevent that. At his silent command, four unwary contestants on the right were moved to the left of the entranceway, and the four slaves there moved to the right to join their fellows. Ali could do no more to influence the games; the sounding of tubas, Roman war trumpets, prevented any further manipulation.

Again the Roman judge addressed them. "Oh ye *mujalid* who are about to fight to the death, we salute you. Do you salute him who has power to save you?" The response of the gladiators, although ragged and uttered in more than a dozen languages, made up in volume and enthusiasm for the lack of rehearsal, many of the gladiators reinforcing their yells by banging with the broadsides of their swords upon their shields. No one needed to coach them on the need to please the man who held the power of life and death over them.

The Moulay was flattered and stood to renewed cheers to receive their plaudits and return their salute, his thin, high-pitched voice lost in the far reaches of the vast arena, "Mujalid, I salute you. Now, let the games begin!"

As trumpets sounded again, the Moulay sat down and commented in a voice deliberately loud enough for Aisha and Ramlah to overhear, "Well, this certainly begins better than yesterday's debacle. I just wish we could make out the competitors' faces better." Swinging around to stare at Aisha, he demanded, "Why do they fight with helmets on? How can we see their expressions when they die?''

Aisha forced herself to answer quietly, ''They fight with strange weapons, the helmets give them—''

Ramlah, seeing from the Moulay's expression that his daughter's answer was not pleasing to him, hastened to interrupt. ''But the ones who fall, the ones you consign to death, they'll have their helmets removed first, so you can see their faces. Isn't that right, daughter?''

Aisha behind her veil clenched her teeth in anger, but the Moulay, mollified by Ramlah's remarks, didn't wait for his daughter's answer. ''Well, that's better than nothing. But if I get too bored, the helmets come off! Maybe the shields, too!''

Aisha said nothing, but signed her command to Ali ben Zaid who passed it on to the rest of his troop that the fallen gladiators have their helmets removed before perishing.

Even as this byplay was going on, two of the gates that had slammed shut, once all the contestants were inside, slid open and the gladiators, without the persuasion of the whip-bearers' scourges, hastened to exit, one half through one gate, the other half through the other. Those in the audience, seeing this, began whistling and stomping feet and shouting for the games to begin. The Moulay waved his gold-embroidered handkerchief in gay concert with the crowd. Since the Moulay was as agitated as the rest, he did not notice that the crowd grew ugly when the gladiators did not reverse their course, but continued out. Aisha and Ramlah exchanged looks. Ramlah recognized in the sounds the same horrifying blood-lust she had heard nearly twenty years ago on the day the Moulay had murdered all his male relatives. And Aisha, for the first time, understood why centuries before, the Roman emperors had built al Djem to propitiate the crowds and satiate their mad hunger with more and more bloodshed.

Ramlah whispered to Aisha, ''Don't wait, do something.'' More than her words, the hint of hysteria in her voice convinced Aisha to signal Ali ben Zaid to move the schedule up. With that the tubas sounded and the silent ones gestured for yesterday's winners to leave their posts at the Gate of Death and advance to the center of the arena. There Gilliver and Cameron had their swords taken from them and replaced with wooden ones that could injure but not kill. The Roman judge announced, "O Moulay, in the tradition of your revered imperial ancestors, Julius Caesar and Hadrian and Marcus Aurelius, we offer you a foretaste of today's games. Upon your command, O mighty Caesar, beloved ruler of Ifriqiya!"

At the Moulay's squeaked, "Fight! Go ahead, fight. I, Caesar, command you, fight!" Cameron and Gilliver fell to.

They were good. Gilliver, in particular, as Drummond had mentioned, pursuing his fellow with vigor. The mock battle was a swordsman's delight. But it wasn't bloody, and soon the crowd, seconded by the Moulay, grew impatient.

"Let the blood flow," the Moulay demanded of his daughter and wife and all within earshot. And again, the schedule was abandoned, the next event moved up. Even as Gilliver and Cameron were resuming their posts, still armed with their wooden swords, another gate opened and with the sharp points of the silent ones' spears urging them forward, two women entered. Young, healthy, presumably strong and remarkably pretty, they were two of the women supposedly transported from al Djem to Sfax. When the pair arrived beneath the royal box, they fell to their knees crying and begging for mercy, but the Moulay, confirmed woman-hater that he was, had none. Nor had Aisha and Ramlah for whores.

The Moulay's eyes sparkled, the corners of his lips bubbled with spittle. "What now? What fun have you planned?"

Before they could answer, the Roman judge did so. "O mighty Caesar, in al Djem centuries ago, your forebears amused themselves gladiatorially not just with weapons, but with wood, as you have just seen . . . and with women such as these which appear before you!"

He had to shout to be heard above the sobs of the women. "With your permission, O mighty Caesar, the women of your house would set free . . ." The sobs ceased as the women, hearing the word *free*, looked up and gave the judge all their attention. ". . . the women of your house would set free the woman who wins this match; you, O mighty Caesar to be the judge. Does this win favor with you?"

The Moulay clapped his hands with pleasure, and at this, two silent ones cast Gilliver's and Cameron's short sharp swords upon the sand. The women were on their feet instantly and seized the weapons. As the two warily circled each other in the sand below the royal box, Ramlah leaned forward to speak into the totally absorbed Moulay's ear. "You see, *rafi as' sa' n,* your word is our command. No helmets. No shields. Now you will see blood, I promise you."

On the sand below, the women exercised their primary weapon, the tongue. From first one, then the other, and then from both simultaneously poured taunts and vile threats aimed at intimidating the other. The thought of instant freedom had turned friend to foe. And neither doubted she would at last escape slavery, though whether dead or alive to enjoy that freedom neither could be sure.

But swords, not words, would have to be the great decider. And soon realizing this, the pair had at it, each trying to emulate the swordplay they had witnessed often enough, but never before attempted. The crowd chuckled at the inept display, content for the moment to watch the gyrations which stretched their billowing harem pants tightly across undulating buttocks and set their scantily haltered bosoms to bobbing and weaving.

At the first drawing of blood, the spectators turned savage. Now the roar was for the kill. But it would be long minutes before the trickle turned gush. Fighting at long range, as was the way with beginning swordsmen, the arms bore the brunt of the early blows. And soon both *houris* had wounds of their sword arms, serving only to make them the more wary. The feet slowed, the thrusts became less frantic and more deliberate.

An overhead slash got through to the left shoulder of the smaller of the two, severing both halter strap and tendon. It was the first serious wound of the combat. And the perpetrator pressed her advantage with renewed courage, while the wounded one retreated and parried with her still good sword arm.

All the while, the shrewish shouts never ceased, to the delight of those within earshot. Blood ran freely down the back, and soaked the flimsy material still covering most of the wounded one's left breast. More than one spectator hoped to see the rest of the halter give way, the sight of blood dripping from her breast exciting them to new frenzy.

The next advantage went, however, to the desperate wounded combatant. She lunged, her sword point stabbing into the midsection of her larger opponent, though not penetrating enough to inflict a mortal wound. Blood flowed again, soaking her groin area and both pants legs.

A delighted Moulay clapped his hands in glee and shouted a bit too loudly, "Look, 'tis her time. She bleeds like it is her first day."

A disgusted Aisha pretended not to have heard.

Both combatants, realizing their strength was ebbing, tried for a telling stroke or blow. No more retreating. No more footwork, now it was toe-to-toe. Each was too tired to do else than stand and meet her fate, be it victory or death. Swords clashed, swords drew more blood. Tongues now uttered only occasional oaths, gasping breaths alternated with grunts and sharp outcries of pain as blade pierced skin again and again.

The once bright and billowing pants hung in shreds, blood-soaked and grimy with dust. More than once, when sword hilt met sword hilt, the bloody bodies closed in on one another, loose hands grabbing for hair or eyes, and feet trying to trip up the other.

The appreciative spectators gasped audibly as, in one of these grappling encounters, the upper covering of the larger woman was ripped away entirely, exposing her generous breasts for all to see. In a world where such sights, except in the privacy of one's bedchamber with one's own wives, were forbidden by Allah, this was indeed a most glorious moment. The most devout averted their eyes; the less devout quickly decided it was the will of the Most High that they be shown this pleasurable sight and leaned forward in their seats or stood, the better to see more.

Still holding the garment in her left hand, the smaller combatant—now the crowd's favorite—seemed to make those two bouncing globes the target of her attack. First one and then the other felt the point or the sharp edge of her blade, spilling blood.

The duel ended suddenly, before many of the spectators were ready. Their favorite, in a move that was executed as quickly as it came to mind, flung her garment into the face of her taller opponent, blinding her momentarily. Just long enough to lunge for the unprotected and already wounded belly. Straight through and out the back came the red blade. The smaller woman closed in and held her mortally wounded opponent close against her own body, all the while thrusting and sawing with the buried blade. Only when her opponent stopped jerking and writhing, did she release her grip on sword and body and allow the dead woman to slump to the sand. Looking down on what she'd wrought, she sank to her knees and threw her body across and her arms around her victim. A mournful cry penetrated the ears and hearts of all but the most jaded witnesses. The Greeks would have called it a three-act tragedy. A friend-to-foe-to-friend trilogy that freed two of Allah's servants from slavery. One to make her own way down a new and strange path. The other, by dint of dying in battle with sword in hand, already breathing the sweet perfume of paradise.

If Gilliver and Cameron had been properly armed, the Lady Islean's teaching would have forced them to intervene, to stop the farce before it began. Helpless as they were, neither had the stomach to watch, instead pretending not to hear, resolutely looking elsewhere—at, for example, slaves drawing circles of salt upon the sand. Both eventually turned their attention to the royal box where the Moulay was animatedly enjoying and mock-emulating every clumsy hack and high-pitched shriek. At one point, only the quick actions of the young hermaphrodite kept him from leaning too far over the wall of the box and falling to the sands beneath.

In the end, slaves pulled the victor from the victim, while one of their number, a burly slave carrying a hammer, ritualistically assured and reassured the fact of death with a sharp blow to the dead woman's forehead, splitting the skull open, spilling more blood upon the sands. Other slaves ran forward to drag the body across the arena and out the Gate of Death. Cameron and Gilliver carefully averted their eyes and watched instead as other slaves, bearing baskets, strew fresh sand over the bloodstains.

Again trumpets sounded, and now the two gates slid open and the combatants advanced into the arena: the Samnites proceeded to the circle closest to the Gate of Death; the Thracians went to the other end, near the Gate of the Gladiators; the fishman and net-wielder paired off in the center ring before the royal box.

When the first pair showed reluctance to engage, the whip-bearers brandished scourges and persuaded them. Then, suddenly, the arena rang with the honest clash of sword on sword and the crunch of shield on shield. Silently, the net flew through the air again and again. The crowd surged to its feet with delight shouting *"Affirin"* or

"*Ma'dan*," the sixteenth-century Arabic versions of the ancient Roman cry of "*Habet!*" When, within minutes, the first man went down, the mass of spectators gave voice to such a roar that the gladiators down below the arena surface heard it.

To the Moulay's delight, two of the first three matches did not result in instant death. With the fallen ones' helmets removed, as Aisha had commanded, he could watch the piteous faces turn pasty white and contort with anguish as each watched a downturned thumb signal his death.

Only when the last match of the three was complete and a leather-lunged crier announced the results did slaves drag the dead gladiators out through the Gate of Death: "The winners!—from Venice, the Samnite Corosco . . . from Egypt, the Thracian, ben Duailan. From Greece, the Fishman, Koropolus. May the peace of Allah descend on those who lost."

As slaves passed among the audience with refreshments, others scattered fresh sand within and salt around each circle. Thus was the pattern set for the day. First the fights, then the dead dragged out, then audience and arena refreshed.

Gilliver and Cameron had lost count of the matches when the next fighters entered the arena. Both immediately recognized the man in the high-crested helmet with the sharply angled brim who carried both scutum and long sword—John Drummond—they would have known him anywhere. A flick of his head as he entered the circle nearest the Gate of Death showed that he, too, was aware of their presence. Drummond was not a small man nor slight of stature, but the Sicilian he faced was so large he made him seem so.

Each was too good a swordsman to wade into battle without testing out his opponent's reflexes, moves, and defenses. Long the two circled and sparred, until suddenly the Sicilian pressed the attack. After a furious exchange, he fell back, and again they circled. Drummond, professional swordsman that he was, realized he had drawn too tough an opponent, a man who outreached him by a good six inches. His only chance was to husband his strength, hoping to find an unexpected opening or land a lucky blow. Again and again, the Sicilian sprang to the attack, only to be forced to fall back. Long after the matches in the other circles had come to a bloody end, Drummond still held his own. But Gilliver and Cameron, watching critically, soon began to detect signs of tiredness. Drummond held his shield ever closer and closer to him, blocking rather than parrying thrusts; his sword moved in smaller and smaller arcs, making not so loud a clatter on his opponent's shield. Yet, though he bled copiously from both arms and a gash in his side, he still matched thrust for thrust, swing for swing, despite sword and shield growing heavier by the minute.

Ali, pleased by one of his protégés' showing and personally fond of Drummond as all who knew him were, signed to Aisha silently begging for the slave's life if he fell. She had already come to such a decision. Such dogged determination struck sympathetic sparks among the warriors looking on, but not from the Moulay who found the match interminably boring and urged the Sicilian on to the attack. Drummond just barely beat back each new sortie. Clearly his opponent had made the long sword, or its like, his specialty, so deft and practiced was he in its use.

Gilliver and Cameron, watching, found themselves yelling at Drummond to go down, to concede defeat, to save his life. No way did he show he heard. Barely holding up his shield and his sword hanging limply at the end of his arm, Drummond still stayed on his feet and circled wearily, dragging his feet in retreat about the circle and keeping the Sicilian always before him.

Tears blinded Gilliver's eyes as the bloodthirsty giant moved in for the kill, dropping his own shield and two-handedly launching such a whirlwind of arcing blows that none but an expert or a man big as himself could have turned them back. One sweeping blow sent Drummond's battered shield flying, the next—on his helmet— sent him to his knees, the third partially separated Drummond's head from his neck, blood spewing over victor as well as victim. The young Scotsman slumped forward to the ground; his head connected to his body by but a thin strip of flesh, and rolled over to stare unseeingly at the brilliant blue sky so hard and different from the soft blues of his native Scotland.

The victorious Sicilian, with a maniacal cry, placed his foot heavily on the chest, forcing a gush of blood to spout from the dead man's throat. His upraised sword acknowledged the plaudits of a crowd that fickle-mindedly forgot its admiration for the fallen foe and now paid the victor his due. Cameron refused to look upon his fallen friend; Gilliver, retching, couldn't, as two slaves dragged Drummond feet-first through the Gate of Death, his head bouncing along behind.

Fionn, entering with the next group, didn't need to be told that Drummond had fallen. One look at Cameron still supporting a Gilliver racked with dry heaves, told him the whole story. Anger surged through the young giant, transforming him into a merciless avenger.

He never really saw the young Cypriot athlete who faced him within the circle. Forgetting caution, technique, everything but revenge, Fionn sprang with a cry of agony at the nearest object. Using his sword like an ax, he literally folded the scutum around his opponent's left arm, leaving the torso bared for the thrust that found a vital organ. As the breath gurgled hideously within the young Cypriot's throat, the anger cleared from Fionn's brain. With a cry he dropped shield and sword as if red-hot and fell to his knees to beg tearful forgiveness of the man he'd just killed, the first ever.

Gentle, lovable Fionn had intended if given the chance to knock the weapon from his man and ask the Moulay to decide his fate. Too late, he remembered his plan. And there, beside his lifeless opponent's body, he buried his face in his hands and cried—for himself, for Drummond, for the young Cypriot whose name he didn't know.

In the center circle, John the Rob circled warily as he twitched his neatly folded net and crouched behind the tri-points of a trident longer than he was tall. His partner in combat was a battle-scarred dark-skinned veteran of many a war, who had nothing but contempt for the funny-looking three-pronged spear and the flimsy net. John the Rob had cast the net but once, and that so awkwardly, that the fishman easily warded it off on his buckler and made John the Rob scramble for his life, dragging the net behind him. Only the swift intervention of a silent one backed up by the whip-bearers kept a suddenly terrified John the Rob from leaving the salt-enclosed ring. Forced to turn back and face the fishman who stood arms akimbo roaring with laughter, he grew deadly calm. Laughter he knew . . . all his life his monkey-face had inspired mirth at his expense. Laughter for him was like a cold shower, dampening emotion, restoring determination, leaving his mind keener and sharper.

Crouching slightly, John the Rob reeled in the net and shook it, preparing for another cast. The whip of the net stopped the Moor's laughter; he fended it off not so quickly as before. More deftly did John the Rob gather up his net this time, shaking it out for another try. Not ten times had he thrown the net, but already his dextrous juggler's hands were learning to control it. Now, he knew confidence. No muscle-bound lout would defeat the man who had escaped King Hal's warders, not to mention the Mayor of London's guards, a good hundred times over. He had been caught the only time he was off guard—while in bed with a wench. No wenches were here today to slow him down or keep his mind off his work. All he needed was an opening that would give him a bit of an edge.

The Moor was in no hurry, preferring to wait until the net was cast, then he planned to pounce on the monkey-faced one as he busily reeled it in; or better yet, yank and cut the net from his hand.

Another quick toss of the net. A hurried sidestep. The deadly net slithered off the Moor's shoulder to fall harmlessly to the ground and be pulled back instantly by the wiry little cut-purse.

John the Rob swiftly gathered in the net, shaking it open with one quick jerk. He was realist enough to know that in a fair fight he had no chance against his bigger and stronger opponent; his only chance was to trick the man. Circling, he teased and tested his opponent, flicking the net first left, then right, then right again. While the Secutor watched, almost hypnotized by the movements of the net, John the Rob studied the fishman's movements. Finally, when he thought he detected a pattern to the man's habits, he feinted with a juggler's speed to the left and instead flung the net where a heavy foot should land. And snared himself a fishman.

Yanking with all the muscles in his right arm, he threw the fishman off balance. The buckler swerved to one side and the three-pronged fork rammed home, skewering navel, groin, and right thigh. The impact knocked the man off his feet and onto his back, John the Rob following and planting one foot upon the man's sword, the other on the base of the prongs, ready to drive it deeper into the man's guts if he showed any sign of battle. But the Moor had no stomach for more this day. Throwing aside his shield and releasing the hilt of his sword, he sued for peace. "I concede you the better man, friend. Only spare me to fight another day."

John the Rob had the feeling this same life-saving favor had been asked many times before; the man was too facile. Not trusting the Moor an inch and without moving his feet from atop sword and base of the still-buried trident, he looked over his shoulder toward the Moulay, who stood and surveyed the crowd. A sea of downturned thumbs confronted him, emphasized by cries of "Kill him" in a dozen different tongues.

The Moulay raised his thumb slowly into the air, only to reverse it and throw it downward as he screamed *"Iugula!"* the deathcry of the Roman Emperors. John the Rob, seeing it, did not wait for the slave with the hammer—"Sorry, *friend*, the man says no"—and jammed the trident home. As the man screamed and arched his back in agony, John the Rob reached down, picked up the man's own sword and said, "Next time, *friend*, don't be so quick to laugh." With that he deftly traced a bloody smile from ear to ear across the man's throat.

With fully half the matches complete, Aisha and Ramlah suggested a break for food, but the Moulay wouldn't hear of it. "Have food brought here. The games continue."

"We may run out of contestants at this rate," Ramlah cautioned.

"Then, get more. Use slaves or those half-men your daughter surrounds herself with. I don't care whom you use or where you get them, but the games will go on until I say stop!"

Mother and daughter exchanged glances. If anything, the Roman games were proving too successful. Steps must be taken to ensure that fresh combatants not be thrown into the arena, especially not Aisha's bodyguard, for its ranks could be cut in half by the Moulay's apparent refusal to spare a single victim's life.

Both women swung into action. Ramlah sent for food, giving instructions that every dish be heavily seasoned with *hrisa*, that hot red pepper-cumin sauce that made the eyes tear and the mouth cry out for water. But Ramlah would have the Moulay's thirst quenched not with water, not even wine, but with *boukha*, that potent native brandy distilled by Jews from figs. Let the Moulay empty a few goblets of this and he would never know when the games ended.

As for Aisha, her agile fingers sent silent instructions to Ali ben Zaid to stall for time and why. It was Ali ben Zaid's idea to hold back the one gladiator–slave whose life he wished to save. Thus, one after another of the companions bade farewell to de Wynter and stepped forth to face his fate in the arena.

The first was Carlby, who made John the Rob look clumsy with the net. Carlby's opponent was overweight and overmatched. Within minutes Carlby realized that he could kill his man at any moment. But he chose to play with him instead and make of the fishman a buffoon whose trident-inspired antics might amuse enough to save his life.

Thus, when Carlby cast his net and yelled, "Jump!" the frightened fishman leaped as if galvanized. When Carlby yelled, "Duck!" he dove and sprawled on the ground. When Carlby said "Back up," the man retreated so fast he tripped over his own sword and went sprawling. When Carlby said, "Move," the man crawled on his heels. When Carlby said, "Get up," the man buck-jumped to his feet. When Carlby said, "Down," the man tumbled to the ground.

And with every ludicrous move the lumpish fishman made, the crowd roared with laughter. They were genuinely sorry when the Englishman, running out of comic commands, drove his trident through the netting that encompassed the fishman's head, shoulders, arms, and waist, catching the man's head between two of the forks of the weapon and driving him to the ground. Carlby had but to continue pushing the prongs into the ground to strangle the man . . . or pull it free and drive it through his heart.

As the two men froze in a tableau of death, the Moulay looked about him and saw only upraised thumbs; the crowd had laughed itself into a benevolent mood. Still the Moulay would have rejected mercy, but the her/him put a soft hand upon the Moulay's arm and said, "O master, save him for me that he may amuse us further, I beg this—" His voice of its own accord suddenly descended an octave and the her/him dared not speak more lest it play him games again. But the Moulay, already partially besotted with brandy, did not notice. For this lovely creature beside him, he was prepared to do most anything.

As Carlby and Pietro di Zecca watched anxiously, the Moulay played with his lower lip a bit in contemplation, then finally, slowly, the right hand, made into a tight fist, was outstretched. All eyes stared raptly at that fist. And then it opened, the thumb thrusting up. The man was saved. The first that day.

To the crowd's delight, once freed of the trident but still draped in the net, the fat man crawled after Carlby and attempted to kiss his feet. And then the chase was on, as the fat man pursued his savior, the savior tripping over the fishman's forgotten shield and landing on his behind. No one but Carlby heard Pietro's promise: "If ever there is aught I can do for you, you have but to ask. I, Pietro di Zecca swear it, or may my mother sleep uneasy in her grave."

Ogilvy was the next of the slaves to enter the arena, saluting his fellows at the Gate of Death at the other end of the arena from the ring of the Thracians. His was a typical thrust, parry, engage, disengage, slash, smite, hack, close. It was rhythmic, it was deadly, it was nothing extraordinary, simply a repetition of workmanlike swordsmanship. The same swordsmanship that had been seen over and over throughout the day.

Eventually, Ogilvy's hard conditioning wore down his opponent, and the match ended, as others had before, with Ogilvy finding an opening and taking advantage of it to skewer his opponent below his wide leather belt. A half-turn of the curved sword and his opponent was disemboweled. While Ogilvy watched, no expression crossing his dark saturnine face, the hammer-bearing slave removed the mortally wounded man's helmet and gave the blow of death.

The next occupant of the Thracian circle was Angus. Those within the crowd who had gulped deeply of the *lagmi* poured so freely by slaves began to wonder if perhaps they had had enough, so much did Angus look in build and swordsmanship like the Thracian who had just competed.

Indeed, this match ran much the same course as the previous one, with Angus also wearing out his opponent and finding an opening in his guard. A swift slash of his curved sword and, with a piercing shriek, the man's left arm went flying. As he dropped his now-useless shield and grasped at the stub of his shoulder in a vain attempt to stop the bleeding, the crowd turned thumbs down in imitation of their Moulay, whose eyes were really seeing double. But Angus did not wait for the hammer-bearer, instead matter-of-factly stopping the man's shrieks by driving his sword to the hilt through the man's gaping mouth. He would have continued on over to see his friends at the other end of the arena, but the scourges of the whip-bearers dissuaded him from that course. He had no choice but to turn and leave by the Victor's Gate as had the others before him.

Two groups later, it was Menzies–Gilliver's turn to enter the arena. His double recognized him immediately and only Cameron's restraining hand kept Gilliver from leaving his station at the Gate of Death and confessing the deception. But before he could, Menzies had moved quickly into the fighting area to face an opponent a head shorter than he. And despite the fellow's persistence, Menzies's quickness stood him in good stead as he effectively kept out of the net wielder's range. A disquieting thought crossed his mind. Any injury or visible wound on himself could make the transition back from Gilliver to Menzies all the more difficult.

The next time the net hit his sword arm, he deliberately entangled it by swirling his arm, then gave a mighty pull and relieved the man of one of his two weapons. Throwing the net out of the ring, he concentrated on blocking the trident with his buckler and countering with sword thrusts.

The net-man, bleeding from half a dozen superficial cuts by now, desperately jabbed and lunged at Menzies with the trident. But still the net-man refused to take the one gamble that Menzies feared—the trident used as javelin when his shield might be out of position.

Another furious rush. Menzies sidestepped and ran his buckler up the shaft of the trident as he charged forward, thrusting his short sword into his opponent's naked chest and holding him up by the uptilted blade until he was sure he was done for, then letting him slide down it onto the dirt to writhe in agony until stilled by a hammerblow.

It was past midafternoon when the last of the combatants entered the arena and saluted the Moulay, who sprawled in his chair, eyes closed, breathing raucously through slackened, drunken mouth. With but three circles for four pairs, one of the two pairs of Samnites had to fight in a narrow corridor, directly below the royal box, which was bounded by the solid wall of the arena on one side and an invisible wall created by the combatants' circles on the other. Shadows infringed upon it, those created by the high arches on the upper tiers of the colosseum . . . and one enormous one caused by the protective awning stretched across the royal box. The longer the contest went on, the greater the advantage the man had who stood with his back to a descending sun. By the luck of the draw, de

Wynter and his opponent were given the corridor in which to fight. Slaves with metal-tipped bars stationed themselves between them and the other gladiators to prevent their straying into one of the circles and interfering with the combatants there.

Under other circumstances, the Thracians in the ring to the left of center would have drawn all eyes to it, for here was being created a sadistic cat-and-mouse game as Eulj Ali with a lucky thrust had early on disarmed his opponent and kicked his weapon outside the circle to lie tantalizingly just beyond the swordsman's reach. Now, Eulj Ali amused himself and prolonged the fight by incising bloody patterns on the man's hide, the small round shield offering little protection from the lightning swift cuts and slashes of the redhead's curved sword, a sword not unlike the scimitar with which he had fought all of his life.

The two in the center ring by some mistake both turned out to be net-wielders and their combat turned into a wrestling match as each became entangled in the other's net.

The Samnites in the ring to the right were both big, hulking, slow men who traded hammering each other's shield with loud but ineffective blows of their swords. Bang. Bang. Bang. The noise and the blows echoed slowly, monotonously through the arena. "I dare say," Ramlah remarked, "if we left now and came back tomorrow, they'd still be banging away and not have moved an inch from the spot or come one blow closer to ending the match."

Aisha perfunctorily agreed, ignoring all else but the two men below her. One she knew was the silver-haired one. The other, smaller than the slave and more wiry, also looked suspiciously familiar, especially his thick mat of red chest hair.

He was a stranger to de Wynter, who sized him up as perhaps five years older, slightly heavier, possibly not quite as quick or agile, but probably a more experienced combatant in this type of match.

At the signal, they circled and tested each other with ringing blows that bounced harmlessly off each other's scutums. De Wynter tried a roundhouse swing to see how his opponent would counter. Easily. Then a short, low thrust. Blocked. A series of feints and thrusts delivered one right after the other and parried systematically. A worthy opponent, de Wynter decided, one who knew his defense, the lack of which was often the undoing of many a good swordsman.

Very well, let's see what he's got in the way of offense, de Wynter thought, beginning a slow backpedaling designed to bring his opponent aggressively to him. Not bad, he said to himself, as he countered a thrust with his shield and tried unsuccessfully to knock the invading weapon high with an upward swing of his own sword. Then in rapid succession he was forced to ward off a series of good moves that might have broken through the guard of a less experienced swordsman. This was going to be a long battle, he decided. A typical battle. The first mistake would decide the winner.

Five minutes into the fight, the crowd and the occupants of the royal box—all but the snoring Moulay—knew a classic duel was underway below them. The footwork, the good use of the scutum as well as the sword, the attacking on both dexter and sinister—all these testified to many years of expert teaching and practice in the art.

With a furious rush, the red-haired one tried driving de Wynter out of the corridor and into a circle. But at the last moment, de Wynter nimbly sidestepped and almost drove his opponent out with his own countercharge. Urged back to their own strip of sand by the scourges, they feinted and thrust and parried, filling the arena with the ringing of sword on shield.

Aisha had followed every move of the two with the knowing eyes of a warrior queen and leaned ever more forward to see even better until she found herself on the edge of her seat, her bejeweled hands clenched in her lap, her dark eyes flashing above her veil. Ramlah watched her daughter and wondered how she could be so fascinated by the play of sword on sword. And why? The fighters below did nothing, so far as she could see, different from the scores who had fought before them. Could it be, she wondered, the swordsmen themselves who made the difference?

Though Ramlah admired her daughter's inventiveness and daring in setting up the games, secretly she found them repulsive—an unfit way to pick a husband. But if that were what Aisha wanted, Ramlah could only hope the man could awaken the passions she felt sure must be there inside that beautiful body.

The Samnites down below were not aware of their royal audience, nor of the "mouse" that "cat" Eulj Ali had already killed, nor the fall of one of the Thracians, nor of the two silent, net-covered forms entwined in each other's arms and nets and bleeding to death from hammer blows in the center ring.

Not a quarter was given by either man. De Wynter paused occasionally to catch his breath; his opponent a little more often it seemed, though perhaps that was but a trick. Feeling strong, de Wynter pressed the battle. For the first time he thanked the oarmasters and slave-drivers who had pushed his body beyond its natural limits of conditioning. They just might be his saviors. A ringing blow on his helmet reminded de Wynter to concentrate on the battle. Soon, he drew first blood with a nick on the other's sword arm. Not enough to cause him any trouble, de Wynter decided, but a bleeding arm might eventually weaken him, or the blood befoul his grip. The immediate effect was to spur his opponent on to an even more furious effort to penetrate the Scot's defense.

Good, de Wynter thought; let him tire himself out a little more. A daring plan was formulating in his mind, but the time wasn't yet right. The older and more experienced man had to be a bit more tired than he was now, or it would never work. As the classic yet creative battle went on and on, the spectators cheered wildly, the object of these matrimonial games watched with rapt attention the longest match of the day.

For another half hour the battle raged, the two men trying to maneuver each other into facing the sun. Back and forth in furious charges, and sometimes standing toe to toe, pummeling each other with great blows that made the fine Spanish steel ring and crash and clang.

The crowd was becoming restless, growing impatient for the kill, and screaming for the blood they felt they deserved. Still the officials showed no sign of calling a halt to the confrontation.

The Scottish earl made his decision. Sun and shadow must make the difference. He knew he was tiring, which was dangerous. He knew, too, that his adversary was even more tired, not moving his feet as much, preferring to stand and do battle where his extra weight could stand him in good stead. He watched for the right moment, and seeing it, flung his scutum from his left arm, grasped the broad sword in both hands, and in great criss-crossing swings battered the red-haired one's sword and shield so fiercely on the left that he must turn more and more, in spite of himself, to the right.

De Wynter did not dare let up his fusillade until he had his opponent positioned just right. If he let the other bring his own sword into play, the Scot was lost without his shield. How long he could maintain this attack he didn't know, but two more steps to the right, then one back, and it was all over for one of them.

The sword was what he had to get. He watched its every move as he continued to pummel the man's shield, driving him back out of the shadow cast by the great awning and into the bright westerly sun. Momentarily blinded, his opponent raised his sword hand to shield his eyes. In that instant, de Wynter swung his sword with all his might, hoping to catch the other's near the hilt and knock it from his grasp. But the redhead's grip was too secure; instead, the blade snapped in two. De Wynter's gamble had paid off.

With terror in his eyes, the unarmed man flung aside the useless handle and grasped with both hands the shield now dented and battered from the heavy, two-handed blows of de Wynter which drove him in whatever direction the Scot chose.

"Throw down your shield. I won't kill you!" de Wynter yelled.

But the redhead understood neither the words nor the intent. The crowd screamed for the kill they felt was imminent. But still de Wynter stalled. Watching for an opening, he thrust his sword between the backtracking legs and tripped the redhead onto his backside. In a flash the Scotsman was on top of him, kicking aside the scutum and placing the point of his sword at the base of his throat.

"Ma'dan!" "Affirin!" "Al rabb mujalid!"

Slowly, the cheers of the crowd penetrated the pounding in de Wynter's ears as he gasped for breath. Without moving his sword, he turned to face a crowd on its feet, stomping and clapping rhythmic applause. Even the two women and the her/him in the royal box joined in. De Wynter found himself staring into the bright sparkling eyes of Aisha. In spite of himself, he wondered if the lips beneath that veil ever softened and parted with passion. Then, he caught himself up short. He was not interested in this woman, he reminded himself. Tearing his gaze from her, he looked instead at the Moulay, aroused unwillingly from his stupor by the noise about him. Shaking his head in confusion, he called for more wine and without looking at the scene below in the arena, he gestured imperiously with downturned thumb, then covered his ears with both hands to stop the noise.

His actions were not popular. The crowd renewed their cheers, thrusting their thumbs violently into the air and yelling, *"Mitte! Mitte!"* Still holding his ears, the Moulay looked wildly about and screamed for silence, but the crowd could not hear him over their own noise. Anything to stop the noise, he thought, and wrapping his left arm about his head in a vain attempt to cover both ears, he quickly put his right hand out to save the man's life. Before he could give the signal, he felt a hand on his upheld arm. It was his daughter, desperate that the redheaded son of Barbarossa die.

"Are you ruler or subject?" she demanded deliberately. "Is your will the law or do you let that rabble bend you to theirs?"

He only stared at her, mouth drooping in surprise.

"You made your decision. Let it stand. Lest those within the stands think you weak. Unkingly. And decide to replace you with one stronger."

He dropped his hand, the noise forgotten. "Replace me? I'll have all their heads first!" Drawing himself to his full pouter-pigeon dignity, he repeated his thumbs-down gesture.

At Aisha's command, Ali's shrill whistle sounded over the din . . . once twice, and again. Immediately, the silent ones turned, spears at the ready, to face their commander, in so doing of course, facing the crowd. The crowd got the message. And though scattered throughout the crowd came cries of disapproval, most kept their mutterings to themselves.

De Wynter couldn't believe what he had seen. Even after the Amira intervened, still the Moulay persisted. What kind of monster was he to condemn this man who had fought so valiantly? Withdrawing his sword, de Wynter strode halfway to the royal box. There, raising his arms in appeal, he silently asked for the life of his fallen opponent.

The crowd roared its approval, but both Moulay and Asmira rejected his appeal. The former with both thumbs vigorously stabbing the air. The latter with what de Wynter took as a dejected shake of her head.

Turning on his heel, de Wynter defiantly walked back to the fallen warrior, scooping up that man's shield as he went by. "Here, let me give you a hand up," he said to the older man, who, although he didn't understand the words, rightly interpreted the outstretched hand.

Handing the man his shield, de Wynter gestured for the man to get behind him. "If they wish to kill you, they'll have to kill me first!" Back to back the two men stood, challenging the silent ones and whip-bearers to do something.

Gilliver and Cameron started forward to join them, but the lances of four silent ones stopped them in their tracks.

The Moulay jumped up and down, screaming with anger. First, the crowd defied him, now a lowly gladiator. "I'll have their heads, all of their heads! Before I'm through those two will beg for death!"

Aisha ignored him as did Ramlah. The two women exchanged looks, Ramlah marveling at the slave's bravery in refusing the Moulay's orders, Aisha marveling at his foolhardiness. Only Ali acted decisively to break the impasse. Shortly thereafter, silent ones entered the arena bearing armfuls of the nets of the *retiarii* and surrounded the pair. Although the nets were inexpertly thrown, one sword could not cut in every direction, nor could two men who spoke not the same language coordinate their movements to stay together while dodging nets. Within minutes, the silent ones had trapped themselves two gladiators.

The Moulay would have seen them both killed, but Aisha intervened. "A king can and should be merciless. Cruel. Dispassionate. But a king if he would have his subjects' respect as well as fear goes not back on his word. You promised the winners would live. Keep your pledge." Her voice crackled with authority and the Moulay couldn't meet her scornful glance.

Mustering what little dignity he had left, he turned, gesturing for the her/him to accompany him, and stormed out of the royal box. Ali, down below, patiently waited the royal pleasure. Aisha hesitated a moment, then raised her hand, index finger pointing up, thumb down: one man must die. De Wynter, within his envelope of confining cording, could not see the byplay in the royal box nor who it was who condemned his fellow to death. But he heard the results: a long, shrill scream of sheer agony cut short in mid-crescendo, only to be replaced by the fearsome deep-throated gurgle of a dying man drowning in his own blood.

De Wynter froze momentarily, then renewed his mighty but futile struggle with the net. But he was caught fast and left that way to shout himself hoarse threatening, taunting, pleading, cursing. Finally, he fell silent and after what seemed hours, he was hoisted high on the shoulders of two silent ones and carried back to his cell, there to be dumped none too gently on the floor at the feet of his companions.

Immediately, many eager hands set to the job of disentangling the giant knot of webbing that held the captive as if in a cocoon. While they picked at, tugged, bit, twisted, disentwined and unraveled the cording, he badgered them with questions. Questions about themselves and their fights. Questions that no one rushed to answer. Growing suspicious, he twisted his head about and searched among the anxious faces surrounding him for that of the one he could count on to tell him true. Where was he? The others knew for whom he searched, and none could sustain his gaze. Finally de Wynter locked glances with the sympathetic gray eyes of Carlby. It was the younger man's eyes that gave way, his fears confirmed. Then, the nets came free and warm hands helped de Wynter to his feet. Still no words were said. Not then, not during the night when muffled cries disturbed the stillness, not ever.

CHAPTER 31

Involuntarily, her fingers curled as the *asira* lightly stroked the henna brush across her palm. Tonight, thanks to that hand, Aisha was content with the world. For the first time since Ali had alerted her to Eulj Ali's presence in the games, she could think of the outcome of the competition with anticipation, not trepidation. Squirming deeper into the soft cushions upon her couch, she permitted herself a small smile of satisfaction as she admired her free hand with its deceptively slender fingers that could control the unruliest of stallions . . . the buffed nails filed short to give her freedom with bow and lance and throwing dagger . . . the thumb that with one gesture proved itself greater than the rest, by ending a man's life and a princess's fears.

Stretching elegantly, Aisha smiled fondly at Ramlah, who lounged on a couch opposite, busily soothing herself by puffing from her waterpipe, the one decadent custom of her Arab in-laws that she had adopted wholeheartedly. Looking upon this woman who had selflessly sacrificed so much for her country, her people, her daughter, Aisha vowed to do as much for her. If that meant sitting through what seemed to Aisha to be a semisavage pre-wedding-night ritual, then so be it.

The bath ritual last night had been enjoyable. But then, it was merely an elaborate version of her own usual bathing habits. But this senseless dyeing of hands and feet, barbaric! But not by word or glance or gesture did Aisha reveal her personal opinions to her mother.

Ramlah, who had been awaiting a repetition of the outburst of two nights before, noted her daughter's smile with relief. Finally, Aisha had reconciled herself to her marriage. At least, Ramlah hoped that was so. Deep down inside there was the nagging fear that her daughter's content might have been caused by the selfsame thing that always calmed the Moulay: the sight of gore. Resolutely, Ramlah put that thought from her mind as the euphoria of the smoke from Zainab's special blend of tobacco spread throughout her system. As it did so, her smile grew wider, her eyelids dropped, her eyes glazed. For almost twenty years, the waterpipe had never failed to give her solace. She came awake with a jerk. She must not forget the *hafiz* sitting behind the latticework screen. A word to the white eunuch serving the coffee, who passed it on to the black eunuch guarding the screen, who respectfully requested the *hafiz* to begin the night's readings from the *Koran*.

Ramlah, once she'd assured herself that he was reading the right passages, leaned back and gave herself over totally to the smoke of the *nargileh*. Aisha, engrossed in her own thoughts, watched disinterestedly as the *ama* finished repainting the egg and gathered up dye-pots and brushes preparatory to moving to the other side of the couch to begin on the other hand. But first Zainab must inspect her work and then summon a young cherubic castrato to dry the dye on the Amira's hand with an ostrich-plume fan.

All seemed apparent domestic docile bliss until Aisha suddenly sat up, tearing her hand from the *asira's* grasp. "Holy man," she called to the figure hidden from sight. "The blessings of Allah be upon you."

"And on you, my daughter. Why stop you me in my reading?"

"Holy man, I thought I misheard. Read me those last words again so I may be properly instructed."

"From where should I begin, my daughter . . . at the beginning?"

"Nay, holy man, from where you said, 'Men are in charge of women.'"

There was a rustling of vellum as the *hafiz* turned over the pages he'd just read and looked for the proper verse. Then, his dry inflectionless voice began anew:

"Men are in charge of women, because Allah hath made the one of them to excel the other, and because they spend of their property for the support of women."

"Is this the verse of which you spoke, daughter?"

Ramlah and Zainab held their breaths, waiting for the explosion from Aisha. But it didn't come. Instead Aisha laughed. Exuberantly, genuinely, almost girlishly. From what she had seen in the camp of the contestants, she had no fears in this respect; those men had no property to use to support a woman much less the only daughter of a king. Just let one of those penniless adventurers attempt to be in charge of the Amira Aisha; he'd live only long enough to regret it.

Ramlah knew not what amused her daughter but prayed the good humor lasted through the rest of the readings which she was sure would not be to her daughter's liking:

"So good women are obedient, guarding in secret that which Allah hath guarded. As for those from whom ye fear rebellion, admonish them and banish them to beds apart, and scourge them. Then, if they obey you, seek not a way against them. Lo! Allah is ever High, Exalted, Great."

Ramlah waited with bated breath for the explosion, but though Aisha no longer looked merry, her expression was more thoughtful than angered.

Ramlah was right; Aisha didn't like what she heard. It was time to face facts: to elevate a man to rank of consort was dangerous; the *Koran* gave a husband too much power. Under the laws of Islam, her consort could indeed banish her from her own bed. As for lawfully scourging her? Never! She it was who would wield any whip. The *hafiz* continued his readings and she made up her mind.

"And if ye fear a breach between the man and wife, appoint an arbiter from his folk and an arbiter from her folk. If they desire amendment, Allah will make of them one mind. Lo! Allah is ever knowing, Aware!"

Aisha smiled; then Allah must know her plan. Ali was right. A slave was the answer. A slave had no power, no rights, no family from which to find an arbiter. With a slave as a husband, she'd be free. With the decision made, she was surprised to experience a great feeling of relief, tinged even by a degree of anticipation. Looking upon the eventual victor as a husband had been wrong, she decided. Think of him, instead, as a jewel to grace her tent: to complement her own good looks, to inspire envy among others, to add to her prestige. And to impress her people. That he was a slave would be no detriment in a world where slaves had been elevated to stand next to Suleiman's throne and exercise power second only to the Sultan's. As to which one, there was only one practical, realistic, unemotional, logical choice.

Aisha, once she had made up her mind, was quick to put her decisions into action. Even as the *ama* finished painting the arrow on her hand and moved to the foot of the couch to rework the *ukda* on her feet, Aisha summoned Zainab to her side. "Send for Ali ben Zaid. Tell him I was wrong and would speak to him tonight. Tell him, further, I have made up my mind."

Zainab would have questioned her mistress, but Aisha hushed her; the *hafiz* was still reciting. Zainab bit her lip and left. Whatever Aisha had to say to Ali could be worth handfuls of gold to the Moulay. And as Zainab knew far too well, it had been some time since she had been able to please her master with substantial information about his daughter's actions. He, in turn, had refused to send her fresh men for playmates. Zainab decided one way or another the conversation between Amira and Amir *l'al-assa* must be overheard.

While Zaniab delivered the message, first to Ali then the Moulay, Ramlah smoked and the *hafiz* singsang from the *Koran*. Aisha was again lost in thought. Again she relived the day's events. Most of the encounters blurred together into one long scene of bloodshed. But one thing, besides the death of that last one, stood out: many of the men she had thought would win had fallen to defeat. Maybe the games had been a mistake. How could this chaotic, complex charade possibly result in the elimination of all but one single suitable marriage partner? Even with Ali's help, how could she be sure that that particular prospect would get through another four days of competition? She could only hope that having drastically and dramatically winnowed down the field by way of the sword, she could exert influence on the outcome. There was, of course, always that unpredictable factor to consider: the Moulay. And though tomorrow's competition would be less personally and individually risky, there would be losers. Fully a third of them and their fates would be decided by the Moulay and limited only by his imagination. Aisha had no doubts that that imagination would be equal to the effort.

Her musings carried Aisha well into the half hour it took for the *hafiz* to read *"An-Nisa"* in its entirety, not just that portion dealing largely with women's rights as revealed at al-Madinah in the fourth year of the Hejira. None of it seemed particularly relevant to a marriage such as the princess envisioned. And certainly no verse or passage roused Aisha's ire as had the reference to men's superiority over women. Sometime, when there was time, she would have to take her mother to task for having chosen that reading for this night. Aisha smiled as she thought of the spirited argument that that would prompt. Poor, sweet Ramlah . . . so obviously superior to her own husband yet forced by society and religion to espouse a tradition which her very life contradicted. Lovingly, Aisha would have blown her mother a kiss, but the sight of the dark red symbols on her palms stopped her action in mid-thought. Aisha loved beauty. The very thought of having such ugliness upon her person made her clench her fingers until her painted nails dug deeply into the discolored palms. The pain refreshed her and drove thoughts she considered unforgivingly feminine from her mind. Let Ramlah think what she would, but Aisha was not prepared to shed her blood willingly in any bed, especially childbed. And no one could make her change her mind.

Zainab's hesitant cough broke into her thoughts. "Ali ben Zaid awaits your pleasure outside, Amira."

"Good. Stay you here and keep Ramlah company. I shall return." Aisha sat up and took Zainab's cloak from her arm.

The handmaiden surrendered it reluctantly. "Would you not have me join you? To be alone with a man during a night of ritual, it is sacrilege."

Aisha only laughed. "Ali ben Zaid is no man. He is my uncle." Throwing the cloak about her shoulders, Aisha strode from the room leaving an unhappy but determined woman behind her. As Aisha left the inner tent, Zainab followed right behind to listen through the hangings, but to no avail, for Aisha took her uncle by the arm. "Come, Uncle, let us walk and talk." Of only one thing could

Zainab be sure: their talk couldn't be important, it would be too short, for the clear starlit beauty of a desert night is equaled by its bone-chilling cold and discourages long walks.

Ali was content to be led anywhere by Aisha. When he was with her, he saw nothing else. Though their kinship might negate his gender for her, it had no such effect upon Ali. To him, there was but one woman in the world. And tonight she looked more beautiful than she had in months. A smile softened her haughty lips and warmed her tawny eyes.

"Why?" he wondered aloud.

"Why what, Uncle?" she asked almost mischievously, holding his arm even closer.

He could feel, he thought, the swelling of her breast through his robe. He knew he should draw away, but he didn't. Instead, when she repeated her question, he could think of no response. "Why what, indeed? I don't remember if once I knew. Unless, yes, of course: Why summon me?"

"Uncle, you were right!"

"Really? Right about what?"

"About choosing a slave as consort."

He was bewildered. "I thought that was settled some time ago."

"Ah, but not which one."

The fragrance of her bath perfume surrounded her like the moonlight and filled his nostrils with a scent all her own, one none of his concubines had ever been able to duplicate although he'd had them try. Somehow, tonight, in the moonlight with her holding him close, the last thing he wanted to discuss was who should share her bed, especially when he wanted so badly to be that man himself. He tried to change the subject. "And what brought this on?"

"The death of the redhead!" she answered triumphantly.

Totally confused, he stopped in mid-stride. "How so?"

"I am free of that barbarian's get. Now, I have naught to fear from—"

"Princess, wait. You rejoice prematurely. The man you condemned today—"

"Eulj Ali, you mean."

"No, I don't mean Eulj Ali. Eulj Ali is alive and far too well to suit my taste."

Aisha pulled her arm away. "You're wrong. Eulj Ali was a redhead, the only redhead among the contestants. The man who died had thick *red* chest hair, I saw that for myself. That's why I put my thumb down."

"My dear, Aisha," Ali said, shaking his head sadly, "many a dark-haired man has red body hair. I grant you the two looked much alike, but the man who died was Latin . . . not barbarian."

Aisha's lips tightened. Her eyes grew dark with anger. Her face settled back into its carefully controlled mask. Ali ben Zaid knew his princess too well to imagine she was feeling remorse for the death of the wrong man. He was right. Already, all thoughts were on plotting the death of this one.

Thus, when Ali gently prompted her—"You've chosen one of the slaves?"—her reply was short, almost disinterested: "Yes, the big one."

Ali was surprised. Fionn was a handsome man, but to the Berber's way of thinking not in the same class as de Wynter. Then again, the two were much alike: brave, honest, proud with a certain similarity in bearing. They were even built much alike, although one was on a far larger scale. Ali decided, in a close fight, he would not mind having either defend his back.

However, Aisha had still another man on her mind. "Eulj Ali. He must not win. Ali, you must promise me. I care not who else wins or loses, but this man must die. How you do it is not my concern, but do it. Pledge me Eulj Ali's life."

To Aisha's surprise Ali did not immediately agree. "Are you sure you want him *dead*, or just removed from contention for your hand?"

"Dead!" But she didn't sound positive.

"Wouldn't it be better for your country to have Barbarossa's son as a hostage, rather than a corpse? No, don't answer hastily. Think a moment. Now, I grant you the man is not the Beglerbey's heir, but he is Marimah's favorite."

"What difference does that make? Marimah is but one of the four wives."

"But she is the Beglerbey's favorite. That makes a difference. Let me put it to you this way: If you were in Eulj Ali's position and Ramlah in Marimah's, don't you agree that your mother would make her husband's life hell on earth until you were back?"

"Yes, I see your point. But how do we save him and still save me from him?"

Ali did not answer immediately; instead, feeling the chill and noting how far they'd gone into the desert, he suggested they retrace their steps.

"Well, you haven't answered me. Or"—and her voice reeked with sarcasm—"are you one of those who can pose problems but not solve them?"

Stung more by her tone of voice than her words, he responded curtly. "I have the answer, but I want something in return."

"You would bargain with me?" She was too shocked to hide her surprise. Always before she had need but express a desire to Ali, and it was hers.

"I would. Is it not worth something to you to be free of Eulj Ali . . . and to have the giant's life assured?"

She studied her uncle intently for a moment, considering his words. "And what would you have as reward?"

"The *jamad ja'da* to do with as I please."

"To what end is that?" She didn't really need to ask. Ali had made no secret of his attraction to the slave. Without thinking, a mental picture of the two men, one fair, the other dark, flashed through her mind. The two laughing and riding and hawking and—unbidden, other thoughts came to mind: the two sharing one of Ali's concubines, or, worse yet, entwined in each other's arms. A pang of jealousy went through her.

Ali had hesitated but a moment. "That is no concern of yours. Is it a bargain?"

She was undecided. That strange feeling of jealousy, was it for Ali or the other? She couldn't tell. Besides, she detected a degree of uneasiness in Ali, which might be used to her advantage. "What you would do with him would matter not a whit to me. But suppose the giant does suffer a mishap?"

"Then the bargain is off, of course." He was uncomfortable. She

494

could see it in the way he shifted his weight back and forth and chewed his lower lip.

"Suppose I change my mind about the giant and want the other?"

It was his turn to consider her. Rarely did Aisha change her mind, he knew. It was a matter of pride with her. It was a safe wager that she wouldn't in this case: "Agreed. But you won't."

He was so sure of himself, she almost—out of sheer perversity—challenged him there and then. Instead, she merely smiled. "A bargain it is then, Uncle. So what is your answer?"

"Why content yourself with one winner? Instead, have several. A handful even. Then, you are not at the mercy of the fates and may do with each as you please, except the *jamad ja'da.*"

"It has appeal. But I wonder what the Moulay's reaction will be when he finds out that more than one will escape his clutches."

"Don't tell him. Not until the end. Then give him the whole of the tent-city to play with. Even the spectators, if you wish. Just withhold this small group. He'll never miss them."

She nodded her head. It might work. "If necessary, I could offer the Moulay something he has wanted for years. Then again, I might threaten just the opposite. Who knows? In any event, leave the Moulay to me."

When she smiled, Ali could see that she was her father's get.

Zainab, just within the entrance to Ramlah's tent, overheard the last remark and wondered what the Moulay might make of it. And what he might pay for it.

When Aisha, having bid the Amir *l'al-assa* good-night, swept into the tent, Zainab was nowhere about. Ramlah was. She had indulged too frequently and deeply of the solace of her waterpipe. Her daughter's fond kiss on her forehead did not wake her, nor did the black eunuchs' carrying her to bed, nor even the white eunuchs' disrobing of her.

When Aisha left the tent, Zainab appeared and would have followed after her, but Aisha directed her and the *asira,* with their towels and bowls and pillows, to go on without her to her tent.

"But the henna? Don't you want me to scrub it?" Zainab protested.

495

"I think it just ingrains it deeper. No, you and the maids seek out your own beds, I will walk awhile."

The two groups, Zainab and the *asiras* on one hand, the Amira and her silent escort on the other, went their separate ways. Aisha headed toward a secluded tent in an inconspicuous site where scribes toiled, mapmakers charted, and spies waited with their reports on the strange doings of the tribes of Tunisia. Reading one, on the supernatural beliefs of the Dyaks, who settled disputes by the diving ordeal, it occurred to Aisha that not only did she not know if the blond giant could swim, she didn't even know his name; nor that of the *jamad ja'da* either. He, she decided, would know how to swim; he had the sleek body of one used to water.

Chapter 32

The third day of the great competition was blessed by Allah with more of the burning sun that had marked the previous day. Outside the huge amphitheater, the tent-city sprang to life with the sun's first blood-red rays. There were animals to be fed, baths to be poured, aches to be massaged, pummeled, rubbed, and subdued, so that the contestants might continue. The less than 90 of the original 180 contestants who remained roused themselves with difficulty, wondering what the day held for them. After yesterday's combat, almost anything else would be tame, an anticlimax, most thought. But little did they know what the clever mind of the Amira Aisha had arranged for the survivors.

Within the walls of al Djem, last-minute preparations were under way as whips urged slaves to work more diligently at spreading and raking fresh sand over the bloody debris of yesterday.

Within the bowels of the arena, a dejected group of nine went mechanically about their early morning routine. They were still stunned by the death of Drummond. Only reminding themselves of their success in substituting Cameron for Gilliver served to keep them from being totally despondent—that plus a desire for freedom that verged on monomania.

This was not the first time Carlby had seen men defeated by their own emotions. It had happened at Rhodes when, despite their prayers, the Knights Hospitaler appeared destined to defeat by the heathen led by Suleiman the Magnificent. They began questioning their God and fought not with the strength of ten but that of less than one. They made their defeat inevitable. Carlby wasn't willing to see that happen again, here. He would have to fill the void of leadership de Wynter's grief had created. No one would resent it, no one would question it; his rank insured that. He prayed God to inspire him with the right words to motivate these men.

"I think I know how all of you feel," he said, addressing the men, sitting, lying, standing passively about the cell. "To know John Drummond was to love him. But he would not forgive you if you were to allow sorrow to get in the way of the survival of the rest of the group. If he were here, you know he would say, 'Forget me. I am dead. Your grief cannot help me. Help yourself. Think of yourself. Do not make my death meaningless!'" Carlby paused to check the reactions of his listeners. Some seemed encouraged, others guilty, still others resolute. Only de Wynter remained impassive, lost in his own thoughts. "Yes," Carlby continued, "it is right to mourn him. But not now. Later. When all of this is over. Then we will mourn him . . . hold a requiem for him, a proper one, I promise you. But for now, you honor him and his memory most by living. And you dishonor his memory if you value your own lives so cheaply that you will not fight to keep them. He didn't. He fought to the end. John Drummond was proud of you. Proud to be a companion. Mourn him as he would want it—by living. And may one of you return to tell his family that he died bravely. Amen."

What Carlby didn't say, but John the Rob also realized, was that unless Carlby could incite his listeners to continue to fight to survive, that delayed funeral service would be for more than one.

Gilliver, the one the companions looked to for religious guidance, said, "John would have wanted it that way. Anything John wants now, God will surely grant him. For his is a martyrdom."

De Wynter, sitting on his pallet, head buried in his hands, was the cynosure of all eyes. Finally, he sighed and looked up, his face composed, his cheeks dry, his eyes unnaturally bright. "All right, then. It's decided. We go on. For John's sake. Best prepare yourself for another rugged day. I hate to think what atrocity we face, but what they devise, we can circumvent. For John!"

"For John!" Nine strong masculine voices pledged themselves as one.

498

Not until they joined the now much depleted group of competitors, did they realize how much carnage had been wrought the day before. Again it was Ibn al-Hudaij who addressed them. "Welcome again to the games. Today, I am privileged to announce that as reward for your courage of yesterday, the contest rules will be changed." There was a murmur within the crowd and contestants. Only the nine looked properly skeptical; they had seen too many "rewards" of the Amira. "Instead of this being a contest to the death for all but one man, the Amira has agreed that many may win free with their lives at the end of the game, and one of these shall receive the ultimate reward, the princess as bride."

The decision was greeted with a great roar of approval from the contestants. Not so among the spectators; however, they had faced the silent ones' spears the day before and, as one, chose not to challenge their ruler's decision again. The fact that the Moulay had not yet arrived did encourage them to grumble a bit. They quieted as Ibn al-Hudaij continued. "Today's games will test your ability to use one of Ifriquiya's finest resources, our great ship of the desert, the camel. And now, let the rules of this competition be announced. The blessings of Allah be on him who competes."

The white-turbaned speaker gave way for Hamad Attis, from Gafsa in southern Tunisia, wearing the traditional red felt tarboosh with its dark blue tassel hanging down in front of his ear. "The man who would win the Amira Aisha must prove his skill with the animal that has played such an important role in the history of this country. This revered animal gives its master sustenance, transports him, his family, his goods. It clothes us against the burning sun and the chilling night winds, and it shelters us in the midst of howling sandstorms.

"Let him who would call Tunisia his home and have the hand of the Amira prove he is master of the humped one. Therefore, today's events will test your skills in three important ways. By luck of the draw, you will be divided into three groups. The first group will milk she-camels—thus can man provide food for his family if he properly cares for his camel herd. Thirty of you will compete in this event. The thirty she-camels available to the contestants include some who have recently calved and have just begun to let down the milk. Others have been suckling their young for weeks or months and are heavy with milk. A few are weaning and almost upon their dry cycle. Again by luck of the draw, each contestant in turn will make his choice from the herd of she-camels, and he will proceed to milk the animal into a goatskin container.

"I caution you on three points only. First, any man who fails to obtain half a container of milk will lose. Second, the milking must be completed before the ram's horn sounds. Third, spilled milk does not count."

The Tunisian judge smiled a bit wryly, then continued. "The second group will be tested in your ability to load merchandise on camels, strapping it on so that a long journey would not dislodge it, nor cause undue discomfort to the animal. Each contestant will be given exactly the same pack and fastenings. And again, each contestant in turn will select his camel and load it, working against the sandglass. I should warn you, most of these camels are green, only a few are used to bearing burdens. Once your beast is loaded, it will make one circuit of the arena at a fast pace. Woe betide him whose pack comes loose, or whose bindings cause injury or discomfort to the camel.

"The third group will select camels to ride, and will compete in heats of three, racing the length of the arena. The ten winners will then race in a final event, the winner to be excused from tomorrow's competition."

The Gate of Death opened, to admit a large group of slaves struggling to drag in three huge copper caldrons. Under the watchful eyes of the whip-bearers, the caldrons were pushed, shoved, and rocked into place below the royal box, where the Moulay Hassan had finally deigned to arrive.

When the caldrons had been placed to the judge's satisfaction, Hamad Attia gave one final bit of advice to the assembled group. "The camel, I warn you, is not a cooperative animal. It thinks for itself. When properly handled and respected, it is an obedient and faithful servant. When it detects either lack of respect or skill, it can be a vengeful beast. Beware, then, of flying hooves and strong-toothed jaws. Let the blessings of Allah be on him who competes. The games begin within the hour. But first, you draw for your contest from the caldron on the right. If it is a disc with one circle, you load; two circles for milkers; three circles, and you race."

As the other contestants milled about with dismayed expressions, Carlby blurted out, "Thank God for Ali and his cantankerous camel."

The words struck the others as incongruous considering Carlby's shower of green cud. They couldn't help themselves, they laughed. Although he hadn't planned it, Carlby was secretly pleased. Laughter can purge one as much as tears, and with lifted spirits, confidence returned.

As the whip-bearers jostled the crowd into a rough line, the slaves drew together. "Let's assume," de Wynter said, "that among us, we will be entered in all three events. What is to prevent us from trading discs and choosing the event best suited to each? The odds are that with ten—" He stopped short, his face remained impassive, but others in the group winced. First ten, now nine. How many tomorrow?

The line moved comparatively quickly as man after man drew his lot and went off to join his group. De Wynter continued, his voice dry and emotionless. "With nine of us, odds are that at least two will be in any event. We must decide now while we have the chance which two shall be which."

Carlby spoke up. "Pray that most of us race in the contest for which we have experience. As far as milking a camel is concerned, I don't even know how many teats the damn beast has."

The others grinned and Fionn chimed in, "At least two."

"Ah, there speaks a man with experience," Carlby said approvingly.

"A little," Fionn admitted. "Mostly with goats."

"I've milked me a woman or two," Cameron boasted, the others scoffing and jeering at him.

Even de Wynter grinned. "Sorry, George, I don't think it's the same. Fionn, we need your help. What do you remember about milking those goats? Can you give us some tips?"

Fionn shrugged his shoulders. "Milking's easy when you know how."

"That much we know. But we don't know *how.*"

"Well, the first thing is that you don't just step up and start yanking on those tits," Fionn explained. "Womanlike, the animal has to be stimulated by some gentle rubbing or squeezing. Watch a young kid starting to nurse. It instinctively gives its mother a few butts in the udder with its head. That's its way of signaling the mother to send down some milk. I would guess a camel is the same way. Use your hands to rub whatever udder is there for a bit, and then go to work on the teats. You should feel them fill up with milk.''

"But how do you pick out one that will give enough milk?" Carlby asked.

"Look for a big udder. But not one that is also hard and lumpy and hot. Not just warm, hot! That means she's diseased. If she feels like a goatskin filled with water, with more than a bit of give to it, that's a good sign. Also, the teats should be enlarged. If she's been nursing, they'll be smooth as a baby's butt, not wrinkled and dry feeling. Personally, I look for big teats. Of a size to get my four fingers around. I hate those you have to milk sissylike, between thumb and forefinger. With woman or goat, I like me a real handful.''

"Not me. I measure by me mouth, not me hand," protested Cameron.

"Whatever makes you happy," Fionn agreed as the others chuckled.

"Can't we get on with the milking?" Gilliver asked. Talk about women always left him embarrassed. The others winked at each other. They knew Gilliver's reticence of old and had been known deliberately to be coarse in order to tease him.

Fionn, however, took pity on the young man. "With a goat, I grab as much of that teat as I can, then simultaneously squeeze and pull downward. Two-handed, you simply alternate strokes, not unlike pulling a rope downward, hand over hand. As for how hard to squeeze and how hard to pull . . . do it too easy and no milk will you get. Too hard and a hoof will let you know.''

"You make it sound too easy," de Wynter said. "I tried milking a goat when in Naples. Not a drop did I get. Nor did anyone else. We ended up butchering the beast. Take it from me, milking's not easy. Of course, I'll bet the packing isn't either.''

More than half of the line had passed before the caldron, reached in, and drawn a disc. Time for discussion was running out.

"What about packing a camel?" asked de Wynter. "Anyone know aught of that?''

502

No one responded, each looking at the other, hoping there would be a positive response.

"I've supervised many a camel train in my time," Carlby said, "but never actually loaded one. If I remember right it always took two men to do it."

"One of us is equal to two others any day," de Wynter said flatly. "Besides, everyone else is at the same disadvantage. Come on now, someone must have paid attention to the loading of the camels on our trip from Tunis to al Djem. Think, men! Dredge your memories and remember!"

After a few moments of silence, Menzies spoke, his eyes tightly closed, his head bent forward, his hands clasped tightly together. "They don't pile things up on top. That I can see. They sling things on either side, well balanced. Then there is a kind of strap that goes around the things slung on either side and passes down under the belly—a little more to the front I think than the rear—right where the belly starts to slope downward toward the front legs. I can't tell how they fasten the strap. It may have some kind of buckle or it may just be tied. Sorry, that's all I can see." And he opened his eyes and stood blinking in the sunlight.

De Wynter clapped him on the shoulder approvingly as the line moved forward several paces again. "That's our Kenneth! The man with an artist's memory!"

Carlby and John the Rob exchanged empathetic glances. Frequently, the unabashed love and friendship the companions showed one another made the other two feel like outsiders. This Carlby resolutely ignored, instead picking up the thread of the conversation at this point. "So much for packing. As for racing, dare we assume Ali's specimen was indicative of what we may face at least in the way of tack?"

De Wynter shrugged. "Might as well; we've had no experience with any other." The others' silence bespoke their agreement.

Carlby continued. "We know Ali's was fast. Suppose we look for its like?"

"Aye," said Angus. "A good lean one."

Ogilvy added, "With a good long length of leg."

"Small hooves," was Gilliver's contribution.

"A refined head," de Wynter noted.

"Big!" exclaimed Fionn.

"For you, yes, you monster. But for us, not quite so," de Wynter replied.

"Disposition would certainly be a factor so far as I am concerned," Carlby said, to be greeted with hoots, jeers, and de Wynter's, "I hear you can tell a fast one by how far he can spit." He gave up. "It was only a suggestion. A friendly beast could be an advantage."

Three more men, and then it was their turn to draw. Sticking together, they managed to exchange discs, most ending up where they wanted to be: Angus and Ogilvy chose to milk, hoping their experience with sheep would be of help. John the Rob relied on his quick hands to fill his bucket also. Cameron and Menzies seemed the logical choices for the only two racing discs. The rest were left to pack the great ships of the desert.

Prodded by whip butt and sting of the thong, the nine, the last in the line, separated and joined their respective groups. As they did, the seats in the lower tier were filling up with silent ones and spectators. Just then cymbals clashed, gongs reverberated, and trumpets brayed; a gate opened and a herd of camels charged wild-eyed into the arena as a stentorian voice announced, "Enter, the she-camels!" Just as quickly many of the beasts wheeled about and attempted to return whence they came. Angus shouted over the sounds of squeals, "Ogilvy, look at the dugs! Damnation! The beasts have just been nursing."

Normally, a female camel won't bite unless provoked. A mother separated from her calf is another story. And more than one man that day gave a sudden scream as eight large, sharp, jagged teeth crunched an arm or shoulder, shattering the bone. One unfortunate was bitten in the rear, the camel gouging a huge chunk out of his buttocks. Fortunately, Angus, Ogilvy, and John the Rob were survivors all . . . and spied a fellow contestant who seemed not at all fazed by the contest. They watched him closely as he approached his beast, speaking quietly and firmly the while. When she had calmed down, he stroked her udder, still talking to her, his words blending together in a monotonous but apparently comforting tuneless song. As she let down her milk, he stood on one leg with his right foot resting on his left knee, the goatskin wedged within the triangle formed.

Soon a rhythmic squishing signaled the success of his enterprise.

Angus and Ogilvy were not about to try that balancing act, but were not above crooning a highland tune if that should make the one-humped lassie cooperative. And it did. John the Rob, mouthing a catch last heard in a London ale-house, would have been equally successful except that at the last moment, his goatskin tipped, spilling some of the precious milk into the sand. Ever resourceful, he simply gathered in a fold of the skin, hiding the excess within his capable hand, thus decreasing the bag's capacity and raising the level of the milk. Since the measuring was done by the judge's eye instead of by weight or liquid measurement, the little beggar got away with his inspired deception.

When the last teat had been squeezed, udder stroked, and dug pulled, the she-camels were driven out of the arena, leaving a full third of the group who were either unable to milk at all or could not eke enough out of their camels. When presented to the Moulay for his judgment, he said only, "Take them away," and waved toward the Gate of Death.

The second group was now herded in through a second gate in the wall. Again, that stentorian voice left no doubt as to which animals these were. "Enter, the beasts of burden."

This group was no better-natured than the first. Some thrashed themselves with their long, sinewy, tufted tail. Others ground and gnashed their eight jutting teeth. Still another group blew large pink air sacs from their mouths, sucking them back in with a slurping sound. One or two here and there even tried to mount his fellows only to be met by a cruel slash of an ugly head at the end of a snakelike neck. One did not have to be an expert on camels to recognize these were all bulls . . . and every one was in rut.

Fionn was first to make his attempt, and his approach was crude but effective. With one hamlike fist, he sledgehammered his choice between the eyes. As the stunned beast wobbled, he hit it again, sending it to its knees. Other than getting the strap under its belly, it was a simple matter to load the beast; in fact, the judges found it far more difficult to get the animal back on its feet. Even then it merely staggered around the arena, never once going faster than a very slow stumble.

Fionn accepted with a wide grin the shouts of "Well done!" from the audience, even the veiled woman in the royal box deigning to clap for his efforts. But then, though as a victor he might leave the arena, he refused to. His purpose became apparent later, after Carlby and de Wynter had quickly, efficiently, almost expertly hobbled their beasts and loaded them. Gilliver was the last of their group to compete. As he walked forward to face his mount, Fionn stood not far behind. Before whip-bearer or silent one could intervene, Fionn charged forward and dealt Gilliver's beast a mighty blow just as he had his own. This time it took a second and third and a fourth blow to fell the beast, but finally it too sank to the ground. Then as Fionn sat on the camel's head, Gilliver piled bundles on top and to one side. Released, the camel lurched to the off-loaded side, yet the bundles did not fall off, although they did slide down below his belly. The crowd was in an uproar. Half applauded the audacity of the blond giant; the rest demanded his punishment. Quickly the judges consulted, their decision being tempered by a word from Ali ben Zaid, "The Amira favors the blond one."

After much shaking of heads and pulling of beards, the white-turbaned one spoke. "Nothing in the rules states a man must load his beast unassisted. The decision is favorable, the man successful."

The decision was not popular with the crowd . . . at first. But as they watched the dazed camel lurch about the arena tripping and stumbling over his belly-load, a titter or two was heard, followed by deep masculine laughs and then guffaws. Finally, even the silent ones could be heard uttering that piteous mew that passed for laughter among them.

Their good humor restored, the crowd settled back for the races. These were, if anything, even more comical. Riders fell off, camels knocked one another over, some even fell over their own two-toed feet when trying to make a tight turn. In one heat, the winner was he who managed to stay mounted throughout the whole of the race . . . the only one to do so. That he was a redhead may have contributed to Aisha and Ramlah's departure from the arena early.

The Moulay, who had plans for the thirty-two contestants who had clearly lost this day, grew impatient to see the day end and so told his wazier. Thus it was that all nine of the slaves, nursing their share of bruises and bites and scrapes, were ushered back to their cells earlier than on the preceding days, later to be let out and taken to the showers; and for the first time in a week or more, the silent ones did not hurry them through their ablutions. Instead, the water continued to pour as the men soaped, scrubbed, and rubbed the soreness from their bodies. Who it was that started the song, no one knew. But suddenly it seemed to leap full-grown from seven Scottish throats:

> Lo! What it is to love
> Learn ye that wish to prove.
> By me, I say, that no way may
> The grind of grief remove
> But still decay, both night and say:
> Lo! what it is to love.
>
> Love is a fervent fire,
> Kindled without desire
> Short pleasure, long displeasure,
> Repentance is the hire; payment
> And pure treasure without measure
> Love is a fervent fire.
>
> To love and to be wise,
> To rage with good advice,
> Now thus, now that, so goes the game
> Uncertain is the dice.
> There is no man, I say, that can
> Both love and, too, be wise.
>
> Free always from the snare;
> Learn from me to beware:
> It is all pain and double share
> Of endless woe and care;
> For to refrain that danger plain
> Flee always from the snare.
>
> Lo! What it is to love!
> Lo! What it is to love!

The snapping of towels against bare bottoms by the intrepid few who, waterlogged, had splashed and soaked their fill, brought the song to a close before it was fully launched on a second singing.

As the last of the slaves left the room, fresh shaved, hair cropped, clean clothed, Ali ben Zaid did not accompany them. Instead, he paused at the side of a silent one who had been standing off to one side during the whole of the water-works.

"Satisfied?"

The head barely moved forward.

"Still the blond one?"

For a long moment, the head was motionless, then it nodded firmly. As Ali had known, when the Amira made up her mind, she did not easily change it.

CHAPTER 33

After leaving the slaves' crude bathing quarters, Aisha and Ali made their way out of the arena and toward the sybarite baths where Ramlah awaited her daughter for that night's ritual. Aisha, before leaving Ali at the entrance, gave her commands for the morrow. Then added, "About the slaves . . ."

"Yes?"

"Shave their bodies."

"*Their bodies?*"

"Yes."

"All?"

"All."

"Tonight?"

"No. It can wait. They wear loincloths the rest of the games. But I do not wish to see all that body hair again. It is offensive to me." Without waiting for Ali's "As you command," she swept into the baths. As swiftly as the baths permitted, she moved through the hot baths and into the tepid one that closes the pores and finally into the restroom where Ramlah whiled away her time with the *nargileh* and where Zainab was ready with the sweet melon slices, the dish of sherbet, the cup of mint tea. Aisha's body fairly shone from its scrubbings and oiling as she rested in the chair carved out of white marble, traced with gold and green veins. Compared to her glowing, alive skin, the marble looked pale and dull.

The room was silent except for the sounds of water cascading in

509

fountains and the occasional gurgle of the waterpipe as Ramlah puffed away. Then, the silence was broken by the voice of the *hafiz*. Aisha's lips tightened in annoyance, and she struck out pettishly at the nearest object. "Clumsy girl, you pull my hair," she said, slapping the young slave sharply. "Get out of my sight before I give you to the silent ones for their amusement. The rest of you. What do you gape at? Get back about your tasks. Zainab, you will finish my hair!"

Zainab's own lips tightened. To work Aisha's hair into hundreds of braids took hours and exhausted hands, eyes, and back. But in the Amira's mood, Zainab knew better than to protest.

As she took the place of the slave, the *hafiz*, who had stopped reading when he'd heard Aisha's voice, cleared his throat and began anew. "Oh, you woman who would enter into marriage. Know you that like him who prays, you must be in a state of ritual purity from *hadath;* that you, your clothes, the bedding of your marriage couch, all must be free of uncleanness. So say the *Ajwiba.*"

Aisha, of course, knew well her Islamic catechism, having first heard and studied portions of it as a young student in the Prince's School in Tunis. But tonight for the first time, she was to hear those teachings reserved for the bride-to-be. Determinedly, she ignored what she heard, instead rehearsing in her mind the route she planned to take four days hence; south to Sfax, home of the sponge-divers, and the opposite direction from that gorge near Redeyef and its sweet memories of what might have been. Thence to Gabes and the ancient chariot road leading into the Saharan nomad country, especially Matmata, those Berber tribes who had given up their perpetually wandering ways and settled underground. From there, she meant to travel to Medenine, region of the granaries of the *ghorfas*. And after that— Try as she might, the insidious voice of the *hafiz* intruded upon her concentration:

"Know you, woman, that there are two kinds of uncleanliness, a lesser hadath and a greater one. Know you, too, woman, that women are more susceptible to some hadath, men to others. But both to the causes of the lesser hadath which include: first, anything coming out of the rectum, and anything but semen from the genitals. Second, sleep, except that possible while sitting upright. Third,

unconsciousness caused by anything, drunkenness, sickness, madness or faint. Fourth, touching the human pudenda with the inner palm or the fingers, but the back of the hand is lawful. Fifth, the coming together of the epidermi of man and woman who have reached the age of lustful desire. For any one of these, purification is necessary. And until purified, it is unlawful for you, woman, to pray, to listen to the Friday sermon, to touch the Holy Book, to carry the book or, if in Mecca, to circumambulate the sacred shrine. Remember this, woman, the morning after your wedding night. These five things are forbidden to you. But there is more.

Know you, too, that, in marrying, you are, as woman, subject more than men, to even greater hadath. Of these, there are six. The first is emission of semen, which may be recognized either by its actual ejaculation or by the presence of its smell, which when it is moist is like the smell of dough and when it is dry like the smell of white of egg.

The second is intercourse by the insertion of the penis into the vulva or anus, whether of human or animal, and occurs even if no semen descendeth.

The third is childbirth.

The fourth menstruation, namely blood which comes from the vagina of any female who has known nine years or more and whose shortest course is a flow of a night and a day and whose longest is fifteen days. Rest assured, Allah who created female knows that usually it lasts six or seven days, but he knoweth, too, that women have their irregularities.

The fifth is also bloody. Afterbirth. Namely the blood which comes as a result of giving birth to a child, the shortest flow being of but a moment and the longest sixty days, though usually as Allah well knows, it lasts forty days. Know you, woman, that you who experience it and he who knows you during those days, both have experienced the greater hadath and need purifying. If you would save your man from uncleanliness, remind him that his tilth is resting and needs no plowing. So save you he from hadath.

The last, the sixth, comes to all and is death.

And for each of these, greater purification is necessary before, for the first three, eight things may be done: prayer, hearing the Holy Day sermon, touching or carrying the book, circling the sacred *shrine, reading the* Koran, *tarrying in a mosque, even frequenting one. Menstruation and afterbirth render twelve things unlawful: the eight already mentioned and four more: fasting, divorce proceedings, marital intercourse and fondling between the navel and the knees. Know you all this for your sake and that of your husband.''*

The *hafiz* paused, having completed the first part of his exposition. Ramlah signaled for an attentive slave girl to bring him a fruit drink. She drank deep of her own goblet as did Aisha from the cup handed her by Zainab. The sharp taste that greeted her tongue told the princess that Zainab had personally mixed the beverage and had happened to include a generous portion of a heady wine. Aisha smiled fondly on her handmaiden and then on Ramlah who was, through her daughter, living through the pre-wedding ritual she had been denied as bride of the Moulay.

The *hafiz*, refreshed, again took up his reading:

Know you, woman, that once known by man, you must perform the lesser purification or the greater depending upon your hadath. For the lesser, wudu is necessary: cleansing the teeth with the tooth stick, washing the palms of the hands, and the arms up to the elbow, the rinsing of the mouth, snuffling water up the nostrils, wiping the whole of the head, washing ears and face, wiping ears and face and the whole of the head, all with fresh water. If one is a man, one must finger comb the thick hair of beard and cheeks, if woman, the hair on her head and facial hair, if she has any, as well.

One should while performing the purification, say the creed: I bear witness that there is no God save Allah, the One who has no partner, and I bear witness that our Master, Mohammed, is servant and his apostle. Allahumma, make me one of those who repent, make me one of those who are purified. Glory be to Thee, Allahumma! so did our Master Mohammed teach us to praise Him.''

Aisha gave a start as a sharp nail-cleaning stick penetrated too deeply under her cuticle. With a flip of her wrist, she punished the guilty one, cuffing the girl lightly and matter-of-factly, as would a lioness with an errant cub. Animal-like, the girl swiftly dipped forehead to floor, and uttered a low moan. The cuff had no more than momentarily stung; it was fear of banishment from the presence of the much-adored mistress that frightened the girl so. Absentmindedly,

Aisha dismissed the child, meaning to summon her back later, but the princess forgot. Having abandoned her mental exercises about the trip, Aisha was too busy reviewing in her mind the day's events and the unusual spectacle she had planned for the morrow. As near as she could tell, all of her favorites had survived the tame, but potentially risky, camel contests. The crowd, however, had not found the relatively passive contests to its liking, having been spoiled by the bloody gladiator matches of the day before. Tomorrow, Aisha thought to herself, the crowd would experience the biggest surprise of the games. As would, she chuckled to herself, the hapless contestants.

Behind the screen, the *hafiz* drank. And again Ramlah directed her handmaid to light her waterpipe. Coughing, clearing his throat, humming and hawing, the *hafiz* began reading again:

For the greater purification, bathing the body with pure water is required. However, when water is unavailable, one must perform the tayammum, which is the use of sand on the face and hands and body to take the place of water. Know you that Allah in his mercy accepts that when water is needed for satisfying the thirst of a venerated animal, or when there is fear of harm arising from its use in case of sickness or wounds, sand makes a satisfactory substitute.

Know you, woman, that if you be desirous of being cleansed, your man must be also. For Allah although recognizing each to his own responsibility lays special stress on the wife and mother. Know you that if he who comes to your bed keeps not himself clean, you are neither. So must you practice istinja, and insist your man do the same. Thus the cleaning of the anus or the genitals after every voiding of excrement, but not in the case of semen. For this, keep you water and stones nearby for the combination of the two is best. However, water is preferable if one must confine oneself to either. For if the istinja has been by means of stone, purification is conditional on five things. First, that the excrement not be allowed to dry or be transferred from the place where it came to rest, this includes staining of loin clothes. Second, that there be no foreign matter added thereto, so woman, I charge you, inspect your husband's piles for parasites and other grossness. Third, that the rub by the stone does not proceed beyond the orifice in question. It is not lawful to receive illicit pleasure from purification. Fourth, that it be a triple wiping, each one of which goes over the place with three clean stones or with three applications of one clean stone. And know you that if the cleansing is not accomplished by three applications, then as many more must be applied as will effect it. It is no matter that some trace be left which can only be removed by water or small pebbles for that is pardonable and you are charged with inspecting same and so seeing to it."

Aisha gagged at the thought of having to check a man's asshole for cleanliness, and each time he squatted, to inspect his dump for worms. With a thump the *hafiz* closed the book. The reading was over for the night, he wished his pay. Aisha could only pray that the games come to an end soon, and she escape this oppressive atmosphere for the clean air of southern Tunisia.

Ramlah had listened carefully to the *hafiz* readings and wondered if it were the uncleanliness and pollution of their wedding night that had affected the Moulay's mind. She sighed deeply. If only she, too, had had the benefit of these readings as had Aisha. However, such regrets fled her mind as eager hands dabbed and rubbed towels lightly over her body. Then other hands dressed her in delicately scented undergarments, a magnificent robe, and tiny sandals.

The same had been done for Aisha. So pleased was the daughter to be released from the *hafiz*'s spell that she almost invited her mother to come and see the preparations for her wedding trip. Then, Aisha checked herself. The more who knew of it, the less long it would remain secretive. Not even Zainab had been admitted to the small pavilion where the scribes worked making lists and writing invitations and proclamations under Ali's direction. Regretfully, Aisha stifled the impulse as side by side, mother and daughter walked from the room, down the long tiled hall and out the front entrance of the magnificent Roman bath into the serenity of the night. As the two women approached the waiting litter in a glow of goodwill to the world, the stillness was shattered by an inhuman scream. The two women froze. Neither said a word. They didn't need to. Each knew what was in the other's mind: the Moulay was at play. To wish each other a good-night would have been facetious and factitious. Each knew the other would sleep only when the last of the Moulay's thirty-two playthings had uttered his final scream.

514

Of all the city of tents, only the slaves within their stone walls slept quietly unaware of the fate of the losers. All except de Wynter, who was the victim of his own nightmarish dreams. Gilliver, on the pallet nearby, stirred but kept silent when a low, familiar voice pleaded, "Drummond, don't go. Wait for me. I, too, am coming home."

CHAPTER 34

The next morning when ever fewer survivors came out from the now-dwindling tent-city of the contestants, they saw for themselves the source of last night's screams. The Moulay had decorated the entrance to the amphitheater with his handiwork: two red-raw bodies, skinned alive; a dozen corpses scorched and charred and blackened by fire; headless, armless, legless, sexless bodies propped in second tier archways spilling their guts down the now red-streaked pinkish stone walls. Neatly stacked to the left of the gateway were the missing arms, the legs piled to the right. Some of the heads had joined the now-picked-clean skulls of the deserters atop the classically beautiful Corinthian columns. Others were simply impaled on spikes. All stared, wide-eyed, straight ahead.

Trying not to look anywhere but at their feet, the contestants charged through the gate of the colosseum, their sandals clattering noisily on the stone floor of the ramp as they ran down to the dressing room below. Those in front had scarcely reached the room when they pulled up short and tried not to enter. But the mass behind prevented that. Those in the second and third rows, peering over the shoulders of the men ahead, saw that the room was not empty. Two of the contestants had preceded them and now sat silently on a bench on the other side of the room. Despite the noise, the commotion, those figures didn't move. They couldn't—pieces of straw protruded from eyes and mouth and nostrils and ears. There before them sat the ultimate example of the Moulay's perverted sense of humor: two human skins stuffed with straw. Once word was passed, there was a wild melee as men fought to get out of the room and into the arena floor, to be joined shortly by the slaves.

What Aisha's purpose was in dreaming up today's outlandish contest, Ali ben Zaid feared to imagine. When he ventured to ask her, she only laughed. There was a hint in her laughter that reminded Ali uncomfortably of the Moulay. But then, so did the contest itself. Yesterday's events had made sense. Any man fit to wed the Amira should be able to handle camels. But today's would prove little or nothing about these men who had already survived so much. Except perhaps that they could take a tremendous kick in the stomach. Poor devils, Ali thought, if they don't hate her now, they will before this day is through.

Trumpets, cymbals, and ram's horns called for silence. "Today," the Moulay's *wazier* announced, adjusting his white turban so that it perched on his head just so. "Today is ostrich day! With permission of our great and gracious Moulay Hassan, let the order of events be announced. The blessings of Allah be on him who competes."

Al wazier Yahiba, of Marrakesh, stepped forward, leaning on a walking stick. A magnificent white and pistachio green burnoose covered him from his hooded head to the tips of his yellow babouche-shod feet. The folds of his hood concealed his features from most. Only those directly in front of him made out the sharp nose, cruel mouth, and small black eyes.

His voice was harsh, his accent guttural, his words startling: "First, there will be a fight between two of the giant beasts who have been pestered, starved, and not watered for three days. Following this, an exhibition of lassoing the big birds from horseback, and of hunting them by an expert archer. All of this to give you contestants a foretaste of your fate later in the morning.

"Your first event of the day will be to lasso or otherwise bring under control any one ostrich from the wild ones unloosed in the arena. You will then break your bird for riding. Later there will be ostrich races in heats, with the heat winners meeting in the final race of the day to determine the champion.

"The fate of those who cannot catch an ostrich nor take one away from another contestant will be decided, as usual, by the *rafi as' sa'n*, the Moulay Hassan. Let the blessings of Allah be on him who competes!''

The spectators sensed that this was going to be an exciting day. Most of them knew of the cantankerous nature of the great birds, of their fierce kick, which could knock a man over or break his bones. And there were stories, true or not, of their pecking the eyes out of a man's head. The audience chuckled and snickered—there would be many a bruised, scratched, and battered contestant before this day was over.

Two giant cages were wheeled into the center of the arena, each containing a stomping, darting, black-plumaged ostrich. Standing chest-high to a man, its naked neck and reddish head stretched half again as high. Carrying sticks with which to beat back any ostrich that might try to break through the ring, blackamoors formed a ring around the cages. A small crock of water was set midway between the two cages; the cage doors were flung open and out stormed the two gigantic birds, both bound for the same water. Thirst-maddened, the birds set upon each other, each attempting to keep the other from the water. In their battle, they upset the crock, the water sinking immediately into the parched earth and sand that was the arena floor.

Now, totally enraged, one sailed into the other, pecking its head and neck, clawing at it with his two-toed foot, driving it away in a flurry of legs. At the circle's edge, the slaves beat them both back with great shouts and clubbings, which only further infuriated the huge feathery combatants.

The spectators loved it. They cheered and made wagers on one bird or the other and laughed every time the ostriches, coming near the slaves, clawed savagely at them. Steel-tipped whips in turn forced the slaves to close ranks and tighten the circle. Feeling hemmed in, the ostriches forgot one another and attacked their encirclers, only to be beaten back again and again. Here and there a slave went down, slit from neck to gullet by the ostrich's single claw, but another unfortunate quickly was whipped into his place. Slowly but irresistibly, the slaves tightened their circle until it was hardly large enough to contain the two pecking, kicking, gouging birds. Now the slaves stood three and four deep at all points around the perimeter. Sticks rained blows on the birds, who countered with mighty legs, thrusting taloned feet into the front ranks.

It was a grand and glorious opening event, the crowd agreed, as, by sheer numbers, the slaves beat the giant birds into a bloody pulp, at a cost of a few dead or nearly dead slaves plus dozens more with broken bones, cuts, and bruises. Triumphantly, the slaves dragged the huge carcasses from the arena, it being their only victory in weeks . . . perhaps years.

A blast of many ram horns cleared the arena. Through an entrance charged six more of the feathery beasts to gallop, stomp, and glide about the arena. A single archer entered on horseback; his huge bow, lying across his saddle, stretched a meter to either side of his horse. Fitting a shaft from the quiver strapped on his back, he took aim, and dropped his quarry with a shot into its huge chest.

Now the archer trotted his horse to the other end of the arena, the birds spreading out and watching him warily. Then at full gallop, he headed straight for them, scattering them in full flight, drew his bow and drove an arrow through the neck of a moving target. To clapping and cheers and huzzahs he rode proudly out of the arena.

In came another mounted tribesman—an ebony-hued Negro from Ifriqiya's great desert country with a single coil of rope held in his right hand. Charging into the midst of the squawking, flapping birds, he twirled the rope in a neat loop above his head, then flung it with a snap of his wrist. The lasso snaked through the air and dropped over the head of a startled ostrich in mid-flight, drawing tight and pulling him off his feet as the horse quickly braked to a halt. Like magic, a dagger materialized within the rider's hand and flew, in a blur of silver, to skewer the long sinuous neck; the strong, dangerous legs clawed once weakly at the sky then fell, still, to the ground.

Again the horseman set his horse at full gallop, recoiling his rope as he rode. Again he twirled it high and, charging into the scattering birds, flung it out along the dirt where it fairly danced across the surface before snaring a pounding leg. The archer reappeared as if by magic and drove a shaft into the exposed chest, stilling the raucous squawks and the flapping wings.

Once more the horseman recoiled his well-trained rope and herding the remaining two birds in front of him, chased them the full length of the arena, all three at breakneck speed. The lasso leaped and circled both heads at once, tightened instantly, binding the birds together in its death grip. The birds in a frenzy turned to one another, clawing and pecking, further tightening the constricting rope and forcing it up the long necks until the bulging heads stopped it short.

For long minutes the death struggle went on. Again the spectators roared their approval and placed their wagers. And when one finally crumpled to the dirt, a talon having pierced its heart, the thumbs went up and the shouts of *"Mitte!"* rang out for the victor. When the Moulay Hassan stood and raised his thumb as well, the loser's neck was cut in two, and the survivor was dragged and chased from the arena, its head still caught in the loop along with the flopping head and bleeding neck of its vanquished foe.

The Moulay Hassan was enjoying himself. He hadn't thought much of the Olympic events, nor yesterday's camel competition, although he had delighted in its aftermath, as he had the gladiator fights. Yawning, he hoped today's events continued to be exciting; if not, he was going back to bed. He had had an exhausting night last night and stayed up much too late. Which reminded him of Zainab's message.

Imperiously he gestured for Ali to step forward and said, "Today, I would know who competes. Have their names announced!"

"As you command, *rafi as'sa'n,*" said Ali, bowing and looking askance at Aisha. Her shrug and raised eyebrow conveyed without words her own bewilderment over the Moulay's orders. Even as Ali left to relay those orders to the officials, the crier called for the contestants to take their place at the starting line at the south end. Of the original 180 men, only 57 were left, survivors of three grueling days of competition. One look at them revealed no paunches, no flabby muscles. Only the strong remained. Some blistered and peeling from the sun, others bronzed and golden; only the blacks and Gilliver were apparently untouched by the sun's rays. The frail Scot's skin refused to tan, reddening, then peeling and returning to white. Nor was his body as smooth-muscled and sleek as the rest of the group that now lined up for the start of the fourth day's competition.

As the men approached the line marked in salt on the sand, horns sounded, gates swung open, and in stormed a thundering pack of ostriches, herded by men on horseback and club-bearers on foot. As the last of the big birds entered, the men retreated and the gates swung shut, the arena left to the birds and men.

As the dust settled about the birds, it was Carlby who first noted the not readily obvious: "Dammit, the devils didn't give us enough birds to go round." De Wynter, peering at the darting, stomping, angry birds, hazarded a guess that there were no more than fifty and more probably forty in number.

"That must be their game," Carlby continued. "If you don't get a bird, you're out of it."

"We'll have to work as a team," de Wynter replied, thinking rapidly what strategy to employ. "For each two we get, one man will have to hold them while the others go after more until we have enough."

"Aye, but you can bet there will be trouble when it gets down to just a few," Menzies said.

Cameron agreed. "These fellows will do anything to survive at this point. If they see one of our men with two, they'll try to take one."

"True," said de Wynter. "We'll have to assign our strongest to do the holding. Fionn, of course. And Angus and Ogilvy. We have no other choice but to chance it."

Officials now passed up and down the line handing out pieces of rope, each carefully measured at only two meters in length, one rope per man. At the end of the line, one man was left with no rope which set off an uproar, each official blaming the others for not counting right. Finally another rope was found, and the contest could begin.

Carlby and de Wynter reminded their fellows to stay close; the strategy was to catch birds as a team, not individually. "Would an extra rope help?" John the Rob whispered to de Wynter.

"Not again?" said de Wynter with a grin. "Those hands are going to get you in trouble some day. Right now, I'm glad to have them. Where have you got it?" he added, looking searchingly at John the Rob who was as near naked as he. John the Rob pulled down the edge of his loincloth to reveal the missing rope, wrapped neatly around his waist. De Wynter shook his head in wonderment.

The caller cupped his hands and shouted the commands of the

Moor from Morocco: "You may start when the ram horns sound and continue until they sound again. There are no restrictions on what you may do to get yourself a bird. Those without a bird, when the horns blow the second time, lose. Winners continue on to the race events in the afternoon. Let the blessings of Allah be on you who compete."

Pray God, de Wynter thought, there are no experienced men at this strange game. If so, with good teamwork and a little bit of luck, we should come out all right. Provided somebody doesn't get kicked or maimed.

The trumpets sounded. Fifty-seven men leaped from the starting line. The great birds saw what was coming and ran helter-skelter. Quickly, the men were among them, trying to corner them against the wall, throwing looped ends of their short ropes at heads and feet, and picking themselves up off the dirt when flattened by a kick or tripped by a fellow contestant's leg.

The nine took off together, following the lead of Cameron, who was their fastest runner. Isolating a pair of the feathery beasts, they formed a semicircle and herded them toward the wall. Then Fionn leaped on the neck of the first and held on while de Wynter roped the fiercely darting head.

"Hold that one while we get another," de Wynter yelled to Angus. Then Fionn was upon the second. Soon it, too, wore a halter. And off they went to repeat the strategy. Again it worked, but not without Carlby taking a fearful kick in the stomach and John the Rob having his arm gashed. As a group they chased and dragged their third bird to where Fionn held the first two.

"I don't think I can hold three!" Fionn shouted desperately. "It's all I can do to keep the two under control."

"Tie their bloody necks together," Carlby grunted, holding onto his aching stomach.

"Here, use this," John the Rob volunteered, handing over his extra rope.

De Wynter quickly made a large loop and by tugging on the two ropes already secured, managed to get the third rope over two heads and tighten the noose.

"Hang on to them," he yelled at Fionn as the pack sped off for more. It was more difficult now. Half the birds had been captured, and the others were the biggest and strongest and wisest of the flock. And these remaining twenty were being pursued by three dozen eager huntsmen. Several bodies—both bird and human—lay stretched out on the arena floor, some moving, some not.

Their fourth bird was handed over to Ogilvy to hold. And a fifth was finally roped, John the Rob quickly producing another rope to tie another pair together.

"Where did that come from?" de Wynter asked in amazement.

"Just happened to find it," John the Rob said, raising his hand to show three more looped in his grasp. "I'll tell you this, friend, there's some fellows out there hunting birds with no ropes."

De Wynter allowed himself an appreciative smile at John the Rob's feat. There was no time for anything more, since four birds were still needed, and only a dozen left loose with twice that number of men pursuing them around the arena—each working independently.

That gave the team a distinct advantage. For one thing seven could corner the speedy, cranky critters more easily than one. And seven could herd it into a wall, where it had to turn and try to fight its way out. And, thanks to John the Rob's extras, seven ropes would find more targets more quickly than one rope.

They roped the sixth bird around one leg, ignoring the furiously pecking head, gang-tackled it, and trussed both legs together. Ogilvy was left to guard it while the rest went back for others.

Cornering the seventh, Gilliver took a glancing kick on his right leg, the talons raking deep gashes in his thigh. But the group subdued the squawking bird, and de Wynter looked around for John the Rob to hold this one while they went for more.

A strange sight greeted his eyes. Down the center of the great amphitheater came a bird running full tilt, dragging a man at the end of a rope. It was John the Rob and they ran to his aid.

"How did you catch this one?" de Wynter asked.

"Some fellow decided he didn't want it any longer," John the Rob shouted, spitting dirt from his mouth.

"Oh," said de Wynter. "I suppose the one heading this way has simply changed his mind and wants it back."

The others looked where de Wynter was pointing, to see an angry contestant bearing down on them. With Carlby holding the eighth bird, five of the group lined up to face the irate man.

"That's my bird, and he stole it," he screamed, pointing a finger at John the Rob.

"Forget it, friend," de Wynter shouted above the din, tossing the man a rope. "Go get yourself another one." As he spoke, the five stepped forward menacingly toward the man; he held his ground for a long minute, then decided he didn't really want that particular bird.

"Just one to go," de Wynter cried. And the five sped off looking for another ostrich to subdue.

The crowd had watched the spectacle with fascination, especially the teamwork. Some thought it clever. Others considered it unfair. The judges, too, had frowned, conferred, and found that there was nothing in their rules to prohibit such action, though they certainly had not expected it.

Of the five birds still speeding around the arena, they needed but one. At that moment they heard a shout—Gilliver's charge had gotten away. All turned to run this one down, Cameron making a dangerous and daring tackle of one leg, with the others then piling on before the beast could seriously hurt him. Gilliver, whose right leg was still bleeding, was again put in charge of the bird. Now de Wynter, John the Rob, and Menzies could set off to track down their final prey. Horrified, de Wynter looked around the arena to see that there were no more ostriches on the loose. "Now what?" he said.

John the Rob said, "I'll get us another one. Watch." Twirling the rope about his head, he finally let go, and the rope found its target, wrapping itself about another contestant's neck. Startled, the man let go of his bird, and it took off for freedom. As one, the three took after it, as did every other contestant without a bird.

Desperation showed on every face. Anyone who got in someone else's way was jostled, tripped, shoved, or belted. John the Rob concentrated on stripping contestants of their ropes, many of them never knowing whad had happened. The result was that out of the eleven pursuers only five had ropes: two others besides de Wynter and Menzies and John the Rob.

Still moving as fast as his legs would take him, John the Rob knotted his extra ropes together, making them into one long rope. Tying knots at each end, he threw one end to de Wynter and shouted, "Grab hold, milord, we've got to slow these fellows down a bit."

524

So saying, he darted off at an angle, taking his end of the rope with him, so that it stretched out on the ground between them. De Wynter took only a moment to see what was on the other's mind. Then with a grin, he carried out his end of the plan. Circling around one end of the group pursuing the ostrich, he dragged the rope behind him, the other end of which was held tightly in John the Rob's hand. Now he cut sharply back across their path, and yanked the rope tight at knee level. Down went the pursuers in a heap, wondering what hit them. All except one. Kenneth Menzies leaped over the rope and sped after the bird, with de Wynter and John the Rob right behind him. The long rope was hopelessly tangled in legs and bodies and had to be abandoned, but both Menzies and de Wynter had theirs. What's more, the bird still trailed the one by which it had been held captive.

Menzies caught up to the bird by anticipating which way he would turn as he reached the end of the arena, then cutting him off. Cornered by the three contestants, the bird decided to stand and fight. Too late. While two men made a feint to one side, Menzies dived for the rope. Scrambling to his feet, he pulled with all of his strength. As the bird answered the tug, de Wynter tossed another rope over his head, then pulled it taut, and dragged the creature back to where the rest of their group awaited them, fighting off other contestants as they went.

Now to figure out how to get the still kicking and struggling birds under better control. "Hobble them," de Wynter decided. "It works for horses and camels." By combining their strength and talents, one by one they trussed the birds' legs together with about a hand's breadth between.

"Check all the knots on those loops," de Wynter said. "We don't want to lose any at this stage. Damn, there should be a way to keep these together without each of us holding one."

"As you command," said a grinning John the Rob, producing from around his middle the long length of rope used to trip up their competitors. It was short work to join all of the neck ropes with the long rope. Now, to steal one, all must be stolen. All but de Wynter and Carlby were assigned to sit on, pin, or otherwise control the still irritable but tired ostriches until the ram's horn blared again.

"So far so good," de Wynter said as the pair squatted several paces in front of the group, ready to do battle with any birdless one who came too close. But their aspect was too formidable. They were left alone.

"Are we really going to try to ride those creatures? We must be mad," Carlby said, rubbing his sore stomach.

De Wynter ignored both words and gesture. "We've got to fashion some bridles to steer the bloody beasts. Damn. If we didn't need the extra rope to hold the birds, we could use it for bridles."

"Suppose we bury one's head in the sand while you turn his rope into a bridle," Carlby suggested facetiously.

De Wynter ignored his sarcasm. "You have the makings of a good idea there. Suppose we blindfold one with a loincloth then use the neck rope to make the bridle? Come on, it's worth a try."

Before they could experiment, a loose ostrich went screaming and flapping down the arena, squawking shrilly as its captor chased it, six men chasing him. No one lifted a hand to help. At that moment, the ram's horn sounded and the silent ones entered the arena, herding the birdless ones, including the seven would-be captors of the loose bird, inexorably toward the Gate of Death. None went willingly. Some tried to scale the arena wall. Others tried to take shelter among the captive birds. At this, the stentorian voice announced, "He who harbors a birdless one will sacrifice his own chance to compete." At that, the luckier ones expelled their fellows, allowing the silent ones to round up all the others. As the Moulay had commanded, each man's name was announced as he was shoved through the Gate of Death. The Moulay, satisfied that the one he was interested in was still in the arena, announced, "I am tired. Hold the games until I return from my nap." Before Ramlah or Aisha could protest, he had left the royal box on his way to the couching room prepared by the slaves days before.

The slaves, for one, welcomed the chance the delay gave them. While Fionn and Ogilvy wrapped themselves around the hobbled legs of one bird, de Wynter gave his loincloth to Carlby to blind the bird. The bird struggled once, then lay still while de Wynter experimented, knotting the rope various ways. Eventually, he devised a double loop: one for the top of the neck, a smaller one for around the beak. The two free ends would be grasped like reins, one in each hand.

"No good. It's not quite long enough," de Wynter said. "We're going to have to use two ropes for each bridle. Otherwise, when they stretch out their necks, they'll pull the reins free."

Redoing the two loops closer to one end of the two-meter rope, de Wynter had Gilliver untie one length from the tether, and tied it on the long end of the bridle. Now the reins formed a long loop of their own, one which the rider could tie behind his back and still have plenty of rope to rein with. Putting it on the bird was not easy, but as Carlby said, nothing had been these last four days.

"We still have a problem," Carlby pointed out. "Only six extra ropes and nine birds."

"The three of us with the longest arms will have to make do; we have no other choice," de Wynter said. "Let's get started."

Over the next hour, the group painstakingly, and painfully, put bridles on each of their plumed steeds, tying the reins to each other to keep the big birds tethered. When the last one was done, de Wynter rescued what was left of his loincloth: a shredded rag.

"Thank God, I'm not proud," de Wynter said, holding it up.

"Nor modest," Fionn added.

While the others laughed, John the Rob disappeared, only to return with a fresh loincloth.

"Now, how did you do that? Strip a man naked without his knowing it? I don't believe it."

"Believe it. It was Eulj Ali's I stole, and he doesn't look too happy about it."

"I'll lend him my rag; it might remind him of his good times rowing."

"If you two are finished chatting?" Carlby prodded them. Then the men were all business; it was time to learn to ride their winged, two-legged beasts. It took two men to control one in the beginning. While one clambered aboard, the other held the bridle and then led the bird.

They soon discovered riding an ostrich was not easy. To compound matters, they dared not exhaust the beasts, for the birds must race that afternoon. By the time the ram's horn sounded at the Moulay's return from his nap, the dust-covered men were exhausted, and none was absolutely sure he could stay aboard his rolling, jolting steed, let alone guide him or urge him on faster.

"With the Moulay's great and glorious permission," the crier shouted, "there will be five races. Plus a final one for the five winners, this winner to receive an advantage in tomorrow's contest. The slaves passing among you bear pots. Within them are discs to draw for position. Yellow races first. Then red, followed by blue, white after that, and black racing last. The blessings of Allah on him who competes."

De Wynter, first to draw, drew yellow. Cameron and Menzies, drawing one after the other, both came up with red discs. Angus and Ogilvy found themselves in the third and fourth heats respectively. Carlby's disc was blue, Fionn's white. John the Rob, whose dextrous hands managed to take one disc and palm a second, came up with two white ones, to his disgust; there were already three of them in the fourth heat. Gilliver drew last and prayed it wasn't a sign, for his disc was black.

De Wynter, seeing Gilliver's face, put an arm around his friend's shoulders and quietly reassured him, "Henry, don't worry. The main thing today is not to get injured. If you have a chance to win without taking any risk, fine. If not, don't worry. They may have already done their winnowing for today. So just cling to your bird and stay on. Understand?"

Gilliver nodded and smiled tremulously. Whatever Jamie said, Gilliver believed implicitly, religiously.

De Wynter took his own advice and approached the first heat with a lighthearted feeling that was not appropriate for the occasion but totally in character. He loved competition, the element of danger only adding to the excitement. The ram's horn signaled the start, and de Wynter, who had been given a boost up by his fellows, kicked the feathery beast in the sides and took off in a cloud of sand along with seven other angry, rambunctious ostriches. Most of them went as much laterally as forward, fouling everybody's well-laid plans and bumping one rider unceremoniously from his perch to crash upon the sun-hardened sand.

The bridle that de Wynter had fashioned was superior to any of the crude halters the others in the heat had managed, and it gave him an advantage that served him well. By tugging with all his might on one rein or the other, he could actually steer the headstrong beast. His biggest problem turned out to be getting it to move fast enough.

But enough kicks in the side and enough shouts of encouragement brought him to the finish line before the others. In fact, only three of the eight managed to get across the finish line within the time allowed.

"Nothing to it," said a sweat-soaked, hard-breathing de Wynter as he rejoined his friends at the starting line. His steed had been led away by slaves to be held until the final race of the day.

"I would suggest that you two," he said to Cameron and Menzies, "delay your start just a few seconds. Let the crazy birds get spread out a bit heading in the right direction, and then you can take off. It might save you a spill."

"Good idea," said Menzies.

"Makes sense," George said, not at all confidently. He was more than a little worried because he, like de Wynter and Fionn, was using the short reins.

At the blast of the ram's horn, five of the eight birds leaped from the starting line in a melee of bumping, jostling, and shouting. One refused to move, instead, to his rider's horror, squatting down as if nesting. Cameron and Menzies, who lagged behind, saw their openings; they kicked their birds into action and sped forth in a near-straight line, soon passing four erratic birds. But the fifth stubbornly held his lead, streaking down the length of the arena. It was a three-man, or ostrich, race, and Cameron and Menzies lost in a close finish.

Angus and Carlby fared no better in the third heat. Carlby not only wound up eating dirt some three meters into the race, but his bird broke loose and he ended up chasing the flapping creature halfway to the finish line to no avail. To add to his discomfort, the winner of his heat was a naked redhead, a man watched intently by more than one observer from within the royal box.

Fionn redeemed Carlby's disgrace by winning the fourth race. Ogilvy finished in the middle of that pack and John the Rob brought up the rear, a position that Gilliver barely managed to equal in the fifth race.

To no one's surprise, all of those who met in the race of winners were not strangers to the crowd, each having made his presence known consistently during the last three days of competition. Besides Fionn, de Wynter, and Eulj Ali, the *muezzin* identified the Taureg, and the Nuba wrestler. As the men angled their birds toward the starting line, de Wynter leaned over to Fionn and said, "I'll bet you Dunstan's next colt I beat you."

"You're on," said the younger man. At that moment a ram's horn split the silence and the race was on. Within minutes, it had degenerated into a farce. Perhaps the beasts had decided enough was enough; more likely all were exhausted. Whatever, they were totally uncooperative. At the start, the Nuba and de Wynter were promptly dumped. Halfway down the course, the birds of the Taureg and Eulj Ali took a dislike to each other and began fighting, their riders pulling futilely at them. Fionn's took ten paces, stopped short and wouldn't budge. Fionn kicked and shouted and hit his beast with the reins to no avail. Then, slowly, deliberately, the bird folded its legs and crouched down on the ground, laying its head down on the sand, leaving Fionn standing, straddling his mount. By all odds, he should have been out of the race but he wasn't. The other two birds, after much pecking, both called it quits simultaneously, turned, and ran—back toward the starting line. The crowd loved it. Even the other competitors, including the Nuba and de Wynter, joined in the laughter. Up in the royal box, the Moulay began urging Eulj Ali on, shouting advice at the top of his lungs in a most unkingly way. At that Eulj Ali's bird forgot its wings were useless and attempted to fly out of the arena, taking enormous and futile hops up into the air, while beating its wings furiously. Aisha and her mother had a most difficult time concealing their delight at his difficulties. The Taureg's bird then stopped short, as if to see whether the hopper were onto something successful. And still Fionn's bird lay there motionless, its eyes closed, evidently hoping the whole thing would go away. Fionn, in desperation, leaned down, grabbed the surprised bird around the middle and staggered with it across the finish line. Not till he sat it down did it give any sign of life, then it took off kicking and flapping and squawking indignantly. A dismayed judge looked at the officials and the royals and, seeing no help from them and no other contestant anywhere near the finish line, halfheartedly declared Fionn the winner.

As his friends pommeled and thumped him congratulations of his victory, Fionn reminded de Wynter, "That'll earn me a horse, remember."

"As soon as we get back to Scotland, these others are my witness." Fionn would get his reward much sooner than either he or the others expected.

CHAPTER 35

The Moulay and the her/him, with Pietro the ex-gladiator dancing attendance, led the royals from the box, only to part with his womenfolk at the first ramp. Aisha and Ramlah proceeded on; the Moulay remained behind to examine at closer range the losers in today's contests and to decide their fate as he had those of the night before. The Moulay felt energized by today's events, titillated and inspired by the behavior of the strange birds. Back in Tunis, he vowed, he would have Ibn al-Hudaij procure a flock of the most ferocious known to men, have them taken to the Bardo and pitted against one another. On second thought, he wondered if, enraged enough, the birds would kill a man. What better time, he decided, smiling unpleasantly, than now to find out.

Aisha and Ramlah, once they had left the amphitheater behind them, parted also; but only over Ramlah's objections, Aisha faithfully promising her mother to be prompt for the fifth nightly ritual, this to be held in the queen's tent.

Once Aisha had assured herself that all was in readiness for the morrow—for a contest to which she had looked forward all week—she, Zainab, the cheetah, and a small retinue of *asiras* and silent ones made their way to the luxurious tent Ramlah preferred to a villa. Within the second chamber, its walls were hung with lengths of heavy, richly embroidered, multicolored woolens, her mother lounged on an equally commodious and sumptuous divan, as slaves spread out thimble-sized glass-lined copper cups for the thick mint tea.

Approaching a cushion-strewn couch covered with fur, Aisha unloosed her long hair and stretched like a cat; sitting down, she looked directly into the blank eyes of a man. A short, brown, ageless man—but a man nonetheless—sitting cross-legged, hands on knees, upon a small varicolored rug. A man in her mother's innermost quarters! Aisha was too self-possessed to protest . . . and too startled to hide her surprise. Ramlah was amused. The girl was not so untraditional as she pretended.

"Tonight, my daughter, in accordance with Berber custom we will hear, from the lips of this honored storyteller—" Aisha relaxed with a perceptible sigh. Berber storytellers were as safe as eunuchs in women's quarters. They were blind, frequently deliberately made so by their families.

"He was sent by your honored grandfather, upon whom may Allah smile, so you may hear how Allah—exalted be He—created Eve from one of the ribs of Adam, and how he caused them to be married. Even as he speaks truly the words of the Prophet—upon whom be Allah's blessing and peace—Zainab shall transform you into a proper Berber bride, applying harcoos to palms and fingertips, obliterating those ugly Arab symbols. The *ukda* on your feet shall remind you of the other royal bloodline joined in you and your eggs. Zainab, bring the tray . . . Sarifa, my casket."

Aisha was not loathe to lose the egg and arrow that she had attempted to scrub off on more than one occasion, but she feared the harcoos might be worse. However, she watched with interest as an *asira* set up an ebony stand for the tray Zainab brought. It was intricately beaten, punched, and worked copper with precious metal inlays. Upon it, Sarifa, Ramlah's handmaiden, placed an equally elaborately wrought copper box whose latch Ramlah took several minutes to undo. Then, reaching into the depths of this small casket, she brought out another smaller, golden pyx. From within it, she took a brush, a sponge, a tiny agate dish, an ancient simpulum, and two amphora, one smaller than the other. The latter she unstoppered to pour its black contents into the tiny dish, adding a dollop from the larger of the two jars and mixing the whole together with the ancient utensil. Aisha watched intently and with curiosity.

Then the blind man began to spin his tale, making of the creation a suspenseful story, pausing at significant points to hear the expected "what then" from his audience. When his story ended, the storyteller sat silently, his beautiful voice stilled, his listeners spellbound by his description of the only marriage truly made in heaven. Even Aisha had been so caught up in the web that magnificent voice wove that she had watched with unseeing eyes what was happening to her hands.

Freed of his vocal magic, she really looked at them and gave a strangled gasp. The red egg and arrow were indeed gone—replaced by solid black palms and fingertips. Horrified, she leaped to her feet, sending the brass tray with the tea cups flying, and fled the tent, her cat bounding after. When Ramlah followed, she had to penetrate the circle of silent ones surrounding Aisha. There, in the midst of them knelt a hysterical child, weeping convulsively and desperately scouring her hands with sand. A word from the queen made the men draw back. Then she knelt protectively by her loved one. "Hush, Aisha, don't cry so. It is only a Berber bridal tradition."

When Ramlah reached out to take the girl in her arms to comfort her, Aisha pulled away, the tears streaming down her face totally ignored. "How could you, my own mother, do this to me?"

"The dye will wear off, I promise you."

"I don't care." She gestured with those fearsomely dark-stained hands. "It's not this I'm talking about."

"Come, let's talk about it inside where there are fewer ears."

Aisha shook her head; she wasn't going back in there. Not now.

Ramlah was not about to argue. After all, the *Ikwan* had no tongues to repeat what they heard. "If it's not the dye, what then?"

"The whole thing. I don't want to be a bride. Not a Berber bride, not any bride. Mother, I beg you, get me out of this. Don't force me to go through with it. Help me escape this horrible marriage."

Aisha looked at her mother expectantly, trustingly, as if a little child again.

"Dear one, please dry your tears. Everything will work out all right."

"Then you will help me?"

Ramlah wished she could lie. "I can't, my dear. Women, especially women in your position, must marry. It's the right, the natural thing, to do."

"Without love?"

534

Ramlah looked at her daughter with wise eyes and spoke very quietly. "I married without love."

Aisha, remorseful, quickly hugged her mother. "I know, I'm sorry."

Now it was Ramlah's turn to pull away. "As a Berber princess, I did it for my tribe. You must do it for all of your country."

"I didn't ask to be a princess," Aisha retorted defensively, as if Ramlah were accusing her.

"No," Ramlah conceded, "but you've enjoyed the benefits of it. Now, you pay the price."

"Why? If I were prince, not princess, I should not be forced into this travesty of a marriage."

"That is beside the point and *you* make of this marriage the travesty, not me, not your country—you! These games are your idea, not ours."

"What would you have had me do, marry Barbarossa?"

"No, child. Like my marriage, that one would have held absolutely no chance of success. This one does, at least your husband-to-be risks his life for you. And if nothing else, you, too, may be blessed with a loving child. Aisha, accept what you cannot change. In two days, you marry the winner of your own great games. You made the law, you must abide by it. Now, please, let us return inside. I could use one of Zainab's brews."

Arm in arm the two women walked back toward the tent. They had not gone far when Aisha spoke again in a subdued voice. "I have chosen a slave, you know."

"Have you? I thought you might. Which one?"

"The blond."

"Really? I thought you might have chosen the other."

"You, too? Ali also. You have listened to the readings. Probably closer than I. Tell me, if a man is a slave, does he have the same connubial rights as a freeborn man?"

Ramlah looked thoughtful, as Aisha waited expectantly, then shook her head. "No. I shouldn't think so. Only those you grant him."

"Good. I wasn't going to check his backside, anyway."

Ramlah laughed. And secretly pitied the poor slave who married her daughter.

CHAPTER 36

"Allahu Akbar," God is most Great," the age-old cry of the *muezzin* awoke the remaining contestants within the tent-city. They had slept almost soundly, the night being comparatively quiet, interrupted only twice by mercifully brief outbursts of sharp thin cries, so painfully high-pitched that on hearing them, one's throat ached emphatically. Of the men still eligible to compete, only twenty-nine threw back their fur bedcoverings and answered the call. The other's wound—a deep gash from neck to pelvis—had been infected by a disease that birds' feet harbor and had festered overnight. So he kept to his bed, sending word by a slave to the Amir *l'al-assa* of his condition and begging leave to be excused from the day's contest so as to be treated by a physician. The reply was brief and to the point: a silent one's stiletto mortally enlarged his wound and permanently excused him from the games.

The others, unaware of this and having eaten heartily, started off toward the amphitheater in good humor. They ached less than previously. They had proven they were winners in a game so execrable and bereft of reason they could not conceive that even a totally deranged mind could come up with anything more harrowing. If it were not for the gruesome reminders of the fate of losers exhibited at the contestants' entrance to al Djem, many would have actually looked forward to today's game, daring the Moulay to do his worst, especially since the games ended on the morrow.

The nine slaves did not share the others' attitude. They were

536

spared, because they were incarcerated within the arena proper, the preview of a charnelhouse that greeted the others each morning when they arrived at the arena. But the slaves were motivated differently. They fought for freedom. Not for one, but for all. Their goal was simply to survive the next two days; however, the pragmatists among them knew that the odds against this grew greater each passing day. They had lost but one man out of ten, while less than one out of five of the other competitors survived.

On this morning when the contestants entered the arena, they found, to their surprise, that the galleries were already filling up, mostly with men in gray and red striped caftans and white headcloths held in place by coils of black braid. The Taureg standing behind de Wynter clapped his hands suddenly and explosively. Startled, de Wynter turned about to see the Taureg staring with a frown up into the throng.

"Berbers," he whispered to the silver-haired one whom normally he avoided out of fear that such hair was magicked. "They ride with *djinn,* but loud noises frighten them away."

"The Berbers?"

"No," replied the Taureg with a disgusted, exasperated look at the ignorant one. "The *djinn.*" When de Wynter still looked bewildered, the Taureg, an Arab, explained. "The *djinn* must continually search for new human lovers. I do not wish them to choose me."

"Why? What do they do?"

"They kill their lovers with love." The Taureg looked uncomfortable as if he wished he had never deigned to explain.

But de Wynter, curiosity aroused, pursued the subject. "With love? How?"

Now, the Taureg was truly embarrassed. "You know."

"No, I don't." De Wynter said, managing with great effort to keep his face impassive and stifle his smile.

Finally, the Taureg blurted out. "By forced, continuous, never-ending coupling." Having done the unthinkable, spoken of sexual congress with an infidel, the Taureg impatiently waited for de Wynter's reaction.

De Wynter nodded knowingly. "Ah, yes. We have those kind of djinn, too. We call them mermaids."

Just then, Carlby interrupted them, drawing de Wynter aside. But Fionn, who had overheard, took it upon himself to satisfy the Arab's curiosity by describing the history of the house of Seaforth and its initial meeting with the mermaid. He did not of course, omit the story of the Mer-Lion and the Mer-Lion ring nor the many sightings of those supernatural creatures at sea. "I saw them myself," Fionn concluded with more than a hint of pride in his voice. "The last time, just before we landed at Tunis. Let me tell you, if al Djem were anywhere near water, the Earl of Seaforth would only need cry for assistance and we'd all be rescued. Just like that," and Fionn snapped his fingers. The Taureg would have questioned him further, but the blaring of tubas silenced all conversation.

Again, it was Ibn al-Hudaij who introduced the contestants to the schedule of events. But first, taking note of the increased number of new spectators, he addressed his opening remarks to them. "Welcome to the fifth day of the Great Games of the Moulay Hassan, may Allah shower favor upon him and increase his *baraka*. Today shall be a day of beauty, grace, and magnificence. Today is Horse Day, a day devoted to those descendants of the five mares of the Prophet—upon whom be Allah's blessing and peace—the true royalty of the desert: our glorious horses. Our júdge today is Sheikh Beteyen ibn Kader, of Arred. The blessings of Allah be on him who competes."

Carlby and de Wynter exchanged glances. Carlby had said he thought he'd heard the distant neighing of horses; but before the two could speak, a man stepped forward from among the group of judges. He wore a burnoose, a hooded full-length robe, of pure white, belted tightly and widely about the waist with a dagger's hilt protruding from it. His headcloth was also of white, but wound about with the green cord of the *hajii*.

"I, too, welcome all to the games of His Highness the *rafi as' sa'n*. Today's game, like that of yesterday and the day before and yes, the day before the day before that, is designed to test the worth of man. Just as the horsebreeder weeds out the weak, the infirm, and those who do not breed true, so do these games eliminate all but the fit, mentally and physically. You who compete today have proven able to ride the ostrich and utilize the camel. Now, you shall prove your ability to select, to train, to ride, to tame, and to be one with the horse. Your instructions are simple. Be not deceived, they are not easily followed. Soon, you will be faced with a wild Arabian stallion. He has never known bridle or saddle or rider. You must correct that deficiency . . . by tomorrow, when the final contest will be held, on horseback! A word of caution: today, every man must capture his own horse. Any two or more contestants seen working together will be eliminated from further competition. And now, with the great and glorious permission of the Moulay—'' He broke off, for the Moulay was not in the royal box although his wife and daughter were.

The Moulay, having heard what was planned for today, had decided against attending. He did not share with his half-Berber daughter her enthusiasm for horseflesh. As a matter of fact, he had never ridden a horse in the whole of his life and had no intention of ever doing so. So, in lieu of joining his hated, dreaded Berber relatives now crowding the first tier of the amphitheater, he chose to amuse himself in his own way in al Djem's other arena: with ants, sun, wet leather strips, poles, tongs, and the remaining losers from yesterday.

Sheikh ibn Kader was only momentarily at a loss for words, then continued smoothly on, ''With the permission of the Moulay Hassan's beloved daughter, the Amira Aisha.'' At her nod, he gave his orders. ''For each man, a length of rope; for every other man, a horse. A stallion from the stables of Aisha bint Hassan herself. The blessings of Allah be on him who competes. Throw in the ropes and open the—''

He was interrupted by Ali with a message from an agitated Amira. Fionn, she had reminded Ali, was to be given his advantage. ''What? Ah, yes. Of course. As the Amira commands. The blond giant shall choose first. Only when he has made his choice and seen it captured will the others compete. Throw in the ropes. Open the gates!''

Even as a mass of ropes was tossed into the arena to be caught or fought over by the contestants, gates at the far end of the arena sprang open, and in thundered nearly a score of the most beautiful horses de Wynter had ever seen.

Black, bay, brown, chestnut, dun, sorrel, and one gray so light he looked white. All solid-colored animals. Not a skewbald, piebald, or dapple, not even a roan, among them. They entered, heads held high, nostrils flaring, manes and tails flowing. Charging, driving, whirling . . . biting, rearing, kicking. They were all in beautiful, powerful constant motion. Straight into the center of the amphitheater these two- and three-year-olds streamed. Then, sensing the danger at the far end, as one, they wheeled left and right, heading back whence they had come. Only then was the striped one seen. Its neck and head were banded in brown and off-white, the stripes gradually fading out to a murky solid brown just behind the shoulders. Its legs and belly were white, its mane roached, its tail tufted.

"That's no horse," Carlby exclaimed. "For God's sake, it's a zebra. Stay clear of it."

Fionn, who picked first, laughed humorlessly. "No chance of my choosing it, it's too small. God, give me a big horse, a tall horse, not one of these small things."

"Don't underestimate them," Carlby cautioned him. "They can carry heavier burdens than many war-horses and turn like a cat."

"I hope you're right. Since you seem to know them so well, suppose you pick me one?" But it was de Wynter who spotted the brown, a mousey-colored horse among his more brilliant brothers. The horse had substance, a good barrel chest and legs in proportion to support it all. "That one, the quiet one to the right. He'll give you the steadiness you need without being fearful. Take him, Fionn."

The Amira, smiling behind her veil, nodded approval of Fionn's choice. She too would have selected the brown for him. This was her own private test of him. If he had chosen badly, she would have had to seriously reconsider him as her own choice.

While the silent ones tried to catch the brown, John the Rob, whose experience with horses had been confined to dodging their hooves in the unpaved lanes of London, quizzed Angus and Ogilvy. "What do I look for? What do I do?"

The two Scots looked at each other, considering, then tried to compress a lifetime of horsemanship into a few moments of advice:

Angus: With these thin-skinned ones, you can almost read the expressions on their faces.

Ogilvy: Watch the ears. Pressed back, he's going to fight.

Angus: And the neck. Arched, it's threatening; outstretched, about to attack.

540

Ogilvy: Cocking a foot, that means a kick is coming.

Angus: So does hunching the back.

Ogilvy: The horse that retreats from you, even though pawing the air and snorting, he's submitting.

Ogilvy: Don't be too afraid of the horse that kicks with his hind feet. He looks more ferocious than he is. Besides, such kicking puts his head down low, in a good position to be snared.

Angus: Watch out for the one that fights with his forelegs. He's vicious. And the head will be too high to rope.

Ogilvy: Beware of those teeth. They can break a man's bone as easy as snapping a stalk of hay in two.

Angus: Let one of those stallions get his teeth on a small man like you, and he'll throw you across the arena.

The two had said all they had to say, so they stopped talking.

But John the Rob was more desperate than before. "Is that all you can say?"

"What else would you know?" Angus asked, looking at Ogilvy with some surprise. He thought the two had been very thorough.

"For starters, how the hell do I get close enough to rope one of those beasts?"

"They're not beasts, they're horses," Ogilvy protested.

"Horses to you, man-eating monsters to me."

Angus was more helpful. "Can you make a running noose?"

"Of course."

"And throw it?" asked Ogilvy.

"Throw it? No, don't think I can."

Angus tsked for a moment. "I suggest you learn. Unless *you* want to be thrown."

Ogilvy considered a moment then delivered his opinion: "It's clear you cannot catch a horse on your own."

"I know that," John the Rob said, his voice rising almost to a scream, "I know that. Tell me something I don't know."

De Wynter's quiet voice forestalled the Highlanders' reply. "If you can't do it yourself, use someone else to do it for you."

"What?"

"Yes, what do you mean?" Gilliver echoed.

"You, too, Henry. Listen carefully. The rest of us can't help either of you through outright teamwork. Whatever we do, we're suspect. We're too well known as a team. But you can take advantage of another's tactics. Say somebody throws a rope at a horse's head. The horse sees it coming and dodges or slips it. In that instant while the horse avoids one rope, he's vulnerable to another."

"What would you have us do? Follow one of you about?"

"Not one of *us*. The best and strongest horseman you can find. Let him make the first move; you catch the horse with the second. I wouldn't be surprised if you two have yourself mounts before the rest of us do."

Angus and Ogilvy turned and gave their leader a stare that was a mixture of surprise, shock, and disbelief. Highlanders have a certain look that without words questions your ancestry, your sanity, and your veracity.

De Wynter laughed. "Prove me wrong, I dare you."

Carlby rubbed his chin and said quietly, "Don't worry about them or John the Rob. He's a survivor like the rest of us. Worry about Gilliver instead."

"I do. Constantly."

"Wouldn't he be better off staying close to one or two of us—not teaming up exactly, but staying nearby. In the melee, we should be able to slip him the rope of a captured horse. He need only hang on until the horse tires."

"You might be right. Especially if I tire the horse out first, before switching with Gilliver."

"'I'?"

"Henry's my responsibility. Always has been. If anyone is going to risk his life, I am the one."

"I believe you'd get seven dissenting votes on that."

"It's my decision. There will be no voting on it."

Carlby said no more, but personally vowed if he were first to get a horse under control, he'd head for Henry himself, exchange ropes and keep going. After all, Gilliver was a religious like himself.

Once the brown was separated out for Fionn and the two taken from the crowded arena to work in private, the remaining stallions banded together, obeying the herd instinct, to face their adversaries. Occasionally one would rear up on hind legs, front hooves knifing the air, and give voice to great neighs of defiance. Then up and down the line there would come answers in whinnies of high-pitched

542

excitement. The zebra, shunned by his hot-blooded brothers, replied with a barking high-pitched cry, "Quag-ga! Quag-ga!" which set the horses to shying and snorting.

Eventually, when the men kept their distance, the horses quieted down and began trying to establish dominance among themselves, neighing, posturing, and prancing, their ears pricked forward, their nostrils flaring. One dun finally defeated. That started the procession. When a stallion was forced to give way by a bigger or older or fiercer male, he would charge to the dung pile, blow loudly and exaggeratedly, then cover the previously made droppings with his own dung. One after another the stallions marked, until there was no question that the pale gray with the silver mane and tail was the dominant stud in this group. The dun, in the meantime, the first to cry quits, was left in peace and actually began sniffing the sand looking for forage.

"That's the one," said Angus.

"Aye," agreed Ogilvy. "John the Rob, if you're ever going to catch a horse, that's the one that will stick his head in the noose for you."

John the Rob stared intently at the yellowish horse, trying desperately to memorize him, but all horses looked the same to this beggar chief, except the striped one, of course.

The Berbers in the crowd could have watched the stallions for hours on end. Already they were engrossed in discussing their fine points. However, the rest of the crowd was growing restless. At a signal from the sheikh, slaves bearing clay vessels slopping over with yellow liquid came running from four directions at once and headed straight for the grouped stallions. The horses turned and pawed at the gates, trying to escape. Then turned to face their attackers. In their momentary confusion, the slaves were upon them, dousing the stallions with the liquid and thoroughly wetting down the dirt in a huge semicircle about them. Their amphoras empty, the slaves scattered, dropping their vessels, scurrying for their lives. Two did not make it, going down under the mighty kicks of stallions suddenly made frenzied.

It took de Wynter but a moment to figure out what was going on. "Oh, no," he said to no one in particular. "That's urine from mares in heat!"

"My God, no," Ogilvy muttered. "Now there won't be any way to calm them down, even after we catch them."

Even as he spoke, the stallions were bearing out his words. None of their kind wants another stallion around when that smell is in the air. The pecking order forgotten, they turned on each other, kicking, biting, and head-butting in a frenzied show that few but the Berbers in the audience had ever seen before. The judges let it go on for a time, knowing the thrill-hungry crowd was enjoying the sight of stallion trying to mount stallion amid the kicks and squeals of the rest. The spectators soon were exchanging remarks about the size and length of the rampant staffs that flashed in the melee.

Suddenly, the Gate of Death flew open and in came one mare, a round of sharp cracks on the flanks driving her forward at full gallop. As suddenly, she locked her forelegs and skidded to an abrupt stop, facing the angry and excited group of stallions.

"I'm afraid that poor thing is in for a bit of a rough go," Carlby said to de Wynter.

"They'll kill her," de Wynter replied. Ogilvy and Angus grunted their agreement.

The stallions spotted the mare and took off after her. She, in turn, with the screech–squeal of the virgin, headed back toward the gate, only to find it closed. On she went seeking to escape, fear making her fly like the very wind. The stallions gained with every stride. Catching up to her before she had circled the arena once, they fought, still in full-stride, to sniff her pungent genital area. As some of the excited stallions passed her and crowded her, she was slowly forced toward the wall. Finally she stood her ground, warning with shrill screech and lashing tail, arched neck and hunched rump, "Stay back or I kick." Ignored, she launched kick after kick with her hind legs. Like the virgin that she was, she defended herself as nature had intended. In truth she did not know what her body was telling her it wanted, and she saw the stallions only as enemies out to harm her.

If one of the frenzied stallions got in position to hold her down with his head, and thus avoid the flying hooves, several others would drive him away, trying to get in position themselves. Now and then a stallion would scream and limp away from the melee, only to return, the pain overcome by his mad desire. The action made its way

544

around the arena in fits and bursts, the mare breaking out and running whenever she could. The crowd thus got a close-up view at one point or another, and showed its enjoyment of the wild scene by standing and shouting.

In the royal box, Aisha found herself on her feet, screaming, "No, stop it. Don't let them do it! Please, for the love of Allah, help her! Somebody help her."

But her words were drowned out by the masculine roar of "Take her, take her, go get her, mount her."

It was only a matter of time. When enough heads and necks were weighing her hind quarters down from either side, the gray stallion threw his forelegs over her rump and, with rear legs prancing to get him in position, rammed forward several times before seating himself fully in that sought-after tunnel. The mare screamed and kicked, but the gray sunk his teeth savagely into her neck, holding her fast. The stud's nostrils flared, his mouth relaxed, his tail twitched with each pulse of his penis. Then, he was still resting peacefully on his precarious perch despite thundering kicks and bites from his fellow rapists. Finished, spent, he slid from her back and, wrinkling his muzzle, urinated copiously then trotted off.

His replacement had just as much difficulty, suffering the blows that reigned on him as though he felt them not. A third, a fourth, and a fifth stallion had his way with her, she now standing with legs set wide, her head lowered, and her tail swishing high over her back. As others jostled for position, the Gates of Death opened, and in rode half a dozen mounted camelmen. Riding directly into the melee, one roped the mare's head, while the others scattered the stallions as best they could. Dragging and beating the mare, they were out of the gate before the stallions realized they were losing their prize.

The shouting, stomping crowd showed its appreciation with standing ovations that soared and ebbed, only to be renewed by the excited and titillated viewers who wanted more of the same. Aisha, white-faced and dry-eyed beneath her veil, had long since ceased screaming and resumed her seat.

"I prefer to think you, of all people, did not arrange that exhibition," Ramlah said quietly.

"Men. How I despise them," was Aisha's tight-lipped response.

Ramlah, realizing she would get no coherent answer from Aisha, turned and summoned Ali to her side. "And what do you know of this?"

The Commander of *al Ikwan* shook his head. "Not much, revered daughter of my father. I gather it was he, our father, Sheikh Zaid ben Sadr who decided it would please the crowd."

"And the mare?" Aisha interrupted, still staring unseeingly into the arena. "What of her?"

"The mare?" He was bewildered. "If she did not take, we shall have her serviced again in her next season."

"Think you she will stand more docilely the next time?" Aisha asked bitterly.

"Of course. What else? As you should know from your times with the tribes, once a mare is mounted she only puts up a token fight thereafter."

Ramlah decided it was time to intervene. "Ali, the sheikh our father was indeed right. The crowd was pleased."

"It looks as though their pleasure will result in some empty seats. At least for the next hour or so," Aisha said scornfully, pointing out to her mother the number of men hurrying from the arena.

"Really, Aisha, you know not where they go," her mother scolded.

"One need not be a sorcerer to guess."

The contestants were now lined up across one end of the arena, and at the sound of the ram horns, they charged toward the still fighting, biting, and kicking group of stallions, their short ropes clutched tightly in their hands.

Gilliver tried hard to stay a few paces behind de Wynter. The others went their separate ways, or so they hoped it would appear to the judges. Meanwhile, the stallions bolted in unison for the far end, no longer fighting among themselves, thinking only of escaping from the fast advancing men, who turned and pursued their prey.

The fleetest men caught up to the milling stallions just as they encountered the far wall. Momentarily they stood their ground; then a group broke, spreading to each side, running through and over the defenseless men on the perimeters. At this the rest of the stallions broke through the ranks and bolted the full length of the arena. Turning, the men started the long run back to the other end.

"Enough of this," de Wynter shouted to Gilliver. "They can outrun us all day long. We'll have to do something different." A number of other contestants had come to the same conclusion, as, winded and gasping for breath, they stopped running and started walking.

For the next minutes, the action slowed considerably. Even the horses were glad to get a breather, but they still bolted away as soon as a man got within a few meters. Now it became a stalking game. How close could one get before the quarry wheeled away or charged right through his path? And slowly but surely, the tired men were getting closer and closer, some even attempting reckless throws of their ropes. One stallion now wore a rope around his neck, but there was no man on the other end.

Eventually, the stallions would decide to stand and fight, de Wynter knew full well. Only then did the men stand any real chance of success. But which horse would first decide to make that stand? That was the one he wanted. His horseman's eye picked out two likely ones.

Ogilvy, by luck, although he called it skill, was first to score. Wrapping the rope quickly around his waist, he threw his weight downward, only to be dragged the entire length of the amphitheater to the delight of the crowd, who found his progress funny. He found himself breathing dust and sand as his body bumped and skidded painfully along. If he could only hang on long enough, he knew, the stallion would tire and try to shake the rope by rearing, pawing, and kicking at his antagonist. Ogilvy also knew that, in the end, exhaustion would break one or the other.

Back the full length of the arena Ogilvy was dragged before he was able to regain his feet. Digging in his heels, he was alternately dragged and forced into long loping strides, clinging desperately to the short rope. Finally, the stallion decided it would rid its neck of its heavy burden only by fighting. It wheeled and, rearing up on its hind legs, lifted Ogilvy off the ground and jolted him back down hard as it tried to stomp him. But Ogilvy had fought his share of unruly horses. Unwrapping the rope from around his waist and wrapping it instead around a wrist, he kept the rope taut at all times. When the stallion reared, he moved in closer to gain the slack needed to keep from being lifted off his feet, back-pedaling quickly when those flying hooves started down and giving the rope a fierce tug often enough to let the animal know who was in command.

Inside half an hour, Ogilvy had himself a conciliatory if not docile stallion that was willing, most of the time, to stand and shake its head. Now the biggest problem was keeping his catch out of the continuing fracas going on all around the arena. Aside from a handful of other roped stallions, the remainder were still fighting back, occasionally breaking out and running for freedom.

Ogilvy had a moment to look around. With relief he saw Angus, stallion in hand . . . and further on, Gilliver holding tentatively to a rope wrapped around his waist, and on the other end an Arabian that had somewhat less heart for fighting than some of its mates. One thing he was convinced of—someone had been able to make a switch, for Gilliver was no match for one of these brutes until its spirit was broken, or at least subdued. Slowly, Ogilvy worked his stallion closer to Gilliver, hoping that he could somehow help out if Gilliver's catch got its wind and decided to make a break for it.

Then, he saw two bodies lying on the ground near the wall, where they had been dragged either by horses or silent ones. His horse shied and would not approach them. Ogilvy did not dare force him, lest the horse get away. Instead, he made a wide circle in order to see the face of the nearer corpse, one he feared he already knew.

His forehead smashed so badly that he was almost unrecognizable except to a brother, Kenneth Menzies—God rest his soul—lay crumpled in the blood and dirt of al Djem, the second of the group to fall victim to the outrageous games of Aisha of Tunisia. One glance told Ogilvy that Gilliver knew, too. "Snap out of it, Henry," he shouted above the noise. "There's nothing we can do for him. Keep your weight on that rope all the time."

Carlby, leaning against the wall of the arena, realized he was too old to outrun stallions or younger men. He had to find another way. Then something moved under his outstretched grasping hand. A piece of stone. One not wedged securely in the wall. Feverishly, he worked it loose. Just then, a rope settled over a thrashing head and snapped taut around its neck. At the other end of the rope, the huge Nuba went to his knees, putting his sizable weight into the rope. Here was Carlby's chance. Deliberately closing his mind to what he was doing, he ran toward the man. Up his hand went, high in the air it hovered, then swooped down to end in a dull thud against kinky hair and black flesh. Blood spurted from the neck as Carlby grabbed the rope from dying hands.

Four of the group desperately clung to their prizes and watched the spectacle avidly, fascinated in spite of themselves, especially since three of their number were in a race not only against horse and man but time. De Wynter, having already snared one horse for Gilliver, had found his attention attracted, as had many others, by the single gray white stud in the pack. Already the horse had taught some of his captors respect for his ways, for his small but sharp hooves were covered with blood, with more flecks of the same copiously covering his shoulders and withers. The horse was a beauty. Its head was fine, well set on the neck, its withers high and laid back, well developed, not too narrow or thin. The back was short, surprisingly so. Its loins were powerful, croup high, haunch very fine, tail high-set, and dock short. More than that, it was obviously intelligent: the horse feinted only with its rear legs, striking with its forefeet. Then as he watched, the horse slipped one rope, and another. In lieu of doing the same a third time, it deliberately lunged at his third tormentor and bit hard; one could hear the bone of the offending arm crunch. But the horse didn't let go. Instead, with a flip of its powerful neck, it tossed the man ten feet across the arena, then followed after and tried to trample him. Approached from behind by another man, it leaped into the air, kicking out with its hind feet and landing catlike almost within its footprints. De Wynter had seen war-horses do the same, but only after training, months of it. Here was a horse that, whether by instinct or reason, used a supposedly man-made maneuver to incapacitate his tormentors.

Two men were down in almost as many minutes. How many before? De Wynter wondered. How many more? Already the circle of men about the pale horse was dissipating. Many of the men had lost their appetite for this struggle and moved on to more promising ground where the horses were predictable and the competitors could do the savaging. De Wynter did not take his eyes off the horse that now stood quietly, catching its breath, its sides heaving, its nostrils flaring. But he knew the horse was not exhausted. It held its head too high, its small, pricked ears moving rapidly back and forth, sorting out those sounds that should be ignored. Its black eyes were calm, showing little white. That worried de Wynter. But he had made up his mind. This was the horse he would have.

Draping his rope about his neck, he moved sideways, circling the horse, hoping to come up on its rear and catch it unaware, but his steps in the loose sand betrayed him. Swinging its head about, the horse took its opponent's measure. Something about de Wynter disturbed the animal. Maybe it was his silver white hair . . . or the air of confidence the man exuded. Enraged, the horse quickly pivoted to face his opponent, then rumbled—a deep chesty neigh. The man did not flinch or stop, but continued forward. Suddenly uncertain, the horse took one step back. A good sign, de Wynter thought. Still the man moved forward, hands at his sides. Again the horse retreated. That was the plan. To back the horse at least partially against the wall. Again the horse retreated but not before kicking sideways at another man. De Wynter was glad; the horse was keeping his fellow competitors honest.

The tension between the two white-haired ones grew more palpable by the moment. It was the horse, once so masterful, so sure of himself, so disdainful of men, that fidgeted and shook his skin nervously. De Wynter clapped his hands sharply. The horse jumped straight-legged. With that, a rope caught his leg and tripped him up. Within seconds the horse was down, hooves flying wildly. A man's weight on his head, a hand cruelly twisting his ear, another curling his sensitive nostril—the pain was too much for him. With a squeal of hatred, the horse conceded defeat and lay still. But de Wynter's problems weren't over. He had lost his rope in the struggle. Resourceful in his desperation, he unfastened his loincloth and used it as he had done with the ostrich as a blindfold about the white's eyes, then let the horse back up on its feet. Tugging painfully on its ear with his free hand, he led the horse over to where his rope lay abandoned in the sand. Then, though it took some doing, he managed to work his toes about the rope, and, standing one-legged, the horse actually supporting his weight, he brought the rope up to where he could grab it with one hand. After that it was an easy matter to make a noseband-halter out of the rope and lead his horse back—to applause and cheers from the Berbers, especially—to where his friends waited.

John the Rob, totally unsuccessful in every attempt that he'd made, found himself near the zebra. Desperate and taking a lesson from de Wynter, he too undid his loincloth and threw it over the beast's head. But instead of calming the animal as had happened with the white, the beast went berserk. Jerking the loincloth out of John the Rob's hand, it turned and twirled and kicked in every direction at once it seemed. One of its hooves landed beneath another stallion's chin, and knocked that animal off its feet. There was a mad scramble among the nearby contestants for the fallen animal, most getting there before John the Rob. Unfazed, he simply looped his rope around the necks of his competitors. The next thing they knew, they were tied together and stumbling over one another while a small, monkey-faced man calmly walked away with a horse.

Only Cameron now was without a horse, and there were not many horses left. One by one, all but four of the horses had been roped and brought under control, though often not by the man who had originally thrown his noose about the animal's neck. Fighting had been going on almost from the beginning, but now it was rampant. Many a horse changed hands as his successive captors were overpowered, each replaced by another. Eulj Ali was no horseman, but he was a good dirty fighter. Maybe one of the best. Cameron was no match for him. A feint, some sand in the Scot's face, a kick in the groin, and when the long-legged one looked up from the sand where he lay doubled over with pain, a redhead was calmly walking off with his horse. De Wynter handed the rope of the white to the nearest man, saying, "Here, hold this." Whatever his intentions—to go to Cameron's aid or to take on Eulj Ali and get the horse back—it was too late. The ram's horn sounded. Silent ones dropped down into the arena from their stations on the first tier. Some rounded up and surrounded the walking losers. Others grasped the dead and the wounded by their heels and dragged them toward the Gate of Death. Still others leveled their lances at the group of slaves over by the wall, preventing de Wynter and the rest from coming to Cameron's rescue. The last they saw of their friend was an arm waving in the air. Whether deliberately, as signal to his friends, or by quirk of his rough treatment, no one knew. Gilliver, however, preferred to think George was waving them farewell. Fortunately for him, once all attention was on the losers, Angus and Ogilvy had each grabbed for the rope that a grieving, unthinking Gilliver dropped. The judges now, they were sure, could not complain about teamwork.

De Wynter, looking about him, suddenly realized that they had lost more than one man this day. Menzies too was missing. "How?"

"Kicked in the forehead by a horse. He went down without a sound. Never moved once." Gilliver's strained voice supplied the details. He forgot to mention, and Ogilvy chose not to say, that the horse that did it was gray white. For now they had other business at hand, and de Wynter needed that horse for the morrow.

The six men swallowed their grief and numbed their minds with work. Expert hands turned lengths of rope into crude but effective halters. Then, it was a hand up and onto the stallion's back . . . and usually as quickly down on the ground again.

Rubbing backside ruefully or gasping for the wind knocked out when landing flat on one's back, each man had no choice but to get back up onto his unruly mount. Actually, the horses were more exhausted than their riders and most capitulated after only a token battle, but not the pale gray. The struggle between it and de Wynter went on for what seemed hours. To free itself of the rider, the white reared, bucked, sidewinded, fishtailed, fell to its knees, did the capriole again, deliberately fell on its side and attempted to roll over. But though de Wynter was dislodged more than once, he remounted immediately and, biding his time, waited for the horse to rear once more. Then, the white-haired man pulled the stallion back and over, jumping clear of the horse at the last minute. Falling, not by its own design, seemed to take the fight out of the stallion. For when it struggled back up to its feet, its ears were upright, its face relaxed and void of tension or expression.

Gilliver, who had been watching while holding the reins of the Highlanders' mounts as Angus gentled one for Gilliver (Ogilvy doing the same for John the Rob), suddenly spoke up: "If white is the color of purity, then that horse is pure evil." He said it without emotion, without inflection, as if stating an obvious known fact.

De Wynter, inclined to agree, felt the hair stand up on the back of his neck, but it was too late to do aught other than live with the situation. Mounting again, he pressed the horse into a gentle walk. The pale gray went forward like a lady's hackney, as if he'd been ridden all his life. A slight squeeze of the legs and the horse broke into a slow trot. Urged faster, he moved on into a canter and then controlled gallop. De Wynter couldn't remember bestriding a smoother-going animal. Suddenly, the animal swerved and tried to brush his rider against the wall. But the man was too alert. He threw himself over to the side, pulling his leg out of danger. When he regained his seat atop the horse, the gray was once again going smoothly along. Only one twitching ear revealed any sign of nervousness.

De Wynter smiled grimly. It was going to be that kind of a battle, was it? Then the gray had better learn it had met its match. Kicking the horse savagely, he put it at a gallop and headed straight for a wall. Taking advantage of the animal's poor depth perception, he forced it on long after the beast would have swerved away. Only at the last minute did de Wynter pull the horse's head about, letting its own momentum carry its haunches bruisingly into the wall. There, he thought, letting the horse move at its own pace, discover that two can play at your game. That will give you something to think about.

"Ma'dan!" A compelling voice interrupted his thoughts. *"Ma'dan. Mutajasur!"* A man in caftan and headdress sat atop the wall of the arena and leaned over.

De Wynter bowed his thanks for the Berber's kind words.

The man smiled at this *mujamala* by a slave. "You speak Sabir?" the desert chieftain asked, the lingua franca uncomfortable on his tongue.

"That or Arabic, whichever you prefer," de Wynter replied courteously. There was something about the hawk-faced man with his gray-tinged beard that inspired the same respect one accorded royalty.

"Good. We will speak in Arabic. The horse—you fought it bravely. What do you think of it?"

De Wynter looked down at the animal, its head cocked and slyly watching his every move. "A beauty in all but manners."

The sheikh laughed silently, without showing teeth. "Agreed. But the silver-haired one may have met its match. We shall talk again. For now, I look forward to the contest tomorrow. May Allah look upon you with special favor." Even as de Wynter was replying in kind, the desert man rose and turned away in a swirl of robes, others similarly dressed, rushing to join him.

If de Wynter had been surprised by this encounter, he was astonished by the rest of the afternoon. As he schooled the horse, many were the Berbers who abandoned their seats in the gallery and came down to the first tier to hail him, compliment him, give him advice, ask his advice—all pertaining to the horse he was working. Some of the onlookers, drawn by their almost fanatical interest in the Arabian, actually leaped lightly down onto the sand to look the horses over more closely.

Although much of the attention centered about de Wynter, none of the others failed to get his share, for every horse represented a stable known for the purity of its lines and the beauty of its get.

CHAPTER 37

A very subdued Fionn returned to the cell beneath the arena. So dejected was he that he didn't notice the gloom within the cell, nor the absence of two of his companions. In fact, he never looked at the others, instead going straight to his pallet and throwing himself down upon it, burying his face within the crook of his arm.

DeWynter exchanged glances with the rest of the men, then went over and squatted down beside the son of his long-time friend. "Fionn, what's wrong? The work with the horse, did it go badly?"

"No," came the muffled reply. "It went just fine."

"Then what's wrong?"

There was no reply for a long moment; then, Fionn heaved over onto his back and looked straight up into de Wynter's concerned blue eyes. "Jamie, I mean, milord—" Fionn broke off in confusion.

"No, call me Jamie."

"Jamie," Fionn whispered, "do you remember the head they had on the pole? On the second day?"

"Yes, all too well."

"I saw dozens more like it. Outside the arena. Rotting arms and legs, too, lying in heaps outside one of the gates. The smell makes you sick. And Jamie, some of the bones had been gnawed on."

De Wynter put a comforting hand on his friend's shoulder. "Don't think about it. The dead are dead. They have no care for what happens to their bones."

Fionn ignored de Wynter's words, gripping de Wynter's arm

tightly. "That's the point. I don't think they were all dead first."
Horror permeated his voice, showed in his eyes. "And, Jamie, I
recognized one of those heads."

"Drummond's?" de Wynter asked.

"No. He's probably there, too. But the one I saw had its forehead
smashed in. I think—I swear I knew that face."

De Wynter sighed, grimacing in pain. "Yes, it was Kenneth.
They tell me he died instantly. Probably, he didn't feel a thing."

Fionn said nothing, merely closing his eyes. De Wynter couldn't
tell whether his words gave the boy any relief. Many times he had to
remind himself that Fionn was so many years younger than the rest.
His vast height was deceiving. Now it was de Wynter's turn to bring
up a difficult, unpleasant subject, but he had to know. "Fionn, think
back. The heads up there. Did you recognize another one?"

Fionn searched his memory and shook his head. Then, the
meaning behind the question struck home. "Who?" But de Wynter
didn't have to answer. Fionn's searching glance had already discovered
the missing face. "Cameron?"

De Wynter only nodded.

"Dead?" Fionn almost sounded hopeful.

"We don't know. We hope so."

"Jamie, tell me, do you think we'll survive this?"

The others could not avoid overhearing, the cell was so small, the
room was so quiet. In spite of themselves, they turned toward de
Wynter and Fionn, as if by staring at the two, they would hear
better.

Normally, de Wynter would have weighed his words carefully,
considering all positive and potentially negative reactions. But this
time, he spoke with his gut, not his head: "Yes, Fionn. We'll
survive. I can't tell you why or how I know. I have no logical
reasons for saying so. But I know it. Tomorrow night, we'll be out
of this cell and on our way, believe me. As sure as I am sitting here,
I know this is the last night we'll spend like this."

Fionn did believe him. He smiled tremulously. Then, realizing he
had de Wynter's arm still tightly in his grasp, he grew confused.
Releasing the arm, he would have apologized, but de Wynter
wouldn't hear of it. As he had just said, tonight was their last night
in the cell. He, for one, wasn't going to spend it despondently.

Tomorrow was the last day of the games. Five days had they survived, against all odds. One more day and freedom!

Carlby, as if reading his mind, smiled and asked softly, "What are you going to do when Ali sets you free?"

"Can't you guess? Head for the nearest boat and back to England I go."

"And the order? What of your vows to the order?"

"Carlby, be reasonable. You know my vow, all of our vows were made under duress. Would you really hold us to them?"

Carlby didn't answer directly. "You didn't get your men out of the Tower, the order did. Those vows saved all of your lives. Don't you think you owe the Hospitalers something?"

De Wynter sighed. "Maybe so, but I'm tired of being obligated to others." At Carlby's disbelieving glance, de Wynter tried to explain. "You don't understand, John. I'm in love with an English lady. And she with me. That was a crime for which my friends and I were arrested and sent to the Tower. Should I have to pay for the rest of my life because I love the same woman the king does?"

"Anne Boleyn?"

De Wynter nodded.

Carlby rubbed his chin. "I don't know the answer to that, Jamie. I do know that Malta is the last bastion of Christianity, a haven against the barbarity of the Moslems whose cruelty we of all people know so well."

"Tell me about Malta," Gilliver said. Carlby acquiesced quickly, as if as glad as de Wynter to end that conversation. Soon, urged on by Gilliver's real interest and enthusiasm, Carlby forgot all else but his description with love-blinded eyes of an essentially barren island.

While those two pursued this mutually engrossing subject, the thoughts of the rest ranged far afield. Angus and Ogilvy argued about a new formula for the Scotch whiskey they planned to brew back in the hills. Fionn reviewed the tales he'd have to tell to his family. He could imagine the admiring looks Nelly and Devorguilla would lavish on him . . . and the envious ones Dugan and Derry couldn't resist. Mostly, though, he savored the thought of Seamus putting an arm about his shoulders and saying, "Well done, son. You brought the earl home. I couldn't have done better myself."

In de Wynter's thoughts, Anne Boleyn was all. Slowly, exquisitely, he undressed her . . . and kissed her . . . and caressed her . . . and knew her. When he did, she confessed her love for him, and begged to be his wife.

It wasn't a new daydream. He had savored every moment of it many times. Of course, always it ended the same way—with an excruciating ache in his loins and an erection that refused to subside.

Aisha, too, was thinking of the future. But not with anticipation or arousal. Nor was she to be left alone with her thoughts much longer. Aisha and her mother had spent two hours here at the baths, and now, their bodies soaked and oiled, their hair cleaned and plaited, their makeup applied and dried with an expert hand, they were ready to be dressed. Almost reverently the *asiras* came forward, carrying the garments upon their outstretched arms. Weeks, nay, months had seamstresses toiled over these costumes, embroidering and re-embroidering in spun-gold thread on the finest fabrics ever to be sold in a souk in Tunis. Only one night would they be worn—for the traditional feast of the relatives—and then, tomorrow, seamstresses would start in again, picking out each strand of gold thread for future use. The jewels, too, would be saved. The fabric itself put aside to be burnt the first morning of her married life. Supporting themselves by leaning on two *asiras*, each woman stepped into a pair of long, full drawers. Ramlah's were of thin, rose-colored damask brocaded with flowers and reaching down to her ankle. Aisha's were white but striped with thousands of minute chain-stitches of gold, and they were tucked into high white boots of the softest kid, absolutely plain except for their solid gold heels and soles. The queen's slippers were more modest, of red leather, gold bells on the toes. Over their heads, the *asiras* carefully slipped smocks of fine white silk gauze, edged with gold embroidery and closed at the neck with jewels as large as hen's eggs. Ramlah's was a ruby; Aisha's a tawny diamond close in color to the hair that an *asira* carefully lifted free of the smock and allowed to hang in one thick fall down the center of the amira's back. So thin were both smock and drawers that they veiled little and concealed nothing. Over these went still another garment.

The queen chose a sleeveless full-length waistcoat, form-fitting and fastened at the waist with a pair of rubies made into a buckle. The skirts of the coat were so long, trailing three feet behind her, that two young blackamoors waited outside to hold the coattails from dragging. Aisha found such a coat too cumbersome, and so she chose an equally form-fitting robe that reached just to the top of her boots and fastened up the front, from hem to neck, with a procession of gold-set diamond solitaires. Over this went her girdle, about four fingers wide and so thickly embroidered with gold thread and diamonds that the fabric could not be seen. Within it, she concealed the small throwing knife she kept with her always; as part of her parure, she also carried a bejeweled curved dagger. Ramlah's hair, like Aisha's, was long, but she wore hers loosely plaited, with a string of pearls woven through the strands. Aisha's mane was left unfastened, confined only by a small cap of rich velvet, which she wore at an angle and held in place with a circlet of tawny diamonds about her forehead.

Ramlah, looking at her child, caught her breath—the girl was a glittering vision in white and gold. "Your grandfather will be proud of you!"

"And my father, will he be there, too?"

"You know better. Not once since my wedding morn have my father and your father met. Be glad he won't be there. Tonight, you will be a Berber bride, not an Arab one confined to spend her night within the harem listening to the festivities through the tent hangings," Ramlah said, sipping from the petite coffee cup Zainab served her.

"At least there's *one* thing I can thank him for," Aisha said, refusing the proffered cup.

Ramlah rebuked her sharply. "There are *many* things you can thank your father for. To begin with for not exposing you on a mountain when an infant—as he had the right. Instead, he made you his heir."

"He had no other, remember? He butchered every other possible one."

Ramlah ignored her daughter's rejoinder. "He allowed you to be educated at the 'Prince's School—'"

"The graybeards were in need of someone to teach."

"And to let you visit the tents and cities of your grandfather each summer—"

"He was glad to get me out of the city."

"He could have married you off to Barbarossa or some other man of his choice."

"Never. I am a princess. I should have the same right to name my husband as did Marimah, daughter of Suleiman. She named hers. And he wed her not of his free will. Suleiman simply called him to the Sublime Porte one day and informed him that he was to marry the princess the following day, but that he must divorce his other wives first."

"You sound holier than she," Ramlah said, growing irritated with her daughter. "Is what you are doing so different? Did you not make men divorce their wives—"

"They didn't have to, they could have left. No one forced them to stay and compete."

"And what of the slaves?" Ramlah asked.

Aisha couldn't meet her mother's eyes, but she tried to bluff her way out. "They, too, were given a choice—"

"Indeed? Die or compete. What choice is that?"

"It was Ali's idea—"

"Don't blame that on your kinsman. He loves you, and you know it. He sought only to find you a husband worthy of what he *thinks* you are."

There was a long silence as Aisha paced the floor, then spoke, not looking at her mother. Her voice was quiet and questioning. "Am I truly not worthy, Mother? Am I less than he thinks I—"

She never finished. Ramlah caught her child up in an embrace that said more than words what a treasure she thought her daughter was. Then, brushing a tear carefully from her daughter's face without disturbing the makeup, as Aisha did the same for her, Ramlah giggled. Girlishly. Aisha looked surprised.

"I was thinking. If your father hadn't killed all those men, you would have had a proper wedding ritual like a proper Arab girl. Instead of taking your ease up there in the royal box and watching the games these five days past, you would have spent them underground."

"Underground? You mean, buried alive."

"Not quite. The proper Arab girl, just before her wedding, spends at least a week in a bridal cave."

"What on earth for?"

560

"To get the right unearthly paleness, a desirable state of complexion for a young girl. It shows she has grown up protected. Your cheeks, my dear"—and Ramlah tweaked one gently—"are much too golden and healthy-looking. Be glad you're part Berber."

"Mother, do you ever regret marrying the Moulay?"

"No. You made that worthwhile."

"Didn't you ever wish I were a boy?"

Ramlah laughed. "You should have seen the steps I took to make sure no boy was born. However, at times like this, I could wish I had had a son also."

"Why?" Aisha signaled Zainab to refill Ramlah's coffee cup and bring her one, too.

"To become a proper Arab mother-in-law to a proper Arab daughter-in-law."

Aisha laughed. Ramlah proper? Impossible.

"You laugh. I resent that. I would make an excellent mother-in-law to some docile Arab girl."

"Really? Tell me more." Aisha was in no hurry to get to this feast of relatives. Let Ramlah talk instead.

"Well, to begin with, once my son reached marriageable age, I would cast about among my proper Arab friends for suitable candidates for my son. I would even search the harems. And when I found just the right one, I would describe her to my husband, who would investigate the child's family as well.

"Now, if all seemed satisfactory, I would arrange for a party to be held at the best public bathhouse I could afford—"

"Why not the royal baths?"

"You're right. We'll hold the party there."

"And why are you holding this party?"

"To inspect the child in the altogether, to make sure she has no physical defects to pass on to my grandchildren."

"Of course, I should have realized. So, you hold a party, what then?"

"You get ahead of yourself. First, I must prepare for that party.

"The cooks of both families will be busy for several days before the bath party. And both families will be readying the grandest fashions we can assemble. Eventually, the great day comes. The girl wears her finest dress and arrives at the bath accompanied by her

561

mother and all the women of her house and her servants. The presence of servants denotes wealth and eligibility, so many are on hand. I will be properly impressed.

"Compliments abound. Food and drinks are served, and I attempt to draw information from the nominee. I probe her character. Question her tastes. Test her intelligence. When I am satisfied I have found out all I can, I suggest that she might like to take a bath. Naturally, she disrobes under my watchful eye. Then, she is wrapped in towels and escorted into the interior of the bath. Here the towels are removed, her hair unloosened—I check its length—and she seats herself on the marble floor, where her servants wash her head and body, liberally applying soap and washing off the suds with basins of water.

"During all this time, I'll stay close at hand. If any facet of the nominee's body is flawed, including her teeth, her breasts, or her feet, I want to be sure to spot it so I can report dutifully to my husband.

"Before leaving the baths, all of us dye our nails and palms with henna, as was done for you, my dear. To continue, the festivities move to a cooling room where the banquet is held. I seat the guests on a rug in a circle around a low table on which, one after the other, the serving dishes are placed. I even supply a long, continuous napkin of the finest linen for the laps of everyone in the circle. The napkin in common signifies unity and friendship."

"Will we have that tonight?" Aisha asked, almost envious of this imaginary girl Ramlah was describing.

"Of course not. This is a Berber feast. Now where was I? Oh, yes. The girl gets to taste each dish first, the others eagerly dipping their henna-dyed hands into the food immediately thereafter. For perhaps another three hours the party proceeds, before everyone parts with promises to soon renew the festivities. The future mother-in-law—that's me—then dashes home to report to an eager husband.

"If all is well, I contact the girl's mother within two days and suggest the marriage. No answer is given immediately. The girl's father must be consulted. Two days later, the girl's mother comes to visit me with her answer, which, if affirmative, paves the way for actual wedding plans." Ramlah smiled at the picture she'd painted in her own mind, then turned to Aisha. "Well, what do you think?"

"It sounds like fun." Now it was Aisha's turn to hug her mother. "And I agree, I think you'd make a truly proper Arab mother-in-law."

"Do you think so?"

"I know so!" Aisha assured her mother.

"Tell Ali ben Zaid that in case he ever decides to marry properly, I'll act as his mother."

"I'm sure he'd be delighted."

"I'm not. But enough of that. What I am is a Berber mother. Mother of the most beautiful daughter in the world. Tonight, our Berber relatives expect us. Let's not keep them waiting any longer, shall we?" Aisha shook her head. Then the two women left the bathhouse and entered their litters to be borne to the tent of Aisha's grandfather.

The man who came out to meet their litters was the selfsame desert chieftain who had spoken to de Wynter earlier that day: Sheikh Zaid ben Sadr. Lovingly, this fierce-looking man greeted the two women: "My tent is your tent."

"And mine yours," Ramlah said.

He then led them into the tent, across thick carpets to low divans, piled high with cushions, brass trays arranged before them upon carved stands. Once the guests were seated, introductions were made ceremonially, although Ramlah and Aisha had known these men all of their lives. Then, the first servers rushed in carrying hooded wicker baskets to keep the soup hot. Following the soup, which was drunk from handleless cups, came a pastry of eggs and chicken. Each pastry arrived on its own large dish and was predivided into five or six portions—the sugar mounded in the center was to be sprinkled at the diner's discretion upon his portion. Pigeons stuffed with pistachios and rice came next from more covered baskets . . . and chickens stuffed with two kinds of nuts . . . and, as they were Berbers, a whole roasted lamb. Crisp on the outside, juicy within. No feast would be complete without couscous, but Ramlah, as hostess, served it near last so that the guests might feast on the delicacies first. After that came the sweets! Among them a confection of ground almonds, dates, and pistachio nuts, dribbled with oil, shaped into balls and dusted with pounded sugar. Within one of them was hidden one whole almond. He who got that, by tradition, would give the next wedding feast for relatives.

Finally came the hot and cold: ices to refresh the palate . . . thick, black coffee and sweetened syrupy tea to refresh the mind. Now Ramlah basked in the compliments of her male relatives on the quality of the house she ran, the foods she presented. Although such compliments were traditional, she knew from the way her guests ate and ate, licking fingers to get the last drop, that her cooks had done her proud. As well they might, for they had been cooking for over a week.

While they waited for the entertainment to begin, Ramlah, her daughter, and the sheikh talked. Actually, the sheikh talked and Ramlah responded.

"My daughter, let me compliment you on your daughter; she will be a lovely bride."

"My father, she wishes only to bring honor on her house."

"My daughter, let me compliment your daughter on the horses of her breeding."

"My father, she wishes only to continue the bloodlines established by her house."

"My daughter, what of her house's own bloodlines? Have the games produced candidates worthy of adding to our house?"

Ramlah suspected Ali had been talking to his father. "My father, she is aware of her obligations to her own line. As to candidates, the games are not over yet."

The sheikh continued his relentless questioning. Aisha, for once, did not regret that she must keep silent unless spoken to directly and let Ramlah answer her grandfather.

At last, the sheikh spoke his mind. "Today I saw one that impressed me much . . . as he has my son. The one known as the *jamad ja'da*. I should be pleased to welcome sons of his loins into my tent."

Ramlah and Aisha exchanged glances. They had not expected the old man to state a preference so early. Particularly a preference for a man the women had not chosen. Ramlah cleared her throat. "My father?"

The sheikh held his cup out for more boiling hot coffee. "Yes, my daughter?"

"My father, there is another. One you did not see today. A giant of a man worthy of your attention."

The sheikh only harumphed, then slurped from his cup noisily, cooling the coffee as he did. Finally, he turned to his daughter and inclined his head graciously. "My daughter, I shall look for him on the morrow. I promise you that. But the silver-haired one, I am sure, is *ajmal!* If she chooses the other, so be it; I have another granddaughter. Your sister Khadija's child."

There was no more conversation. The fire-eater had arrived with his band of musicians. To the banging of metal rods on metal strips, the man stuffed candles and coals and burning twigs in his mouth. Lastly, he produced an enormous candle—a long, thick, black one that burned, when lit, with a sputtering, flaring flame. This one, too, after suitable build-up, he swallowed, but when he removed the candle, the flame had transferred to his mouth. Blowing flames, he relit the candle, then swallowed it again. Again the flame left the candle for his mouth. This time he lit handkerchiefs, dung chips, and wood splinters; the whole while the guests, especially the women lining the walls of the tent, sitting or squatting behind their menfolk, oohed and ahhed.

The fire-eater was followed by a troop of acrobats, who walked on their hands . . . on one foot and one hand . . . upside down on all fours . . . like a human wheel, spinning across the floor. Their act was cut short, however, when they built a human pyramid that fell. However, the guests clapped heartily for them, even after the fall.

After the acrobats, a young lad entered leading the old man who had told stories to Aisha the other night. The blind one leaned heavily on his staff but more so on the shoulder of the dark-haired beauty. Aisha cynically guessed from the looks he received that this lad supported his grandfather in more ways than one.

Carefully, the lad seated the old man upon a thick cushion placed upon the edge of the rug; the staff he placed across the blind man's lap. Then, he squatted behind his grandfather.

Aisha looked at her mother quizzically. Story-tellers could drag out their entertainment for hours, eating and drinking their fill at their hosts' expense. Naturally, the longer the tale, the greater the *tajziya* they received. However, Aisha consoled herself that the man had not taken overlong with his tale of the marriage of Adam and

Eve. With the very first words out of his mouth, she wished he'd embarked on the longest and most boring tale he knew:

> "Come, Aisha, fill the goblet up.
> Reach round the rosy wine,
> Think not that we will take the cup
> From any hand but thine."

To Aisha's dismay, her guests expected that she do just that. Servers were handing out goblets, others stood by with ewers, waiting for her to hand round the rosy wine. Gracefully she did what was necessary to do.

> "A draught like this 'twere vain to seek,
> No grape can such supply:
> It steals its tint from Aisha's cheek,
> Its brightness from her eye."

And this was only the beginning. All of the man's poems were addressed to Aisha. It was an age-old tradition that not only Ramlah had known, but every other woman in the room as well: to temper the poetry and make the selections to honor or tease the bride. Of course, the groom, too, at the traditional wedding would have come in for his share of fun. Tonight, he, whoever he was, received his in absentia.

> Aisha, with too successful art,
> Has spread for me love's wicked snare;
> And now, having caught my heart,
> She laughs . . . and leaves me in despair.
>
> Thus the poor sparrow pants for breath,
> Held captive by a playful she
> And while her heedless hand deals death
> The thoughtless child looks on with glee!"

Aisha had no choice but to smile, to look pleased, to playact in response to the old man's poems, which went on and on, as did her guests' teasings. After a while, her face mindlessly reflected the proper mood of joy or pride or whatever. The only thing it refused to do, while Aisha's thoughts were elsewhere, was blush.

She was thinking on her grandfather's remark, "I have another granddaughter . . ." Aisha knew the girl. Fat, fatuous, flabby Fatima, aptly named. Not an intelligent thought in her head, not a brave bone in her body. Aisha was determined that that girl would never have the *jamad ja'da*. Not if she had to marry him herself first. Aisha's eyes widened as she realized what she'd just said to herself. Then she blushed. And just in time, for the old man had launched into still another poem.

Aisha had heard enough. She needed to get to her tent and think through her strange thoughts about the *jamad ja'da*. She knew he was not the wise choice; the tractable, good-natured giant was. That one she could wind about her finger, throw him a crumb or two, and have a slave for life. The white-haired one, on the other hand, would be a challenge she was not sure she wanted to accept . . . nor one she would win! Why, then, she asked herself, did she even consider it. Was she mad and would this feast never end?

Fortunately for her, the grandfather, too, wished the evening over; the poetry had awakened fires within him that had not been stoked in weeks. Hot-blooded Ramlah was not averse to leaving early, before her passions awoke too far and couldn't be controlled the usual way. Thus the feast of the relatives ended quite early, as such feasts go.

CHAPTER 38

24 January A.D. 1533/
16 Jamad II A.H. 939.
The sixth day

Day dawned magnificently. Rays of light misted the African night. The desert clothed itself with a rose red hue. The tents in the city loomed larger and yet softer than ever. Then, suddenly, the sun seemed to surge forth into the sky. But the competitors in the city had no eyes for the sky. Nor did they taste the food they ate, nor notice the macabre remains they passed by. Today all was right with the world. Today was the sixth day. The last day. And for those twenty men the adrenaline flowed, for today the prize was in reach.

Fear may be a powerful incentive, reward even stronger, but the two pale when compared with freedom. So it was that the sadness of the seven slaves was replaced by determination. To survive this final day. To win their freedom. They never dreamed such a freedom was as illusory as the mirages that people the desert. Only the thought of freedom had brought them this far. They needed it as a reluctant horse needs spurs—to keep them going.

The nineteen contestants who had survived yesterday's wild stallion event, plus Fionn, gathered for one last time in the room of the gladiators. Twenty out of 180. The rest? Known or presumed dead, courtesy of the Moulay Hassan.

Looking about them, the seven slaves had to admit the cream had risen to the top; the best had made it to the end. All except Eulj Ali, of course, who was either the luckiest man there or had friends in high places. Everyone avoided looking at the poor man who'd roped the zebra. If yesterday afternoon had been frustrating for those working with the stallions, for him it had been futile. He knew, as the others did, that in capturing the zebra, he had merely postponed the inevitable. However, the others on entering the arena suddenly had qualms as to their accomplishments the previous day. After a night of rest, would the stallions be wild again? Another thing: the stallions had been removed en masse. If they returned the same way, how would they match up horse and owner? Or would they? Perhaps all of the hard work in each breaking his own animal might benefit someone else. The corollary, of course, was that each might get a horse that someone else had only half-broken, or worse. Questions tumbled through the minds of all. Only time, or the judges, could answer them. Thus, when the judges entered the arena, the contestants crowded as close as possible in their eagerness to find out what was happening.

Ibn al-Hudaij, the head judge, spoke first. "My congratulations to all of you who have qualified for the events of the final day. The blessings of Allah have indeed been with you. May His face continue to shine upon you, for by the end of today, one of you shall be named consort to the Amira Aisha, daughter of the *rafi as'sa'n*, the Moulay Hassan—may Allah look upon him with favor.

"As for today's competition. You will be participating in an adult to-the-death version of an ancient game that children play known as 'Follow the first.' We call ours, for lack of a better name, simply 'Horse.' The rules are fairly simple, but listen closely. You horsemen are the attackers, you will be given targets. Men on foot. From these targets, each man will select one. The first man to ride forth *names* a feat which he will then perform on his target. In turn, every other rider must follow the first and do the same with his living target. Those who fail to do so to the satisfaction of the judges, within the very brief time of this sandglass, will forfeit one of these three rings that will be given to each of you before the game officially begins. Lose all three rings and you lose your horse, becoming no more than a living target such as these.'' The judge pointed. As one, the men turned to see nineteen men enter the arena from the Gate of Death through which all had exited the arena before.

The six slaves would have looked for Cameron but the judge was continuing. "A target may become a horseman by simply avoiding attackers three times, thus winning three rings. For the first five rounds, the feat selected by the leader to perform on his target may be anything at all short of death. Any rider who kills a target during these first five rounds forfeits his horse and takes the dead man's place. After the fifth round, there will be no restrictions on the feat that you as leader or first rider may select.

"The first leader will be selected by the Amira. He will remain the leader until he fails to properly execute the feat he has named. He then loses his horse, and becomes a target but one with two rings.

"The other riders will perform in order according to a drawing of names by the judges, moving up one place in the order each time a leader is replaced.

"The leaders must select feats that do bodily harm to the targets. All riders will be given a short sword and a dagger. Any use of these weapons other than against the human targets will result in the forfeiting of the horses of those riders involved, and the riders will become targets.

"As your turn comes up, each rider must call out the number of his intended target. Each man on foot wears, as you may have noticed, a disc around his neck, bearing a number. When a target's number is called, he must, on penalty of immediate death, move into the huge circle drawn in salt in the middle of the arena. The target must remain somewhere, anywhere, within that circle during the draining of the sandglass.

"The games will begin upon the arrival of his excellency, the Moulay. The last man on horse wins. Use this thinking time wisely, and the blessings of Allah be on him who competes."

Then, they settled back to wait. Aisha was furious with the Moulay. How could he, on this day of all days, make all wait. "He's being spiteful toward your grandfather, my dear. Ignore him," her mother advised.

"I can't. We can't start the games without him."

"Then, Ali ben Zaid, I suggest you take a message to him. Come close while I tell you exactly what to say," Ramlah said, then whispered something in Ali's ear. Meanwhile the six slaves gathered together away from the rest of the contestants. "Did you see him? Is he there? Did anyone see him?" Gilliver asked.

Fionn nodded. "He's there all right."

"Well, that's a relief," de Wynter admitted. "Now, let's see what strategy we can come up with to save Cameron's life as well as our own. First, we need ways as horsemen to do bodily harm without killing anyone for the first five rounds. Any suggestions?"

None had ever participated in a more grisly or distasteful discussion, but necessity forced a list of cruelties from their rebelling minds. Among the feats agreed upon were such as marking an X on an arm with a sword, cutting off an ear, slashing a cheek with a dagger, cutting off a finger, marking the target's back with a sword, etc. All agreed that the loss of an ear was worse than losing part or all of a finger. And, if they had the choice, they would avoid any act of amputation, trying to confine the first five rounds to marking each arm, each cheek, the target's chest or back or thigh.

Carlby, in the meantime, thinking on the game from Cameron's— that is, the target's—point of view announced he had found a loophole in the rules—nothing had been said about the target's unseating the rider from his mount and thus evening up the match a bit. How, as a target, to stay away from the sword or dagger for three minutes? They agreed that staying on the left side of a right-handed swordsman would help, as would using the horse's head as a kind of moving shield. No rule had been made against grabbing the horse's bridle and hanging on or using that advantage to unseat the rider.

During all of this talk, it was apparent to the others that Gilliver had little stomach for the day's events and would have difficulty keeping his mount. And all knew that after the fifth round, the targets would not live too long. It was imperative to keep the seven on their horses, and, if possible, to get a mount for Cameron, by dint of three wins within the first five rounds. Not an easy task, they agreed.

Then the Moulay arrived, his escort the commander of the Amira's bodyguard. Wave after wave of trumpeting filled the arena and filtered upward into the already searing sky. Clamorous cheers, too, except among the Berbers. As the *wazier* to the Moulay fulsomely welcomed his master and briefly reiterated the conditions of the contest, silent ones escorted the twenty riders-to-be through the gates at the far end of the arena. There they were instructed to pick a horse from those held in a huge fenced-off area. As they had suspected, there was little chance of getting the same horse one had caught and broken the day before, and with only three minutes to accomplish each designated feat, it was crucial to have a horse that handled well.

Rearing and kicking and biting, the mounts seemed as intractable as they had been the day before. But today they had real bridles, meager saddles strapped on their backs, and stirrups flapping against their bellies; and they fought as much to rid themselves of the frightening, offending restraints as to escape the men.

Into the melee plunged de Wynter and the other six, each, except John the Rob, heading straight for his mount. Now the purpose of the wild card, the zebra, became clear. The man who had caught it would seek another steed; if he succeeded, then that horse's rider would search out another and so forth until the last man must try to ride a striped, unmanageable mount. Grasping for reins draped over necks or dragging on the ground, while avoiding flying hooves and flashing teeth, was one thing; getting aboard was quite another. Time after time, would-be riders were thrown off, sometimes directly into the kicking, stomping legs or into the heavy timbers that ringed the enclosure. John the Rob was lucky. When he was thrown, he landed on the back of another horse. Scrambling into the proper position before the surprised stallion could figure out what to do, John the Rob got his feet solidly into the stirrups and hung on to neck and reins, outlasted several bucking and rearing attempts, before his gift mount settled down. Fionn's brown—tamer than most—was easily caught by someone else. Fionn simply tore the rider from the saddle and mounted himself. De Wynter, of them all, had the least competition for his horse. No one else wanted his life dependent on a potential killer.

Gilliver was among the last to come up with a mount, which meant it was one of those that fought strongest and longest against capture. Ogilvy managed to work his way alongside and help get the steed quieted down. Even as de Wynter was fighting the gray for control, he momentarily wondered if the others felt the same rush of excitement he did with all that power and spirit gathered between his legs and tugging fiercely at the reins.

Twenty riders were herded back into the arena and managed to line up in a fairly straight line. The nineteen targets were gathered at the center of the arena.

The trumpets sounded in a long and pretentious salute. The head judge made his way across the dusty surface, stopping in front of the royal box. The princess was being asked to select a leader. Only a formality. The princess had previously narrowed it down to two, and Ramlah had made the final choice.

With a bow, the head judge trudged back toward the lined-up horsemen. There he extended his arm and pointed a finger at de Wynter: "You have the honor of being the first of the firsts. See that you do nothing to discredit her wise choice."

As ibn Hudaij read off the order in which they would perform, as predetermined earlier, too, de Wynter thought it only fair. The Amira had caused the death of Drummond and Menzies. Now, whatever her reason, she had made it possible for him to save two other of his boyhood friends.

Then a horrible thought struck him, one that he hadn't even considered. If he picked Cameron, and Cameron cooperated so that de Wynter could remain the leader and thus control the bloodshed, Cameron would be lessening his own chances to earn a horse by evading a rider three times. My God what a quandary.

Aisha was not unaware of the dilemma de Wynter faced. She, after all, had seen to it that Cameron was saved from the Moulay's torments and included in this group for just this purpose: to test de Wynter. She sat on the edge of her seat, watching his every move, wondering what he would decide. Her mother watched her intently and decided the child liked the white-haired one more than she would admit even to herself.

"Leader, select your target!" came the shout from the head judge, and de Wynter's horse fairly leaped forward, rider wrestling to keep

573

the excited stallion under control, the gray eager to run and escape the strange weight on its back and the harsh restrictions of bit and cinch.

Straight at the targets came the prancing, sidestepping gray white Arabian with the handsome white-haired rider. As the others scattered, one stood his ground, Cameron, proving his faith and offering his help to de Wynter in remaining the leader of this fear-crazed and power-maddened collection of contestants.

Close enough he rode to read a number on a disc before the Arabian shied and pranced away, raising a small cloud of dust. As he rode back, a silent one waited to give him sword and dagger and three gold rings. The rider ignored him, instead, urging his horse forward.

"What number did you choose?" the head judge asked. De Wynter rode past him without saying a word, and the judge went on, desperately, "Then what act do you choose to perform?"

"I choose none!" de Wynter shouted in defiance, and rode at full gallop straight for the royal box. Yanking his mount to a skidding halt, he addressed the princess as her bodyguards gathered around the royal family, judges and whip-bearers running toward the errant horse and rider.

"By all that is holy, Amira, I call upon you to end this farce," he shouted above the turmoil. "Select your marriage partner from those who have already proved themselves worthy. Do not, I beg of you, force us to maim and kill helpless individuals."

"You will return to the ring immediately and proceed with the games, or I will have your target's head cut off where he stands," the angered princess replied, her dark, flashing eyes looking over her veil straight into his.

With a sinking feeling, he realized she meant it and that there was no further reason to plead. She was too cruel and hardened. Again he wheeled the horse, just as the mounted judges caught up to him, and he dashed through them back to the silent one, grabbing the weapons and rings and proceeding on to the circle, signifying his compliance with her order.

Again came the request to name the target and act he would perform. This time he replied: "Number seventeen, an X on his right arm."

At the signal, he rode the Arabian into the ring at half speed, circling the wary but determined figure of Cameron. "Sorry, my friend, but I must remain the leader as long as possible in order to control the game."

"I know," was all Cameron said.

"Then make it look good, but at the right moment hold that arm as still as you can." With that he kicked the horse into a feigned chase, while Cameron leaped and ran and feinted. For more than half of his allotted time, de Wynter practiced getting the horse close enough to Cameron and in the right position so he could mark him without cutting his arm too deeply or, God forbid, amputating it completely.

"Now, George," he called, adding under his breath, "Pray let's make it quick and easy." Cameron feigned a slip, and as he rose, the Arabian sidestepped and backtracked close enough for the Scotsman to flick his sword. It was over in an instant. Blood barely trickled from the clear X which covered more than five centimeters on his bicep. Cameron stared at his arm in disbelief. Then he flashed a smile at de Wynter and said, "God bless you, Jamie, I owe you one."

The next rider was promptly called forward and instructed to select his target. The horseman finally accomplished a crude X on his target's arm, though the blood poured freely through the fingers that sought to stem the flow.

One after another, rider matched wits and skill with target. Gilliver, in fourth place, got one mark on his victim's arm, but could not complete the X within the time limit. He was first to give up one of the precious rings that kept him a rider. Angus had a fairly easy time since, as he'd made sure, he rode the same horse he'd broken the day before. John the Rob's luck continued to hold, or perhaps it was his skill at sizing up an opponent. At any rate, he got one mark on early and cross-hatched it just before his time ran out. Fionn again used his great size to advantage; that, plus the docility of his mount. He simply reached down and grabbed his smallish target by the back of the neck, threw him over the saddle, zigged and zagged with the dagger, and dropped the man down to the ground properly marked. The audience roared, even the Berber sheikh shouting his approval.

The next five targets successfully protected their arms and took rings away from disappointed and frustrated riders. One of these was Cameron, who—on the basis of de Wynter's ride—had been taken for an easy mark; he soon proved the rider wrong. Ogilvy, in the next to last spot, also selected a previously used target, a slow-moving giant of a man, one whose arm had been badly slashed early on and who had lost considerable blood. The way Ogilvy figured it, the man had undoubtedly lost some of his stamina and probably much of his stomach for swordplay. Ogilvy was right. His sword soon added a second X to the man's bloodied right arm.

As was expected, the man on the zebra, who went last, could not even stay on his mount the prescribed time.

With no letup, the officials called for the second round to begin, asking de Wynter to choose his target and his act. This time the Scot picked a heavyset man whom he thought moved not too swiftly the first time round. He was right. De Wynter easily drew blood in the manner he said he would: slicing a furrow across the top of his target's left knee.

Gilliver survived this round and retained his two rings, but he shuddered as his sword slashed too deeply across the target's knee. Two riders lost their second rings. A few lost their first, including John the Rob. But most carved up their targets' legs to the satisfaction of the judges and the delight of the bloodthirsty crowd. Cameron took a slight cut on his left knee.

For his third target, de Wynter took a lesson from Ogilvy and picked the target whose right arm was badly sliced with two Xs, and whose left kneecap was badly damaged by an errant blade. It tore at his guts to do it, but he knew he must try to remain the leader to save his fellow slaves. There were grumbles from some of the contestants as he announced his intent to draw blood on his target's left cheek with the dagger. Most wanted to cause more damage to the targets to ensure their own success.

In less than a minute a neat nick with but the point of his dagger drew just enough blood to satisfy the unhappy judges. He could only hope that the rest of the riders would be as compassionate. And he hoped that if it were inevitable, Cameron would let the blade do its work neatly, rather than risk losing an eye or ending up with a big scar by attempting to avoid the injury.

He need not have worried. George scrambled and ducked and grabbed the bridle and pulled every trick he could think of to outlast the clock. Eventually, he took a cut on the shoulder, but won a ring. As de Wynter had surmised, the short-bladed dagger would be easier for the targets to avoid, especially against a man on horseback.

Gilliver lost another ring. Carlby his first. Angus and Ogilvy, veterans of mountain fighting that they were, had no real trouble in getting to their respective targets. The zebra-man lost his third ring, and joined the targets, the zebra being held aside to reward the first target to get three rings.

Sadly, the giant, weakened by loss of blood and hobbled by the bad kneecap, was selected by several of the riders as an easy target, while the stronger and more agile did not get picked. For while they did not have to face slashed cheeks, they also lost their opportunity to win three rings and thus gain horses.

The fourth round was marked by shouts of derision from the Arabs in the crowd and a growing disfavor among most of the other contestants of de Wynter as the leader. The judges, too, were not pleased, the pleasure of the crowd being their measure. But they had to live with their own rules, short of Aisha herself making a change.

His target selected, de Wynter called for the riders to duplicate his feat of cutting his target's skin from shoulder blade to shoulder blade with the dagger. There was open opposition now. Most of the riders were tired of what they considered child's play with grown-up toys. They hooted and shouted at their leader, who paid no attention, moving quickly on his target and chasing him madly around the large circle. When he grabbed the reins and used the gray's head to stay just out of reach, de Wynter took a calculated risk rather than let time run out on him. Vaulting from the saddle while still holding the reins, he slit the back of his surprised opponent and was back on the horse's back almost before either horse or target realized what had happened. This feat drew applause from the Berbers for his horsemanship. But the Moulay booed.

Gilliver's long arm made the difference as he fought gamely to keep his final ring. Aided by a now-tamer horse that responded well to his urgings, he carved a bloody streak across a tired and aching giant's back.

Angus lost his first ring. John the Rob his second. Ogilvy and

Fionn kept their perfect records intact. Cameron was bloody but still very much alive, with two triumphs.

For one more round de Wynter could delay the inevitable, but he had not time even to consider what he would do when the rules changed to allow—nay, demand—more than just bodily harm. He knew the pressure he would be under from fellow riders, judges, and the crowd to speed up the elimination process. And who knew when the Moulay would intervene and decide things were not moving fast enough? That mad ruler was perfectly capable of dictating the very acts of violence himself.

A fifth time de Wynter selected his target and braved the wrath of the other riders by calling for a relatively harmless piece of swordmanship. He signaled that he was going to drive his sword through the fleshy part of his victim's right thigh, making it clear that the blade must both enter and exit the flesh.

Cameron's thin long legs, he hoped, would make a difficult target, while his running ability should help him escape. If he could hold out again for three minutes, he would gain a horse. But first, de Wynter wished with all his heart, let some other target get a third ring and, along with it, the zebra. Most of all he worried about Gilliver losing his third ring and becoming a target instead of a rider.

He skewered his target in short order, his stomach convulsing as he felt the sword enter and slide through flesh and muscle. No bone, no tendon, he felt sure from the feel. And in a show of friendship, he reached down from the saddle and helped his victim back on his feet to hobble out of the ring holding his punctured thigh with both hands.

Gilliver couldn't do it; he lost his third ring, and tears welled in de Wynter's eyes. For six days now they had fought, schemed and prayed that this, their physically weakest member, could somehow be spared a wretched death in this burning desert country so far away from his beloved homeland. Cameron had even begged Gilliver to select him as his target, but Gilliver had shaken his head and named a healthy one, one who had an excellent chance of avoiding the sword. Gilliver's kind heart would not let him pick on the weakest, and he had drawn a formidable opponent.

Handing over his third ring to an official, he dismounted and walked slowly into the gathering of wounded targets, not really surprised or disappointed . . . more resigned to the inevitable.

Whether or not the other riders felt pity for this quiet man with the frail frame who had just moments ago been one of them, who could tell? But somehow he did not get picked as a target for the rest of the fifth round.

Some of the crowd had long since grown bored with the competition; they were tired of sitting on uncushioned seats and feeling the sun's heat beat upon their heads. Ramlah was prepared for this. She sent Pietro, the fat and the funny and the former contestant, with a message to Ali. Soon, servants passed among the crowd with trays of food and pitchers of drink. As the crowd munched and gulped the free viands, they consoled themselves with the thought that, with the start of the sixth round, things would get exciting.

They couldn't have been more right. Aisha herself intervened. Irritated that the white-haired one, given a golden opportunity to impress the Amira and the Berbers, had thought more of the targets than himself, she decided to teach the *jamad ja'da* a lesson he'd not soon forget. Again it was Pietro the Funny who was sent with the message, this time to the head judge.

De Wynter was lined up at the edge of the circle to start the sixth round when tubas stopped him. Ibn Hudaij had the *muezzin* next to him call for silence, then announced a new rule. After every five rounds, the leadership was to change, the first becoming the last, the second becoming first.

With a surge of his powerful stallion, the new leader, a redhead, charged forward to the edge of the circle. Aisha bit her lip. In her anger at de Wynter she had not paid attention to who would take his place. Now, she could only pray Eulj Ali would go quickly down to defeat. He didn't need to look the targets over, he already knew the number of the man he wanted.

Why he selected George Cameron was difficult to imagine. The Scot had been barely touched by the sword and dagger, and his athletic ability had stood out for all to see throughout the day. The two rings he wore on his left hand were proof of that. Perhaps the rider's past successes made him overconfident, wanting to face only what he considered the best. "Number seventeen, I'll slit his throat." A roar of approval went up from the now revitalized crowd.

Carlby moved his horse next to de Wynter's gray and the two conversed in guarded tones. "This doesn't look good," Carlby said, trying not to move his lips and not looking directly at de Wynter.

"If she would have let me be the leader for just a few more rounds, we could have stalled this thing until Cameron won, maybe even Gilliver, if three of us sacrificed a ring."

"Not your fault," Carlby said, "and there's nothing we can do but sit here and watch. Pray God, George can stay away long enough."

The butchery took no more than two minutes. Only Carlby's restraining hand kept de Wynter from riding into the ring and slaying the man who had, in one terrible flashing moment, drawn his blade across Cameron's jugular vein, then roared in triumph as the blood spurted out in great pulsing streams. Cameron looked stunned, disbelieving, then blank as he sank to his knees, and slowly rolled over onto his side, his legs drawn up tight to his belly, full circle from the womb to the dusty floor of al Djem.

Slaves hauled his body roughly, like butchered meat, from the arena, even while the next in line moved up to the circle, looked over the targets, and called out a number. The intended victim and his fellow targets were still in shock, so monstrous was the memory of that first young, athletic body slumping to the ground in the last throes of death. Woodenly, the selected target moved into the circle. Briefly, he went down on one knee and bowed his head in a silent prayer to whatever God he believed could hear him.

Gilliver added his own fervent prayer . . . not for himself, but for the man now facing death. As an afterthought, he asked that John the Rob, who now had only one ring remaining, be granted success if the Creator could see it that way.

Another rider won. A second body was dragged away. The crowd loved it. This was what they had come to see. Soon there would be an end to the long day, and they would know who was going to marry the princess.

By the time it was Angus's turn, four more had died but two had escaped their fate for at least one more round. Three riders, including the Taureg, had lost their rings and become targets, but two of the targets had become riders, so there were more riders than targets and the ratio was increasing with every ride.

Angus succeeded against a courageous but outmatched competitor. The next two targets took rings, but one only because the judges ruled that the slash across his lower throat and chest while bleeding profusely, did not qualify as a properly slit throat.

John the Rob seized the opportunity to pick that same man, knowing that the blood he was losing would make him vulnerable. To the one ugly red gash was added a second that split the man's Adam's apple in half and ended his misery.

A rider lost his third ring and joined the living targets. Two more targets could not escape the flashing swords. Then it was Ogilvy's turn. He called Gilliver's number. De Wynter, riding next, realized instantly what Ogilvy was going to do. De Wynter had been planning the same thing: to sacrifice one of his three rings, that Henry might live.

"Make it look good," Ogilvy said fiercely to Henry. "We've got to show them you are a bad pick." And he winked at his friend as he wheeled and went to the edge of the circle to await the starting signal.

Horsemanship brought it off. Ogilvy always managed to have the horse in the wrong position when the target was vulnerable. Yet it looked to all the contestants, the judges, and the crowd as though his mount was being unruly. And Gilliver ran for his life. There was no faking his mad dashing back and forth, his feints and leaps to avoid hooves and slashing blade. No two players ever acted out a more desperate scene. When time ran out, Ogilvy gladly handed over a ring, the first he had lost. And Gilliver, panting and tired, but trying not to show it, mingled in with the other targets, hoping to find anonymity and a welcome respite.

Gilliver's exhaustion was apparent to de Wynter at least. It called for a change in plans. Henry, tired, would not be able to put on as good a defense as he had playacting against Ogilvy. Whom to choose? His gaze swept the group and fell on the Taureg who wore gold rings on two fingers of his left hand. Making a quick decision, de Wynter called out the man's number. Never, so long as he lived, would he forget the fearful expression on the nomad's face, replaced, almost immediately and by sheer determination, with a half-smile of calm acceptance.

The Taureg had correctly read his fate. De Wynter and the gray, working at least temporarily as a harmonious team, were easily the match of any man afoot. But the Taureg was determined to put up a brave fight. At one point, in desperation, he even went so far as to throw himself under the horse's hooves, praying the animal's killer instincts were confined to its rider and that the horse would instinctively jump a fallen man's body. The horse wouldn't, but de Wynter would. He made the gray rear and saved the Taureg's life. But only for a minute. Even as he was getting to his feet, the horse was upon him and he found himself pinned against the gray's side, a dagger firmly held at his throat. De Wynter paused only a minute, then, remembering the man's smile, he removed his blade, pushed the surprised victim away and tossed him a ring, his third. While the Taureg, trembling with emotion, ran to claim a horse, de Wynter turned in his saddle to face the royal box and raised his sword high in a mocking salute.

Damn him, Aisha thought. Is he fearless or is he afraid to take another's life? It did not help her emotional state to notice that the sheikh was applauding the man's compassion. And why not? The man he'd saved was a fellow Bedouin. De Wynter, she realized, could not have done anything that would have pleased the Berbers more.

The seventh round began with Eulj Ali electing to run his sword through the guts of a target. He was, to the Amira's annoyance, successful. At this rate, she began to wonder if she would have to supply fresh targets. Of course! That was it. Against fresh men, the riders would not be so successful. Again, Pietro the Funny was pressed into messenger service to Ali whose eyes couldn't be attracted for her signed orders.

Most of those who followed succeeded, but two lost their third rings and became targets, four gave up their second rings, a few their first. Angus was a winner; Fionn wasn't, he gave up a ring to save Gilliver's life. One more ring and Gilliver would be back on horseback. Again, de Wynter rode last. Who this time? he wondered. He dared not give up another ring; he needed one to save himself and one in case he might save Gilliver. This time his gaze dwelled speculatively on another man—the zebra-man, who of all the riders had come into the arena this day prepared to die. And die he did with de Wynter's sword through his belly.

The Moulay was again growing bored. To watch the same way of killing, time after time, rider after rider, was no fun. "Besides," he gleefully pointed out to his women, "you are running out of targets."

Aisha knew it. Where, she wondered, were the fresh ones she'd ordered Ali get? And where was Pietro the Funny with Ali's answer to her orders?

"Well?" The Moulay waited for an answer. But not long enough for her to explain that fresh ones were on the way. Instead, he shouted instructions to his *wazier:* "All the riders with only one ring left now become targets!"

John the Rob's curse was heard above all the rest. After all of his hard work, and even killing two innocent men, he was to be deprived of what was rightfully his—a horse, a sword, and a dagger. And his life.

But John the Rob chose not to die yet. Turning to the rider next to him, he rode up close and extended his hand in a farewell gesture. "Good fortune," he said to the surprised combatant. And he passed down the line of those still with two rings, clapping them on the back, shaking their hands, chattering away like a magpie in a show of bravado. Only two, Eulj Ali and a Sicilian, disdained him. Suddenly he wheeled his mount back into the line in his assigned place and waited for al-Hudaij to check rings.

As he approached, each reached for his rings: one untying his tunic belt where he'd strung his for safekeeping; another feeling along his horse's reins for his; another grabbing for the bag that hung from a chain about his neck and held his *ukda;* others thumbing the rings they wore on their left hands. The rings were gone! Vanished. All but those owned by the six slaves, the Taureg, Eulj Ali, and the Sicilian. And among seven of these, certain rings had been redistributed to ensure their safety.

All hell broke loose as nine men realized they were to be made targets. Many would have mobbed John the Rob, accusing him of stealing their rings. While his friends gathered about him and the judges conferred, the Taureg began clapping his hands sharply and frantically. *"Djinn!"* he shouted. "I see *djinn*. They did it. Beware the djinn." John the Rob and his fellows joined in, clapping and shouting *"Djinn."* The noise and the suggestion was infectious. Soon, Arabs among the crowd began clapping, stomping and yelling to scare the *djinn* away.

The confused judges rushed to consult with their master, even as Aisha and Ali spoke silently with their hands, she asking what to do, he saying let matters be. The Moulay had come to the same conclusion. He was not eager to delay the games while they searched out a culprit, if there were one. Secretly, he, too, feared the *djinn* and kept stealing anxious secretive looks about. However, again the rules were amended. "A rule change. Judges now will award rings. Still three rings make a target into a rider," al-Hudaij announced. "As for the riders—failure to duplicate a feat immediately makes a man a target."

"Can he keep his rings?" cried one rider.

The judges consulted, "He can."

It was settled. The count? Nine riders, twelve targets. And again Eulj Ali started it off. "Number eleven, to be beheaded." Off he charged. He struck true, but he had underestimated the strength of the neck before him . . . or else his blade was dulled. Whatever, the head did not come off, the sword wedged in it. While the man bled to death, the judges consulted and awarded the target a ring posthumously. But Eulj Ali had fallen from first. His horse he must forfeit, but his two rings he could keep. The slaves quickly consulted, the Taureg listening in. "For God's sake, don't take on Eulj Ali as a target," was de Wynter's whispered advice. "He's too devious to risk choosing now."

"Besides," John the Rob added, all practicality, "he already has two rings. A third and he'll be back among us."

The Sicilian, who would be first—if he beheaded a target—was a brute of a man who had obviously fought many a battle, judging from his scarred hide, and killed unknown numbers of men. He lopped off a head with ease. Angus, Ogilvy, and Fionn were equally, savagely successful. Fionn, in fact, struck so hard that the head flew up into the crowd. The Taureg failed and returned to the pack. John the Rob knew from the beginning that he had not the strength to do the feat, but he tried. Slashing and stabbing and swinging away, he gashed his target a bit, sliced his mount, and nicked his own leg. When his few minutes were up, he, too, joined the targets. Carlby, also, avoided the niceties of combat and tried to disable a target, so that he became stationary and would then lose his head easily. Time defeated him, too, and Carlby joined the targets. De Wynter finished off the man that Carlby had started.

Then, while the Sicilian was deciding on his next feat, the four slaves consulted together. They were being boxed into a corner. Of the seven targets left, three were companions and the fourth—the Taureg—a brave man they respected. The contest could not go on much longer before they were faced with butchering their friends or else joining the targets.

The Sicilian, not unaware of the conference among his fellow horsemen, interpreted it as fear of him. He gloated and decided to reinforce that fear by coming up with the most impossible stunt he could think of, for he already knew his next target. While he savored his triumph, he kept glancing up into the royal box. Why the hell did the woman have to go veiled? He laughed to himself. What difference did it make? His way with women, he never saw their faces anyway. Besides, bedding her was only part of winning. Mostly he was here for the power. Once he had broken her to his ways, he'd be next in line to the throne. Let her sit on her butt on the throne, he thought, he'd skewer *her* butt and make her love it!

He named his next feat: "Daggers only! I shall skewer the man whose number I call through the neck." Before he named him, however, he threw aside his sword and waited for the rest to drop theirs. Only when that was done did he call out his target: number seventeen—Gilliver.

Even as the Sicilian clapped his legs against his horse and moved him forward at a trot toward the circle where a somewhat dazed Gilliver was being pushed, the other horsemen moved forward as one, only to be checked by Ali and his mounted silent ones, who interposed their horses between the four other competitors and the circle where the conclusion of this game would be played out.

The Sicilian had been right in his choice of target. Poor Gilliver didn't even think to pull his shoulders up to protect his neck. He simply ran. And ran. And ran. Within seconds of riding into the circle, the Sicilian knew he could have his man whenever he wanted. So he played with him, as a ferret would a mouse. Only when Gilliver was about to drop of exhaustion and could run no longer... only when he turned to face his pursuer and the last grains of sand were about to fall through the funnel within the sandglass... only then did a dagger whistle through the air in a blur of silver and pierce the poor young Scot's neck, entering in the front, exiting in the back.

As his friends watched, Gilliver grabbed ineffectually at the weapon that was killing him, then his knees buckled and he fell forward to the ground, his head staring at them, held up grotesquely by the hilt of the dagger that had killed him.

The four companions didn't move, paralyzed by horror. Then they heard a voice from among the targets: "I am the resurrection and the life, saith the Lord: he that believeth in me, though he were dead, yet shall he live: and whosoever liveth and believeth in me, shall never die."

As Carlby continued, de Wynter knew what he had to do. He kicked his horse forward, "Angus, Ogilvy, if you love me, dismount and join the targets. You, too, Fionn. Pray for me."

Angus and Ogilvy did not ask why. They simply kicked off their stirrups and slid out of the saddle. Fionn hesitated. "What do you do?"

"I win our freedom and mayhap avenge Henry Gilliver, too. Wish me luck. Now, go." De Wynter smiled at the giant reassuringly.

As the giant dismounted, the crowd screamed its displeasure. Coward was the kindest word shouted at him. And when words seemed to have no effect on him or the two black-haired men who went before him, looking neither left nor right, many in the crowd reinforced their screams by throwing food into the arena. The three Scots ignored that also, instead joining Carlby and John the Rob where they knelt and kneeling with them, blending their voices with theirs: "The Lord giveth and the Lord hath taken away; blessed be the name of the Lord. I will lift up mine eyes unto the hills whence..."

As de Wynter sat his horse, watching the silent ones try to quiet the crowd and clear the arena, he, too, spoke the words of the psalm and found them peculiarly fitting: "The Lord is thy defense upon thy right hand; so that the sun shall not burn thee by day, neither the moon by night. The Lord shall preserve thee from all evil; yea, it is even he that shall keep thy soul. The Lord shall preserve thy going out, and thy coming in, from this time forth—"

Ali interrupted him, shouting, "*Jamad ja'da,* do you continue to compete?"

"Aye, Amir *l' al-assa,* I still compete."

"Know you that if you skewer your target, there will be another round, but if you fail, the man from Sicily wins?"

"I know. And if I win, do my companions go free?"

Ali hesitated a minute. "As free as you!"

"Then I ride."

"Name your target's number."

He shall not be warned, de Wynter thought, urging the gray forward, taking him from a standstill to a full gallop within a few strides. Straight for the Sicilian he went. "He has no number . . . he was the first!" The Sicilian could not believe his eyes for a moment, then weaponless, turned and fled. De Wynter's dagger caught him fair in the neck, the point entering through the back, exiting from the front of his neck.

The games were over. The fickle crowd went wild with joy. Even the Moulay applauded the audacity of the Scot's coup. Ali and his father exchanged knowing looks. As de Wynter slowed his horse down to a canter, someone in the crowd started the chant: "*Jamad Ja'da! Jamad Ja'da! Jamad Ja'da!*" On and on it went, echoing and reverberating through the stadium as the rider went where his horse would go, tears blinding his eyes. It was Ali's firm grip on the reins that brought the gray to a stop, and Ali's bronzed hand that gently wiped tears from the other's eyes.

"Come, my friend. You have done well. Now, it is time to rest."

De Wynter felt too drained emotionally to protest; he let his horse be led off without lifting a hand. Before they left the arena, he roused himself long enough to say, "And my friends?"

"They shall soon join you. Come, you are tired and dirty and in need of food and drink and rest. We go to my tent."

As the silver-haired one on the gray left the arena for the last time, silent ones, rounding up the rest of the horses, would have escorted the other survivors out of the amphitheater. However, all but Eulj Ali refused to leave. The rest would accompany their dead friends' bodies and see them properly buried.

As Ali and de Wynter left the arena by the Gate of Death, Aisha and Ramlah hurried out of the royal box. There were wedding preparations to be made. The crowd too, the games over, gathered their belongings together and prepared to make their way home. Only the Berbers and the Moulay lingered. The former because they were in no hurry. They and their sheikh would not leave until the morrow when he hung the bloodstained sheepskin upon the pole outside the wedding tent. Besides, here where the events were still fresh in their minds, they could compare and rehearse the stories they would bring back to their campfires, there to be retold, fact after fact, from beginning to very end—the six days of the games of the Amira Aisha.

The Moulay lingered longest. He was still there when the galleries emptied of all other spectators, and slaves entered carrying in huge stakes and armfuls of wood. Where the target had been dug for the javelin throw, fresh stakes were sunk in the ground. Where the three circles had been for the gladiator fights grew a ring of more stakes. Where the camels had waited to be milked or ridden or loaded, tall empty stakes stood waiting. Where the two ostriches had been beaten to death a pair of stakes were pounded into the ground. Where Gilliver had bled his last, and the Sicilian had taken the dagger through his throat . . . there the two largest stakes were sunk through the red-colored sand into the ground.

The Moulay looked on approvingly. Now the arena was ready for games of his kind. And through the gates at the far end came men bound together by ropes about their necks. Some had been losers in the actual games; others were losers by association—the servers and slaves who had inhabited the camp of the contestants for the last six days—they were here now to lose a final time and give up their lives for the amusement of a madman.

CHAPTER 39

While de Wynter slept as if dead in Ali's tent and hundreds of other men died the death of the damned in fire and torment within the arena, six of the remaining survivors watched as the silent ones dug two graves and gave Cameron and Gilliver Moslem burials. In its shallow grave, each body, washed and wrapped in a simple shroud, lay curled on its side, facing toward Mecca. As an *iman* spoke the simple words of the Islamic faith, attesting to their belief, too, in a life after death, Carlby's church-trained voice, beginning quietly, gained momentum and soon overpowered all others:

"Man, that is born of woman, hath but a short time to live, and is full of misery. He cometh up, and is cut down, like a flower; he fleeth as if he were a shadow and never continueth in one stay. Unto you Almighty God, we commend the souls of Henry Gilliver and George Cameron departed, and we commit their bodies to the ground; earth to earth, ashes to ashes, dust to dust.

For a long moment, there was silence, none daring to breathe deeply or rasp sand by shifting his weight from foot to foot. Then, Fionn's deep voice began, "Our Father who art in . . ." He spoke—as Gilliver and Cameron and Drummond and Menzies would have wanted it—not in Latin but in Scots-Gaelic, and Angus and Ogilvy joined in.

John the Rob, like Carlby and the Taureg, knew not the words of this language other than a scattering of oaths and obscenities learned

589

the hard way: alongside the Scots toiling in the galleys, crossing the desert, rebuilding al Djem, fighting in the games. Thus, though keeping his head properly bowed, the beggar chief had time to study the row of silent ones surreptitiously. And out of the corner of one eye, he saw one man's lips move in concert with the Scots. It gave him something to think about as he and the others joined Eulj Ali in the baths. Now—in the latter's presence—was no time for serious conversation; however, there would be ample opportunity later. Only three of these—Eulj Ali, the Taureg, and Fionn—were ordered by Ali to attend the nuptial feast.

Ali did not allow de Wynter to sleep long. There was much to do and not much time in which to do it. "Come, my friend, it is time to be up." A sleepy, yawning de Wynter stretched and sat up, looking about, trying to orient himself. He was in a tent . . . not large but lavish. The walls were hung with a kaleidoscope of carpets, woven in shades of green and brown and blue and the earth reds of Ali's beloved iron-rich mountain homeland. The divan upon which de Wynter sat was covered with another rug, one woven of wool as soft as silk; his feet rested on still another that made the ground seem soft. Ali, watching de Wynter take it all in—the trays set up here and there, the plush cushions and ottomans scattered about the floor, the elephant foot that held scrolls in one corner—said quietly, "My tent. It is yours, it and anything within it."

It was the desert-dwellers greeting and Ali, de Wynter was sure, at that moment meant it. De Wynter at another time and under other circumstances might have allowed his sense of humor to take control and have asked for the gift of the owner of the delightfully feminine voice he could hear speak in bits and snatches. But not today. "My friends?" was all he could summon up the energy to ask.

"They have already bathed. And if you are ready, we shall go there, too, to cleanse your body inside and out." Ali took de Wynter's silence as assent and gestured him to lead the way through the hangings he pulled aside.

At first, he thought night must have just fallen, for the sky to the west was still reddened by the setting sun. A second glance—taking in the stars—made de Wynter wonder. He would have been horrified to learn that the Moulay's games this evening were being lit by more than a hundred dying human torches. Ali preferred not to discuss the subject and so hustled his charge toward the east and the Roman baths, where Aisha and Ramlah had spent the last hours. Ali headed for a different section. These rooms were set aside just for men and were much more modern and Tunisian than ancient Roman. In an outer room empty except for divans built against the wall, de Wynter and Ali stripped, handing their clothes to a servant. Each took the measure of the other's well-modeled body and decided he was in better shape. Each then was given a *foukah* to wrap about his hips and high wooden clogs to protect his feet from the hot floors. "The water and the floors are heated from beneath," Ali explained, leading the way into the first of three hot rooms. De Wynter was prepared for the difference in temperature, but not for the silence broken only by the splash of water in a marble fountain and the faintest scuffling of the naked feet of the male bath attendants.

"If you need to relieve yourself?" Ali tactfully suggested, and de Wynter nodded, following him into the latrine. It was a room such as he had never been in before. The basins carved of marble stood at many different heights along the wall, so that each man might relieve himself without undue splashing. Gold animal heads served as water faucets to wash the urine away.

"Another need?" Ali asked, pointing to a series of marble seats, again of many heights.

De Wynter shook his head and the two returned to the hot room. There they took their places at opposite ends of a long, narrow marble tub, filled halfway up with extremely hot water. Immediately an attendant began ladling in boiling water, gradually raising the temperature of the water until de Wynter swore he was about to be parboiled like a prawn. But if Ali could take it, so could he. Leaning back, each man rested his head against the tub's ledge, attendants carefully lifting his head to put towels beneath to protect the neck. Then, each was left with his thoughts. Ali thought of the night yet ahead when he would gain the *jamad ja'da* but lose Aisha. De Wynter daydreamed about his loving reception by Anne Boleyn in England short weeks from now when he disembarked from the first ship he could find heading that way.

How long the two men rested there, de Wynter had no idea. But too soon Ali murmured, "The water grows cool," stepped out of the tub, and led him to another room containing two marble slabs set

591

upon pillars. He stretched out face down on one and gestured for de Wynter to take the other. Then, two masseurs went to work, rubbing the men down with a glove of fur. No part of de Wynter's backside was missed, from his neck to his anus to his big toes. And when he thought he'd been rubbed to death, the real massage, bare-handed, began. Was this, de Wynter wondered, just a continuation of the games? Powerful fingers worked the shoulderblades until they cracked; the backbone was pressed on, hard, here and here and here and here, until de Wynter listened for the telltale crack of a broken back. Abandoning the back for his arm, muscles were prodded by persistent fingers, the elbow jerked, the fingers cracked, the arm itself stretched until de Wynter thought he'd have to yell, "Give it back." In fact, only the sight of Ali being put through the same torture, arm for arm, leg for leg, kept de Wynter there. Then, the agony was over. The masseur took thick, soft, perfumed soap and lathered it in from head to toe, turning his victim over so as to do the front. Their work finished, the masseurs disappeared to let the two men rest.

Again, it was Ali who finally sat up and led the way into the steam room. Compared to this, the water in the marble bath was cool. Now, the cleansing from the inside out began. As de Wynter sat sweating, gentle hands began scraping the lather and sweat off his back . . . his arms . . . and legs . . . working up to his chest. Then without warning, someone emptied a bowl of water over his head . . . and another and another. He sputtered and stood up protesting, but Ali, laughing, said, "Relax, it's part of the bath."

From the hot room, they made their way through a series of cooler rooms, gradually accustoming their pink skin to normal air. Then, on another marble slab where he was toweled dry. Turning over onto his back, he discovered the toweler was, as he had suspected, a woman. A naked woman. At that moment, she reached down and pulled off his *foukah*, leaving him as naked as she, with the expected results.

Ali, watching, laughed. "So you are a man with a man's desires after all."

But de Wynter couldn't answer, his face was being lathered up. The almond-eyed, dark-haired girl then took up a straight razor and prepared to shave him. Nervously, he awaited the first stroke. It was smooth and firm and gentle. Relaxing, he felt but could not see other hands on his body. More lather or oil or something was being rubbed into his armpits and on his chest and about his outstretched manhood. Why, he didn't know, and with the razor on his neck, didn't dare ask, lest in moving his mouth he slit his own throat. Another head bent over his face to look into his blue eyes, then gentle hands began working his hair, combing and, judging from the scraping sound, cutting and shaping it.

The man who stood up when all this was done—his body washed off and oiled, his nails paired and pumiced, his teeth scrubbed and gums rubbed—did not look as though he had spent the last months rebuilding an amphitheater under the burning sun, except of course for the bronze of his skin. Nor did he look like a man, he thought with shock, looking down where his pelvic hair had been! Even as he stood there staring, the slave girls took giant puffs and began powdering his body, powder making little clouds that tickled his nostrils. Fresh puffs patted the excess off. At last, he and Ali were ready to return to the room of the divans, where male servants waited for them with fresh clothing. Ali's were the garb of the silent ones, but the fabric was the finest wool. De Wynter's garments were of silk, the trousers so thin he was almost glad there was no hair there to show through. Over them hung a long loose wool robe, embroidered at hem and cuff and neck in silver and edged with smoke gray pearls. The slave wrapped a girdle about his waist, and about that a rope of pearls. As two more men brought white leather slippers for his feet, de Wynter commented, "You dress your guests well."

"It gives me pleasure," was Ali's diplomatic answer.

"Why?" De Wynter's eyes narrowed as he waited for the reply.

"Why does it give me plea—"

"No, why do you dress me this way?"

Ali had hoped to avoid such questions until they had made their way at least as far as Aisha's tent, but he realized he now had no choice but to answer and pray that Allah guided his tongue. "You are to be a guest at a banquet tonight—"

"The Amira's?"

Ali reluctantly nodded.

"I'm not going. Take those sandals away and bring me back my old tunic. I shall go nowhere near that woman."

The slaves, in a quandary, looked to Ali for instructions. He gestured for them to stay as they were. As de Wynter began to shrug the heavy robe off, Ali shook his head, and the two attendants firmly pulled the robe back up onto de Wynter's shoulders.

"You have no choice, my friend—"

"Don't call me that. You are not my—" de Wynter continued to try to disrobe.

"But I am. Believe me, I do this for you." Ali's claps brought reinforcements for the attendants, de Wynter kicking and squirming within their grasp. But he was at too great a disadvantage. When de Wynter's futile struggles finally ceased, Ali had the man bring the slippers forward again. "Put them on him," Ali commanded, and the two men squatted to do so. The first one picked himself up with a howl of pain as de Wynter's heel caught him on the side of the jaw. The other avoided such a kick only by falling back on his haunches. Two more attendants entered the fray, wrapping their arms around de Wynter's legs and using their body weight to prevent further kicking. Now, he was lifted bodily, the slippers placed on his feet. Silken ties, brought at Ali's command, bound his wrists and ankles. Rather than risk losing him or mussing him, Ali decided to carry the man to the Amira's tent like the trophy he was—slung like a dangerous cat from a trophy pole fashioned from a cluster of the silent ones' spears. De Wynter's arriving like this, Ali guessed, would set the Amira's teeth on edge and do more to further the selection of Fionn. Ali was not adverse to influencing her choice right up to the very end.

A dozen guards accompanied the "guest of honor" and the Amir out of the baths and down a completely deserted street of a city, two thirds empty tents and one third abandoned ancient ruins. They needed no torches to light their way, for eerie red light still emanated from the amphitheater itself. Ali, seeing the sparks soaring above it, found himself wishing that the fires would burn out of control and trap their instigator in his inhuman campfire. Waiting to let the silent ones go past with their burden was a large contingent of roped-together slaves who had belonged to the losers, fresh fuel for the huge funeral pyre.

The black in front, who had gray scattered liberally through his tightly kinked hair, stood still and looked at the man hanging from

594

the pole, taking him for one of them. "Take heart, my brother. Allah's blessings upon you."

"And you," de Wynter answered, bewildered anew by a country that could produce such dignity and bravery in the midst of utter depravity.

Slaves were not the only ones destined for immolation; scattered among them were groups of better-dressed men who had been spectators at the games and now were to become part of the spectacle themselves. These men, judging from their torn raiment and disheveled appearance, went not so stoically to their deaths. Ali, whose idea it had been to so sacrifice them, watched these, too, herded toward al Djem without a twinge of regret. He would have slaughtered hundreds and thousands to save the life of the one man he now escorted to the Amira's white wedding tent. And whose messenger came to hurry their steps.

It was his genuine regard for de Wynter that forced Ali to make an offer essentially inimicable to his own cause: "I shall, if you like, cut you free. Then you can walk in like a man, the victor of the games that you are."

"Never. Never will I willingly have aught to do with that woman."

With anyone else, under any other circumstances, Ali would not have been gainsaid, but for once, one single time, he chose to be self-serving and temporized, "You may be wise. In the meantime, give me your word—"

"No. The only way you'll get me in there is trussed like game and hanging from this pole. And even then, Ali, you'll not keep me there. Not unless you tie me and hold me down."

"So be it," Ali said, waving Aisha's messenger aside and gesturing to the pole-bearers to proceed.

While de Wynter had slept and been groomed, Aisha had not been idle. With her mother's assistance, she, too, had spent hours being bathed, buffed, perfumed, and groomed for her wedding—and torturing herself over her choice for consort. Logically, sensibly, intelligently, practically, by any measurement she could devise, the giant remained the proper choice. Yet something within her rebelled at her own practicality, and perhaps the same aspect of her personality made her long for love where love could not possibly exist: not in a *mariage de convenance*. Nevertheless, she knew it was true. Besides, the sheikh had made his preference for the *jamad ja'da* undeniably known. While the giant's feats had won plaudits, the daring and imagination of the final coup of the *jamad ja'da* was the fabric of which legends were made and stories woven. Still, she could not ignore her own certainty that the white-haired one would never be as malleable as the other.

At one point, in desperation, she was prepared to reject both in favor of another. Which other? The Taureg? She laughed cynically. Might as well choose the monkey-faced one; neither inspired more than mere admiration for their ability to survive. As for Eulj Ali—never! Besides, she had other plans for that braggart.

The garments she wore this night were almost identical in cut and color to the ones she'd worn the night before, except that upon these were lavished more embroidery, more diamonds, and more gold. Looking at herself in the mirror, she wondered how he could resist smiling upon her with favor. He? With favor?

With a cry, she threw the mirror from her. The song birds in their cages, startled, scolded her loudly. How dare I, she thought, think of him again? And why always that one? Why not the other one, too?

The mirror was retrieved and returned undamaged by a frightened *asira* and Aisha patted the girl on her head as if she were a pet, then touched her own fingertips to her lips, to show the server that the thanks were not just of the body but of the soul, too.

None too soon was she ready. Her mother headed the procession to the white wedding tent where Aisha would await, as a proper Berber wife should, the coming of her husband. There would be no elaborate wedding ceremony such as the Christians and Jews knew; marriage among the Moslems is a civil matter. And that had been accomplished by the signing of the scroll some seven days ago by 180 men. Whichever candidate she chose tonight was, by law, already married to her and had been for a full week.

Beyond the diaphanous curtains, beside the soft, fresh-made bed with its perfumed silken coverings and telltale white sheepskin, she waited alone save for her cheetah, al Abid.

Finally, voices and vague shapes seen through the curtains announced her time was upon her. Even as the men settled down onto the low divans placed for them, she swept back the curtains and strode into the room, her long skirts swirling, her eyes taking in the whole scene at once. Eulj Ali was there in rich robes of red and rubies, in sharp contrast to the twice-married Taureg in his black robe and black sandals, with a black scarf covering his lower face, its ends tied behind his ears, then hanging down his back. The giant, who took up most of one divan, wore robes of blue. Lapis lazuli around the border picked up the color of a man's eyes, the eyes of a man who wasn't there, the *jamad ja'da*.

Then, too, neither was her Amir *l'al-assa*. Had the two lingered too long at the baths? Or was Ali prematurely enjoying the other's favors? Her eyes grew stony as with a snap of her fingers she brought a slave running. A word or two and he was off to find the miscreants.

The slave was back almost immediately. Ali came first, and behind him a richly dressed human trophy dangled from a pole. A word from the Amir and the carriers gladly lowered their burden to the floor, there to lie on his side. Seeing Aisha's obvious displeasure, Ali tried to explain. "He would not come of his own doing. We had to tie him."

"Untie him," she ordered, frowning down upon the man who lay there, his very bindings his final insult and affront to her person.

"But he—"

"I said," she said, enunciating every word distinctly, "untie him."

Ali shrugged. Stepping forward, he pulled his own knife and, rolling de Wynter over with his foot, bent down and sawed through the silk ties that bound first ankles, then wrists. With one catlike movement, de Wynter rolled over and sprang to his feet and leapt straight for Aisha. He was stopped in his tracks by the pounce of Aisha's cheetah. The snarling al Abid would have given any man pause.

Although Ali had instinctively lunged after the prisoner, it was Aisha who, taking advantage of the *jamad ja'da*'s hesitation, sprang forward and, baring her own small blade, pressed it hard against his jugular.

"If you move," she informed him, trying hard to keep her breathing even, "you drown your lungs in your own blood. Heed me and heed me well. You are an invited guest at my table. Now act the part. Or else you shall never sup again without the food and drink flowing freely through a slit in your neck.''

She had never killed a man. She wasn't sure that she ever would. But she was sure he did not know that, and, rather than have him test her resolve, she stepped back and removed the knife from his throat as Ali moved in between them.

Just as quickly, a frustrated de Wynter went for Ali, knocking him to the ground and narrowly missing taking the princess with him. On top of the two struggling men sprang the snarling cat. More in fear of what al Abid might do to the *jamad ja'da* than of what the two men might do to each other, Aisha waded into the fray, catching her pet by the collar while signaling her guards, with her free hand, to move in and restrain the white-haired one.

Then, though words to her men were unnecessary, she spat them out, her eyes dark with rage, her voice as deadly as an icicle; ''Bind him again. Bind him fast to the tent pole.''

While her orders were being carried out, she soothed, scratched, and calmed her cheetah . . . and noticed the gaping faces of the other three men. Idiots. Useless. Slow-witted dolts. He could have been hurt while you sat there, she charged them silently. Typical men. In so doing, she dismissed all three from further consideration.

Al Abid began purring under the gentle but thorough cheek-scratching of her mistress's hand. Now it was safe to turn her pet loose again and retreat to her own couch. A casual gesture with her right hand and the cat slowly sank to the floor at her feet. A wave of her left hand and slaves entered the room bearing platters heaped high with aromatic foods. Between each two men, a tray was placed, overflowing with fragrantly spiced meats, crisp exotic vegetables, fresh-baked breads. The men, not having eaten since breakfast, were ravenous and set to with a will.

Not Aisha. She picked at her food. Tossed tidbits to her cat. Every now and again she stole a glance across the room to where the *jamad ja'da* sat propped against the pole, his eyes closed, his face stern. Even tied tightly in what must be an uncomfortable position, he looked as elegantly at ease as . . . as al Abid.

Suddenly, she realized she did not know his name, his real name. Always she had referred to him as the *jamad ja'da* as she had called the other the blond giant. In fact, of the three men, only one name—that a hated one—came readily to her lips: Eulj Ali. It was time to rectify all that. Waiting until the giant, seated between two trays, had satisfied his voracious hunger by helping himself, with two hands, first to one tray then the other, Aisha decided to introduce herself.

Deliberately she made herself speak softly and beguilingly, in direct contrast to the haughtiness of her words, for it suddenly became important to her that the *jamad ja'da* look upon her favorably: "Allow me, O victors, to introduce myself: Aisha Kahina Amira of Tunisia, twenty-third in line of direct descent from Dido, daughter of Belus of Tyre and founder of Carthage. Daughter, too, of Ramlah bint Zaid, daughter of Zaid, Sheikh of the Berbers, who is descended from Kahina, the great Berber princess–prophetess who first drove the Arabs from our lands. Now, I would know you and your patronomy as well."

She had spoken directly to the *jamad ja'da*, but not by a quiver of his eyelids did he indicate he heard. Could he be sleeping? she wondered. Or, worse, hurt in the struggle. She clapped her hands sharply. When his eyes flew open, she said, *"Djinn,"* and smiled skeptically at him. Her smile, a suggestion of mutual sophistication rather than superstition, was more than that. It was also an invitation to forgive, to forget, to ally. While the Arabs in their midst—the Taureg and Eulj Ali included—joined in the clapping to scare off the *djinn*, de Wynter slowly and deliberately closed his eyes, refusing her invitation. Never would he forgive nor forget Drummond and Cameron and Menzies . . . and Gilliver. Let Fionn eat her food and share her couch—in any manner he chose. Once this farce of a feast was finished, this particular Scot was going to find the gray stallion, if possible, and if not, walk back to Tunis to find a ship to England.

When the clapping died down, Eulj Ali with typical braggadoccio and ignoring the known fact that he was grandson of a washerwoman and a janissary-turned-potter boasted, "Eulj Ali, beloved son of the Beglerbey of Algiers, Uruj Barbarossa, whose very name strikes terror into the hearts of Allah's enemies and who now commands the fleet of the Sultan of Sultans, Suleiman the Magnificent."

The latter was news to her. That Eulj Ali's father found favor at the Sublime Porte might conceivably influence her plans for the son. That would need discussing with Ramlah and Ali.

In the meantime, the Taureg, finally over his concern with the *djinn,* spoke next: "Ben Duailan, of the tarik el Taureg"—he smiled gently, the smile making a sharp countenance soft, a stern visage boyish—"whose ancestors welcomed Dido to our shores and sold her all the land she could encompass with one bull hide."

Aisha could not resist the sweetness of the smile and the gentleness of his message. Dido, as she well knew, had cheated the Tauregs out of their land by cutting the bull's hide into the thinnest of strips and laying these out end to end, encircling all of that promontory to the northwest of the city of Tunis. She smiled back. And captured at least one man's heart there and then.

"Ben Duailan, of the tarik el Taureg, welcome to my tent." She meant it. She also meant to cheat him of the reward for which he had risked so much, just as Dido had done to his ancestor centuries before. And both men she knew would always consider themselves fortunate to have been favored by such a beautiful woman.

Fionn, through all of this, chomped steadily away. Finally, Aisha addressed herself directly to him. "And you, tall man, do you go nameless?"

"Nay," he replied, grinning broadly at her. "I be Fionn, son of Seamus and Nelly. The first is the Seaforth's captain of the guard and me mother be the best cook in the land."

Cook? Captain of the guard? She had considered consorting with the son of these? Not a suggestion of her thoughts found its way to her face or her manner. Instead, she smiled even more sweetly upon him.

"And your friend over there, is he too the son of a cook, maybe even your brother?"

It was Fionn's turn to be shocked. "Him, brother to me?" He chuckled at the very thought and could imagine Nelly's reaction if he revealed that someone thought she had put horns on Seamus's head. "Nay, he be my master, Jamie Mackenzie, Earl of Seaforth and Lord de Wynter."

This sounded much more promising. "And what might an earl be?"

Fionn was at a loss. He knew what an earl was, just as he knew what the sun was, but not how to describe it. A glance at Jamie

600

revealed no help there. Other than a slight tenseness of his shoulders, de Wynter sat as if of stone.

"An earl?" he echoed, buying time. "Well, it's a lord of sorts. Not so high as a prince mind you, although Jamie is the grandson of a king—"

"Really? Tell me more," Aisha urged.

"Jamie isn't a prince; he's an earl because his mother was a bas—"

De Wynter suddenly came alive. "Fionn, that's enough," he said with a voice so imbued with authority that Fionn dared not say another word.

But in silencing Fionn, he had left an opening for Aisha. "It is not enough," she said. "If you prefer he not tell me, then you do it." It was a royal command, and de Wynter, out of mixed pity for Fionn and a lifetime of gallantry toward women, gave in.

"An earl is a title of nobility so ancient that it goes back to antiquity. It yields precedence only to royals, dukes, and marquesses, and has a position above viscount and baron."

Hers was a hollow victory. He had used the English titles, not the Arabic equivalents. But she let that go. "You are grandson of a king?"

"Aye, many a woman spread her legs for James IV." He got perverse pleasure out of being coarse.

"And the de Wynter, what's that?"

"French. An honorific. Like your *jamad ja'da*."

"*Mais oui*," she replied, "for your hair."

It was his turn to be taken aback. A barbaric semisavage princess speaking French in the middle of nowhere. Aisha continued her probing, in French, "I thought you were *Anglais*, not *Français*."

De Wynter had had enough of idle curiosity. "Neither. I am Scots. Now, it is your turn. When do you let us go free as you promised?"

Aisha looked at the man coolly. "You are wrong. I did not promise to let you go free. I promised you would be free of me. There is a difference. Today, once the games were over, I gave over to Ali a document. It conveyed to him the ownership of some slaves, and that, de Wynter, is the only freedom you'll get here."

He was incredulous. They had been tricked. For this, all had risked their lives and four had given theirs. "Why, you—" For a moment he was at a loss for words; then they came gushing to his mouth in his native Scots.

Fionn, who did not understand French, wondered what inspired his friend's invective, but he grinned broadly at the familiar words. As de Wynter cursed daughter, damned mother, reviled father, shifting with ease from obscenity to profanity to blasphemy in order to encompass all aspects of this debauched country, Fionn's admiration at this bravura performance led him to the conclusion that, in de Wynter, Seamus had had an able pupil now grown to surpass his master's stature.

Ali, on the other hand, did not need to know the exact meaning of the words to catch their gist, and he moved swiftly to dam the flow, using a firm hand as a gag while a cloth was ripped from a robe. But de Wynter slipped his grip and fastened his teeth in the other's fleshy palm. Tearing loose with a cry of pain and a spurt of blood that splattered de Wynter's wedding finery, Ali too found surcease in words. And while these were not as inventive nor as masterful as the others, they too were heartfelt and at least these all could understand. Not a moment too soon the cloth was handed to Ali, and, ignoring the blood dripping from his hand, he ripped it again in two. One piece he fastened round de Wynter's mouth, tightening the gag cruelly and more than need be. The other half he wrapped round his own wound.

Eulj Ali who had watched this byplay with great interest, decided that de Wynter had destroyed all chance of being named consort. The giant he dismissed out of hand; he had bungled his chance by revealing that his family was low-born. As for the Taureg, he and Aisha had smiled one upon the other . . . and Ben Duailan was a fellow Berber. Yet, somehow Eulj Ali could not see the Amira choosing this tall, stern-looking warrior who wore a veil, now pulled down beneath his chin when she could have someone as handsome as himself. Thus, arrogantly, Eulj Ali rose to his feet and strolled toward the Amira. Even as silent ones came forward to prevent any more acts of violence, and al Abid half rose to her feet, the redhead, ignoring the hot feral breath of the cheetah, knelt at her feet in a much-practiced, well-perfected imitation of humility. From his experience with his four wives, he was sure no woman could resist him when he smiled boyishly and literally threw himself at her feet.

"Oh, wondrous Aisha," he began, "Oh, magnificent Aisha. Waste not your perfection on these unworthy specimens." He gestured widely about him, making the cat still more nervous, but a firm female hand restrained her. Aisha was curious as to what this cockerel might have to say. "These lacklusters know not that they are favored by Allah merely to breathe the same air that you do, much less actually come within your exquisite presence. While I"—he paused for dramatic emphasis—"who can offer you more than any wife ever received from a husband, would be content to simply kiss your feet." He smiled again, more boyishly than before.

Aisha smiled back. And extended her foot for him to kiss. The boyish smile faded as he stared disbelieving upon it. Although he had offered before, no woman had ever called his bluff. But taking a deep breath, he restored the smile to his face and gingerly lowered himself so that his lips might brush her instep.

Behind his back and over his head, Ali and Aisha were conversing silently:

Shall I stop this charade?
No, I enjoy it.
When he finds out you play with him, he will be dangerous.
He shall not find out until too late. By then, I will have defanged him. Send for the wine.

Eulj Ali, swallowing the gorge that rose to his throat as he kissed her foot, vowed to himself that one day she would use her own lips to please him in his own way. But first, he reminded himself, she must be won.

"Oh, Aisha, I would lay the riches of the world at your feet if you would have them, and take you upon the finest ship ever built by man to search out those riches. From one end of the world to the other we would go seeking gold to be shamed by your hair, yellow diamonds whose sparkle would fade next to your eyes, rubies to pale close to your lips."

Aisha was enjoying this. Never before had she heard such flowery

603

language used by a man toward her. She had to fight her compulsion to laugh. "And my teeth?"

"Pearls," he declared, "never gleamed so brightly. Together, you and I would sail the seven seas, then return to a palace I shall build for you high on a hill overlooking the sea!"

"In Tunis or Algiers?" she wanted to know.

He thought fast, but first favored her with another boyish grin. "Half and half. For you and I shall join these two kingdoms together in one as Allah has destined them to be."

Behind her apparently pleased facade, a cynical princess was thinking, As Barbarossa has destined them to be.

At that moment, the slaves appeared bearing flagons of wine and amber goblets as well. Looking down on the redhead with well-feigned mock indecision, she said, "It does sound delightful."

"It's settled then." He didn't ask, he declared it.

"Well . . ." She was more than willing to dally with him as a spider does a fly, but he gave her no real chance.

Instead, with a hearty "Good!" he sprang to his feet, ruffling al Abid's composure again, then, spying the wine, commanded, "Let's drink to it. Pour wine, slave. We would drink a toast, your mistress and I, to our future." Grandiosely, he gestured to Ali and the Taureg and Fionn. "You too may join us."

Seizing the first two goblets, he waited impatiently for them to be filled, then brought one to the Amira. Then, he watched as the others were poured and handed round. Aisha stared down at hers and feared to drink, for the wine was drugged. But she needn't have worried. Ali, pouring himself a cup from another flagon, came to her and secretly exchanged goblets as Eulj Ali turned toward de Wynter. Then, before anyone could stop him, he'd pulled free the gag. "And, you, too, shall drink to us, oh man who was my master, who bought me and my carvings with a pearl.

"Bring the *jamad ja'da* a cup," he said to a slave. "And what of my carving, do you still have it?"

De Wynter, spitting the lint from his mouth, couldn't speak and only shook his head.

"A shame. It was one of the best I did. Here, Ali, help the slave to drink," he ordered.

Ali was furious, but not Aisha. Eulj Ali, unwittingly, was playing

604

their game for them. Let him think himself risen to great heights; it will make his fall even harder, she thought, nodding her approval for Ali to do as he was bidden.

As Ali held the goblet to de Wynter's mouth, Eulj Ali vaingloriously intoned his toast: "To the great games of the Princess Aisha, the greatest spectacle ever held in her land."

Aisha sipped politely as the other drank deep, all but de Wynter. Instead, with a head-butt that might well have chipped a tooth, he sent the goblet and its contents flying in all directions.

"Fill it up," the princess ordered. "I would that he drink to my games, too. Ali, see to it. As for the rest of you, I promise each shall be rewarded with *tajziya* worthy of your courage and skill, especially you, son of Barbarossa." She smiled winningly on him. "Drink with me until we see the bottoms of our glasses." With that, she and the others drained their goblets. Even de Wynter joined in. He had no choice. Ali had used his good hand at the back of the man's jaws to force his mouth open, as a bit would a horse's teeth. When the teeth parted just a crack, he slipped a knife blade in between and twisted it. The struggling captive could do little to eject the blade as his head was held securely by the guards. As de Wynter's head was forced back against the pole, the glass of wine was poured unceremoniously down his throat as he sputtered and choked.

Not releasing his pressure on the knife blade, Ali asked, "Would you care for another? We have plenty."

Aisha's startled "no" was drowned out by Eulj Ali's "Good idea!" Before Aisha could countermand the suggestion, the goblet had been refilled, its contents poured down a reluctant throat. Only when de Wynter had gulped the last drop did Ali release the head to lean again against the tent pole.

In the meantime, the others had drunk as deeply of their second pourings of the sweet and heady fluid.

Too late Eulj Ali wondered why de Wynter no longer struggled and why his eyes looked so strange. His own head felt so heavy he could hardly hold it off his chest. Just then, the Taureg toppled over. Far away in the distance Eulj Ali could hear the Amira's mocking voice, but it faded and swelled alternately, and her words, no matter how he struggled to understand them, made no sense. The last thing

605

he remembered was seeing Fionn stagger to his feet, waver unsteadily, then crash to the floor, knocking trays of food over and strewing their contents over divan and carpet.

As al Abid rose to help herself to some meats, Aisha looked about her with disfavor. The tent was a mess. Even as her slaves hurried forward to set things aright, Aisha turned with a frown to Ali. "What say you? Are preparations ready for my departure tomorrow?"

Damn her, she's determined, Ali thought. He had looked forward to a few days of rest before undertaking the journey. "Ready as they can be in such a short time."

His noncomittal answer was not at all to her liking. However, the thought came to her that here was a solution to one of her problems. "Then you have the rest of the night to get them ready."

"But—!" he protested, glancing at de Wynter. He had had other plans for this night.

Aisha cut him short. She knew what that glance meant, but sooner or later he would have to know that de Wynter was not for him. And business can be healing. "As for the spectators. Did any leave here, except for our Berbers and the storyteller, who may be relied upon to glorify the games wherever he goes?"

Ali, who had the road to Sousse blocked upon Aisha's orders and all travelers turned back, shook his head; he could guess what happened to those hapless people once they were back within the reach of the Moulay. The sky above al Djem could not be lit this long with only slaves as its tallow. Others must have lent their fat to the huge conflagration.

"I pray you are right. It will make what I do less dangerous. Word of the fate of Eulj Ali must not get to the Sublime Porte. Nor can he, for the sake of our country, go free to tell what he knows." She looked down at the sprawling redhead and spat at him. "Even the name leaves a bad taste in my mouth. Take him, as planned, to Tunis under heavy guard. I have had the prince's cage restored in the Dar al Bey. Keep him there, dressed and fed as I have ordered until such time as I can make best use of this pawn in the game his father and I play.

"As for the Taureg, I wish him well. Take him to the third tent east of here. It is already prepared for him. Do not bind him, for he is one of us, but leave a strong guard outside his tent to assure his sleep is not disturbed. When he awakes, tell him that he is free to return to his tribe and his former wives. Tell him I would hope that he would take them back. Tell him also that my grandfather has another granddaughter, Khadija's daughter. You need not tell him, of course, that the girl is fat and fatuous. Let him find that out for himself. If he chooses not to visit the tents of the sheikh, do not obstruct him. Give him horse or camel—he may choose—and an escort—"

Two men disposed of, two men to go.

She hesitated a long while, choosing her words with care.

"Ali," she began but he stopped her lips with one finger of his bandaged hand.

"I know. You have changed your mind. And it is right. For both of you. He is descended from kings, as you are, and his destiny is not to be a plaything in someone's bed, but to father kings. As for you . . ." His voice broke. Then he recovered. "If it cannot be me, then I rather it be he. He is the best, the winner of the games, the champion of champions."

Tears welled within her eyes. "Ali, I'm so sorry. Always I am the one who hurts you. And you are the one person I would hurt the least."

The two looked deep into each other's eyes. Then, she rose up on tiptoe and kissed his lips gently, fleetingly.

Somehow, from somewhere, from the depths of his soul, he summoned a smile and a lie. "You make more of this than there is. He would have been my *anata*, a mere receptacle for my lust. And within weeks I would have cast him from me, as the lowly slave I thought he was. No, you do us all a favor by choosing him. And twice over you please my father. By selecting a worthy man as your consort and by sending me back to my concubines. Now, enough of this. What would you do with this one?" He nudged Fionn with his foot.

Aisha wanted to believe Ali. Even if she could not, she could pretend that she did. Thus, she forced a mischievous look to her face. "Take him to Zainab's tent. For one with a gargantuan appetite, a giant should satisfy."

"As for the *jamad ja'da—*" She bit her lip. "It is so easy to say

607

what his fate will be, but it is my experience that he goes not willingly to fulfill it. I may marry him, but how do I make him marry me?''

She had a point. Never in Ali's life had he met a man more determined to fight fate rather than accept it. He confessed defeat.

''Then what I cannot have willingly, I shall simply have to take. Untie him . . . and the spears as well that made up the trophy pole. Then follow me.''

She held aside the diaphanous curtains so that her men might carry their burden through. At her direction they thrust the heads of the spears deep into the sand, two at either end of the bed. The silken ties that had bound him first to the trophy pole, then to the tent pole, now tied him hand and foot, spread-eagled across her sheepskin-draped bed, but not before all of his wedding finery had been stripped from his limp body.

Then she and her drugged husband were left alone, except for al Abid, the cheetah, who took her usual place beneath the rattan cage that housed the Amira's birds. Al Abid considered these her rightful prey and could not understand why they were denied her. With the patience of the hunting cat, she waited each night for the cage to fall and present her with her just deserts.

Suddenly, Aisha did not want to be left alone. She wanted desperately to call after Ali, ''Come back, don't leave me here with him. I'm afraid.'' But she bit off the words before they were voiced. Ali would not have come back, and if he had, he would not have understood. Instead of the determined, decisive princess he believed her to be, he would have seen a spineless child, afraid of being alone with a man utterly helpless to do aught against her will. She smiled wryly. Determined, decisive princess, indeed. Instead, she was one caught in a trap of her own devising with no way out. The fact is, was, and always would be that she needed a husband. To block Barbarossa, to depose the Moulay. What she had secretly wanted and prayed for was that he be a husband in name only. That was why she was so willing to entertain the thought of his being a slave. What she had obtained—chosen, she had to admit, of her own free will—was the one man truly worthy of being her consort. His exploits in the games would make him a legend at the oases and aid her cause. He also happened to be the one man who had refused to bend to her will—the one man who would never agree, she knew, to being husband in either fact or fiction. Unless she were willing to give him up and forfeit all chance to be queen, she must before daybreak find a way to elude her own ensnaring and impose her will upon him. Otherwise, she had no choice but to accept defeat.

Damn you, she thought, looking over at him where he lay, a motionless, magnificent golden brown statue against the white of bedcoverings, all clean limbs and symmetry like one of the life-sized Roman bronzes recently pulled from the deep off Djerba. "You lie there drugged, unable to speak, bound hand and foot, totally helpless, and still you defeat me."

There she had said it. Defeat. The very thought was foreign to her nature, and she chided herself. "For Allah's sake, Aisha, are you going to give up without a fight? Does being queen mean so little to you? Are you so impervious to this man that you would willingly let him go free on the morrow? Can you ignore his audacity, his absolute genius in the arena today? The picture he made astride the gray? Admit it—just thinking of him makes your blood race. He has captured your imagination and you want him. And you want to be queen. The two go hand in hand. You must have a plan. You can not simply lie down there beside him and wait like some sacrificial lamb for the morning to come and the sheikh to arrive to find the sheepskin unsoiled and unsullied and the marriage unmade."

She tried to argue with herself. "What I don't want is to be married.

"Neither did Ramlah. And she, like you, was raped by the Moulay.

"With me, it was different.

"Different, yes, but no worse!"

It wasn't, she had to admit. Ramlah had known what was going to happen to her, Aisha hadn't. Ramlah had foreseen the pain, the agony, the degradation, Aisha hadn't. Nor had Aisha had to live through a nine-month-long consequence of her deflowering. Ramlah had, and against all odds Ramlah had loved the child born of that rape. Ramlah wanted her child and her child's children to rule this country. Would she now nullify all of Ramlah's sacrifices and dreams? No. Never. Not if it meant getting down on the ground and groveling at this man's feet and begging him to marry her.

The very thought took her aback. Her chin went up, her back stiffened, her shoulders squared. Make her beg, would he? She'd show him. Hadn't she been trained by the most talented odalisques in the land to seduce men's bodies to her will? How many men had she practiced on? Men who had been warned their lives were at stake if they responded. Yet they did and begged for release until in her mercy she had them castrated. Was this man any less impervious to her wiles than they were? All she need do was arouse him. And if he would not take her, then she could take him. It was not, after all, as if she were a virgin or unfamiliar with the mechanics of the act. She knew both all too well. Her pacing had brought her alongside the bed and she stared down at him, daring him to wake up, to unsheath his manhood and know desire.

But despite her resolve, her throat constricted, her lips were dry, and something within her, protesting at the thought of self-imposed rape, tightened into a cramp. However, she had made up her mind. If necessary, to keep this man and to be queen she would mount him and ride him until the sheepskin below them reeked of his seed.

She found herself praying as she paced back and forth, that although not cut as Arabs were, he would react physically as other men did.

How long, she wondered, before she could find out? He slept the sleep of the drugged. He had been first to succumb. Would he be first to revive? She had no way of knowing, yet she needed to know. She feared she was in for a long wait. Wearily she attempted to remove her garments, but she had never done this by herself before. With her hair caught in a jeweled clasp, she was helpless and called for Zainab. Then she remembered her handmaiden had her own plans for the evening. Of course, she thought. Why didn't it occur to me earlier?

She clapped her hands, summoning the *asira* as she watched for some response from the man. Nothing. As she gazed down upon him, she did not feel the tugging of the *asira* as they untangled her hair, nor was she conscious of her heavy garments being removed and a thin gown slipping over her head. When the well-trained *asira*, as a matter of course, handed her the throwing dagger she was never without, it was purely instinct that made her take it and throw it into a tent pole. Instead, she was painfully aware of the man's beauty, the curve of his cheek, the line of his chin, the set of his lips. Suddenly, she realized that she was not the only one who gazed upon him longingly. That she would not have. Immediately all the *asira* were dismissed, except one that she remembered had been useful to her before. It was the girl who had retrieved the mirror. "Child, I would ask of you a kindness."

"Anything, highness, anything."

"I would ask you to torture yourself for me." The statement was misleading but deliberately testing.

The child swallowed once or twice, then spoke the simple truth. "You have but to command!"

"You know the blond giant who survived the games?"

"The one who now occupies Zainab's bed?"

"The same. I see you do know him well."

The girl did not look up but her cheeks dimpled.

"Would you know him better?"

The *asira*'s kiss on her hand was Aisha's answer. "Then, I should like you to listen by Zainab's tent, and let me know when he awakes."

"How, highness," she asked ingenuously, "will I know?"

"You'll know. Zainab will unwittingly see to that. And if you come promptly to tell me, I promise you that when Zainab is through with him, he shall be yours. Would you like that?"

The girl's eyes shone. "Oh, yes, a man to oneself—that would be better than almost anything else."

Aisha chose not to pursue that subject further.

Once the *asira* left, the only sound in the tent was the hissing of the coals in the braziers and the rasping of the cheetah's loud breathing. In the flickering of the torches, the gentle noises were soothing. The bed looked so soft, so fresh, so inviting. The man upon it so handsome yet helpless.

She drew closer and studied that face once again. Unlike Eulj Ali's of only an hour ago, under the drugs his lips had not sagged disgustingly open. Nor did he snore loudly like the giant had done, nor did bubbles of drool appear in the corners of his mouth as they had the Taureg's. He slept peacefully, like a child. Suddenly she realized she did not even know how old he was. With that strange gray hair, she assumed him to be old. But looking down at him, she was not at all sure. Asleep like this with his lips set in a half-smile, he awoke in her a fierce maternal instinct. She wanted to hold him and protect him. She half laughed aloud ruefully. The person he most needed protection from was herself. Carefully, she sat down on the bed next to him so as not to disturb him, then caught herself up short. The one thing she wanted to do was disturb him, to wake him up. It was essential to her plans. Encouraged, she reached out to touch that mass of ombré gray hair. Would it be wiry like Ramlah's occasional gray strand? At first, she was tentative, stroking with a single fingertip. Then, when he offered no resistance, she plunged all ten fingers into the curls of his head. They were soft and smooth and ran through her fingers like silk embroidery floss.

Now her hands seemed to have minds of their own. Not content with playing with the curls on his head, they made their way lower. One finger traced the arc of those startlingly proud black eyebrows, another lightly ran down the length of his aquiline nose. Two fingers on his chin and his head moved side to side within the frame of his outstretched arms. Yes, he was young she thought. Perhaps as young as she was. They would have many years—she caught herself; she had almost thought to grow gray together, but he was already that. But of all the features of his face, the one that fascinated her most was his mouth. Tenderly she brushed those lips with a fingertip. And this time he reacted instinctively, like a baby when first presented with its mother's nipple; he followed the caressing fingertip.

What, she wondered, would be his reaction to her own lips? Leaning over, she proceeded to find out. Well she remembered those lips that had haunted her dreams for nights. And now, kiss for kiss, they were returning her caresses. If she demanded more, his met hers and gave as good as they got. If her lips parted, his did also. If her tongue ventured forth to lick and taste his sweet, soft lips, his did the same. Eventually, however, even she had to breathe, and she sat up, sighing, to rest a moment before returning to the sweet combat.

Then the magnitude of what had happened struck her. He was drugged, but his lips responded! Might not his manhood as well? And if so, might there be a third way out of her trap? One that would spare her from self-ravishment, yet bind him just as fast to her as if she had indeed mounted him!

There was only one way to find out. Down over the muscles of his broad chest her hand moved, fingering the scars, some old, some new, that proclaimed this a fighting man's body. Slipping beyond the ribs and down to his abdomen, stopping only momentarily to explore his navel, her sensitive fingers detected just the faintest trace of down leading toward his *uyur*. Those damned slaves in the baths would be punished, she vowed, for letting those hairs escape their razors. As her fingers explored, he groaned and attempted within the bounds of his bindings to move away. More important, her questing hand had evoked a response from his manhood. His *uyur* jerked as if just coming awake. Another caress of his abdomen and still greater response.

Aisha smiled in triumph. Her plan would work. She would win. This man who had refused her everything up to now, on this night could refuse her nothing. Then, suddenly, she remember the *asira*. If the girl should come back prematurely, the plan would fail, as it would if the man awoke too soon. She must make her move now. Determinedly she reached for his *uyur*, not quite knowing what to expect, for in its loose-skin sheath it was different from those of the slaves she'd practiced on. But like theirs it was warm and smooth to the touch. More than that, it responded like any other man's to every move of her hand. Like a man milking a camel, she forced his *uyur* into the first stage of the *kadill*, its natural cycle: to stiffen. And now, to surrender its ejaculate. Any other time, she would have played with him and delayed him as long as she could. Not tonight. Only by spilling his seed upon the sheepskin could she defeat him. Eventually, it spurted. As it did, his body arched, he cried out in exquisite anguish, and his eyes came wide open. She held her breath. Did he recognize her? But his eyes, those startlingly blue eyes, remained soft and unfocused. Whatever he was seeing, he was not seeing the Amira Aisha.

She was right. In his stupor he was back in a cold bare room at Hampton Court and the face looking down into his was dark-haired, the eyes black and sparkling mischievously, the lips demanding to be kissed. He tried to rise up, to take her in his arms, to drink deep of those lips, but he could not. Some unknown force kept him lying there helplessly as that beloved face moved even farther away. "Come back to me, my love," he called out in French, the language that had, during his exile, become his mother tongue.

Aisha's heart leapt. Was he conceding defeat at last? Had he succumbed so easily as that? Was he but one of those whose heart follows wherever the penis leads? Leaning over him, she smiled lovingly and reassured him, "I am here my *rawa*, my *jamad ja'da*, my husband."

"Anne, please dear Anne come back!"

When Aisha realized that his words had not been meant for her, but someone else, her smile swiftly faded. Someone else was his love, was she? Aisha's eyes darkened with anger. How dare he? Lying there in her bed, with her lips and her hands giving him pleasure, how dare he think of another?

Well, let him dream of this other love tonight. Tomorrow he would wake to the reality that he belonged to the Amira Aisha. In one supple move she was on her feet, putting the last part of her plan into action. As the cheetah watched attentively, she opened the large wicker cage. Crooning softly under her breath, she soothed the sleepy songbirds. Then, she chose one, one whose feathers had grown scant and whose song had been stilled for weeks. A finger nudged it awake and then made a perch for the bird to hop onto trustingly. At the last moment, as she withdrew it from the cage, it fluttered its wings anxiously, but a fingertip stroking its forehead soothed it again. And then her hand pinned it tight. It struggled once, then lay quiescent, but she could feel its heart pounding fiercely as she brought the warm body to rest against her cheek. "I am so sorry, little one, that I must do this to you, but your life is drawing to its conclusion and mine has yet to begin!"

Pulling her dagger lose from its seat in the tent pole, she held it against the bird's throat, but hesitated a long moment. This plan of hers was not without its obvious disadvantages. With one swift stroke of her knife, she would release her hold on the Moulay and put Ramlah's life in peril. The sheikh, when he saw the bloody sheepskin in the morning, would believe she had come to her marriage bed virginal, and so she would have lost her chance to depose the Moulay swiftly and easily with little bloodshed. But if, by shedding this bird's blood, she bound the *jamad ja'da* to her forever, was the rest too much to pay? On the morrow he would wake to believe that the marriage had been consummated, himself raped and taken by a conquering virginal queen who had impaled herself upon his staff and thus triumphed over him. After that, he would have to accept defeat and acknowledge that he was hers for the rest of their lives.

Deftly, she cut the bird's throat, and let its blood spill over her consort-couchant and run convincingly down onto the sheepskin below.

De Wynter stirred and pleaded with the girl in his dream, "Anne, I love you. Don't cry. Please, Anne, no more tears."

Tears there were, but they were Aisha's. For the bird, for Ramlah, for herself, for all of them. But they did not keep her from milking the bird of its last bit of blood, then throwing the corpse to the cheetah, whose patience was finally rewarded with one crunch and a satisfied gulp. Then, blinking the tears from her eyes, Aisha dipped a finger in the gore and smeared the insides of her thighs with the final, absolute proof of the consummation of her marriage.

As she lay down beside him, her fingers seeking under the pillows the talisman she kept there, she realized that her tears were not just for herself but for that unknown girl of whom de Wynter dreamed. And who had lost him now forever. But if that Anne thought she might some day regain him, she was wrong, Aisha vowed. Anne might have his dreams, but Aisha had his body, and she had proved this night that she could control it. Eventually, she knew, Anne's memory would fade before the reality of her own warm body and then Aisha should possess him in his entirety. The thought was bittersweet but had to suffice.

When the *asira* stole into the tent later with word of Fionn's awakening, the tent was quiet. Aisha slept, her head pillowed on the *jamad ja'da*'s chest and a small scrimshaw carving of a Mer-Lion rested within the curve of her outstretched black-painted palm. Two heads turned as the girl entered. Two pairs of eyes studied her seriously. The brilliant blue gaze of the man caught and held her breathless; the green yellow slits of the cheetah, accompanied by a coarse cough of warning, sped her departure.

"He was awake, you say, yet lying quietly?" Ramlah asked her

615

spy when the girl came next to the queen's tent. "And what of your mistress?"

"Sound asleep, her body pressed against him, her head upon his chest."

"Could you see the sheepskin?"

The girl shook her head no, but quickly added, "However, I saw him."

"And?"

"He was dark with blood."

"You are sure it wasn't hair?"

"Yes, mistress, I am sure. I saw him earlier; he was shaved clean."

Ramlah smiled sadly. Her daughter had found and secured herself a man, but at what price? Now, Aisha, the *jamad ja'da*, Ali, Ramlah herself, were in danger from the Moulay. Yet Ramlah would not have had her daughter otherwise. Ramlah knew far too well what price was paid in a loveless marriage. Bending down, she patted the *asira* upon her lips. "You have done well, my child. Now, seek you your bed."

The *asira* hesitated a moment, wondering, then deciding against telling the queen that besides the bloodstains on the *jamad ja'da*'s body, she had seen tear streaks upon the Amira's face. Aisha had cried herself to sleep.

Poor proud, purposeful princess.

So ended the last day of the Great Games of the Amira Aisha on the 17th Jamad II, A.H. 939.

Epilogue

On that same day, the last day but six of the first month of the year of our Lord 1533, Thomas Cranmer was called upon to officiate at the marriage of Henry VIII and Anne Boleyn. The only witnesses were Anne's immediate family, including her brother Rochford and her malicious sister-in-law, and also her family priest.

"She looked," Lady Rochford later cooed, "absolutely terrible. Her face was swollen; whether from fat or bloat or crying, I'll never know. But Henry was excited and grinning like a cat that drank the clotted cream. Believe you me, in less than nine months, we can expect a new heir to the throne of England.

GLOSSARY

Adnan	call to prayer
affamsu	the sun
affirin	bravo
ajmal	more beautiul
albahru	the sea
al ifranj	europeans
al jalala	the exalted one
al Jununi	the madman
al Ikwan	the elite
Allahu Akbar	God is most Great
al rabb	the lord
amira	princess

Amir al-assa	Commander of the Bodyguard
arrajulu	the man
asira	handmaiden
baraka	blessing
hafiz	reader/reciter
hajii	pilgrim who has visited Mecca
iman	holy man
jalala al-malik	the king
jamad ja'da	hair of ice
janab	title of respect
jima	sexual intercourse
ju'al	dung beetle
kafir	unbeliever
lailat al-jilwa	wedding night
ma'dan	well-done
majanna	madness
muezzin	caller to prayer
mujalid	gladiator
mujamala	act of courtesy

mujmil	trader
mu-min	believer
muraqib	master
mutajasur	very daring
paynun	eye
qa'edi	loafer
radika	small gift
rafi as'sa'n	title bestowed on rulers of Tunis
raqisa	female dancer
rawa	beauty
ruqba	gift
tajziya	reward
tarik	a berber
ukda	charm
uyur	penis
xamrun	wine
yadun	hand

BIBLIOGRAPHY

Barber, Noel, *The Sultans*
Bradford, Ernie, *The Great Siege*
————, *Mediterranean, Portrait of a Sea*
————, *The Shield 'n Sword*
————, *The Sultan's Admiral*
Braudel, Fernand, *The Mediterranean*, Vol. I and Vol. II
Davidson, Basil, *African Kingdoms*
————, *Lost Cities of Africa*
Ferguson, Charles, *Naked But Mine Enemies*
Fisher, Godfrey, *Barbary Legend*
Flaubert, Gustave, *Salammbo*
Joseph, Joan, *Black African Empires*
Lane-Poole, Stanley, *Barbary Corsair*
Latham, Norah, *Heritage of West Africa*
Ludwig, Emil, *The Mediterranean, Saga of a Sea*
Payne, Robert, *Holy Sword*
Pollard, A.F., *Henry VIII*
Rowse, A.L., *Elizabethan Renaissance*
Seward, Desmond, *Prince of the Renaissance*
Sik, Endre, *History of Black Africa*
Sitwell, Sacheverell, *Mauretania*
Sylvester, Anthony, *Tunisia*
Trupin, James E., *West Africa*
Vlabos, Olivia, *African Beginnings*

BEST OF BESTSELLERS
FROM WARNER BOOKS

___**RAGE OF ANGELS**
by Sidney Sheldon   *(A36-214, $3.95)*
A breath-taking novel that takes you behind the doors of the law and inside the heart and mind of Jennifer Parker. She rises from the ashes of her own courtroom disaster to become one of America's most brilliant attorneys. Her story is interwoven with that of two very different men of enormous power. As Jennifer inspires both men to passion, each is determined to destroy the other—and Jennifer, caught in the crossfire, becomes the ultimate victim.

___**SCRUPLES**
by Judith Krantz   *(A30-531, $3.95)*
The ultimate romance! The spellbinding story of the rise of a fascinating woman from fat, unhappy "poor relative" of an aristocratic Boston family to a unique position among the super-beautiful and super-rich, a woman who got everything she wanted—fame, wealth, power and love.

___**CHANCES**
by Jackie Collins   *(A30-268, $3.95)*
                                                       (August 1982 publication)
Handsome, hot-blooded, hard-to-handle Gino Santangelo took chances on the city streets where he staked his guts and brains to build an empire. He used women, discarded them at will...until he met the woman of his dreams. The greatest chance he ever took led him to America to escape prosecution when he entrusted his empire to Lucky Santangelo. Jackie Collins' latest is a real sizzling, sexy, action-packed national bestseller!

___**LOVE'S TENDER FURY**
by Jennifer Wilde   *(D30-528, $3.95)*
The turbulent story of an English beauty—sold at auction like a slave—who scandalized the New World by enslaving her masters. She would conquer them all—only if she could subdue the hot unruly passions of the heart.

___**SILVER JASMINE**
by Janet Louise Roberts   *(D30-224, $2.95)*
Slender as a reed, and as ready as a fawn to flee at a man's touch...yet seventeen-year-old Tess had mettle too, though it could not prevent her cruel stepfather from gambling away her honor in a card game—or Morgan Hamilton's forcing her into his marriage bed.

INTRODUCING
THE RAKEHELL DYNASTY

BOOK ONE: THE BOOK OF JONATHAN RAKEHELL
by Michael William Scott

(D30-308, $3.50)
(Available August 1982)

BOOK TWO: CHINA BRIDE
by Michael William Scott

(D30-309, $3.50)
(Available August 1982)

BOOK THREE: ORIENT AFFAIR
by Michael William Scott

(D90-238, $3.50)
(August, 1982 publication)

The bold, sweeping, passionate story of a great New England shipping family caught up in the winds of change—and of the one man who would dare to sail his dream ship to the frightening, beautiful land of China. He was Jonathan Rakehell, and his destiny would change the course of history.

THE RAKEHELL DYNASTY—
THE GRAND SAGA OF THE GREAT CLIPPER SHIPS
AND OF THE MEN WHO BUILT THEM
TO CONQUER THE SEAS AND CHALLENGE THE WORLD!

Jonathan Rakehell—who staked his reputation and his place in the family on the clipper's amazing speed.

Lai-Tse Lu—the beautiful, independent daughter of a Chinese merchant. She could not know that Jonathan's proud clipper ship carried a cargo of love and pain, joy and tragedy for her.

Louise Graves—Jonathan's wife-to-be, who waits at home in New London keeping a secret of her own.

Bradford Walker—Jonathan's scheming brother-in-law who scoffs at the clipper and plots to replace Jonathan as heir to the Rakehell shipping line.

BEST OF BESTSELLERS
FROM WARNER BOOKS

THE CARDINAL SINS
by Andrew M. Greeley   *(A90-913, $3.95)*
From the humblest parish to the inner councils of the Vatican, Father Greeley reveals the hierarchy of the Catholic Church as it really is, and its priests as the men they really are. This book follows the lives of two Irish boys who grow up on the West Side of Chicago and enter the priesthood. We share their triumphs as well as their tragedies and temptations.

THE OFFICERS' WIVES
by Thomas Fleming   *(A90-920, $3.95)*
This is a book you will never forget. It is about the U.S. Army, the huge unwieldy organism on which much of the nation's survival depends. It is about Americans trying to live personal lives, to cling to touchstones of faith and hope in the grip of the blind, blunderous history of the last 25 years. It is about marriage, the illusions and hopes that people bring to it, the struggle to maintain and renew commitment.